JONATHAN BLAZER

Beyond These Fences

For all those that are in the dark—there's a way out; keep going.

Preface

Revisionism in the loosest sense of the word has always come off as plagiarism to me. We are copying a moment of time in history or someone's life. How can anything possibly live up to such a thing as being a part of history? Words will never be able to capture that because we were not meant to repeat those moments. Fiction is meant to capture the painful, nasty, or inspiring moments of real life in a rhythmic parallel.

Put simply, my words are not theirs; their stories are more significant than fiction. Therefore, revisionism is a pale copycat of the original events. So, when history is used at all in conjunction with invention, it must be met with a balance that tugs between being banal at best, or at worst, historically inaccurate demonization. We must have respect, or nothing can be written about those moments.

My story focuses on post-traumatic stress disorder in an era of history that I've been heavily invested in my whole life. It is infinitely easy to be mistaken in history, to be flat-out wrong. This is why, in these pages that you're about to read, I stretch that moral conflict and the kick-ass battle is, in this story, not fact. Anything I wrote in these pages wasn't meant to demonize any group, only to paint a story. Their stories—anyone's stories, really—can be written as heroic or villainous depending on whose fingers are on the keys. This story is just a story about fighting your past, present, and future. Inspired by real-world events, yes, but not at all historically accurate. Just a story—no historical facts. Thanks, everyone, for understanding this. Now, enjoy!

Acknowledgement

Now to the more personal bits. Skip if these kinds of things annoy you, either way, shut up. To my editor, this time, we got it done in three drafts—next time just one! My cover designer, you truly have a way of keeping me glued onto this Earth. Thank you to my brothers for believing in me when I couldn't even finish a sentence. Alex and Meg, for helping me through my addiction. William, for telling me I didn't have to lie to my best friend. Dan, for telling me to keep writing as long as I had something to say. David, for being my brother during my darkest days of depression and PTSD. David and Brandon, best test readers ever. Seth, for listening to a friend as he lost his mind with endless patience. Jordyn, for unbelievable encouragement. Jeremy, for understanding an artist's pain. My sisters Jaime, Riki, and Shelly, for being the best women in my life. My parents. The SCOO space cat team and the Seattle Cyberteam, thanks for giving me homes. Lastly, bird, for being the only person in the whole world that I'm pretty sure could kick my ass. Countless others helped me during these last few years of absolute darkness—thank you all. Without you, I would never have survived. Thank you. I was able to move beyond those fences.

I

Part One

"Whoever fights monsters should see to it that in the process he does not become a monster. And if you gaze long enough into an abyss, the abyss will gaze back into you."
Friedrich Nietzsche

1

Chapter 1

"I have always seen the devil in the ash. Even now. And I wonder now—I wonder if it was the elusive figure burning in the smoke that was the devil. Or, far more likely and far more terrifying: was the figure none other than me? I was always the devil inside the smoke, the demon encrusted in the gray of the ashes of those around me, dying in a fiery pit, one by one."

"That sounds pretty dark, to be honest with you, man. I was merely asking if you would pass the smoke," said Huey. He was one of my cellmates inside the California State Penitentiary, block D, cell 162.

I looked at him and shrugged, turning back to the narrow window overlooking the fried brown grass, on what would most likely be another beautiful day trapped inside. In the distance, I could see the iron fences stretching out toward the sky like the gnarled hands of the damned reaching to a savior above. I sighed deeply; this was going to be another depressing day.

"Avi, I know white people are some greedy folks, but rotate—especially since you didn't roll the damn thing and lost half my tobacco on the damn floor," grumbled Huey.

I took another long drag, ignoring Huey as I took in the deep shadows disappearing into the morning blaze.

My cigarette ran dry—*shit*. I looked out the window for a minute longer, observing the men below as the sun rose higher and higher, burning the

3

brown grass until the ground resembled a sea made of moving mud below me. It was like watching little ants running in the dirt. I turned back to my cellmates sprawled out on their respective bunks. A light-skinned Asian man lay on the lower bed, shoving a pack of cards back and forth through his fingers. He was chisel-jawed, without a trace of lines or deepening in his skin, which reflected bronze in the light through our barred window. Adjacent to him sat another man, his skin wrinkled and haggard from age, and a stump of a missing hand. He had a long, grizzled beard, misshapen and singed off in sections that were peppered white and a light auburn—a sign of its former color.

An unusual pair, but California was full of curious people. Best to go about your day—you were fucked anyways: welcome to prison, who cares about anyone else? They had become my cellmates a week ago, after my former mates and I had... well, let's just say in prison that you do things you don't want to do, or things will be done to you. New cellmates were always popping up for one reason or another. I lost track of the number after a while.

For the most part, the pair kept to themselves, which was all right by me. I wasn't in the mood for making friends today, and they both looked a lot more dangerous and rough to be playing games. Especially the old man—his eyes were always cast away, looking out as if he wasn't there, lost in some faraway place and time. The few glimpses I caught made my spine tingle. A deep gray, so iced over that you would think there was a world that never knew what the sun was like inside them. He had seen something to make his eyes like that—I knew that all too well.

I passed by the two and flipped myself onto the top bunk next to them. A nap was in order. I would need to get some sleep before yard time—it was the first of the month and the beginning of the month was when you would likely get your ass kicked for no other reason than it being the first of the month. I wanted another cigarette. Just one more taste before I heard the dash of the butt on my walls. It always felt good to be finished. It was like the end of toe-curling sex: a real time that was filled with all the right emotions to send you on a trip into the bliss, but over way too

4

soon. I closed my eyes, dreaming of that sweet embrace of filter tips and the smell of burning tobacco.

I felt a tap on my shoulder. "Hey friend, got any idea when we go out into the yard? I got an itch, you know." It was the Asian man asking. He was twitching in the shadows cast by the rising sun across our cell.

Great, I thought, *another junkie*. I had been in and out of prisons for as long as I could remember, and met all kinds of people. The worst ones were always the junkies. You couldn't trust them not to try and stiff you on some kind of deal, or to steal from you the first chance they got. Hopefully, I could get rid of this guy before show time. He was a small man for his stature, with good shoulder posture though. He held himself way too well for a junkie or someone in prison. Not only that, his old friend with the stump hand looked frail but wild. I made a quick mental note of the pair—the only way to survive behind the fences was to know your enemy.

The old man seemed disinterested in everything. He hadn't spoken a word since coming onto the block. Maybe he wouldn't get involved, maybe he would. There was no way to be sure. His eyes unsettled me with their sky clouds pouring into my every thought, even as I looked at the cracked ceiling above. I sighed and prepared myself for the fight that was about to come—junkies had one thing that they at least did predictably: they were always working an angle and would strike if they thought they could win. And judging by the red of this one's eyes, he had been on something strong and somehow was so high it was still in his system. I turned, preparing to strike, just in case. "How about you—"

I never got to finish as the cells doors slid open. "Wake up! Roll call starts in two!" shouted the voice of the head guard below as the stir of inmates all around us started ringing out in the early morning hours.

I grunted. "I would say *now*, man. Yard time starts *now*."

The heavy steel door slid away as easily as a sharp skate on ice. It always amazed me how fast automatic cells could be closed, or how fast a door could be opened, and you could be granted a moment of freedom. Only, like most things in life, it would be just a for a second because even as we exited our cells, all of us lucky inmates at the California State Penitentiary were being flanked by rows of security, all aching for a chance to use their clubs in some way.

Being lead out to the yard through the tightly constructed maze of iron and concrete was smooth as always. One thing was for sure: death camps, prisons, or anything else that involves people with guns, they always seem to be quite efficient. Never any mistakes made—well, only by those in the chains. As we made our way down the first flight of stairs leading outside, one inmate was getting wild. It's never a good idea to get crazy when someone else has a gun and you don't. Just like clockwork, though, we were all on the floor, in a barrage of shouting and banging of clubs on the old metal railings of the prison, sending a ringing through the steel and concrete, which shook my cheeks as I lay down on its cold surface.

We all knew the drill. Even the new guys behind me could figure out to drop to the ground and put your hands behind your head. It didn't pay to look around when the guards were getting a high of their own from the opportunity to become heroes. People with guns guarding animals all day get bored, and it becomes even harder to stay entertained when you're forced to get your kicks from somewhere. I kept my head down flat. I didn't need to look around as I heard the inmate who was making the noises go down in a hail of thumps and brutal cracks from the butt of a gun.

"Just another fucking day in paradise," I muttered. In the confusion, with all of us dropped to the ground, I was now facing the one-handed old man, his glossy, almost silver eyes staring hard into my own. I never liked looking into people's eyes. My grandmother told me once as a child that staring into the eyes of another is like seeing a mirror into their soul. Yet my grandmother believed souls were actually real, and if they were, they had long since left this place. No soul would stay around here if they had a choice. So I never put any stock into what Grandma said. I'd already had my doubts, and as the guards dragged the half-dead man away, still bleeding trails of blood thicker than his words, he was still muttering curses somehow. Yeah, if souls were real, they were smart in leaving this place, I thought.

I ignored the old man's brief but far too intimate look. I couldn't see anything in his eyes anyway, just a sadness that filled me like gas inside a balloon. You would be hard pressed to not find that in human beings trapped behind walls. It was easy; don't stare into the eyes of those who are caged. Want to see sorrow? Look into the eyes of the imprisoned.

After we were all lined up again and led outside in single file, the warmth of the sweet summer air felt like heaven on my face. A disturbance such as that man had created was commonplace—I had seen a lifetime of guards beating on someone else, or even me. The smart thing to do was to distance yourself from it. You can't be beaten if you aren't a part of it. I tilted my head up and for the scarcest of moments, I was a free man again somewhere beyond this place of iron and tears.

The yard was already a buzz of men laughing, arguing, and generally going about their lives the best they could. It's a jungle when you're in the pen, and the best way to survive, as I had found, was to avoid the center and keep to yourself as much as possible. Some groups were making diesel, though prison tea would never seem good to me. No matter how much the guys from F-block claimed it to be mostly made of real ingredients. Others were rolling little fellas, and the yard was full of the standard black markets. Must stay busy—must stay protected as well. It also didn't hurt to keep something sharp on you—I had some form of cutlery in almost every sleeve in my faded gray clothes. Which isn't excessive by any means—Huey had double that in just his left boot.

I saw the nearest benches toward the end of the yard and made a beeline to their safety of rotten, splintered wooden boards, yet still durable enough to sit on. The drama of this morning seemed all but forgotten by everyone in the yard. Blood and gore is just life. That was all I had ever known—or rather, all I could remember. I took my seat away from everyone else, huddling tight into myself on the pews, the sermon playing out across the concrete jungle—I was being preached to on a glorious sunny day. This was the best part of my day, enjoying the sunshine and what little openness I could find. I imagined it must be like what a fish feels when they're moved from a smaller bowl to a larger bowl. More room, but still trapped in a bowl, with just the dream of a bigger ocean.

Still, as I sat, I just focused on the sun. It kept everything from seeming so close, and took me miles away. I thought of Linor's black hair. It was a splendid tangle of wispy curls, flowing in every direction. I had often made fun of her as a kid, yet I missed those tangles now. I missed the way they seemed to move with her mood. I wondered if she was still alive, and if she would be seeing the sun in the same way that I was now, and whether her hair would still be in waves.

Huey interrupted my thoughts, a fresh cigarette already rolled as he took his customary place next to me on the bench. I liked Huey. He talked a lot, but he knew when to enjoy the sun. Huey had been in prison about two years longer than me, for inciting a protest—or, as he called it, "cracker knocking." Either way, it ended with him in jail with little old me on the first sunny day of the year. We had both managed to stay out of a gang. That was soon coming, though. Everyone got into a gang. Everyone. From the straight-laced type who never dreamed of deep-throating a man's junk or getting beaten to death. You joined a gang. There was no choice in the matter. So far, since we were roommates, we had decided that when that day came, we would do our best to look the other way. So far, we were left alone. So far.

"Beautiful day, isn't it?" asked the red-eyed man as he sat with his back near me, staring off at some unknown object in the distance. To the left of him sat the one-armed man, his mutilated stump of an arm being used as a blocker for the sun. I ignored the man and continued to look at the sun. I wasn't about to lose my train of thought for some asshole.

"It's the hair—you never quite forget what the hair looks like. How it smelled, how it looked like the kernels of the yellowest of ears picked in the summer," muttered the man with one arm.

That managed to stop my thoughts. That managed to pull me from my isolated world. I hated when people interrupted me. I especially hated it when people were making a scene. From a mouse fart to paper notes, someone in this yard had just heard what he said. Believe me, when you're in prison, the new guys make a scene with everything that comes out of their mouth. Someone nearby was probably listening and could use anything they said against me.

"What the hell are you going on about, old man?"

He turned to look at me, a pleading look that someone would expect to get from a disciplining mother and not an old man trapped behind walls of iron. "Don't waste your life in here, kid—don't let the things that are inside consume you before it's too late. I've been there—I am still there now. You have to run young man, run as fast as you—"

"Enough of that now, James. You know that we can't change what's in motion. Only they can change that," said the red-eyed man, his tone much more revealing of his accent, but carrying an authority to it that matched someone of a much older age.

The old man glanced at the Asian man, whose back was turned to us with an eerie stiffness that I couldn't place. A sternness that shaped his shoulders into pride: a free man's shape. The old man continued, moving closer to me, "Listen to me, please—everything must change. Everything must change with you if you're to get through this. If you want to see her hair again, you will need to put to sleep the beast."

"This old cracker man is nuts," muttered Huey, eyeballing the two with a look of unease.

I flinched from the old man as he got closer. What was he trying to do? Was he insane? Someone could think the three of us were together. In prison, you only touch people if you're meaning to settle business with them. His hands almost touched mine and I flung myself back from his touch, pulling out a sharpened comb from my pocket. I had been saving the sharp plastic for a bigger threat—you never know how many strikes you'd get before guards took you down—and something told me this old man could take a few. The comb would break fast, but the bladed end was sharp, quick, and precise. I have a lot of experience at using blades.

He flinched. I could tell he knew what was coming as I slid from the bench as his one hand reached out toward me. "Please, don't lose someone who loves you—someone who will keep your heart warm on a cold night. It's not worth it. You are not an animal—"

"What kind of liberal platitude are you uttering, you crazy old man?" I asked, reaching for the comb.

"Shut up now, James," snapped the Asian man, turning toward us, his eyes the color of blood, his eyes like those of a dragon.

I had seen eyes like that once as a child, and I knew only one thing that they could mean. Images span their way into my head, crawling from the safe place I had made as a little boy. *Keep the pain away, keep the red away!* I was screaming inside my head, tortured, and facing the fire, peeling away my sanity like the skin of an apple.

I turned to flee, and collided right into the body of someone massive. My comb was out, and it had gone deep into his flesh. Hot blood splattered around the puncture wound, fighting for a chance to flow out, aching for a chance to erupt. The man I had stabbed was in shock, and emitted a small yelp. I had taken him right in the heart, and he fell down a few breaths later, what felt like an eternity lasting through the moment.

"Great, James. Well, you might want to get to running, my friend." The Asian man motioned as all around, the yard whistles blew and guns were fired. I dropped the knife, putting both my hands up, as guards flew almost out of nowhere in my direction.

"Avi, what the hell, man?" shouted Huey as he dashed his cigarette, jumping to the ground. The world was spinning, and I felt the blood from the large faceless man spill slowly to ground. It had otherwise been a fine day.

"Fuck, fuck, fuck," I stammered, dropping to my knees as someone hit me from behind. My head bounced off the tough, cracked earth. *Don't bleed, don't bleed!* I swore and closed my eyes as the person that had hit me dragged me to my feet. I felt another smack on the side of my head and I fought to stay conscious. All the while, I chanted inside my head not to bleed, over and over again. A voice shouted back to me in the darkness. "*Yes!*" I replied, looking at the benches. Both men had disappeared into a sea of people. Huey was nowhere to be seen, and everything was suddenly getting very dark.

I snapped open my eyes and saw the looming stretches of concrete all around me. I sighed deeply, knowing how lucky I was, how lucky everyone else was that it had been me who had woken up in this small cell. My legs were cramped in toward myself. I had just enough room to stand up and could only lie down with my legs curled in. I was in solitary, but that was okay. I felt my head and face for blood. I was bruised, and lumps were forming on my head. I was still me—I had not become the monster.

Take a breath, take a big deep breath. I wasn't sure, I wasn't sure if the walls around me were moving. I could feel flames, a heat rising inside my mind and in the very air itself. I could hear their laughter. I could feel their gazes on me.

The feel of their sharp fangs ripping into me, my fellow brothers and sisters. I was drowning, I was drowning in images. I fought my way through the haze as a banging came from the door to my cell.

"Avraham Aleksandrovich," said an unknown voice. It was like a lifeline, though, pulling me from the fire. I didn't respond. Instead, I took that moment to focus on calming my heart. It was running fast, burning like the flames of a wicker candle.

"Avraham Aleksandrovich," affirmed the voice from behind the door. Or at least, what I thought was the door—the voice seemed muffled from its veil as I lay in the darkness.

"Yes?" I muttered, afraid to speak up for fear of exposing my dreams out loud.

At the response of my words, a flap was lowered and a blast of sunshine came through a small opening across the room. Bewildered, I turned to the sun. It hurt my eyes, but it fed my soul. Almost greedily, I moved toward the light.

"You've been charged with the murder of one man. The repercussions are death. Death by firing squad, until the time that you expire in a pile of lead and a pool of your own blood. Do you have anything to say in your defense?"

I couldn't see who was speaking. It was as if the light was the only thing that was talking in that moment. "Wait—death? That is a little extreme, don't you think?" I asked the voice, trying to peer at whom was talking.

"I say again, sir; do you have anything to say for yourself, Avraham Aleksandrovich?"

That made me pause. Americans never could pronounce my name on the first try. Most people in general couldn't say my name right. In fact, my name was butchered so much it was why I went by "Avi" instead. It had been a long time since anyone had spoken my name—not with such clarity. I was reasonably sure when I came here the guards didn't bother saying my name, they just said "A" and pushed me along. This was queer. This was something where I needed to know how he was doing that. "Who are you?" I asked the voice. "No one gets my name right." *No one living, that is.*

"That is all you have to say? Your last words and the most you can say is 'What?' You people are always the same, so brassy and noble. At the end of the day, saviors end up the same, though, filled with mirth and self-loathing, with everything always having to be about them. It's such an odd complex, I suppose. You would think a person could only wholly be one or the other. Oh well, that must be why your type is always picked to save it all, for whatever reason."

I was confused, lost in the man's words as I saw an object shining in the light and gleaming as only something designed to kill would gleam.

"The way I see it, you have two choices, my friend. Either stay here and die, or take this knife and slit your wrists. Let the beast out and take control of your life. Or not: let some bullets enter you. I wonder if they would even kill that thing inside you. Time is ticking, and you're still hooked on what I've said, rather than what you think you should be doing. Sheep, every single one of you! Goodbye, sir. This will be the last time we meet. Good luck. You have ten minutes before they come for you." The voice cajoled, then left, and the flap closed.

And like that it was dark again; it was dark inside my mind and I was all alone. This is insane—who the hell was that? One moment I was out enjoying what little sunshine I could ever have, now I was in this shit, waiting to be executed. I looked down, somehow seeing the outline of the blade in the dark. How did he know about—about *him?*

A rumble started, a growl and a roar. Clawing, biting, thirst-ing for blood. It sprang from somewhere deep inside my mind. "*Use—the—blade—free—me!*" boomed the voice from within. *It's him. It is the beast.* "*Free—me!*" growled something just below, like a lurking shark waiting for a bird to land at sea. Patient, hungry, ready to feast on the unknowing.

"No, I'm not going to let you lose," I called back weakly, my voice sounding strained in the thick air. I could hear footsteps approaching—so many, coming from somewhere. They were coming; they were coming to get me.

"*Do—it—fool!*" echoed my own voice, along with the beast, as I reached for the knife in the darkness. It had been a long time since that animal had come out, a long time since I had unsealed him. I had thought that by going to prison I would be safe—or more importantly, everyone else would be safe from me.

I took the knife, holding it against my arm. My hand shook. I only needed to apply my strength; the rest would happen on its own. "Forgive me," I whispered into the darkness as the blade punctured my arm. I pulled the blade up, dragging its sharp edges until I reached my bicep. Hot syrup rained down from my arm. My clothes soaked fast in blood. It quickly dried, steaming and rolling from the heat, bursting beneath my skin. *He is coming.* The air was heavy with hot iron, melting and moving in tendrils of fire.

Instead of cold, I felt hot. I felt fire, I felt rage boiling to the surface. And then the drum started: *drum, drum, drum.* My heart pumping to the beat of the fools coming to my cage. I could hear their footsteps approaching—*he* could hear their footsteps. *They should be running,* I thought as the drums reached their highest tempo and my ears begin to flush with heat. The monster started his cry: *Freedom at last!* The blood from my wound started flowing, flowing all around me, turning the air into a thick red gas. He was coming. There was no stopping the demon now.

My body continued to burn, as my bones started to crack, shake, rip, tear, snap, and dislocate themselves from my body. The pain caused me to cry out as my voice mixed with that of the beast. *The more brittle the bones, the darker the hole*, I screamed into the darkness of my mind.

The drums continued, and the solitary door flew open. In front of me were five flabbergasted guards.

"Run!" I howled as my skin peeled away and the madness broke free.

2

Chapter 2

So many times in my life, I had gone to sleep, drifted away, and had not rested. So many times had I seen the palest of moons light up the night sky and wondered if I could be among the stars, be among those above, so that I might be spared from the horrors below. But sleep was never a slow drift into an ecstasy of pleasure and rest. It was a plunge into a red sky, blanketing out everything else, all dreams of being above replaced by a primal fear. A fear of being eaten alive, for the sky was deceiving. It was not a pale moon crowned with a sheen that only purity can provide; it was merely the teeth before they came to devour you.

And I awoke, my eyes still closed, whenever I had the dream of the monster. The great *Devour*. I had learned it was best to give it a minute to open my eyes. My skin was still tingling under a thick sheen of sweat as the beast roared his words one last time into his body: *soon, Avi.* His sinister growl reverberated, causing me to shake.

I just wanted another cigarette and a long fucking nap. But my eyes were forced open as my head was jarred against the top of something hard and made of metal. I snapped my eyes open and looked about. I was in a car moving fast, very fast. My clothes were completely gone and I could feel something warm coating my skin. I glanced to the front seat. In the front was the old one-armed man, pointing and yelling about something out the window. I didn't have the strength to see what the old coot was going on about. Next to him was that red-eyed crazy man. He was driving the vehicle, switching gears in an almost casual and bored way, despite the panic that was written on the old man's face. I went to speak, but my voice was raspy. It felt as rough as sandpaper gliding over metal. It was always like this after *he* came out. Nothing worked, and it was as if my body had forgotten how to work—how to be human. Huey leaned forward through the middle of the car, joining the shouting from the front seat.

It all flooded back to me after that—the memories. The sights, the sounds, the tastes. I had transformed into the monster, and I had killed someone. It wasn't the first time I had found myself in such a state. I wish it had been. *Waking up somewhere covered in blood was my true identity,* I thought. I chased away the images of me consuming flesh, ripping men to limbs and shredded meat.

I felt vomit coming to my mouth and I leaned over the seat and threw up onto the dirty floor below, the smell causing dizziness to set in. The whole car seemed to start moving a lot slower.

"Dude, what the hell? That smells awful!" shouted Huey as he flared his arms in the small car.

I closed my eyes, trying to chase off the images. If it weren't the memories of the creatures, it would be the fences. I could never tell which ones were worse. I was always stuck behind something. I could never tell where the fences ended anymore. In some ways, I was still trapped behind them. Just instead of metal bars, it was now fur and anger.

The two in the front became aware of my consciousness. "Oh, good evening, young man—boy, I've seen some monsters, but yours takes the cake," quipped the red-eyed man from the front seat. I could see in the mirror an almost happy smile stretching across his angular cheekbones. I shuddered—he was like looking at some demon from the sea, a monster that should never be viewed on land.

"Hey kid, are you okay?" asked the old man, concern radiating from his voice. This was off-putting; a part of me wanted nothing more than to tear both of their collective heads off and feast upon their innards. I gulped. The old man made me mad, but I knew it wasn't me that was wanting to cause the two of them harm. "Be easy, young wolf—the hunter is gone." I mumbled my father's prayer in the darkness of the backseat as we continued to flash along on a dark road leading somewhere.

Huey glanced nervously at me. "I got you a blanket, man—after you calmed down." His words trailed off as his eyes darted away from mine. I didn't blame him; I haven't met anyone who wanted to look into my eyes.

"What?" the old man responded to my words.

"Nothing you would understand," I shot back, almost as a snarl.

The red-eyed Asian man looked less than impressed in the front seat as he adjusted the mirror. "Boy, some kids just don't know respect. None at all," he said again, in an even greater form of disinterest for the whole conversation. His body language was far too relaxed for the situation and the way he talked came off as though he had known me for a very long time, and that this whole thing was nothing more than some kind of joke...

I was quiet, steadying my heartbeat as it charged along faster than the car we were in, with the hammer of the day's events causing me to flush in a wave of sickening heat. Besides the carnage and mayhem that had been caused, the worst part was my senses. I could always smell whoever my victims were, know everything about them from their taste. From a security guard with the smell of his wife's perfume, to some poor janitor's musky and damp cotton shirts, long since worn in with his smell. His smell was the only thing that was left of him now.

My stomach threatened to come rising to the top again. I couldn't remember the exact details of everything I did when I was the beast. I could remember those I had sank my teeth into and I could remember those who had died. I coughed and splinters of bone came out onto my closed fist. The pieces of someone I ate—or maybe pieces of my own. I felt Huey's hand on my back as I leaned forward and emptied my guts into the floorboards of the car.

Handcuffs littered the ground before me. We were in a cruiser; how did we get in here? With my eyes lowered in the car, I could see the light coming through the jagged tears in the door. Something big and nasty had clawed the metal like a toy. I gulped.

"I would definitely give you a smoke right now, free of charge. I didn't have the time to get my papers. Do me a favor: when you're done making this tiny bottle of a car smell worse than it already does, can you tell me what the hell is going on!" Huey whispered. It sounded like a bag of bricks breaking over my head.

I looked at the front seat again. The old man with his cold eyes was staring right back at me, never blinking, never changing his tone. It bothered me to no end, that look inside his eyes. It was a look not of fear—that was something I was used to from many people—it was a look of understanding, or closer to pity, even.

We continued to trade gazes until I lowered mine and a frown edged its way into the old man's wrinkles. Quietly, the old man spoke to the Asian man. "I don't get it—we could just..."

He stopped at the gaze from the red-eyed Asian man. "James, that's not an option. You know what awaits everyone if you do not do this," he said, his tone suddenly very serious.

"How—how can we know that what we are doing is anything that can be justified?" asked the old man.

The Asian man sighed deeply, casting his glaring red eyes at the road ahead of us. "It's not justification, James, it just is. There is a balance," he said sternly.

I blinked, perplexed from their discussion, as the car continued to speed along.

"That's the other thing: why did you two assholes shove me into the backseat of a car with a naked white boy covered in a sheet?" Huey shouted above the engine.

In the rearview mirror, the red-eyed man visually sighed, muttering something indiscernible under his breath. Huey held his gaze, not flinching from the man's impossibly red eyes.

My senses slowly started coming to and I could hear sirens wailing in the distance behind us. I snapped up out of the back seat, looking in the direction of the sirens. An armada of police were chasing after us. In the darkness, I couldn't make out the numbers as we flew by. We were hunted

18

prey by a unified force. My heart was racing, racing fast. I could have become the beast at any time to have escaped the prison, but I didn't want to go back and they certainly would pull the animal back out again. I just wanted to be left alone, I had spent years alone, not after the night I... I cut that thought off. I shuddered and turned, hoping one of the whack jobs in the front had a better idea than I did.

"Hey, I don't know if you two haven't noticed. Right behind us now—are a fuck load of police. Can this thing go anywhere faster?" I asked, panicked, as the lights got closer.

The red-eyed man looked at me coolly, seeming madder that I had interrupted than anything else. As if annoyed that the police were forcing him to drive fast, on what was an otherwise normal drive for him. "As I was saying, there is a balance, James—that balance starts here. It starts everywhere, and this planet is supposed to end," he said simply to the old man.

I blinked, unable to comprehend what he was getting at. "I get that—but we've seen who he is. He's a good kid. A little misguided—I don't blame him though. I don't see why this place has to be the one; I don't see why it has to be him," James replied, gesturing to me as if I weren't a foot away from them.

"The balance, James—the balance. Remember what I told you. Remember what will happen," the red-eyed man said to him, his tone much softer than before.

"You keep talking about that 'balance,'" James mumbled, looking out of his window.

"If it makes you feel better, it does get easier, I promise," he responded.

"That's the thing—I would never want this to get easier," James mewled, looking at the dashboard as if all of life's mysteries could be solved from a coffee-stained dash, in a car whose interior was slowly fading away due to an uncertain amount of spilled drinks and miscalculated ash from cheap smokes.

His eyes ablaze, the red-eyed man cleared his throat and looked in the mirror. I could see his eyes drilling into mine, burying their glow into my

19

soul. "Are you ready for this? You have a very important road ahead of you. Can't be having you locked up when your destiny awaits!" he exclaimed, laughing.

"What the hell are you two fucking talking about?" I shouted, over the roar of sirens and now gunshots splattering past us. Huey glanced at the cars behind us, frantically looking for a way out of this mess. I knew what he was thinking: if we got caught now, we would both never see the open world ever again.

The old man James turned in his seat, taking my hands in his one. I recoiled from his touch, his fingers as ridged as sandpaper. "Look, kid, remember what your grandfather told you. Remember his stories: you can change your destiny," the old man pleaded.

Instead of taking his advice, my mind just tried its best to figure out what the old man was going on about. What did he mean by his words? He couldn't have known my grandfather. He'd died long before the camps.

My grandfather was someone I thought about a lot, but mostly only during my nightmares. It was a struggle just to remember what his face looked like, let alone what his words may have been about. I simply muttered, "I don't understand," and moved myself against the seat. Despite the violence behind us, I was more worried about what the man had said. His partner, on the other hand, was glowing with a rage, and shaking.

In the red-eyed man's hands was an object glowing with a white light, images moving very fast. His crimson eyes flashed with inhuman speed as the images blurred before me. "God damn it, James, look what you did." He sighed, turning his head toward me. "Well, looks like we have us a hero now. I was planning to see if we couldn't get that beast out of him some more. It's been a long time since I've seen a good rampage. Oh—well—take old James's advice here now, son. You have a lot of work ahead of you now. Oh, one last thing." He paused as a shot came through the glass shattering the back window.

Huey docked and swore, tossing one of the vomit-soaked handcuffs, flying into the night. *Disgusting—might actually work,* I thought. I was so enthralled, so caught up in what they were saying, I didn't notice as the pieces of glass cut my skin and the red gas started to form.

"To save a place, you need to end up being one of the good guys. So, best start working on yourself a bit," the red-eyed man consoled.

As my body shook and the rage inside me began bursting through, I heard shouting between the two and the passenger door was somehow thrown open. "Good luck kid," the old man muttered as I was ejected out of the car by some invisible force.

I bounced off the ground, my skin tearing away and blood oozing out of every inch. The cars chasing us hit me, and I heard snaps and pops from within. I watched the speeding car carrying the two men off into the distance—Huey came tumbling out a few moments later. I felt the heat rising inside me and I felt the flames start to take hold. I was back in the pits, back in the furnace that had consumed me so long ago. I cried out in pain as everything went red.

3

Chapter 3

"Are you ready for this, Avi?" shouted my *bruder* Zevi as I stood before my *foter's* watch store, on one of the few sunny days of the year. I was taking aim at my *bruder*. Zevi never missed, but I was sure that today would be the day I finally took that smug smile off his face. I looked to the shorter girl behind him with long black hair. It was a midnight tar color in the summer shine that morning. That was only overshadowed by the angular roses that were her cheekbones. I was sprouting in those days. Even then, I knew that she was beautiful.

I nodded toward Zevi—or rather, he thought it was toward him. As I moved the tattered remains of my ball back and forth through my hands, I kept my eye on the girl behind my *bruder*. I could see impatience. Exactly where I wanted him, confused and not ready for the greatest pitch of all time.

I wound my hand back in a curving method just like Zevi and I had seen on a book cover once. My *bruder's* eyes grew wide. As I prepared the wind-up, Linor shot forward, her hair whipping like the black flags of a pirate ship high at sea in the wind. Nothing could slow her down—she was the fastest thing on the sea!

He was caught completely off guard. Linor had his pants pulled down and the ball hit my *bruder* square in the shoulder, bowling him over. Both of us burst into laughter, as Zevi quickly stood up, pulling the strings on his pants and standing.

"That's not funny, Avraham!" he shouted, red-eyed, with his cheeks already puffing up. My *bruder* was a little chubby, his thick barrel neck puffing out as his tears rolled down his full cheeks. All round us, the other *kinder* forgot to mind their bases, forgot we were in the middle of the championship, and started laughing. Nothing was as funny as seeing someone get pants. I couldn't stop laughing as my *bruder* stormed off, kicking the ball and taking his bat. Linor and I continued to laugh; we laughed until tears came from our eyes.

"Avraham," rang the stern voice of my *foter* from behind me. I knew that sound whenever I was in trouble.

Linor flinched, moved, and kissed me on the cheek as she ran away in the direction that my *bruder* had gone. It was still morning; the sun was shining bright off of the few cars in our city. That was my first kiss. I was done laughing. I wasn't even afraid of what *foter* was going to say. A girl had kissed me—and not just any girl! The most beautiful girl in all of town, maybe even the world. *Definitely the world,* I thought. I was blushing from the kiss, but more concerned about what my *foter* would say.

"Yes, *foter*?" I asked, turning toward his voice. My *foter* wasn't a tall man; he had fading brown hair like mine, only not as thick. *Muter* always complained how my hair seemed to never stop growing, and *foter's* hair seemed to only ever want to grow. His eyesight was getting bad, so whenever he wore his glasses, I always pictured him like a crow, with small black eyes and a long-hooked nose. Yet, my *foter* did have something that made him seem a lot larger than most men, despite not being that tall. His voice carried, so when my *foter* did speak, I knew to listen always.

"Avraham, you should know better than to treat anyone in such a way," my *foter* scolded sternly.

"Yes, *foter*, I—"

"Stop talking, Avraham. Do you know what happens when you don't treat others with respect? It comes back to haunt you always. It always does," my *foter* said, staring off into the sky as if there was some kind of far-off object only he could see.

My *foter* placed his hands around my shoulders and steered me around back toward his shop. "Look, my *zun*, love everyone as if they're your *bruder*, no matter how lost or strange they may seem. We are all equals under the sky, as the Lord teaches us. Promise me that you will remember this, *zun*."

"I know he is my *bruder*, *foter*. I didn't mean anything by it," I said defensively.

"Mean anything or not, he is your *bruder*, just like anyone who comes into our watch store today, or anyone else that you've ever seen walking upon these rocky streets. We are all equal, do you understand my, *zun*?" He stooped in front of me, peering into my eyes. My *foter* had deep black eyes, eyes that could be the very image of a night sky on a cloudy, overcast day.

I didn't understand why my *foter* was so mad. I had messed with Zevi plenty of times. He was always lecturing me on not picking on anyone, especially my little *bruder*. I knew that my *foter* wanted my eye contact—he always demanded that when he asked questions. I don't understand why he insisted on that so much. I looked up in his eyes and responded, "Yes, *foter*."

He continued looking into my eyes until I felt uncomfortable and turned my eyes away. "Let's go, my *zun*. The day is getting longer, and the shop needs to be swept. We will be busy today."

"Yes, *foter*," I replied, mumbling, as we made our way into my *mish-pokhe's* watch store.

My *foter* was wrong; he was very wrong. There were a lot of people on the streets that day—not people that would be looking to buy a watch, though. Instead, it was people running past, some walking with families and bags stocked to the brim with what looked like clothes. And various other goods. I had walked to the store's front window to see what all the commotion was about, when my *foter* said to me. "Avraham, step away from the window, *zun*."

Outside, a horde of trollies rushed before us, swiftly moving past our humble store. At the apex of the trollies were many carriages, pulled along by misshapen and flamboyantly colored horses. The carriages were just as fantastical in their appearance. Waves of colors and boards decorated the boxes at odd angles, some even having their carriage tops ladled with rows of crested gold and rubies. A jubilee of sound and noise rose from the roaming train of Gypsies—the *kumpania*, or the great band of families, as Linor had once told me. Whenever the carriages went into town with that much noise, it meant only one thing: tonight was a show.

"Why are they always so loud..." my *foter* scoffed, taking the broom from my still hands. "Go on, boy, I know you won't listen anyways. Be careful of them—boy," my *foter* cautioned.

I knew if I mentioned anything, he wouldn't let me go out tonight. He was still mad about what I had done to Zevi, but he also was highly suspicious of the Gypsies. *Foter* had spoken many times to my *bruder* and me on the nature of Gypsies, saying they were the fleas to us fleas. I never saw how it made a difference though: we had set up our own community us the *zuns* and *tokhters* of Abraham. Our community was amongst each other, vast and resilient on the fringes as well. *Foter* considered them thieves and moochers on the town, but *muter* says *foter* was only like that because one of them had tricked *foter* during a card game. I wasn't sure about moochers and all the other things people said; all I knew was they had the best songs and dances... and Linor.

"Finish sweeping, boy, then find your *bruder* and you can head to town," he said. I barely heard *foter*. All I could feel was Linor's hot kiss on my cheek. I tried to be a good *zun* and honor my *foter*, but that evening, the store's floor remained dirty as I hooked up my apron and ran into the streets.

4

Chapter 4

That night, the whole town had gathered around the square by the time I found my *bruder*. He was mad. I gave him some chewing gum and told him about how good the kiss from Linor had felt. Zevi was simple; he forgave way too easily, as I thought. I snatched a wad of the thick, sugary goo from the pouch in my pocket and jammed it into my mouth. Gum was a hard thing to come by in town these days. I savored the sweetness. Like a lot of things lately, the town was seemingly drying up of all things good.

I dropped that line of thought once the bears came out. Two bears, one long and thick snouted, with baggy brown fur and a small red cap on his head, was standing on two feet and waving at the crowd of people near him. We all waved back, cheering in unison and smiling and throwing shouts in Yiddish and Polish. Two male Gypsies danced near the bear, feverishly twirling in their garments. Their necklaces were woven with pieces of bone, beads, beans, shells. Anything that could possibly have a string fastened through it was tied lightly around these men's necks. The men smiled, throwing shakers filled with small pieces of colored paper into the cheering crowd. Around them sat more Gypsies banging on drums and various other stringed and wooden instruments that I had no name for.

In the center was an old woman, her hair long and black, curled like the wings of crow with talons and a nose to match. She had in her hands an outstretched cap as she walked around the circle, and many families dropped coins into the hat. This was Linor's *bubbe*. She cackled and smiled, teeth gleaming in the bright light of the many lit torches and street lamps around us. I shuddered near my *bruder*. The old woman did not like me. Anytime she saw Linor and I together, she would just hiss in my direction. *She is a crazy old lady, a coot,* I thought, as she made her way around the crowd. Near her danced the *kinder* and my *bruder*, and we instinctively dropped our hands to our pockets.

The little ones always went for the gold. Adults never noticed it because they were too busy clapping like seabirds, but Zevi and I were just short enough to see what they were really doing besides dancing. Linor's *bubbe* waved and distracted, along with the other dancers, until the *kinder* approached the adults. The adults were unguarded and unaware of the small hands worming their way into their pockets. Snatching anything they could pull, like birds pecking small bugs from the dirt, the *kinder* quickly looted entire families of everything they had in their pockets.

I watched the *kinder* until they had passed by my *bruder* and I, not falling for their fake smiles this time. Last time, I had nearly lost my pocket and was left with only lint! That's when I heard her voice—it was Linor and it was the closest thing to the sound of water hitting the sandbanks on the beach *foter* took us to as *kinder*. A sudden pull and a slow crash that was so rhythmic and tranquil that I felt I could drift away into the sun, as it set on the moving glasses of blue, pulling back on the rocks of gold.

Linor was singing and with every lyric of her song, something twirled inside me. She was a bird swaying in the light and all eyes held on her as she shook the crowd to tears, her slow Roma language foreign, and yet so natural to my ears. She was decorated in red, with swirls of gold and a crest of yellow tied through her midnight black hair.

She was what love is, I thought. Actual and genuine love that flowed and twirled balanced in a way that made only the sense to the insane—she was my heart and even in those moments, I didn't know much, but I knew I could listen to Linor sing every day for the rest of my life. When she finished, she looked into my direction, a small smile tugging at her lips as her piercing black eyes found mine through the crowds. Through the darkness, we found each other's eyes.

5

Chapter 5

The next morning, *foter* and I were sweeping the front of the store again. I was in trouble for picking on Zevi that morning at breakfast, knocking my *bruder's* bread unto the floor. *Foter* was mad—he hadn't spoken much to me the whole day as we worked. I thought of Linor's voice and that made me smile, even as *foter* piled on more chores. There was only so much floor to clean before he would release me. I just had to stay on his good side.

We continued to work when a crowd of people stormed past the shop's windows. I stopped sweeping and turned toward the people as they frantically made their way through town. My *foter* shouted something. I couldn't hear him over the crowd—their volume increasing at an alarming rate and the sound deafening us in the small store. My *foter* said something again—I think he'd told me to move from the window.

I ignored my *foter* as the groups of people became a wave. It looked like the whole town. I turned to my *foter*, and his eyes did something else that I never seen in them before, as he searched out the window. My *foter* was afraid. "Where is *muter*?" I asked him, scared by that look in his eyes.

"I don't know *zun*, I do not know. We need to find her." My *foter* and I closed the store in a hurry as more people kept coming past the front of the store. We closed the sign to the shop and that was the last time my *foter's* watch shop would have the open sign. In fact, I wouldn't know if it even stood there to this day.

My *foter* took ahold of my hand as we made our way through the crowd of people. They crashed and I felt like I was being surrounded by moving walls on all sides, as we made our way to the front of the crowds.

As we passed through my town, I noticed the newspaper clippings scattered on walls, tossed to the floor, words sprawled all around me during all the chaos. I wondered then if they had always been there. I felt a silent note of terror all around me. One stuck out to me, only because it showed a picture of our town, a very angry man on the front and near him, two men with rifles.

My *foter* hated guns, hated the sight of them, and hated talking about them, He told me once that was why he made watches, to remind people that we only had so long to live, and that there was no point in wasting our time killing each other. Next to the guns was a caption: "Mazurik." I didn't know what it meant.

And in that winter of 1939, I was unsure and utterly unprepared for the horror that would soon befall all of us that day. We made it out to the town square. All of us people together. In the center of the mob of people was a small podium, plain and unimpressive with a likewise individual standing behind its flimsy wooden rail.

It was an older man. I had seen him in my *foter's* store several times, though his name I couldn't remember. The noise from the crowd was too much, and my mind was reeling from all the sound. It was as if I had been dumped into a moving ocean made of glass, crashing all around me. I placed my hands over my ears, drowning out the sound—or rather, I just caused the sound to feel like I was trapped inside a shell. I looked around frantically and my *foter* was still near me. I could see Linor next to some old man, her face locked in the same confusion that I imagined mirrored my own. I looked from her back to my *foter*. He was staring ahead at the old man.

The old man cupped his hands around his mouth, trying to stretch his voice over the gathering. *It was useless*, I thought, *this wasn't a crowd of people*. This was a living ball of sound.

The old man kept at it, kept shouting and waving his hands to quieten the sound down. Slowly, ever so slowly, everyone started to quiet. I was thankful—my ears rang and I couldn't imagine there ever being anything else in the world that could possibly be louder.

"Everyone!" I heard the old man cry above the noise.

The crowd around me began to quieten, the dull thunder of their voices subsiding into the whimper that our *mishpokhe* dog makes when he is scared. *That was us,* I thought, *a crowd of people scared, despite being around each other.*

The old man cleared his throat, his face flushed and red from the discomfort of yelling. He had pulled out a white cloth from somewhere and started dabbing at the sweat pouring down his face. "Um—hmm—yes, thank you, everyone," he mumbled, his face quickly disappearing under the salt of his sweat, as his skin began to grow redder, despite the cold weather of the day. "I know things—" the old man started to say, but he never got to finish.

It was like looking at a clear and sunny day that suddenly turns to rain. You just couldn't have predicted what would happen next.

A loud shattering noise boomed across the town square. And the old man slumped back, never to rise again. A lot happened at once. My *foter* swept me up into his arms quickly, as the people around us scattered like the flock of birds in the park, after my *bruder* and I chased after them nearly every morning on the way to school.

Everything happened in a blur, the wave of people crashing around me, turning into a tsunami. My *foter* was a tall man; he was strong for someone so long of body and narrow of shoulders, yet even he had trouble keeping us together. My eyes were cast in the faces of fear—yes, fear.

The first time I had ever seen blood was when my tooth had fallen out as a younger child. I remember the metallic taste in my mouth as the blood oozed into the furthest reaches of my tastebuds. I remember having stopped what I was doing as a young child. Not feeling any pain, just feeling this strange taste inside my mouth. My little fingers slid around until I found the source of the taste—something sticky, warm to the touch. I pulled my fingers away. They were covered in blood. I cried for a long time when I had seen the blood—not just because of the pain, but because it was my transformation. The first real pain that is life—now vivid, staining and tarnishing the very nature of what I thought I knew about reality. From that moment on until the end of my days, I would understand life's hardest, most important lesson: pain.

What I saw now as my *foter* finally scooped me up into his arms was blood. An ocean of it, compared to the amount that had been in my mouth so long ago. The old man was crumpled over, a gaping hole stretched from his chest like some kind of monster, rows of jagged bones for teeth. And a never-ending river of red saliva. I looked away, only to see my *foter* run into someone in front of us. I never got to see who it was—my *foter* pushed me down as I tried to rise. Staying low, I looked under the many legs before me, like swaying trees all covered in cotton and dust from the busy crowds. I kept trying to pierce the veil of legs until I came to their opening and I saw what was stopping the ocean of people. Dozens of gray uniformed pants; black boots, and large tires, only a breath away from the crowd. I held my breath and I felt my *foter's* hands on my back. "No matter what happens, *zun*, do not move," my *foter* urged firmly. My *foter* had never been like this. Why was he covering me? Why was the old man—dead?

A loud voice sounded off, breaking my thoughts. The voice spoke in a language that I couldn't understand, rough and harsh. Loud and fierce—convoying malice with absolute authority. The voice continued and I got lower; flat to the ground. My *foter* hovered above me, crouching near me. "Be easy, my *zun*, Our *Foter* will not let something happen to us today," he whispered. That was something my *foter* always said when he was angry or worried. I think it was meant to comfort me. It did not help today.

I closed my eyes and prayed as the shouts grew louder. *Foter, please, if you're listening—help us!* I screamed into my mind, afraid to open my mouth. Afraid to open my eyes. I heard the loud noise again, this time met with screams. The ocean had come alive, the sharks had gathered to feed.

The loud noise from earlier was dwarfed by a hail of what sounded like glass being broken by rocks, all around me. People screamed, twisted, convulsing under the weight of their own voices. I could feel my *foter's* hands over my ears as the noises continued. I could hear their screams, and I finally let my own scream out. A ball of pain that was forming inside of me, threatening to blow open—just like that old man's chest. I wondered then if that would be the same for me, if one of those loud sounds would explode my chest, causing a monster to come from within.

I felt bile in my throat and I started to vomit. The air was thick with smoke; it was hard to breathe and everything was hot. It started to rain. I felt droplets of something land on me, I felt something heavy and warm pin me to the ground.

The rain soon got into my mouth, relentless in its pursuit of soaking me. Only it wasn't rain, it was that metal taste that I had tasted from long ago. *It is blood, I have blood in my mouth.* My eyes were still closed, but my heart had never been more open. I started to cry, wondering what was going on, wondering where my *foter* was. Wherever I was, I wasn't in that town square anymore. I was in hell, I thought. I had skipped too many of my prayers, picked on my *bruder* too much. I thought of him and my *muter* in that moment. Where had they been? After the baseball game this morning, my *bruder* didn't come back to the shop. My *muter* either. I hoped they were both all right. I thought of my long-haired friend, her silky black hair flapping in the wind in our many times playing outside. I longed for her—I longed for her with all my heart and soul.

I let my voice out in that moment, let it rage from my body. My *foter* had said to be quiet, but I couldn't do it anymore. My voice soon joined those that were in agony all around me. We were singing a brutal song of demise, and somewhere, somehow, the deceiver was smiling from all this terror.

My voice croaked and I couldn't scream anymore. I was dried out and my mouth was full of the blood from someone else. The loud noises had stopped. I knew now that it had been a gun I was hearing. I didn't want to think that, though. Only good people used guns, right?

I wanted my *foter*, I wanted him to sweep me up and take me from this place. I thought of my *muter* and *bruder*. *Where were they? Were they some of those at the front who had been shot?* I shook from that thought, I shook all over. Around me, I could still hear moaning. People were dying. *Where was my foter?* I thought again.

I was about to call out for my *foter* when I heard his voice from next to me—as silent as the whispers of leaves in the wind. "No."

That was all he whispered as the gray boots appeared in front of me. My eyes had come open. I was staring at the bodies littering the square; no longer human beings now, just garbage that had been left behind. Like seeing me and my *bruder's* toys scattered about. Only, I had doubts that my *muter* would be yelling at us to clean these up. There was no cleaning up such—such a mess, when all the world is red around you. All I wanted to do was cry. Tears, though, tears could not scrub away the sight of blood. They could not wash away the twisted and mutilated forms of the living, now put through meat grinders.

I was so stunned I didn't hear the footsteps of the approaching gray pants until they were only an arm's length away. I could hear their language again, gruff and utterly careless for the lives that they had snuffed out. It was German—I could make out just the shapes of their words, but I hadn't paid nearly enough attention when I was in my classes for it. Actually, none of my classes. I hoped my teachers and classmates weren't in the square...

What monsters—what devils they must be. Long had my *muter* and my *foter* talked about devils of this Earth to me. Here before me were plenty of them. And yet, I was not scared—not as scared as I thought that I should be.

Instead of crying, I kept quiet like my *foter* told me to. I kept quiet even as the men in gray turn some of us over and began to shoot us. Those who tried to run from the crowd were shot as they fled for their lives. And as the day trickled away, ticked away like the countless watches inside of my *foter's* store, the moans of our dying all ceased. There was no mistaking it; we were all dead, those that were here. None of us were ever going to see the light of another day. None of us would enjoy honey cake again, or chasing frogs down by the river. Being kissed by our *muters* at night. Or the smell of our *foters'* pipes when they came home from work. The feel of a ball being thrown between my *bruder* and me.

That is what made me cry—knowing that I was as good as dead, lying like a fish caught from a river. There was nothing I could do but gasp for life, as the fish does for water.

I never dared closing my eyes, even when I was turned over by one of the gray pants. I looked up, expecting to see the face of a demon, a monster twisted and horned, ready to devour my soul. Instead, I saw a man—he was long of face and skinny. In fact, I would say he wasn't that much older than me at all. His helmet looked almost too big for his head. His shoulders were slumped from the weight of his straps. His gun was gleaming in the last few hours of the day. I looked up—he had brown eyes, brown just like my own. And when I noticed his eyes, he noticed mine. I didn't blink—I didn't move. I stayed silent like my *foter* had told me too. But something registered on his face; it pulled into itself in a thick brow of concentration. I knew in that moment: he knew I was still alive.

Covered in the blood, smeared in gore as I was, he still knew that I was alive. A voice came from behind him and he gave me one last quick glance and turned away. I stayed sprawled out in the position that he had left me in long after their voices had trailed off; even longer, after the sun had trailed off into the night. My body ached from staying so still for so long, staying that way—the dead boy trapped in a square.

I felt a touch on my shoulder—a simple pull. I did not move though; it had to be the demons coming back to finish the job. That young gray solider had changed his mind and was coming for me. I breathed in a small amount of air that I could take in through my nose, and then I heard my *foter's* voice again. "Be easy, my *zun*, it is your *foter*."

Only when I heard *foter* did I look, my eyes stiff from being open for so long. They cracked and burned. I felt them tear up like someone had thrown handfuls of salt into them; like Zevi and I had done once when we found a slug. We had both dared each other on the count of three, but I tricked my *bruder* and did it on two. While I laughed, some of my own salt got into my eyes.

"I can't see you, *foter*—" I blurted, before I felt his hand covering my mouth. In the darkness, I could see his finger. The soldiers had lit lights from somewhere inside the city; there was enough now that I could make out the outline of my *foter*, but only when he was close to me. I nodded and he removed his hand slowly, still holding one finger up to his mouth. His attention was far ahead of us—he was thinking about *muter*. As was I, I wanted to see her so badly. I just hoped that she hadn't been here when all this had happened.

My *foter* crawled past me, over the bodies. Gesturing with one hand to indicate that I should follow him. I understood, I flipped to my stomach, my whole body feeling like a sack of flour. My *foter* lead the way and I followed. We went slow and it felt like hours before we reached the end of the bodies. A sea of blood and limbs, an endless ocean of death. They say hell is a lake of fire—I think it is a lake of the dead.

When we made it out of the center mass, my *foter* crawled to his feet, his legs shaking, and I worried that he would fall. He stopped cowering behind the coverage of a ruined wall. Chunks of cement were missing from the spray of bullets; chunks that I realized could never be put back. My *foter* turned back to me again, his finger placed toward his mouth, and he went around the corner. His movements were quick and low to the ground, as we made our way across our city. In the distance, I could see fires burning. Light was coming from somewhere and I could hear screams.

I wanted nothing more than to somehow make them stop, make the screaming go away. The bodies all had screams frozen on their faces, even in the darkness. Now, the screams were walking all around us.

As we approached the end of the road, a loud convoy of metal on tracks started down the street. My *foter* pulled me into an alley as the tracked machines, slow and clambering, passed by. Each was painted in a dust gray, with symbols stretching from its long nose all the way back to its open compartment. They were bigger than any car I had ever seen in my life, like moving boulders.

I shook so bad that the tent my *foter* and I had hidden behind started to shake. My *foter* gripped my legs with one of his hands, his eyes never leaving the moving boulders. The soldiers continued to scan with a searchlight from behind and on top of the boulders, as they passed down the street. Eventually, my *foter* let go of my leg and turned to me, motioning again with his hands for us to keep moving.

When we were out of the sight of the building lines in the back alleys, I asked my *foter*, "Foter—where are we going? Home is not this way from the square."

"Be quiet, *zun*, we are not going home. We would never make it through all those soldiers. We are heading to the shop. Your *muter* will think to go there as well," he said earnestly and out of breath. We were both getting tired from the journey.

It took us a few more times of hiding in the alleys and even hiding under a vehicle at one point, to back track to the shop. Smoke was rising the next street over. My *foter* peered at the rising smoke, his gaze deep in thought.

He turned around and clasped my hands. "Avraham, unlock the shop. Keep low and stay out of sight. If I am not back in one hour, make your way to the next city over. Along the path that *zayde* once showed you through the woods. Do you remember?" he asked me, placing his modest keyring into my shaking hands.

"Yes, but—" I whimpered.

"No, son, don't argue. Go now and remember to stay out of sight. I will return," my *foter* whispered, turning and disappearing into the darkness of the city. I blinked, feeling a very cold shiver run up my back. I was alone—as alone as I had ever been. I felt my eyes sting, the water all gone, and all that remained was salt. I fumbled the keys and almost dropped them as I unlocked my *mishpokhe's* watch shop, entering into the darkness. Once inside, I crept low to the ground, just like *foter* had told me to.

I walked behind the counter at the end of the store, coming around the door-flaps. I faced toward the window. *Foter will come back, I know he will, he always does*, I thought.

"Av—" someone started to say in the darkness and I jumped. Flinging myself back against the store wall.

"Stop, *zun*, it's us. You're safe now," my *muter* cooed from the darkness of the other side of the counter.

"*Muter*?" I asked the darkness in disbelief.

"Yes, it's us, honey. Where did your *foter* go?" my *muter* asked, coming up to me and snatching me in her arms. I was pressed so tight against her bosom that I couldn't breathe. My hands were crushed into my pants leg, unsure of what I should do as she pulled me tighter into her. I finally submitted and buried my face back into her. We didn't talk, we just cried, the both of us.

My *muter* began to hum a song she called *Caged Bird*. "If that bird cries into the hand, if the hand clutches for the talons. Oh, the hold that cannot bind those soliloquized thoughts." She sang lightly as my tears stopped. "If that bird cries into the hand, let bird fly free into love," she finished, kissing my forehead. I could feel the wetness of her kiss through my blood-soaked hair. My *muter*, she could sing the saddest tales, the happiest of hymns. *Muters are supposed to be that way*, I thought, *they're supposed to always be able to sing and make their kinder feel better*. My *muter* always had that effect on me at least.

"Not to interrupt this here, but we need to get going," my *feter* commented, coming from the darkness. He looked like my *foter* in almost every way, only his face was not framed by glasses and middle age had yet to set in. He was my *foter's* younger *bruder*.

"For the last time, Azhi, we are not leaving until Avi returns," my *muter* said sternly.

My *feter* stammered, mumbling, grudgingly accepting that he could not move my *muter*. My *foter* had always told me I took after her in that regard. "Well, what will we do, then? We've been hiding out here ever since that mass—" my *feter* started, until he looked around. Suddenly he became aware that it wasn't just the three of us in the store. Zevi sat on the floor, his back against a wall, his form low and out of sight.

I wanted to hug my *bruder*, to kiss his brow. I had been holding my breath in worry for him, I realized. Dread that was flowing inside me, flowing with a strong and powerful grace, was slowing down now, knowing my *mishpokhe* was alive. *They're alive: muter, foter, bruder.*

My *feter* caught my gaze upon Zevi. "Yes, young man, we were worried sick about you." My *feter* haphazardly pointed at my *bruder*, whose attention was resting on the door leading from the store. At the mention of his name, my *bruder* kept his gaze on the floor. I had never seen Zevi like this—I had never seen myself like this. It repulsed me, thinking what I must look like to all of them. It must have made things that much harder.

"Glad you're back," my young friend Linor whispered in my ear from behind me, and squeezing my fingers, which had already started to shake from her voice. All the troubles in the world were forgotten in her touch. I paused, thinking of her fingers, while outside the world was falling apart in a hail of ash and night. I wished *foter* would return already, I hoped that we could all leave this place.

As we sat, my *muter* and *feter* spoke to each other in hushed voices. I think they were trying not to worry us, but it sounded like they were more scared than us *kinder*. "We are not going anywhere until he has returned!" my *muter* reiterated frantically to my *feter's* pleas once again for us to leave.

"At a certain point, my *bruder* would want us to be safe. He would want you to be safe." My *feter* comforted my *muter*, moving closer to her as uncertainty formed on her face in the darkness. As they spoke, small pockets of light burst near the shop, causing a collective holding of everyone's breath, until the lights passed by the area.

"Our *foter* told me to wait one hour," I stated to my *muter* and *feter*.

"I understand that, *zun*, but at a certain point..." my *feter* responded.

"Our *foter* told me to wait one hour. We will wait," I hissed back to my *feter*. I turned away, tears threatening to spill down my cheeks. I couldn't understand why my *feter* wouldn't wait. Why was my *muter* even listening to him talk like that? She had to know that *foter* was on his way, that we had nothing to worry about.

I walked past Zevi, making my way to the very end of the counter; I crumpled to the floor as I slid down, hoping that the darkness would cover up my tears. My *feter* and *muter* continued to argue in quick, lowered voices. My *feter* had ahold of my *muter's* arm, while pulling her closer to him.

I turned my head back to the floor. All the watches around me but no light to make out the time. It had only been a few minutes since *foter* had left—right? I just wished he would come back before we had to make the choice to leave. It was an easy choice. My *muter* would never leave our *foter* behind.

I pulled my knees into my chest, feeling no comfort in my wet clothes. The blood of those that I had crawled over had stained the cotton, staining far deeper than just my clothes.

I shook when I felt Linor's delicate hands on my back. "Are you okay, Avraham?" she asked. Her words hypnotized me, I thought. I looked at her, feeling like all my worries were thousands of years behind me. Like nothing else mattered except the time that her and I spent together. She had tear lines running down her cheeks, and I felt horrible in that moment. She was here—where was her *muter*, where was her *foter*? But I knew from the way she stood. I knew before I gently asked her what happened. I simply hugged her tight. She was tense in the hug for a while, until she was coaxed back to life in my embrace.

"Is your *foter* really coming back?" she asked frantically, searching for an answer of hope, as we both looked away, drying our eyes.

My *foter* had always told me to never lie—I wasn't good at listening to him, sometimes. I was even worse at listening to *muter*. I mouthed, "Yes—he will come back," as the shooting in the distance moved off. We were safe for now, but for how much longer, I honestly couldn't say. No more questions were asked after that. Even my *muter* and *feter* were now quiet, as the clocks in the store slowly ticked away. Each movement of the little hands showered us in a wave of rocks, smashing rocks in our minds, as the weight crawled ever on. Unease started to set in. If *foter* did not return soon, we were going to have to leave. It had only been a few minutes—maybe longer. I wasn't sure; all those timepieces around me and not an ounce of will to fix the light issue. *A fish without air*, I thought, *a fish without air was just like a watch salesman's son being unable to see what time it was.*

My *feter* cleared his throat. "It is time. We have to leave. My *bruder* has had over an hour," he informed us. My *muter's* face sank at his comment as quickly as my heart did. My *bruder* remained glued like a statue, unmoving and still staring at the floor.

I started to protest when my *feter* spoke again. "Avraham, this is not the place for a child to interject. Your *foter* would not want us to wait for him like this." My *feter* gestured to the surrounding shop. It was true—we were liked trapped mice that my *muter's* cat would play with. Stuck with the cats outside, just us little mice stuck inside a watch shop.

I stared at the floor, as if some answer to the situation would appear in the hardwood floor. I felt hot. I just wanted to crawl into bed and let my *muter* tuck me in. That wasn't going to happen again—I had a feeling that I would never see my old bed ever again. "I won't let that be the same for *foter*," I declared.

"What's that, Avraham?" Linor asked.

"Yeah, what is that Avraham? Speak up, young man." My *feter* was hostile as he approached me.

"I don't care what you think. I won't be leaving without *foter*. He didn't leave me, so I won't leave him. Besides, where were you when everyone started dying, *feter*? Where were you when the world became blood? You were here, cowering in our shop," I screamed, rising to my feet.

"Why you—ungrateful, spoiled little child," he stammered, reaching to his waistline to seize his belt.

I stood in defiance. My *foter* once told me that if I was going to say anything—anything at all—I had to stand by it. Or at the very least, if it was dumb, I would have to pay for it. My *feter* growled, becoming larger in the shadows, and his form flaked with red rage as he wheeled toward me.

My *muter* caught his elbow with the belt in it, stopping him long enough for him to turn around and shake her grip loose. "Let me go. The boy needs this," he fumed.

"That is not for your place to decide. Stop—too much has happened already. He is just frightened. We all are," she proclaimed.

"Unhand me, woman!" he roared, cocking back his hand, and slapping my *muter*. The blow was louder than any of the gunfire that was outside. A silence filled the shop as my *muter* almost fell from the blow. Something wet fell from her face as she turned.

I gasped. My *eltern* didn't hit each other. Not people in my *mishpokhe*. They especially didn't hit my *muter*. No one would ever hurt her. Zevi, however, wasn't as taken aback. He sprang from the ground, rushing toward my *feter*, the anger carrying his chubby form faster than it would have been expected for someone so large. He lunged at my *feter*, taking his hand firmly from my *muter*, though he lacked the weight to topple my *feter* over.

"O! Both of you two, stop this!" my *feter* shouted, picking my *bruder* up and sending him sprawling into the counter. Zevi bounced hard and fell to the ground. "I am so sorry I hurt you like that, Shiel," he said, approaching my *muter* again.

"Get out," she stammered.

"But I—" he started.

"No—get out, I don't care where you go. You can't stay here. Touch me again and I will kill you," she snarled, with a ferocity and malice I had never heard or thought my *muter* was capable of. My *feter* was as taken aback from this as the rest of us were, as she reached down, helping my *bruder* to his feet.

Her eyes never left my *feter*, her face a hardened mask of emotion. "Leave us now," she directed, her voice infinite in the old store. He stood in silence, my *feter* with his hands at his side, his belt all but forgotten as it slid to the floor. Some men wanted to only love, some wanted only to control—in those moments, I could no longer tell what my *feter* wanted, but *muter's* will was greater.

He lowered his head, his shame hanging in the tornado of emotions that already whirled within the store. "I'm sorry," he mumbled.

"I do not care—be gone and never darken the steps of this *mishpokhe* ever again," she harshly stated.

"Okay—goodbye," my *feter* said somberly, picking his belt from the ground, looping it back into place. "I—" he started to say, before he shook his head, hung low as he made his way around the counter and out toward the front of the store. I looked at my *feter*, as if seeing him for the first time in my life. As if seeing the world in red had somehow opened the truest sight of this existence around me that I had been unaware of this whole time.

I couldn't feel anything as he opened the door leading out into the alley, away from the store. I couldn't feel anything as he left my sightline in the darkness of this long and neverending night. The darkness would run you down into the night, and things that you never thought to be possible would happen. Things I would wish had come only from nightmares and tales of far-off places in far-off times. Like the books Zevi was always reading, full of darkness and creatures of impossibilities. The night swallows those who walk into it, those who are never to return—that was my *feter* now. I gulped, hoping that this would all be over soon enough.

I turned back and my *muter* had my little *bruder* pulled tight into her, her head resting on top of his. He was crying, his tears soaking the front of her brown coat. I turned back to the front of the store, afraid to look toward them lest I started to break down in tears myself. "Just hurry, *foter*—wherever you are, hurry," I spoke into the darkness as the clocks continued to tick by.

Something whispered into my ears, a thick strand of invisible fingers tightening around my shoulders as they slumped forward under the weight: "I don't control the darkness."

"People get what they deserve, is what my *foter* used to tell me all the time, when we worked in his fields." Linor said. "When my *muter* left, my *foter* left in his own way, now that I think about it. We always worked the fields and he would constantly say that we would get what we deserved. I think, in a way, that isn't fair. No one deserves to be unhappy. And that's all we did, work the fields and pray for a better tomorrow. Watching everyone pass us by, day by day," she whispered.

I turned, looking at my friend, her black hair darker than the shadows around us. "I don't know—does it really matter?" I asked, shrugging.

"Most likely not. Nothing else better to do than to speculate on the meaning of happiness when we could die, I suppose. I don't want think we deserve this," she said, genuinely concerned with the dilemmas of her statement.

"Girls are weird," I declared.

"Boys stink," she rebutted, sticking out her tongue.

I smiled thinking about her, glad, even as we stood so close, to have her by my side. It was a feeling that I wanted for the rest of my days, I decided.

As she and I looked at the darkness of the alley, lit by the explosions coming from far, a face came from the darkness. I jumped back—my heart beating in my chest. It was the gray men—they had come to shoot us as well. My movement caused everyone else in the shop to suck in a deep breath; not a single sound to be heard other than the ticking of the clocks. As we held our breath, more faces appeared from the darkness. An endless sprawl of time, our breaths unable to outlast their movement forward.

Many of them were covered in dirt, old, young, narrow cheeked, or round and innocent. They all came from the shadows, like floating ghosts in the darkest of nightmares. Their faces soon gave way to the rest of their bodies as they stayed low to the ground, heading in the direction of the watch shop. All the while, their movements the sure footing of individuals who had lived in this city for a long, long time.

And behind them appeared the hooked nose of my *foter*, his glasses missing, his face smeared with blood and dirt. It was him, though, lean and wary of the world and all around him, with his deep eyes. I let my breath out, the fear in my chest leaving. Everything was going to be all right now; my *foter* was back. My *foter* gestured to an older man nearest him. The older man tapped the person in front, a young woman, who angled herself in the direction of the shop.

I turned looking at my *muter*. Her jaw dropped in the cold night air as I bolted over the counter and moved toward the door, unlatching the slides, and pulling the glass slowly open. A loud screech stretched from the old wooden frames, causing the glass window portion of the door to shake.

"Come, *foter*—over here." I beckoned with my hand, hoping he would see me showing him the way. If he had seen me, I couldn't tell. His pace did not change as he led the group up to the watch shop.

"Avraham, did I not tell you to leave after an hour?" he growled, as the people nearest him looked desperate to be out of the road.

"Yes *foter*, but I—" I started.

"No time for it, my *zun*, we have to go. This area will not be safe for long. They're going building to building. Rock to roof. We need to leave now. Make our way out to *zayde*, out in the country. It is the only way. Hurry, it is time to be on our way," he said, pointing at the line of scared individuals behind him.

"Alright, let me get *muter* and the others," I replied, turning back to head inside the store.

My *foter* blurted out, "Your *muter* is alive?" His face was alight with hope that I hadn't seen all night. Fire or bullets, *mishpokhe* will always be a strong grace that can bounce anyone out of the deepest of holes, I thought.

I smiled and waved to my *mishpokhe* inside the shop. My *muter* came out first, tucking my *bruder* against her leg. His lip was bleeding from where my *feter* had struck him, his eyes watering behind the red and puffy cheeks only a child can pull off without the fear of looking too weak or pitiful.

My *foter* rushed into the doorway and embraced my *muter* into a tight hug. Their bodies close, allowing for no light or distance to separate them, as even their voices became joined in their bliss. They stayed that way for what felt like to long to me. *Foter* was right, I could hear the voices of the soldiers near us.

Linor came up to me, speaking aloud what was on my mind. "We need to be going soon—I can hear them getting closer," she stammered.

The other adults and group members mumbled similar agreements. "*Foter*," I reminded him of our existence and situation.

He slowly became aware of the world again, like a lost puppy forgetting where his play-toy was. "Yes—of course. We have to get moving. Don't worry about anything in the shop, my *zun*, it will be here when we get back," he assured me; his words didn't have the effect I think he was trying to achieve. I never understood why adults felt compelled to reassure us. *I am eight years old now—I am almost a man; I can take any bad news.*

"What about food, what about our life? Can we really just abandon everything we own?" my *muter* pleaded with my *foter*. An old man stepped forward from the darkness of the others, his face long since showing lines of worry—worry so deep that their groves appeared as snakes on his face in the shadows. "Your life is here now, on the run. Do not think of the past or material goods as something that you have. You have never had anything but the gift of God." The old man spoke with such confidence and absolution in his tone. He seemed to be the leader of our Shulkhan Arukh, our Rabbi.

My *muter* blinked, staggered from the man's comment. Understanding came into her features and she nodded. "Regardless, we still need food for the kids—I count lots of *kinder*; they won't be able to go far without food," she declared.

At the mention of food, my stomach began to rumble, my bowels twisting into knots of pain from the lack of nutrients, but mostly from the image of gore that I had witnessed in the town square. I wasn't sure if I would ever want to eat again after that.

My *foter* hesitated before speaking. "Hurry, then. Get what you can. Quick though—we still have to get my *bruder* before leaving here."

My *muter* turned from my *foter*. "He won't be coming with us," she stated, heading inside the shop.

My *foter* stood stunned, his face twisting into itself before he turned it back into stone. I wondered then what happened to my *feter*, but that thought was chased away quickly after what he had done to my *muter* and my *bruder*. I just felt anger toward my *feter*. Just because he was *mishpokhe*, didn't mean I couldn't hate him. If you can learn to love someone, same thing must be true for hating someone.

My *muter* came out a minute later, flushed and out of breath, carrying a large sack over her shoulders. My *foter* took the bag over his shoulder, pulling the loops tight. I wondered what she had packed in the bag, as my stomach was growling from the hunger. The old Rabbi beside me went back to the group of people, his white hair whipping like candle light in the darkness. I had never seen the man; he didn't go to our gathering, who was he?

I shook it away; more important things were going on and my *mishpokhe* would need me. My *foter* gestured for us to follow him, taking point at the front. "Keep low, everyone, and remember to be as quiet as possible. We must not be found," he said, hurrying ahead as the rest of us followed. I couldn't tell how many of us there were, but the whole way, I felt that our steps were too loud, too unsure in the darkness, too easy for us to be picked off by the gray soldiers.

We made it out of the city faster than I would have thought possible with our pace. My *foter* knew this city well—he knew every corner and every twist. As we left the city, I could hear more gunshots in the distance, screams echoing out into the darkness. One long scream after another in the longest terror of my life.

Our pace continued to be fast as we crossed into the countryside. We all stayed low, going as fast as we could, pressing on like mad beasts in the woods. The night dragged on until early morning lights showed from somewhere ahead. I didn't know my face was pointed to the ground until I ran into Zevi, my nose jamming hard into his back from the impact. My first instinct was to push him. As I looked up, though, I could see how exhausted my *foter* looked, how beyond his wits' end he was. *Everyone must be*, I thought as I looked around the group of people. We were all at our end. "We need to keep moving, everyone—we haven't put enough distance between us and the city," my *foter* said through puffs of breath, his air showing in the cold morning mist. It was the first signs of fall approaching, with our breath turning into ice and the leaves of the trees becoming yellow and gold.

"We need to stop; look around you, young man. The rest can't keep up," the old Rabbi heaved, his voice crackling from the cold and something else. It was as if it was wood popping in a fire. I looked at him. For an old man, he was bigger than my *foter*, his shoulders broad and his chest long.

The old Rabbi and my *foter* talked, as they conversed, the rest of the group slowly collapsed to the ground. My *foter* looked around, concern on his face, and he reached into his pocket, pulling free a handkerchief. "My *mishpokhe* is all I have, elder. I would do anything to protect my *mishpokhe*. Therefore, I will get us to safety, no matter what the cost," my *foter* said sternly.

Calmly, the old Rabbi spoke, as if testing the words he was going to say before speaking them. "I understand that. You wish to protect your *mishpokhe*. I assure you that you're doing the best thing, as I told you yesterday. These monsters are everywhere, in every city and every farm. I've been on the run from them for weeks. If you do not help those around you, your *mishpokhe* will be as good as dead. Survival is much higher when there are more of us," the old Rabbi said.

He stepped toward my *foter*, placing his right hand on my *foter's* shoulder. "Like it or not, we are all in this together, and you're leading us now. A good leader needs to know when to push his people and when to let his people rest: that takes real talent." His voice popped like wood on a fire again. He walked past my *foter* to a log that had fallen over and squatted down on it.

I looked at him as my *muter* took pieces of bread and cheese from the bag on my *foter's* shoulder, gently pulling it from him as his shoulder sagged from the weight. *That had to be heavy,* I thought, *heavier than myself. My foter is a hero; he is an amazing man that cannot be stopped.* My *foter* leaned up against a tree as more food was produced. Without having to speak, we all took turns gathering pieces of food that we had collectively brought together. I greedily wolfed my bread and cheese down. It was the longest I had ever gone without food in my entire life.

Foter looked at me with a tired smile before speaking. "Too fatigued to walk, but not enough to eat food, huh my *zun*?"

I looked at him, feeling shy as I looked around at the others in the group. They all looked as hungry, but none of them were eating as the food was passed around. The collection made its way to the old Rabbi, who only took a slice of bread, and finally my *foter* was handed food. He took a modest amount. I could see his eyes grow big with worry as he looked at my *muter* handing him the bread. "We have to make this last, dear—we don't know how much food we can find from here and at *zayde's* house."

"Just eat dear and rest. We will figure out the rest later," my *muter* said, smiling at my *foter*. My *foter* grumbled before relenting and finally taking a bite. I bowed my head at that moment, suddenly thankful for my chance to have what little bit of food we possessed. I ate much slower when I opened my eyes, looking at the faces all around us. The old man on the log stared at me as I ate, his eyes never leaving me; *gray like the wind*, I thought as I finished my bread and cheese.

My *foter* caught my gaze, following it to the old man. He sighed wearily, "Don't stare, my *zun*, it is very rude." I flushed in embarrassment, as my curiosity had got the better of me. "I would think after everything you've seen, everything that has happened, you would be as worn out as the rest of us are. You were always a curious one, though," he said, finishing the last remaining bites of his bread, a dejected expression overriding any indications of enjoyment. "Go on, I know what you want to ask me, son. You can," he stated.

"Well—I am just curious who he is. I've never seen him in the shop before. I don't think he is from here," I responded.

"Not everyone can afford a watch, *zun*. You're correct, though, he is not from here," my *foter* said, turning away from me to address the rest of the group. "Everyone, get some rest. We will each take a shift of watching for an hour. Rest, eat, relax. Just do not make fires. We don't know how far away we are from the town."

Some responded, but most had already fallen asleep. My *foter* turned his head back to me and told me, "Go to bed, my *zun*. Leave the man alone," before he walked back to where my *muter* lay next to a log. Zevi was pulled tight against her, his face hidden. I could hear his snores and I fought back a giggle. He could saw logs with how loud he was. Out here in the openness of the woods, though, it was a welcoming sound.

I put my head against the tree my *foter* had been on, the sun's light just starting to appear over the horizon. I felt tired—beyond tired, unable to even understand what it was like to feel this way.

My eyes narrowed and the sun wheeled overhead—it was still cold. Still so very cold, though inside I could feel something warm. Something angry, something that shouldn't have been there in a small eight-year-old's body. And the more I thought about it, the more I delved into the confines of my mind. I could hear the cracking gunshots of the previous morning, the smell of black powder and death. Above all, though, I could feel heat rising from somewhere inside, like I was sitting too close to the fireplace at home.

Panicking, I opened my eyes. The sun was still rising above the tree line. It hadn't been that long since I had drifted off. It felt like I had been lying there for a thousand years. I looked up; the old man sat with his legs crossed on the same log as before, his ashy gray eyes pinned on me. His eyes were the color of charred boards, the color of an old sea. They were full of fire—they were staring at me.

6

Chapter 6

"Wake up, Avraham, wake up," my *muter* urged, shaking my shoulder, her voice only slightly above a bird chirping from somewhere nearby. I rolled over, ignoring her, my back feeling the heat from the sun. "Avraham, wake up," she said again.

This time I responded to her. "Just a few more minutes, *muter*."

"We can't wait any longer, boy, we are leaving this place," she urged again, pulling on my shoulders once more.

Place, I thought, tasting the word inside my mind. That is right—I wasn't in my bed. My *muter* wasn't waking me for school. My *bruder* wasn't taking up most of his side of the bed. Instead, I was sleeping in the woods, like a frightened animal. I turned my head to my *muter*, her face ashen and sunken from her sleep in the woods. She appeared to be much older—as if she had aged a hundred years while we slept. Crows feet were peeking at the corners of her eyes, with more gray than I remembered in her fine black hair.

She looked away from me, worry in her features. I realized at that moment that my *muter* would someday get old—a lot older. Which was something that a young boy never thought about. A part of me just always assumed that she would stay that happy woman who made me honey bread and kissed my forehead at night. Parents didn't get old; they didn't die. Then again, those people in the town square... they were all somebody's parents, somebody's *muters* and *foters*, *bruders* and *shvesters*. I shook the images out of my head, looking at my *muter* again. Seeing her like this—that made the fire in my belly rumble again. It just kept rumbling like an animal clawing its way out.

My *muter* gave me one last long look before stepping away. I stood up, stretching, my body feeling like it had been pulled like a piece of gum.

"You really should hurry it up," Zevi said from behind me. He was kneeling, hunched on his heels nearby. A stick in his hand that he jabbed into the ground. On his face was the tattered remains of a potato sack my *muter* had once made into a mask for him. It was slightly too big for his head, hanging lopsided around his ears. On the bag was a charcoaled smile. That smile always bothered me and gave me the chills. My *muter* had told me once to leave him alone about the mask, though. It comforted him and he would always wear it whenever he was scared. "We are all packing up to leave. Don't slow us down, *bruder*," he stated, jabbing his stick back into the ground.

My *bruder* had always been a quiet boy. I had spent too much time picking on him, teasing him about his weight and curly red hair. He looked like none of us in the *mishpokhe*, save for my *feter* with a round face and red hair. The rest of us were tall and lean, dark of hair and hooked noses peering down at the world. I felt bad for having done that. I felt bad for my *feter* hitting him like he had done. "You know—try to angle the stick more; it will go in the mud deeper," I said, gesturing with my hands in the motion of poking the ground.

"Just like you, Avraham, always thinking you're so much smarter and better than everyone else," he growled, hitting the ground harder with his stick.

I looked at Zevi, feeling anger flood inside me. I was just trying to be nice to him for a change. Where did he get off trying to talk to me in such a way? I was about to snarl back when my *foter* came up to our log. "Are you two boys ready to go?" he asked, bending down, taking the stick from my *bruder's* hand. He pulled me next to Zevi and took the sack from his head. My *bruders'* eyes still showed puffy and red. He had been crying. I felt even worse, my anger for him not accepting my help depleting fast. My *bruder* had to be twice as scared as I was. I really should have let him hit more balls when we played together. Maybe then he wouldn't have needed that odd sack of his.

"I need you two to promise me something before we start our journey. Look after your *muter* if anything should happen to me—okay, care for her as you would each other. And if anything is to go wrong, keep on running and don't stop for anything, unless it is each other," my *foter* stated, standing up. His knees popped, his eyes were the deepest of us all.

Both Zevi and I remained quiet.

"Answer me," he said sternly.

"Yes *foter*," we both replied in unison.

Foter nodded. "Good. Now go find your *muter* and help her pack. We are leaving in five minutes," he stated, moving past us to a group of people huddled by a tree nearby.

As Zevi passed me, he bumped into my shoulder. I almost responded by hitting him back, if the old man with the ashy eyes hadn't been watching me. His eyes followed my movements like smoke to a flame. I pulled my *bruder's* shoulders, ignoring the old Rabbi's gaze, Zevi stopped, snapping his head toward me. "Let go of me, Avraham," he warned.

"Zevi, do you remember that time that we were running in the woods at *zayde's* house? How we got lost?" I asked my *bruder*, hoping to bridge some common ground back to him.

His back was still turned to me, but I could see a small smile creep along his face. "Yeah, we were lost for days in the woods, trying to find rocks for our dam."

I laughed. "Yes, and then we went off into the countryside, ignoring what *zayde* said. Then it started to rain and we both cried our eyes out, trying to find our way home. We were so lost and thought we would never get food ever again."

Zevi laughed. "You were the one that cried. Not me, Avraham, I'm brave."

I nodded in agreement, not wanting to upset Zevi again. "When we were finally found by *zayde* on the second night, after spending it trapped under that log, he was so mad. He yelled at us the whole way until we made it back to *bubbe's*."

"Yeah, but she made us lemon cake," he said, savoring the tasty treat.

At "cake," my own mouth started to water. I pressed on. "Do you remember what *zayde* told us on the way back, about if we ever came across a beast?" I asked my younger *bruder*.

He paused, searching for the answer. "That we shouldn't be afraid of the beasts. Even if they're about to devour us, we are to plant are feet. And if we are to be eaten, then we shove our hands in its mouth—not that the beast won't be able to swallow with hands on its tongue, but then the beast will know that we aren't afraid to meet our death."

"Exactly, my *akhi*, exactly. I think we need to remember *zayde's* words. There's no reason to be afraid," I assured him, clasping his shoulder. I smiled at my *bruder*, but in that instance, there was a moment that I had never seen from him, even when the two of us were trapped in the dark pouring rain on a long night, many years ago. I saw something different from him. He wasn't afraid; he was angry, and he had hate his eyes.

He shook my hands away from his shoulders once more. "I'm not afraid, Avraham. I'm the brave one; you aren't," he sneered, putting his sack on, his green eyes gleaming through the holes. My *bruder* looked nothing like me—in that moment he didn't even act like my *bruder*. I let my hands fall to my side, defeated and flabbergasted by what my *bruder* had told me.

I shivered—frightened almost, when the old Rabbi met my gaze, his eyes tracking mine as I watched my *bruder* walk away. That got me moving. I kept a distance from my *bruder*, though. Something was off about him. My own anger was taunted into submission for now by the old man's eyes. I wondered why he kept looking at me—I soon became distracted from those thoughts as the group started moving.

We made our way out of the forest. It was close to night—*foter* said around 6 pm and in the distance, I could see the sky darkening behind us. The temperature began to drop as we walked. Sticks cracked under our heavy and slow footsteps. Light coughs matched the footfalls and groans escaping from the old and the young—we were fatigued, we were dying.

Our steps echoed in the dark as the sun gave way to night, the night giving way to the freezing cold of our country's climate. We took no breaks as we walked closer and closer to my grandparents' home. People moaned in the line, and the old fell behind, but still my *foter* drove us on. A small song broke out at one point amongst the group—singing to the angels to come and save us.

I thought about it. The angels couldn't like the cold any more than we did, and that must have been why they weren't showing up. That had to be the reason for why, otherwise I just didn't understand why we were marching in the cold so far away from our homes. Surely by now whoever those men in the gray were, they had picked up and moved on. We wouldn't be on their minds.

Whenever we came near a road, my *foter* would have us wait inside the tree line, wary of any vehicles that might have been approaching the roads. We never saw any, though. We never saw the soldiers in gray. That was something I felt relieved about. Some amongst us whispered that they had been kicked back by our own army.

To this, my *foter* said, "We will know soon enough. Let's be quiet for the remainder of our journey. It is only a few more hours and there are too many roads here."

As we moved on, the group's movements grew slower. Our only light was the moon from above. We had all formed a line, holding on the person in front of us, with my *foter* at the very front.

It wasn't until a kid fell from the line that my *foter* finally stopped. People shouted for him at the front. "We have to be quiet," he hissed back.

"We need to keep moving is what we need to do," the old Rabbi with gray eyes replied, somewhere from inside the line. I knew that he was probably gazing at me from somewhere in the group, his eyes a dull shine.

"No, we need to stop—we've been walking for hours. We need food and rest," stated someone. It was hard to tell who was saying what in the line, as we were a mass herd of animals fleeing for our lives—no longer people, just animals.

"Yeah!" echoed back others in the group.

"It's not much further. We are almost there," my *foter* said reassuringly, his voice straining to remain low as voices around us started to complain.

"You've been saying that for hours!" a woman shouted.

Cheers of "yeahs" went up around me. My ears started to hurt from the noise and I feared we were being too loud, like my *foter* had warrned. I cupped my ears from their noise and went to the ground. I just wanted the loud noise to stop. I wanted so bad for everyone to stop yelling, for their voices to go away. For everything to just go away and leave me alone in this place, in this field, so that I would never have to hear the sounds of voices or the sounds of screams.

I felt tears running down my cheeks, their wet trails pulling the mud that was coating my face down. I could taste it as I sat hunched in the field, adults all around me becoming louder and louder.

Too loud, too loud. All of this is too loud, we need to be quiet—we need to be quiet, I thought in vain as the adults continued to shout. I saw something move quickly between the gaps in my fingers. I looked up, and coming from the tree line on the other side of the road came the gray soldiers. Charging from the woods—like a flock of angry gray pigeons swarming after a morsel of food scattered on the ground. I knew, then, that we were the morsels of food—we were going to be devoured by the birds.

I shook—the whole world exploding around me as vehicles came pouring out of the woods like water running off leaves, plows on the front, painted crimson from their victims. In the center mass of one plow, I could see a man. He was tall of stature, short red hair, and he looked almost like my *foter*, only a rounder chin and less gray. It was my *feter*; chained to the front of the plow, naked as the day he was born. His body was riddled with small cuts, crossing his body in every direction. Agony—a feeling of life that every man and woman will experience in their life. Only I did not think anyone could ever understand the amount of agony that my *feter* had on his face—his agony was something that no person should ever understand.

I froze, my mind screaming for me to move from this rolling hell tearing its way toward me. Shots rang overhead, but I remained in place. Fear glued me to the ground. Strong hands lifted me, taking me into the air. My face stayed on my *feter*—the truck with the plow holding him getting closer.

"Get to the woods and run!" my *foter* yelled as he continued to carry me from the danger coming for us.

My gaze stayed on my *feter*—his body racked in pain as the truck plowed forward at an endless pace, determined to catch us. Above, the bullets were so numerous, that in the dark sky they appeared as swarms of bats flying in the air.

One of the bats came close to my *foter* and I, the heat from the bullet burned at the tips of my hair as it flew somewhere ahead of us, hitting a man fleeing for his life. It was luck—or intervention. We should have been killed twice over as we hit the tree line. I could feel my *foter* start to slow down, the strain of carrying my dead weight in his arms for so long taking its toll on him.

"*Foter*," I whispered as a bullet ripped into his legs. He grunted, staggered a step, and dropped me to the ground below. I landed hard in the mud, tasting blood in my mouth as my *foter* let out a contained scream. He fought hard not to yell out.

"*Foter*, come on," I pled with the old man, as fire erupted around me, a mix of gunpowder and screams.

In the dark light, my *foter* said to me, "Stay calm, my *zun*, we will rise soon enough." He smiled before his chest convulsed forward, his body shook, and he fell into the mud of the wooded area.

My mouth opened, but nothing came out. No sounds, no words for the bravest man I had ever known, now bleeding out before me. I could see the small holes in his back. Now smeared in gore and blood. If he was dead, I couldn't tell. I didn't want to find out the ending to my *foter*. It wasn't like a book or a story I had read in bed. It was a painful horror that I couldn't just pretend that my favorite character was in peril. I couldn't just skip to the part where they magically woke up. My *foter* wasn't getting back up.

I placed my hands on his back, I felt him pull away—croaking like the frogs outside my *zayde's* lake, their throats almost choking on something vile. "Get up, *foter*," I implored, hesitant to touch him again.

He coughed, spitting blood on the ground below, turning his head up to me. His glasses were broken, shattered within their frames. "Go, my *zun*. This isn't the end of your tale today," he wheezed, pushing his hand into my shoulder. He collapsed after that into the dirt below. I could still see his chest heaving in and out as my body turned on its own and started running.

My *foter* had always told me before bed, when I was a child, that my tale wasn't ending. I think he meant it as a way of telling me to not fear falling asleep. I always had dreams of wolves and fire at night. When I woke, my *foter* would tell me that I had nothing to fear from anything for it was not the end of my tale.

I faced my head forward, tears trailing down my face. "Yes, my *foter*, today is not the end of my tale." The words fell out as I sprinted forward, outrunning their pitch, outrunning the other members of my fleeing group, outrunning the devils in gray, outrunning hell itself as it unfolded all around me. Fear was the linchpin to my movement. Soon I was out of the woods and running forward, the woods giving way to another open field. I had no idea where I was running, with just the sounds behind me propelling me forward.

For *foter's* sake, I was not going to let my tale end. I wasn't going to let my tale end today. I ran further then I had ever thought was possible, until my chest felt as though I was a ball being hit by my *bruder's* bat. I ran until the fields disappeared altogether, until the trees returned.

The ground and the woods blurred turning into images of gray and green in the night sky. My legs carried me long past the point of when my tears ceased, long past the salt that stung my eyes as I ran. By the time I finally stopped, bent over vomiting, my shirt and pants were drenched in sweat.

I wiped my mouth, feeling nauseous from the smell, my heart beating out of control like a rabbit running from the dogs—they way my *foter* and I hunted sometimes during the summers. I placed my hands on the nearest tree, trying to steady myself, not trusting my body to hold itself up without support. When my breath came back, my heart stopped beating as fast. The image of my *foter* still played in my head, his words haunting me to keep me moving forward.

I started to step forward, but my feet gave out and I collapsed into my own vomit. I coughed, fighting to keep my own fluids from getting in as well as from more from leaving me. The smell was causing me to lose all the fight that was building in me from my *foter's* probable death.

Not even my *foter*, with all his strength, could have survived that. But what of my *muter* and *bruder*? I had forgotten them once again. I had forgotten my charges, in my selfishness to save myself.

Worse than the vomit, that made me want to throw up more. My heart started picking up again. I could hear its beat, but it was rhythmic, slow, and loud. Like the splintering of trees, like heavy wheels rolling through the woods. That wasn't my heart it was coming from around me.

I listened. I could hear voices not too far off from me. It was in that language of the soldiers; it was also the language of my people. They were near, near to me. I looked around. I could hide where I was. They would go right past me—probably would never find me. I could find my way to *zayde's* home. I could find my way there and find him. Bring him back and stop all these vile men.

That wasn't true, though. I could find my way through these woods, after all, even as far as I had run, I knew these woods. What would *foter* think, though? What would he think if I ran now? I had already let him down by abandoning both *muter* and my *bruder*. I had left them to die.

I am a coward, I am no better than the monsters that had invaded my town, I thought. I had to rescue my *bruder*; I had to rescue all of them. My *muter* always told me I was her wild one. I had more fire in me than I had boy. It was time to go live up to her words, I thought. I picked myself up, brushing the vomit and forest debris to the ground.

My belt had loosened in the last couple of days. I tightened it, bending down to secure the laces on my shoes. Their soles were worn almost all the way off—one shoe was pretty much gone. I took off both. thinking of all the times that my *bruder* and I had snuck around our room at night.

We were much deadlier and quieter without our shoes on. Plus I was the neighborhood champion of running. I ran faster with nothing on my feet.

In the darkness, I searched for a branch. My hands found one thicker than my arm. I gave it a practice swing. Satisfied with the girth, I put the branch forward as I made my way in the darkness, following the sounds of their vehicles.

I traveled in the direction of the sounds until I could see their lights shining a path through the dense woods. I stopped once I could see the trucks. Men were spread all around them as they rolled forward. The lights made the shadows of the men appear immense in the darkness, like massive sharks hiding underneath the swells.

I looked at my branch, suddenly feeling like an infant in the face of their machines. I gulped. I could maybe get in one swing before I was overtaken, but there were just too many of them. And unlike in the books I read before bed—bullets wouldn't bounce off me.

An idea shot into my head, galvanizing my heart for what I would need to do. The heroes in the books I read as a child didn't always use their muscles to stop the bad guys—they used their heads. If a man in underwear could fight off criminals with guns, a kid with a big stick could certainly take them on.

Fire erupted in my belly again. I hated everything that these monsters had done to my *mishpokhe*, what they had done to my town. What I hated the most was the fear that they were causing me. I hate bullies, and I hate people who try and tell me what to do. Most of all, I hated feeling like I couldn't do anything against them.

I curled the branch tighter; I would show them what happened when you messed with Avraham Firwoolf. I waited in the brush, hidden from their lights and from their trucks as they slowly moved by. I counted twelve vehicles, all different shapes and sizes. I even spotted the one that had held my *feter*. He was no longer on the front of the plow, but its blade was coated in something violet.

The memory of my *feter* suffering on the front of the plow caused my eyes to sting—after a certain point, tears just can't come out. *That's right,*

I thought, *it is time to stop crying and start doing for your feter and your foter.*

At the end of the line walked two soldiers. Both had rifles, but it was the truck they were guarding that concerned me the most though. In the back, I could see men and woman—most importantly, the old Rabbi with the gray eyes. Even in the darkness I could still see those steel-colored eyes.

"It's them," I whispered, creeping from my hiding place as the line of trucks and men continued their path through the woods. I made sure to keep out of the sight of their lights as I followed behind the men, always just out of their eyesight. They never became aware that I was following them. I was like a ghost in the shadows.

They continued to travel along in that line for what felt like hours. I was worried that the sun was going to come up before the men finally stopped. They stopped sooner, coming upon a railroad station out in the middle of a lonely field. Men walked back and in-between the various boxcars that were connected, all shouting in that gruff language and waving their hands in the air.

The trucks soon parked and the men rushed to the back of the last two trucks in line. They pulled down the tailgates, and using their guns, they pointed at the people in the back of them, gesturing for the people to exit. From the distance of the last remaining trees, I couldn't make out the faces of any of the people. I said a silent prayer for my *muter* and *bruder* as I made my way into the grass outside of the safety of the woods.

The grass turned out to be hay, its stalks long and coarse, cutting into me as I crawled my way toward the train. My movements were made quick by my small size, and I imagined if anyone was seeing me, they would think I was a cat or the wind. I made my way to the train by using the sound of the men, not daring to lift my head, or they would see me in an instant. The hay cut deep ridges into my hands as I crawled along on the ground, but still, I held onto my stick. The rocks tore into the tattered remains of my pants, while my stomach yearned for some of my *muter's* honey bread. Or any food, for that matter. I had never felt this famished and exhausted in my life. I kept crawling, though, knowing that my *foter* would have kept crawling. I could not stop until I freed my *mishpokhe.*

My path reached its end when my fingers found the metal railing of the train tracks, their thick wooden beams set deep in the ground. I rubbed my hands on their bare surfaces, glad to finally feel something other than the harshness of the hay beneath me. I looked ahead. I was only a few meters from the last boxcar. Anxiety started hitting me—what if I got to the trains and my *muter* and *bruder* were already...

I burned that thought out of my mind before it could take hold. If I thought about it any more, I would end up staying in the hay. I looked back at the woods I had come from. They weren't too far away. Perhaps I could make a run for it and I wouldn't have to crawl again.

The guilt, though, that would get me if the soldiers did not. My body shook from the fear of being so close to the soldiers. I started thinking of my *muter*, how she would bake for me and kiss me. The many games that Zevi and I played, so often ending in *foter* separating us. And lastly, I thought of my *foter*, always strict, but always kind. He wouldn't run away from anything.

I moved completely onto the railroad tracks, trying to keep low, as the sun began to rise behind me. On my neck, I could feel its early morning flares dancing heat across me, kissing me good morning and good luck on my task. The soldiers hadn't noticed me so far. Their backs were facing away from me.

The nearest group of three were all smoking and laughing. Their guns were thrown over their shoulders. Carrying my branch, I hid under the boxcar, pulling my body tight. From my angle, all I could see was their legs. In the distance, I could see one boxcar still open, a lone soldier shouting at the people inside the box. His rifle was out and pointed toward them. I crawled under the boxcars until I reached the soldier facing the open carriage. He was shouting, his voice spewing saliva as he yelled.

I glanced at the three soldiers at the end of the railcars, their backs to the lone soldier, still laughing and puffing on their tobacco. Slowly, I pulled myself out from under the railcar, my hands guiding my body along as I came out from under the car.

Once all the way out, I pulled the branch to my shoulders, twisting the wood until I was pointed toward the man in the stance my *foter* had taught me for when hitting a ball. Shoulders high, chin tucked, my eyes on the ball—in this case, my eyes on the man. I swung, just like in the many games we had played outside of my *foter's* store. Swung with everything I had. The branch connected.

The soldier doubled forward, his weight causing him to hit into the side of the boxcar. His reply was a fierce cry of pain. I swung again, this time at his legs to shut him up quickly. A popping sound erupted forth into the night when the branch connected with his knee. He fell to the ground, letting out a torrent of screams. I took the branch overhead and slammed the wood down on the man's head. The screaming stopped, turning into whimpering.

This only angered me. I swung again on the man's head. And again. Over and over, I repeatedly slammed the hunk of wood into the man's head. I felt something splatter my face, and all I could think of was what this monster had done to my *mishpokhe*. What he had done to me. I wanted nothing more than to keep hitting him. To keep punishing him for what he had done to me and my people. I wanted him to be unable to move, like the crowds of the dead in the square of my town. I wanted him dead, I wanted him to hurt. Time and time again, I continued to hit this man beneath me, feeling nothing but the splinters of the now-broken branch in my hand. My vision had blurred red. If it had not been for the gasps coming from the open boxcar, I don't know if I would have stopped.

The anger was coursing through me—that fire like a piece of dry timber in the middle of an inferno. Voices brought me back, voices brought me back from the blaze that was building inside of me.

"Get his keys," whispered the harsh voice of the gray-eyed old Rabbi. His tone took me more than a few deep breaths to register as an actual voice. I looked at him, confused and perplexed about where I was. This wasn't supposed to happen. Had I killed a man? A weight gave way in my stomach and I felt vomit shoot its way from my mouth. I heaved through the stinging tears. I had committed the worst sin: I had killed a man.

"Hurry, boy!" urged the Rabbi.

"Right—one second," I lamented, feeling regret for my actions. *I had just killed a man in cold blood. I had just committed the worst crime,* I repeated to myself. I shook with fear as I dropped the remains of the branch, feeling around on the man without looking, my eyes cast far away.

"On his belt, hurry!" The old man pointed. I felt my fingers tighten on metal rings, and I unlatched them and started to stand. I felt the hot whack of something on the back of my head. My fingers could no longer hold on to the keys. My legs gave out and I fell on the man I had just killed. Everything faded to black. Everything...

7

Chapter 7

Frosty stinging shocked my cheeks. Each jolt happened in sequence, causing my body to shake. My body felt as though I had been dragged and beaten, as though I had been wounded beyond repair. *That is true, though—I don't think I am my* elterns' zun *anymore, I don't think I am God's child anymore.* I could hear a fluid sound coming from somewhere nearby. Was it me? Was my head bursting open like a too-hot pie that had been left inside my *muter's* oven?

Panicking, I tried to sit up, only to be held down by an unknown force. "Be still, Avraham, save your strength," cooed my *muter*, like a bird would her *kinder*. In this case—like a *muter* would her own *kinder*.

Hot tears started flooding down my cheeks, a stark contrast to the otherwise frozen surface of my face. "*Muter*," I whimpered, turning into her hands. She pulled me into her bosom as I reached up, taking hold of her in my arms. She held me tight as I cried. I had never cried that hard in my life. Not even when I had dropped one of my *zayde's* hammers on my toes. Tears are a funny thing. I would never have liked to be seen with tears in my eyes. But when the water finally started to flow, it didn't matter who was watching. Some pains just go beyond the care of any and you couldn't keep them in any longer.

My *muter* was the only exception in the world whom I would allow to see me cry. If Zevi had seen me now, he would have laughed. Mocking me as *bruders* do.

"It's okay, Avraham, I am here for you. I am here for you always," *muter* said quietly.

"Don't spend your time crying. It will bring nothing to you besides lamented pain, over and over again," *foter* replied.

I started at my *foter's* voice, pulling away from my *muter*, along with the cloth that had covered my face. With the cloth gone, my eyes adjusted to the darkness. I was in a small railroad car, the sides held in place by flimsy planks of wood. Slits on the side provided little light and highlighted pitiful faces. The faces of the group I had been traveling with. Their features were masked by sadness, dirt, and blood. Animals by any other name—not people. No, people weren't supposed to look like they were about to be slaughtered. We were animals. On my *muter's* face was the same look: feeble and defeated.

My eyes began to sting again as flakes of ice drifted through the wooden slits, melting from the heat on my red cheeks. I sniffled from the cold, turning my head in the direction from which my *foter* had spoken, puzzled if it had really been him or if it had been inside my mind.

Near the end of the tight compartment was a body stretched on the ground below, the form indescribable inside the darkness. I moved closer, through the compact group of people, the air becoming hotter as the tight space pressed all around me. Like the people were made of water inside of a balloon waiting to pop. Hands and legs moved to let me pass, my short height making it easier to move amongst the adults.

I found my *foter*, huddled on the ground with many coats covering all but his face. The adults around us all stood in what they hadn't placed on top of my *foter*. Across his forehead was a wet cloth placed tight against his hairline. Gray stretched like a morning fog on his face, his cheeks hung low—the skin loosening before me as I watched the life slowly leave my *foter*.

When I was younger, my *foter* had bought both my *bruder* and me a bicycle. I had struggled with the balance, the pedals always seeming to spin to fast. *Foter* had told me that balance would come with time, that once I figured it out, a part of me would just know. A part of me would just become aware of what I would need to accomplish it.

He was right, my *foter*; at some point during my many attempts to find balance on the metal frame of spokes and wheels, I found balance. Now surrounded by a wooden prison, amidst strangers, I found balance in knowing that my *foter* was going to die. The shot he had taken to his chest had been brutal, it had been mutilating and visceral, but a final end to my *foter's* fears.

Tears didn't slide down my cheeks as I knelt down next to my *foter*. He reached a hand up to my face, taking it in his. "My *zun*, it's good to see you," he drawled before falling asleep. His hand fell, and a dull thump echoed inside the railroad car.

I stayed with my *foter* for hours after that, as the night gave way to a longer day. The train we were in never slowed down. We could only catch flashes of green and yellow through the wooden slats. Sometimes, we would see orange, followed by a thick plume of black smoke, which would drift into the car.

The air tasted on fire as the day went on. There was no room to lie down, with my *foter* spread in the middle. What little food any of us had was passed around, water being the one notified absence that seemed as if it was a death warrant. Soon, people pulled down their pants or dresses, spewing their bowels in a rush of relief and shame.

The smell caused many to throw up as the train continued through the day. At the first signs of darkness, I found myself separated from my *mishpokhe* at the farthest corner away from them. My body shook with the rhythm of the train, shaking with the shallow gasps of my *foter*.

"It was your *feter* who had revealed our direction to the soldiers. Though, if it had not been your *feter*, I suspect we would have been found anyways. All the noise that we were making wasn't hiding any of us," the gray-eyed Rabbi disclosed. He was in the corner, crouched with his legs folded in tightly, closest to the "bathroom." The stench caused me to place my shirt over my nose.

"How do you know that, old man—when I am his blood? Blood does not betray each other, no matter what the circumstances may be," I objected back to the old Rabbi.

His gray eyes flashed my way, peering at me as if he was reading a book with the tiniest of letters. "Perhaps, perhaps not. Either way, in this case, he did betray your *foter* and especially you, little boy. I suspect that blood may turn out of love, or the breaking of love," he said, before coughing into his hands. It rang over the rumble of the train.

I shot back, "What does an old man know anyways? He is just some old man covered in piss and shit!" I snarled at the man, coming to my feet.

Bemused, the old man cackled as a fit of coughing spewed from his mouth. "*Zun*—I was dying before I was placed inside this train like a lamb to the slaughter. I was dying the moment that I was born—the moment that my *foter* was born, the moment that his *foter* was born and so on. We all die, covered in shit, or covered in dirt. The only difference is one of them feels warmer than the other," he declared.

Confused, I looked at the old man, his words nebulous to me. "You are crazy, old man—stay away from me," I stated.

"If you think that I am so crazy, why do you not run away from me? Why not attack me with the same rage that you used when you killed that soldier?" he asked, his voice still in the darkness. Despite the car being filled like fish in a barrel, many of the passengers had drifted off into a confined sleep. I was trapped with nowhere to run, even if I wanted to.

"I have nowhere to go," I sighed, putting my head between my legs.

"That makes two of us—or, as my count goes, forty-three. Forty-three souls all squeezed into a railroad car." He said this almost as a joke that one would tell at dinner.

I looked up at the old man, his face passive and as blank as a carved piece of stone. Throughout the last couple of days, it had been his eyes that I always found watching me, his voice that always jested me, almost at every turn. "Who are you, old man?" I asked.

He remained silent for a time. I almost asked him again, before he spoke, "I am a dead man—that is who you see before you. One of many in the forty-three." He explained this like my *muter* did when she went over my *bruder's* and my writing lessons.

"No one is going to die here," I shot back, but that I could not promise to myself. Through the slats, I looked at the moon high above the train, its silver rays casting light into our tomb, like some kind of vengeful god watching its sacrifice.

"You don't believe that—I can tell by the sound of your voice that you know we will all die soon. Just like you know your kin betrayed all of us," he interjected.

The old man was right. Even as the words left my mouth, I had doubted them. If you can't lie to yourself, what good is your lie when it comes to other people? I remained silent, picking my words slowly before I spoke to the old man. "Why do you keep saying my *feter* betrayed us? How do you even know this?" I queried, trying to confirm the facts.

"Before you came to, your *feter* was presented in front of all of us. He was broken and bowed. The soldiers had turned him into the lowest form of a man that I had ever seen, or perhaps it was his true form. Either way, he admitted to betraying everyone, under the pain of physical torture. Maybe even emotional. I think that realization hurt your *foter* worse than the actual shot he received." The old Rabbi paused, pointing his silver gaze in my direction.

His words caused a mix of emotion within me—I was struggling to keep up with the world around me. At a certain point, your tears dry and when they dry, there is nothing more to do but to face the reality of the situation. It was possible that my *feter* had betrayed us, in return: we were all doomed. I sunk deeper into the railcar, trying with all my willpower to become part of the wooden frame. The wood was no more than a few hands thick, laid on top of flimsy metal, from what I had seen. A few pieces of wood and metal were all that was keeping me here—the animals on my *zayde's* farm all must have felt this way. To be trapped by so little, yet so much.

"If what you're saying is true—what does it matter now? We are all about to be led off to our deaths. At least with bullets, it will be quick," I muttered, looking out the slit of the railcar as the wilderness outside flew by in a blur of gray in the dark night. "What do you do when blood betrays blood?" I asked the old man.

The old Rabbi dug his eyes into me—their power unquestionable. It was like staring at your reflection in the mirror, your eyes might recognize that it is you staring, but the person on the other side is still a stranger. "Tell me, boy—does the man that you murdered earlier haunt you? Do you feel his death on your hands, stained and engraved like the deepest of grooves in a tree?" he asked, his tone direct and startling in the night.

His questions struck instantly. I wasn't sure why I hadn't thought about what I had done to that man, the weight of killing someone who had harmed so many. He had deserved it, hadn't he? He had killed so many. But—what if he had not killed anyone? What if he was only in the background? Not everyone could be that evil.

I begged my mind to come up with an image of him harming one of the citizens of my city. I dredged the darkest corners of the events. No matter the twist, no matter the turn, I could not find any time that man had killed anyone. I had killed him in cold blood. I had killed him. It had been to rescue my *mishpokhe*. Most likely, he had a *mishpokhe* of his own, though, his own *bruder* and his own *muter*.

I would have thrown up again, had I eaten anything. My stomach had never felt so stretched before in my life. Its growls bordered on the edges of hurting me. "I can tell by the look in your eyes that was your first man. It pains you. That is a good thing: you don't enjoy killing," he stated.

I looked up, perplexed by his statement. "Why—yes it was my first time killing someone. God forgive me," I cried into my hands, placing my head down.

"Dry your tears, boy. Our *Foter* has forsaken us this day, and I suspect for many more days still," he stated, taking my hands away so that my head fell. I tilted my head back toward his, his head shaking in disapproval.

"Have you killed many people?" I asked, suddenly feeling isolated in the rear compartment.

"Yes," he answered.

Silence stretched out between us, the air warm from the compressed feel of the railroad car. I was surprised no one else had tuned into our conversation by now. A woman and a man lay huddled together in the cold night air, one of their elbows jamming into the side of my leg. Otherwise, we were our own little island in a sea of people.

When spaces are that tight, it's hard to feel alone and sad within your thoughts. Even if I wanted to, I couldn't break down the way I wanted too. That was a blessing at least. Even though we were so close, it prevented me from breaking at the worst of times. I looked at the old man, and his face was vacant of any emotion. "Maybe we are both being punished for being killers," I stated.

"Not everyone in this carriage is a killer. Not everyone who put us in this train is a killer. All are capable of it. Tell me, boy, have you learned of Cain and Abel?" The old man positioned his body so that we were both at eye level.

I shook my head. "No," I muttered, confused what this had to do with our conversation.

The old man peered through slit outside the train, his gaze miles away, as if searching for words from cross an ocean of letters. "You see—the first murder by man was committed by a *bruder* unto another *bruder*. The first time man had taken the flesh of one of our own, spilling their blood into the ground from which we carry our hearts and souls," he said, turning his eyes back to me, their smoky gray coming alive in that instant.

His words didn't cause me to shrink away, which surprised me. I wasn't afraid of the dark like my *bruder*, since my parents had never told us stories about people dying, about murder. But then again, my parents never told me to kill someone either.

He continued, "There are many different versions of this tale. Ones that deal with wives, with lambs and sacrifices. But all of them come back to that same road made of the vital fluid pumping so quickly through your body—even now, boy."

When he said "blood," my heart began to thump, to crash against the bones in my chest like the metal wheels on the tracks below. I pulled my knees close to my chest as the old man continued to talk.

"Whichever version of the story you choose to believe is not important—what is important is the message: blood, or divine reasons, we all kill for what we want. We all can do horrible, horrible things. Look around you in this train, the whispers of sleep barely taking hold of the group. I promise you though, if this train were to stop, if this train were to give us permanent freedom right now—there isn't a man, woman or child who wouldn't fight tooth and nail for what is most important," he grimaced.

"What is most important?" I quavered, the words coming from my all-too-small mouth.

"Your life, boy!" he spat, his gray eyes lit like the moon.

"Believe me when I say this, believe me when I give you these words. Your *feter* brought us all to this demise. We are all going to die, we are all going eat at the table of blood, dining in hell. That is what happens to those that are led to the slaughter," he shot back, venom spewing from his mouth.

I crawled back as far as I could go, pushing myself into the lap of a sleeping man nearby. With a surprising speed that I wouldn't have thought possible, the old Rabbi took hold of my hands. "Hear me boy when I say this: if you want to live through the night—if you want to live, you must listen," he pleaded. "The beast is coming. So much hate in this world has to find a home—he is coming to you tonight, and he will devour you if you let it. Man can create any monster if they hate enough!"

My hands shook in his talon-like grasp. "What am I supposed to be listening to?" I hesitantly asked the man, trying my best to keep the tears out of my voice.

"Let go of my *zun*, or the soldiers will be the least of your concerns tonight," my *muter* said calmly. Behind her stood half the train of people, now awake, the fire in their eyes matching the sparks flying from the metal on metal below.

The old Rabbi looked at me, his silver eyes almost pleading with a desperation, a fleeing fear, which was hidden by the time he turned his head to the gathered group of people. The inside of the train was warm and unpleasant, the smell causing me to choke on the very air. He turned away, facing the corner of the train, muttering, "Say your goodbyes while you can. Say them..."

The uneasiness of the train increased tenfold, like blankets my *muter* would place on me during winter, smothering me into a hot sweat during the coldest of nights. So many, in fact, that it was too hot to breathe, the weight causing me to suffocate.

After the old man's scene, the train went back to silence. No one was sleeping anymore, just coughs and low moans in the hot air.

The train braked, shuddering as its rails came to a grinding halt during the fall of a cold winter.

"Say your goodbyes to the day, *zun*—you will never see them the same way again."

8

Chapter 8

Huey took a long drag from his cigarette. True to his word, he had remained silent while I told him my story. We were inside the men's bathroom, to the best of our guess somewhere between twenty and twenty-five miles from the prison. Not nearly enough distance. We had to make do. Huey had dragged and helped me for about a half a mile across the desert in the middle of the night. Despite being completely naked with a man who had transformed into a monster and eaten an unknown amount of people, he remained surprisingly calm, all things considering.

We broke into the local repair shop, found two pairs of worn-down jumpsuits, and proceeded to change our appearance as quickly as possible. A few hacks later with a knife we found in the shop, minus a few curse words from the two of us trying to cut each other's hair, and we were both now more or less clean shaven.

Huey sat rubbing his head, with his cigarette never ending in his mouth. Somehow, out of all the things we could have taken with us, he didn't forget his smokes. "No one can cut a black man's hair except for another black man. This shit is as bumpy as a lawyer doing pro bono," Huey said, rubbing his head.

I shrugged, drying off my face, as the night's transformation came sprawling back. I gripped the sink and steadied myself, avoiding the mirror at all costs. Some things just waited for a chance to jump at you through the mirrors, and now was not the time.

"So, you're going to finish your story on how the fuck you turned into that—thing," Huey stated behind me.

I turned, glancing at him. "Yeah there's a bit more to it. We have to hit the road before I can tell you the rest," I responded. I looked past Huey to a collection of key rings. I took the jeep keys—reliable, and most likely not the mechanic's. I felt bad enough that we had broken through the glass door leading into the shop, not to mention stealing most of the work clothes and someone's leftover soup. I took an extra pair of keys before turning back to Huey. "We can go our separate ways, now. No sense in us both getting caught," I stated.

Huey walked up and snatched the jeep keys from my hands. "Look, pecker head, we just escaped from prison and multiple guards were eaten up like dog meat—we are going to fry and then fry again for that. Much better chance if we stick together. Also, I will drive. You look like shit," he stated while opening the driver door and helping me inside. I crawled into the passenger seat.

"Your funeral," I muttered as he slammed the door.

Huey finished rolling up the garage door before slamming the driver's side door, and we reversed out of the garage. "Yeah, well, if you ain't living you're dying anyways—you just can't tell because you're too close to life," he stated as we started down the California road. "I think we would be a lot safer if we booked it out of California. Maybe make our way up north to Oregon or Washington."

I turned in the seat with what little energy I had. "We aren't going to fucking Washington," I affirmed.

"Alright, sounds like you also have some more history there. By the way, we were cellmates for three months. You never told me you're a Jew," Huey responded cooly.

"That doesn't really matter now. No Washington though—please."

"No Washington it is. I guess we can try somewhere else in the West. I know just the place. We have to get to moving fast before they find our sorry asses, because every pig in this state is going to be gunning for a price," Huey remarked. "And you also better finish telling me about you know..." Huey trailed off. We had both refrained from talking about the escape. I had told him to wait until the story was told before anything was asked. "While you're at it, tell me why the fuck we can't go to Washington. Tell me why I don't just kick your pasty ass out of this jeep and let them take you in," he said contemptuously.

"I would transform into that beast and eat you," I casually stated. Huey didn't know how much it hurt me to turn... to feel my bones breaking and ripping apart. Huey was a good enough person—no one was truly my friend, but for now, Huey could be relied on. I had no idea why he wasn't running for the hills, but beggars can't be choosers and I needed the help.

"Yeah, yeah, you've said that six times already," he mumbled nervously.

I sighed deeply as we started down the road, my shoulders hurting from the transformation, everything hurting for that matter. "Okay, well, I hate going to Washington because it was where my brother and I ended up after the camps, traveling with a group of Gypsies."

9

Chapter 9

I coughed, spitting into my hand as the bile from last night's "meat and spit," as my brother called it, threatened to come charging up my throat. It was a cold morning in the camp. Combined with the rot in my mouth, it was already promising to be another wonderful morning in the valley.

I groaned, sitting up on the tussled blankets around me. Somehow, whenever I made to set camp, I always picked the one spot that had a rock. I grumbled, pushing hard into the firm surface of what had to be a boulder, if my back was any indication of the level of discomfort.

I stretched, looking at the bare walls of my tent. We had been camped here for six weeks now, in the lower valleys of Washington, the longest we had stayed anywhere. as far back as I could remember. Yet in the six weeks that I spent here, I had not bothered to hang anything on the walls of my tent. A true vagabond—or maybe I was just lazy, as Linor put it.

Either way, it's just a fucking tent, I grumbled as I fumbled for the straps of my jeans, pulling them high up my waist in the cold morning. My boots were still wet from the night before as I slid into them, squeezing the water from their soggy leather, just as my tent flap was pulled aside.

"Avi," snorted a pig-faced boy, whose ears flapped down toward his brows like a dog, with hands almost cloven into hook-like pincers that only further highlighted the dough around his face as swine-like.

"Put my flap down," I sneered at the boy.

Schwein snorted again, dropping the flap as his hands fished out the bottle of "Spit," as my brother had named his choice of liquor. It was too early to be drinking, too early to be getting mad at someone, I thought. But Schwein, like most of my brother's group of friends, made me uncomfortable. In general, most people made me uncomfortable. I tossed on the ragged remains of my checkered shirt. I smoothed off the leaves and brushed off the flaked blood. I paused, looking at the long stain going around the bottom part of my shirt. *This is my favorite shirt,* I grumbled, tucking in the soiled part into the waistband of my pants. Schwein had weaseled out my brother's bottle while I was focused on getting dressed. Great, I thought, now I would have to face the day sober.

I left the tent and stepped into the cold morning air as the sun was rising into the valley of the Forgotten. That's what we were, the nomads of a world long forgotten, even before we had been kicked out. We were called God's chosen people, which basically boiled down to God's chosen fucked. So, naturally, the forgotten would flock to the only group that was just as cast out as us: the Roma.

I spat, tasting more of my brother's liquor from last night. *What in the world did he put in that stuff?* I pondered as I stumbled my way through the camp. Even in the early hours, children flew past me, their giggles only matched by the flair of their mismatched clothes. Most of us forgotten failed to match even the most basic clothing conventions—why should we? As far as we were concerned, down here in our valley, or any other place we chose to make camp at, we were the masters of our faith; let our colors shine bright in the brightest of days.

Around me, people were coming and going, swiftly moving through the packed and conglomerated tents arranged all around us. In an instant, we could build a city of made of silk, tarps, car doors, and stolen house doors. Then, just as quickly, we could be gone, like the light snuffed from a candle.

The noise was causing my already pounding head to trample like the massive hoofs of the horses tied to that lonely orchard tree. I made my way over to a red-flapped tent, propped up and combined with the remains of a rustic station wagon, still gleaming with its stolen plates from Louisiana. *It's good to be home,* I smiled, as I went to knock on a sign attached to a twisted oak branch jutting from the ground, which read, "Don't bother knocking; in fact, just go away!"

I read it in Linor's grandmother's voice. The old woman was a gloomy, sour old lady, who insisted on being left alone, but at the same time, her hooked aquiline nose would undoubtedly find its way into any business that was going on in our shanty town.

I could hear her lecture now: "Boy, why do you come at all hours of the morning? Did you not read the sign?" I grumbled to myself and went to pull the tent flap open, when the nylon door was snatched away, revealing Linor.

Her face was dusted in a light coating of early-year freckles, webbed over a heart-shaped canvas. In every moment since I had first seen her, I had known that I would always love this girl, no matter the changes of the seasons and the long years. She was framed by dreaded and beaded tussles of midnight black hair, flowing like oil in a sea. At the end of her long bangs was hanging what appeared to be a faded yellow pocket-knife, which she had twisted into her curls, along with many assortments of beads, clothes, and everything else under the rainbow—as she put it.

The dubious yellow knife flashed in the morning sun and I shielded the reflection as Linor stepped fully out of the tent flap. "You're late!" she snapped, placing her hands on her hips as I squinted my eyes through the blaze.

"Yeah, well, I came as soon as I could—" I started, before she yanked my chin down and pulled my hands near her face.

"Avi, are you ever not covered in blood? Look at you, you're a mess. I am sensing a pattern with you. What am I going to do with you?" she asked with a dramatic sigh that I knew was entirely too fake to be real. "I mean really. Let me clean your hands, at least—you animal.

I grumbled as she jerked my arms and body in the direction of the tent. Already, Linor was taller than me, in fact, taller then most of the boys in the city. She was long-legged and thin, like all of us, with the exception of Schwein, of course. I began to protest about being jerked around and pulled, but the feeling of her hands on my face had blistered my cheeks into a high noon red that was working its way through my body. *Maybe I should be late more often—when a pretty girl had ahold of your face, there shouldn't be many words.*

We went through the flap, Linor still pulling me forward, somehow getting us both through the door and zipping away the world before I even had time to register we were moving. I almost tripped over the mounds of shoes piled at the front of the door.

Linor scoffed and eyed me with murderous intent. "Watch out for my babies, you stupid *offt*, before I stab you." She gestured with her free hand to the knife in her hair. I rolled my eyes, knowing full well that her "babies" were nothing more than an assortment of various daisies and other flowers, shoved into the dirty sneakers and old boots. Most were not even matching, but all were filled to the brim with soil, the laces twisted and flowing with colors of birds and creatures that could never exist anywhere outside of the mind of Linor.

"You know, you probably shouldn't stick them in the doorway if you don't want them to die," I retorted.

She sighed, "Everything is always death with you Avi. Besides, I need more, find me some, but no more boots please. I need ones with laces," she responded, ignoring my tone.

"That's right. You only need to flood the rest of the city with your flower shoes. You could at least get matching pairs," I smiled.

Linor shrugged. "Where is the fun in a world that is filled with matching shoes?"

"One that is probably easier to walk in," I snapped back, trying to pull her out of her head before she got too deep. It was always some unseen universe of color that Linor lived in, where it was her world and her world only. The rest of us were just shoes waiting to have some dirt and flowers placed into us—as she had put it to me once. Despite how odd and down right off-balanced she made me feel sometimes, her energy and power were enough to sweep away any of my thoughts and make me just want a glimpse of the world that she inhabited.

She scoffed before responding, letting go of my hand as we made it into her living room area. "Pull your opinions, Avi, from things that haven't been extrapolated from incomplete information," she said matter-of-factly.

I arched my eyebrows at her. *Understanding her will take the rest of my life,* I thought. As if coming back to our world, Linor beamed, "Okay, let's get those hands washed up!" she cheered, snatching my hands, pulling us through her massive living room. It was propped up by poles of wood and steel, even a growing willow tree that had its limbs sheared back as support beams for the heavy flaps of tarps and nylon tent pieces used as roofing for her and her grandmother's home. Like the shoes, everything was coated in colors which, despite the dreary nature of her grandmother, reflected a home of happiness at the very least, on top of the general insanity.

I took it all in, breathing deep the smells of fresh flowers, honey, and something festering with a fungus twist somewhere in the maze of tarps and wooden poles. That had to be her grandmother. I wondered in which of the many curved hallways she was lurking. Compared to Linor, her grandmother was short, hunched over so far that her back resembled a round boulder propped upon a degraded log. Her skin was darker than the root tea Linor insisted upon me drinking every day, and flanked by the heavy lines on her skin and her long silver hair, which was tied upon her in an almost comically perfect bun on her head. The bun was way too big to be on the old woman's skull without causing her discomfort. But you would be a fool to ever comment on her appearance. In fact, you would be a bigger fool to ever say anything bad to her grandmother.

Linor must have sensed my unease, "Don't worry, Avi grandma, isn't up yet," she snickered, pulling me to the kitchen.

"I'm not worried," I voiced, doing a doubletake before that troll of a woman spawned from the shadows. She always seemed to appear out of nowhere, appearing and disappearing like snow in the early spring months; completely unexpected, terrifying with the possibilities.

Linor stopped, turning just her upper body toward me, her right eyebrow cocked and a thick frown falling into her features. "Avi, come back to reality. She isn't that bad and while the doom and darkness is certainly only moments away, we have much more important things. Such as Pirogo, and leaves falling into a creek right before an autumn rain. Speaking of which! We should go to the creek tonight. There's these interesting growths that kind of look like miniature turtles growing from the dirt. You just have to squint your eyes—you will see them, Avi." Linor rambled on as we made our way deeper into her and her grandmother's home. I smiled. Linor was the only person that I would ever let me forget "reality," as she called it. Call it young love, but there was no reality more interesting than the one I shared with her.

"Well actually, instead of the creek—" I started, before she cast her eyes, one brown and one green, in my direction. Whenever her other form showed up, I could tell she was losing her concentration—she was distracted. I pushed on, digging deep for my confidence. *You can do this, Avraham,* I thought. "I was thinking we could go into town—maybe steal a few of old Pete's good beers and shoot off some of those firecrackers I have been saving since last year's festival," I stammered.

Linor beamed at me. "Thought you would never ask, Avraham."

"Oh you do—I mean awesome," I replied with my cheeks surely as red as the sun above us.

"But first! We need to start making those pies!" she said, through mouthfuls of air as she bit into a circle she drew into the air.

"I thought you told me we were making Pirogo?" I asked, bemused as she pulled me into the kitchen. The words had hardly left my mouth before a tight blue apron was tied around my waist and the head hole quickly fell over the mess of my curly hair.

"No, I didn't," she sneered as the apron top momentarily got caught in my hair. I was happy with it. It was the closest her face had been to mine in at least a few days. "Honestly, Avraham, cut your hair already. Jeez," she scoffed, letting go of the apron top and turning to a cabinet shelved on top of two poles, lined up to discolored bricks of bright red to fading concrete gray. We set about after that, making noodle pudding. Linor joked about my inability to do anything right as I sprayed her with water when we were washing the fruit. It was these simple moments between us that made me forget about the past—the only time I could do it sober.

I looked down at one point, glancing at the raisins in the draining bin. The water was flowing through the raisins, turning them, washing them into puffy shapes about to explode. Suddenly, I was back in the cage—the bars tight, a festering smell eating my sanity bite by bite. The cold causing my skin to stick to the bars, while my skin slackened from lack of food. Almost trying to eat the metal as it wrapped so tight to the alloy against my naked skin. I was hunched in the corner of my small cage, keeping to the furthest corner from anything that was dangerous. My thoughts racing, shifting, grinding, and tumbling into rage repeatedly as I shook from the hunger, as I shivered from the cold, as I shuddered from the terror.

A man in sharp black trousers and even sharper-edged shoes gleaming like black tar, save for a scarlet sleeve up his left bicep and a golden, gleaming belt buckle, stood before me in his Allgemeine uniform. I kept my eyesight down. The last time I'd glanced, the hose had nearly killed me and the cage was already cold enough. The man produced a small bowl of silver, containing a heap of dark, raw meat and bones churned together to look like raisins too wrinkly to become grapes again—but not wrinkle-free enough to be anything else. Only I knew it wasn't raisins and I knew I was long past my qualms of being picky over food. *Muter*, I thought, as I started to cry. Only dust and pain came out as I thought of her.

The man bent down near me. I flinched, bolting to the other corner when I hit my head on the top of the metal cage. He smiled wide, a bright light reflecting from his capped teeth in the back, and a wide hole where his front teeth parted like Moses did the Red Sea. It was Albert, his sneer and his peppermint-colored eyes lined up under a tussle of thick auburn hair, combed back with more grease than the blubber on most fish. Albert started talking in his thick German accent, and gone was the confusion I had felt when they had first entered our town. It was the Germans. German had never been my best subject in school. *Muter* and *foter* had insisted for me to practice, though I had just wanted to play games. It seemed so long ago now and I had trouble grasping onto the memory—maybe I just didn't want to.

It frightened me though, that I couldn't remember the night they attacked. Maybe because I couldn't see anyone doing something so awful and still remaining human—Albert at least, he wasn't human. And listening to it over the last several... but I wasn't sure how long I had been here, how long since the trains had landed us in this never-ending hell.

He cackled, his breath reeking of foul onions and ham. I covered my nose, glaring at him through gritted teeth. A fire burning, rising, as the logs of anger began to stack on top of each other.

"I know how much you love your meat—wolf boy," Albert chuckled through his parted teeth. "Yes, you like your meat. Here, don't you want it?" Albert asked, pushing the bowl through a small opening in my cage. I hesitated, shrinking back into the cage, the bars unmoving against my force. "What's wrong, little wolf? Little puppy," he sneered, tipping the bowl until the meat fell at my feet. "Oops." His laughter shot through the cage, causing my skin to prickle against the icy metal.

He pulled back his hands and the bowl. I paused, looking at the meat on the ground. The floor below us was stained wood, covered in my urine from the previous months and the remains of other tipped-over meals. I gulped, my stomach wider than the ocean as my thin arms slowly reached for the meat. When I got the first chewy and dripping piece without being struck, I yanked my hand back, taking the piece into my mouth. I was tired of meat; I was tired of being hit, though. The chunks were so red, that the meat had turned purple and shriveled in blood—like raisins. Greedily, I stuffed the meat into my mouth and swallowed without chewing. I kept my eyes on Albert—no secret hose behind his back this time, no chain to choke me with until I passed out. I was in the clear; he wasn't getting my food this time, or hurting me.

Quickly, the meat was shoveled down my throat as I watched Albert, my eyes never leaving him as his smile widened on his face. "Wow, wolf, you're an animal. I didn't know you liked human so much," he jeered.

My mouth stopped moving before my brain fully understood the implications of his words. That was... human meat. I spat the meat out and immediately began scraping my tongue with my hands. My eyes started to water, tears rolling down my cheeks as Albert laughed at my misery.

Anger flooded my veins, seeping into my eyes, and I wanted to kill this man, *had* to kill this man, as I struggled against the bars. My hands found hold and I pulled with all my strength. It was no use. Albert continued to chuckle at my pain. I braced both my dirty feet and broken hands against the bars, pulling with everything, until I collapsed into the pile of my own filth below me.

As I lay catching my breath and Albert panting from laughing, the entrance way into my holding area opened. In walked a man dressed similarly to Albert, only his top was a thick brown and he had a tussle of golden blonde hair. His face was young, lacking any of the age that you would expect of someone who did what they do. His features were guiltless and youthful, leading up to a small button nose and a noticeable notch in his right ear where the top portion had been taken away.

"Stop laughing already, Albert," urged Joseph as he came near my cage. "Joachim is on his way," he cautioned. His angelic features caused his hay-colored hair to almost bristle in the sun with a darker gold. Albert straightened up, his laughter all but forgotten. He sniffed, adjusting his uniform, pulling his tie twice to center before checking that it was aligned with his trousers and belt buckle, before coming rigid as a fence post.

Joseph stepped near my cage, whispering, "It's not meat, don't listen to Albert. Honestly, it's the leftover *Rinderbraten*." He smiled as the door to my cage opened again. This time, both Joseph and Albert stood erect, with no more noise being made. Before, they were just boys pretending to be soldiers, I thought. Now they looked like men at war as their bodies became a picture of discipline.

The door lazily reverberated off the adjacent wall as Hans strolled through. Like Albert, his uniform was coal black, save for the crimson strip across his bicep. Unlike Albert, though, I gulped as did my torturers. I knew that Hans's stripe was earned—it was soaked in blood. He was pressed and clean, his uniform tailored to the edge of a blade and his shoes shined a murky black which showed your death when you glanced upon them. It was his face that haunted me the most. His face showed what his uniform did as well—he was a man of focus; he was someone that should never be trifled with.

His head gleamed bald in the low light, showing his scars. From his cheekbone on his right side to the tips of his ears, the right side of his face was peeled back, like the skin from a deer. Hans's exposed flesh, his ruined burns resembled the rocky roads my *bruder* and I would walk when we visited our *zayde*. Even his eye had not been spared, as the lid was gone, leaving in a scarred-over hole where his matching cruel black eye should be. Instead, a tussle of flawed meat stretched to his missing nose and hatchet face. Jammed under his arms was his hat, crisp and rounded edges like the rest of his uniform. I didn't dare make eye contact. Neither did the other two.

Hans stopped, examining the concrete walls around us with his one eye slowly turning his head around the empty room of aging dust where a spicket with a long yellowed hose lead to the mouth of a red dragon in the corner. I flinched from the sight of it, the memories of being hosed down, the battered soreness of every muscle fiber in my body feeling like I was meat being beaten by a hammer. I prayed silently that it wouldn't come to using the hose again—only as I had been learning more and more: God had already forsaken me.

I averted my eyes back to Hans as he stood near my cage, his back straight as a board, the other two, straighter. Dr. Joachim strolled into the room, clean shaven like the other three, face long and narrowed-up chiseled cheeks with the furrowed lines of someone who had spent many years studying material inside a book, seeing very little sunlight on his milk white skin and bronze color hair, which was thinning to a coarse white underneath.

By all accounts, Dr. Joachim was a full-faced and pleasant to behold man, seemingly polite, like a fresh *zayde* giving a treat to you during a ballgame. His eyes, though, were worse than Hans's. They held the real secret to the men before me. The real dragon was only a small man in a lab coat, but his words and pursuits would terrify the bravest of men. For behind his pale blue eyes, there beat an endless void, that calculated and would shift you beneath his tides in an instant—not because he felt no pain, but because he genuinely relished in it. His name was pain, his name was death, and his face was that of a vicious old man. My spine felt fingers crawl up it, strangling my veins in an icy grip of terror. It's not the torture that is most feared, it's the person who inflicts the torture and smiles while you scream who causes the true ending of all hope.

Dr. Joachim stepped in front of my cage, a clipboard buried behind his back, his black uniform nowhere near the state of cleanliness of the others, but no one would dare to comment on his uniform. His thick square glasses lurched to the point of almost falling off his face, as a wide smile spread across his lips, causing even his forehead wrinkles to smile at my pitiful state.

"Good morning—well evening now, young man," invited Dr. Joachim, his tone exposing nothing of his insidious nature. I started blankly at the doctor, pulling my legs into my arms as my heart started beating faster—I should have eaten more of the meat before he came in.

Silence stretched out between four of my deep breaths before the doctor cleared his throat to speak again. "Well, I see you still won't respond to pleasantries Avraham," he jeered.

I shot out of my embrace onto my legs and pushed closer to the bars. *He knew my name, how did he know my name?* Since entering my cage, my new world, I had refused to speak to anyone. No matter the pain, I wasn't going to call out, I wasn't going to speak.

How did he know my name? The thought burned like a torch to dry leaves at the ending of a brutal summer. I swallowed, searching for my voice. It had been so many weeks since I had last spoken. Just before my cries could escape, a voice roared deep within, causing my teeth to rattle, my heart to burst from my chest and my skin to feel as though it was going to melt away. I was on fire, only beneath my skin. It was the beast. *"No!"* was all it said, and I clamped my mouth shut. They wanted me to speak. They wanted me to finally cave. I wouldn't grant them that. I would fight,

I would claw, I would resist. Only, as my thoughts gathered and my heart slowed, how did they know my name? It crept like a spider across my brain.

Someone had to have told them. I wasn't sure how long I had been here or who was even left from my friends or family. Not since the night we arrived… I let the thoughts burn away, like the flames that had taken so many of the people I once knew, and I felt myself weep for their pain, weep for their liberation from this hell.

"That is your name, right? Avraham? Yes, that is your name. What a beautiful name for such a creature as you: you the Jew, you the wolf!" he sneered, grinning wildly.

Anger boiled under my skin again and I gritted my teeth against the rising tide that was forcing me to speak out. His smile finally disappeared at that as he squinted and got closer to my cage.

"Even when I taunt you, you dare not speak. I make your bones feel like rubber pulled to breaking point, but you will not tell us how you got such wild power," he pondered, ignoring my existence. He continued, "You must be an animal, more that than boy—which is of course true for the Jew. I hurt so many of your friends in order to learn your name, Avraham," he taunted and my rage boiled over until a scuff of a sound made its way from my throat.

He snapped to attention from his hunched-over stance. "Did you hear that, gentleman? He can speak, and if he can speak, he can tell us more!" He gravitated back to me as Albert and Joseph snickered at his comment. Hans remained stoic and was no more taken by the situation than someone watching a pigeon fly overhead.

"Not just a wolf. No, more than that. How do you transform, wolf? How did you get your powers?" He slammed his clipboard into his right hand. "Answer me. It is not the moon, as if you're a nursery rhyme. It must be in that magical blood. Oh yes, I've gotten far off your blood. So have your friends," he sneered.

I jerked toward him, banging against the cage, when in a flick of movement, Albert had the long yellowish hose pumping full of water.

Joseph unhinged the mouth of the dragon. I was blasted to the other side of the cage, debris and filth passing me as what little remained of my tattered clothes were beaten from me. It was a feeling that cannot be described to those that have not had the sensation, but there is a panic, an endless wave.

And then there is a silence that stretches, as you feel as though you had never any sense before—nothing, nothing but a void. Many times, the hose had sprayed me with such intensity that my mouth shot open. My tongue would be swollen, and my teeth would rattle to near breaking point. My body could only hold so much. I was never thirsty; hunger had become my friend, but not thirst. No, I no longer wanted water, as the blackout was coming—I would soon pass out as my chest fought for air, as I fought for life against the beating pain that was forcing me to scream. My mouth wide open, no voice to the screams.

It hurt, it hurt so bad, worse than the time that *bruder* had popped a highball into my stomach. That pain had left me bent over for what felt like days, a perfectly circled welt that was purple and blue. Though, thinking back now, my *muter* crying when she saw my stomach was worse than the pain— I just never liked to see her cry. This was different, though. I would get no lemon cakes when it was over—and my *muter* would never cry for me again.

I sucked in my teeth the best I could at that thought, the water choking me. *Was I dying?* I thought...

And just as quickly, the water stopped—shut off from some unknown force. The suddenness of the pressure being gone caused me to fall to the bottom of the cage. I spat, trying to eject all the water from my body. I was filled up like a vase about to break.

I collapsed onto the ground, my body no longer remembering what it was like to not feel pain—to feel something else. My *zayde* would tell my *bruder* and I stories when we visited—*zayde* would speak often of David fighting Goliath, or strange creatures in faraway lands. Things that seemed so far away—such ideas of pain, though I could never understand what the heroes must have faced. I wondered now if my feelings of pain were something that *zayde* could have put into his stories.

I coughed as Dr. Joachim approached my cage. He sighed deeply, rubbing the bridge of his nose where his glasses sat. "Every day, Mr. Avraham, every day we go through this over and over again. I ask my questions; you refuse to be a good young man, and I have to come up with new and inventive ways to torture you—without breaking that skin of yours. That monster can't come out without that, huh?" he asked, turning his back to me, glancing out of the only window in my small room. I couldn't see much through the gray clouds outside; *they seemed to never end,* I thought, as I looked for something, anything, out that window.

"You want to kill me," he stated, turning back toward me. "You want to see me die. You want to see me drop dead, to cease to be someone that you have to see every day. It brings me no pleasure doing any of this—harming such a fine young man like yourself—well, fine enough for what you are," he sneered.

He clapped his hands in front of his face. "Just tell me: what are you, wolf." The doctor's voice and eyes were strained to the point of almost popping out of his head.

I sucked in my breath, seeing the raisins floating around in the water near my drenched head. "I... am... the... w...wolf..." I enunciated, wishing each "w" could have been stronger.

The doctor smiled, pulling out his clipboard, and writing something down as he chuckled. "There may be hope for you yet, wolf." He gestured to Albert and Joseph. "You two, come with me. Fetch this young man a proper dinner. He will need his energy for what is next."

Joachim hooted, like an owl in the darkest of woods.

I spat more water up in response to the doctor. His smile only got bigger.

Albert and Joseph snapped straight as trees, dropping the dragon hose, and I let my breath out as the monster fell to the ground, a small trickle of water leaving its wide nozzle. That thing wouldn't hurt me—not for a little while, at least.

"Many, many more plans for you, Avraham the boy wolf," the doctor trailed off. He almost skipped, leaving the small gray room. Only Hans and I remained in the room as the cold silence I had begun to get used to sank in. I had never been around such quiet in my whole life; not at night, when everyone else was asleep, when I would stay up playing with my tops hoping to not wake *foter*, or the night that had almost taken Zevi and me, with its dark claws and neverending stampede of terror. No—it was true silence and what scared me was that I liked it. It meant no more pain; I felt so alone as I pulled my naked legs to my chest, tucking my chin on top of them, clamping down the chatter of my teeth that clicked like the shoes of the Gypsy dancers, that last night in my town.

Hans walked toward my cage. I ignored him, keeping my eyes on the farthest wall away from me, expecting a blow at any moment. Instead, I heard the rummaging of papers and metal. A small object caught the light and fell from Hans' hands through the cage slats, near to my feet. I gasped, realizing what it was, as Hans placed his hat on his head. "The strong only survive when they're willing to make sacrifices. Stay here and die a slow death, or take your own faith into your hands," Hans said coolly, adjusting his hat.

I fumbled for a voice before speaking out. "Thanks," I muttered.

Hans didn't say anything, didn't show any sign he heard me. He just walked toward the door. "It's how I saved myself, kid," he informed me as he disappeared.

I was alone with the knife: small, with a wooden handle and a retractable blade. I tenderly picked up the knife and a surge of heat rushed into my fingers. The beast wanted me to use the blade—he wanted me to. Could I do it, though? Could I let the monster come back out? The pain from last time caused me to shudder and vomit at the memory, small chunks of the raisin meat coming out. The pain of the beast was greater than the dragon hose—*I would rather have that for hours*, I thought, as I could hear laughter approaching the doors.

My heart skipped into overdrive. If they found the blade, I would surely suffer in ways that would redefine my understanding of pain—with vocabulary I did not even possess. I was quickly learning that maybe I should have been a better student in school. Or perhaps not, though.

I shuddered, thinking about what had happened to me since arriving. Having better words for pain didn't change the pain—it only gave me a new meaning of it. Small bumps appeared all over my arms, the hair standing like the whiskers on our old neighbor's fluffy gray cat.

I snatched the blade into my weak hands, unsure what to do as the doors almost opened. Then I shoved the blade under me as the doors swung open. Albert and Joseph strolled in, carrying a long metal chain...

Even now, in Washington, I could feel the beast—he had remained dormant for so long. *That didn't mean he was gone,* I thought, as I stared into the sink. He was always there, waiting, watching, and lurking for a chance to come out. He had a mind of his own and he would devour anything and anyone—Linor included.

I was back in Linor's kitchen, the faucet spraying water. The memory of my time in the cage drifting down the sink of my mind, just like the raisins floating down the drain.

I clenched my knuckles, digging my nails into my skin as I felt something hot start to burn inside me. So brittle, I felt, so little and surrounded by a never-ending blast of noise, noise that played endlessly until my head was about to explode. *Those monsters! All that they had done... I would eat all of them, I would kill all of them. Just let it go, let the animal come out and all of this pain would go away.*

No, I was never going to let anything bad happen to Linor. Not after last time. Not after—

"Avi," Linor soothed, gently putting her hand on mine.

I felt the built-up tension resign back to the dull pit it had lurked in before. *Next time,* it howled from within. I shook with fear. Just then, he had fought, clawing his twisted form to the surface. I had almost lost control again! I shuddered. He was getting closer and closer to coming out every day—a river of hate and heat flooding like a flame that is never smothered.

"Avi, relax. It's okay," Linor whispered, coming behind me and placing her hands around my waist. I didn't know my body was shaking until she was tight against me. I let out my breath, not trusting myself to talk, as she held me.

10

Chapter 10

I let my hands fall from the sink, slapping like fish on dry land, useless things that had lost their purpose in life. It didn't matter to me. I was thousands of miles away in that moment and as my tears streaked and burned down my cheeks, I felt myself struggle into the mindset—an image of what my thoughts should be. Just a small idea, a self-inflicted virus that could gnaw and wriggle its way to the front of my mind and take me away from this pain. There's nothing worse than when you can no longer be saved by the love another, no longer feel the light within yourself. It was all a long night and I was searching for a candle in the darkest of storms.

I felt something moist and soft on my shoulders, a calm but steadily growing affirmation of love.

"Avi, we're here now, in this place, away from all of that. No more fences. We are beyond them," she whispered and I hissed back my voice as fire threatened to come out of my mouth. It was always like this when the memories came back, when *he* tried to take over. One moment, my mind was as straight as a pop-flyer above the roof of my childhood home, the next it was like diving into a pond, only to be sucked into the mouth of the ocean beneath its surface, and jagged teeth that bite, never letting go.

Fuck that, fuck all of that. I felt my fist tighten into my palms. Linor's arms were still around me as I started to shake again. I wasn't going to let them win. *I am better than that, I am not their bitch, I am not their animal!*

As I shook, a small golden-winged butterfly, with traces of silver and teal, flickered its mighty wings fluttered near my nose. Tiny legs stretched on the tip of my long nose. I blinked, and the rage I was building inside me deflated like a busted ball after a long summer. I narrowed my eyes at the small creature on my nose, its long black body overshadowed by colors vast and changing. Inspecting the wings, Linor's face appeared in them, slowly dissolving into the colors in the small smile she wore, only when I saw her planting her plants, or those times she hit me with her tambourine when I was being too flirty. I blinked several times and the butterfly popped before my eyes.

Behind me, Linor giggled. "See? No one can be mad after seeing one of my flies. Small wings can change even the worse of moods, grumpy," she teased, letting go of me and turning back to cutting up fruit. She hummed silently as I stood gasping like a slackjawed frog that had its meal escape after rolling it deep inside its tongue.

Linor had a special power—in a way, we all did, all of us children who had survived our time in the camps. Some people in the commune called us gifted and lucky. I say the ones who came back normal were the lucky ones. None of us really did come back. I shivered but smiled, thinking about her butterfly. Linor could make anything—shapes of vast and visceral, pure creativity. Linor, told me it was like peering into a world full of paint. All of us were like statues, rigid and unmoving. Her world was one of twisting colors and never-ending creation, which could appear almost out of anywhere and stay for hours. There was no telling how long. Linor could never be bothered to explain. I just took her at her strange word that the rooms were yielding to a force that I would never understand.

It did make for one hell of a drinking game, though. Many times she and I would throw rocks at animals that couldn't possibly exist, weighing nothing and floating like bubbles in the wind. I smiled at her, my cheeks flushing, as I realized I was covered in sweat. Linor said nothing. She just hummed and whistled as if it was just the two of us, cutting fruits and vegetables.

She was the best. None like her, I thought.

"Avi, quit being lazy and get to work, unless you like looking like a skinny widget," Linor chimed, lifting a knife with the skills of an expert, as she peeled the skin of an apple like a seasoned hunter.

"Yes ma'am," I responded, turning back to the sink, this time washing the raisins quickly with no thought of the past. *Just simple work, the way I like it; keep things stupid.*

"You know, the moon will be out tonight, maybe even a full moon. Nothing like those silver rays shining down. Like a personal lamp riding above us, you know, Avi?" She scampered to a cupboard on the other side of the kitchen, her long legs billowing out of her flowered dress. I watched her for a moment as she rummaged through the cupboard.

How about instead of lighting some firecrackers, we go for a dance?" I proposed.

She stopped moving, like a lighting bolt had shocked her in place. She turned toward me, a huge smile spreading from corner to corner. "You really mean it this time? You aren't going to chicken out and let your *bruder* tango with me instead?" she teased.

I flushed. Zevi had come a long way, smoother and more confident, his childhood pudge and weakness long forgotten.

"I think I can manage. No need for Zevi—but I was thinking something more private. Just you and us, the grocery store in town, you and me at six, tomorrow night," I puffed out my chest, speaking with a confidence that I hoped she wouldn't notice leaving my small frame as the embarrassment ran through me. It wasn't that I didn't like to dance—just what should I do with my hands?

Linor jumped, covering the distance between us in only a few steps, throwing her arms around my neck. "Thought you would never get the courage, Avi," she laughed.

I laughed too. Yeah, I was full of surprises today, and I wasn't going to lose to the memories. Not today, I thought, as we both laughed.

She suddenly got more serious. "Wait, why can't we go tonight?" she asked silently.

We both knew the answer. I set down the knife. "You know why," I said silently, hoping to avoid having to talk about it.

Linor sighed. "This time—I want to come, Avi. No ifs or buts. Don't think I didn't notice the blood on your hands before you washed it off," she stated.

I hung my head, ashamed. It was true. I had gotten the blood on me from doing the same thing we did most nights. All of us "gifted," we went out and hunted those who had harmed us.

We hunted Nazis—not much more to say on that.

11

Chapter 11

In the distance, I could hear the train coming, roaring its concrete jungle roar over the vast landscape. There was a time when if that roar had been coming from a mountain lion, no one would be standing here at this train station—everyone would be fleeing like tiny ants in every direction. However, the lion would soon have the same problem the train had today in our modern times. After a while you just become so used to the sight and sounds of the train—no king of the jungle could even get the homeless man near the end of the tracks to stop pissing on the rails, I thought, as I watched two local cops harass him.

Linor sat with her feet dangling over the platform, as the train on the opposite side picked up passengers heading in a direction out of our small town. I wondered what that must be like, taking a train somewhere out of this town just for fun. Sure, I'd ridden plenty of trains, but never one that led anywhere new and exciting. It was always on some mission, fleeing somewhere or even worse—arriving at a place of fire. I shivered at that thought and decided to walk up to Linor who was humming deeply into the afternoon. *Better to not ruin the day,* I thought.

Her legs swayed over the ledge. I sat beside her. Neither of us was talking as crowds of people moved along the station. I noticed more than one or two stares our way as people hurried by, turning their kids' heads or pretending to be talking about something else as they walked by. They took one look at our tattered clothes, our general look. Linor was decorated more for a fair than for casual wear, with her beads and bones crisscrossed in odd places along her dress. That was just Linor, though. Her *mishpokhe* held on to old traditions of the Roma, which did little to help the already unhealthy amount of misconceptions people had about us. If they were to ask her, though, she would simply smile and tell them to "Fuck off." That was her way, one of the things I liked about her.

Still, I felt a little self-conscious, so I tried to rub the dirt from my face and look a little cleaner than the homeless man pissing off the side of the rails had. This was just how we looked; we came into this country with nothing, after the camps. Years struggling and moving hadn't left time for clean clothes. Most of us didn't steal—most had more education than anyone would find in those cheap boxes they send kids to. However, our camp had it rough, on the outskirts of town: it didn't leave many options. With the way cops seemed to confuse us with the local homeless population, just because we were darker and poorer, that pretty much summed up our troubles. Thankfully, with the Roma, us survivors had a place. Though, with the Roma, the true Roma, the ones whose family came out of North India, life was tougher, even in our small community.

They were hated long before they came to America, hated for being Jewish, hated for being Gypsies. That was just a sad fact of life; some people will just hate you regardless of where you were at that moment. Some people would just hate; it was a thousand times easier to do that than to understand why they hated in the first place.

Who was I kidding? I thought as I jammed my hands in my pockets, pretending to whistle and kick an invisible rock on the platform. Linor laughed, "Why are you always acting like a complete dumbass, Avi?" she teased.

I jeered, "It takes one to know one, dumbass." She smiled at me as we both waited for our train. The police officer stopped harassing the homeless man and found his new target: us. He approached us slowly and cautiously, his baton out, mustache gleaming brown in the high sun. "Oh great," I mumbled as he approached.

"You kids taking the train?" he asked, already positioning his body so that Linor and I couldn't run away without side-stepping him first. I rolled my eyes and dug into my pockets until I pulled out a bent cigarette and a matchbook with the cover completely worn away—I had spent every free minute tearing off the sticker on the front. I think it had been a woman on a bomb. Wasn't sure; didn't pay for it anyways.

I flicked out my last remaining match, striking it as I held it to the cigarette. I took a long puff, inhaling deepening as I rolled my eyes deep into my head. "I think we are all taking a train somewhere, officer," I stated, trying to sound tough.

Linor covered her mouth, hiding a giggle, but my antics worked. The officer shifted in-between us, focusing all his attention on just me. He snatched my cigarette from my mouth and threw it on the ground. "Feeling like a wise ass, huh kid?" he rumbled, grinding my smoke into the dirty platform.

"Why, trying to learn a lesson from my ass, huh?" I countered.

He pulled me by my collar at that comment, growling as neck veins stood out down his throat. "Listen here, punk, I see little Gypsy shits like you all the time, playing tricks on the good people of this town. I better not catch your ass on a train, or you will be sorry you ever set foot on this platform, you understand me?" he snarled.

I put my hands up in a defensive gesture. "So, what you're saying is—you've been watching little Gypsy children. That doesn't seem very smart, wouldn't want to have it known you like them young, huh?" I stated, not nearly confident enough to stop my beating heart.

He loosened his hold on me and set me down on the platform, his face utter bewilderment. The officer was dripping sweat by this point, glancing in both directions for an unknown bystander. A few people thankfully on the other side of the tracks were looking on. As the roar of the train's brakes came to a grinding halt at that exact moment, steam bellowed out from under the massive machine, which distracted the officer further. Linor slipped by unseen through the open doors of the train.

After a moment, the officer pushed my chest, light enough not to knock me over, but hard enough to make the point clear. If I ran into him again, he would remember. Without saying anything more, he turned, adjusting his cap and shirt.

I covered my giggle and got onto the train as the doors closed at the last moment. I jumped into the nearest empty seat, popping down the sliding window. Nearby, the officer had his head high and shoulders rolled back. The train started moving forward, and I shouted, "Hey officer!" The policeman turned to see me halfway out the window. I cupped my hands over my mouth, shouting, "No ticket!" His face flushed red, and he stupidly gave chase to the train, but we were already in motion, steaming down the road.

I turned back into my seat, laughing, and a woman sitting across from me scoffed. I pretended to not hear her and got up from the seat, moving into the cluttered aisle. I was covering my mouth the whole way as I crossed the next car over. This one was mostly empty, save for Linor. The city had paid an aberrant amount for the train a long time ago, anticipating a boom in the population. It never came—instead, the area became filled with people fleeing their homes and staying as far away from the rest of civilization. Truly, after the war, the world had become one giant flight of people leaving.

I settled next to Linor, sinking into the soft leather of the train seat. Linor was pulling on one of the many necklaces she had around her neck. This one was made of seashells and broken glass. I took a deep breath, letting the laughter flow out of my chest.

"Did you have fun?" she asked, beaming.

I grinned at her. "It's always fun when we are together, admit it," I stated.

She looked amused, glancing up at me for a moment. "Neither confirm nor deny. Besides, that cop was a dick—he had it coming. He was the same guy that comes around grandmother's shop that one time I told you, where someone had smashed one of her balls. The cop blamed it on her. It isn't grandmother's fault that her customer's wife is cheating—she just reads the cards," Linor told me.

Her grandmother owned a fortune teller's shop in town. Most of her client base was poor and desperate people whose significant others were cheating or strung-out druggies running away from home. Either way, it was some of the more honest work in town. I never bought into the "visions" she saw in her ball. Mostly, just because anything that came out of that old woman's mouth about me had to be bad.

"Is that right?" I said nonchalantly, pretending that there was something stuck under my nails.

Linor sighed deeply, "You know, one of these days you're going to have to get over it with my grandmother—she isn't so bad." She hesitated.

I glared at Linor for a moment before shaking away my anger. It wasn't just Linor's grandmother—it was everyone in the community. I was regarded as the outcast amongst the outcasts. The demon walking among them. It was a beautiful day out, and I didn't want to ruin it by sulking, especially since we hadn't gone out like I promised her we would.

Instead, we were going to meet up with my brother and his friends. Nothing we were going to do tonight would be pleasant in the slightest, the thought already making my stomach do dances. We pulled into the next station, and as Linor and I sat, she was humming a soft song, while I had stretched out my legs across the seats. Neither of us had talked while we sat. I was normally the talker of the two of us, speaking endlessly, any chance I could get anyone to listen, but only Linor ever got anything out of me that wasn't an attempt to fill the void of the universe. It's such a horrible, awful, wretched thing, the silence that germinates spreading across our world. We miss so much, and we feel so little when everything is so loud, so pointless. And for what? Because we are afraid of the quiet, we are afraid of what we might just hear in the void.

I shivered at that thought. I knew what was in that silence—it was the beast. It was the things that loomed, ghastly apparitions in the darkness. I talked to keep from hearing them. I talked to keep the silence away. It was a crashing wave louder than anything that could be made from any fire.

"Hey Linor," I said before the onset of a negative wave swept me back out to sea. Once today was enough for me and I would have to change my shirt from how much sweat it seemed to have cost me.

She looked at me, her brown eye deep as Mother Earth. "Yeah, Avi?" she asked back. I smiled at her as the doors opened and in strolled my brother, his red hair curling in every direction, like a beacon for lost sailors at sea.

I stopped before speaking more. *Another time,* I thought. "Nothing," I muttered as Zevi saw me, a look of contempt momentarily flashing over his long face before he walked toward the seat next to my own. The rest of the crew showed up with him. It was time, already. Part of me wished that the train had kept going, that we hadn't stopped here.

But as Sophia entered, followed by Tir, Bug, Schwein, Arnold, and Solly, I knew that it was too late. Sometimes, you should just get off when you see the danger, even if the faces may seem innocent, may seem friendly. All of us were survivors from the camps: the children that were made special somehow.

Zevi gave me a long look before switching to a smile. Even though his features weren't completely grown in, his large muscles moved under the shirt he wore, and freckles danced down his arms and legs, cast over his tall body as if he was the night sky. Sophia sat in his lap, an air of boredom about her. She seldom spoke, and rarely was apart from Zevi either. Her long brown hair was tied up in a tight bun. Across from them, on the red seats, sat Arnold and Bug. Arnold was still small framed, so thin his bones almost seemed to be see-through. He had struggled to gain weight the most, after the camp, so much that under normal circumstances, might have made you feel sorry for him.

To make up for his lack of body, Arnold was a bully. Point in case as I was meeting Zevi's look, Arnold tossed a paper ball that smacked me in the face. I rolled my eyes as he slapped Bug's hand. Bug grinned, his teeth having completely fallen out, his goggles so tight on his head that his pale skin puffed up red around the rubber bandages.

I heard a sniffle from behind me. It was Schwein. He had my brother's bottle in his hand, taking a big pull before belching loudly. "That's disgusting, you twat," Solly sneered as she sat next to Linor. She gave me a half smile and a wide birth—even amongst us special kids, no one wanted to be seen talking to the wolf.

Tir rolled his eyes and sat in the seats behind Linor and Solly. His long hair flowed past his shoulders. He had a book about local plants in his hands.

"The gang's all here," I muttered.

Zevi took that as the time to start his plans. "Let's keep this private, everyone, shall we?" He turned his head to Bug. "Make us go, Bug," my brother shouted to the strange boy, his cowboy hat and gloves he wore was tough to take him seriously, up until you could see what was capable of.

Bug skirted around Arnold pulling down their window, "All aboard!" he screamed out the open window. The sound vibrated the whole train car as the boom carried off into the distance, louder than the real notification. I saw then that Arnold and Sophia had covered their ears as the young boy's voice had caused the train to power up and start rolling forward. Zevi was grinning ear to ear, unaffected by the amped voice of Bug.

Bug turned back, flashing his gums as he sat down in the seat adjacent to Arnold. I grimaced but did my best to conceal it. Zevi looked at Sophia. "Get the doors, will you, sweet?" he stated as Sophia got up, walking in front of the door that led into the train. She held up her finger, and veins sprouted throughout her body, flashing in neon colors, just before bolts of electricity shot from her fingers, melting the locks on the door. She turned around, smirking, as the rest of us covered our mouths from the smell of burning steel.

The train was moving as she sat back down on Zevi's lap. He was quiet, a slow smile creeping over his face. "Alright before reach our destination, we need food, everyone!" my brother exclaimed. I rolled my eyes. This raid had already been planned the other night; at this point he was just being boastful and gaining the favor of the others. All of this just so everyone would like him more—*what good would that get a person anyways?*

"Schwein, throw me the bag." He directed toward Schwein, who suddenly flushed red and looked embarrassed about something only he knew. When he hesitated, Zevi turned his head toward Schwein. The pig boy looked down before reaching over his shoulder and throwing the bag that he wore on his back to Zevi.

Zevi looked inside of the bag, a deep frown on his face. "Schwein, there's barely anything in here—once more, it looks like some kind of animal has eaten one of the straps." Zevi pointed at the missing chunk of the backpack. Zevi gave a cold glare to Schwein, and the big boy retreated into the seat. "We will count all the snacks you ate as yours, Schwein—I mean, even the strap?" Zevi questioned. Schwein rolled his shoulders in response. Another shake of his head and Zevi stood up, opening the zipper of the bag, "Easy enough; I will play a game, I guess. Let's see, I think I know what everyone's favorite snacks are," Zevi stated.

He turned toward Arnold first, who sat with a pose of someone trying to be a lot more popular than what they were. He had greased back hair, drenched in so much product that I thought I could cook a chicken with all the gel he had. A heavily buttoned black leather jacket went along with his rolled-up blue trousers. Zevi smiled, pulling out a piece of Blackjack taffy and tossed it toward Arnold.

Arnold looked like he was going to be sick, either from his Brylcreem-slicked hair or from the taffy. I wasn't sure, but when he saw something on Zevi's face, he quickly changed his grimace into a smile.

Zevi nodded and turned toward Bug. "Let's see, Bug, I feel like you're the only one here that could plop, fizz, and fizz again better than anyone. How about you have some Fizzes," my brother stated, throwing a pouch of the dissolving tablets to Bug. Bug snatched them, taking one out and sucked on the candy instead of pouring it into anything. A smile played across his face. No sounds came from his mouth as he did this. Bug always had to be careful. He could mimic anything, but as for volume control, it was very much an effervescent punch if he let lose too much.

Next, Zevi turned to Sophia, smiling at the stern girl. She was beautiful, but that wasn't an invite. That's why when Zevi pulled out a packet of Rocky Road, the two shared a smile that I might have understood for the first time. Sophia and Zevi would never be separated. When we had first got to America, a group of bullies tried picking on her, claiming her hair was cut to look like a boy. It was Zevi who came and chased off the bullies—after they had already hurt her. I wasn't around to see it, only to hear about it. But, whatever they did to Sophia, when Zevi saved her, Rocky Roads or not, she was sticking with him.

Zevi then turned toward Tiresias. He was the more approachable of my brother's friends, and kind enough to me. He would at least smile instead of running away. He spent his time talking to plants, always smiling about something. Zevi threw him Necco Wafers, saucer-shaped discs that had been around for a long, long time. Just like the plants that Tiresias smiled at.

My brother then looked at Solly, the other redhead of our group, a dusting of freckles riding along her nose. She was the only one of us that wasn't Jewish before she entered the camps—her family had been on vacation in Poland when the Germans had invaded. Thus, she had ended up like the rest of us now.

"Solly, the red headed tamale," Zevi stated as he handed her a packet of hot tamales.

Solly flushed pink before responding, "Yeah, yeah spit your cinnamon somewhere else, you wanker."

Zevi smiled and moved on to Linor and me. His face twisted for a moment, before he pulled out a multicolored candy necklace. "That's you, Linor, always something new about you every time I see you," Zevi commented.

Linor looked confused by Zevi's words, stating, "Thanks."

Lastly, Zevi looked at me. We both stared each other down, a glare forming on his face as I knew mine was doing the same. Zevi thought he had everyone figured out, that he knew everything. It was true, my dopey little brother was becoming something I'd never dreamed of him being. He walked around playing games like this—playing tests. Like he was trying to learn everything about everyone.

The thing that made me the angriest about it all was that I couldn't figure out why he was doing it. Why he had to be in control over everything—it creeped me out. My brother had changed so much since we were kids—he was now the stable and strong elder brother. I was the weak and confused one now. I thought about fighting him over his game. I imagined for just a moment slapping my brother in the back of the head like our mother had done so many times when we were children. My hand stayed at my side; my head lowered. It was better this way—I wished I believed that.

He stepped in front of me, and I heard Linor draw in a deep breath. I moved my head up, matching his gaze. This was insane; I was the elder brother—our relationship adamantly hadn't always been on the best of terms, especially since coming to America. You wouldn't have thought we were brothers. He was lean, of course, like everyone in our family, but when he had filled out, his muscles had come in ways that mine never would. A wide back and a barreled chest greeted anyone that Zevi came upon. He had once had piercing green eyes—now, he had one dull, lifeless brown one that seemed like the eye of a monster, while the other was a green inferno dancing like the tops of trees in the forest.

I shivered at his eyes. They were in my brother's skull, but they weren't the eyes of my sibling. That angered me to no end: here I was taking a beating from him without any words even being passed between us. Fire began to pour into my stomach, slowly, like tiny flames on the back of fireflies lighting the night sky. Drumming started in my ears and I could hear the beast growling somewhere in the pit of my stomach.

He sensed a challenge—even if I wanted nothing to do with it. Zevi gave me a look, a small smile stretching over his fair skin, pulling out to show shark teeth. In that moment, I knew that Zevi was sensing the unease building inside me. But why? Why was he trying to provoke such a thing? Such a monstrous creature that would surely kill him and everyone else on this train with zero remorse. I chased that thought down. Zevi was just being tough; no one could be that stupid.

But still, in the corners of my mind, I felt his claws. Felt his ripping at the edges. I remained seated, and a sweat broke out on my face, sliding down into my eyes. I bowed my head to keep from throwing up. I think Zevi thought that was a sign of me acknowledging him. Zevi chuckled and I felt something drop on my head. I kept my eyes narrowed to the ground.

As the anger from his action swept through me, pushing like a relentless hate with its own mind.

What Zevi had dropped rolled into view: it was a packet of Atomic Fireballs. I paused at that one, feeling my face flush red. I left the candy on the ground as I pushed back into my seat. Zevi was smiling the whole way to his seat.

"Hey, what's yours?" I blurted out, feeling embarrassed that I was being a hothead as my brother's candy suggested.

Zevi pulled out a packet of yellow M&Ms, stuffing one of the big candies in his mouth. "Easy: peanut and chocolate. The king around here." He smiled as our train trudged on.

12

Chapter 12

He ran down the hall as we all gave chase in the small apartment complex. A thunder of sweat and curses. Most of those whom we found were generally in awful shape—their time in the military physically, at least, a thing of the past. He was young, old enough to perhaps be one of our elder brothers.

I fell through the wooden door that led to the hallway where the others were chasing the man. After leaving the train, we waited until nightfall before breaking into this man's apartment. We used the information gathered from Bug, who spent most days using his powers of voice mimicking to prank call people, and the rest of his time researching where the Nazis had gone off to after the war.

Zevi, though, was a different story. Most of us played some role in tracking down the vermin, but my brother was a different story. Like the hard walls of his tent, when he went to work, it was methodical, his focus absolute. He didn't half-ass anything, from setting up a proper shelter every time we moved to the news clippings and research he did on our former guards. That was truly Zevi's superpower, a focus that never wavered, never stopped. It chilled me, thinking how far he would go. My stomach was doing flip-flops by the time I stood up.

With a loud bang and a short scuffle, the others had caught the fleeing man. I had avoided his face since we broke down the door to his apartment. The inside was like any other home that you would find these days.

Low-hanging walls, base-level fixtures, including a small television that Schwein took an extra moment to steal, once the man had somehow slipped past nine teenagers standing in his doorway.

On the way out, though, I had noticed his photographs on the wall. He had a lot, mostly images of hillsides, and glowing trees. He seemed to pull their very moments out, frozen like raindrops on a windowsill, forever in place for everyone to see, even if it was not their natural state.

Those hadn't bothered me as much as the ones nearest his bed. He had many frames, of a younger version of our quarry, standing with a tall and plain woman. A rosy-cheeked elderly man, and a version of the guard that had to be a younger brother, hooked nose and mud brown hair. It was his family. *People like this—had family,* I thought, as we chased the man, and a feeling overcame me. By the time I reached the kicked-in door that led to where others had gathered around the man, my stomach had just about fallen out.

I wiped the sweat that was globing up at the top of my forehead, my shirt little more than a washrag. In the middle of the floor sat the young man, his arms bent behind his back by Schwein, who was grinning a devilish grin that stretched from horizon to horizon, like a dark omen promising blood from a red sun. Linor stood closet to me. She looked like she wanted to speak. I shook my head—trying to tell her I was fine.

Everyone else gathered around the man's room, Bug tore down the frames on the man's walls, dropping them to the ground and bursting them into pieces like cracked eggs. Zevi smiled and kicked the man in the face hard enough to send him sprawling into the opposite wall, the cheap paneling collapsing from the force. Blood spattered the ground—a plague out of Exodus. I turned away as I heard Sophia approaching the man, her fists hitting something fleshy and meaty and him groaning. There was a small bathroom to my left. I went inside the little room, which was about the size of a driver's seat. The walls were uncomfortably close, convulsing, moving toward me as if they had a mind of their own, squeezing me into a tomb forever.

I gripped the sink, sweat rolling off of me like a stream—I was dizzy.

I tore the shower curtain down from the metal hooks, sending them shooting around the room. The noise did nothing to keep me from hearing the fists in the other room, the whimpering moans as a man was being beaten. *What was happening?* I thought as I looked into the mirror. We've beaten plenty of these people up since the war—they deserved it. They had to deserve it. Didn't they?

A cold chill swept down my back, dousing the fire that had been burning since I had entered the building. In the mirror, nearby in the smoldering corners, burning to black glass, was the wolf. A growl escaped his mouth as he opened his mouth wide.

13

Chapter 13

"Well, that was pretty fucking weird—friend," Huey grunted as we both took the end of a heavy load of bricks inside a bin.

"Oh, trust me, you don't even know what you're in store for with this one," I woofed as we tipped the collection of rubble to the edge of the building. It rained piles of stone to the ground far below, shattering uselessly like a red rockslide. I shivered, as the huge chunks became pebbles from this height. A sense of vertigo causing me to flinch from the ledge.

Huey snickered. "You're a flaming wolf demon thing—but you can't stand to be a few floors off the ground?"

"We aren't just a few floors off the ground—more like twenty-eight, but who's counting? Not me, that's for sure." The acid and contempt was only partially fake at Huey's comment.

"Yeah, who's counting," he jested as we both walked to the pile of broken blocks on the adjacent wall. We had managed to land a construction gig on the outskirts of the town we had settled in. The perfect place for two people who wanted to be left alone without anyone batting an eyelash. Construction workers were drifters, just like hobos on trains—only difference was our train didn't move as fast. But when you are on the run and you need a decent paying job with zero qualifications—just bring your hammer. America was always building, we had thought. It had been building in every direction since I first came here in the 40s.

It was the only job where the manager could be pretty sure every one of his employees was a felon. He didn't care: he had an endless supply of material, not with so much being constructed. The sun was setting, and our shift would be over soon. I took my helmet off and wiped the sweat from my head, and a cool breeze shifted, continually bringing the dry Arizona heat, even this high up.

Huey sat down on the rocks opposite of me, his face a blank expression of lines that had been formed from something I would never understand. We didn't ask each other anything unless we needed to, and when we did, Huey spoke with few words and was direct enough.

He complained about my long stories, and I complained about being stuck in a single-wide mobile home with a man who insisted on smoking more cigarettes than Cool Hand Luke on a long bender, with an empty day ahead of him.

Sweat slowly trickled down my head, stinging my eyes as the sun started to set. We were both silent. That was the best part about this job—we were both drained at the end of our days and conversation seemed little more than what it always was—a way to break up the moment so we could be distracted from what we were doing. By this time of the day, everyone else had gone home to friends and family. We didn't have that; extra pay for extra hours wasn't bad motivation.

"The man with his face pulled off—Hans—you said he gave you a knife?" Huey questioned me.

I glanced his way with one eye, wiping more sweat from my brow. Even at night, this place was still on fire. I sucked in my breath before responding, "Yeah—he gave me a choice to use it. Seems to be the case every step of my life: just one more choice between being fucked and getting fucked," I mumbled.

"What happened to him?" Huey asked, his hands shaking the ash from the cigarette.

I paused before responding. He wasn't shaking because of the light breeze up here. His eyes were drilling holes into the freshly layered floor below us. Without even seeing his stare, I knew that something about Hans was making Huey rage like the flame from the smokes he dragged on all day. We had been in Arizona for a total of three months at this point and in the months we had known each other, the most Huey had told me about himself was his name. I held my head in shame at that, and a slight ping of isolation came creeping back in like the waves of cold over a lake in a long winter.

I had spent so many years on the run by myself, that I only understood what it was like to be alone. I had doubts Huey and I were friends. We were at least roommates, and accomplices, and easily the most sought-after criminals in the west, if not the whole of the States. That made very little sense to me. Somehow, we hadn't been found. Which only left Huey and I feeling uneasy every day. We didn't say it, but we both showed the signs. Spending time snagging any amount of food off our plates with our hands, no time to eat normally, just a break a piece off and prepare for flight. Nights were the worse, though. Prison is loud—filled with the broken whimpers of men and an unending overhead of bright lights, mixed in with the languages of the jailed.

"I will get to that part—might as well continue with the rest of the story first," I joked.

Huey didn't laugh. He remained the way he was, stiff and unmoving, for a moment longer before bringing his gaze back up to mine. His brown eyes showed only an infinite darkness and I shivered. We had both been to jail for something. I never found out what Huey had done, but you don't get those kinds of eyes from stealing televisions and radios.

I ventured to find out more about my former cellmate. "Do you know him?"

The wind almost ceased for a moment as Huey drew in a thick amount of air before speaking. "Yeah, I knew a guy like that once, head all sorts of roadkill-like. Slender body, tall and gaunt like a thick gust of wind would blow him over. He wasn't the kind of man to do something for anyone, though—not without wanting something in return. One dangerous motherfucker," Huey grumbled as his fists balled up.

I started to say something, then decided it was best to stop, as Huey crumpled his cigarette to the ground. Those things were like a holy cross to that man—must have hit a nail.

"I was in a war once. Senseless as shit—I suppose they all are." He shook, as he searched for the words, almost as if they were hidden in the dust at our feet, before continuing. "Just a big ol' track through a swamp-ass jungle, cutting veins and those nasty-ass peckerwood mosquitoes every few steps," he snarled. "To make it all the fucking worse—there wasn't a fucking reason for any of use to be there, not one fucking reason. Just me, hiking my ass through brush only to be fired upon in every direction."

He paused, spit sliding to the ground, his head still bowed, when his face snapped up and faced toward me. "I love the fucking jungle, man. It's my fucking home. I've seen white boys just like you lie on the ground, butchered like fresh meat before being shipped off to fancy folks with big-ass hats. And you know what, I fucking loved it, every goddamn minute of being in the jungle, watching men turn into pieces of roadkill." Huey's voice cracked, and tears flowed down his face.

"The jungle is where I am from. My parents worked hard to get me to this country, only to be shipped off before I even knew how to roll a cigarette or wipe my ass." He wiped his tears on his sleeve. I looked away. *Don't ever watch a man cry; it was the fastest way for you both to die.*

He snorted and blew his nose, adjusted his hat firmly over his eyes and waited to speak. I didn't hurry him. Huey had done the same. "My momma—she worked hard to put food on the table, worked hard to put my brother and me into school. You wouldn't believe it, but I used to be the biggest bookworm you ever met. I even practiced my Machado, and I got to go to a few classes before we moved to America. Once here, well, you know. The same ol' story: speak right or look right. If you can't do one, you best learn before people throw your life into hell." Huey stood, suddenly knocking over one of the stacks of bricks near us.

"I studied hard, Avi, I studied really hard. Both my mind and my body. Without it, I wouldn't have survived that damn jungle. Without it, I wouldn't have survived that dogmeat-headed cueball when he and his goons came prowling in the jungle," he sneered, fiercely gazing off into the distance.

I stood as well, my heart pounding, what were the chances that Huey had run into Hans? I suppose it was possible. A lot of them got away after the camp burned down. It wasn't that I doubted Huey, it was just that I had doubts that anyone could survive meeting Hans. He was the angel of death in camp: when Hans came around, everyone died—except me. I looked down at my feet, too ashamed to speak, as the wind picked up and nightfall found its way to our lofty throne, too high off the ground, over a barren town filled with broken dreams and tumbleweeds.

I cleared my throat before speaking. "If you keep crying like that, Huey, I can find you a diaper. I think they make them for babies your size," I jabbed.

Huey turned toward me, a smile floating over his face, "Finish your damn story, dickhead."

"Asshole," I joked.

14

Chapter 14

The following day had come and gone the same way as most days. After we had finished finding our quarry, it was round after round of my brother's homemade drink. And with each shot, the image of the man's face nailed deeper into my mind. At some point I left, taking the bottle with me, dragging myself to my tent. I slept on the floor; a rock jammed itself into my back. I wanted to die; I tried to kill myself. Linor came and got me in the morning. I cheered up once it was the two of us cooking in her kitchen. This was our life; Linor never knew how I felt every night, a fact I couldn't have been more thankful for. It was worth the risk of running into her grandmother just to spend time together, the two of us—the rest of the world be dammed.

The sun was hanging high in the sky by the time we left Linor's tent. We had managed an entire pie without seeing her grandmother or killing ourselves in bizarre crust accident. We exited the home, and I covered my eyes. The camp was jovial and kicking into gear—if you're ever feeling blue and need energy, come to a Gypsy camp after tea time. That will raise your spirits or at least get you to a nice "transformative feeling," as Linor put it. There was nothing as invigorating as watching the colors and drums beat for folks just glad to be alive for one more day, happy to have another night to look forward to.

Linor took my hand, yanking me between the rows of mis-matched tents, trees, cars, and structures that couldn't stand up to a cough, let alone an earthquake. We didn't care—this was our home. After spending so long behind fences, all of us, we made our own land away from everyone else.

We sped along dirt paths stumped bare under the movement of the camp, past my tent by the eucalyptus tree. I hesitated for a moment in getting the firecrackers—*women love explosions,* I recalled, thinking of the advice Elder Adahy had told me once. Elder Adahy was the go-to man for any kind of advice. Come to think of it, Adahy was who you went to about anything.

When we got to America all those years ago, most of us were senseless and shell-shocked, a piece of bread and tattered hand-me-downs given to us by smiling Christians, ushering us into America with one wave and completely disregarding us once they found out we had nothing of value. Of the hundreds of us who had boarded that train so long ago, only eleven children and thirty-seven adults survived. Everyone else was gone—flat-out lost, like grains of sand falling through fingers on a wet beach. The tide came in and swooped us up, and we never came out of the water.

I shook my head, clearing my thoughts, and focused on Elder Adahy—or Ad, as we often called him.

Confused and with nowhere to go, us Jewish people went to the only logical places a group of displaced people could go: society's outskirts. Jews are used to it; it's been that way since Abraham first entertained the idea of sacrificing his son, since Moses decided to listen to a burning bush. Some of us called it faith. I called it hypocritical bullshit. Once in America, with those of us who were beyond just normal toilers, who showed some level of artisanship, we were snatched up fast. All our doctors and educated individuals had been the first to die in the camps. Those who happened to be unfortunate enough to survive the whole ordeal soon discovered that America wanted usefulness, not neediness.

Lost and with very little room to go anywhere, we strode out to the outskirts, this time with the Roma people campmates. Like us, they had suffered in the camps. However, their blights were far less well known and far less remembered. As Linor's grandma had put it when we were first on the road: "The world has always seen us as traveling cartoons—dancing bears and fancy cakes. Reading your palm one moment, stealing your automobile the next. We are the Roma people, and we stay standing—we don't take handouts and we take what we can, even if it's at the thinnest reaches."

I shivered, recalling the glare in her eyes that day. I was much younger then, wide-eyed and scared of my own shadow. *The only thing that has changed is your eyes,* whispered a very cold and powerful voice that caused my ears to burn red. Linor led us out of the camps, past my tent, past my firecrackers. I gulped hard; I was going to need those. *Girls like explosions,* echoed Elder Ad's words.

Elder Ad had taken our caravan in, not too long after we made our journey west. With very little money between us, and those of us alive in the group serving as the only family any of us had left, we had to take one final train. After spending days trapped in people's feces and the stench of those that were being led to the slaughter, most of us were reluctant to get on a train again. Some rides, you just don't know if you will ever get off again—I suppose that is true with all rides. Any moment might be your last. Only, when you've been on the train to hell, you know that the fancy carriage compartments with long individual velvet rows of comfortable chairs can easily be replaced with a human for every meter until you are packed tighter than fish in a can.

We rode in the fancy new aluminum and COR-TEN steel car compartments across a foreign land, displaced people starving and fearing that when that fancy metal train with smiling servants and lavatories with doors finally stopped, they might open to the flames again. I didn't sleep a wink the entire ride. Linor smiled, pressed her face against our window, and snorted at every barren rock and murky river all the way west.

That first year was the roughest, just because we were now a part of the Roma people. Other groups shunned us. Everyone was hurting, they would say. Some of our elders in the group protested, but Linor's grandmother just waved us forward—that woman never stopped. We kept moving, kept surviving, as she put it every day. Until we came to Oklahoma, a land of fertile grassland, rolled into neverending mountains that stretched all the way to Colorado, down to New Mexico.

It basically looked like one giant field with some mountains to me, too warm, and with weather that caused me to sweat even now, thinking about it.

We went with it until we came across one of the local reservations—Elder Ad was still tan and leathery in those days—a few less gray hairs, but still long of face, dotted by long indentions that were weathered into his skin. His face had once been a smooth earth, only to be shaped by the passage of time and water. Elder Ad took us in, our group of mismatched and half-starved lambs who were used to being shipped from slaughterhouse to another. Finally we had somewhere where we could rest. That was the thing about Elder Ad taking us in; it made sense, I realized now in hindsight. The only place for outsiders to go was to the outsiders—be with the Indians, who were the only people in the world who probably felt like aliens on their own land.

Our short reprise from constant vagabond life was brief and burned like a sparkler, so beautiful and just what the soul needed, only to end in darkness. Oklahoma was growing, and so was our camp, and as the 40s gave way to the period of high-demand goods of the 50s, roads needed to be built.

Our camp was in the way of progress, and progress waits for no one. It just builds a road, endless and covered in hot tar, burning the countryside. You can drive on progress, you can walk on progress, but you don't stop progress. Treaty or not, we had to hit the road. When we did, Elder Ad came with us. By that time, he had taken a liking to a thick-haired blonde woman named Alice. She was long hipped and broad shouldered, despite all the lack of nutrition we'd had over the years. Most importantly, though, out of those of us tested at the camps, Alice was the only adult to have survived the treatments. May have been something in her wide hips—or as Elder Ad put it, "That damn woman will mess you up, boy, if you stare too long."

Whatever the case was, she lived relatively unscathed until childbirth.

The thought made me wince. It had been a long time since I thought of Alice, since I had thought of anyone from the camps. That was how it went; you forget those that had left before you to survive. Only sometimes—more like all the time—it was the bitter truth that when those who die before you are taken, those who love you will always remember you. *That was the truth,* I thought as we stumbled deeper onto the dirt path, the thick green grass clumped over by the steps of countless feet.

Girls like explosions, I thought again as my pulsed raced, trying to stay in the moment with Linor. We came to a creek bed, the water flowing swift with a clear current that played with brown leaves and droves of small stones in its shallow movements. I looked at Linor: she had a thick smile spread across her face. I knew what she was thinking and before she knew it, I took three steps back, bolting forward with all my speed, and flew across the creek to the riverbank on the other side.

My feet clipped the muddy ledge and my boots became caked in mud. Linor laughed, slapping her knees. "Honestly—I never thought I would see the day when you would finally jump something! Avraham, congrats, I'm proud of you. Too bad you just couldn't make it." She gestured with her fingers, pulling them close to her eye, taunting me.

I turned red, feeling very silly despite finally jumping the creek. The thought alone caused me to shake in my legs, but by now, mud-soaked boots kept me firmly in place. The last time we had come this far down this path, Linor had easily jumped it, and so had my brother and everyone else we were with. I couldn't though—the idea of missing the creek bed and somehow flowing down the river kept crawling its way into my head, like some king of spider gliding across the water.

"Shut up. I would love to see you try and land as good as me," I said smartly, though I knew what was about to come. Linor simply smiled, pulled her dress up to her knees, bent slightly, taking off like a rocket, and landed a feet away from me as if she were simply stepping over a crack in concrete, rather than a fierce creek flow, threatening to steal us both in an unending tide down to a watery grave.

She smiled again, dropping her dress, and arched her back until a loud "pop" came out and she sighed heavily with pleasure. I shook a little as a stiff breeze came through. "You think way too much, Avi. No point in being so smart if you end up freezing up all the time. You weren't like that when we were kids; you always were willing to bust a knee or—"

I cut her off. "That was before—*him*. You know why." I grumbled, turning away from her, and started down to the dirt path leading away from the creek bed and out to an old gravel road.

"Avi, I wasn't trying to make fun—I understand, I'm sorry," she started to say. I ignored her and kept on walking, feeling anger boil within me. She was right, though. I used to be more than willing to fall as a kid: heights, speed, danger, I loved it all. It was the quickest way I could get my mother worried sick or my father scolding, spanking me when he knew I wasn't listening to anything they told me to do. I knew my behavior upset my parents—made Zevi scared. I just didn't care in those days. Life seemed so much different. Like a sun smiling on a crisp spring field, everything was going to be alright and there was nothing that could harm me. After the camps, though, I shook often. I was now afraid of heights, moving fast, anything that could potentially bring—*him*. It only took a moment; a drop of blood, and the monster was free. Hell would follow, and I wasn't going to subject myself to that ever again.

I dropped my shoulders though, turning back to Linor. "Don't be sorry, Linor, I shouldn't have gotten upset. Still want to go on that—date?" I hastily asked.

Linor beamed, walked up to me, kissed me on the cheek, and I flushed cheery red. "You don't have to be worry about being scared of nothing anymore, Avi—I will kick its ass. But you should watch out for that bear!" she shrieked, jumping back.

I snapped my head back to the left, fast to see a golden-brown bear, long limbed and as tall as a train compartment, standing only inches away from me. I fell back in the dirt, throwing one hand in front of my face, shouting, "Linor, get behind me, now!"

My heart pounded and nothing came. I waited; my eyes closed tightly, waiting for its thick paws to level me. Another heartbeat, another breath.

Nothing came. I moved my hand to see Linor bent over, covering her mouth as tears of mirth raced down her cheeks. I hated when she did that—never took anything serious. Everything was a joke to her.

I flushed with anger and palmed a handful of mud and took aim, throwing it on her dress. She stopped laughing and it was my turn to start giggling at her.

"Hey Avi, that's not funny. I really liked this dress—you jerk!" she screamed, kicking my boots and feinting, as if she was going to punch me.

I threw more mud. This time, it became entangled in the unyielding mop of her long black curly hair. I kept laughing, Linor kept muttering many curses in a few languages I understood, a few that I only ever heard her grandmother say to her.

"Not so funny now," I giggled as she came close to my face. I stopped laughing long enough to notice her lips near mine. I was afraid to jump a creek bed, I was afraid to ride my bike to quick, I wasn't afraid to kiss this fiery woman, though.

I went for it, slamming my mouth into the top part of hers as our teeth ground together. My heart started to panic. Unsure what to do, I sucked in my lips and tried to match hers. Linor didn't move her mouth for a moment, before a smile broke into her lips moving across mine, wet and tender.

"Glad you can have some fun," she whispered as her lips moved with mine. The initial awkwardness was all but forgotten in moments, and I felt lightning shooting through my body. I started to sit up when she gently pushed me away. "Easy there, tiger, we still have a date. And you're going to pay for ruining my pretty dress," she said, annoyed, and outstretched her hand toward me.

I took her hand and stood up. She brushed the dirt from my back. "Let's go, already. I have the perfect spot for us." I took her hand, this time with more confidence, and led us onto the gravel road.

15

Chapter 15

We found bikes at the end of the gravel road. The nice thing about the reputation of the Roma people being full of devil worshipers and thieves was that people tended to stay as far away from the camps as possible. We were miles outside of Tri-Cities Washington, in a sectioned-off piece of greenery that was more forest than civilization. However, with the postwar boom and the building of the Alaskan Way Viaduct last year, that was quickly changing.

We had been camped in Washington for about two to three years now, and with most of our group becoming batcavers, Elder Ad and Linor's grandmother felt it was time to start moving before the boom took full swing. For now, though, we decided to enjoy the perks of being able to leave brand-new bikes lying on the side of an embankment, while the rest of town thought we would steal their souls if they even looked at our stolen bikes the wrong way.

Though "stolen" was subjective, really: we just liberated them from the store front before the hippies following around all the goth bands in the freezing rain had time to waste their money on something other than fake herbal medicine and the "natural wonders" of the Gypsy people. Linor rode her bike in a rhythmic silence, next to mine, the big golden rims juxtaposed by the flank of green grass either side of us, streaming like a river made of emeralds. I smiled; the world was our playground and things were never so bad as when she was around. I pedaled faster, cutting her off with my glowing red bike.

Behind me Linor, scoffed, "Trying to be funny after I embarrassed you back on the river?"

"You know I'm funny. Just trying to show you the butt you will be kissing once I beat you to the store!" I shouted, pulling ahead of her and pumping the pedals as fast as my legs could go. The road was flat up until we came to the lake. By then, I knew Linor would beat me with her long and powerful legs.

Had to at least give her a challenge. I heard the quick pull of her tires scraping on the lose rocks below us and saw the gleam of her bike as she sped ahead of me, laughing the entire way. I smiled, standing on my bike and chasing after her.

We continued that way until we came to town. Small shops dotted the one lane of the downtown region. Buildings made of brick and timber from long-fallen trees crested by the clear lake. We stopped in front of the general store. The sun was still high in the sky as we got out and entered Pete's grocery.

The clerk was a balding man, thin gray hair slinging down to horn-rimmed glasses and a hunched-over back from many years of working behind a counter. With a puff he glanced at us, then quickly adverted his gaze when Linor looked his way.

"So, why are we here?" I questioned her as she pulled her bag pack in front of her.

"You know, this and that. Grandmother wants me to pick up a few supplies," she responded, pulling jars of peanut butter into her bag.

"Uh-huh," I muttered, keeping my eye on the store clerk, who was watching Linor quickly fill her backpack full of peanut butter, clothes, a twine of rope, and then stop in front of the bags of charcoal.

"Avi, I'm going to get the coal. You get the ice—and be ready to run," she remarked, putting the small bag of coal in her bag.

The clerk decided that was enough, making his way abruptly from behind the counter. "Hey, you kids!" he started.

"Now, Avi!" she proclaimed, and the store became filled with glowing red smoke. Birds of golden and purple flew in every direction, some bigger than the bikes we rode in on. The clerk dropped to the ground, covering the back of his head as the birds swooped close to his fingers.

"Holy shit," I blurted out, as Linor bolted to the glass doors leading to the streets. I froze for a moment, transfixed by the show of birds, and remembered to go for the ice. I ran to the counter, stepping over the clerk as the birds flew and cawed near his head. He swatted at them with his face down—had he opened his eyes, he would have noticed his hand flowing through them, turning the birds into thick colors of smoke when they connected.

"Sorry," I muttered, glancing at his belt which gleamed with a thick ring of keys. I had them unclipped and was moving around the clerk before he even noticed that they were gone. I flipped through the ring until I found the one marked "Ice." I went through the glass doors, the chime of me leaving barely audible over the hysteria of the birds.

Onlookers in the street gawked at the scene, as I raced around the corner of the store and came to the cooler marked "Ice." My hands shaking, I inserted the key, pulling two bags from the ice cooler. I left the keys in the lock—the old man was going to have a hard enough time as it was after all of that.

I shook my head and ran back to where Linor and I had stashed the bikes on the other side of the store. Linor was humming, her eyes miles away—as if seeing a different world. It was hard to tell with Linor; she always seemed to be seeing a world as if it was a moving canvas and all of us were just sharing in her world. When she brought out the creatures made of smoke, her eyes would glaze over, burning with a thick glow of silver. Her mismatched brown and green eyes were both completely gray as she concentrated. I hesitated to touch her as I hoisted my bike up right off the ground, securing the bags of ice on the back of the bike. "Linor, it's time to go," I urged, shaking her shoulder gently, as more people began to show up outside of the general store. I felt a hum of power run through my fingers when I touched her bare shoulder.

Linor responded slowly, her song increasing in tempo. Her eyes suddenly cleared. She looked at me, unsure at first and slowly awakening to remembering whom I was. "Avraham." She beamed.

I looked over my shoulder, both our bikes were close by. People came running out of the store, pointing in our direction. Time was up. I could no longer see the birds flying in the store, which meant what Linor was doing had ended. I swore. That was the longest I had ever seen one of her "creations," as she called them, stay around.

I looked back at her; a small drop of blood fell from her nose onto her hand.

She wasn't going to able to ride like that, I thought. "Come here," I grunted, helping Linor off of her bike. I placed her on the front of mine. She clutched her bag in her hands as I gulped in a big burst of air and started us in the direction of the lake, as we left the area. People shouted, swarming in our direction. The nice thing about small-town crime was that you could get away with a lot, and people would see you, of course, but excitement such as strange birds showing up in a convince store was something you just didn't see every day.

I pedaled hard, feeling my legs burning from the added weight of Linor and the goods that we had taken. I turned my head every couple of seconds, expecting sirens to be blowing behind us. Things were quiet as we rode deep into the thick green woods near the lake. Once we had gone long enough for me to think that no one was following us, I slowed down, taking the road nearest us, leading back into town.

People would most likely look for us on the main road. It was seldom that any criminal would ever turn around and go back to the scene of the crime. Which is exactly what I had planned for our getaway. I rode us silently to the back of the general store; the sun was setting closer to the side of the building. I still had time. Out front, a police officer was frantically trying to piece together the story being told to him by the old man. I caught snippets as I pulled in: "I'm telling you, those weren't normal birds, they were huge—beasts; dinosaurs, even! Wings bigger than your car!" the old man shouted, gesturing toward the police officer's car.

"Giant colorful birds; got it. Tiny men riding dragons..." the officer muttered as the old man turned red, flustered by the officer finding him completely incredulous.

I snickered, covering my laugh as I pulled up to the back porch area, a massive canister for loading and unloading the story blocking us from anyone on the other side of the building who might have been looking. Linor came back as soon as I hoisted her down from the front of the bike.

"How are you feeling?" My concern was turning into an intense uneasiness that I worried would cause me a nosebleed as well. Linor sniffled, more blood coming out of her nose. She took the end of her dress, hesitated for a moment, and decided it was the right thing to do, blowing her nose into the cloth. I looked away, giving her some privacy before lecturing her.

"That was crazy, you know. All that for some coal and peanut butter?" I asked, pointing toward the store, trying hard to not sound overbearing for a change. Today had been a good day, better than drinking more of the "meat and spit," just to end up doing something stupid, and sleeping in a ditch again.

Linor just shrugged. "You will see later. So what's the plan? Why bring us back to the scene of the crime?" she asked, pointing at the building.

"Good question," I said, while moving to the building. A ladder was attached to the side of the red brick, leading to the roof. "We are going up that," I pointed, forcing my body to keep moving as I started to shake. *Just keep moving Avraham; one step at a time. You've already measured it—no taller than some of the trees you climbed as a boy. Only that was different,* I thought as my hands touched the cool metal. In those days, if I fell the worst that happened was a busted head or broken arm. Now, it would mean the death of everyone. I gulped as sweat ran down my head.

I could feel Linor's concerned gaze through my shirt. "Are you sure about this, Avi? I mean, I appreciate the thought, but we can do something el—" she started, before I cut her off by climbing the rail and pointing my face toward the top.

"Yeah, I'm pretty sure this is dumb—everything is pretty dumb to me, though. What's one fucking dumb thing more?" I mumbled as I put my hands over another rung, climbing to the top. My eyes were stinging as the sweat came dripping down my face like a fresh spring storm. *All it would take is one misstep and down, down you will fall.*

I spat at the wall, closing on the top. "Not today," I grumbled, climbing higher until I came to the last step, hoisting my body over it and onto to the roof. I landed on the roof just a few inches off the ladder, but my body was drenched in sweat. I was gasping for air when Linor came over the top of the ladder. She was breathing slightly hard—otherwise, it seemed to take nowhere near as much effort out of her.

She looked at me, a frown forming on her face. "Are you alright, Avi? Way to be a little solider." She stretched her hand out to my shoulder, comforting me.

I smiled at her, sweat trickling down. "Well you know, if I didn't get up that ladder, I would have to look for a new girlfriend by the time we got back to camp," I stated.

Linor feigned being stunned. "Girlfriend? Wait, pump the brakes, Avi," she jabbed back, but helped me stand up. "Okay, so what was the point of coming up here?" she gestured.

I slicked back my long black hair, wishing now that I had gotten a hair cut before deciding to go on this date. *Roll with it,* I thought. "Just relax, set the coal down, and wait for the music," I replied.

"What music?" she asked, perplexed, as she sat her bag down. I took a deep breath and moved my hands to her hips. "When did you get so bold?" she whispered, as I took her hands and placed them around my neck.

"Been taking some classes three times since we left Texas," I stated.

I could see her thinking of the logistics of that before it dawned on her. "Avi, that was over a year ago. Are you crazy?"

"For you, totally," I said, my voice sounding in my head to be barely over a croak.

She smiled. "I like the new bold you. Your shoulders aren't as hunched for a change."

"Huh." I looked down to see if my shoulders were in fact hunched. She smirked at me and I smiled back, my cheeks turning red. "Baby steps," I muttered.

"Baby steps," she whispered back.

"So, where is this music?" she asked again.

I hesitated, my pulse pounding, I thought the hard part was going to be the ladder, not the dance. "Just keep waiting—do you trust me?" I asked, unsure as to what her response would be.

"Ever since I first met you," she responded.

We were quiet for a moment after that. I could feel her breath on me, and I was trying not to sweat more than I already had. If it bothered her, she didn't seem to care. My shirt felt as if I had taken a shower, as it clung to me like a wet rag.

It was little more than a rag, anyways. A rag I was probably going to have to set on fire at this rate, as more sweat dripped down my back. I started to mumble something, when a slow drum started being beat in the distance. Followed by another hit to the beat, and then the tempo started to roll, invigorating us in a quick whiplash of funk.

Linor's face lit up instantly, an element of pure enlightened ecstasy that I had never seen on her face before. "Avi," she whispered under the joyful funk.

"Just enjoy it... you're welcome. Some of the old guys play here every Tuesday night by the gazebo near the lake," I informed her, smiling back, as the two of us quickly moved from our spot.

My anxiety about the evening washed away, and I was no longer afraid of falling off the roof. Of somehow tripping and cutting myself. It was just the two of us, and to top it off, I hadn't stepped on her foot one time. As we danced to the energetic music that picked up in a rapid and gradual beat, we were both smiling so wide that I wondered if my jaw would ever be able to close again.

It was great being close to her. It was even better seeing her so happy, as rows of colors began to come out from under our feet, slowly. I was concerned at first that Linor was going to exert herself again. If it was causing her to be fatigued, I couldn't tell. She was smiling so wide and as the smoke around us, it changed into shapes of cats, dogs, birds, and even a long green dragon with golden talons instead of wings. The roof became our playground.

All the world was at play, and for the first time in fifteen years, ever since that long night when the train doors opened, I let my armor go, I dropped my sword and shield. I thought that in my life, I would forever remember the smoke, the food being pressed between my bars of my cage, the scream of small children in the distance, and the long time I spent trapped behind the fences, thinking I would die there. Alone, separated from my family, mixed in the ashes of those who had once been there.

I didn't realize I had stopped moving until Linor's leg kicked mine. "Oops, sorry Avi," she giggled, until something in my face made her change her tone. "Are you okay, Avi? Do you need to rest?" she asked, shaking my shoulders gently.

I shook my head, clearing the vision that had started to climb its way into my mind. The only thing that actually climbed any height, any danger, no matter the place or who I was with, my memories found a way to overcome any obstacle and made sure that even though I was no longer behind those metal poles streaming electricity, I *was* still behind them—I could never leave completely.

I was shaking when I felt Linor's hands climb up my back. The creatures around us were still dancing waves of smoke, visible as the sun started setting. We would have to leave soon, but the funk players would be at it all night. If I could just make one happy moment, just one for once, that lasted longer than a few minutes, it would be the best thing in this life.

She suddenly stopped, her eyes glazed over in almost tears. My heart skipped a beat and all I could think was *don't do anything stupid.* "Did I do something wrong?" I cautiously asked.

Linor blinked, laughed, and exclaimed, all in the span it took for me to blink my own eyes. "Just shut up, Avi, and hold me," she urged in her most level tone, which still came off in a flirtatious way. In that moment, under the night sky, my heart beating because of fear of being caught or falling off a grocery store, I went in for a kiss.

It was long and deep, and even though I felt my lips shaking, she didn't quit. Neither did I. At some point, I think my heart must have exploded, as I could no longer feel anything other than her mouth, the feeling of her bare flesh beneath my own. I'm not sure who broke away first, just that when it was over, for once I wasn't the sweaty one.

She stood there, a small smile in quiet amazement, a controlled grin forming even bigger, as she said, "You're just full of surprises today, Avraham, thank you." She jumped up and hugged me. I almost fell from her added weight, but I balanced myself, remembering that it would be getting dark soon, and Elder Ad wanted everyone back at the camp for one of his "spiritual talks."

I turned, taking her hand. "Come on, we need to be going soon," I urged gently, walking us to the direction of the ladder.

"Do you remember the first time we finally saw each other? In the..." she asked. She didn't need to finish her sentence—I knew what she was talking about. We all did, no matter how vague or gentle one of us tried to put it—we knew.

I sucked in a deep breath, settling myself onto the edge of the building, my fear of the height keeping my eyes glued to the ground, so very far away.

"What about it?" I asked venomously.

Linor winced before speaking. "Sometimes, this all seems so surreal: dancing on rooftops, robbing grocery stores, kissing on bikes in the middle of blistering summers. I never thought—thought that there would be anything besides cold wires and endless ash. It's like we are waiting for someone to pull a hood back from over our collective heads and boom, the joke is on us."

Linor sighed, and my anger dissipated once more. It was so hard controlling it when I got mad. Just the mention of the camps and my skin would itch.

I looked out once more at the setting sun, smelling the sweat on us both, even the sweat of the old men playing their funk into the long summer night. I was half the world away from the camps, but in that moment, I was back. In a long listless hallway, being dragged across the floor, like a mop more than as a child...

16

Chapter 16

"That was pretty touching. I didn't know you were capable of saying more than five words at a time to someone," Huey jabbed, as he pulled two bottles of beer from the tiny icebox in our trailer. He gestured to them.

I grunted, turning my head back to the sink, dipping my fingers in the water to wash the dust from work away. After a few splashes and nearly suffocating myself when trying to get dry with the towel, I stepped outside on the porch with Huey.

Huey sat on a small wooden stool, its blue legs chipped away to the bare brown underneath. I took a place in the broken lawn chair opposite him. If I always kept my weight shifted to the front right, I could just manage to sit down without falling over—just.

Popping the top of the dark beer Huey gave me, I drank slowly and looked out into the open field before us. Even though it was some time after nine, the night had already settled into its thick blanket, blocking out most the stars. I could still see a fox chasing a rabbit a few hundred feet away from us. An owl sleeping in a nest, the smell of the summer weeds pollinating in the light breeze. The wolf was always in me, and slowly but surely over the years, I had gained more of him than I could ever admit to Huey. I could see, smell, hear, move, and taste more than I had ever wanted to, ever since that day in the camps. I kept that information to myself; the less Huey knew, the safer we would both be. The less I knew, I think the safer everyone was.

"I think it's pretty cute, all that with your little girlfriend. Still, doesn't answer the questions, though. You sort of suck at telling stories. So many flashbacks and long, long pauses," Huey stated, sipping his beer.

"It's easier to be meta in hindsight about any story, okay? Besides, name one story you ever told anyone, besides some broad you were trying to impress, or a poop joke to a bunch of felons that lasted longer than two sentences, then tell me if you were satisfied with how it was told," I responded.

"Touché." He sipped again.

"That's what I thought, smart ass. I just needed time to enjoy that moment, that's all. So many things happened pretty fast after that. Up until that moment in my life, I had no happy memories. Linor was always at the center of the good ones, even in the camps. And let me tell you, Huey, once you've entered into a night where you're praying for anything, anyone, to help you out, then the terror has only just begun. When there is a chance to breathe, take it, because life has no finish line, and we never leave our long nights."

We both sipped in the sober night before I started my story again, picking up all those years ago as I was being pulled from my cage...

17

Chapter 17

I squeezed my knuckles, digging my nails into my skin, as I felt something hot start to burn inside me. So brittle, I felt, so little and surrounded by a never-ending blast of noise, one that played endlessly until my head was about to explode. Those monsters! All that they did... I would eat all of them, I would kill all of them. *Just let it go. Let the animal come out and all of this pain will go away.* But I was never going to let anything bad happen to Linor, not after last time. Not after—that first night we had arrived at the camps.

It seemed an endless amount of time ago that had passed. There were no windows in the room I was kept in, just the gray walls, the bars behind the coverings, the rage kept within the falling of an all-seeing timescale. As I had learned, people were wrong about time travel. I remember once, as a little boy, my *foter* reading a story to my *bruder* and me about a man who had built a time machine. The story was full of whimsical devices, tubes of fantastic colors, machines bursting with pipes and gears of unimaginable sizes. Bolts of raw electricity, streaming through bulbs bigger than our beds!

Such a device was needed for a man to go back in time, in that story—it was all bullshit, as I realized. You didn't need a machine that could only be built by mad scientists, you just needed a gray room with no windows, and no sense of day or night, under the blanket of a twitching yellow glow, hanging centimeters above your head. That was enough for me to time travel, enough for me to spend hours, curled up, flying back to the memories of playing ball games, sweeping *foter's* shop, eating my *muter's* cake, laughing with Linor. I clung to those memories—those cherished good times that I just couldn't hold onto, but which would stay with me, no matter my place and time. However, unlike the man in the story my *foter* read to us so long ago, I couldn't choose always which time periods I could go to—like now for instance; my mind remembered the thick doors opening on the train and the chaos that followed.

Storms of light shot into the darkness of the compartment, all of us becoming one-handed or blind, trying to keep the light away. We had become what they wanted us to be, creatures of the night, stuffed into a tiny cage reeking of piss and shit.

"Nothing could ever compare to how it feels knowing you'll never taste the sun again, but the winter can't last forever," the old Rabbi whispered as I stepped back from the lights. I turned, seeing tears in his gray eyes. I wanted to say something, to acknowledge that I had heard him, but I never got the chance as guns above us opened and fired above the train compartment.

We cried out shrilly in response, but to no avail. I flinched in my cold bars as I remembered the way we were cattle, led out of the car, lines forming in different directions, being struck from countless directions. A man shouting in German nearly every step, someone else lost in each step. It was a mass panic, a sea of people, yet we were somehow being shepherded to our doom.

Two men, one holding a rifle, were jamming, bludgeoning, striking, hitting anyone that came near them, while another man, sharply dressed in a gleaming uniform, fiercely examined everyone who passed them, as we were quickly put into a line. I turned, and felt a hard thump across my brow and heard the shout, "Face forward!" I never saw who it was that shouted at me, as my head was spinning, and I would have fallen had I not felt hands on me. They were wrinkled, yet strong. I knew it was the old Rabbi; he was keeping me up. I felt something hot trickle down my face, and I tasted metal and earth. I was bleeding, enough to cover my eye. I wanted to cry, to cry so badly again. But my eyes were open, and no tears would come.

I stumbled over my feet; I felt the Rabbi's hands on my arm. Where was *muter*, where was my *bruder*? My thoughts ceased instantly, throttled into an unmoving crawl of the white frosts of snowy hell—but the snow was ash, ash of the people that I once knew; my people.

I jerked back in the Rabbi's hand, my eyes taking in the massive pit burning just beyond the two German soldiers sorting people. We were heading right to it, a path to the end with no way out except forward. Hands pushed from behind, silent prayers of fear carried me, one step, two steps, three shaking steps.

"This is monstrous—no words," choked the Rabbi through thick tears. I could see land on the ground below us, quickly swallowed by the footsteps of the damned. "All any of us ever have is segments, segments of our life before it's snatched out," mumbled the Rabbi, before he suddenly turned facing me, bending to my level. "Boy, remember what I told you on the train—if people believe enough, hate enough, some truly monstrous creatures can be born—"

I never got to hear the rest of what the Rabbi said. A shot rang out and blood sprayed on my face. A moment later, the Rabbi slumped forward, nearly knocking me over, if it wasn't for a solider gripping me, yanking me from the hold the Rabbi had on my forearm. His grip was so tight, my skin was burning, melting even! It was such an intense heat that I cried out.

My skin crawled, my flesh running from the burning sensation. Something awful was being done to me—there was nothing I could do to stop it. The solider pried more on the old Rabbi's arm, until finally another solider stomped on the arm of the old Rabbi. A few kicks, and my arm was free. I pulled my arm to my chest, the pain like molten bricks touching my bare flesh, pressing hard, burning until even the bone was ash.

I looked, and my arm was a furious red, a network of veins shooting in all directions. I wasn't sure if it was the blood drifting into my eyes, but I could have sworn I saw something black, swimming along my veins. Like a dark cloud flooding a tunnel. I gasped at the snakes swimming up my arms, my skin a blistered red, borderline crisp in some parts. As I examined my arm in terror, I was shoved forward again, tripping over the old Rabbi. I never learned his name, never learned how he got to the city. Instead, I watched as his body was trampled into the dirt.

I pointed myself back toward the fire, I wondered if it would be quick. I neared the two sorters—the older of the soldiers looked almost bored as he mumbled, "Rechts und links," pointing at the flush of people's cheeks, the color to their skins, the shine of their eyes. Who was healthy, though? I wondered what awaited those that went to the right. Ahead of me were a *muter* and child. I blinked, thinking of my own *muter*, of my own *bruder*. Where were they?

I could hear the soldier with the clipboard. "Too weak. Filthy," and the *tokhter* was sent left, the *muter* right. The *muter* pulled from the arms of the soldier pushing her right. I panicked. What could I do to help? What could any of us do? I clutched my arm to my chest and closed my eyes.

I opened my eyes as I was shoved again, nearly falling over. Both the *muter* and *tokhter* were being pushed left to the pit—now I could smell the hair burning, clothes, boots, and shoes. I could see piles of jewelry and *mishpokhe* heirlooms thrown in a heap that was almost as tall as the fences. I couldn't breathe, couldn't walk. I choked on the screams all around me and I heard the crackling of fire but knew there wasn't wood in that pit.

Maybe this was just how it was supposed to be? This was the only way it could end? I missed my *foter* terribly—I had already let him down. I stepped up to the two guards. One was young, close enough that I wondered if, in a different life, he could have been my older *bruder*. His helmet was slightly too big, his uniform sagging off him as well, down to his gray trousers jammed deep into his boots. He gripped his rifle, thumping his fingers along the wooden butt as if he was nervous, while his eyes constantly shifted from us to some far-off location.

The other man, the one with the clipboard, was older, hair thinning and as gray as the uniform the men wore. Eyes long and peering through his glasses, as they gazed down his long beaked nose. He looked tired, as if he had been examining those before the gates of Erebus before sending them to their destination. *It must be exhausting*, I thought, judging all these people, killing us before our *bruders* and *shvesters*, *muters* and *foters*.

I want to hurt this man—I want to hurt him so bad, punish him and send him to his own gates of hell, like he is doing all of us. The burning in my arm began to move, flashing, sheering up my arm, like it had a mind of its own and its only goal was to consume me in fire. That was alright, though—one way or another, I was going into the fire. I had always been a good boy—someone my parents sometimes had to chastise for being to mean to my *bruder*, for not picking up my toys, doing a poor job of sweeping the store—I was a good boy, though I was afraid that boy was no more.

"I'm sorry, *foter*," I mumbled as I approached the two men. I knew the blood coming down my head would discount me from whatever was right. They seemed to be only taking the strongest, the healthiest of us.

For some reason, though, when the old man with the clipboard looked at me, his exhausted blue eyes froze on me. He didn't shift them around, only stayed focused on my face. I clutched my burning arm to my chest, my whole body building heat, like I was a furnace and my skin was the house for the fire. Blood continued to flow down my face, past my eyes and into my lips. I sucked my lips in, tasting the metal of my blood, afraid to open my mouth because I might scream otherwise. His stare had an intensity to it, an air of darkness that swelled as he moved his eyes over me. I met his gaze; this was the man responsible for so many people's death.

My *zayde* once told me that when you meet the devil, you hold his gaze, no matter what—you were about to be in pain anyways, unimaginable pain. Might as well face him on your own terms. Though I think *zayde* was referring to something in the woods, but who knows? I just wished he was here. *Zayde* seemed to always know what to do, just like my dad did. The thought of my dad caused me to lower my chin, tears coming out—I couldn't pretend to be tough anymore.

The old man cackled. "For a moment there, I thought we had found us one we couldn't break, there, Corporal Philip."

"Yes, Herr Mitz," the young solider mumbled, facing toward me finally. His hands still shook, and his eyes were wide. He was just as scared as I was, just as lost. Why were we here, here in such an awful, awful place? I wanted to speak to him, to ask him for help. Maybe he would help me. Maybe he wasn't as bad as the Mitz person, with his judgmental blue eyes, like bombers waiting to find their target.

Only my voice never came. Herr Mitz smiled, nodded his head, then wrote something down on his clipboard. "We have no room for those that can't work, but you seem to be of strong stock, though you would just get others sick, as much as you're bleeding. I'm afraid it's the pits for you," he sneered.

I felt the young soldiers' hands on my back, and with a hard shove I was sent down the walkway that lead to the burning pit. Double sets of metal fences surrounded me, shooting electricity to their barbed fingers above. I looked out beyond the fence line and saw only darkness, as if those metal arms, those metal webs glowing blue and dancing with the pale orange of the flames on their shining metal, were the only thing that existed now.

The ground beneath me held the footprints of so many, the weeping steps of people going to their faith. Flames crackled high, and I flinched, knowing what was coming. It was silent near the flames. Soldiers gathered in the distance, their uniforms bleached crimson by the pit. It was a lake of fire—a dragon with its mouth agape. I looked at the pile of goods that were teetering on overflowing over the fences. I had no goods, no *mishpokhe* treasure tucked away.

A soldier nearest one pile of clothes motioned for me to take my shoes off. I slid out of my loafers, a heel missing on my left one from all the running, smudges of dirt so thick that my *muter* would have had a heart attack had she seen it. I tossed my shoes on the pile of others: boots, heels, loafers, and too many small baby shoes.

The soldier once more pointed to another pile. The remains of my trousers and shirt came off, the smell until that moment I hadn't realized would be so strong—so potent. Still, though, my *muter* had made those clothes for me, she had stitched together my pants many times after I tore them. And the shirt, though long since covered in blood from too many sources, had somewhere in its fabric, in its stiches, the last bit of my *foter*.

Like that, I was naked in the dark, nothing but dirt and the smiles of the devil between me and a lake of fire. Finally, I started to sob. I just wanted to be back at home again, in my bed listening to Zevi snore, playing with my tops or playing ball. Anywhere, even back on *zayde's* ranch cutting wood or peeling potatoes with my *bubbe*. School didn't sound that bad, even. Fighting sleep, being forced to read the Torah and other books. I hated it all; I just wanted to be outside to play.

"Move!" shouted a voice from somewhere in the darkness, and my thoughts were sent flying like a popfly into the night. I moved my legs stiffly, robotically, near the fire. I could feel a heat so great that the blood on my face dried, and the hair on my arms started to burn. I was already burning, I realized. Under my skin, the festering heat was building intensely, crackling like some kind of mad animal fighting to break out.

Firm hands gripped my shoulders once more and I knew that it was time. I would see my *foter* again shortly. I closed my eyes as multiple sets of hands took hold of my shoulders, of my back. I had no idea where they came from, who they belonged to, but I knew where they were sending me. I was lifted, quickly, with the experience and efficiency of people that had done this many times.

My body sailed through the air, and I kept my eyes shut, hoping this was all a dream, this would be over. I felt the heat first, then the breath was taken from my lungs, pulled out screams that vanished into the flames. The pain was beyond words, beyond anything that I could ever describe.

Something was angry, though. In the flames when I should have died, I heard the roar. My bones crackled, steamed, tore, and ripped to pieces. My skin peeled away, and a thick smoke covered me. Somehow, I had hit the ground of the pit, and torches continued blowing out a toxic fume that combined with the flames. It washed over me, my eyes rolled back, and I was hanging on by a breath.

I was shivering in the darkness, when I heard the yelp. I looked down. Before me was a puppy. Its ears were pointed high, small horns jotting from its head, only mere knobs of bone. Its fur was pure midnight, a body of lean muscle, even for something so young. It turned its head toward me, and the same gray eyes of the old Rabbi met mine, gray old eyes full of a hatred that was deeper and hotter than the flames eating me. I wanted to be afraid of this small beast, but he was young, just like me. I reached down and rubbed his fur, petted his head. The small puppy turned toward me; I became lost in those deep crimson eyes.

All the pain stopped in that instant. Like a light switch, the flow of pain ceased, and I ended, along with the pain. And out came the wolf.

18

Chapter 18

My time travel was done for the day, I decided, as I remembered the first night in the camp. It all felt like a dream—or so I would have thought it, had I not awakened to being surrounded by guards, their guns pointed at me. I had been stuck in a similar cage to the one I was in now—much smaller, though. I was naked, strapped down under a pile of chains, the metal so cold to my skin. I had never felt so fatigued in my life, drained out like an apple sitting on the windowsill for months.

Since waking up, I had spent many days seeing the good doctor, too many days being asked to speak and explain what I was. I didn't know what I was, or how I had done what I had done. I just remember the images, the grizzly shouts as men died. Fire, fire everywhere, that seemed to never end. My fangs and claws—no, *his* fangs and claws. The puppy was growing, getting bigger and stronger every day. I could hear him sometimes, calling me, wanting to come out. To meet him back down in the flames.

I shook, my throat dry, the bars only growing closer and closer every time I looked at them. The doors to the room opened slowly as I looked at the bars of my cage. I saw Hans's black-fisted gloves, tight to his massive hands and crisp uniform. Dr. Joachim almost melted into the low light of the room as Hans held the door for him. Dr. Joachim was clad in his deep gray lab coat, wrinkled and untidy, like it hadn't been taken off in days. His glasses were hanging by a chain around his neck. I had never seen Dr.

Joachim disheveled. I crouched back in my cage. This couldn't be anything good. He always seemed like something was cooking under the surface like a pie made with a living chicken instead of one already butchered.

Joseph and Albert came in afterward, their brown uniforms untidy as well, with Albert's shirttail untucked in the back, and his face looking to be breaking out in a sweat. Both had a rifle tucked onto their shoulders, the long barrels tied with a strap. That was even worse—that meant I was being moved. Sure enough, I noticed the long chains over their shoulders, links as big as my fists. Out of the four, Hans was the only one calm, looking almost bored, his one eye glancing at the adjacent wall. Usually, when I was being moved, there would be hordes of guards flanking them, just in case I got wild.

Dr. Joachim spoke once the doors were closed. He held a black journal, with markers on nearly every page, a thick black pen in his right hand. His sword, which, when pressed to a page, could do untold amounts of damage. "Good morning, young wolf—I must profess that I do apologize for not coming to see you sooner. These last few days have been"—he paused, searching for the words—"unfortunate," he said with an air of disappointment that I couldn't understand. It was true that I hadn't seen the doctor or any of his men, other than Albert and with the rare appearance of Joseph.

I simply looked at Dr. Joachim. What difference did anything that he was saying matter? I was still stuck in this cage. "It seems that the Jewish-lover Americans have landed—they may even get this far." He huffed and there was a collective sigh from everyone, except for Hans. "It seems that our time may not be as long together as I would like, dear wolf. These past two years have been some of the best research that I could ever dream of. Such wonderful things I have learned from studying you. I think I haven't even started it yet; there is so much still left to be learned." His eyes sparkled with pride as I felt like I was going to throw up. It was the most terrifying and disgusting thing I had ever heard. Two years—two years trapped inside of a metal cage, two years since I had seen another living soul, besides guards with guns. Guards with food, guards with chains, guards with needles, guards dead from whatever was living inside me. Two years of constantly being nearly drowned by water, shocked until my teeth and bones rattled, that smug look on the doctor's face seeming to never go away.

But two years, two years of this. I looked at my fingers; they were prune-wrinkled and bruised. I wondered how I must have looked. My nails had grown jagged and long, sharp like talons. I felt my mop of hair that was thick, matted, and dried to the point of feeling like horsehair, like I used to brush from my *zayde's* horses growing up. It hadn't felt like two years had passed, so much time spent here… I wondered if Linor was okay, if Zevi was doing well, if my *muter* had made it.

I looked up at the doctor as he continued, "I'm afraid we are going to have to rush things along—we need to find the catalysis for what you are. This facility doesn't have the manpower to cut you open again—" he exclaimed.

Albert muttered behind him, "Not yet, at least."

The doctor rolled his eyes, motioning with one hand to Hans. Hans nodded once, and in a blur, moved toward Albert, yanking the rifle from his hands and butting him with the metal end in his stomach. Albert lurched forward; Hans sidestepped to let Albert fall to the ground. He then very gently placed the rifle back into his hands. "On your feet solider. Be quiet." He spoke with confidence and yet still conveyed an air of disjointedness about him.

Dr. Joachim started again. "As I was saying, we need to do something else. So, I am feeling particularly magnanimous today, my young canine friend. Very, very confident that today is the day you finally speak, finally crack, and tell us what you are. I think you will be so grateful for what we are about to do for you that we won't ever have to use the hose again."

Joseph, who had helped Albert back to his feet, almost looked sad, almost. During most the beatings, he would keep track of how many hits I would take on the yellow notepad he kept in the back of his trousers. He wrote in it first thing at the end of every one of the tortures. Quick to jolt down whatever he was gaining from all of this, a small smile would play out over his lips. In a lot of ways, Joseph scared me the most out of the four. Hans was the fiercest one in the room, but he seemed to be in control—there was nothing hiding there. He was the number two in the room, the fist for the doctor. With Dr. Joachim, I never knew what to expect from his sadistic mouth. He was consistent, though; he only cared about whatever was inside me.

Albert was a moron who seemed to love torturing me, yet I could see him a mile away every single time. Joseph, however, he was friendly first, and smiling—he would sometimes even talk to me about his wife and kids back in Mintz. When the curtain was drawn and the play was no longer in effect, he would smile at the pain inflicted on me, looking forward to it, and even when things got most brutal, he would be almost eager. Something was off with Joseph. In a room full of monsters, a monster that was hiding was the scariest one.

I shook, glad for the first time that my bars separated me from the monsters. Math wasn't my best subject, but I knew no subject besides reading. I could even read anything but certainly couldn't write to save my life. As my teacher had told me countless times, "Your writing is horrendous, and your spelling is atrocious." So I couldn't read the passage of time, and my skills with keeping track of the days was meaningless. Maybe it had been two years—that was two years without the Purim, without Hanukkah. Useless skills, I thought; none of them were saving me now—I had no idea when or where I was.

I thought on that. Had I noticed snow on any of the guards? Maybe it was close to December? Maybe Hanukkah was still going on and somewhere Linor was celebrating it with my *mishpokhe*.

"Young wolf—are you ready to see the outside world?" Dr. Joachim inquired. I looked at the man, searching for any signs in his face, the deep lines of age, the thick gray eyebrows that were so busy, I think he would put a bear to shame! Dr. Joachim gestured to Hans with his right hand, his eyes never leaving me. "Say the words, 'I want to see the outside world,'" he urged, and his voice fretted on the line between cracking and holding it together, like he was a potpie about to explode. "You get to see your—friends... you get to see them all." He almost sounded like he was pleading as he neared my cage. Hans came around to the front of the cage and opened the door, unbolting the heavy padlock that I had tried breaking so many times. The lock dropped to the ground, hitting the dusty floor below. I tracked it with my eyes, not believing what I was seeing. Every instinct in my mind screamed to run, screamed to shout with joy: *I was finally free!*

Don't... the beast growled. I flinched at the suddenness of his voice. He had been quiet for so long that I almost thought for a moment, thought for a moment that maybe it was gone, and I was a normal boy again. He would never be gone, though; he was a constant overgrowing scar that would never fade away, only develop until it consumed me. Yet, this time, despite the fear that shivered up my back, I stayed where I was. Even as Hans opened the door, swinging it wide, Dr. Joachim smiled at me. I kept my body still—despite the urge to bolt, take off, and never be around these people again. I was the fastest when we played ball. I could run fast: just put my head down, pump my arms, and be gone. Just—I knew I wouldn't make it far. Somehow, out those doors, I knew that nothing good was waiting for me. Even if I could leave here, what could I possibly do? I was just a kid.

"I promise you, this is no trick. You get to go see the outside world. Just say the words," Dr. Joachim pleaded once more. He sighed heavily, turning his back to me. "Surely I would think that a little boy like yourself would want to someone else other than me and that ugly grimace of Hans. Plenty of girls and boys your age. Lots of Jews and Gypsies," Dr. Joachim explained, before I sprang from my corner to the hinges of my feet.

It was Linor; it had to be her. She could still be alive. If she was alive, all the others would be as well. Surely that must be so. There were only so many Gypsies. There couldn't be that many of them here at the camps. There was hope, just a little bit, but a little bit was all it ever took. My *foter* told me that a lot, whenever I would get stuck on something in my homework or when I complained about sweeping. Both seemed like such minor things now, that I truly missed. He would well me, "Just a little bit,

Avi, that's all it ever takes is just a little bit, and you will be surprised at what can be done with a little bit."

I remembered my *foter's* words well. Without thinking, I parted my lips and spoke the first words that I had in what was years now: "I... want... to... see... the... out-side... wworld," I croaked through weak lips. I had spoken a few words here and there, during the long and lonely nights. I had needed to hear something, even if it was a whimper, something besides the cold dark walls. But these words now, they didn't feel like my own—they were edges in a stone, showing the outline of a creature long ago. Sure, it had existed once, may have even been similar, but it wasn't me. It was the same with my words.

The doctor smiled; I could feel it even before he turned around. "The wolf speaks! Yes, the wolf speaks." He beamed, I had never seen the doctor so happy. I coughed, my throat sore, feeling like it had forgotten what it was like to make sounds other than hisses or growls. "Albert," Dr. Joachim stated.

"Sir," snapped Albert, his whole body going rigid.

"Be a good lad. Fetch the young wolf his water bowl... and get some clothes. Can't have him going outside in this weather like—that." Dr. Joachim gestured toward my chains and lack of clothes. I had long since accepted that I was without what I used to have: not even a bathroom, nor a shirt to keep me warm. The chains had long since torn the skin from my wrists. Despite being metal cuffs, they were the closest things I had to clothes now.

"Come on out of the cage. No one here will hurt you—you get to see your friends." He emphasized the "friends" and ushered me out of my cage.

I was slow at first, unsteady, and my legs didn't trust the feet that were moving them. Every step felt like it could be my last. Sway too much to the right and I would break something, too much to the left and it was all over. Hans had stayed by the door of the cage as I crawled out, his face as impassive as ever. Joseph remained out of sight of the doctor; a strange smile played over his face. More alarms started going off in my head—I ignored them. I was finally free.

I almost fell twice. Dr. Joachim outstretched his arm. I took hold of his sleeve, and the doctor helped me walk a few more steps. My legs felt weak—I staggered like a baby lamb. Both Hans and Joseph looked repulsed by this, an old man helping a boy walk. It was the vilest thing they had ever witnessed.

It's because of what I am: not that I am a monster, but because I am a Jew. To them, I must have seemed like a double monster—something out of a nightmare. Whatever was inside me, whatever was outside me, I was hated; I was looked down upon with every step. I thought of my *muter's* embrace, I thought of seeing Linor's sweet curly black hair once more, and I used their images in place of the stares. I may have been lower than the dirt on the floor I walked to these men, but they couldn't take away what I was seeing inside my head. I couldn't be lowered that far.

We soon reached the double doors as the end of the room, Dr. Joachim and me. It was the furthest I had been away from my cage since I had first come to this dreadful place. All the other times that the doctor had experimented on me, they would bring some kind of cold metal contraption that they used to tie my hands with leather straps. They would place a belt in my mouth, and I would gag from the taste of worn leather. I could see the tooth marks that had already been worked into the groves of the leather. Like it had been used on someone before me. I could taste whoever had previously had this belt in their mouth. I prayed that whomever it was, that they had not suffered worse than I had.

I had a feeling though: if they had suffered less, they would still be here. I shook those thoughts away. I wasn't getting any yellow cake from my *muter*, but I would get to see her again, finally, after so long. That was better than cake, and I could live with that, just being able to have her hold me again. Tears came down my cheek. Dr. Joachim pretended to not notice. He just smiled that large smile of his and hummed some strange song that made my skin itch as we waited at the doors.

Cold air was coming from outside. Somewhere beyond those doors, it was winter. I hoped that Albert would come back with a thick coat—knowing Albert, though, that wasn't likely. I was shivering, my body rattling when the double doors finally swung open. Albert had in one hand a dog bowl that was filled with water, in the other a simple pair of overalls, with a faded striped shirt.

"Sir!" snapped Albert coming into the gray room as the doors closed behind him.

Dr. Joachim scoffed, rolling his eyes deeply. "Albert—dear boy. I want you to think just for once in that tiny little skull of yours. The temperature is cold enough to freeze water outside, so you bring back, out of all the clothes in this facility, something that looks like it was stolen from a bum?" Dr. Joachim shouted.

Albert avoided eye contact. "Sir, there was nothing else. I had to take this from one of the *untermenschen*," he mumbled.

Dr. Joachim reeled, dropping my hand from his sleeve like I was a dry leaf holding on in the wind. "You're paid to serve, solider; you're paid to do what I say when I say it. Exactly as I mean it to be done. Do you understand me?" Joachim snarled, spit flying onto Albert's face. "Now move your incompetent ass. See to it that you find the boy some shoes! We already know how he reacts to the cold. Are you deaf or are you trying to kill the most valuable asset in this camp? Yes, I mean the most valuable—even for a filthy Jew, he is more important than you can realize, you monkey!"

"Right away, sir, yes!" snapped back Albert, dropping the clothes.

"Leave the water," shouted Hans as Albert started to turn away. Albert jerked back as if he was pulled around. He turned slightly and dropped the water bowl on the ground.

Dr. Joachim wheeled back, facing me once more. The snarling was completely forgotten, and he was the good doctor again. "Sorry about that, my boy. Good help is just so—well, you can always find help..." he hummed to himself. "Drink up—get dressed," he directed.

I eyed him, keeping an eye on Hans and Joseph as I moved toward the bowl. Greedily I stuck my face down in the bowl, trying to fumble it to my mouth. Thankful for the drink. It hurt at first, my throat creaking and cracking. Other than the hose and the occasional meal, I couldn't recall the last time that I'd had this much water. I gulped it down, licking the bowl of all droplets. When I was finished, I dropped the bowl and went back to my watch of the three of them.

The doctor's smile seemed to have grown, stretching from ear to ear. "Get dressed," he commanded. I hesitated, picking the shirt up gingerly, and put it on quickly. The fabric itched—smelled like sweat. I was thankful though. Just that thin layer of cotton made standing in front of the doors better. The overalls came on quickly; they must have belonged to someone my *foter's* size. I had to roll up the legs for my feet to fit. When I finished, I stood in the cold room, just me and the only people that had spoken to me in the last two years.

Not much longer, I thought, *soon I will have muter and Zevi... even Linor and this will all be a dream.* I wouldn't have to see that cage ever again. I glanced at the gage, remembering where I had put the knife. Looked like I wouldn't have to make that choice. The beast wasn't going to hurt anyone ever again. I said a silent prayer—thankful that no one else would get hurt.

"Oh, Joseph, get the camera ready," Dr. Joachim directed.

What does he mean, "camera?" I kept my eyes averted to the ground, I may have been free of the cage, I wasn't free of this place, though. I was drilling holes into the floor, when the metal doors slung open and Albert strolled back into the confines of the gray prison.

I looked up; Albert tossed the shoes at me. I closed my eyes as the tattered boots hit my face. The boots were falling apart, the leather shattered and crinkling. If it had been new, it would have hurt more. Bending over, I kept my eyes on Albert as I reached for the boots.

"Stop," snarled Dr. Joachim. "Albert, pick the boots up and place them in the wolf's hands. Now," he commanded, his face a torsion of absolute authority that may have been wrinkled by time, yet reflected the lines of a man that was used to getting what he asked when he spoke.

Albert stood stiff for a moment, slowly nodding his head and reached down, scooping the boots off the floor like they were a newborn baby. With a slow and tender grace, he outstretched his arms until I took the boots from his hands. I snatched them quickly, my long fingernails scratching Albert as I pulled away. His face momentarily contorted in pain—I was going to pay for that later. Good, I thought, any amount of punishment was worth getting to see my *mishpokhe* again.

The boots were about two more of my feet, just as oversized as the overalls. I remembered how many clothes I had seen piled up when I first got here. Where were all those now? They had been good clothes, maybe soiled a bit from the train, but what I was wearing now was little more than the pillowcase that had lined me and my *bruder's* sheets.

As I laced the boots, my fingers shook from the effort. It had been two years since I had tied anything. When my hair got in the way, I would simply chew the bits that extended into my mouth. Fingers could forget memories, just like the brain. That was unfair, though. Why should the hands forget things, but the heart never forgets? Why was it easier to hold something than to love? I relived the pain of that long night, my own gun that fired bullets into a never-ending nightmare that couldn't be forgotten; its target was my heart and the boom could still be heard after all this time.

Slowly, I stood back up with my oversized clothes. I smoothed down my shirt, tucking the tail in. My *muter* would often get mad if I treated my clothes disrespectfully. As she'd put it: "Do you think we are wealthy, Avraham? You need to take care of your clothes. Your *foter* and I worked too hard for you and your *bruder*—to be so filthy," she would gripe. I missed that so much now. I would gladly take her scolding. Soon, soon, *muter* could complain all she wanted about my appearance. I just wanted her to hold me—hold me with only the warm embrace a *muter* can provide.

"Are you ready to go, young wolf?" Dr. Joachim inquired, moving to the double set of doors.

"Yes—sir," I added, thinking that to placate the doctor was the safest bet to ensure I didn't end back up in the cage.

"Good," he responded, gesturing to Hans.

Hans came to the doors and motioned to Albert and Joseph, who had returned with a camera. It was unlike any I had seen back in my hometown. It was smaller, the metal frame looking sleeker, and had two big barrels like things on the back. A small tank—just another weapon of these people.

Dr. Joachim started toward a long hallway, more gray-lined walls that had never had a happy soul walk through them, just these guards and wherever they might have gone after that. Behind me walked Joseph and Albert, their boots clicking loud down the barren hall. Hans flanked behind Dr. Joachim, who strolled like he was a man entering a park. I suppose he had finally gotten what he wanted from me. I didn't understand why, all these months, years, that he was so obsessed with getting me to talk. Why he was so drawn to me? That night I arrived was a blur, just the flames and the aches I had when I awoke. As if my body had been flattened by some train. My skin a fiery red, that peeled for days, worse than the summer months at *zayde's* lake. Though that wasn't the thing that was the most confusing—those first couple of days strapped to that table, and all the people staring at me. When I had awoken to their eyes, unblinking in the cold darkness, the flames seemed like a candle to a much larger inferno.

When I had finally stopped crying that first day, I had coughed up a wad of blonde hair, thick and bundled into a ball. When I could go to the bathroom, the nurse with her pan, shoving it under my bare body, and the endless stares continued. Watching me shit and piss unflinching, constantly writing that first few days. They looked on whatever came out of me. They gasped, and it was the most painful time I had ever relieved myself, like I was passing something hard, shredded and yet brittle. I shook my head at those thoughts, and at the frightful temptation of being lost in memories that had, by now, become almost a comfort—because out of all the things that had happened while trapped behind those metal bars, I could be sure the bad memories were at least mine.

That was the twisted thing I was learning quickly. So many bad memories could just stack like blocks of stones until they were taller than the pieces of wood that were the good ones. But, as we walked the poorly lit corridors, a faint small spark burned—just a few more steps and this nightmare was finally over. I noticed there was no one else in the area besides us, our steps clanking on the hardwood floor beneath us until we rounded the corner and passed an open garage door.

The door led to a loading dock that was filled with tables bearing stacks of clothes, shoes, watches, bags, necklaces, food utensils, and many jewels, the light reflecting from rubies hitting my eyes as we neared the door. We were in a massive loading dock, where gigantic trucks with train-tracked backs filled the area nearest the tables. The front of each truck was coated in gray, with curved crosses painted on the doors, while the back looked like bicycle wheels trapped between thick tracks of metal.

I had seen very few vehicles. Some would come into town, blowing smoke, louder than a ball shattering a window! Most of them were just tractors, and the only big ones I had seen close to the ones in the garage had been in Warsaw, but we had only gone there to see my *tante's* wedding—that had been years ago. Still though, none of them in that city had even looked... so terrifying, like metal dragons that had been made for the purpose of destroying, devouring the world under their armored tracks like flowers under a boot.

Shivers raced up my spine. The doctor stopped turning into the garage's doorway slightly, to peer at the many soldiers rifling through the piles on the tables nearest the huge trucks. Their uniforms were black like Hans, only their lapels were stains of red, with emblems of lightning bolts on them. There were a few woman guards as well—one who even looked like my *muter*, her cut shorter and angled like a knife's edge, her longer neck and limbs coupled with eyes that burned like a hazel hayfield.

I had seen her once before. She had fed me once when I was on the table. She wasn't as cruel as Albert taunting me with the food, but no guard here gave me food without at least some level of scorn. To them I was less than the boards we walked on. There were clothes of more value which remained unused on the metal tables, memories forever frozen in the shapes and sizes of those they used to belong to.

I avoided her eye contact, hoping that she would move on as I gave a silent prayer to the ground. Hopefully, the others were better off than I was. I prayed Yahweh was listening below as above, with as many prayers as I had to make with my head bowed.

"Dear Jutta, what is the status of the patients?" inquired Dr. Joachim as he walked up to one of the tables, picking up a small pair of pants with the tip of a long black pen, a small smile traced over his lips.

"We lost three of the adults last night, Dr. Joachim. Two males and one female. All bled out from their corneas. A thin film of blood again, doctor," Jutta responded quickly, standing along with the other guards in the room. I would never understand the bearing of the military, to go from a moment of living to hardly moving at all. It was the strangest thing to see, and made me feel like I wasn't around people—I was around some kind of machines dressed as men and women.

Dr. Joachim grimaced, his face creasing in a moment of anger. I had seen that look before. I stepped back until I hit something hard and unmoving. I turned around; Hans was looking down at me as my too-big shoes stepped on his boots. I stepped forward quickly and kept my head down, thankful that it had been Hans's shoes that my feet had landed on and not someone else's. Hans carried a weight to him that gravitated fear. It wasn't just his monstrous looks—his body was thin, but toned. His looks though didn't convey the fear; it was how he did everything. From walking to breathing, he was always like a bear in the woods waiting to attack—compared to the others, he was the only one that wouldn't hurt me for a simple mistake like that.

I thought about the knife he had given me. I knew where it was still in the cage, hopefully whoever found it wouldn't suspect how it got there. I doubted any of the guards would dig too thoroughly through my cage. Joseph and Albert kept at arm's length whenever it was time to clean out my small metal box.

On those occasions, such as now, when the doctor's face made that look, things were only going to end badly for everyone in the room. I wanted to bolt, feeling suddenly exposed without the comfort of the bars. I knew what the smile of the devil meant; I was about to be hurt.

Only Dr. Joachim blew out a puff of air and turned back to Jutta. "That is unfortunate. That leaves just one adult and ten children, counting the wolf. But I think we've made a breakthrough that cannot be understated. The wolf has spoken." Dr. Joachim grinned, turning toward me with his arms outstretched, like a proud father. Jutta and the rest of the guards all turned my way, their faces ranging from general shock or a cursory glance while staying in stances. That was making me shake. Not to mention: who were the people that the doctor was talking about?

I think part of the reason why I didn't listen to my *elterns* as much wasn't that I hated them—far from it. My *muter* was doting on Zevi; he was always a sick boy. As for *foter*, he lived for work as much as he lived for taking care of us. I would act out, break more things than I should have, make a bigger deal out of being told to do something. In a way, it was the only way my *elterns* would both look at me. It made me feel like I was getting their attention finally.

This, though, I hated this. The stares that drilled holes into every part of my being. It made me feel that even though I was clothed, I was naked back in my cage, back on the table, with long tubes being forced down my throat, scraping against my skin with blades of metal pulling my blood forth. I was owned by them; that was what those stares meant. It meant that every fiber of my being belonged to them.

What they hadn't figured out, though, but what I suspected Hans knew, was that when they made me bleed, any at all, I turned into the monster. I think they thought extreme pain was causing it—I don't know—but everything got hot when I bled, a torrent of fire building inside me. I looked down at the floor, avoiding their glances. *Just stay seen but not heard, Avraham, this will pass, and you won't get hurt anymore.*

"That is wonderful news, Dr. Joachim," Jutta said dryly. The doctor didn't catch it: he was staring at the celling, the small smile back on his face, his arms crossed behind his back. He had gotten what he wanted, I had finally spoken. I was their science experiment? Fine, I only had to play by their rules, and I got to see my *mishpokhe* again.

"What are you doing with all the contraband?" Hans inquired, his slow raspy voice coming out as if he had injury to even his voice box.

Jutta turned nervously, slowly and with even more reverence for Hans than she had showed Dr. Joachim. "We were sorting through the items from last night's arrivals, sir. Taking inventory as requested, sir." Jutta repeated, like a well-oiled machine. Hans must have been satisfied, his face passive and disinterested.

All of this was from just last night? I thought in horror; some of the piles extended to multiple tables, reaching to even the heights of the trucks. How many families had this been, how many had gone into the flames? I shook, tears on the verge of becoming the only thing that I could do. I could only pray that my *mishpokhe* had made it—that Linor had made it.

"No sense in it going to waste. Take what you want, Jutta, and burn or bury the rest. I don't care," Dr. Joachim said, turning to leave through the garage doors.

"Yes sir!" replied Jutta, as everyone in the room, saluted from their chests with one arm to the air exclaiming, "*Sig Heil!*" The enthusiasm so high that my ears rang in the confined space of the garage. I wanted to leave that place more than any other I had ever been, my legs shaking in my oversized shoes.

I'd heard those words too many times and it was always the last thing they did whenever Dr. Joachim left a room. Every time, it rocked me to the core. How was doing this to people leading anyone to victory? Whoever it was that was winning, I hoped they would come soon, I hoped they would stop Dr. Joachim. Some things can just be hoped for—this one was one I was daring to hope for.

We turned back to the hallway, suddenly feeling a lot longer than it had before. We came to the set of doors with windows, and outside I could see a gray sky, a dusting of dark mixed in to soak out the sun's rays. Through the doors I could feel the cold draft, but it was still wind; it had been so long since I felt wind, since I had felt anything besides dampness. I paused, looking at my hands. Beneath the grime, my skin was as pale as the flakes of snow falling through the windows. Hopefully the others were getting more sunshine than me.

I sniffed the air and immediately covered my nose. The air was thick with something I could have likened to when my *muter* singed a chicken. As if the very air was on fire, a furnace in the middle of winter. I panicked. Were they taking me to the fires again? Had I been tricked? I shuddered and stepped back, but I felt hands shove me forward.

"Welcome to Auschwitz-Birkenau, your home, dear wolf," Dr. Joachim said with pride in his voice. We went outside and I was bombarded by sensory overload. The night I had arrived in camp, it was dark, an endless night of muck that I couldn't see a light above. But in the daytime, somehow the world seemed darker, colder, and far more sinister than I'd ever thought possible. In the distance, I could see railcars, with the wooden sides coming and leaving the train station. Mounds of chimneys jettisoned from the ground, spewing a continued stream of black smoke, like the very earth was pushing toxic air out, blowing in pain. Men worked, carrying loads of rocks, while others hammered into rails of iron as it was being laid across steel columns. Groups of people in striped clothes and thin coats. I could see their breath in the cold air, sending up puffs of frozen wind at an equal pace to the black smoke, creating a moving monster of gray that was reaching toward the ground.

Everywhere I looked, people were working, even small *kinder*, and for every step, the guards were shouting, beating, attacking. It was vicious, it was unending, and I knew that I was seeing among the buildings marked with skulls that this was the land of them, this was the land of death. A real hell here on Earth.

If I wasn't being pushed forward by someone behind me, I would have curled into a ball right there, and that would have been that. Just held my knees to my chest and cried—tears of oceans for the people lost, for my *mishpokhe*, for the world. What was happening? Why was any of this happening...?

It was a question that I just didn't want the answer to, even if someone would have answered. A sinking pit spilled into the bottom of my stomach. Where was my *mishpokhe*? Where was my *muter* and *bruder*? I started to turn around too, when Dr. Joachim pushed my face back forward. I wasn't going to be able to ask anything, let alone convince any of these men around me to answer what happened to my *mishpokhe*.

My tears stayed in, though, as we walked, heading toward a row of wooden buildings that were separated by more barbed wire and fences. I could see the lights again that I had seen the first night when I had come to the camp. During the day, they looked like snakes peeking over a cage, their mouths shining down like a wide cave, full of a never-ending light that froze you in place. I shivered—not because of the cold, though.

We kept walking along the fence line nearest the buildings. Guards would pass us by, pausing momentarily from beating prisoners to salute Dr. Joachim. The prisoners would keep their heads down, the look on their faces like a stone; nothing was there. Like all light and hope had drained from them, and what remained was simply bodies. I saw it everywhere: walking corpses, I truly was in the land of the dead. Men, women, children—no one had a face that was not grim, that was not in pain.

I decided to keep my head down. I couldn't look anymore. I just hoped that where we were going, we would get there soon. After a few more steps, we came to a gate, where we stopped, so I looked up. Hans and a guard talked in hushed voices, the guard pointing west in the direction of more of the wooden buildings I had seen earlier in the distance. Hans said something, gesturing back toward Dr. Joachim and me.

I kept my head down and pretended that I hadn't seen the guard point in my direction, as Hans came back to the group. "Are they all ready?" asked Dr. Joachim with a sudden drop in his voice, almost as if he wasn't genuinely sure. I figured Dr. Joachim to have absolute control.

"It is, sir, the cage just needed to be cleaned out after last night. They know that we are on our way," Hans responded, and I saw Dr. Joachim take a breath before shaking his head.

"You see, young wolf, I have been waiting a very, very long time for this moment." Dr. Joachim turned toward me, his eyes a blaze with some far-off memory as he spoke. "I will accept nothing less than the very best in this moment. All of you children mean so very much to me." He patted my head, stroking my wild curly hair to the side before it bounced back to the position it was before. "We need to do something about that hair of yours, dear wolf," grumbled Dr. Joachim.

Periodically, I was held down after being sprayed by the high-pressure hose or shocked by their strange rod devices, and Albert or Joseph would shave off my hair. I screamed the first few times, which scared them. But after that, I would wake up in the middle of the night to them cutting strands of my hair as I slept. I had no idea why they were doing that. Or why they would collect anything that came out of me with more care than a newborn child. *They're evil, Avraham; evil and weird just go hand and hand,* I thought to myself as I shrugged at Dr. Joachim.

He smirked at me before we started moving again. The uneasiness in my stomach was only made worse with every step and I wondered if I might have been filling up with rocks on the inside. Spend enough time indoors, strange things could start happening to you, my *zayde* would tell Zevi and me, whenever my *bubbe* wouldn't let Zevi go outside. Zevi was always sick, always pale, and looking at any moment like he was about to start coughing.

So, my *muter* and *bubbe* kept him inside, kept him reading books or helping my *muter* cook. Which is probably why he never could hit a ball further than I could. I smiled at those memories, keeping the spark from that to help with the feeling inside of my stomach. I couldn't wait to pick on Zevi for sucking at ball games again. He wasn't my favorite to play with and I was to mean to him, but I missed the way his face would turn the same copper red as his hair whenever he was mad. Thinking of his red hair made me notice the little bit of sun that was breaking through the clouds above me. My skin was feeling like I was being burned. I looked down at my hands, and they matched the snow we were walking on. I stuffed my hands in my pockets.

I had turned paler than a glass of milk since being here. *Too much time inside,* rang my *zayde's* words in my head again. I had taken more after my *muter*, the same darker Slavic and Romanian skin. I wondered now if, when I saw my *muter* again, she would recognize me, since I was so dirty and pale now. She would though, I hoped.

We passed many of the wooden buildings. They had no doors, just a wide-open entrance way where people huddled next to the frame. But they weren't people—people couldn't be straws. Everywhere I looked, people's clothes were falling from them, their bodies similar to the worms that I had seen in the ground. Some so thin that I could almost see the red in their blood under their skin. It was like looking at tissue paper. If anyone pressed them, their fingers would go right through the skin of these people.

In all my life, I had never seen anyone that was so starved, so inhuman, and suffering from the loss of so much. To see people thinner than a roll of dough stretched across my *muter's* kitchen counter—I had no words for it. Their eyes, though, hollowed out to the point of black deeper than any animal eyes, were that—they weren't human anymore. I wasn't sure what they were, but as the disheveled and broken faces viewed me, the deepest pit of dread came forward in that moment. Just what was awaiting me, once I finally got to see my *mishpokhe*? Would they look just like all these people here, a moment away from a breeze being able to knock them away?

I averted my eyes. I couldn't see any more, or their ghostly images would haunt my thoughts until the end of time. *Think positive*, I mumbled as we continued to walk. In the many nights that I had spent inside the cage, in the blackness, I'd had to remind myself that I wasn't some kind of beast of burden. I was still Avraham, I was still the person that I was meant to be. Now, though, I was feeling far older than a boy, far sadder than I ever remembered being.

It was true that our heads can only stay up for so long without the aid of the heart, that some pains tore the heart into so many small chambers that the mind could never navigate through the darkness ever again. That's the thing I realized now, as we came to another fence line, but this time there was a concrete compound, bigger than the one that we had come from. I would never find my way through the dark ever again. Its doors were massive and long, clamped tight under big locks, like they were keeping something inside.

We approached the gate, and Dr. Joachim said, "Stay here, boy. Albert, go tell them to let one through ten have some yard time—it's good for them to see the outside world on such a fine and beautiful day." He hummed as a stiff breeze went through the yard. I was inches from the fence, but

I could hear the electricity riding the metal links, waiting for an unlucky soul to regret touching the separation piece. I was breathing hard, but I tried to calm myself. With my newfound hearing, I could hear the three men behind me breathing. I could hear the guard that Albert spoke to as he gained access to the compound behind the fence.

The voice I could hear, somewhere in the distance, was Linor's. The silent way she tucked in air when she was nervous, sucking her bottom lip inward. It would always make a sound that was somewhere between a whistle being blown softly and a cough. I kept my jubilee of happy thoughts inside as I scanned the building, looking for any signs of her. The compound was vast, windowless, and above all, only had the one door that I could see with the lock on the outside, and the massive garage doors, which had of those truck tank things parked inside it. Otherwise, I was unable to see deep into the shadows of the garage, as if whatever was back there was hiding itself from the world.

Where was she? I sniffed the air, while doing my best to keep my ears open for any sound that she made. Snow started to sprinkle upon us, and my hopes of finding Linor fell just as fast. The building looked like a castle, with its long chimneys and solid walls. Maybe she was one of the ten that the doctor had mentioned—I could hope. There was always hope. I was unsure of where that might have come from, or what form it would take once it had gotten here.

Albert made it to the compound door as the guard took a ring of keys, unlocking the massive lock that was holding the door. Albert went inside, and in the distance, I could see two guards on the inside of the building behind the door. Still, no one else that I recognized. Everything was checks and balances with these people. Everything was behind a closed door, off to another unforeseen spot, as if it was so kind of game, a cruel trick to get our spirits up, only to dash them down.

I had heard her, though, that was true. Even now, I smelled something in the air. I'd never understood it until that moment—but she was someone as important to me as my *mishpokhe*. She had her own smell, which must have been what love is, when you can smell the person you want to see so badly that amongst a void filled with gases, there was one above them all; that was love.

Fresh cut hay and a forest drifted to my nose, and I looked down. Nearby, in the shadows of the fence line, only inches away from me, the snow was pushed in, like there was weight from a footprint. I couldn't see anything there; I rubbed my eyes as a dense fog floated at about my height. It shimmered for a second and snapped, away revealing Linor's tussle of black hair. I stepped back, gasping. How did she do that? The fog was gone and now I could see Linor shivering in the cold. She wore a medical gown, her bare legs exposed, her hands held tight to her chest, with her head bowed, obscuring her face.

I tried to turn my head to get a better look. Linor just tilted her head in response to my movement. My words burst forth before I could contain them. It had been so long since I had seen her—seen anyone else other than them. "Linor!" I exclaimed, my heart racing, warming me up as the snow melted on my cheeks. She kept her head down, still facing the dirt, not responding to my words. I noticed she had gotten a lot taller since we had last seen each other. She stood above me, even if I stood on my tippy toes.

I bet she could probably beat all of us up easily. I grinned, speaking again. "It's me, Linor—Avraham, your favorite knuckle-head."

Linor still remained unresponsive, her frail body shaking in the wind. My grin started to feel extremely out of place in that instant. The snow whipped up harder and faster, as if the very clouds were angry that I would dare to smile in such a place.

I turned around. Hans and the others had retreated a distance behind me. Joseph had the camera assembled in place on a tripod. While Dr. Joachim frantically took notes on his pad, all three men breathing huge puffs of air in the cold. They were watching us. I started to reach for the fire that was always burning within me, when I shut it down. There was no point in getting mad now—they had given me what I had asked for by finally speaking. This was worth it; this was worth leaving that box. I got to see her; that was all that mattered. I looked down, seeing the snow start to melt near Linor, small droplets forming in the crisp powder.

She was crying. Linor was crying when she finally said, "I know it's you, Avraham—I—we thought you were dead. I saw you get taken left—I saw you get thrown into the flames, but then, then I saw that thing which came out of there!" Her voice shook, dredging the memory from a place that I could have only imagined. In the chaos, I had lost track of everyone that night.

Linor snapped her head up finally. I saw now why she had been avoiding eye contact with me. Over her right eye was a thick mound of bandages covering from above her eyebrow down her lightly freckled face. My eyes went wide as I noticed her one eye she had showing, shifting uncomfortably to make eye contact.

"I thought you were gone, Avi. I thought I would never get to see you again," Linor sniffled. I clenched my fists, the fire burning hot enough to make my fists start shaking, and suddenly, I wasn't cold anymore.

"Did they do that?" I prodded through clenched teeth. I was trying to breathe, trying to keep my mouth closed as much as possible, afraid that if I opened my lips somehow, I would blow fire. Linor ignored me, looking past me, the fog around her slowly starting to come back, obscuring her slightly from my view—even though she was only inches from me.

I could hear the shock of the fence, see the electricity bolts racing back and forth, taunting me to touch the wires. I hesitated. The fire, though, the fire that gets created when you see someone you love in so much pain that you know you would stick your hands through any pain that comes your way to comfort them. I reached through with my fingers—inching toward Linor, when I felt my body suddenly start to tremble, and voltage streamed through my body with a current that was stronger than any wave. I shook, trembling in pain—screaming, but I kept reaching through the metal toward Linor.

I had been shocked plenty of times while in the cage. It was the only thing that kept me from bleeding, besides drowning me. It was the sound of something racing through your body, an invisible pain faster than light, that made my mind scramble to let go, with a will I never thought I had before. That is what hurts when you're shocked, an invisible snap shooting through your body. Every ounce of me hurt, like my mind was filling with false information. I grunted, pushing forward, when an explosion of energy shot from the fence, sending my hand free and my body flying into the air.

I landed hard on the ground, my head spinning, everything hurting, the rage still burning. It took all my effort to get my body upright. I looked to Linor, and her mouth was wide, gasping. With the hand that I hadn't used to touch the fence, I gave her a thumbs-up as my body shook and jerked. I looked at my right hand. My flesh appeared normal, just slightly pink where my fingers had touched the fence. The hair was singed along my forearm—this happened every time a flame was held toward me now. It was like my skin sucked in the heat—and defeated the fire with an even bigger flame.

Within moments, my skin was no longer pink, though my bones shook, and my thoughts still seemed to scramble in every direction, searching for a way out of the pain. Shaking, I managed to stand myself back up. I was no longer cold, though the snow fell more and I wiped it off me. I glanced back behind. The doctor and Joseph were furiously taking notes. I don't think even they knew about how my body would react to that much electricity.

I shouldn't have been alive. Not just from that, but from multiple things. Whatever was inside me—it wasn't natural, it had changed me in ways I didn't want to understand. I found myself clutching my stomach, the weight of my worries pressing down on me with a force I couldn't understand. *Her face, though. Must get to my mishpokhe,* I thought, trudging in the snow, making my way to the fence line. The snow was almost covering my too-large shoes, making my walk slower and clumsy. I reached the fence line and decided not to try my luck a second time at touching the fence, as I could see where a piece of my sleeve was sticking to the electrified metal, slowly turning to ash.

"That was crazy—Avraham," Linor gasped.

"Speak for yourself—are you creating that fog?" I grinned while questioning her.

Linor's head stayed pointed down, but she slowly nodded. "I can create all kinds of things—anything I can imagine," she replied her voice shaky and unsure.

A long silence stretched between us. I cleared my throat. "Think you can put that fog around the two of us? I don't want them looking at us anymore, just for a moment." I almost pleaded, realizing how much I meant what I had just said. It had been so long since I was not under their eyes. I could never be sure when I wasn't being watched. Privacy, shame—those were things I no longer had anymore, if I'd ever really had them at all.

But what I did have was right there in front of me, separated by an electrical fence. Linor was quiet again, looking at the ground. I was about to say something else, when she spoke up, "I can try... sometimes, the bigger I make things, the harder it is for me—everything gets fuzzy, like looking into the water in a creek," she mumbled.

"Does it hurt?' I pointed around her as I asked my question.

"A little bit. Nothing I can't handle, though," she smirked in response.

I smiled back—Linor was the toughest out of all of us; she could do this. A small gray fog started to shimmer and appear from Linor, as if the very air had suddenly become filled with a void of smoke. Veins started to appear on Linor's face, straining like webs as a small droplet of blood slid down her nose.

With an exclamation, I shouted, "Linor!" just as the fog rapidly shot from her to all around us, leading all around us to be completely enveloped by the fog. I gasped, unable to see anything besides just her and the fence in front of me. I wondered if the camera would be able to see through it, though. Its lens seemed to be the kind that could see through anything—all the way to your soul.

I shivered through the fog and looked at Linor, her silence seeming to be the norm in her personality. I tried to fish for something that could bring her back—bring back the Linor that I was used to. Now that it was just us, I was suddenly drawing a blank.

Luckily, Linor broke the silence after covering her nosebleed. "I have no idea how I can even do this, now... they hooked me up to a bed, strapped all kinds of tubes and needles in me—and they..." she stammered.

"Go on," I urged silently.

With a deep breath, she whispered, "They did something to your *bruder* and me, Avraham... something awful that hurt so badly." Tears rolled down her cheeks and I found myself choking back a heavy feeling inside my throat. She had mentioned Zevi. *Was he okay? Was my muter okay?*

My *muter* wouldn't have let anything happen to Zevi and me without putting up a fight—it was what our *foter* had told us many times. It was what my *muter* had showed us, many times, that she would claw tooth and nail for her *kinder.*

"*Muter,*" I whispered to myself before speaking to Linor. My voice felt small and weak, like it had suddenly aged to be an old man, like Linor and I were no longer *kinder.* We were young in body—our minds now endless as the graying sky above us. "What happened, Linor? Where is Zevi, where is my *muter?*" I asked, summoning what little courage I could in the cold. The fog kept us hidden but did nothing to keep us warm, I noted, as Linor sucked in her bottom lip.

"Avi, your *bruder*—" she started before I heard a bang. The bang caused both of us to jerk our heads in the direction of the building. The fog dropped and we could see again. Joseph and the guard stepped out of the building, the guard holding the door wide as Albert kept walking. Behind him followed a series of kids, covered in bandages and some walking with crutches. I could see Zevi right behind Albert, his red hair glowing like a beacon in the snow. He was now thin, half the size of my former little *bruder.* Like Linor, his right eye was covered with a massive bandage, only his looked brown and dirty. It needed to be changed, and a long trail of stiches rode up his head, showing a deep parting in his hair that went up half his skull. It was his face that made me shake—it made me wonder who I was looking at, even as I recognized my *bruder.* His face was now long and gaunt. The wide nose of our *muter,* but his left eye that had always been a deep shade of green like fresh summer grass hung down like a frosty icicle, a depth that was born of pure malice. That wasn't my *bruder's* eye, it was the eye of a monster, the eye of someone who had changed.

After so many years of not seeing someone—someone you had spent countless hours getting to know and spending small moments together with, to see how much they had changed, it was like that time machine again. Only what they don't tell you, when you go messing around with traveling in time, is you can't control what happens to people. You can only travel through time, like looking through a thick glass pane, only to watch a river become an ocean, while you get so far apart from what you used to know that even though it looks the same, you can no longer understand what you're seeing—because it's not part of your time, you're from a different time and there is no going back in time. Just forward, relentlessly.

In that moment, I just wanted time to go back. I wanted to see the same chubby and dumpy little *bruder* of mine I would tease relentlessly. There was no time machine, there was no going back. As my *bruder* walked, nine more followed. None of them I recognized. Most had bandages covering their whole body. One boy had a wired contraption going around his mouth and head. At the end of them was a frail woman, her body shriveled, with the bandages covering her seeming to slide off from how thin she was.

Albert marched the group out to the yard, stopped, and turned to the guard. Whispering something to him. Even with my hearing being better, I couldn't hear what they were saying under the now heavy fall of snow—or the pounding in my chest.

Small bits did manage to come through, though: "Let them have some yard time. Do not miss anything," Albert directed to the guard. The guard threw his salute and phrase, Albert returned his salute back. From there, Albert walked to the gate, locking the door behind him, and the guard outside the gate saluted Albert. I scanned ahead at the group that had come out. They staggered around the "yard," mostly looking like lost animals in the snow, their clothes peeling and falling off. Bandages sagging from the globs of ice forming on their bodies, showing rows upon rows of what looked like miniature train tracks running all along their bodies.

For some of the kids, I saw more tracks than I saw skin—I shuddered at the boy whose skin almost looked yellow under the low gray light, his fin-ger tips and forearms laced with stiches that promised an insurmountable amount of pain had been inflected upon him. Another was a girl with long red hair that drifted down her back as if it was flames crawling up her. She was the only one that didn't have a shaved head, I noted. Her hair seemed to be crawling and growing as I stared, constantly moving in a twisting pattern, and when I blinked, I could have sworn that her hair had grown even longer.

The strangest, though, was the woman. Not just because she was out of place with the rest of the kids nor that she looked so starved, it was because of the thick tussle of black hair on her arms, her legs, and if I was seeing correctly, even sticking slightly out of her shirt. I had never seen anyone with that much body hair—not even from my *foter*, who had almost seemed to grow a beard overnight. I glanced back to Linor, doing my best to smile at her. She needed me now more than ever, but what do you say to someone in this situation?

Zevi looked in our direction, as the others stayed silent in a general crowded area. Then, Zevi marched in our direction. That gave me only a few moments to say something to her. I sucked in a deep breath and looked at Linor. "Snow sure is pretty—always looks nice and fluffy," I trailed off, looking at the ground as my face heated up. Linor was staring at the ground, but she didn't have the smile I hoped she would have had.

I cleared my throat, thinking about how this might have been the last time that Linor and I would ever see each other. That made my knuckles clench, but I sucked in my anger again. That was becoming more and more common, being only seconds away from breathing fire. The thing that worried me the most was that Linor was right there in front of me.

My breath turned into ice in the wind and I took an extra moment before speaking. "Sometimes, I like to think that when air gets this cold, I like to think it's the same with drops of snow, that each one's just a tear falling from God's face," I whispered, my words trailing off. *That was just as dumb as the first one,* I thought.

She lifted her head, though, looking me in the eye for the first time since we had seen each other. "You really think that, that snow is like the tears from God?" She hesitated, her voice on the edge of a plea.

"Oh yeah, it can't be rain. If God was to cry, it would be a cold day—so cold that it snows," I smiled.

Linor grinned, flashing a wide smile that quickly faded to a smirk. "That is probably a pretty dumb thing to think, Avi—but thanks for trying to cheer me up. We wouldn't be here if God was crying," Linor trailed off.

I shot back, "Yeah, if it was up to you, we would probably be painting those dang rocks of yours—you would just get mad at me for hitting them with my bat anyways. This is probably for the best," I joked.

"You and that bat!" she snickered back, and for the briefest of moments, I think we were kids again. We started to laugh, a strange thing now in such a distant land, that I noticed caused everyone around us to look in our direction. Their eyes were on us, sharper than razors, as their gaze seemed to cut all the way through us. I squirmed under their gaze when Zevi walked up next to Linor. Seeing my *bruder* up close, I could see the long lines of stitches that were poking out of one of his sleeves. Unlike Linor, Zevi's bandages were dirty, festering, and had a stench to them. *This isn't my little bruder,* I thought—it was beyond a thought at this point. Without even speaking, I could tell that Zevi had changed in a way that I would never fully understand.

"Why are you here, Avraham?" Zevi probed.

I was so taken back by the directness of my *bruder's* question that it took me more than a few moments to respond. "What do you mean, why am I here? Why else would I be here, Zevi? We are all stuck here," I blurted back to him.

Zevi darted his eyes side to side, checking as if for some invisible and terrible force that might have been listening in to our conversation. "You should not be here, Avraham. You're supposed to dead," he stated matter-of-factly.

"What do you mean, dead?" I responded.

Zevi looked around again, inching closer to the fence line than I would have dared to have ventured again. I could survive that shock once; I didn't want to test my luck again.

"That night, the night that we were in the camp, we all saw you, Avraham. We saw what you are—that animal." My *bruder's* words hit me square in the chest and I felt myself gasping. A part of me had hoped that the first night had been a dream, that the subsequent time had been a part of an elaborate dream that was going to end at any moment. I would have been okay with even waking up in my metal cage, if the thoughts I had of fangs and claws, blood and gore hadn't been real. That it had all been a nightmare. The thought of my cage, trapped with only bars in every direction, was far less frightening. At least in the cage, no one could be hurt; it was just me. There were no monsters in the cage—just me.

Looking into my *bruder's* eye, I saw the truth and the feeling of the pit in my stomach suddenly gained teeth, so that voice I was hearing, it was real there was something awful inside of me. My spine tingled and I shook my head at my *bruder*, not daring to speak.

"That night—we were told you were gone, Avi. It's because of you"—he paused, his eye full of tears—"because of you, *muter* is gone," he growled.

"What do you mean? Did I hurt her, that night?" I hesitated to ask, my words cold as the ice that was forming on our clothes, frozen in the day.

Zevi shook his head. "No, it was later. You disappeared that night—so they took it out on us. Most of us thought it was just another way to shame us." Zevi was shaking, his wiry frame looking as if it could have blasted off to another planet if he had wings. "But no, they lined us all up, the ones that were left on that train, number seven hundred and forty. From our small, small town. None of us knew why at the time, but they knew," Zevi snarled, his body no longer shaking.

"That was the start. Then they beat us and beat us until people started crying out. Then, that one back there"—Zevi stared past me; I didn't dare turn around—"that one with the scar, he got his answers for that—doctor." Zevi spat, as if even speaking of them was as vile as the blackest night. Fear shook me, and a feeling of dread reared with such force that I felt myself gripping my heart.

"And as they beat us; they got what they wanted. They found people that knew you; they tortured us until someone spoke. So, they sought those that knew you, those that could have been related to you..." Zevi stopped, turning his face away, finally showing emotion other than rage.

He jerked his head back to me. "Someone spoke up about how the watchmaker's son had been seen without clothes, without hair, lying in a pile of rubble. So, when they came for me, as the easy-to-spot redhead in a crowd full of dark hair—our *muter* wasn't going to let that happen. Not to one of us, not to me." Zevi finally started to cry, his face breaking down in pain.

"They killed her—Avraham, then they took me, and they did things to us. Now you're here. I was told you were gone, Avraham. I was told you were gone and now you're here!" Zevi's rage boiled over. Veins begin to bulge from his body, crisscrossing over his stitches, making them seem as though if his anger grew anymore, it would surely force the wounds open.

"I'm sorry, Zevi—this was all—all my fault. If you guys hadn't known me..." I didn't dare finish my sentence. I sucked in so much cold air my nose started to burn.

Zevi growled, snarling almost as an animal. "Don't be so thick, Avraham! Something bad was going to happen to us in this place either way—no, they're to blame!" Zevi's hands shook at his side, and more veins and muscles, that my *bruder* shouldn't have had on such a small and young body, formed before my eyes. "I hate them! I hate them, I hate them!" Zevi screamed.

I was feeling frightened. If he didn't keep it down, they were going to hurt us. Dr. Joachim would never be this forgiving. "Zevi, you need to be quiet little *bruder*," I pleaded with him. Linor had inched away from Zevi, her body trembling in fear.

"Keep it down? Don't you tell me to ever be quiet! Don't you ever tell me to calm down! You know what? This is your fault, Avraham. If you had such a creature in you this whole time, why didn't you save us all?" he spat.

"I didn't have—" I started, before Zevi turned, his body away from me, with just part of his face looking toward me.

"You're the weak one, Avraham. I would have turned into the monster and eaten them all by now," he stated with absolute conviction that left me stunned and unable to move.

The last bit of the memories of my conversation with Zevi faded off and I looked at Linor's concerned face, her black hair decorated with yellow ribbons blooming like a flower in the lowering sun.

"Did you just leave me again?" Linor whispered on the windy rooftop.

I smiled, looking at her, her eyes dropping into a gaze that pulled me from my self-centered little world every single time. "Leave you? Hell, Linor, I've been trying to get rid of your stinky butt for years. Glad you caught on," I joked.

She snorted and elbowed me in the ribs. "I'm stinky? Please, when was the last time you heard of the words 'shower' or 'soap,' Avi?" she returned, standing up and stretching her arms over her head in a way that made me pay more attention than I should have. "You're close to being just as bad as Schwein if you keep that up," Linor pointed at me and waved in front of her nose.

I narrowed my eyes, shooting up. "Now I know you have to go. No one—I mean no one stinks as bad as Schwein," I retorted.

Linor nodded. "Yeah, that's true. Well, come on, Avi, we have to get to making these crystals before my grandmother turns us both into lumps of coal. Trust me, she might try," she stated, climbing back down the ladder.

I paused before going after her. Considering the things that Linor could do, along with the others, that may have been a valid threat. Her grandmother held me in as about as much distain as you might with sticky sap lodged between your toes. I gulped and turned toward the ladder, my legs shaking from either the memories of my time in the camp or what was about to come next.

19

Chapter 19

Voices were coming from the hall, and my heart caught within my chest. I was unsure of what time it was, but I knew it was late—far too late, and the shadows that stretched between me and the door were long, casting edges of frightening midnight into the gloom of my soul. I was afraid, easily, that my bed, soaked through with my sweat, lay flat on the ground.

As I stirred, raising my head, peeping at the noises coming from the shadows behind me, the ones in the hallway called my name, whispering for me to come out, calling me a wolf. I froze. It had been many years since anyone had called me a wolf. The last had been Linor's grandmother. It was *them*—they had finally found me. It was either the doctors from the camps or worse, it was my *bruder* who had come for his challenge, like I always knew he would. Blackness danced under the doorframe, drowning the light from the moon, and I felt my mouth open. A deep curdling scream stretched forth, deepening into a howl of pure fear.

I sat up in my bed. The dream I just had drifted out of me like a plastic bag at the mercy of a vast ocean. The door to my meager bedroom slammed open, the lights snapped on, and I covered my eyes, groaning. Huey came in, and a thick piece of wood that had been carved and taped by Huey himself was in his hands. I'd told Huey a few times, when I had seen him performing some kind of bizarre dance with this staff, that it looked like a broom handle, just minus the broom. Huey would just smirk and continue his dance, claiming that the weapon was him; the staff was just for stretching.

Whatever he meant by it, I had seen Huey use that broom handle on many occasions, whirling and twisting with even a few flips—it was something. Huey had the staff braced, his hands raised up with his elbows tucked, his feet wide apart and his body lowered. He scanned the room quickly and then sighed.

"Again, Avi?" he asked, exasperation in his voice.

"Kiss my ass."

Huey snorted, looking around the room, grunting as he pulled out a stool that was in the corner, sweeping off the pile of clothes that were tossed onto it before he sat. With a quick twist, Huey laid his staff across his lap and pulled out a cigarette, the wrap close to bursting, but still tight at the ends in its brown paper. I eyed the cigarette. Huey caught my eye, and offered the cigarette to me.

I sighed, taking it from him, as I twisted in bed to a sitting position. I threw off my soaked shirt, picking up off the ground what I hoped was a clean sweater. We were both quiet in the silence of the yellowed room. The walls were caked in gray dust and the singe of unwashed clothes permeated throughout the space.

"Do you have a light?" I gestured with my thumb. Huey lit his first and tossed a silver lighter with a faded eagle inside an emblem, with the chipped word "AIRBORNE" scribbled across the top. "Fancy," I mumbled, lighting the rolled tobacco before tossing the lighter back to Huey. He caught it expertly and flipped it back into his pocket.

"That was the third time this week, man," Huey announced.

"So what?" I retorted, noting the bags under Huey's eyes as well. Neither of us was sleeping much. As much as I knew Huey would hate to admit it, he couldn't sleep for his own reasons. It wasn't just the fact that we were finally sleeping in our own rooms, away from a cellmate trying to brutally murder us or steal everything we owned. Or the fact that the lights remained mostly off at night. Everything felt off. We were switches that could never be placed back on, no matter how much time and effort was put in. Thus, nothing in this new life felt normal. Not even the feel of a bed that hadn't held men losing their minds, as the fear of what was coming the next day soaked into the very fabric.

Freedom was largely a misunderstood thing. It's so sought out, but when it's been denied for so long, so far removed from anything that could be a reality, then doubts flood your heart with the pictures of fields, knowing full well that those fields are someone else's freedom, not yours. Your freedom is a long way gone, and it crushes you into an infinity of endless strokes of paint, made up from those that could never be anything more than a caged bird ever again. I would never be free again; I felt it in my bones as my mind started coming back fully to the situation.

I groaned and took too long a drag on my cigarette, before coughing. Huey was eyeing me, his legs crossed, and I knew this was going to be a conversation that he wasn't letting go. "If you're going to lecture me again, can we get a drink, at least?" I asked, dashing the cigarette on the ground.

Huey sighed again, reaching down and picking up the butt of the cigarette as I grunted at him. "My mother used to say a messy room is the sign of a messy mind," he stated.

"My mother used to say to change my soaks and underwear daily. It's pretty common sense; same with the messy mind," I stated back.

"So, you admit finally."

"Yeah—yeah, I guess I do. Again, so what?" I questioned, hoping that Huey would leave soon, and I could at least attempt to get some amount of sleep before the night was over.

Instead, he stood up and placed his staff against the wall, turning to leave the room. "Get your coat. We are going to get that drink," he directed, turning to leave the room.

"Don't we have work tomorrow? You never say yes when I ask."

"Just get your coat. We are going to finish this once and for all, you punk ass," Huey leered at the door.

I got my coat and brushed off my jeans. It was going to be a long night.

20

Chapter 20

Grimy bars have their charms, beyond just dark bottles stacked in a seemingly endless order of color or design. A bartender, polishing a glass constantly, towels appearing as if from thin air, as the counter remains in a never-ending battle of keeping it dry. It was a war that no bartender would ever win.

Still, though, who was I to complain, as I sipped a beer with Huey at the bar while the bartender fought to keep it dry, grunting for us to use a coaster? I flicked him off, and he just shook his head and went back to cleaning glasses.

"You know, ever since you started telling me stories about those camps, I've had trouble sleeping again. What was done to you"—Huey paused as I kept my eyes on the countertop—"that was monstrous, no doubt about it. But I think what you're doing to yourself now is way worse, just as monstrous and downright evil," Huey remarked, in the silence of the bar. We were the only three inside the small area.

The bartender threw a white towel over his shoulder and shuffled off with a stack of dishes to another part of the bar, pretending to be too busy. He had been around long enough to know that two people alone drinking in a bar either meant sex, a fight, or worse: a long incoherent rant about someone's life, and them spilling out an uninvited history of their life onto you.

"So, what?" I muttered my catchphrase that seemed to keep coming out of my mouth more and more as it went on.

"So, what it describes to me is a lot of things. Mostly, what it tells me is that I still have peace—for a moment there, I thought maybe I was hiding it again," he replied, casually passing the bottle back and forth between his hands.

"What are you, some kind criminal-philosopher-vet type?"

"If that is the moniker that you feel is best, sure thing, jackass."

I smirked at Huey. "Well go on, lay your ideas on me. I've heard them all and let me tell you man, you and I both know that every joint and slumdog yard has someone spitting this and that—if you ask me, it's all bullshit. I used to be a Jew, remember? And you know what that got me? The stuff that makes me end up in a shitty bar talking to you in the middle of the night, for two fucking years now," I muttered, eyeing the barkeep as he frowned at the shitty bar comment.

"Yeah, good point—I met a few of those types, but I ain't pushing some dogmatic hoky-poky religion on you. No snake-oil here. Take it more as one fuck-up to another. Wisdom, if you will." Huey tipped his beer to me.

I eyed him. Huey was long and wiry, his hands were heavily callused, and I noticed for the first time that unlike me, he wasn't just lean with no muscle. Huey had put his swirling of his staff to good use, his hands coated in scars to prove it—his posture too upright to be a person that didn't take care of his body.

"Don't get angry, Avi, I could probably kick your ass," Huey asserted.

"Yeah probably, but you can't kick *his ass*," I fired back.

"Point. Let me continue though with what I was saying, or is this going to take all night just to get a simple sentence in with you?" he stated.

"Be my guest," I replied, gesturing with both my hands that I was going to be quiet now.

Huey turned back to the bar for a moment, closing his eyes before turning back to me. "For a long time after I got out of the war, I saw shit, shit you wouldn't believe. Hell, I saw shit during the war while I lay in those trenches, bullets flying overhead. Young people losing everything that made them young in a flash. These were dudes that I drew the cards with. We all were so nervous. From screaming messes before the battlefield, to on the battlefield. When you see so many people having their souls torn from them, that breaks a man, because you know yours is gone right along with them," Huey told me.

We were both silent at that. He didn't need me to agree or say anything, to know that I agreed.

I started to speak, then stopped myself, and pulled from my beer until it rattled empty. The bartender slid another one on the black countertop, the lights in the bar dancing off the glass in golden waves. "Well—" I started before Huey cut me off.

"I'm not finished yet. There's a lot of things that came home with me after the war—things that, well, they just had no place existing in this life, but they do. I spend many nights just fumbling through the images, imagining people at my door when no one is there. I kept waking up and thinking that there had to be someone, that I know I heard them—even smelled them. I kept running over to the shadows on the floor, Avi. I think you might know what I mean when I say these things to you. There was this quiet, every so often. Just the quiet, when I didn't have some stuck-up sergeant with a stick up his ass yelling at me every time I stopped to take a piss. I could finally lie down in an actual bed, one that I knew where it had come from and it wasn't made of leaves or my battle buddy's smelly old back. No one was shooting at me, no one was trying to kill me—I wasn't killing anyone else. Yet, for some reason, nearly every night, my head buzzed with noise, this white noise that stayed constant, and I couldn't get it to shut off." Huey gestured with his hands.

I cleared my throat, thinking about all the times my room was quiet, and that scared me more than anything else. It reminded me of the cage, being alone with no one else. In prison, at least, I may have not been able to blow my nose without someone watching. That meant I was never alone, which was oddly comforting, in its own way.

Huey stopped, taking a long pull from his drink. I did the same with mine, hoping this conversation would die soon. For some reason, every part of me was beating faster and faster as we continued to talk.

Huey finished, tipped his beer, and continued, "It was all too much for me—being afraid all the time. Half the time, I didn't know if I was about to be bombed, the other half, I thought I should get a gun to defend myself from old people staring at me wrong as I walked by. Fear is such a terrible thing. Not that it isn't needed, just that fear can be such a powerful thing that you become controlled by it. I tell you, man, more than sex, more than drinking, nothing takes hold of a person like fear does. That was me, Avi, every day living in fear. I stopped going out after a while, ignored my momma when she called, pretended like I wasn't home when my brothers came a-knocking.

"I found myself—sitting around tossing a gun around the room like a fucking beetle attached to a thin string during a hot-ass summer. In my damn house, blinds closed, clutching a half-empty bottle of booze. As you can imagine, my dumb ass toting around all drunk and shit with a big ol' gun, might as well say 'Take me to jail now, coppers.' Sure enough, they found me, and I spent many months in and out of the joint.

"And you know what, Avi?" Huey queried, turning to gaze at me for the first time since he had started talking.

How could I respond to that, when it was so close to home? So much of what he described I dealt with after the camps—after being kicked out of the group back in Washington. I didn't trust my voice to speak, so I opted to just shaking my head no.

"It was all my fucking fault—every bit of it. All the dark times I spent beating myself down, entrenched in that hole, seeing the shadows behind every curtain, carrying a knife in my heart as if I was going to go to war at any moment. Horrible shit happens to us all, and wonderful shit happens to us all the time—we just don't notice it. But, when that bad shit happens, when we go through those dark times, they're over and gone, just like the good times. We keep those scars open. When I was done dying and the lights stopped spinning, I came to that conclusion, inside the walls of a jail cell somewhere in Brazil," Huey stated coolly.

"Brazil? How did you end up there?" I responded.

"I think a few lost bets and hell of a lot of whiskey. Shit happens, man, when you start mixing your drugs." Huey shook his shoulders and I let the question die.

"So then what happened? You trained with some monks and got sober? Sounds like something out of a graphic book at the newsstand," I stated.

"Those books tend to be based on something, wiseass, but you aren't too far off. Something like that happened. Got stronger, gave up weapons, no more killing. Got me sober, gave me some time to start talking to the person that mattered: myself. Take it from me, kid, you need to have those conversations and you need to have them now. That or you can spend the rest of your life with a gun under the pillow." Huey calmly finished his second beer and set the glass down on the counter, smiling at the bartender.

"I am telling you all this as a friend. Let it go. You're the only one hurting yourself anymore," he declared.

Fire erupted within me, and the roar of the beast started to growl—no, it was me, not the animal, I thought, after some steadying with my hand on my stomach. I lashed out, though, directing my anger toward him. "Wait, I saw how angry you got when I mentioned Hans. I doubt you gave up your anger," I said skeptically, ignoring the heat smoldering inside me.

"I didn't say I gave up my anger, and I will make an exception for him—just him. Though I will kill him with these fists." Huey balled his hands, and the color drained to a white in his knuckles. We were both silent, listening to the dull music inside the bar, the polish of the wet rag on the glasses and the heavily dusted ceiling fans above us. It took me a while to catch my breath. My thoughts raced because of Huey's words and I wanted to be anywhere else in the world than there. I had nowhere to go; neither did Huey. After hearing his story, though, I knew Huey would be fine wherever he was. I didn't think that was why I was staying now. I would still see shadows under my door.

I downed my beer again, the cold foam dripping from my mouth like a dog.

"Might want to slow down there, cowboy. We do have work in the morning," Huey cautioned.

"Yeah, well, moderation is for cowards. I'm not afraid to have a few more before work—*foter*," I shot back to Huey, slurring my words as a burp from the massive amount of beer I had consumed already started to bubble within.

"*Foter?*" Huey questioned, his eyebrows raised, as if I had either insulted him or I had somehow put a curse on him.

"Yiddish... it doesn't matter," I grumbled, drilling holes into the bar table with my eyes.

Huey took a deep breath. "On your 'moderation is for cowards' comment: keep in mind that stupidity is for the arrogant, you shit-head," he retorted.

I let out a long breath finally and turned back to Huey. "This isn't how I pictured the rest of my night going, but it never is," I joked.

Huey laughed. "Yeah, it never does. Go on with your story, man. Why did you leave Washington? Sounds like you were head-over-heels in love with that Linor girl, ever since you were a boy."

"Yeah, she had me at 'dumbass.'"

21

Chapter 21

"You're such a dumbass, Avi," Linor joked as I stuck my tongue at her, both our hands dug deep into a bowl of ice. I was complaining that I'd got the short end of the job. All Linor had to do was put peanut butter on coal. I then had to take the coal and bury it under a pile of ice. My fingers were quickly losing any sense of feeling as they slowly became numb to this daunting and terrible task.

"Why are you always calling me names? You're the one that can't even spread peanut butter right. Who uses a knife?" I jabbed back at her.

"Watch it, I've cut people for less," she snapped.

"You've never cut anyone. Maybe a loud fart—that's about it," I snickered.

Linor turned red. "That's it, you're going to be the first person I cut, Avi!" she shouted back, a huge smile on her face as she slapped at me.

"Yeah, you already do that every time I come around you—" I started, before Linor's grandmother came into the room.

The shadows seemed to move with the room. I heard her cane on the floor before her croaky voice. "Dumbass—you be careful, boy, before you knock that coal over," Linor's grandmother huffed before she staggered into the room. She was hunched over, a tall woman, like her granddaughter, but time or something else had brought her down to about the table level. Her nose was long, crooked, and pierced with three different noserings, the largest being a bone pulled through the top of her skin. Her skin was deep olive brown like Linor's. Even in her advanced age, her hair was blacker than the coal we were coating with peanut butter.

Her eyes, though, they had a deep hue of brown that was the same color as those found on wild animals, almost like her narrow eyes were camouflaging themselves from some hidden danger, or more likely concealing herself before going to attack her favorite prey—me.

"Yeah, old lady—what's so important about coal, covered in peanuts, put into a bowl of ice?" I asked, snarkily puffing out my chest and throwing back my shoulders—which were far too thin, even compared to someone as old as Linor's grandmother.

"Watch your mouth, boy." She shot her faded lime green cane forward, hitting my knee. I kept my mouth shut not wanting to give her the satisfaction of seeing me in pain. Her prune-colored long sleeves came up, revealing a long line of numbers, tattooed onto her right forearm. It was prefaced by the letter A, followed by 23,478 was scribbled down below it.

I averted my eyes, as I caught Linor instinctively moving her hand to her arm. Even though it was a warm summer, Linor still wore long sleeves covering her numbers, sometimes even using her abilities to keep anyone from seeing her do it. I don't think she realized that I knew she was doing it. I had only seen her numbers a few times, but I remember a triangle at the end, followed the numbers "02" in conjunction with the triangle. All the prisoners from the camps had the tattoos. Some even had the triangle, but only the ten that had been in that building that day had the 01-10 tattoos next to the triangle. Everyone had them, except for me.

Sometimes, when I walked around camp, I would hear whispers of people calling me a beast, calling me an animal. Those served to only make me angrier. The one that stung the most, that made me feel like I was branded and could never be undone, was when I was called "Numberless." It was an instant separation that made people who had known me for years view me differently—keep me at an arm's reach, despite everything, as if I had not gone through the same hell as them. Funny, human beings can go through such misery and a sorrier state, and still find ways to separate themselves from each other.

Linor's grandmother continued. "If you must know, boy, we are going to use it to bring in some much-needed funds into the camp. You would know this, you bum, if you weren't always drinking with that shifty-eyed ginger brother of yours," she hissed.

"Why you—" I started as she held up a hand to me.

"We are making diamonds, boy, or crystals. Dumb tourists love these things." She stated this as a fact.

I blinked at her, looking down at the coal covered in peanut butter. "That doesn't sound right. No amount of peanut butter and ice will turn a coal into a diamond," I countered.

"Precisely, dumbass. We shall use my precious granddaughters' powers to make it appear that way. Once they've bought into our sale, it will be like taking candy from children. All people want is a get-rich-quick scheme. So, we are only providing the tools for them, the secrets. Easy copper, boy," she declared.

I'm sure more than just granddaughter—most likely great, great, great granddaughter, you old hag, I thought. Out loud, I said, "Way to be a supporting grandmother, using your granddaughter like that."

Linor gasped, as a violent wave of energy shook her.

"You ungrateful numberless—" her grandmother snarled, with her cane pointed at me.

Linor intervened. "The dumbass didn't mean it, grandmother. It's late and you need rest. He is just being dumb—like you always say, grandmother."

Linor's grandmother shifted her eyes between us two before reluctantly nodding and shaking her cane at me, as Linor took her arm, walking her out of the kitchen. I let out a deep breath and gripped the table. *That old bitch, saying whatever comes to her mind, who the fuck does she think she is...* I felt the fire first, leaking from my hands, before I noticed the table burning in my grip. I withdrew them and quickly shoved them in the bowl of ice.

"Calm down, calm down, please don't get mad," I stammered, my heart beating so loud I didn't hear Linor come back into the room. She froze, looking at the burn marks on the table, my hands in the bowl of ice. One wrong word, one wrong step from either of us, and the beast would come out and everyone would be in danger. Like threads of fire, my veins bulged, burning everywhere on my body, like something was frying away the brush in a forest to clear a path. I knew why that path was being cleared; it was for him.

Just a little cut—a dash of blood, Avi, and I can make her go away. His voice whispered as a chill colder than the ice sliding up my spine, swimming like an eel in the murkiest of waters. I cleared my throat, which felt like something metal and thick like mud was crawling up it. Chaos was flooding through my mind, through my body, as everything Linor's *bubbe* had said washed away. It had been many years since I had spoken back to *him*. My legs trembled, my neck was sweating.

What do you... want? Go away... I whispered to the monster that had taken hold of a part of my body that I would never understand. He was my parasite—Linor's *bubbe* may have called me Numberless, and the others did as well under their breath, but they all feared him. Feared what they had seen in the camp. They knew the monster was inside me. He was endless and a void of terror built into the very fabric of the night. He was my mark, the tattoos I was missing on the outside.

I want you to tell that old woman off, to shower her in your hate, Avi. She doesn't talk to you like that. No one does, he growled, and I felt the inside of my skull shake with his words.

I can't, I can't do that. Linor would never forgive me if I hurt her bubbe—

Do you think Linor wants a coward? A twig of a boy sniffling like a rat, scouring for scraps of love? No—she will want a man, a strong man that will wrap her up and—

"No!" I snarled, my hands digging into the charred piece of the table, as my body shook with a rage that I had never felt before.

"Avi," Linor whispered. She was standing back from the table, the knife from the peanut butter jar held toward me. I blinked at her, realizing that she was afraid. We were both afraid. I cursed under my breath.

A heavy silence fell between us, neither of us speaking as the table crackled, and the ashes from where I had burned it started to drift to the floor below.

Linor sighed. "I will get the broom." She took the knife with her. I nodded, not trusting myself to speak. Linor disappeared down the hallway, moving past the large oak tree support piece and out of sight. The beast was quiet. He wouldn't talk for a while; this was what he did. He caused me to get angry upset, to lash out when I didn't mean to.

I don't cause that; you do, Avraham. He snickered as his voice fell to the background of my thoughts. I shivered. Maybe, in a weird way, he was right. Maybe I was the one that was being angry. What did that mean, though? Why was I so mad?

Before I could divulge deeper down that rabbit hole, Linor came back into the room with a large brown-handled broom with the inscription carved on the side. "Careful, this is my other car" written along its wooden length.

She thrust it to me and I let go of table, taking hold of the broom just inches from my face. "Well thanks Linor, I appreciate it," I scoffed.

"Avi, it's okay to have emotions—we have to let it out sometimes, but remember we always have to clean up the mess afterward," she stated, taking the apron off. I looked down, avoiding her eye contact. "Chin up, bucker-roo, I think Elder Ad is having a bonfire night—I know how much you love his little speeches," she snickered.

I rolled my eyes. "Let me tell you, I can't wait for another one of his stories. Maybe this time he will actually remember what he was saying." We both laughed as I started to sweep the floor. The slow work calmed me, as Linor danced about the kitchen, humming a tune into the silence between us, the distance that was there now forgotten.

Once the kitchen was clean, I took off my apron, noticing the singes along the fabric and black dust coating the white cotton. I sighed—it was a somber realization, every time I let the anger come out. I would feel awful for it—feel lost within the hate. It was never far from my mind. I re-tucked in my shirt, smelling my armpits while Linor had her back to me. My eyebrows shot up and Linor laughed.

"Yeah, yeah, okay. I need to get a new shirt before we go out tonight," I grumbled.

She turned back to me, a small smile on her face, catching the light, making her glow like a flame inside the dark den of her tent.

"I will see you tonight—I had fun today, Avi." She beamed and I knew in that moment that she genuinely meant it. She was about as easy to read as a book underwater sometimes, but in that moment, she was clear as the page inches from my nose. "Even if you were acting like a dumbass again," she joked, rolling her eyes.

"Who's the bigger dumbass? Me, or the person hanging out with the dumbass?" I jabbed back to her.

"Get changed—hurry back," she giggled, leaving me in the kitchen, my hands on a broom, and a feeling that I had somehow lost that conversation.

I will never be gone long, I thought as she left my sight and I followed after her.

22

Chapter 22

I was rummaging through my tent. Old bottles and wrappers from too many endless nights on the bender littered every foot of my meager home. "Why is it so hard to just find one stupid thing in this fucking place?" I grumbled as I looked for a belt. It was fruitless and with a heavy sigh, I tore off a corded wire sleeve that I had "liberated" from the construction men while they were wiring a new store.

I smiled at the thought: *I am a good thief. Yeah, world's greatest thief who can't find a belt to match his black pants*, I thought as I stood up, tucking my shirttail back in. Why did I even bother—what difference did tucking my shirt in make anyways? My father had insisted that both Zevi and I had our shirts tucked in, our shoes looking glossy even though they were ragged with the wear and tear of little boys long before we had gotten them. He even made us comb our hair, and I wondered what the point of that was as well. Once the day got hot, my curls would just come out and break down any shape I bothered putting my hair in anyways. I sighed. My parents were a pain in my ass, but they wanted what was best for Zevi and me. That was all they ever wanted and I had been such a prick to them. Acting up or throwing a fit. Zevi would study, stay quiet during sermons, do exactly whatever mother would tell him to do.

Anything father told him to do, though—that was a different story. Zevi would listen, but the most basic tasks like sweeping or taking out the trash were somehow hard for him. Anything he had to do with his hands suddenly became as if he was being asked to build a car out of straw. Father would be perplexed and just utterly flabbergasted most of time, often losing his patience with my brother. Give him a book, though, and Zevi would have it consumed like it was the last bite of lemon cake in an instant. Knowing the pages inside and out, the beats of every character, the place of every comma and noun.

Often, I would catch Zevi playing alone when we were at home, supposed to be doing what father had directed us to do. Zevi would try—fidget and flay around like a fish on land, but he would at least listen to our parents. I would usually take breaks to throw my ball, watching my brother as he failed to sweep up even an eighth of what I would do in a minute. That lead me to do his chores after him—I would grumble about it, get mad, and pick on Zevi later for it. Yet, when father would come to inspect our work afterward, he would actually pay attention to Zevi instead of overlooking his work. Zevi tried. What could I do though? Sort of help without any conviction, or deliver the most tepid responses to our parents at every bend? I shook my head, tucking in my shirt like our father had taught us.

I doused the candle in my tent, glancing at myself in the mirror first, the long leather jacket that Linor had found for me a summer ago in Texas still holding up and looking fresh.

"Looking for this, Avi?" said Tiresias from behind me, and I nearly jumped out of my skin. Tiresias could sneak up on anyone—anyone. Not even with my heightened smell or hearing could I tell where he was coming from until he chose to be seen. I turned back to my friend. He was the meekest of us all, never gaining back the weight he had lost during his time in the camps. He had olive-colored skin, wooly hair, and golden brown tint to his long stringy hair that I almost could have sworn was red, and it made him stick out even more in our camp. He was Greek, and somehow had ended up in the camps, though. It was not surprising that undesirables from across Europe were brought in—that seemed to be everyone, from what I could tell.

I snatched the brown belt hanging in his hands, a smirk touching his

191

eyes as he giggled like a small child over my anguish. Tiresias may have been the smallest of us, but he was the only one of us who never showed any sign of being sad. He had shown up in the camps alone—a scared ten-year-old boy that didn't speak any language that was recognized from us. I could only imagine how terrifying that must have been for him.

But, if it frightened the boy, he never showed any sign. Even as a teenager, he showed no remorse, no malice, no anguish. Which just isn't natural for any teenager. Either way, he was the closest thing to a friend outside of Linor that I had. The only one who never called me Numberless, hopefully out of respect and the fact that Tiresias had no eyes.

He kept his eyes closed, his dark eyelids shut, obscuring anything that could be discerned in that manner. Instead, you had to listen to his voice, look at that smile he always wore. It was like Tiresias was seeing something that none of us could at all times—which he probably could—resulting in him being able to find almost anything. Including my belt.

I grumbled my thanks, pulling off the wire. It tore one of the loops on my pants off. "Damn it!" I snarled, lacing my finger through the hole where the cotton loop used to be. "You get way too upset about the smallest things, Avi. Just relax—you have a belt now," Tiresias pointed out.

"And you see too much into my business you blind bastard," I jabbed, pulling my belt through the rest of the loops. This was my favorite pair of pants. Tiresias laughed and pulled up my tent flap. "Come on, Avi, we are all meeting at the lot before seeing Elder Ad. Try not to get too worked up before we got there like last time," he smiled, gesturing me to follow him, a metal pole at his side lightly tapping the ground.

"There won't be a last time—it was a small fire anyways, Tir," I mumbled, following past him out the tent flap. He took hold of my elbow as we walked slowly across the uneven camp walkway. The camp was quiet at this point, most people having just returned from their jobs out "salvaging," or getting ready for dinner. We were on our way to the lot—the best place to play a game of baseball in a small town. Mainly because the local paper mill—that was churning as much smoke in the atmosphere as it was dumping strange globs of sludge into the rivers—was lit up like a Christmas tree all year round. The resulting area always had enough light to do whatever you wanted. Capitalism at its finest: the smell of burning money at the expense of the environment, that only benefitted the poor because the town's mayor didn't want to invest in lighting, and instead opted to look the other way as half the town died of some mysterious growths—good times.

"You know, a couple of Elder Ad's kids are going to be playing tonight with us. Might make the teams a little uneven, if you don't play. It wouldn't hurt for you to be second base or something like that. Maybe even outfielder," Tir said as I yanked my elbow off of his and we stopped suddenly along the dirt path.

"I don't play anymore, Tir. You know this," I responded, jamming my hands in my pockets. Tir stood up straighter, his lengthy hands looking like veins attached to his metal pole as he bent down to the small grass nearest our feet. He planted his hands in the grass and his smile widened to show all his teeth.

"I like grass, Avi. It can grow just about anywhere and tell us so many wonderful stories." He continued to pet the grass, whispering something I couldn't hear.

"Not all of us can talk to plants, Tir. Besides what can they tell you anyways? That a dog came and pissed all over a fern earlier?" I responded.

Tir turned his head to me, his smile gone and his mouth tucked in a look of confusion. A moment passed and we both started laughing.

"You joke, but you aren't too far off. Most of the time, the grass only talks about being cut or being peed on—so many little voices, so hard to keep up with," Tir stated, standing up again and flaring his hands in the air.

I scoffed at his comment and watched as he pulled his long metal pole in, with various rivets and slides, until it looked like a baseball bat.

"I love coming out here. It's the only time when I can see the most clearly," Tir stated.

"I know the feeling—away from camp finally, away from it all." I turned, placing my hands behind my head, and we both started walking through the tall woods that would lead us behind the paper mill's tall fences to our old and forgotten field.

We walked through the darkened woods, our path twisting and branch-ing over the tendril-like legs of the forest floor. I could see in the night—almost as clear as the daytime. Better, even. Tiresias had no problems walking through the thick canopy. This was his home and I was reasonably sure his campsite was the deepest in the woods. Without us saying anything, we both soon started an unofficial race through the woods. We were both at a slow jog by the time the baseball field came into view. I stopped, as I looked at the mill lights in the distance, glowing like a metal bonfire, illuminating the world around it.

Tir pulled up next to me, perfectly stepping over a limb that was jutting out from a fallen tree in the path with ease. I smirked at him as he glided over, a huge toothy grin on his face. We both loved running through the woods at night—one of the few times when we didn't feel like freaks. Even in our camp, made up of survivors and society's degenerates, there were plenty of people that felt uneasy about us. I mean, I got it: Tir could talk to plants and somehow see anything as long as it was near one of his "friends," as he called it from time to time. Naturally, that made even the Roma people more than a little uncomfortable.

But that compared little to the overwhelming uneasiness people felt when I came around, their discomfort nauseating and thick, almost as if the very air was made of their anxiety. Which I would think would be the worst thing about having a hyper-sensitive nose, being able to smell people's literal fear; but nothing was worse than bean night in the camp. On those nights, I left far out into the woods—a direction that wasn't downwind.

"I wish for once we had a more permanent place to stay," Tir whispered next to me.

"We've been here for almost a year now—that's pretty good for us," I replied.

"You know what I meant, Avi."

"Yeah, I know what you meant, Tiresias, but that kind of thinking is wishful at best—the dreams of the elders in camp."

"The dream of your brother, Zevi," he stated, more than a little bit of hopeful thinking coming through.

I scoffed at the mention of Zevi's name. My brother and I, that was one relationship that I wasn't sure could ever be more than name alone.

Tiresias must have caught my reaction to Zevi. He said, "You two still aren't getting along, huh? I mean, I guess I could see why Zevi is like that toward you. It's been, what, five years since the camps? I guess time only heals wounds in stories," he said somberly.

"No—time heals wounds, just you're never supposed to forget what caused them in the first place. Zevi has a stick up his ass—one that isn't deep enough, if you ask me," I growled in response.

"I don't know about all that—just maybe you should consider things from his point of view, Avi. I mean—"

I cut off Tiresias before he could finish his statement. "I know what Zevi would say. The same thing all of you would say, every one of you in this damn camp, Tir. It's a curse, what I am. I know what he wanted me to do; I know what he is still mad at me for not doing." I shook, feeling hot tension run up my veins, flooding my arms and legs up like a balloon.

He shrugged in the light from the mill. "I get it, why you didn't act sooner. We were children. You can still do something about it now, though," Tir stated before quickly changing the subject. "Come, let's go play some baseball." Tir turned, touching my shoulder, before continuing down the path to the field.

I called out to him. "I won't be playing, Tiresias. Don't waste your time."

"Why not?" he asked, confusion in his voice. The same question he asked every single time we went to this field. "Because—it's too dangerous," I replied, walking past him.

"It's a game with a wooden bat and some leather gloves. What are you worried about? Getting glove oil in your eyes?" Tir joked, fanning his hands over his eyes and pantomiming being unable to see.

"Eat a dick! Because I said so, Tir!" I growled.

23

Chapter 23

"PLAY BALL," boomed Bug's voice. It was louder than any speaker could possibly hope to be, his voice carrying all the way to the mill. I grumbled on the sidelines putting my pinky in my ear to clean out the noise. Bug giggled in the outfield. I flicked him off as my brother stepped up to the plate. Zevi was no longer that chubby little redhead I used to pick on—in fact, he was now the tallest out of all of us. He had the same hook nose as my father—the piercing green eye of my mother, complimented by a chocolate brown eye. His red curls still shot in every direction, but that's where his younger resemblance ended. He was taller than even Linor, with long and lean limbs that were toned and pumped up like he was some character out of a graphic novel—our camp's very own Superman.

In the back pocket of his blue jeans stuck out the potato sack mask our mother made him and a pair of batting gloves. He never did explain to me how he got the mask back or how he even managed to keep it. Our conversations over the last few years had been little more than grunts at the most. The mask creeped me out anyways—I was comfortable not knowing how.

His face held a long toothy grin, which matched his alabaster skin as it bled to an almost bronze color from the light of the mill. Zevi held his bat high with his shoulders tucked in. Gone was the little brother who could barely lift the bat over his head. Now, at a year younger than me, it was

Zevi who looked like the older brother—looked like a man. I crossed my arms and shifted uncomfortably in the dirt of the dugout cage. The only one standing against the wall as the rest of the team sat on the bleachers, ready for their chance to play.

Linor had a red cap pulled tight on her head, decorated with a yellow flower with the words "Catch you later—pop fly" bolded and showing a fly with a ball in its center, flying off into the distance. I never could understand where she had the time to make all the things that she did—let alone how she came up with it all.

I smiled at her. Linor stayed focused on Zevi as one of Elder Ad's kids approached. Bipin looked just like his father, only with gangly features and a look of everything being slightly too big for him. He was a few years younger than us, but all Elder Ad's kids had grown to our size. In fact, they were only six years old but stood at our height. His six kids served well for filling out a baseball team.

Bipin stepped up to the plate, looking both ways before sizing up Zevi. My brother held his grin out in front of him like a predator feasting in bloodied waters—he knew exactly how to hit the ball. Bipin's best bet would be to try to walk him. I watched Bipin nod to his brother some unknown signal and I knew already that it was a mistake. Everyone was silent except for Linor who kept blowing a big wad of gum, popping it loudly.

I turned toward Linor. "Where did you get that gum from?" I asked, genuinely interested, because I thought I had seen everything we both took.

She blew a bubble, her eyes fixed on the field. "I got it from the gum place, Avi—duh," she stated matter-of-factly.

"Fair enough," I grunted back.

"Bipin is about to make a mistake, isn't he, Avi?" she whispered, trying not to make the others more uneasy than they already were. I kept my head down, grunting again. "Most likely—the kid just doesn't throw fast enough to strike out Zevi."

"But you could," Linor said, turning toward me.

"I couldn't even if I wanted to, Linor, you know that," I affirmed.

Her shoulders slumped. "Well, looks like we are buying the beer again."

I chuckled. "When have we ever bought the beer?" I pondered.

She shrugged. "I don't know. When have we ever bought anything? Besides, charging for beer is just un-American, just like for water and bacon. You don't charge for the good stuff," Linor stated.

I blinked at her, smiled, and turned back to Zevi—there was no arguing against that point. I caught Bipin's wind-up just as he sent the ball rocketing toward Zevi. To his credit, any normal player wouldn't have been able to hit a ball moving that fast—from the speed, it had to be the boy's wolf-form taking over, like all Elder Ad's kids. But Zevi wasn't a normal person either. As the ball neared him, in one fluid motion of inhuman speed and precision, Zevi hit the ball. I could see it busting at the seams as soon as the ball connected with the bat. In a loud display of yarn and hot rubber bursting under intense heat, the whole thing exploded as it took off into the air like a jet. I could see where the bat had cracked nearly in half. Zevi smiled, throwing down the bat, and gingerly walked to first base.

Every time Zevi got up to bat, we lost both a bat and a ball. Every single time. Stealing baseball equipment wasn't too hard, but the local store was running out of balls because we had to take so many. When the ball went flying, a massive spike of grass and stems shot from Tiresias's hand. The spike had to easily be fifty feet or more. Only it wasn't enough to stop Zevi's ball; the ball veered up as if willed on its own and took off, fading to the mill on the other side of the river, which separated the field and the factory. I listened for a moment—straining my ears for the ring of the ball hitting the metal wall. After a few breaths, I heard a ding as what was left of the ball shattered glass, implanting itself into steel.

On the other side of us, his team let out cheers as Bug cupped his mouth. "Attention, everyone—we have a high-flyer rocket man!" His rhythmic voice rattled my ears again, and I knew that even people inside the mill most likely heard his voice. In fact, we had tested his voice once. Not only could he mimic any sound—even sounds that some of us had never heard and that I wasn't even sure nature had heard—but his voice could be heard with my ears almost a mile away. I cringed though, mostly from the noise of his voice, but mainly because I just didn't like my brother's friends. And Bug was accurately named. Even when I'd met him as a kid, his eyes shifted like some kind of praying mantis, his skin a pale gray that matched most tree trunks, and hair that looked more rubber than human. His eyes were too big to actually be real, jutting out from his skull, but contained behind a pair red-framed goggles.

I shook as I thought about his beady little eyes, as Zevi finished walking his last trip around the bases. Once he crossed home, he slapped the waiting hands of Sophia, a girl who was just as tall as Linor, but lacking the awkward teenage limbs. She had reddish brown hair that was closer to strawberry than auburn.

She was beautiful—in a viperous kind of way, with a heart-shaped face, and cold blue eyes that from this distance looked to be frozen pools of water. Sophia had never spoken more than five words to me in these last few years—she usually held the same generally judgmental look that most of Zevi's friends did. I was the Numberless to them; I was the wolf to them. Sophia caught me looking at her. I shifted my eyes down, as the next batter came up to the plate.

Arnold was average in almost every aspect of typical Jewish boys from our town. He had the darker skin tone of us Eastern Europeans, brown hair, brown eyes. A body no more filled out than mine—in fact, I think Tir and I both edged him in terms of height. What Arnold did have though, was a demon. As he stepped up to the plate, he dropped his bat and a massive shadow shot from his feet. A hulking monster came forth, standing at almost the top of the fence line. His skin was a deep oily black, with hollowed eyes and a thick hairline covered in spikes. As the creature took the bat, Arnold behind him mimicked the same movement, causing the shadow creature to follow everything Arnold was doing.

The shadow's eyes, black as coal, gleamed in the light, and a thirsty grin bordering on the edges of insanity trickled from his black teeth. I kept my eyes on Arnold as Bipin prepared to pitch.

Tir shouted from the outfield suddenly. "Linor, Avi! Will you guys please take your positions!"

"Oh, yeah, right!" Linor took her glove, running toward the third base. I sighed heavily—there was a time when pitching wouldn't have been a question for me, but now, if I even held a bat or a ball, I shook. I walked to the outfield, not putting on my glove, and put my back against the fence.

"Thank you!" yelled in unison everyone on our team.

"Yeah, yeah," I muttered back to them.

I went back to watching Arnold. I made it point to keep an eye on anyone who was trying to show off that much bulk with clear insecurities. People that insecure can be the most dangerous thing. You come to expect certain behaviors from them, only for them to do the exact opposite of what you thought they would do—and now you're the asshole for assuming. Fortunately for all of us, Arnold's shadow was a dumb brute. As for Arnold, I still hadn't figured out yet if he was just a greased-up idiot or not. But if his shadow was aware, capable of cognitive functions, I didn't want to think what would happen if it could ever leave Arnold. All of us had powers in some way, thanks to what was living inside of me; none of us understood exactly what that meant.

"Do you still not want to play, Avi? I mean, Linor forgets to come out to the field every game, but come on, it would be fun!" Solly shouted from the right of me. I turned to her. She was a tall and slender redhead with hair that flowed to below her waist, like a fire rushing to overcome her. Somehow, a tall Irish girl with red hair had managed to find herself captured and held in such an awful place. Whatever it may have been, having her around was always a wonderful feeling.

"Probably not today. Sorry, Solly."

"That's a damn shame. You're as useless as a chocolate teapot, Avi," she jabbed.

I stuck my tongue out at her and resumed my post on the fence. I was the king of being a party pooper at not wanting to play—I probably should have found someone to take my position, and that made me feel guilty—against Elder Ad's kids and Tiresias, everyone had pretty much resigned to our team losing. We hadn't won a game yet.

I watched as Bipin took aim and threw a curve ball—I swore under my breath. That wasn't going to work on a big brute like Arnold. Arnold smiled, squaring his shoulders, and leaned into the pitch. The ball smacked center of the bat and went flying with ease into the air.

Desperately, I could see Tiresias trying to figure out where the ball was. His powers were impressive, but if something wasn't in range of a plant, he was blind. Linor had thrown down her glove and was lying in the grass, while Solly joked with the rest of Elder Ad's kids. I could hear Schwein and Bug laughing at us in the distance. I curled my knuckles in, popping them as my fist tightened. I took a deep breath, letting it out as I tracked the ball in the air. It was going to land near the back right fence, but it was going to land. I dug deep and took off, running toward the ball, pushing away my thoughts of the last time I had handled a ball or bat. *Ignore that, press on*, I thought as I ran hard toward the ball.

When I could tell I was right under the ball, I shouted to Tiresias, "Launch me into the air, Tir!" Tiresias understood, slamming his hands onto the dirt. The ground below me suddenly shifted and a tangle of vines and plants came sprouting out from the dusty soil, forming what looked to be a basket. I was propelled within seconds up toward the ball.

I went wide with my arms as I flew into the air to slow me down, so I wouldn't overshoot the ball. The ball flew to me like a meteor gaining speed hurtling its way toward my face. I stuck out my hand, and the ball hit my palm and I caught it midair. My team below me cheered as I started to fall. I had just enough time to realize that at this height, there was no way I could fall without cutting myself.

"Don't bleed, don't bleed!" I whispered, as my feet landed and I shifted forward. I tucked myself into a ball and rolled. I tumbled over once, twice, and finally stopped on my side on the third roll over my shoulders. I let out a grunt, the ball falling out of my bruised hand—I watched it roll away and my heart stopped. Was the beast about to come out? Everyone here was in danger. I closed my eyes, waiting for the fire to erupt and the change to start. Nothing came, just footsteps moving toward me. I opened my eyes to see my team around me.

"Avi—what the hell, man! That was a good catch!" shouted Tir, extending down a hand.

I looked at it, unsure if everyone was still safe, before I unfolded my hands and took his. "Well shit, Avi, you're as useful as a cigarette lighter on a motorbike," snorted Solly, running up behind me, slapping my back. I flinched, expecting to be hurt—I felt fine, though. That was stranger: the beast never went out of his way to keep me from being hurt; in fact, he usually encouraged it.

Linor ran up to the group that was gathering around us, a concerned small frown pulling a black mole on her cheek down, making her seem far older than she actually was. I gave her a small smile back. She was the only one who knew how my powers worked, the only one who knew how dangerous what I'd just done was. With all Elder Ad's kids around me as well, I was feeling trapped, like the confines of my old cage. A feeling of overwhelming urgency to distance myself from this many people around me hit, and I started to push some of the kids to get free.

Shoving my way through, I looked off into the distance. There stood Zevi, a look of pure contempt on his face as he slung a bat over his shoulders. I stopped, meeting his stare, waiting for him to say something. I had risked a lot by playing in this game. Not only everyone's lives, but most importantly, I had just challenged my brother.

A toothy grin shot from my brother's face. "That was a good catch, Avraham, good catch indeed. Wouldn't you agree, Arnold?" My brother stayed facing me, his words being a command, rather than a question.

Arnold looked to the two of us, a small smile playing on his face, "Sure, Zevi—I completely agree."

Zevi span around to his team. "Let's go out to the field!" he shouted, and his team rushed from the dugout onto the field.

Tir turned to me as we gathered our stuff to take our positions to hit. "We will need you to bat, Avi. Does this mean you're in?" He almost pleaded for me to play. I looked at Zevi again, his grin causing me to want to run into a very deep hole and pull dirt over myself.

I walked off the field into the dugout as Bipin went up to bat. Zevi went to the pitcher's mound. We never had their team on base, except at the start of the game. I gulped, feeling like electricity was rushing through my body. Plug me in and I could probably power the entire baseball diamond with enough light for a year. Bipin raised his shoulders as my brother released the ball with such blinding speed that I lost track of the ball when it hurtled its way toward Bipin. Bipin stayed still, his bat never moving as the ball flew past him into the glove of Schwein.

Schwein snorted, lifting his mask to spit teeth from his mouth—I grimaced as the yellow pulp landed in a pile next to him. Schwein truly was a disgusting creature, I thought, as the rest of Zevi's team cheered. His roster was made up of generally everyone in the camp that I wouldn't go near. It shocked me still to this day how comfortable people in this camp could be with a catcher that could spit out a pile of teeth and a strange forest man propelling a teenage boy fifty feet into the air.

That was the Roma people, though—they had seen many things on their travels, countless generations wandering the world, so who would believe them anyways if they sought to tell what they had seen tonight? No self-respecting Gypsy would talk to the police—no survivor of the camps would ever trust authority ever again. I think people in the camp just accepted that some of us came back with more than just scars, some of us came back freaks—maybe that is what we always were.

Zevi threw another pitch, easily sailing it through Bipin's bat. This time, Bipin was half way through his swing at least. More cheers went up and I knew what was coming. Bipin was sweating; the poor boy knew that he stood no chance against Zevi. In fact, aside from Solly and Tir being walked a few times, no one had ever hit one of Zevi's rocket pitches.

A moment later and Zevi served Bipin his third strike. The young boy threw down his bat, kicking the dirt as he left. It was useless to try. My brother was throwing with inhuman levels of speed and skill. I looked down for a moment, hoping the game could be over by now. A boring story from Elder Ad didn't sound that bad in comparison. At least than it would be warmer than standing here in the cold. I brushed my arms over my jacket. When I looked back up, Linor was skipping her way to bat.

Panicked, I started to fear what could happen to her. You never knew with Zevi—he could play the game fair and easily win, but sometimes, he liked to be a downright demon with the ball. Linor made it to base and Zevi smiled at her, tucking in his chin and leaning his body to the side.

Both my hands shot to the fence in the dugout—Linor was far less spacy than she pretended to be, and when Zevi made that look on his face, I knew exactly what it meant. My brother these days terrified me—almost as much as the beast. In a lot of ways, I had witnessed my brother change so much that I no longer knew him. I suppose that was life, though. In a sense, we think we are entitled to understand and know everyone around us just because we spent time together, while in reality, this is about as disingenuous as it gets and an impeccable false equivalence to ourselves. I struggle most mornings even to know who I am when I wake up, spending most of my time thinking about Linor, fighting off the memories of the camps, or hiding from the beast.

I felt shame in that moment. Something stayed, pulling me to be afraid for Linor from Zevi. I may have had no right to still claim to completely know my brother inside and out, but I did know when someone was up to no good. It helped with Zevi smiling wide—like a shark seeing a seal in the water. I watched as Linor squared her shoulders, elbows dipped, an intense focus on her face. I held the cage in my hands, squeezing into the metal as my heart slowly began to pitch forward into my chest.

Zevi pulled back his hand, releasing the ball as if his arm was made of metal, his hand a muzzle as the pitch became a cannon. Linor smiled as she very nearly hit the ball. I let go of the breath I was holding. To date, no one had ever hit one of Zevi's balls—no one. Linor was a better player than me, or she had been, before the camps. Going up against freaks like Zevi and I was not a fair fight in the slightest. From what I could tell, Linor's cloud powers only gave her the ability to make things appear—even if I sometimes wondered if she could read my mind too.

The second pitch jetted from Zevi's hands. The bazooka had fired as the ball nearly hit Linor. Effortlessly, she moved her hips out of the way, the ball becoming lodged in the fence behind her. Schwein pulled the ball free and threw it back to Zevi, shouting, "Ball one." Both Linor and Zevi were smiling at each other. I gripped the fence tighter into my hands.

"Look boyo, your bird is going to be right as rain—stop your gibbering," Solly stated from behind me, taking a pinch of pink gum from a pouch that one of Elder Ad's kids had been offering everyone. They offered it to me, but I growled, missing the third pitch that balled Linor again, and she narrowly escaped being hit. Furious, I pulled the fence line so hard that it was starting to come torn off the metal poles.

I knew if I couldn't calm down soon, I would have to leave for everyone's safety. I tried changing the subject to ease the growing fire in my belly. "What the hell is a bird in this context, Solly?" I asked her, keeping my eyes on Zevi. The smile on his face now showed one of annoyance. Zevi had balled players before—on purpose, every single time, when I was sure he just felt like hitting one of us. In fact, he had done it to everyone at least once. "Everyone except Linor and I," I muttered to myself.

"What? Bird—it's your girl, mate. Relax, she's got this. No need to worry," Solly said with a tone in her voice that I thought was not warranted for this situation at all. As if to confirm it, Zevi reared his arm well behind his shoulder and shot the ball from his hands, sending it directly at Linor, hitting her square in the shoulder. Linor cried out, clutching her shoulder, and I felt my fingers heat up and suddenly my hands were through the fence, as if the metal was made of butter. I pulled my hands free of the fencing and bolted from the dugout to Linor. She was sitting up and rubbing her shoulder as I came toward her.

Her face, a mask of pain, looked up as I reached out my hand. "I'm fine, Avi—your brother is a—" Linor paused as if searching for the right words.

"A brutal bucket of fucking snots," Solly shot hotly at Zevi, who looked to be bored at the whole exchange, as the rest of the team came out of the dugout.

I growled at Zevi. "You did that on purpose!"

"The ball slipped out of my hands—she should have dodged." He shrugged his shoulders and let them fall. I growled again, this time from a much more primal place.

"Let it go, Avi—I'm fine don't need you sticking up for me, but thank you," Linor stood up, brushing the dirt from her dress. I stopped my reply, looking from her to my brother. For some reason, even with the beast inside me, I wasn't entirely sure I could fight my brother and win. It was something about how calm he always was.

"We need to hurry this up already—Elder Ad will come looking for us soon. What do you say, Schwein, was that a ball?" Zevi pointed at Linor while talking to Schwein.

Schwein snorted once more. "Yeah we can let them have one."

Feeling anger running through me, my eyes bulging and full of fire, I thought for a moment I might have been able to light the world aflame. "How about we settle this in one hit? Me against you, Zevi—right here." Everyone around us got quiet, turning toward me as I pointed at my brother.

I felt my cheeks flush, the anger subsiding only a little bit. I had to sound like a complete jackass. Zevi laughed. "You're joking, right, Avraham? When was the last time you picked up a bat? Full of surprises today—brother," Zevi gibed at my attempt to play.

I looked at Linor's bat. She had dropped it after being hit. *I won't let him get away with that,* I decided, steeling the anger inside of myself. "Yeah, if I can get a hit off of you, we win by default. What do you say—or are you too scared?" I challenged him.

Chants shot up around the field and my cheeks heated up again. In books, when someone declares a challenge, they always look so confident. I felt like at any moment the dirt beneath me was going to give way and I would fall into an endless pit. Probably better than being stared at.

Zevi laughed. "Sure, I will take that, but on one condition: one hit equals one throw. Sound good, brother?" He leaned toward me, pulling his glove deeper onto his hand.

"You're on," I replied as I picked up the bat and stood on the home plate.

Everyone on my team had scattered to the dugout, and Zevi's team had cleared off as well. It was just the two of us now. Years ago, I'd loved playing baseball—the thrill of sending a ball flying off into space, running around the bases with a trumpet of laughter and cheers. What I hadn't told Tiresias, or even Linor, was why I had quit playing. It was hard to enjoy things like baseball anymore, not when it felt like someone else's life, like I was living in a world that I didn't belong to every time I picked up a bat. Like putting on old clothes—at one time, you probably did feel like a different person, but you outgrow clothes, outgrow everything in your life for better or worse. I gulped, trying to steady the stream of electricity flying through my body. I hoped that I still remembered how to play. I got to the plate, hitting the bat against the ground, hearing the heavy "thump" of the metal on the ground. In my stance, I glared at Zevi. He had hit Linor, and I was going to teach my brother a lesson right here and now.

Zevi held his toothy smile at me, belittling my anger. I just got hotter under the lights of the mill. His face had changed: though calm, the ego had washed away and was replaced with a serious glare that I had never seen on my brother. *What was he thinking?* I wondered as Zevi placed his finger on the inside seam in the middle, his elbow and arm forming an "L" shape. His wrist hooked, and pulled down in front of his body. He had two fingers along the middle now, which reminded me of what our father had taught us as boys—I remembered the long summer nights when we could actually get father to stop working and take the time to throw a few balls our way. He would say, "You don't want your arm angled too high because that will take away the ball's bite—you want to maintain a three-quarter arm slot and feel the ball, instead of focusing on just pitch speed." I could still hear our father's soft voice. Zevi and I did not fully understand at all what he meant by arm speed and lowering our elbows, but we were just happy to be playing baseball with our father. All any of us knew were the images from magazines and what the radio played for us. Baseball hadn't been a sport in our home town, but it did become something that we loved.

But why, though? Why would Zevi use father's two-fingered throw when he knew that our *foter* had taught us both the same exact pitch? I had time to think this as my *bruder's* pitch looped its way toward me. I got into my stance, lowering my hips and shoulders and swung with all my might at the ball.

Zevi had put heat on the ball—no one besides me would notice that it wasn't as fast as the one that he had thrown Bipin. Before I could register that completely, I hit the ball, busting its seams and sending it flying over the fence line, into the dark of the river separating the mill and the field.

"Holy shit, Avi, where has that been?" shouted Tir.

Bug called out in his reverberating voice, "That's all folks!"

I ignored them both and started walking toward my brother, who hadn't even turned to see where the ball had gone. I walked up to Zevi, my younger brother who now stood taller than me, my younger brother who now stood completely apart from me. Maybe not completely. He had done all that deliberately, and now was the time to find out why.

Sophia beat me before I could get to Zevi. The two embraced in a short but deep kiss, both of them grinning, I narrowed my eyes at the two, but kept walking. "We need to talk, Zevi, just you and me," I ordered. The fire I had felt still was burning bright, and I wasn't sure why either. Zevi hadn't done anything, I had just hit his ball and our team had won our first game. I should have been happy, but something was completely off about the whole thing and he knew that I knew that.

Zevi gushed at Sophia, nodding his head toward her, and she smiled at us both, before turning and walking away. "Okay, Avi, we can do that. Good hit by the way," he praised me as the two of us walked off the field.

24

Chapter 24

"What the hell is wrong with you?" I shouted at my brother, disgusted by his actions and pushing his shoulder as the two of us stood behind the dugout.

He looked at my hand and his face contorted to anger. "You get one, Avi," he responded, stepping back from my arm's length.

I shook my head, trying to think through the haze. "There was no reason to hit Linor like that," I condoned him.

Zevi sighed deeply. "Fair—that was uncalled for, I shouldn't have done that."

I didn't respond for a moment as a whirlwind of anger, animosity, and general confusion flooded out of my body. "Okay, good. Why did you do it?" I asked, uncomfortable that the conversation was going this route rather than the direction I thought it would go.

"Because, Avi, I wanted to talk to you." Zevi stretched out his hands, letting them slap his thighs as he spoke.

A rush of anger brought the flood back in and I found the words to say to my brother much sooner than I had before. "Have you tried saying 'Hey,' you asshat? There was no reason to have hurt Linor—none at all—"

"Look at the way you're speaking to me now, *bruder.* It doesn't take much observational skills to tell that you're one misspoken word from eating someone. In your case—that might actually be a possibility," he stated, crossing his arms and leaning against the dugout.

I felt backed into a corner, suddenly very ashamed. I had a sinking suspicion that Linor was hiding how dangerous I must have really been—how
much as an angry young man I must have looked to everyone. Linor would
keep that to herself, though; she wouldn't want me to hate myself. I
cleared my throat, pushing aside the overwhelming feelings of the night
and day as they tunneled their way deeper into my body.

"Well we are here now. What do you want to talk about, Zevi?" I
questioned my brother in the darkness.

He cleared his throat, suddenly deadly serious and with a conviction
that I hadn't seen in my brother before. Zevi wasn't that helpless ginger
boy who liked to steal our mother's cookies and cakes every day—I fought
to remind myself that.

"I need you to come along with us tonight, Avraham, on our mission—or
rather, I would like you to come with us; we could use your help," he
declared.

I stepped back, firing my retort. "No, Zevi, it always ends the same way.
We will go out, cause some mayhem, have a little fun along the way, and
then nothing. We are just kids, Zevi, with no way of ever finding anything
on them in a world that doesn't care about what we went through." I
outstretched my hands, trying to make Zevi understand my point of view.

Zevi stepped forward, a disgusted look edged into the hard lines of his
face. "Typical. Even when I ask, you still won't put aside whatever it is
that makes you not give a damn about this community to do anything for
anyone. I thought seeing you finally play a simple game of baseball—which
you yourself would never shut up about as a boy—would make you finally
stop being afraid and help us," Zevi grunted, moving from the dugout and
circling to the side of me.

I turned toward my brother, fuming. "And why would I help any of you
and your friends? You spend half of the time off on your 'missions' doing
lord knows what and the other half generally making my life a living hell
or calling me cruel names! Beating people in the middle of the night—I am
surprised you guys haven't killed anyone yet." I stood tall, meeting Zevi's

gaze, so that even in the darkness, I could see his fire building inside too.

He scoffed, "The sheer arrogance of you will never cease to amaze me, *bruder*. I should have been the elder out of the two of us."

I stepped back, unable to reply. The comment disrupted my thoughts, then the fire that was building within in was dosed in kerosene as I had every urge to punch, kick, and maybe even bite my brother—*yes, shred him with my claws!* A voice roared from deep within my mind. I panicked, feeling guilty of something that hadn't even happened yet. I had let the beast project the images of me attacking my brother sink into my thick skull.

I stepped back, nearly tripping over a rock as Zevi stepped forward, continuing on with his verbal assault. "Nearly every night, nearly every single night, I am up late poring over legal documents, newspaper clippings, anything that could lead us to finding them. When I am not doing that—guess what, Avi, who do you think helps keep this place running? Those half-baked scams of Linor's grandmother? Please. It's my friends that you insult just as much when you think no one is listening and oh, by the way, maybe they wouldn't call you Numberless as much if you would actually show that you care to be part of this community. Instead, you ignore them at every turn." Zevi's eyes shone with a fury as he stepped toward me, closing the distance and pointing at his chest. "I pay off cops not to look too much into our camp. I lead the raids into town to find food for you to eat, booze for you to throw up. Cigarettes for you to dash onto buildings, flicking them away like garbage wrappers. What do I ask for in return? Nothing, Avi, I ask for nothing. Yet, if I wanted to ask you for anything—good luck. You're probably sulking in a corner, or staring at that girl's ass, or sometimes both." Zevi stood before me, his chest out and his voice deep, as I felt like falling to the ground to escape his words.

He took a deep breath as both of us remained silent. "All I am asking for, Avi, is to join your brother just for once. Show the community that you actually give a shit about them and help me find this son-of-a-bitch," he spat, turning away from me. I looked away, staring off into the night, my vision allowing me to see a rabbit running along the outer edges of the fence line. I followed it until the bunny disappeared under the gates to the lot—my anger slowly leaving me as I watched it leave.

Zevi was the first to speak again, cutting the silence like a jagged blade through a wild turkey. "Don't do it for me, do it for this community. Make up for all of it—all of it, by helping us." He pleaded, almost. I pulled my hands in front of me, examining them. Images of the blood that was on my hands, still staining my fingers. Time had done little to remove the memory of what my hands had done, what my hands hadn't done. I remembered Zevi and my last conversation in the camps. He blamed me for our mother, by not acting. He blamed me for not turning into the beast and liberating us from the nightmare. Zevi couldn't understand, though, becoming that thing—the thing that was gnawing its way through me, marching as if to a war drum, couldn't be unsealed. I was in no control, and not only that, but my memories would be almost completely blank, save for when the beast killed someone. Those memories, the pain my body felt afterward, that all stayed with me forever.

"I can't, Zevi—it's too dangerous. I am sorry," I mumbled behind my brother's back.

Zevi hissed and still remained turned away from me before speaking again, his voice steady and undisturbed. "We found one finally, Avi. We found the monster that still haunts all of our dreams, the biggest devil of them all. Dr. Joachim lives just outside of the Tri-City area. We are going to find him, and we are going to get our peaceful nights of sleep, knowing there's one less evil in the world." Zevi shook with anger, his voice cracking, trying to maintain control.

25

Chapter 25

"Nothing lasts forever, not even our little community of artisans and just overall good people," I mumbled as Huey poured me another drink. I held up my cup to his and we clinked glasses with the bartender, who had come over to listen to my story.

Huey grunted. "Yeah that's the problem when everyone shares together in a community. It only works as long as everyone wants to be a community—not to mention there's only so many holes that can be dug. Did your brother actually help the community or was he all talk? I've met plenty of guys just like that in my day. First to stand on a table and preach about the community, last to actually do anything," Huey pointed out to me, taking a long sip from his drink.

I swirled my drink around. I swirled my head around trying to keep hold of the conversation and the story that I was not ready to relive just yet. "To his credit, he did help a lot. Often times finding missing parts for cars, filling out zoning paperwork and getting cash to bribe law enforcement from raiding our camps. To be fair, though, the stigma around the Roma people keeps everyone away, and when most people only know about fortune tellers and button thieves, our reputation did the rest, "I grumbled, emptying my drink. We weren't making it to work today.

"Wait, you can read fortunes?" the bartender leaned in toward me and asked.

I grunted, "Yeah, you will pour me another drink, bitch."

He scoffed, taking my cup. "We are closing soon. You better have the money, Jew boy."

Huey ignored us both and slid his cup away. "I think we've both had enough, but you still have to finish your story Avi," he stated.

I grunted again, "Where was I?"

"You were deciding to help your brother for once, *burer*?" Huey asked in Yiddish.

I nodded. "That was said somewhat right. Good job. Going behind that dugout and talking to Zevi was only the start of my problems for that night. I agreed, though, I agreed to help my *bruder* track down the man that had tortured us so we could make him pay."

26

Chapter 26

The walk through the woods was loud and well lit. Most of the group and camp had come out to the field with plenty of popcorn, peanuts, and way too much of my brother's meat and spit. I lingered behind the group with my steps, as everyone in front of me recounted the game. We had finally won a game. It felt hollow, though. Zevi had let me hit his ball, just like he had purposely hit Linor.

Linor walked beside me, one arm clutching her left bicep. I could see the yellow and purple outline of where the ball had hit her, but my anger toward my brother was like trying to hold water in an unclasped hand: it just kept rolling out. The monster who had hurt so many of us, killed so many of us, was just a few miles over in the next city. Festering hate was opening an old wound that I knew could never be shut—perhaps, perhaps this was the way to finally shut that wound. Part of me hoped for that, pleaded to finally be free of the nightmares, to be free of the catch. Still, though, Dr. Joachim was probably an old man by now. Beating up an old man for turning us into monsters—would that make me feel better?

I looked at Linor. She smiled, then her face turned to concern. "Oh no, you only get those sad puppy eyes when you're lost in your own little world. What now, Avi? You just won a game against your jerk of a brother and you didn't eat him behind the shed like I worried. Between me and you, I wouldn't have told anyone if you bit him—just a little," she winked, laughing, before stopping suddenly and taking my hand. "Oh, Solly says she can give us a fresh mark if you're interested! I have so many ideas!" Linor jumped at the prospect of getting another tattoo. Solly was our camp artist, just as much as Linor. Nearly everyone in camp, save for a few adults, had some kind of tattoo from Solly. Her quick hands would fly over someone as the gentle engine of the needle would puncture into the skin of whomever she was working on.

I shook my head, momentarily being pulled out of my head. "Nope, too much blood for me. I will watch you get yours though," I responded to Linor.

"You're such a wimp sometimes, Avi," she joked.

"Yeah, but I'm your wimp," I shot back.

None of them knew that bleeding was what turned me into the wolf. I felt guilty for having not told Linor that yet. One of these days, I was going to have to tell her. If Linor was afraid of what I was, she never showed it. She didn't care that I was already branded with a scar that would never go away.

Linor turned toward me. "That's okay, I can be the strong one for us both. Are you okay though? You seem quiet. I thought you wouldn't shut up after finally getting to play again. When you were a little boy—that's all you ever talked about."

"Don't worry about me—besides, you were the one that got hit with a ball. How does it feel?" I asked, stepping toward her, taking her arm gently into mine. I could see the purple bruising and swelling in her bicep. It was a vicious bruise that I worried wouldn't heal for a long time. To her credit, Linor wasn't complaining at all. I admired her even more in that moment. She could take a beating and still keep on kicking—that's where real strength could be found, in those of us who could be beat down only to get back up, bloodied but unbowed.

"See something you like?" she jabbed and I dropped her arm.

"Mostly just wondering what you've been eating to get so big and strong—I think you might even be able to hurt me now," I feigned being hit, stepping back from her.

"Shut up!" she punched me in the shoulder, laughing, then suddenly her hand found mine and we were both quiet.

"Thank you for caring," she said softly.

"Thank you for letting me care," I responded, just as soft.

We continued our way through the woods until we made it back to the camp. Lights shown everywhere, people were bustling with stacks of boxes, and somewhere I could smell roasted peanuts as loud cheers shot up all around us. It was a bonfire night, the best time of the month—winter or summer, nothing made you forget about the world like making a huge fire that could be seen from space. Our own pocket of the world made brighter than the sun.

Chimes of music softly swam melodic and rich tunes that drove deep within me—freeing me from the stress of my conversation with Zevi. I wasn't sure how I felt about what Zevi said, about finding such a monster that was nearby, but for now, the tuneful sounds of the camp kept the anger at bay and I found myself smiling, in spite of the deep perforation that I had been feeling so close to just moments ago.

I was home again. Home washes away so much and if nothing else, provides a threshold from the darkness of our own minds. More and more lately, I thought— as we walked through the camp, making our way to the blazing fire at the center, its flames stretching over the tops of the tents—that we put ourselves through so much misery, only to die alone in the end. And that's what I was doing: being miserable, thrashing about like some kind of wild animal. Zevi was right, I wasn't doing enough for the camp. That was going to change now. We had found the devil himself. He would no longer haunt our dreams anymore. Zevi had said that. I believed him, as we approached the fire. I cracked my knuckles. He wouldn't haunt our dreams anymore.

27

Chapter 27

"So, were you going to kill him?" Huey asked, passing me a towel as I pulled my head out of the toilet bowl. I looked at the rag as if it was some kind of flag of an ancient enemy on a battlefield that had thoroughly trounced us. I pushed his hand away and made a deliberate show of wiping off on my sleeve.

"You're a disgusting creature, you know that, Avi? And we spent time in jail. People took bets on who was the biggest douche in there and you're the worst." He grimaced.

"What are you talking about? You're the one that usually won those bets," I smiled.

"You aren't wrong man, you aren't wrong," Huey joked, helping me to my feet.

"So, you tracked down that man right? The doctor?" he asked.

"Not exactly. We first went to the fire—honestly, what happened that night was because of what was said around the fire—what I guess I learned. Its funny, man, I never realized how easily influenced my teenage mind was, you know?" I stated as we both walked to our small dining room, the brown table held up by two of the bricks from work and some stolen tape.

"Easily influenced teenagers with shared traumas and no supervision—who would have thought anything bad would happen?" Huey grumbled as he rummaged through the cabinets.

"Looking for the coffee?" I asked, feeling sick to my stomach. I was never drinking again, I decided. "I drank it all this morning," I stated.

Huey slapped his hands on the counter. "I wanted one thing today: coffee, cigarettes, finally have a better-looking roommate than some coffee-stealing werewolf," he grunted, taking out two cups, filling them with water from our loud sink. The sink shot water in the cups with so much force I was reasonably sure it could strip paint from walls.

Huey placed the cup in front of me. We clinked them and we both remained silent for a spell. The sun was rising, bleeding into the early morning. By all accounts it was going to be a wonderful day—I didn't want to sour it, but I knew what was coming.

Many years later, more than my time in the cages, in those dark days where the only thing getting me through was my promise to not let them win, and not to let the monsters turn me into a monster, all I thought about day by day was that everything that had been Avraham was stripped away like the pages from a calendar.

As the years pressed on, marching ever more on, and I kept traveling, kept being pushed to see more than I ever wanted to see, the pain of my own actions became my niche. Beyond the cages, I was left with just memories. Memories fade, traumas are rooted in the memories—some pains are just so deep that I could never escape them. For me, the things that haunted me the most, that caused me to grip my heart as if it were to burst, were the things I hadn't done. I could always get a new calendar, that was certain, until the pages stopped going. But I could never put the pages back, I could never go back to my actions that caused them to fall to the floor like a freshly fallen snow.

"Elder Ad was a dramatic person sometimes. He really did know how to tell a story with flare. I think you would have liked him."

28

Chapter 28

I could feel the warmth of the fire, Linor's head on my shoulders, her hands around my waist. Any other time, this would have been the happiest moment of my life, just to be with her. But as Elder Ad talked, I was still miles away, still trying to come to terms with what I would do once I saw the evil doctor later—I was going to kill him, I thought. I could do it; it wouldn't take much. I blew out some air and Elder Ad turned his head to me.

"Young Avi, glad you could join us. Welcome, is the fire warm enough for you?" Elder Ad chided and a few people around me snickered.

"Glad to be here," I mumbled and Linor pulled more on my shoulder. I wasn't getting out of this moment. Oh boy, the things I've done to kill a moment of my life. So, strangely, earlier today, my whole world was intertwined with the creature on my arms. Now I was balancing murder while also keeping every urge in my body from wanting to make this a really warm night with Linor. *Stop being stupid, Avi, just focus and breathe, just like you used to all those years ago in the cage.* I decided to give Elder Ad my full attention. Maybe that would help, maybe that would help with murder. *Stop calling it murder; you can't murder a killer—I don't think.*

"We are building a generation of people that want to see the world burn—burn way bigger than even this fire." Ad told his story, stretching his hands wide.

"Not likely, I poured half a bottle of meat on that fire, with some good ol' dust dung for tendering," Schwein snorted.

"That's gross, you pig-foot." Solly rolled her eyes so heavily, I thought she was going to fall off her log.

"You're just jealous that Schwein didn't share any with you, Solly," Bug chimed in, his voice a perfect reflection of Solly's voice.

"I hate when he does that," Linor whispered to me.

"I think Bug hates when he does it himself. Are you comfortable?" I asked her, pulling her closer to the log that we were leaning on.

"I mean, we could be on a beach right now, drinking something other than that nasty meat and listening to stories of Schwein throwing some kind of strange fertilizer on a bonfire," she responded.

"Oh—I'm sorry, maybe we—" I started.

"I'm joking, Avi, there's nowhere else I would rather be." She smiled at me.

I smiled back, leaning in to kiss her instead of wasting time talking. We had the best spot, as far as I was concerned. All throughout camp, there were huge sweltering bonfires lighting the land up like a battlefield. Ours was surrounded by eight or so logs laid near the fire that we had all comfortably sat our lazy asses down on.

Everyone was laughing when Zevi said, "What's wrong with burning it all down anyways, Ad? Maybe some things need to go so that something new can arise." Zevi's words were quiet, but cut through the group like an axe chopping a tree.

Elder Ad's long tan face shifted under his many wrinkles. He looked tired, he looked ancient, and there was no telling how old he was. When I had first met him, I thought he was already on the verge of dying of old age. Now he was a widower and a father to five wolf children. Probably took a lot out of the guy. In the few years I had known him, though, I had never seen his face look graver than in that moment.

"Before anything can rise, before anything can burn, we first must ask ourselves why that is. To take something down means it is no longer needed—okay, fine, tear it down. What are you putting back, though?

What inside you makes you think that you have something better to put there?" Elder Ad asked the group, his strong accent sound close to Canadian or a thick Midwestern as he spoke.

My mouth started speaking before I had time to catch myself. Maybe it was because I had a beautiful woman on my arm, maybe it was the fire: I just had to speak, despite how much my feet were shaking from the fear of it. "Why does it matter, what is inside of us? If it's the better idea, just build it. If it's the wrong idea, build it again," I countered to the Elder.

Without missing a beat, Elder Ad smiled at me through the flames. "You're asking a very good question, Avraham. That is not one that I can provide the answer to. Only you can know that answer," he stated.

I felt crestfallen by his response. Just for once, when some older person started spouting advice, I wished they would spell it out instead of making everything an internal paradox about our inner souls.

"I heard a story once, about why it was important to know what was inside ourselves. A story told by another Elder, for another tribe," Elder Ad announced to the group. The fire popped and he waited until everyone that was gathered was giving him his attention. The outsiders of the camp gathered around a man who was an outsider in his own land. Maybe that's all any of us were—just outsiders.

He continued, "The story went that a grandfather and a grandson were gathered around a fire, much like our own, a long time ago. The night was brutally cold, the air thick with a coming war party the next day. It was the boy's first battle, though the grandfather had fought many wars in his lifetime, and survived countless fights. As he sat back, observing his young grandson, he began to explain to the boy that inside everybody, there are two wolves." Elder Ad held the "w" on "wolves," overplaying it.

I sat up, letting go of Linor—staring into the eyes of Elder Ad. It was like he was seeing into my mind, like he was talking about me and the beast. I listened closer, engaged for the first time in what someone was saying, in maybe my whole life. And I had absolutely no idea why.

"Those two wolves that are inside of us, one is anger, jealousy, envy, sorrow, hate, and all that is bad. The other is love, peace, happiness, joy, laughter, and all that is wonderful. These two wolves, good and bad, spend every day fighting for control. The grandfather finished explaining his story, sat back and watched the fire," Elder Ad did the same thing, pushing down his hat, pulling his green jacket deeper around him, and looked off into the sky.

That was the whole story? I thought, *but it didn't finish; that can't be right.* Eager and with a bit of annoyance, I asked Elder Ad, "Well, which one wins?"

Elder Ad looked at me, his eyes heavy as if looking off into some unknown time and place. "Whichever one you feed," he stated. I sucked in as much air as my body could handle in that moment, and I felt my heart jump to the bottom of my stomach. I couldn't place it, I had few words for it, but it felt like someone had just laid a boulder on my shoulders and told me to walk up a hill. What was I doing? Was I feeding my beast this whole time? Was I the one that was actually causing the pain I felt? Was I the bad beast? Suddenly I didn't want to be around that bonfire, I wanted to be anywhere but there.

I stood up, leaving the fire pit. "Avi, where are you going?" Linor called out behind me as I stormed off. The lights from the fires flickered away and I was alone. I walked to the edge of camp, leaned over, and threw up near the running creek. I felt fatigued, imbalanced, and as if at any moment I was going to implode. I curled into myself, sucking in as much cold air as possible.

Little Avi, growled a voice.

I snapped my eyes open. I knew his inhuman gravelly sharp teeth and claws, anytime he spoke. It also helped or didn't help that when he spoke, my whole mind shuddered under an immense weight.

I closed my eyes again. This time he roared even louder, *Little Avi! Face me!*

My God, what the hell do you want? Can't I just for once have a moment to myself? I came out of my position, sitting up and shouting into the night. I looked into the creek, and the water distorted and flickered as the sediment formed a dark shadow in the shape of a wolf on the moonlit waters. His eyes showed through the murky water, red as the rubies Linor and I had taken from woman's purse once when she wasn't looking. I felt another wave of nausea hit over that—was what happened in my earlier life justification for everything I had done? Even if I never fully understood what it was like to be full, or to have a bed, or to be warm, was I the bad wolf? Who was I feeding?

Which one indeed? growled the beast in the water. "Stop it, go away, I have nothing to say to you!" I snarled back, sitting up on my hands at the shore. He cackled, his voice sounding like lightning bolts, striking the land for some vengeful god. I was tired of this; I was done with every waking moment of my life being stalked by this—this creature. "What do you fucking want?" I growled to the beast.

He laughed again. *Oh, I want a great many things, Avraham. For now though, I am curious. Do you think you can take a life? Plunge your hands into the blood of an enemy—of an innocent?* His voice shot shivers up my spine, my body going cold as his words settled into my mind.

"That man is far from innocent. He tortured me endlessly, tortured my friends, killed people. He is a monster!" I clamored.

What is the conflict then? If you're so sure he is a monster, feast on him, devour him. Better yet—let me do it, if you do not possess the strength to finish your enemies! He barraged my eardrums with such force I felt vertigo. I was closer to the shoreline, so close I could feel the splashing on my fingers, the cool wet of the creek. It felt inviting, like an ending to all my suffering, a nirvana only inches away. I fought that feeling, and pushed it aside with my rage.

I paused. Could I really kill another man? Could I really end another person's life? I wanted so badly to not have this conversation, to paint him as a monster and be done with it. He *is* a monster, Avraham no doubt about it. Just like the stories your *zayde* used to tell you, a hero has to slay the monster. But I was no hero. Heroes are supposed to be sober and wear their underwear out in public.

I can help you—help make it easier for you, Avi, he whispered like an old friend trying to soothe the pain away. It sounded tempting, but why even worry about anything beyond just ending such a vile person as the doctor? Still, though, Elder Ad's words haunted me: the wolf that wins is the one that I am feeding, and killing the doctor felt like I would be feeding that bad wolf. Maybe I could get away with just throwing him in a cage. Calling the police was out of the question—a cop in a Gypsy camp is the equivalent of a bleeding seal in the middle of the ocean. Everyone would fire if the police came. What should I do? Maybe Zevi would know—yeah, Zevi only said that he had found the doctor, he didn't say I had to hurt him. I could just let Zevi do it or one of the others. Zevi, though... Zevi and I might be estranged, but we were brothers. I couldn't shove that off onto him.

All you need is to let me out, Avi, let me handle it! the beast roared from within me.

"Shut up, you!" I snarled, plunging both my fists into the muddy water, punching over and over again into the bottom of the creek bed. On the fifth punch I stopped, fire shooting down to my stinging hands—*this is what he wants, what the beast wants is for me to get mad and bust open my hands.* I looked at my hands. The slimy rocks had left heavy bruises across most of my knuckles. Somehow the skin had remained intact.

I could hear a snarl and the scratch of his claws across the very thresholds of my sanity as he fought to be free. In response, I dove my head face first into the freezing water, screaming into the currents with all my might, only to catch leaves in my teeth. I kept my head under the water until all I heard was the sound of my ears filling up, before I brought myself back up lying on my back.

I was breathing hard, my clothes soaked. I was still me. Still Avraham, just some poor dumb kid sitting alone on a creek bed, soaked to the gills in muddy water and in a desperate need of something to take the edge away. I flicked off the air, hoping that the beast was watching. Inside somewhere, in the deepest roots of my mind, I heard laughter.

I panted—the wolf was silent over my heavy breaths. I looked back into the river, and the images distorted until my father's long face appeared. One word came to mind from his face: disappointment. I tilted my head, tears streaming down into the water like rain. "I'm sorry—I'm so... sorry,"

I wept into a cold night, indifferent to the suffering of a boy crying at the edges of a muddy creek.

29

Chapter 29

I arrived back at the camp, wringing my shirt dry before putting it back on and trying to smooth out my jacket. *That should help, Avi, just twist your shirt and smooth your jacket. Good job, you jackass.* I went through the camp. People were turning in for the night, and most of the twisting walkways and paths were empty. A couple bumped into me, knocking me to the ground. I came up reeling as the woman held sheer terror when she looked at me. My anger deflated—I knew what she was thinking. "It's him—the beast!" she shrieked, clutching her husband tighter. "We—we don't want any trouble..." pleaded the man.

I growled, hissing at the couple. The man and woman turned running in the direction they had came. "Help, the wolf is trying to eat us! He won't just die and go away!" the pair yelled into the night. I considered chasing after them, my heart beating in my ears. No one responded to them; I was all alone. I had always been—alone. A dull ache that never stopped froze my heart over; I would have cried again, but this pain was one I felt everyday. I hated them for it—I could do nothing. I hadn't chosen to have a monster burdened within me. I kept walking for a few more steps until I lost track of time.

I stopped and listened, extending my hearing until I heard the rhythmic buzzing sound of Solly's tattoo needle. That brought me back. I sighed heavily, glad to see that no one had noticed I was gone. I walked toward the sound when Zevi stepped out of the shadows of one of the tents. I hadn't noticed him; it was like he was the night itself. I stepped back, my heart moving fast.

My brother walked out in front of me, looming tall like a statue higher than me. "Oh, hi Zevi, I didn't see you there—" I started.

"Where did you go?" he questioned, his voice direct and his arms crossed. Everything was a challenge with this guy.

"Just... you know... needed some air. Elder Ad's stories absolutely bore me, you know?" I attempted to lie. I didn't believe the wavering in my own voice though. I had my doubts that Zevi would either.

Zevi said nothing for a moment. Even with my eyes, I was unable to see his face clearly in the dark. Something was obscuring it. He stepped forward into a light that was cast down from the full moon above, and his mask that our mother had made him was covering his face. I clenched my teeth. The crude red drawn eyes were faded—still there, though. The smile, smeared by what appeared to be charcoal I could tell had been reapplied recently. I thought back to the last time I had seen Zevi wear his mask. It was when we were children, right after our mother had given him the wicker sack as a gift. For a moment, I wasn't sure what terrified me more, the beast or his mask. My legs wanted to bolt as he walked in front of me, his large chest looming in the light, his broad shoulders dwarfing mine, and for the first time, I was no longer sure if I could beat up my brother. He was the bigger one now.

"I feel you. His stories do drag on with no point." He laughed through the muffled sack.

Awkwardly, I laughed as well when Zevi stepped next to my ear, lowering his head and whispering, "The camp needs you, Avi. I need you. Do not run off like that again. Are we clear?"

Anger and old wounds between us drove their way back into my body, inflating me with an urge to violence. I shoved him hard, but his shoulder barely nudged from its position. Even worse, his skin felt like iron, like I was trying to move a castle, not a person? Did Zevi weigh that much? No, it was impossible for someone to be that big and lean in such a small frame—yet his skin had felt like rows of rows of taut muscle.

I growled at him, clearing my throat and hoping that I sounded tougher than I felt. "Oh, we are clear. You don't control me, *bruder.* I am your protector."

Zevi stayed still, and I felt that behind his mask he was smiling at me, which only made his confrontation more off-putting. He hung his head lower and I tightened my fists. Despite all the times I had been tortured and generally living the lifestyle of being a con-artist, I had never been in a fight. Maybe I was fooling myself. Most people had never taken a punch, let alone thrown one, and they walk around as if at any moment they could be a focus of anger and directed rage.

In reality, it was like my fear of heights. People were imprisoned by a fear of being hurt, only I had been hurt more times than I knew how to describe the word, scars for my scars. That made me feel confident, made me think I had a chance to take someone down if I had to. By the same thought, though, a fight risked bleeding, which was my true underlying fear. So, often, in nearly every situation, my anger stayed buried. Looking at my brother, I wondered again about what I had felt when I pushed him. Over the last few years, nearly all of us nine had shown some unnatural ability. The ease at which he could hit a ball and strike out anyone had proven Zevi's abilities ten times over, but in that moment, I realized I had underestimated him—by miles.

Zevi side-stepped me, walking past, and disappeared into the shadows, calling back, "Don't be late tonight." His tone was clear. He knew he had frightened me.

I waited until I calmed down and wiped the sweat from my forehead before heading toward the sound of Solly and Linor. When I was satisfied that I no longer looked like I had witnessed the end of the world, I walked over to Solly's tent. She had the flap to her "office" open, which was little more than mounds of blankets held up by wooden beams, pulled taunt by what appeared to be ski sticks and one golf club at the corners.

Solly was tapping a pedal rhythmically on the ground, while leaning over Linor's exposed back, pulling down her shoulder blade with one hand.

The other was using the tattoo gun as she periodically looked up at one of Linor's clouds. The cloud was a reverse pinup, a picture of a burly chested man and a bodacious woman sitting on a huge bomb, with the phrase, "Blow things up; plant some flowers" scribbled on the bomb. Solly had done several tattoos for nearly the whole community, although some refused, on account of a tattoo being forced on them being enough for a lifetime. In that moment, I remembered my own arm, how it was so pale and clear of numbers. The one thing that set me apart from all of us survivors. Which left me as the only Jew in camp without a marker. I wasn't part of the Roma people either. They had their own traditions and despite us all having come to America, so very far away from our homes, I was still an outsider. The rest of the camp were other outsiders, from Willy the navy veteran who spent most of his nights sleeping under the oak tree at the entrance to the camp, or Elder Ad and his wolf children. All of us were freaks and outcasts, yet I felt out of place amongst them all, always under the eye of Elder Ad or being put down by Linor's grandmother.

In general, I think the rumors of what happened in the camps just made people uncomfortable—hard to believe in a place with kids turning into giant wolves and a man that could talk to plants—what do I know? I sighed and approached the two. Solly looked up and her face had heavy lines of burden as she examined me. She stopped the pedal. "Avi, you look like you seen a ghost."

"Who me? No—I mean I haven't seen anything. How do I look to you, Linor?" I asked her, and she turned her face to me. Both her and Solly spoke at the same time again: "You look like you've seen a ghost."

"I'm fine, just ate something bad," I gestured toward my stomach.

"Say no more, love. I told everyone to watch out for the damn chili. There's only so many trees in this camp—can't have everyone stinking up the place," Solly commented and I was spared the embarrassment of having to flounder around for an answer.

"That's gross, Solly, besides I helped make that chili," Linor retorted.

"And it's gross. Doesn't change the fact, love, that I love you, but it is shit... which is probably what everyone is doing right now," she confessed as she started the tattoo gun again and slowly pushed Linor's head forward. "Be still. I am almost finished with the outline. We don't have time to do shading tonight and I need some smokes before I lose my gourd," Solly mumbled.

I snorted and sat down, watching Solly work on Linor, amazed at how much Linor had grown with her own powers. When we were kids, it seemed a minute or two was her limit. Now she could make a fully integrated design and hold it for what seemed like forever. I would never have that kind of control with the beast—I didn't want to control such a thing anyways. It was a wild animal and nothing more. Only wanted to kill, and I was cursed with it, so the best I could hope for was that it would die of old age. I mean, how long do wolves live for anyways?

The rhythmic thump of the needles tiny engine was soothing. I became entranced by it, the slow tap of it hitting Linor's flesh. It allowed what had transpired between Zevi and me to come back to the forefront. How did he and I get so far off the rails? We were brothers. That's what we were supposed to be, for all our lives. Now I wondered if at any moment he was going to somehow harm me—maybe worse. In my time in the camps, I had learned what a killer was. A killer wears many faces, comes in every race, gender, and size. But most of all, a killer can be someone you would never suspect, someone close, even. It all puzzled me endlessly—why did life have to make me feel such a long way gone from everything that I knew?

30

Chapter 30

I had been allowed to stay with the others finally. Even in such a dreadful place, the prospect of human contact—of anyone besides Albert, and Joseph's creepy eyes—was a blessing. Often times, during the long nights, I would sing some old Torah songs, in Yiddish or Hebrew. Some nights, the longer nights when time dripped like the waterdrops on top of my cage, drawn-out hours waiting to bomb my face, stories would play in my mind. I recounted the times my *muter* had baked us such delicious treats, reminding myself of how she would make our cakes. Rolling the dough, spreading it thin, using loads of flour. Endless amount of skill harnessed through repetition.

In a way, that was what kept me from becoming the feral monster. The beast was real—there was never anytime I felt he was gone, this hideous thing that only wanted to destroy would always be ready resurface, fierce snarling anger yielding nothing to my heart.

The beast kept me sane. I wasn't going to lose to a devil; my *eltern* had both taught me better than that. I would squeeze my knuckles when there were no more tears to come; I realized that all the water was nourished by those who had cried, or shown strength under the bludgeoning weight of our own thoughts. I cried for many nights, many days, when I had time to be alone. I wiped my cheeks unafraid, unbowed, and unloved. That didn't seem right. *How could I be unafraid and unloved?* I whispered one night.

Nothing ever responded, so I chose my own response, my own mantra. If no one else would love me, if looking inside led to a monster, then I would love myself. If all the world, so vast and far, all the universe so high above, persisted outside my reach, then I would create my own pocket, my own world. Fill it with the love that already existed. It had to exist—what were oceans if not love, what were homes, green mountains, and kisses from your parents, if not love?

Love didn't disappear in the darkness; that's when love was the most abundant, a sea of stars, an endless library whose pages only held letters of the heart. It wasn't much, it barely helped, and just one night afterwards, I had the thought that I was going to say "I love you" to myself every night, in order to sleep. The tortures still hurt, evolved and became more elaborate, and the beast still roared. All those things had not changed, and just like the love I gave myself every night, I saw the light.

When I woke up in the wooden bunk, I shivered. My dreams were of the cages. I whispered, "I love you, Avraham." A small futile gesture, it seemed, like a candle dropped into an ocean.

"Why are you talking to yourself, Avraham?" Bug queried, inches from my bunk. His whole body was wrapped in bandages, obscuring his face as he spoke, his voice rang so loudly that everyone in the room shot out of their bunks. Sleep time was over; a heavy cloud of gray that coughed and sputtered, only to move on to the cold that folded its way into the sleeping area. We were lucky. We had more room to sleep, even if it was still on light pieces of wood that shifted and left splinters in us most nights. I groaned, looking out the window. The night was still in, silent and heavy.

People coughed, spitting and groaning, going back to sleep all around us. I looked at Bug and motioned for him to write. He couldn't control his voice—it would either be so silent you would swear only dogs could hear it, or sound louder than any tractor going off right next to your head. Bug nodded, pulling out a crinkled piece of paper and a stolen brio pen. Its felt tip zoomed over the paper, despite Bug's bandaged hands. I watched him through the scant light from the moonlight, as he slid the paper to me.

Holding it up to my face the note said, "Who do you love, Avi?"

I sighed. Bug was always too close to me here. Having more room to stretch on the tiny bunk compared to the cage, I thought there would be more sleep. It turned out having everyone around me frightened me now. I shouldn't have been afraid of them, but I was. It was funny how I fell in love with a cage—a cage where I died behind metal bars. Now that I was out of it, every wall became another cage.

Every day, if we got yard time or the rare bit of food, they would eye me. I was dirty, sure, by my *muter's* standards. Compared to everyone else, I looked to be some kind of angel that had never heard of the word called dirty. It was because I had fresher clothes than them, and I had at least eaten something other than bread. It didn't help that I was the only one without bandages. I had begun to hear murmurs of curiosity at first and from some, hostility. Someone had tripped me yesterday as we were leaving the building. I fell, landing hard on my face. Linor helped me up. I told her I was fine. I had no idea who had done it.

I snatched the pencil out of Bug's hands and scribbled back, "Go to bed, Bug." I rolled over, hoping that was the end of the conversation, but I felt a tap on my shoulder. I pulled my coat tighter, wishing for what seemed like the millionth time that I had a blanket. At least then, in situations like this, I could ignore people better. The cold was creeping in, cold enough to freeze my bones. Sleep was hard enough, now I had a boy called Bug tapping me during the middle of the night.

I felt a tap again and I shot up, looking at Bug, "What do you want?" I exclaimed, trying to ask my question as quietly as possible. What time was it anyways? It was tough to tell anymore—even how many days I had been with the people here.

Bug furiously wrote something on his small scrap of paper, and he passed it over when he was finished, his red eyes glistening through his eye slits that made the skin on the back of my neck crawl. Luckily for me, Bug was about as imposing as the rest of us, malnourished to the point of looking like a stiff breeze would blow him over. I read the paper: "Why do you not love us?" I clenched tight, abashed by what was written on the crumpled paper.

"What do you mean?" I whispered back, passing Bug the paper for him to write on.

Bug scribbled something again, handing me the note back. I looked at his face, trying to discern his thoughts. It was useless. I read his writing, and this time it was in block capitals: "ZEVI SAYS YOU COULD SAVE US."

A cold chill went up my spine. I crumpled the paper and leered at Bug through the darkness. He stood by my bunk, staring at me for a few minutes, returning my gaze with his all-too-bright eyes.

A moment longer and he made a clicking sound leaving my side and climbing onto one of the other bunks, leaving me alone on the barren world of mine. I swore under my breath, rolling back over. Ignoring his words, ignoring what my *bruder* had said. *None of this is my fault, I couldn't save them anyway—I couldn't.* I shivered not from the cold; from the realization that I had overlooked so many things. All I wanted was to be a kid again, back home playing baseball with my *mishpokhe*. I had hoped things would return to normal. But so much of life was beyond my control, so many things that seemed reasonable never stood a chance of happening. The signs were all there and I had ignored them all.

It's a cruel thing, the misplaced feeling we place in agency—freedom is real, only to an extent, and no matter what we do, we can never be free of all the shackles. What made me hurt the most wasn't the shackles that I could see, but the ones that I was placing on myself now: this was all my fault. Everyone suffering at the camps was my fault. Zevi was right, he was right. I wasn't strong enough. I started to cry, my mental barriers finally breaking. This place was wretched beyond any darkness that could be described. Every morning, the doctors ran tests on the others. Dragging us into a lab, filled with tubs, machines beeping and glowing, fixtures of coils wrapped to massive plugs from above.

They would prod, cut, and sometimes mutilate the others. All the while, I would be left alone in the next room, forced to listen to whatever was happening back there. In the short time I had been there, Zevi was growing in anger. His rage was coming off of his body at every turn and I knew it was only a matter of time until he snapped. What worried me the most was the prospect of him running into the fence, taking the dark way out—a "*fintster veg aoys*." A phrase that the older people in the camps used. I heard my *bubbe* use it once after my *zayde* had told a story of three *bruders* being lost in the woods. The end of the story was the *bruders* choosing to wait instead of taking the dark way out. It scared me. I prayed that Zevi wouldn't do that.

We weren't allowed to interact with the other prisoners. I could see them, though, off in the distance, their faces drawn back in grimaces as they faded like leaves in the winter. That terrified me to no end, the prospect of what was happening to Zevi. He didn't seem gloomy, no more than the rest of us, but his anger was inescapable. It danced off of him like a living thing that was ready to devour the world. I was scared of Zevi, scared for him, and most of all, I was more afraid of letting our *elterns* down than I was anything else. The daily beatings were gone, the weird tests were over, and they couldn't take my blood. They had tried it once and witnessed what had happened.

So one day, when sleep came again and the usual dawn wake-up trumpets on our part of the camp went off, I assumed we were in for another day, another endless day of tests. I was wrong on too many levels. More than I could ever fathom.

A squad of soldiers lined up at our door, along with several of the doctors I had seen over the past two years. Their faces impassive temples of emotion that was impossible to discern anything from. Dread filled my stomach as I climbed down from the bunk. I looked around the room, suddenly aware that last night, I hadn't spoken to anyone before bed. Conversation with most of us wasn't a thing from day to day, when survival was all you could look forward to. I spotted Linor and Zevi toward the end of the row of bunks and I let out a breath of relief. They were okay. This was probably just another test.

Hans came in with the doctors. That was unusual, I hadn't seen him since the day I was brought to this part of the camp. What was even more bizarre was the shape of his uniform. Gone were the crisp lines of a man who spent a great deal of time on his personal appearance. Instead, now he was dissolved, stains of red mixed with his black coat, forming odd shapes of brown across his lapel. He was missing ribbons on his chest, one medal only hanging by a thread. Most importantly, his black boots that normally shone bright enough to see his reflection held thick mounds of dirt. What was going on? A guy like Hans cared way too much about his dress and appearance to ever let something like that show. Once more, most of the doctors were out of their normal uniforms, some not even in lab coats, one wearing just a pair of long brown pants with suspenders pulled over an undershirt.

Compounded with the fact that Albert and Joseph were not amongst those here, I began to worry. Even in hell, nothing spelled out danger more than when the guards looked like they were under stress. I looked around at the eleven others of us in the room, most still groggy from lack of sleep, and the never-ending fatigue that seemed to infect this place; yet no one seemed alarmed, except for me. I looked at Zevi. He was looking toward the ground, his shaved red hair starting to grow over the large scar on his head. I gulped in fear in that moment—knowing something bad was about to happen. It was a sense I had developed since coming to this place. I think it's what all animals most have, a sense that something unnatural was coming their way. That unnatural thing was most likely going to eat them—in this place, that could have been a possibility.

I looked for ways out of the room. The windows were covered in rows of bars—that left just the only entrance of the access door, which was guarded by Hans, who carried a very large gun at his side. Maybe he had enough to put down a few of us, assuming he hit. The way Hans held himself told me he didn't miss even on his off days. My father always told me to respect someone that kept quiet—they could be hiding a monster in plain sight. I had no doubt with a man like him. That was the only way, if I could get Linor and Zevi, the three of us were small, tiny enough to possibly squeeze through the hordes of doctors and escape the building. Only, what then? We would still be trapped in this camp, behind rows and rows of endless fences and guns. My heart dropped at that thought. There was no getting out of this place.

Yes—there is, whispered the voice from within. His voice was groggy and cracked a little, and almost came out as a yelp similar to a young puppy. Only he was no puppy. He was a genuine devil.

Dr. Joachim strolled through the door in that moment. The doctor had never held the same level of rigid uniform standards as Hans, but compared to everyone else, he looked to be in his pajamas still. His thinning hair was blown back at many angles, his glasses hung around his neck, and his shirt held deep sweat stains with no dry areas.

I gulped again, the hole inside my heart widening at what was about to come. I didn't want to die; I didn't want Zevi or Linor to die. I closed my eyes for a quick prayer. One of the kids in our group, Elete, who was a sickly looking boy with hunched shoulders and raccoon eyes, coughed and spat into his hands. Dr. Joachim eyed him with a glare that belonged on a statue, not on a man. Dr. Joachim motioned to Hans. "Fetch me a chair, Hans."

Hans grunted at the doctor. I had never seen him give an order to Hans—the fetch boys were Albert and Joseph, not Hans. Hans disappeared, most likely to another part of the building that we were locked from, and came back quickly with a brown metal chair.

The doctor pointed at Elete, who was coughing again into his hand. He wasn't well at all. I could smell the blood on his hands before I saw it. Elete's eyes went wide at the sight.

"You, sit now," ordered Joachim.

Elete hesitated for a moment before Dr. Joachim growled, pointing again. "Sit, now!" he yelled, and Elete stood tall and quickly rushed to the chair. He sat upright, beads of sweat rolling down his head. Dr. Joachim pointed again to Hans. Hans nodded back, pulling a long knife from his belt, the cold steel glowing red from the dim lighting. My heart cartwheeled and again, I thought about making a dash for the door. Maybe it wouldn't be such a bad thing to just run into the fences and be spared the pain of whatever was about to come.

Time seemed to slow down. The air became thick with a red haze that blinded the already blind, even in the light. The doctor walked next to the man, and Hans walked behind Elete, brandishing the knife in his hands.

"You have one moment, young wolf, to show us the wolf now. Tell us how you came to be, or this man will be the first to die. Then the rest of your friends and *mishpokhe* will be next!" Dr. Joachim yelled.

One of the doctors nearest Dr. Joachim stepped toward him. "Sir, with all due respect—the Yankees getting close or not, we cannot throw away two years of research like this!" he pleaded with the doctor.

Without even turning to the other doctor, Joachim ordered Hans: "Shoot that man, now."

Hans pulled his large pistol from his leather holster and calmly pointed at the doctor who had spoken out. "Wait—please, I was only trying— " he pleaded, before Hans took aim and fired three shots into his chest. He dropped to the ground, his body limp and lifeless. The room's oxygen seemed to be stolen away in that moment, while everyone held their breath, awaiting what would happen next.

Calmly and deliberately, Dr. Joachim stepped around the man and moved toward me, bending at his waist until we were making eye contact. "This will be your only warning. I will not hesitate to shoot all the test subjects. I will not shy from making your life a living hell every waking moment you have on this Earth. You will tell me, you will tell me now!" he snarled, spit dropping out of the corners of his mouth.

He was inches away from my face. The blood seemed to drain away from my body and I wanted to faint. There was no getting out of this, and what was worse of all, I had no idea how to even answer him. I couldn't answer his questions. I wanted to answer them so he would finally leave us alone.

"I don't know what it is— " I stuttered, looking toward the ground.

"Do not say to me again that you don't know," snapped Dr. Joachim. He pointed at Hans, who had secured his gun and now had out his knife. Any remorse for his actions was already gone. He was a killer, and to him it was easier to kill a man than it would be to drink a glass of water.

Elete remained motionless in his seat, his head lowered now, just as everyone else's head was as well. The boy was crying, his tiny chest heaving as if it was a motor that had been pushed to its breaking point.

"Wait, please, I don't know!" I pleaded once again, meeting the cold eyes of Dr. Joachim.

He looked into mine, his dark brown eyes seeming to glow like charcoal in a furnace. With a quiver of his lips, he directed Hans: "Do it."

Hans thrust down his knife into the neck of Elete. I closed my eyes, unable to view what was happening. I started to cover my ears when the doctor took both my hands into his own. "There is no escaping this. You will tell me," he whispered, inches from my face, as I heard the saw of Hans blade against Elete's neck. Elete had been the son of our schoolteacher back in our city, a quiet *mishpokhe* made up of Elete, our teacher, and Elete's two other siblings. I couldn't remember what his *foter* had looked like—I hoped that Elete had, before the end. I couldn't remember their names, but I was sure that he would never forget them. Within moments, the sound of metal being grated through flesh and bone was over. A thick series of was were all I could hear.

Somehow, Elete never made a sound, and that was the hardest thing to ignore. My mouth was closed. Screaming seemed too weak to even try. A little boy had just been killed, no older than Zevi.

I felt a hot slap across my face and the force was enough to make my head turn. "This time, he won't be able to turn his head." Joachim stood up, motioning to two of the doctors. They stuttered and stepped toward me, almost hesitating. The lust in Joachim's face told them to not even dare to question it.

They each took one of my arms, pulling it deep behind my back. I struggled against their strength, but it was pointless. When all I'd had to eat in the last few weeks was bread and snow—since it had been falling every day—I could fight back about as much as a newborn kitten. I struggled more, but they pulled their weight forward and I was hunched over as Dr. Joachim walked toward me.

He stood tall for a moment and looked around the room until he spotted Zevi and Linor in the corner. "Perhaps we can go with one of those two, or even both. You seemed pretty smitten with the girl last time, and the boy—well, we know who he is to you," Joachim pondered.

"No! Leave them alone," I growled, howling until my voice cracked.

"No is not an answer," Dr. Joachim shot back. "Bring the boy. These two are a prisoner riot waiting to happen anyways."

Hans dropped the head of Elete onto to the ground, the blood causing his head to roll in the direction of a few of the kids. They threw up and Dr. Joachim sighed in response. "If you're not currently holding one of the test subjects, now is the time to do so." Most of the doctors were young—about the same age as my *elterns* had been. They went forward and the staff restrained everyone in the room on their knees, except for Zevi and I.

Hans went to grab Zevi, and my *bruder* kicked at his legs. Hans caught one of his feet in his free hands and pulled my *bruder* to the wet chair like he was a lamp. My heart started racing faster than it had the first night in the camps. I thought for a moment that my body was going to explode into thousands of pieces. I broke out into a sweat, the room felt miles longer, the bared windows too far away.

What should I do? My panicked brain swarmed with the images of Zevi's head lying on the floor. The thought was making my knees buckle. They would kill him, they had done it before, many times, inside these camps. Even us test subjects weren't treated any better. Zevi continued to struggle against Hans's arm, but he was just as weak, if not weaker than me in his frail body. At one point, I saw Zevi try and bite through the sleeve of Hans. It was useless and served to only make Hans slap Zevi until he stopped moving. Zevi's face was a bright shade of red, his nose bleeding from the force. I shook with anger and rage on a level I could never understand. I felt so powerless in a world that did not care what was happening. Children were about to die—the world kept on turning.

I can save them, Avi, let me out! The thing inside of me howled, shaking my body in its frustration. I panicked even worse—that thing wasn't natural, it was a demon that had somehow become locked within me. For all I knew, the moment I freed it, everything in this room would be devoured including Zevi.

I gritted my teeth, shaking uncontrollably. The two doctors applied more pressure behind my back while Joachim came up to me. He was standing upright, his glasses pulled down his nose, close to falling off. "Yes, young man—are you going to tell us now?" he asked, patronizingly.

I wanted to growl in frustration, gnaw on his bones, grind my teeth into his flesh. I stopped, suddenly realizing it was the monster making me think those things—or was it? I thought for a moment about once, how a rabbit that was caught in a trap while Zevi and I were helping our *zayde* hunt had turned into a savage creature when we had found it pinned. It was no longer the fluffy big-eared creature dancing across our yards. It was snarling, snapping, kicking, doing everything to live. Our *zayde* told us then that every creature has a fight or flight instinct. Some of us don't know because we've never been in that situation, but when the time comes, when we have to flee or to fight, something has to be done.

I ground my teeth together, ignoring the "no" that was wanting to come out. I wasn't a fighter; I knew that in the back of my mind. I was just wanting to go home. Something—was pushing its way into my thoughts, turning me against my instinct; that I knew I couldn't run from.

"What will it be, son?" Joachim whispered above me.

His comment is what caused the stir inside me to happen. He was not my *foter*, I was not his son. I planted my feet, kicking back, and shoved up until I felt my head hit something soft and square. I heard the groan of one of the doctors behind me. It was enough for them to release their hold on me.

I jumped forward, not thinking, just unsealing all the rage I felt building, hoping to silence the beast, silence Joachim, mostly to silence the fear that I had building. I lunged into the doctor's legs, closing my eyes and tasting his pants before I bit down with all my strength. He screamed first, a howl of terror that was closer to an animal than a man. Then I tasted metal in my mouth. I held on and shook my head, like a dog would savage a rat. Shouts went up all around me, and I felt hands take hold of my shoulders. I held on though, biting again as I was lifted, clawing with my hands in an attempt to chew through this man.

The last thing I heard was heavy footsteps behind me, then a ringing in my ears as I fell over, hitting the ground. Before my eyes closed, I saw the fire in Zevi's eyes from his chair. He looked almost happy—that wasn't right. I glanced at Dr. Joachim. He was clutching his middle section, blood spraying out of him. Finally, my eyes closed. Something else inside me closed its eyes as well.

31

Chapter 31

I awoke back in my metal cage, its stench the same as it had been when I had left, however many weeks ago that was. They hadn't bothered to clean it. I rolled around—hay had been placed on the bottom. I grunted, thinking how nice that felt compared to the wooden bunk. The overhanging light was turned off. That was a new thing.

I looked around the room, seeing that I was in the medical area this time. Trays of metal tools looking like the musical instruments that a devil would use were tossed haphazardly across the room. A long trail of blood led to the doorway. Whoever had brought me here had been in a rush. My eyes found the bare table I had been on, when I first woke up after the beast had come out. I was back in the observation room. My eyes found a long stretch of glass that took up most of the room at the opposite side. I could see figures on the other side of the glass, their arms frantically waving, pointing at something, then back to me.

Where were the others? I pushed my tongue through my teeth and let out a breath. I tasted blood—it was just blood, though. Not the fatty taste of bone I had tasted last time I became the creature. I tried to roll my hands up to look at my fingernails for more signs. I found them restrained. I felt with my fingers until I could feel huge loops of metal tied around both my wrists. I was chained up. In the darkness, I could see that I was still wearing the oversized clothes that I'd had on for weeks now. That meant I had not become the creature. Everyone was safe from me, from my demon. Maybe I had been wrong about how I became that thing. My head ached, feeling like someone was pressing down on my skull with a hammer. I could smell my blood as well. So it wasn't blood that let the demon loose. Or maybe it was? My head was spinning as I thought about how I had not turned into the monster.

I let my tears roll in the cage, just thankful that I hadn't hurt anyone. I could hear muttering coming from behind the glass. I strained my ears to listen. It took me a moment, but I could hear the heavy German of Hans. It wasn't polished like Dr. Joachim, it was crude, slow, and he had a long drawl at the end of his words. I wondered where a monster like him could be from. I shuddered at the ease in which he had killed Elete, the ease at which he might have been able to kill Zevi. What kind of person could kill a child? What kind of person could kill without any more remorse than the time Zevi and I had found a slug, pouring salt over its long slimy body? We had both thought it would be funny at first, until we heard the micro screams coming from the creature, which shrieked louder as its body grew smaller. That day, we both had learned that even something as small as a bug was alive—us boys, such great killers with our salt pinched from our *muter's* baking table. I'd felt so bad that night that I couldn't sleep. I kept seeing the eyes of the slug pop off. I wondered, pondered, and lamented about whether I had killed a slug *foter*. Or if I had killed a slug *muter*, if I had robbed a whole *mishpokhe* of one of its parents. I was thankful in that moment that my *muter* wasn't going to shrivel up from salt. Thinking back to that slug now—it seemed a lifetime ago. It seemed so dumb to think that I would ever get so upset from just killing a slug. Especially when I compared it to the slow death I witnessed every day here.

Hans would pour salt on the whole world, I realized. He was the kind of person that would shrivel us all and show no remorse. I shuddered at his voice, listening closer to the frantic talk between him and a voice I did not recognize.

"That is unacceptable! You know it, Dr. Joachim would never allow us to scrap this project—even if the damned Russian dogs are close! We can't stop the project now!" The unknown voice boomed out from behind the glass, loud enough that even without my hearing, I might have been able to hear it.

Hans cleared a growl from his mouth before speaking, his normal control lost. "It doesn't matter what Dr. Joachim wants. He is in a hospital bed, praying that they will be able to stitch his nutsack back on after what that thing in there did to him!"

"It's not just Joachim's decision. The Führer—" the other man started before I heard a loud pop and a whimper from the unknown voice.

"How much of this do you think was told to that bumbling fool? How much do you think was kept on the books? How else do you feel that all of you white-coat-wearing pansies were paid was allowed? You were picked for this unit as much for your skills as for your hold on reality. None of this research was going to change the tide of war—Joachim knows that. This was all done to help us afterward, to secure a place for the inevitable defeat coming."

"That is treason," muttered the unknown voice before I heard a louder pop this time, followed quickly by a thump against the glass. "Who do you think will kill you first? The Führer who is losing this war, those red bears coming over the hills in a few days, or me?" Hans screamed, followed by the cocking of his pistol. "Here is what you're going to do. Gather all the files, every bit of evidence you have, run it to the tank factory in Kaiserslautern, and await further orders. Before you do that, you will dispose of all the test subjects. Including that damn wolf in there. Throw him in the gas chambers. Sooner or later he will die. Now," Hans directed.

The unknown voice squeaked as his shoes dragged across the hardwood floors of the building. My heart stopped in my chest. All I had done was make things worse. Now they were going to kill us all. Maybe I could lie to Hans, plead to give us more time in exchange for telling him how I became the creature. It would be of no use, though. He was a long way gone as well, and their backs were against the wall.

My eyes flooded with tears, knowing even if I could somehow bluff my way to keeping Zevi and Linor alive until the Red Army was here, I had heard stories in the bunks that red or gray, that army might hurt some of us. Now, after whatever had been done to us, we would end up back in a lab, and this cycle would never end. I swore, thrashing my chained arms against the metal bars, kicking with all my might against the padlocked door. I was a cornered rat with no way out. My hands rolled deeper up my back until I felt a hard lump at the edges of my cage. With my bruised fingers, I dug through my own droppings until I felt the smooth metal blade. My fingers brushed over its metallic point. It was a dull knife; it didn't need to be sharp.

I paused, sitting up. What was I about to do? I swore, knowing that once I started, there was no going back. I was wrong earlier, when I thought I was trapped like a rat. Now I was truly trapped like a rat: if I stayed and failed to act again, everyone would die. If I acted, then who knows who would die?

I looked up at the light fixture above, imagining beyond the darkness that I was back staring at the sun on the cold beaches of Sopot, swimming in the Baltic Sea. The cold black waves hitting the golden sand, a perfect juxtaposition of the dark and the light in this world meeting in a place of peace, if only for a moment. A place where the world wasn't so cruel, the afternoons were long, the birds chirped, and there was plenty of food to go around. It was home, a place I knew I would never have again. I was so far gone, there was no home for me to go back to.

I pleaded, stilling my hand that now had the blade pressed against the back of my leg. I knew it would take a great deal of effort for the blade to go through my thin coveralls, to go through my thinner skin. It would hurt; it would start the fire inside me again. I was already breaking out in a sweat and I paused when I heard the jingle of keys to the doorway at the far side of the room.

There were plenty of people standing outside the door. I could smell them, smell the gunpowder in their guns. The frantic way they were sweating as well. I closed my eyes one last time praying this time to my *mishpokhe*. "I'm sorry, I'm a long way gone," I whimpered as I drove the blade into my leg with what little force I could still muster.

32

Chapter 32

"Does it hurt?" Huey asked, as I placed the cold steak against my head. It was midday and we had built a grill out of a cleaned-up metal trashcan and a pile of wood.

"The steak helps," I muttered.

"Don't change the subject, and tell me you washed your fucking hands before placing that against your damn face."

I took the steak off my face in my hands, shrugging. "Probably did."

"That one is yours, man." Huey turned back to our makeshift grill, placing the battered lid back over a pile of peppers and meat.

"You can't eat pork, right?" he asked, turning back to me with a handful of pig feet.

I looked at the feet, dubious. "I stopped caring about my faith on that last day in the camps. Seemed kind of like a waste of time, when I have a demon inside me," I responded.

Huey grunted and lifted the lid, throwing the feet on the grill. He turned back, handing me a beer. I took it, popping the lid off on the end of my worn boots as he sat down on a pile of wood that the two us had collected this morning. Huey insisted that if we weren't going to work today, we could at least stay busy. That annoyed me for more reasons than just having a hangover. What was the point to all of this?

"Why are you sticking around, Huey? Surely you have your own issues to deal with. Or is this because of some stoic warrior tradition that you feel compelled to do?"

Huey grunted before speaking. "Less to do with having been a solider. Just because you wear a uniform doesn't make you a good person. Just ask all the milk babies being born to lonely subordinate housewives these days. I'm sticking around partly because we are both still wanted more than a picture of Marilyn Monroe's backside, and because I get it, man. I've been where you are, unable to move on. Waking up in the middle of the night pissing yourself because you've heard a loud noise," he stated.

"I've never pissed myself," I leered at him.

He rolled his eyes. "Regardless, I know if someone hadn't taken the time to sit my ass down, I would still be in the fucking joint, dodging gang rapes."

I snorted. "What was it that you needed to hear so bad that you couldn't come up with yourself, huh? Since you're reformed and such now," I stated.

"Nah, I'm not reformed, man. You can't really ever go back to what you used to be, even if you had a magic wish. Everything that has happened to us has happened and is done. The only thing that helped changed my life was realizing that it could not be changed, that was the first step," he responded, pulling pieces of grass out of the ground and let them float off.

By most people's standards, Huey was somewhere between the oddest person I'd ever seen and some milk lady's wet dream. His hands were large enough to crack my skull, but his nose stuck out longer than anyone I had ever known. What stood out the most to me about Huey was how his voice never seemed to be directed at anything or anyone with anger. He was calm, like a man strolling through the grounds of a baseball diamond after dark.

"That worked for you, realizing that nothing could be changed?" I asked.

"What is done, is done, Avi. We go forward, and that is all we can do, brother," he replied.

"I would hold that statement of yours. When I woke up the next day, following my last time in that cage. Most the camp was on fire, and an endless sea of red lay around me. A lot of people died, Huey. Maybe it was all because of my actions. Or maybe it was the soldiers defending themselves from me. Regardless, a lot of people died that day. There was so much ash, blanketing the ground—you would have sworn it had snowed." I started to shiver before speaking again. "You can't just move forward from something like that, not when you were at the center of so much death..." my voice flattened to a whisper, before I trailed off, looking at the field leading away from the trailer. Its silver paneling was falling off in some sections, making it look more like a crumpled can we would kick around as children rather than a place that people were living in.

I paused, letting my words hang between us. To me, there was nothing more to be said. I knew I wasn't largely the cause of much that had transpired. However, I did know that what I did cause, I caused.

"That's good. At least you aren't passing the blame," Huey stated.

I stared at him, perplexed. "What do you mean?"

"This would be an entirely different conversation if you couldn't admit to your wrongs, Avi," he responded.

"Yeah, I may be a terrible person, but I won't lie—often," I grumbled.

Huey snorted. "So, you decimated the camps. What happened after that?"

"Long and short of it, well, thankfully for me, the SS had begun evacuating Auschwitz and the surrounding camps as the Russians got closer. The SS were too busy focusing on the death march to care about the more—sensitive side of camp. That left only the sick and dying, and us special interest people, before the Russians came. Turned out, the day I showed up, the Russians came. When I woke up, I was on railroad tracks. Butt naked and covered in blood, a few miles outside of the camp. It was easy to find again, even through the snow and ash. I just followed the smell. When I got there, I think the Russian soldiers nearly shot me on sight. I kept asking for the others. It took three days before I was finally allowed to see Linor and Zevi.

I found out later from Linor they had all decided to remain silent about what was being done to them. Liberating army or not, our trust of anyone with a firearm was gone now. I also found out from Linor later what had happened. That will live with me forever, Huey," I gulped.

"What is done, is done," he repeated.

"Yeah, right, what is done is done. Either way, a lot of people died when the camp fell. A lot of people died while I tried to help. I should have just let them take me out. Maybe I could have survived whatever it was they were going to do to me, and those people would still—" I started to cry and I put my head in my hands. I rubbed my face, groaning loudly. "See what I mean, Huey? There is no going back after something like that."

"I'm not talking about going back, I'm not even talking about absolving you of what happened yet. I'm just trying to get it through that thick skull of yours that it happened. Two pieces of advice before you finish the rest of your story, Avi. One, accept that you had to transform into that beast—to save you and your friends. Two, and this is the hardest part, forgive yourself. You have to do it. If you don't, you will just continue to hurt yourself and many others. Trust me," Huey told me.

I growled. "Trust you? Trust you to know what? Why should I put any more trust in anyone? I killed people, Huey. How the fuck would you even know what to do?"

"Don't forget that I fought in a war, Avi. Don't forget that we are all fighting in a war, just some of us longer than others," he responded.

I shut my mouth and looked down at the red clay beneath our feet. The grass was always brown here, not the green of Poland. The dirt was always red, the mountains big, but clear and blazing gold in the sun. My home had green: an endless stream of moss-colored hills, leading to many caves that looked like gaping mouths in the ground.

I sighed. "Is there an easier way to do this?" I asked.

"Probably not. You can't just ignore the past by fucking everything that walks or drinking yourself to death. Finish your damn story so I can get on with my day already," Huey stated.

"Alright, man. Don't tell me later that I didn't warn you about all of this," I trailed off.

"I asked for it, don't you worry, man. I already have a good idea of what we should do from here on out."

"Can't wait to hear it," I muttered.

33

Chapter 33

"How do you still not know how to pick a lock yet?" Linor asked, peering over my shoulders as I worked with two paperclips inside the hole of a small lock.

I rolled my eyes. "Look, you could do this, your highness, if it's not going quick enough for you," I retorted.

"I mean, I'm about to step in. It's cold out and I just got a tattoo. But, I do enjoy watching you suffer," Linor giggled.

We were on the outskirts of camp, picking the lock of an old Junker bike that was against a yellow Beetle car. The car belonged to Long Jimmy, a tall hillbilly from somewhere in the southern United States. His donkey, Brianne, snorted as if to add further to the mockery. "Both of you, for the love of God, shut up!" I shouted.

"Keep your voice down, you nit!" Solly whispered behind us. "You know that is Jimmy's house." She gestured to the Beetle that was covered in tree limbs, and what appeared to be wooden sides, but for some reason were carpeted. Jimmy was an odd fellow, and there were a few rules, even in a Gypsy camp: only steal from people outside of camp; though that only applied if you didn't really need it. And it seemed every day we had to get a new bike. I looked down at the rusted red bike with the lock. I think it was one I had stolen two or three months ago.

I shrugged, remembering another rule of living in a Roma people's camp.

If someone lives on the outskirts of camp, they're most likely not to be trifled with. I thought of the last time I had seen Long Jimmy, in one hand a bottle, the other a baby doll. I shuddered, thinking about the memory.

I redoubled my efforts with picking the lock, my fingers twitching too much, though, causing one of the clips to break. "Shit."

"Oh for fuck's sake, give it to her!" Solly swore, smacking my back.

I grumbled, passing the clips to Linor. "Be my guest, Houdini, show me your lock picking skills," I moved out of the way while Linor giggled.

"Here's your first problem, Avi. You're trying way too hard. You need to caress the lock, feel its holes, get to know her," Linor slurred in a sensual voice, turning me cherry red beside her. I was glad that it was nighttime, or I would never hear the end of it from the two of them.

"Yeah okay, I will give that a shot sometime," I responded, flustered and embarrassed, looking away from what she was doing when I heard the click.

"That's why your bird is the best pick in the business!" Solly clapped Linor's shoulders, "Alright, you two love birds hurry up. We are meeting at the grocery store on the east edge of town," Solly stated, taking off before Linor and I had even stood up. She ran into the woods, a neon light flashed, and I knew that Solly was still running. She would be at the gas station long before Linor and I had even left the camp.

"What does she mean, love birds?" I floundered, picking up the bike.

"She means that you should start tying a knife in your hair as well, so we can match. Oh wait, even better, you carry matches in your hair. I will keep the knife. That way, we both have to be together in order to start a fire. Isn't it romantic?" Linor danced toward me, sitting on the handlebars.

"Do you think it's a good idea to sit on the front of the bike at night?" I asked.

"Do you think it's a good idea to shut up?" she suggested.

There just was no winning tonight, I thought, before an idea shot into my head as I started us down the road. The was path rocky, treacherous, and smelled as if Long Jimmy was spraying down the grass with a flamethrower. "You do realize you can't make a fire out of matches and a knife, right? You need flint as well, or I guess you could use the knife to spark the matches," I pondered.

"You do realize that as soon as it rains, the matches would probably get wet. Take a chance, strike a soggy match, and live a little," she responded.

I was completely dumbfounded on how to respond. Instead, I just smiled and pedaled our way forward.

"Did I ever tell you that I want to kiss you?" I asked her as we turned onto the main road. My legs were thankful and my heart more so. I needed to stop smoking and drinking, maybe cut it back to only six bottles on weekdays.

"Did I ever tell you, that as we sit, you're currently only able to see my tush? You're an odd one, Avraham," she stated.

"Would you have me any other way?" I asked her.

"Nope," she responded earnestly. I believed her, wishing I had feelings like this more often. They didn't seem to last forever, but maybe I could just keep having them and make a home out of those feelings, a place where both Linor and I could go. A place where we carried each other's hearts. Maybe, then, it would last. We would both finally be safe.

We turned a corner and the town came into view. The many shops of the downtown district had put up "closed" signs for the night. The Tri-City area was only five miles away. I wondered how Zevi planned to get us there, or where, for that matter, the good doctor was hiding.

I swept that thought away, trying to focus on just pedaling the bike through the dark, listening to Linor hum.

"You know, I read somewhere once about song birds—the males only sing as a territory claim," I told her, trying my best to recall the book without crashing into a ditch.

"Is that so? Afraid if I hum too loud a bird is going to steal me away, Avi?" she jabbed.

I turned red again. "I guess we will be eating some bird tonight if anyone tries that," I stated defiantly, wanting to pound my chest in a display of my strength. But I nearly caused us to crash when I took one hand off the bike. Best to keep focusing on riding the bike.

Linor snorted and continued to hum. I just listened to her, the miles between the camp fading away to the background as my happiness carried us forward. In the distance, I could see the grocery store had piles of bikes piled on the outside, and a red pickup truck. The truck was gleaming with a shine of brand new that said "stolen," even before I could see the scratch marks where the plates had been.

"That answers the transportation issue," I grumbled.

"What issue?" she asked, leaning over the bars just in time for the bike to tip. I fell hard to the side, panicking, praying that my long sleeve would protect me during the fall. My shirt was scratched—no blood, though. Anger shot through me and I watched Linor glide to the ground. I calmed down once she smiled at me. She knew what I had been thinking. I let out the anger, taking a deep breath and picking myself off the ground, when she reached for my hand. I took her hand, leaving the bike in the road. Someone would come along and get it.

We walked toward the same store from earlier. The lights were turned off, with a few more locks now added to the windows, I noticed. We came around the front of the store to find the seven others.

Zevi smiled when he saw me. "Okay, good, let's get this party started!" he shouted, as the others cheered him on. With ease, Zevi took hold of the lock, snapping the metal as if it had been made of a potato chip, the mechanisms inside the lock falling to the ground in pieces.

It's always a party when you don't know the difference between right and wrong anymore. Why did I shy away from such a thing—when someone is who he is? I stopped when I saw Zevi taking a firecracker out of his pocket, lighting it up and throwing it into the air. The others followed suit and a series of bangs propelled the air. I closed my eyes, taking away the lights. The sounds seemed pretty normal and familiar but after hearing it for a while, the sporadic bursts and crackling combustions begin to form an invisible nuisance.

Hell was those sounds. If I was to be asked to listen to this for an hour, or a day, or a week, I would go mad. Everywhere I went to and even when I had to go to sleep, and was forced to even find it in my dreams, those sounds followed. It was unbearable and exhausting. It was as if I was living in a disorienting reality, apart from everyone else. The others were celebrating; I was conflicted over killing a man who had tortured me. Always on edge... at the mercy of the next destabilizing pop... hoping for a moment of silence.

I had stopped, breathing hard, the firecrackers reminding me of the pop that charred bones made once they had become too hot. Joseph had whispered in my ears, through my metal cage once, that bones did that at 760 to roughly 982 Celsius. But even that wasn't enough to completely burn, as Joseph had told me. You needed a second oven to get the smaller bits.

My body was shaking, shook up like a salt shaker, the world tilted below. Linor pressed her hands into my shoulders. We stood there, watching my brother and his friends throw firecrackers into the night's sky. Trauma was a relentless and passive aggressor that fragmented the moments endlessly.

I looked at Linor—her face a beacon of concern. I started to open my mouth, then I quickly closed it. There was no explaining this—I wouldn't even know where to begin.

"They sure are nice, aren't they...?" I stated.

" I don't want to be here anymore, Avi," she stated.

34

Chapter 34

"Do you not like pork ears, Avi?" Schwein chomped down on a sack that was full of crispy pieces of pork. However, I was unsure if the putrid smell was from the expired chips, or from Schwein himself.

I turned toward Schwein. "Get out of here, pig!" I yelled, throwing a soda bottle at him.

He blocked it with his free arm, snorting, "What a freak."

I rolled my eyes, turning back to Linor. With Schwein gone, the two of us were alone in the back of the store. Once Zevi had broken the lock and we had entered the store, everyone had gone to town, stealing whatever they wanted off the wooden shelves. Sophia had sent a bolt of bright lights through the nearby power box—we were going to be alone in this store for as long as we needed. The cops would never get a call, and this store had been robbed so many times I had doubts that any passersby would even say anything. Poor Pete—it was a wonder if he would even stay in business after something like today and tonight.

I looked back at Linor. She was eating candy out of a bag with what appeared to be an orange popsicle. "Why orange?" I asked.

She shrugged. "I mean, he was out of red—and I am halfway sure that I am the one that took all the red flavors."

"That makes sense." I paused, looking around at the store. The others were at the front, digging through the beer and the cigarette containers.

"Can we talk about what you said, earlier?" I asked softly.

Linor shrugged again. "Does it really matter, Avi? There's nothing to really talk about. It is what it is," she responded calmly, continuing to dip her popsicle into her crushed pouch of candy.

"Don't you think you should talk about it, though? You brought it up. You can't say things like that, then not say anything at all," I proclaimed.

Linor stopped scraping for candy with the popsicle and eyed me for a long moment. Her green and brown eyes focused on me in the dark—like a curious owl spotting a rabbit in a field below her perch. "Let's talk about how, day in and day out, you just leave, Avi. I'm not talking about how you're found in a ditch covered in blood almost every other night, or those times you flake for no reason. Those I understand as, well—you. You have a hard time getting out of your own little head. No, I'm talking about those times when you freeze, go miles away. Then get angry, only to never say a word about it. Worse, those times I've seen you buying rope or belts to only lose them that very night. Do you think I haven't seen the belts looped around tree branches? Do you think I like waking up every morning, wondering if my best friend—no my *everything*—is dead? Offed himself in the middle of the night from a hanging, or trying to drink himself to death? I respect that you turn into a little boy, that you're brought back to a place every time you see something awful. How do you expect me to communicate my problems when Lord Avraham can't even be bothered to be in the middle of a conversation for a minute?" Linor said sternly, taking my hands in her face. "Avi, I want to know what's going on in that head of yours, not to be shut out. It's no fun eating all the ice-cream by myself. It's better to share. So, when you're ready to pop that lid of yours, I will tell you why I don't want to be here anymore." She finished, taking her popsicle, and licked the candy coating the side of it.

I moved out of her embrace and landed against the shelf behind me, knocking over the assorted goods to the ground below. "You knew about the belts and the ropes," I whispered.

She kept her eyes focused on the popsicle, "It wasn't that hard to figure out. You kept looking for a new one, only to wear that ragged one you have on now. Every time you did it, you would have bursts of happiness the rest of the day—that would be the only time you would show up to your promises, like you felt guilty."

She had described most of what I had been up to over the last few years. I doubt she knew how often—I never could go through with it, partly because of the beast, partly because of what I'd promised. "I think I only did it—did it to remind myself I was still alive. Things have, well, things are—I never left you, though, Linor. How am I supposed to take it when my best friend says she wants to leave?" I trailed off, standing back up again, brushing my pants off.

"Then why do you lie to me, Avi, if you know it's something that can hurt me? Do you feel it's something you can build a relationship out of?" she responded, her eyes on me now.

"Did you say a relationship?" I smiled.

"Yeah—it's just you and me, wolf boy. We don't keep shit from each other anymore. We don't do that, you hear?" she demanded.

"I promise. I just want to be a good person, Linor, that's all."

"What's a good person to you, Avi?"

I looked at the others, then back to my hands, to the ironwood shelves Linor was sitting on. "I don't know—I mean I do know, I think. I spend a lot of my time wondering what it means to be a good person," I responded.

"Being a good person is hard," she whispered, looking down.

I picked up her chin. "I think good people are those who sacrifice. They do what is right, even if it means putting themselves at a disadvantage, and they do it because it's the right thing to do. That's all I want to do with my life, now, after everything that has happened. After all the shit that has been done—I just want to be good," I whispered back.

Suddenly, we were kissing. It was a deep, sensual touch and we craved each other's breath with every moment of our mouths. I spread my fingers through her thick hair, thankful for her smell, thankful for her. I couldn't tell Linor how I felt throughout my day because truthfully, talking about me, talking about the beast, was something that I was unable to explain. A kiss was simple; it was my way of telling her that she couldn't leave, not without me.

We broke off after a few moments, our breath coming in waves, when I looked her in the eyes. "Don't go anywhere, stinky," I stated.

"I won't, dumbass," she replied.

"Good." Then I begin to kiss up her legs until I moved up her dress. "These are clean, right?" I joked.

"Shut up, dumbass," she responded.

35

Chapter 35

I had my arm over Linor, and she was smiling. I was beaming as all of us started loading into Zevi's truck.

He took a look at us and rolled his eyes. "Love birds, get in the front, everyone else get in the truck bed," he directed. There were a few complaints as the others got into the back, and Sophia regarded Zevi with a long look. "I didn't mean you; you work the pedals, and I will steer," he remarked and Sophia smiled.

"Wait, how did you guys know?" I stopped, questioning Zevi.

"You were in the back of a grocery store. Even without super powers, you guys smell like sex," he replied, calmly opening the door as the three of us slid into the truck. Sophia sat on his lap while Linor and I hunched near the window, both of us too shy to speak. "Afraid so, brother, lets get going!" he shouted, turning the engine on. The truck fired up, peeling away from the parking lot as Schwein and Bug threw empty bottles behind us.

"Do you know where you're going?" I asked Zevi after a few minutes on the road. Whatever shock Sophia had done to the power grid had knocked out nearly every light in town from what I could tell, as we drove through the backwoods.

"I've known all my life," he responded in the darkness. The girls sat between us, no one in the truck saying a thing besides Zevi and I.

"What the hell does that mean?" I asked, skepticism in my voice.

"It means shut the hell up and trust me, Avi. I know where we are going. You just get ready to see an old friend of ours," he replied. I turned my head out the window. In the woods, I could see something running on four legs, its massive form unmistakable in the darkness. It was a wolf, charging into the darkness, easily gliding over the forest floor.

Which wolf was I feeding tonight...? I scratched my pants legs. I felt Linor's hand slide into my own. Her palms were just as sweaty. In an instant, the wolf had vanished into the darkness—I wondered if it had ever really been there. If any of this was even real, half the world away and nearly ten years later, we had found the man who had killed our families.

36

Chapter 36

It looked like any other newly reinvented high-rise apartment complex to me. We stood outside the building, waiting for Tir to pick up the location of Joachim. My palms seemed to stay in a constant state of sweat, and I kept wiping them off on my pants legs while we waited. Tir had his hands planted against the ground. A slow hum was escaping his mouth as the dirt around him seemed to shiver. He was sending his "eyes," as he called them, throughout the building. Anyone or anything that was near a plant, he would know about it. Once, I had seen what actually looked like an eyelid jutting from the trunk of a maple tree near camp, its pupils impossibly huge. It made me wonder if maybe it was Tir that was watching me or if there were other people looking through holes in trees, while you walked alone at night through a deep dark forest.

After a few more moments, Tir pulled his hands from the ground, a small smile stretched across his face. "He's here alright, fast asleep on the twelve floor," Tir said gleefully.

"Fantastic. Now for the next part—cover the exits," Zevi directed. Tir nodded and stuck his fingers into the dirt. Within a moment, the ground shifted near the building. Tree roots, thick as boards, shot from the ground, a tangle of wood webs that stretched around the building, blocking the doors except for the main entrance. As the veins tightened, like leather shoestrings on new boots, Tir turned to Zevi nodding his head.

"Sophia, now it's your turn. Would you kindly, babe?" he asked her as she walked up to the building.

"I am pretty sure this old junk would knock its own power out, with or without me," she stated, moving her hands to the power line pole nearest the building.

"Yeah, but its so much sexier when you do it," Zevi whistled. Sophia's hand seemed to shimmer, distorting, then peeled away until I could see her veins—they were glowing like the neon lights of an amusement park, filled with hot pinks and cosmic blues as a ball of numerous colors sparked from her hand. Faster than I could blink, the few lights that were in the building shut off with a burst of noise, as did the subsequent buildings around us.

"That's my baby," mumbled Zevi as he kept his head pointed toward the twelfth floor. "Arnold, Bug, it's your turn, boys." They snickered as Bug walked toward the building and Arnold's shadow burst from him, its hulking form standing outside the doorway.

Zevi turned toward Linor and me. "Linor, how about you give us some coverage in the surrounding area? Don't need anyone seeing what we are up to, now, do we?" he asked almost belittlingly. I felt a growl coming to my surface—Linor was treated better than I was, but she was guilty by association in their eyes.

"Oh, Solly, love, go around the building and make sure that he doesn't get away," he directed Solly.

Solly smirked. "Too easy, like taking candy from babies," she giggled, bending her head for a moment. I could hear it before I could see it, something pushing its way through her skin. Bones, glittering like diamonds, exploded from her body, incasing her form as she became hunched over, cocooned in a sparkling stone that closely resembled a deer—if that deer had impossibly huge antlers jutting in every direction, like thorns on a bush.

Solly dipped her head and took off into a thick mist that Linor had created around us. The mist obscured even the end of my hand when I held it out toward the road. No one could escape—there was no help coming. A cold chill raced down my back and I suddenly felt very out of place. Linor's nose was bleeding, I noticed. She rarely put out that big an image, especially around a hotel building and a parking lot. I started to say something to her when Zevi sounded off. "Now, Bug!" he yelled.

Bug cupped his mouth and in a perfect imitation of a fire alarm, filled the night's air with the warning. I covered my ears from the sound as Bug called out with the alarm. "ATTENTION RESIDENTS, THIS IS NOT A DRILL. I REPEAT, THIS IS NOT A DRILL. PLEASE EVACUATE THE AREA!" his voice shook the very windows of the building.

"Dial it back on the level, Bug," Zevi directed. Bug nodded and the pitch of the alarm became less likely to make my ears bleed and more just ring. I could hear people scrambling through the noise. Somewhere, someone was screaming about the lights. Small footsteps pattered the hallways and I felt uneasy. There were children in this building, families. I hoped Zevi knew what he was doing.

The first person to leave the building was a confused elderly man, his hair a wisp of gray as he came stumbling through the doorway. He looked at Arnold's shadow, screamed in sheer terror at the fangs of the creature, and took off back into the building. His panic caused people trying to leave the building to panic as well. I could hear the banging of doors on tree limbs as people fought to get out of the tomb, the shudder of windows being impossible to open, due to tree branches holding down the frames like fingers.

I started to sweat. The very air had become filled with fear as families started to lose hope, a building with no lights and no way out. More people managed to make their way to the doorway, pushing and shoving out the doors into the opening, only giving a slight pause in front of the horrific creature guarding the doorway. It snarled, mimicking Arnold's movements, which appeared more beast than man. The snarl caused them to flee faster, like ants scattering from a colony that had been exposed to the outside world for the first time.

This was wrong—wrong on so many levels. The screams, it was like when we got off the trains. The children reaching for parents' hands, darkness followed by overwhelming brightness. *This had to stop now*, something screamed from within me. It wasn't the beast this time. It was me, yelling at myself.

As more and more families piled out of the building, I wanted to be back in the woods alone, back doing my nightly ritual. It may have been harmful, but it was quiet. It was the only way to turn off the world, that brief moment before I thought the lights would go out for good, when I saw the night sky all black with no stars. Then it dawned on me, like a hammer striking an anvil, when I saw a little boy come out of the building. He held in one hand a baseball glove, the other nothing. In the confusion, as families became torn between running into the fog or back from a massive monster standing guard, I realized that what was being done to that boy—to all the boys and girls now—was the same as what was done to us.

That splintered any illusions about the night. Joachim or not, this was not the right thing to do. "Zevi," I spoke up behind Zevi's back. He either didn't hear me over Bug's alarm or he chose to ignore me. I choked for a moment—what could I possibly do to stop this situation.

I stepped closer to him, reaching out and taking hold of his shoulder, pulling him around. "Zevi!" I snarled.

My brother's face contorted in rage for a brief moment when Bug suddenly stopped. Tir called out, "It's him!"

Zevi and I both turned to the doorway. Out stepped a middle aged man, who had on a checkered robe, horn-rimmed glasses and a perturbing hairline that faded back as his gut grew forward over his waist line. He wasn't the evil mastermind who had tortured children, nor any of the sadistic guards that seemed to almost be gleeful to help the mad doctor. It was by all accounts a scared, but normal man.

Arnold's shadow launched forward in one quick motion, pulling the man off the ground by his legs. The man screamed, hitting his head on the ground below him, briefly knocking the wind out of him, before he looked up seeing the demonic face of Arnold's shadow. A few feet away, Arnold mimed holding the man, even making the snarls of the beast—which made me wonder if the beast was in control. I let go of my brother's shoulder.

He rolled it back at the same moment, shaking away my hand.

"That's him, alright. Well done everyone," Zevi smiled, coming up next to the man. "We found you, you little fucker. After all this time," Zevi snarled, spitting into the man's face.

"Zevi, who the hell is that guy? That is not Dr. Joachim," I stated, coming up to my brother, taking hold of his shoulder again.

This time, Zevi looked at my hand like it was some kind of foul beast touching him. "That's two, Avi. One more and you will lose that hand," he calmly stated looking at the man, then looking back at me.

The man wept, snot and tears running out his face as he hung over the ground by one leg, his face turning purple and red even in the dark. "Tir, hold everyone else down," Zevi directed. More roots burst through the hard dirt, taking hold of the many residents of the building that were outside now.

I looked at Tiresias, shouting. "Tir, let them go, man—"

"Shut up Avi. If he lets them go, they will get in the way and could end up hurt. If you really care about these families, help me here and this will all be over," Zevi shouted, keeping his eyes on the man hanging upside down, his body shaking, his shoulders rolled forward like he was holding something from exploding from within his body. I could see, in the dim light of the moon, that steam was rising from his body. I felt an anger I never felt in anyone else besides myself. It frightened me. I always had Linor to calm me down at those levels, but Zevi, he was a bomb waiting to go off. Who did Zevi have? He had me, his brother, his *bruder*. I stepped near Zevi, making sure to keep my hands off of him for now. My heart was beating fast—what was I doing?

"Zevi, who is this man?" I asked, calmer this time.

My brother turned toward me. He was no longer shaking and he stood tall. "Why, this is the guy that forgave Joachim: a now retired but formally high-ranking official in the government. Pardoned lots of good ol' folks back home—one of those people was our favorite scientists, Dr. Joachim Fints. Or, as we knew him in the camps, the doctor of Death." Zevi was beaming like a small kid that had just gotten a gift. I looked to the others.

Most their faces were passive, some looking unsure. No one looked like how I was feeling. Not even Linor—Linor looked calm, like she was busy concentrating on her smoke rather than the situation at hand. That was weird—she couldn't have been okay with what was happening around us.

"Pardoned? Why would anyone have pardoned him?" I asked, shocked by the words coming out of my mouth.

"Good question, brother. Why would someone pardon an evil death-worshiping piece of shit as that bald Nazi asshole. Lets ask our friend, shall we?" Zevi quickly moved toward the man, brandishing a long hooked dagger from his belt loop with practiced precision. It was a blade meant for slashing. It served no other purpose. My stomach pinwheeled. Zevi wasn't that crazy, he couldn't hurt the man. He was rough around the edges, sure, we all were. That wasn't who my brother was, though; he was not a killer.

The way he held the knife at his side, it screamed differently, as he whipped back his hand in a ferocious slash, becoming invisible with such blinding speed. I could only hear the tear and then see the trail of bright red leading from the man's stomach to his shoulders. I heard a man howl like an animal, something that is so natural and can be found in every living person if put under the right circumstances—yet it was the most unnatural sound a human could make. No one should ever be put through so much pain to cry out like that—to languish and grimace with no hope of escape.

A valve within me turned, spinning my blood, crashing against my limbs, as I growled over his screams. "Zevi! Stop this now!" I bellowed at my brother. All other noise ceased, even Bug's alarm.

"What?" he snapped back turning his attention to me, his blade pointed at me.

I could feel the outrage leaping from him. It was fueling mine with every passing moment as every breath I took fumed with fire. "Leave him alone!" I exclaimed.

Zevi narrowed his eyes, and a look of contemplation flashed before his conviction returned. "You see, Avi, this is why I don't like you. Not in the slightest," he informed me. "All that desire to make up for what you did. The promulgation of so much rage—I swear it could be seen in you sometimes. But here you are, telling me not to hurt someone that hurt us! That stole from us. You may have not loved our mother, but I did!" Zevi bent forward again, his back hunched along with his shoulders, his body shaking like a worm on a hook.

"I loved my—our mother," I blurted out, feeling the weight of her being gone all over again at my brother's words.

"Liar! This wouldn't even be a conversation right now if you did! This man let the filth that harmed not only us, but everyone else here, go. Millions of lives torn to pieces, by flames and bullets, like they were fucking livestock! I'm sorry, not even livestock, livestock at least gets fed!" he spat, hissing through clenched teeth.

I retorted, "That may be true. That man, though, he had nothing to do with the camps!"

"Nothing to do! He had everything to do with the camps. He may have not been the one pulling the lever, he may have not loaded the guns, but he is just as much a part of this, brother!"

The man whimpered, looking at me as his glasses fell off his face and he tried to cover the slash with his one hand. "I had nothing to do with that—I swear, I was just following the orders given to—"

Zevi savagely kicked the man in the stomach, so he hunched over. "I'm not so blinded by anger, you rat, to realize that you had nothing to do with the camps until after the war. What drives me mad is how you could look evil in the eyes, knowing you have it, and then let it go! Help it, even, and bring it food and shelter in land thousands of miles away! And for what? For future war information? To better learn about the minds of those that are captured, how to torture children? I am not American, I am not German... I do know what I would do!" Zevi jammed his thumb into his chest.

"That doesn't change anything, brother! There's no reason to hurt him. He may not even know where the doctor is now!" I shouted at Zevi, both of us only feet away from each other.

My words seemed to only tick him off more. "No reason! He knows where that son of a bitch is, and even if he doesn't, I am sick of the 'following orders' excuse. So much hatred is justified in this world based on such flimsy logic. If that's the case, if no one told me not to save a baby from a bonfire, am I supposed to just let it happen? I was just following orders, right!" he spat at me this time, his saliva landing on my feet.

"Avi," whispered Linor behind me. I ignored her and kept my eyes on my brother.

"Shit, if you had just listened to what our parents had said, they would still be here!" he screamed, stepping toward my face. I stood tall; we were inches away from each other, heat coming off the both of us. It was so intense, it was as if our bodies were already fighting each other. A part of me yelled from within to stop this now, stop before things got too late.

I looked at the screaming man, his face pitiful, while his body bled. I thought of our mother, how I never got to see her again. Of the chain of events leading up to this moment. "There was nothing I could have done, Zevi," I stated.

His eyes flashed with a fury of flames before he could speak. "Nothing you could have done, Avi? You have a damn demon that burned down the entire camp! Miles of twisted metal, bent because of you. Hundreds of people died in both nights combined. Don't give me that crap, you numberless coward; you killed them all!" he snarled.

I snapped, shoving my brother hard with all my might. Zevi was knocked back only a few steps before he staggered and stood tall again. A strange toothy smile stretched his lips. "I hope that wasn't all you got. Show me the wolf, brother. I want to see it!" he shouted, flexing his body like a windup toy about to spring.

I suddenly became aware of all the eyes on me—everyone was watching. If I didn't put in an end to Zevi now, something bad was going to happen. *Let me handle this, Avi, I can deal with him,* spoke the monster from within. The anger disappeared at the sound of his voice. *What was I doing? I couldn't fight my brother... letting that thing out, everyone here could die.*

Zevi snarled again. "Show me the wolf, *bruder*!" he screamed, stepping toward me. Elder Ad had spoken about feeding the good wolf. Was this what he meant when he had told me the story? Was feeding into my brother's madness feeding the wolf? I looked at the man. It was true he had let the killers of my family and kinship go—for what purpose, I didn't know. Seeing him now, though, hanging by the foot from a monster, it didn't make me angry. It just made me feel a deep fracture within my body.

Why must we put each other through so much misery when there was already enough that could harm us? I spotted the golden ring on his finger, and my heart dipped the burning fire into an endless ocean. He was married. Somewhere out here, his wife was afraid, terrified that intruders in the dark had unsheathed their daggers, stealing her husband away from her. It was over, then. I couldn't let this man be harmed, and I couldn't fight my brother either—he was my brother. I put my hands down at my sides and Zevi flinched, stepping back. What was I supposed to do here? I couldn't do anything. I was back in the camps, the mornings when I watched the doctors test on the others. Stuck behind chains, stuck behind bars as the people I loved were mutilated.

Zevi drilled holes into me with his eyes before stepping forward, taking my shirt collar in his hands. "Fight me, you coward! Come on, show me the wolf! Show me what is so special about you!" he shouted, picking me off the ground.

I saw Linor outstretch her hand before Sophia took hold of her shoulder. My eyes went wide, taking in Zevi for what seemed like the first time. His strawberry red hair blazing in the low light, his muscles tense, like a constrictor readying to pounce on his prey. I was frightened. Everyone seemed too close, the air was fleeing my lungs, and I felt pressured, with no way out.

"Show me the damn wolf!" he shouted, setting me down on the ground.

I turned toward the smoke. It was fading quickly as Linor was no longer bothering to keep it going. In the distance, I could see all the families that had left in the apartment. I shuddered—they were watching us. They were frightened, terrified in the presence of monsters. We were reenacting the very horrors of all those nights so long ago. I bowed my head and staggered off into the night. My feet kept moving as I walked into the tree line, as Zevi called from behind me, "Show me the wolf!"

37

Chapter 37

Rain never bothered me to any great extent—in fact, it was the few times that I could take any form of solace without thinking. I was resting under a canopy of trees as the heavy pelting of rain splattered the dirt around me, soaking into the wet mud, which seemed to grow with each passing drop.

I sighed heavily, still trying to catch my breath. After I had walked into the forest, I took off at a dead run until I could no longer hear the man's screams. When I could hear nothing besides my breathing, I stopped. The world was a spinning rumble of green all around me. It made more sense than the thoughts in my head. I had left Zevi. I had left my family. That man, he had died and it was all my fault. That mantra played over and over in my head, wounding my thoughts, stabbing my heart.

I didn't know if he was dead—*I don't know that. I need to get back there; I need to see for myself.* I looked up. The moss-covered trees here were confusing to me. They weren't the heavy oaks of our campsite—yet I knew that if I headed south-west, I would be back at the building in a couple of miles. The police would already be there, and there would be nothing to see. "You choose which wolf to feed," echoed Elder Ad's voice in my head.

I stood up, mud falling off me, my body aching from the stress of the night, and I just took off, running in the direction of the building. *Avi—little Avi, what are you doing?* The wolf spoke up. "I don't know—setting things right," I responded weakly as I ran in the darkness, stumbling over tree branches. *You can't do this on your own, you never could. Let me help you!* He hissed in my mind, and I could hear the grinding of his sharp teeth as he spoke. I ignored him, even though I hoped he was wrong. The truth was I wondered now if I could do anything in this situation. I had to, though. There—there were some things that I had to do, even if I was afraid. I was terrified of what I would find; of what I would have to do. Fear was always an option, a thing on a table that people could choose. I was choosing fear now; I was just choosing to go on anyways. So much had been lost because of my inaction; so much of life was a twist and a turn, into a bend that seemed to never end.

No more, I thought as I came close to the wood line that led into the building. I stopped taking a breather. I was out of shape. Too many nights drinking and smoking. When this was over, I would cut back—at least for a few weeks. A few more steps and I was on the road. The building looked completely empty now. Cars were in the parking lot—just far fewer. Heavy tracks of black burned into the pavement as desperate people fled the scene. I walked up to the front. Someone had taken an ax or a saw to Tir's branches around the doors. Piles of wood were chipped and stacked all around the building. I sniffed the air, finding only a mixture of gasoline and fear, otherwise, again, no people.

Coming around the front, I saw why there had been no people. A thick line of red led the way for me. Out front was a massacre—no other words for it. I covered my mouth and took in the scene. The man from earlier was still there, what was left of him scattered across the yard. Someone with considerable strength had completely destroyed his head. Chunks of flesh and bone littered the area, with some having been flung far enough to reach the windows. The only two strong enough would have been Arnold or Zevi. I had a feeling which of the two was heated enough to accomplish this.

I looked at the doorway. A purple blanket was lying under the open door. I picked up the soaked wool and carried it over to the remains of the man. His body was a limp blob, almost on the ground. I covered it with the blanket. Not sure if it helped anyway, but it felt more right than just leaving him there.

I looked around, sniffing the air, and found more traces of blood belonging to someone else. I followed it a few feet to where most the families had been. It was just a few drops, but enough that I could smell it through the light rain. Had it rained like it did in the woods, I wouldn't have been able to find the scent. I was doubtful that the cops were going to be able to find it either. Zevi must have threatened the families that had stayed behind. Which meant any moment now, the police should be coming. As if on cue, I heard sirens blaring in the distance.

I didn't wait around for the police to show up. A good rule of thumb for anyone, especially a soaked teenage boy from a Gypsy camp—don't be around for the police. I threw up when I looked at the body again, bending over to hold it in until I made it to the forest line, at least, before vomiting in the woods. I ran deeper in a different direction from before, this time heading to what I thought was deeper into the town.

It turned out I was correct, after an hour or two of almost aimlessly wandering in the dark woods. I kept seeing that man's body; the way the yard seemed to pool endlessly with his blood, the gore that wrapped into every corner of my mind. Where was Linor? Had she really gone back with Zevi after something like that?

Linor wouldn't have done that, not unless he was forcing her. He must have done something to coerce her back with the rest of the group. But why? Why didn't anyone else do anything? A man had died—for no reason at all, he had died. I remembered how easily Zevi had broken the lock to the store, the ease with which he would destroy a ball. How my best push only sent him back a few feet; I couldn't defeat my brother. Not on my own. I wasn't going to release the beast either. Something told me if I fed into him too much, I would cease to be altogether. It was so hard holding myself back, against what all had happened. Zevi was right, I had killed our mother—I had allowed all of this to happen by not acting. *Feed the good wolf, there was only one thing to do.*

I couldn't let that thought go, and my hands shook, my body shook.

Visions of the dead man splayed out on the ground in such a horrific way. I hadn't even known his name. Someone had, though. So much death—just an endless sea that never stopped. I was exhausted, fatigued beyond my wits' end, when I came to the silver rectangular box of a pay phone. This was where my body had led me as I contemplated what to do. I had caused so much of that pain myself, by not acting. I had caused that man's death as well.

Super-smell, super-hearing, super-night vision—none of that was enough to stop someone as strong as Zevi. I had a feeling that the kind of confidence that gave my brother his bizarre challenge to see the beast last night was about him having more than just strength. He was confident he could win, which somehow made the situation worse. My brother, what had happened to him? What was happening to me now? I choked down more vomit. The anxiety caused me to convulse. It was so hard to breathe. So little room in this tight box called life.

I just wanted to rest, curl up into a ball, and never open my eyes again. Only every time I did, I saw my mother, I saw the man, his golden wedding ring reflecting the moonlight on the chunks of his skull. I fished around in my pockets. I had nothing, just wet pieces of fabric. No money as usual. Frustrated, I fished out the broken remains of the paperclips I had used earlier. Linor was the queen of picking locks, but luckily, the mechanism clicked on the phone box and the tray opened, spilling out hundreds of coins. I swooped up a handful and stuck them into the phone as my heart in pressed with every key. It seemed I had learned enough from the queen, I sighed, hesitating as a voice clicked on.

"Pasco police department," answered a stern gruff voice on the other end. The type of voice that I never would contact, not in any form. It was a voice that had looked down on my kind, a voice that had spent years chasing us, as we spent years dodging them.

I took a deep breath, trying to clear the tears that were falling. "I would like to report—a—crime."

38

Chapter 38

The police got to the camp before I did. In fact, it took me climbing into the back of one truck while the driver was stopped at a station to make any headway with my return back to the community. That took me most of the way, the final leg of the journey. I hopped out of the back, heading to Pete's grocery store. Our bikes were still there from earlier. I left the rest of the coins I had gotten from the payphone on the counter of Pete's store, after taking some beef jerky. It was going to be a long ride back to camp.

My phone call with the police had been brief. I didn't know where Zevi was, but I told them the location of the camp. How to actually find it, and which turns and forests were just a decoy. I hated myself for that—it was already something that I could never forgive myself for. I had betrayed my family. Zevi had to be stopped, though, and it wouldn't stop with that American man. He had the same look in his eyes that Dr. Joachim had held in his eyes plenty of times. It was a look that meant my brother's fire had become an inferno. He would stop at nothing until he had his vengeance. *And what about my own vengeance?* I thought, on the ride home. Did it really matter anymore? The past had already been written and the ones I had lost, I wasn't sure if they would approve of me bashing in the heads of old men during the night.

I pedaled harder. Maybe if I got to the camp before the others, I could get members of the community to help me take down Zevi. I could warn them the police were coming. Getting to them by car was no easy feat—that's why we'd tucked ourselves away in dense woods, surrounded by unforgiving jagged rocks.

I tore up the mountainside over the field that Linor and I had been in earlier that day. If I just moved quickly enough, my mistake of calling the police would be fine. No one else besides Zevi would have to get in trouble. This was a Gypsy matter; I should have brought it before the camps elders, brought it to Linor's cranky grandma even. I could do this, I could talk Zevi down, he could be stopped, and no one had to be hurt. When I rounded the hill leading to the baseball field and camp, I smelled the gunpowder and burning rubber. I stopped the bike. That smell either meant there was a burn pit made to hide the evidence, or...

Or it meant that the police had tried coming into a Gypsy camp that was armed to the teeth. Murder or not, the rule in camp was we did not betray one of our own. Not just because it would mean trouble for that person, but because if one of us went down, we all went down. Family first—that was something my mother told me often, told me every night, in fact. But this was putting my family first—why did it not feel that way, though?

I had the answer when I rounded the hill. The camp had become the aftermath of a war zone. Gone were the many lit bonfires, colorful lights, endless rows of glasses hanging from trees. Now I could only see ruined shelters, torn to pieces. Bullet holes punctured most of the walls. To make it worse were the bodies I could smell before I could see them. In the center of camp, near where Elder Ad had given his talk only hours ago, was most of the town. I couldn't see Zevi or Sophia, or most of his friends. All I saw was Linor and her grandmother, clutching a man in their hands. I saw his long green boots, his tan pants and the brown blanket he always wore draped over him. It was Elder Ad. Across from him lay the nail in the coffin, which put to rest any doubts I had about the situation being fixable.

There was a uniform, his brown trousers soaked in mud, his polished loafers scuffed beyond repair, but most importantly, on his bullet riddled chest, there sat a silver star indicating the sheriff. We were doomed. No one in the camp would get away from this. I hoped off my bike and walked through the circle of people gathered around Linor and her grandmother.

Linor saw me first. Her eyes went wide and the whole story became clear. They had come back to the camp just in time for the police to raid the area. The others had most likely fled or been arrested. The camp, though, we don't give up one of our own. Shots had been fired, and when you're firing on the people with guns, you will get one or two good hits in. In the end, though, there were always more of them, always more guns. Even if Long Jimmy had a rifle that could blow a hole in a tank as he claimed, it wouldn't stop an army of police.

I looked at Elder Ad as he was being held in Linor's grandmother's arms, it registered that he had died trying to defuse the situation. Ad wouldn't have fired on the cops, he wouldn't have fired on anyone. He was a kind old man who loved to tell stories, and always smelled of his pipe tobacco. Now he was dead, not in the making of his own bed, but in the ruins of what I had caused. This was all my fault. Everyone here was done for because of me.

Suddenly I felt everyone's eyes on me in the crowd, as the circle shifted to completely surround me. Linor's grandmother locked eyes on me, and the very air in my chest seemed to get stolen in that instant. "You—boy! This is all your fault. You're a wolf, now get out of here!" the old Gypsy woman screamed; her voice cracking like a whip into the night. The old Gypsy woman had lips stained red—though it wasn't make up and I wondered for a moment how they glowed so red. She spoke to me again, and yelled, "You're a wolf, boy, get out of this town!" Since I was the only one to have not come back into town, it wouldn't have taken many guesses who called the police. For the community could only be found by one of us.

The crowd took up the chant. "You're a wolf."

Gone was the general indifference toward me that the community held. I saw a can thrown from somewhere in the sea of people. I stepped back, letting it hit the ground next to my foot. Many times, I had stumbled into camp drunk at night. People would avoid my eyes, ignoring my presence altogether if it was possible. A Gypsy camp is a shelter for all outcasts, even if that outcast makes them fear for their lives. Now, now I was a traitor.

Linor was crying, and tears rolled down her eyes. She must have been the one that pieced together how the police had found us. Which meant—it meant that she was to some degree okay with the death of that man. My heart sank to a new low, cut to the ocean like a jagged knife, edgy and dull, ending the bliss that I had felt with her in an instant.

She was picking the group over us, over me. I didn't understand. All we had shared and grown with each other, only to end like this.

I was pelted by more small items and chants of "You're a wolf!" that followed me even as I ran into the woods, even as I ran into the darkest of nights with no family, no direction. I had nowhere to go, except into the night. No matter how far I ran, I always ended up hitting a wall, no matter where I went, I would never be free.

39

Chapter 39

"That's rough, man," Huey stated as the sun started to dawn outside our doublewide. I had finished telling my story some time before Huey spoke. We had both remained quiet, sitting still, looking at the golden sun as it jumped away from the Earth.

"Yeah, it wasn't easy. Anyways, after that, sort of bounced around for a few years. Taking work when and where I could. I guess I had become a slave to a trade, riding railroad cars and working long days. The only problem was, I kept getting fired. Can't do most of the dangerous jobs—that only left so many. No education or name didn't help. I went underground man, real underground. Ended up in and out of the joint more times than I had hot meals. That pretty much brings us up to where we are today. I had abandoned my family to save a man who had let go of a monster. Not my best play," I mumbled, trailing off my words as I crumpled the last beer can.

"Now what?" Huey asked.

I burped and looked at the empty beer can in my hand, "What do you mean, 'now what?' We should probably get some rest, I imagine," I said.

"No, Avi, I mean now what are you going to do now? From where I am sitting, it seems like this is the first time in your life where you haven't been behind bars, and where you haven't been running from something."

"I would say, you're sitting on a pretty lofty throne there, Hue." I got up and brushed my pants off, watching the sunset. I liked the sunsets out here. They always splayed a deep gold with the red every night, looking like the celebration of lights: Hanukkah.

"Come on, man, stop ignoring this." He stood up suddenly, I stepped back. "Avi, what do you have to lose? What are you so afraid of?" He questioned me, his face an impassive stone.

"Lose? Huey, look at us man. We are two felons living in an Arizona doublewide. Honestly, if we lose anymore, we will be tied with the homeless people falling into the river down the road every night," I shot back, slightly angry at Huey.

"No man. I am saying to you, Avi, that it's time to do things differently. It's time to move on." He spread his hands wide.

"I am good on snake oil and huckster Bible talk, thank you." I started to walk away from Huey back to the trailer.

He called out, "I am saying, let's be better, man. Let's do something besides waste our lives away in this damn desert." Huey kicked the sand, and that's when I realized Huey's reason for having stuck around for so long. It wasn't just because of us being all each other had, but because Huey still saw the world in a good light.

"I don't think I will ever see the world in a better light, man," I responded.

"Its better than nothing, man. I am not asking you to start going to church on Sunday, I am asking you for us to get clean. To fight back against all that has happened. It stops with us, Avi," he stated.

I looked at Huey for a long time before speaking. "Yeah, it stops with us. Though I think it's pretty pointless. Give it a year and one or both of us will be back in jail, man. Trauma is like being hit by a car. Sure, you can heal to a degree, but you can't change the fact that your foot was dragged under the tires and now you walk with a limp," I responded.

Huey remained silent for a moment. When I was sure that he wasn't going to say anything more, he spoke. "The car hits us, trauma hits us, and we can either live or we can die. The best we can do is ensure that no one else has to get hit by a car either," he said, with a conviction in his voice that was absolute.

"Are you serious?"

"Serious as a heart attack. We are going to do better. Our mommas never wanted us to end up living together in a trailer on the run from the police. Let's put our skills together and at the very least, help ourselves," he said again, the same unwavering tone as before.

I sighed, "Okay, where do we begin? I 'm not doing your damn martial arts at 4am like you have been doing since we got out here."

He snickered. "I doubt I can pull you out that early anyways, but you will be joining me. I think you need to learn how to fight."

"I can fight," I snorted.

Huey just cast me a long look and remained silent.

"Okay you're right, I am pretty punchable. It's a risk, man. There's the beast to consider..." I trailed off, looking at the night's sky as the last bit of the sun left.

"I have some thoughts on that, actually," he stated.

"Such as?" I queried, doubtful that anything that would help.

"For starters, no more drinking and trying to get laid with anything that walks, Avi."

"The first one: yeah, probably for the best. As for the second, don't hate my game, Huey."

This time he snorted. "If throwing up on yourself and crying on a barstool counts as getting ladies you will win everytime," he jabbed.

I turned away. "Yeah okay, what else, what no cigarettes either?" I asked.

Huey looked at the pack he had in his shirt pocket. "Let's not go crazy now."

"That's what I thought—when do we begin?" I asked stepping toward Huey.

Huey bent over, picking up a small rock in his hands. "We start now!" he shouted before he threw the rock right at my head.

II

Part Two

"No man chooses evil because it is evil; he just mistakes it for happiness, the good he seeks."
Mary Wollstonecraft

40

Chapter 40

"Will you just drive!" I screamed at Huey as we sped down the highway, leading away from the Phoenix Zoo, with scores of police cruisers gunning after us. In the back of the van, we had stolen off the lot with a group of activists who were against the idea of a tiger being imprisoned at a zoo, as they put it. Huey and I didn't care either way—tiger or no tiger, things needed be paid, so this job would do.

What Stephanie and her want-to-be boyfriend had failed to tell us when we were driving the getaway van was that the tiger was only mostly knocked out. So, as I sat holding a couple hundred pounds of fur and claws on the ground, in what could only be the weakest headlock a man has ever given a big game cat, I drilled holes in Stephanie. The tiger had clawed her little friend, who had passed out from the sight of blood. Before I had time to help him out, Huey had kicked the van into a new level of speed and we accelerated with every police officer in the city gunning for us.

"I'm just saying if that damn thing scratches you, we are all dead!" he shouted as a cop car clipped the side of the van, sending Huey into the oncoming traffic lane. "Besides, you're doing the headlock wrong. How many times did we train that move and you still can't get it right?"

Over the past two years, Huey and I had gotten up every morning to train. It consisted of lots of rolls, locks, and general time on my ass. I liked to think I was getting decent enough at it. Huey, though, was like an artist—every move, every angle was perfect. Which is why what I said next made the most sense. "Okay, switch. You hold the damn tiger," I yelled, letting go of the beast as it roared, making Stephanie scream. Huey's eyes went wide in sheer terror as I crossed to the front seat. "Slide over, asshole," I grumbled.

Huey, not skipping a beat, bolted over the driver seat as I got there in just in time for the van to skit off the road. I drove us down a hill, bumpy rocks and other unevenness causing everyone inside to feel like a tin can at the bottom of an ocean. I looked in the rearview mirror. Stephanie had plunged another needle filled with lord-knows-what as Huey continued to choke the tiger. To his credit, he was staying down more, but I had softened the tiger up for him.

The police approached in the distance as we sped down the hill, passing roads until we finally came to the city limits. I spotted Huey and my truck. Its rusted brown sides looked like mud connecting to a blue beach. I sucked in a deep breath, flooring the van, and I slammed on the brakes a few feet past our truck. The wheels on the van were smoking, something was on fire under the hood, and I was pretty sure that the brake pads were gone now.

Stephanie's blond hair shot forward and she almost hit the dashboard. "Asshole, you didn't have to hit the brakes like that." She rubbed her head—she had a vicious yellow bruise forming at the crown of her head which made it look like she had grown a third eye for a moment.

"Two jobs in this van, Steph. Do you mind if I call you Steph? I was never good at remembering people's names, so nicknames it is," I stated.

I didn't wait for her to reply. She looked on me with utter bewilderment. "See, job one was to drive, job two was to do something about that!" I yelled, pointing at Huey and the tiger in the back. Huey was drenched in sweat, looking like he had almost been eaten by it.

Huey rolled off the beast, its tongue sticking through its massive teeth, which I realized could have easily made me bleed, then this would have been a lot worse a day. "How are you doing, Huey?" I asked, looking into the back seat. Huey's chest was pounding like a drum. He opted to just flick me off in response.

"See we did our jobs. Now, if you will excuse me," I snapped, exiting the van and walking over to our truck. I pulled out a box that was filled with green and white spray paint. I sorted the white out of the box before handing the rest to Stephanie. "These are for you. Make sure you get the top or else you will never lose the police. Also, there should be a new license plate for you at the bottom of the box. If I were you, though, different paint or not, lose the van fast. The way we went down the hill, I would be surprised if the bumper is still on," I stated, not bothering to inspect the damage to the van as I popped the top on one of the cans and turned toward our truck.

"Wait you guys aren't taking us with you?" she almost pleaded, looking back at the stolen van.

"Not part of the original contract. Plus, to be honest, we don't specialize in animals. I am pretty sure it's on our card," I replied dryly, as I started to spray the side of the truck white. Huey came up beside me, bending over to take out two cans of paint, and he started to spray the side down.

"I read your cheap ass card. It just said 'BMATJ Services.' What does that even mean, by the way? Why do they call you Avi? There's no "I" in Avraham, I think. And this is bullshit! Do you have no honor? Think of the tiger!" she screeched, pointing toward the van.

"You have your boyfriend," I challenged, taking another can and continuing working on spraying down the van. "You might want to hurry. We got lucky with that overpass leading down like that. I think they were more surprised that old junk could go off road. Don't worry, though, we have an old CPD radio with the dispatch channel that will buy you a few hours. A few, though."

"His name is Mark! Thanks to you two, he's knocked out! I want my money back," she screamed again, getting louder in my ears every time.

Huey steadied himself and looked at me. I knew what he was thinking without having to say it. I sighed, putting down the can and pulling out a card from my pocket. "Do you have a pen?" I asked her.

"Oh yeah, maybe," she responded, rummaging into her oversized bag at her side. To her credit, she was wearing all black, including her bag, so she didn't stick out like a sore thumb at least. She pulled out a pen, handing it to me. I turned scribbling something down on the back of the white-and-eggshell card.

"What you do is go down to 23rd Street off of Walsh Ave. Yellow house, third on the right. A guy name Chester will give you a car. Tell him Avi and Huey sent you. He will handle the rest. Don't get attached to the van; he will want to keep it. Go there now, and don't wait!" I handed her the card and turned away.

She read the card, then flipped it over. "Wait, this just has a number on it?" she was clearly confused.

"Yes, I know. Call me sometime if things don't work out with Mark back there." I winked at her as Huey finished spraying the truck down and I shuffled the supplies back into the bed of the truck.

Stephanie turned blood red as we climbed into the truck, closing the doors just as soon as she let out a stream of curse words, which I wasn't sure were real—and I had a met lot of Irish friends over the years.

"Great job, Avi. You successfully succeeded in losing us another client with that stunt," Huey lectured as we sped down the road in our now-white truck.

"Huey, give me some credit. That was Chester's number—do you really think that man would allow a couple of college kids to show up at his place without seeing our card first? Chester likes us; he doesn't work for free, though. I have my doubts he will help on his own—besides, I left the pin on the front for the external account. Chester will take one look at it and understand. I just like ruffling some feathers when I can. Especially with the hippy-dippy types," I stated.

Huey snorted. "Mission accomplished! I say we celebrate," he announced.

"I was thinking the same thing, partner. They just opened up a new—" I started before he eyed me from the passenger seat. "Okay, fine, fine. Don't get your panties in a twist, I was only kidding. I wasn't going to say 'bar.'"

"This is why everyone thinks you're an asshole, Avi," he stated, rolling down the windows as the scorching summer day gave away to the cool desert night.

"What are you talking about? Everyone wants to be my best friend," I rebutted.

"Your left and right hands don't count," he jabbed.

I snorted, taking us back into the city.

41

Chapter 41

"It took me a long time to... come back, you know?" snorted Willy into a blue handkerchief that I swore he never washed. "Things were loud, then they got all quiet. Every single day, it's just so damn quiet here." He finished telling his story to the group of us as we all sat in the dimly lit light of a warehouse, on the outskirts of town.

Huey had been leading these meetings two times a week for the last year, where me and a bunch of other people just sat around talking. Mostly the people that came were old war veterans, or people who had clearly seen better days.

After Willy quit talking, Huey said, "Thank you, Willy. It's true, things are silent here, even in the hustle and bustle of the big city—everything seems so deafening. But that's a good thing, right? Now we have time to silence those voices that aren't our own. We have to learn to search out for the voices that matter, the ones we have within. Remember, guys, even when things get dark—quiet, or far worse; you have exactly what you need to overcome the darkness. I promise you all that. Nothing is as loud as the light within you, Willy." Huey smiled at Willy.

The old man managed a small smile and a nod. He shifted his knee, his faded green uniform still decorated with ribbons. Huey insisted that since we had so many vets in the groups that wore part if not all of their uniforms, that we should all bring in a medal. He told us to treat our suffering as a medal toward our growth. Personally, I thought it was just a waste of time, but I now sat with a yellow ribbon attached to the lapel of my jacket for being a prisoner of war. Which was only partially true. They don't give medals to mass murder victims, I reminded Huey.

"So, whose turn is it now?" Huey slapped his knees, looking around the circle, "Anybody—any new takeaways? Maybe we can get someone new..." Huey turned toward me as the rest of the collective of people looked my way.

I turned red under their gazes, this had happened every time, twice a week, for a year now. A group of men and women looking at me, waiting for me to share. "What do you say, Avi, would you like to share?" he asked, calmly.

"Hard pass. Thanks, though," I mumbled, looking at the celling. The rest of the group groaned, including the woman sitting nearest me. She had shared her experiences almost as little as me. What we had gotten out of her was a story about her husband overdosing accidentally at their honeymoon. Only she had been the one that convinced him to try it. Turns out that her late husband had a heart condition, and now, a few years later, she was here, in a warehouse with a bunch of other forgotten folks. That's what we were—the people that life had landed on, the bad hands, the ball rollers.

These were the forgotten. Sure, someone would take a minute to listen to their sad tales of woe, may even feel a slight pinch of guilt. If you were lucky, you could get them to think about you longer than what was for dinner for a minute. Even if they didn't listen, what were they supposed to do? Why were you forcing your problems on them? Couldn't you see they had problems? That was what made us the forgotten, those who got derailed enough from life, tragic deaths, bad endings, worse choices had made us all into people who were avoided at all costs. Or worse, we chose to avoid people, lurking in a back alley when a sudden panic attack hit. Trying hard not to piss our pants when a loud bang went off. The forgotten are forgotten because we can't move on. Since the rest of the world had already flowed on by, what did that leave us?

"It's not so bad—just try it out for once," she whispered. I looked at her over my folded arms. She barely spoke. That was the first time she had spoken to me directly, now that I thought about it.

I stayed quiet, hoping my awkward silence would cause them to move on. It didn't. That was the story of my life.

I sighed. "If I share something, will you guys shut up?" I asked the group.

"It's not about getting us to shut up Avi. Hell, it's not even about talking. It's about taking some pressure off of those thoughts. Thoughts are pretty weak against the light. Once you expose them out into the open, depending on if they're good or bad, they go right away," he responded.

I sucked in my lip, forcing down a response. If nothing else in the last two years with Huey, I had learned that other people existed around me from time to time. Not all the time, but they were there. After another long moment of deliberation, Huey was about to say something again when I finally spoke.

"I've been getting a telephone call here lately... It's always in the middle of the night. You would think this shit would pick a better time," I said, looking at the ground, fidgeting with my hands. I caught myself, taking a deep breath as I wiped my palms on my pants. "I think, knowing what caused those moments, the moments we can't forget is where it all starts, you know?" I wasn't asking anyone in particular. Everyone in the group was dead quiet.

I cleared my throat after clenching my jaw. "If you were to see me pick up that phone, from the outside, watching me, you'd never know anything was unusual about this. On the inside, though, my heart races so fast, my blood pressure could blow a ship out of the water," I dipped my head even lower before speaking again. "Anyways, I just get this call in the middle of the night. I pick it up—I don't know why, I just do. There's never anyone on the other end. Just me, breathing into this endless void. Sometimes when I ask who's calling—I just hear breathing, crying. I think for a moment that it just might—might be them. You know, the ones that are gone, the ones that are little more than ghosts now. Maybe that is what we always were, just ghosts, living and pretending to be more than a memory. It takes me a while, but after I stop breathing hard, I realize it's just me. Crying into an imaginary phone that's not really there. That's me most nights, wallowing in my own self-pity," I scoffed, looking away from the group.

"Any asshole that tells you you're throwing a pity party after experiencing what you've experienced is lost in their own little world. But is that wrong, though? Do we move forward by staying in the past?" Huey asked the group, taking the attention of me. I was thankful. Huey knew when not to press me. "No, we move forward by being honest about what's happened, being kind to ourselves, then we kick our asses forward—there is no stopping here, folks. We go forward by promising to never be that way again."

"What way is that?" I asked weakly, after clearing my throat again, rubbing my eyes. Something was in them. Must have been dust in the warehouse.

"By not living in fear, Avi, by having hope for the future. Having hope will allow us to build faith to somewhere better. That's what I think, at least. I don't think it would hurt you to have a little hope, Avi," Huey stated.

"That goes for all of us." Huey stood, looking at the clock, "It's getting late, guys. Help me put up the chairs?" Huey gestured to the backroom closet. We all nodded in response, standing up and taking our chairs.

A few people grunted and general small talk was made. I handed my chair to the person in front of me as we all formed a line, passing them to the next person. When it was done, I killed the coffee pot, as Huey approached me. "You know this coffee is piss, right?" I asked pouring out the rest into a sink.

"Well, you know, we work on donations. Plus, you were the one that made it. Did you even grind the beans this time?" he asked.

"Why would I bother doing that? Liquid will come out either way," I responded.

Huey shook his head. "Come on, man, its been a long day, you're saying crazy things."

I nodded, looking back at the empty space in the warehouse. I never shared. The space felt too wide, I decided—maybe that was why it was too open for so many thoughts. Huey and I left the warehouse, driving back to our doublewide up in the mountains. We were able to stay safe for so long with the help of Chester changing our identities, while Huey grew out his beard and I kept changing my hair color every few months. At the moment, it was back to the brown with slight auburn, the first time I'd had my hair like this since I was a boy.

We drove on in silence, both of us worn down from today's adventure. We had been making a decent living with our own company. We offered "discreet" services for the right amount. The discreet part had to be dropped from the Yellow Pages due to how many... let's just say... "Enlightened" individuals there were in the area. All of this was coordinated by Chester for his twenty-five percent of the cut. It was a steep price to pay, but one both Huey and I had come to terms with. Even for me, who begrudgingly accepted those terms, it was better than being behind bars and it allowed us to actually help people. That was something I never realized how much I enjoyed. Folks needed help. Sometimes it was extreme, other times it was finding something simple that was lost. Whatever the case, Huey and I had a wide array of skills that benefited people.

We drove along the back country roads, mostly in silence, when Huey spoke up, breaking the silence. "Can I ask you something, Avi?"

"It's never stopped you before. Shoot," I sighed as I turned us down the path that would lead up the red roads to our trailer.

He laughed, rubbing his eyes. "I don't, man. After all this time, do you think any of this has done you any good?" he gestured at me.

I turned my head, confused. "This whole time, Huey, I thought you had a proclivity to being a pain in my ass—don't tell me you have doubts about your weird self-love mumbo jumbo?" I asked him.

"Humor me. Do you think it's done you any good?" He asked.

"I would say—it's done something. Not to sound weird, but I guess for the first time in a long time, I don't feel like I have to run away. Though, that hasn't stopped the night..." I trailed off. Huey didn't respond. He knew what I meant. The night is never kind to those who have suffered, it's an endless blanket that promises a starry sky, only to bring memories like rain, falling onto the panels of glass. Never truly there, but the world is obscured by darkness, obscured by dots forming an ocean that is deeper than any light dares to go.

"Yeah, I understand that," he mumbled.

"Are you wanting to talk about it?" I asked.

He snickered, "Shit, it must have done you something. Avraham asking someone else how he feels—is the world ending?"

I shrugged. "It's a long drive; don't get used to it. Want to tell me why you shake like a leaf at the sight of a gun?"

Huey curved his eyebrows in. A look of pure malice played across his brows, forming weathered crinkles into his skin. "That's not—that's not important," he almost barked.

I knew better to push someone when they were getting that mad over a question, plus sitting only a foot away from a man who beat me up most mornings during a training session with relative ease didn't seem very wise. But I was never wise, so I decided to push it, "All that talk about opening up and you can't even share that much. If it's just to get women, I will level with you: no one that comes to those meetings should date just yet," I joked, which was always our go-to when one of us said something that got under the other's skin.

After a moment, he relented, and scoffed. "Yeah, not much of a helper if I can't even share myself. The last time I used my gun—it was in the jungle. Things happened in that bush, Avi. It wasn't just with bullets. If you see one person's skin peel off like paper, you've seen too much." He was flexing his fingers open, closing them into tight fists.

"So, you're saying you don't like guns?" I quizzed.

"I am saying I will never kill someone again, Avi. Not with these hands." He dropped his hands in his lap, his head hung low.

"It stops with us," I stated.

That was our phrase for all the terror we had been through, all the times we had been put through the ringer. There would be no more harm. We couldn't change the past, but we could change the future. That was the plan, at least, even if it seemed further and further away every day, like smoke in the wind.

He paused. "Yeah, it stops with us. Just one more question, though—just one," he hissed through clenched teeth. "Who's the one?" he asked.

"He is the bald-headed killer that took all my friends, Huey. Tore through them like a hot knife through butter," I growled. "You said your hands would never be used for war again, you said that once, man. I'm not saying not to kill him—just it's a slippery slope. It never stops with just one. I remember for the first few months after I left the community—it was a blur, to say the least. Well, I would say the whole decade was a blur." I paused, looking at Huey, who still had his head down and was examining the floor of the truck.

"I took a lot of pills and drank way more than I should have, probably did more damage to myself than anyone else. It was enough, though. It only takes once. Then you're rationalizing everything. The next one will be a bit easier to talk yourself into doing. Then the next one after that... 'It's okay, you can quit tomorrow,' you say. But you never quit, you just wake up one day and realize it's all gone," I stated.

Huey turned his head, looking out the window into the deep dark of the backwoods. "It's already all gone," he stated.

"I don't know about all of that, man, we still got this kick ass truck," I replied.

42

Chapter 42

It was just after sunrise, our practice for the morning over. I was throwing up from a long run in the woods. I grumbled to myself: all the things that damn beast had caused in my life and I couldn't get super-cardio as a side-effect, instead I had the ability to know what someone ate last and the desire of a bloodthirsty creature to come out to eat, every time I got near something sharp.

I was hunched over coughing when I heard the tires bouncing over the uneven road leading up to our trailer. I could hear whoever it was coming long before Huey did. Huey came back out of the trailer, two canteens in his hand, handing one over to me as I stood up wiping my mouth. "Someone is coming," I stated.

"I thought you updated the flyers to say we don't open until nine?" he asked, taking a pull from his canteen and snapping the lid back on once he was finished.

I grumbled. "Why do I have to do everything? You know how hard it was to get someone to print something for you with the words: 'Two discreet men for help, no limits?'"

"Well, whoever it is, sure sounds like they are in a hurry. They're tearing up half the mountain to get up here," Huey stated.

I stopped, listening to him, straining my ears to hear any conversation. My hearing was good, but not that good, I reminded myself. Then I heard a high-pitched laugh. Only one person I knew could make noises that loud. I covered my ears, knowing exactly who that noise belonged to. It was Bug!

Huey looked at me, confusion evident on his face. "What?" he asked.

"Just 'fuck me,'" I snapped as a graying jeep came into view of the field leading up to our trailer. I watched through our kitchen window. I peered through the windshield. Inside were Bug and Tiresias. I froze. It had been close to fifteen years since I had last seen those two, fifteen years since that night outside of the apartment complex.

I considered bolting into the woods, running as far as I could, then running some more. Every instinct in my body screamed to run. My feet stayed in place. Instead, it was my heart that ran in every direction. I clutched my chest. Huey arched an eyebrow at me as the jeep came to a stop.

The ignition went off with a rumble and out stepped Bug. He was much taller, thin, with slumped shoulders. His skin was an ashy gray, the color leather turned when left in the rain for too long. He had on a thick pair of goggles that took up much of his face, save for his long beaked nose and greasy hair. Above him was an umbrella hat that extended like a beached whale in every direction.

Tir, on the other hand, was the polar opposite. He held his chest out, his shoulders high. Sunglasses perched over his eyes, sandy blonde hair that looked almost cooper in the Arizona heat. His hair fell to a long ponytail leading down his back, a strange sweater printed with leaves and bright colors, more exotic than a box of seventy-two crayons. A hippie and a pale man in goggles. I was not ready for today.

"Morning, Avi—you've gotten big. It's good to see you," Tir said in a slow irritating way that suggested he wasn't all the way there. He had always been into his plants too much. I had serious doubts he would have smoked them, though. I had a quick thought in that moment about whether Tir had an existential crisis every time he ate veggies.

"Morning. Now why the fuck are you here, Tir?" I snapped, feeling heat start to build up inside me. It had been a long time since I had felt the beast's fire burning, but he must have felt uneasy seeing those two as well. For once we agreed upon something.

Tir looked like I had slapped him in the face. He squinted for a moment.

"Tir? As in Tiresias? The plant guy from your story?" Huey interjected.

"That's the one," I growled. Huey shifted his back foot behind him, tucking his chin while he positioned himself at an angle to Tir and Bug. I waved my hand at the side to tell Huey that wasn't necessary.

"These two aren't a threat like that—isn't that right, Tiresias?" I stated, keeping my eyes on the pair. One thing I had learned from my constant training in the mornings was to never show weakness. After fifteen years, two individuals I had last seen helping to kill a man was a worrying site in the least. Still, though, how had they found me? As far as I knew, Tir's powers were bizarre and frankly borderline terrifying, but they should have had a limited range. Plus, the only vegetation around here was some cactuses and dried grass. Maybe he was talking to cactuses now? Stranger things have happened, I suppose.

"So, I will ask one more time. Why are you here, Tir?" I growled.

Tiresias flinched in response. That was the sign I was looking for: they weren't confident. I eased up the tension that was building inside of me, still keeping my body ready to spring at an moment's notice if need be. "Okay, I feel like you're in a bit of a bad mood. How about this?" Tir took off his glasses, his eyes shut and started wiping the lenses down with his shirt.

"Can you even see out of those?" I asked, keeping an eye on his hands.

"I like the way they frame my face, man. Also this is a godforsaken land of fire—why does anyone live in a place this hot?" he joked.

I ignored his comments, keeping an eye on Bug, who had his hands deep in the jacket pockets of his long trench coat. Despite the heat, Bug looked comfortable. Even if he stood out like a sore thumb under his umbrella, was he always that pale? I shifted my focus back onto Tir. I had spent enough time training with Huey to know he was watching Bug for me.

Tir went on, still cleaning his sunglasses for whatever reason. "Can we get out of the heat and talk? Things are already a little tense—talking inside wouldn't hurt. Besides, we are friends, Avi. At the very least invite me in before telling me to go fuck myself." He finished wiping his glasses as he spoke, placing them back on along with a very pleasant smile. You could find more honest smiles in a graveyard than that one.

I uncoiled my biceps, moving out of my fighter's stance. I had slid into it the moment the two got out of the car. "Sure guys. Let's go inside and have a chit chat." I nodded to Huey, his face hardened to a stoic line that betrayed nothing in that moment. If they were planning something or this was a trap, at least inside the trailer we had a wall between us and whoever was waiting out there. I had the feeling that they hadn't come alone.

Our wooden porch creaked under the heavy steps of our weight as we approached the entrance. I held open the door. Bug had his hands jammed deep in his pockets of his overcoat, and he walked through, followed by Tir and Huey. I closed the door slowly, scanning the horizon for anything that seemed out of the ordinary. Nothing but red rock and bushes for miles, endless and open. The uneasiness in my stomach was only getting heavier with each passing moment.

I bolted the door behind us, latching the chain as well. The four of us walked to the living room. Bug and Tir were already sitting on the yellow couch, framed by wood and mismatched seat cushions. Huey was eyeing them from behind the kitchen counter, through the open area. I stood on the adjacent wall to the two of them, my arms crossed.

"So, what brings you out to see me after so many years?" I growled, my anxiety running ahead of me before I could even get the words out.

Tir cleared his throat. "Okay, I think it's best if I cut to the chase with you fellas," he mumbled, slapping his knees.

"Probably not a bad idea," I responded.

"Okay, fine. Avi... it's... well, to be frank, I wouldn't be here if we had any other option. Part of the problem we are having now is—in part because of what happened that night. You know which one I mean. When the police came, and trust me they kept coming and coming, more than just Elder Ad was caught in the crossfire," Tir stated.

"They wouldn't have had to come in the first place, Tir, had you guys not killed an innocent man!" I growled.

Tir put up his hands in response. "Easy there, tiger. I'm not saying he was innocent or not. I'm not even blaming what happened with the police on you. What I am saying is that a series of, well, unfortunate occurrences befell our little world. I think even you, Avi, can understand that we were your family," he stated again, dropping his hands down to his side.

I took a deep breath before speaking, trying to clear my head as thoughts of life with the camp came flooding back. It was true. I may have been the outcast of the camp, but I was still part of the community. Being away from the community for years, hunting and living on the streets, never having anyone to talk to besides other drifters and societies rejects, that was no place for anyone. People need packs to survive. That was the way of the world. On our own we are weak, fragile, and trivial beings with no fangs or fur. I had never meant for the whole camp to go down that night, just those who had been involved in harming that man. The images flooded back into my head and I felt my stomach rumble in response to the thoughts.

"What does it have to do with me now, Tir? After all this time, no one tried to reach out. More importantly, I never tried to reach out," I responded, feeling lost on the way toward any thought that could shine a light out of the darkness. It was hard to remain optimistic in the face of so much blunder in life, yet it was a social dynamic of living, a requirement that anything that exists does so to carry on for others in some capacity. I felt that, digging into my soul, as Tir began to speak again.

"I can't speak for everyone else, Avi, but we need you. The community needs you—"

"Me? Or do they need the wolf?" I cut Tir off and he closed his mouth for a moment.

He sighed heavily. Bug turned his head between Tir and me, his umbrella reflecting the light from the outside world into rainbows on the living room floor, like they had always been there in the wood since the beginning of time.

"We need family, is what we need, Avi. That's all any of us have, after all that has happened. If you don't want to do it for us, not even for your brother, think about Linor, she was your family as well. We reformed our home, we reformed our group after what happened. It wasn't easy being chased by every officer for a thousand miles. We did our best. Our camp isn't just those of us who survived Germany anymore, it's now made up of other people who have suffered. So many people, Avi—and they need all the help we can give. If we stand any chance of bringing the community back together, bringing us back from the brink, we need you." Tir spilled out.

I unfolded my arms and crossed the distance between us in a flash, saying nothing.

Tir spoke up after a moment. "Anytime something happened in the community—you were there, Avi, to fight. I remember that very clearly. Unless I was wrong and you really are a Numberless—" he started.

Suddenly, I was standing before him, a deep neverending hunger now shot to the surface. "I think you should go, now," I hissed through clenched teeth, every inch of my body flexing, expanding as if I was some kind of animal about to attack a creature.

"She's gone, Avi. Your brother, he's done something awful to her!" Tir shook, throwing his hands over his face. I stood up, pulling him by his shirt—every desire I had inside me wanted to slam him through the wall, wanted to eat him, burn him to a tiny crisp. "What did you say?" I snarled, drooling at the prospect of devouring him. What was he talking about, who was gone?

"Linor. She's been gone for weeks, Avi. No one has seen her. And it's not adding up. Things are crazy back in the community. Your brother... I swear, I had no one else to go to—" Tir started, but I threw him with all my might against the adjacent wall. Tir hit the trailer wall, cracking the faded yellow paint into a web of yellow rivers.

"Where did he take her?" I growled, walking toward him.

"I don't know. I thought you would know. I swear, Avi. I only came because we needed you!" he pleaded, throwing his hands over his face. My former friend's eyes showed not the reflection of an angry man, but one of a beast, waiting to catch fire and burn the world into oblivion for what had been done to him. That froze me. That wasn't me, was it? I shook, a snarl of teeth and claws somewhere in my mind.

"Both of you need to get the fuck out of here, now," Huey urged them, picking Tir off the ground.

He said she's gone, Avraham. Are you going to let her go so easily? hissed a cold, cold voice, deeper than any pit.

"Yeah, that's not a bad idea," Tir whispered, putting his hands up as he stood hunched over from the broken wall. "Don't shoot the messenger, Avi. If you change your mind, we are still in Washington. You know the place.

"And Avi, one last thing. We did find Joachim, we found them all. That's not a lie. Putting aside your feelings for us, they're monsters and you know it. They're still monsters, Avi. I never thought you were the mindless wolf. Zevi never thought that. Zevi wanted me to tell you that—he wanted me to tell you that he was sorry," Tir explained as he walked toward the door.

Bug had already scrambled his way outside of the trailer. I suddenly realized the temperature inside was scorching and I had my doubts that it was because of the heat from the sun.

I followed Tir out of the trailer back onto the porch. "If Zevi wanted to apologize, he could have come here himself, Tir. Not send you two here. He is still trying to control everything, I see."

"No, Avi, your brother is in a bad way—he's been that way since you left. Trust me, he's hurting and is not the same man that he was. We know where that mad doctor is now, this time for sure. You can ignore it or you can come help your family put an end to their suffering. You aren't the only one who is wounded Avi. Keep that in mind and make up for what you did. It beats roasting to death in a tin can, Avi. I would pick helping my family or at the very least keeping evil out of this world. That's your choice. We are extending an olive branch. Either way, one of your family is missing, in trouble. You should care," Tir waved his hand as him and Bug got back into their jeep. Within moments, the engine fired to life and they were heading back down the rocky mountainside.

I watched the two of them go in a deep silence as I waited for their jeep to get down the mountainside. Huey came out standing beside me. I smelled his tobacco before I could see him. "Did any of that sound legit to you in the slightest?" he speculated.

"No—none of what came out of his mouth sounded honest to me. Yet—" I shut my mouth, unable to keep talking, as felt my whole body contract and loosen with every breath.

"If he was telling the truth, it means that the killer of your family is still out there, that someone terrifying is out in the world, and those left from your old life are dealing with it while you're out here. A girl you used to love could be in danger. Your little brother could be in danger. That about what you're thinking, Avi?" Huey asked.

I turned toward him, blowing out more deep breaths. "At a certain point, I think you have to let the past die, Huey. You're the one talking about moving forward—I can't be around them again. I can't." I mumbled as I sat down on the wooden planks at the end of our porch. "Why did any of this have to happen? You always hear about how when people die, they're in God's hands. I keep asking myself, Huey, if that is true, it means that God never cares about us while we are alive. Is there a purpose to anything, Huey? These past two years, we've done so much good—I think I can honestly say that. Does what happened to me, and what I did because of that, make any of this right now? That's what I am thinking. I am thinking that I want to kill the man who killed my family again. I am thinking that I harmed my own family as it tried to grow closer. Who's in the right here, Huey?" I stammered, my voice cracking as I went on.

Huey let out an exasperated breath. "I'm not sure. I can't answer that, man."

I nodded, opening the door to the trailer. "Yeah, I'm not sure either," I stated as the screen door closed behind me, cutting me off from the daylight.

43

Chapter 43

It started with my fingers around the thick leather. I held the belt bundled in my trembling hands—my fingers tracing the loops I had made in the soft leather over the last two years. I was alone inside this whale that was my surroundings. The walls made up of the memories and trauma, which never melted away, never gave way. I was just wrapped its tight coils like a snake, choking me off from my place in the world.

Tears are spread across the stars of grief, and I loathed anything that kept me here. I never chose to be born, to be plunged involuntarily into existence, stuck inside a physical shell that had scarcely seen a day without pain, all tied to an unfathomable time and place and with a family, and to have a consciousness that wouldn't leave. But a family that was gone—as far as I knew, forever. I could never stop feeling their pain.

My hands were now wet from my tears. I wanted it all just to end—no comfort with no consolation within view. However, these feelings were a blanket that I had felt endlessly, an absurd notion that the great cosmic joke of life was why I had never tied the belt to the suffocating point. Even as a teenager, it was true that I had sneaked off into the woods to end it all; I was still here, though.

I'd never cared for the meaning of this life. Just why had I decided to stay when I was in such terrible pain? But, I had to face that question—why had I never finally pulled the last loop around my neck, ended my suffering?

I looked up out the kitchen window, peering into the darkness. That question was legitimate. It was necessary and was the fog that shrouded everything.

In English, linguistically speaking, suicide was phrased as an act that someone committed, as if it was a crime. In German, it was *Selbstmord*, a self-murder. *Zelbstmord* in Yiddish, and in countless other languages. I had a feeling it meant the same. What it meant to me, what it had always meant, was leaving those who still held on. Those who loved me, for whatever reason, even in the darkest of nights, it was trivial, the feelings that they caused me now.

If I was going to stay in the darkness under the argument that there was no other way outside my pain, nothing other than the endless empty lands that were my brain, then I found myself laughing at the notion of my brown belt choking the life out of me. I had stuck around for so long, as I reminded myself, that I would never allow self-pity to leave me in the dark again. The moment I had chosen to use the knife Hans had given me, I had given the middle finger to the universe.

I was going to stay alive. That was my answer to the nihilistic pondering. I looped my belt around my waist. As far as I knew, this was it—it was the only chance at this I'd ever have. Why not ride it to the very end and see what happens? It would have been far too easy to give up, take the easy way out, just because of two people who reminded me of my former life. But I was still here, even with seemingly meaningless moments, life throws something for us all. The simple answer, without any grand thoughts: survival for the sake of survival. I was staying around every day for people like Huey, for those who came before and those who come after. This was what matters most, just hard work for a meaning. I was done losing the battle.

44

Chapter 44

It was just after midnight when the alarm I had set started going off. I had been up for hours, spent most of my night tossing and turning. I had my duffle bag in my hands. What few clothes I had were packed, along with the meager possessions that I'd bothered to hold on to over the years. When I was a boy in the community, I used to envy, in a way, those that had the numbers in the camps. At least they had a thing that could be seen, a common collective and shared marking. What did I have? Sure, I had the dour face of those whose grief was so endless and despairingly profound that tasks as simple as shaving or rolling one's socks up were tiresome tasks. But, I didn't have what everyone else had. As the years ticked off like calendar sheets, grief goes away, if not very well hidden. And still, I remained numberless, a leper amongst the marked. Now, as an adult, not having the numbers on my arm only reminded me I had nothing.

A life on the road is adventure, but no one ever tells you how empty the road can truly be. I gripped the straps on my bags tighter. I only had memories of my childhood, memories of the camps, memories within the community. All thoughts, frozen like water on a photograph, the picture slowly fading to obscurity.

Love, though, love was something that couldn't fade. That was what propelled me off my small mattress, wriggling out of the sheets as I stood. I managed to make my bed before stepping out of my room of two years, bringing some order to the chaos that was my life.

I turned, walking out to the living room, to find Huey with a green army duffle bag, strapped over his shoulders with a sturdy rope. I blinked in surprise, opening my mouth. "We are friends, asshole. Don't say anything," he stated.

I nodded, walking past him. "Good, you can do the driving. I am going back to sleep."

45

Chapter 45

Cross thousands of miles, endless roads and open skies, but home is a place that you can never forget. That was an odd feeling, as we made our way across the country to my old home. I wondered what could have possibly pulled the community back there. I suppose, in the end, coming back to where it all started wasn't a bad idea for them, at least. It remained to be seen for me. I wondered for a moment where they would have had to go. Perhaps maybe even further north—there was no way they could have stayed in Washington. I couldn't understand how they were back now. I felt a hot rush come over me. I leaned on the door. Huey slammed on the brakes, sending me into the dash. "Again?" he asked.

I grunted, opening the door, throwing him the finger, and threw up on the side of the road, somewhere in Oregon.

I wiped my mouth. "Yeah, again. Let's pull off the road for a bit. I need to get out of this screaming metal death trap," I muttered. Huey pulled off onto a ditch in the middle of the back-country roads of Oregon. Massive grand firs and the rough-colored bark of blackwood trees bordered the road, like swaying green statues perched above me on their lofty thrones, judging my every action. Huey got out of our now-blue truck, pulling another can of spray paint from the back and started on the side, tossing me one as he worked.

It was something simple we both did these days. We stopped whatever we were doing and just started working. As I layered the car in blue paint, my thoughts drifted back to what we were doing. Simply spraying down our truck to make sure prying eyes didn't recognize us. "Getting found in the work" is what Huey called it. As he explained, working is the best way to reorganize our thoughts when they go deep into a different direction that is beyond our control. Effectively, it did help—I guess. It made me want to throw up a little less. But, the fear of coming home was still leaving me shaking.

"You know, when you choose to see everything as meaningless—as everything as gray, even you have to admit that it's easy to get annoyed with things. I mean, you're working yourself up to a state of throwing up and we haven't even gotten there yet," Huey stated as he sprayed the other side of the truck.

I waved off the paint that was drifting blue smoke fumes into the wind, like a floating sea of water in the very air itself. "I see this conversation as annoying. Can't I just spray down this stolen truck in peace?"

"I would just let you be, if you weren't spraying the same spot, you jackass," he responded as I looked down, seeing that my hand wasn't moving. Frustrated, I threw the can into the woods, causing the metal to burst open on a rock, spraying the color of the ocean onto the dark ground of the forest floor. I watched the can wheeze out the last few puffs of light blue paint before turning back to Huey.

I sighed deeply. "Fine, alright. Maybe I am acting like a bit of a jackass at the moment—just, you know, sometimes you just want some stories to end. Sometimes, you can't see any good coming from something so dark. Maybe, just knowing how the story might unfold is enough to make me cower in my boots. I don't want to see the rest of this story, Huey, not after so much bad, because how can anything be right again when the world treats us like that paint can?" I shrugged, turning and walking toward the broken metal littering the dark woods.

I picked up the busted spray can. What was left on the inside was very little—but what had been put out into the world, that was something to behold, I thought. I turned back to Huey painting over the missed spots on my side. "I think maybe, Huey, I am worried what will need to happen to make sure this is over. All of this is because I chose to not face down my problems. Now I am running back to entirely new ones with old tools that didn't work before. Maybe I am just kidding myself in thinking I can make a difference."

"You probably won't. Folks always want to be the center of the universe in anything that they come across. If you think you won't do anything, you will either do something useful and not realize it, or do absolutely nothing and the world will continue spinning as it always has. As much as you want your story to end, it doesn't work like that, Avi. You're breathing—so your story goes on because of that," Huey declared.

"Wrong, Huey. Life works like a light switch. You can choose when you want to light it up, and when you want all the lights to turn off forever," I stated, getting back in the truck. My stomach tossed like a ship lost at sea.

46

Chapter 46

Pete's grocery store had expanded, from what I could tell, as we pulled outside to pump gas. Huey went in to pay, just in case Pete somehow recognized one of the many children that used to rob him on a daily basis. Pete now sported a shovel of gray hair, perched above a thick mustache that still held the last remnants of youth just before old age eclipsed him. I wondered if he had recovered from all the things we stole from him. I doubt he trusted his eyes anymore, not after all the smoke creatures Linor had sent flying around town. I smirked at that, remembering a prank we did once where Solly had decorated Tir and I to look like we had been hurt in a devastating attack by aliens. Linor had turned the town's water silo into a walking Martian tripod.

In the distance, I could see the rusting brown of that water silo, still looking like a monstrous form of metal jutting from the land to kill us all. I could leave this place, but I never could truly forget it. Good places edge their way into your life just as much as the bad ones do. Only the places that were the bleakest stand out like an elephant walking on water, leading us to thinking that nothing else could be natural besides the darkness of what we design in our own minds. I shook my head and replaced the nozzle, tightening the lid on the truck's gas cap.

Maybe the community would be better than it was. Maybe I stood a better chance of figuring out how an elephant could walk on water first.

"Nice enough little town. Lots of brick," Huey stated, handing me a soda pop as he opened the passenger door. I slid behind the wheel, my legs still cramped up from the hours of driving we had taken to get here. It was true: the town was layers of red, brown, yellow, and even a few grays lined nearly every home and store. The town may have been small, but it was built to last whatever storm. It was why the community leaders picked this town when we relocated here. Maybe we should have left sooner. *Maybe a lot of things should have happened,* I thought as I grunted back my response to Huey.

We drove on in silence. I looked down at the radio. The cords powering the box still lay pulled out on the ground. I switched on the knob for the first time on this trip. Huey just arched an eyebrow at me. The silence was making me even more uncomfortable than when I was being asked to talk about my feelings. Noise is the one thing in the world that people both need and loathe at the same time. It's either too loud or it's making you sway to the phases of the moon—it all depended on the tune.

The radio sparked out after a few twists of the knob. "The war is heating up, and the North Vietnamese have launched an all-out assault on the cities of Hue, Saigon—" I changed the channel, interrupting the voice before he could finish his statement. I looked at Huey. A dark shadow had fallen across his face. "I should be there—" he choked on his words, balling his fists.

"I know buddy, but like you're always telling me, we have wars to finish here first. There isn't anything else there for you, man, except for more war," I stated, trying to remember what Huey had told me once.

"Would you ever head back? To the camps?" Huey quietly asked me as we pulled off into a massive open field. It was filled with sheep grazing, causing me to slow the truck down to a crawl. I swore, hoping that the farmer was nearby or else Huey and I were about to eat a lot of sheep tonight.

It took me a second to register his question before it dawned on me what he had asked. "No—that is a place that I will not ever return to... The fear, the horror is still there, every time I think of that place... I see all the things that were happening there and I just—I can't walk toward that place, Huey, I can't. I just can't let it go either. So, I guess we never leave our wars, do we?" I asked him.

"I'm afraid not," he replied.

"Well that's just being negative," I stated.

"Most likely, but we can end some wars. Do you want to do this?" he asked as a farmer on a tractor herded the sheep off the road, clearing our path forward.

I peered out the window, watching the farmer lead the sheep away from the road, their bleating sounding like horns going off around us. It was just like the camps, in a way, someone leading us sheep, telling us where to graze, where to go. I had no idea if I could ever escape, and like the sheep, there could simply be a bigger predator right around the corner waiting to devour me in a few bites. If the sheep wanted to be free, sooner or later they were going to have to hop the fence, face the wolf to get freedom.

I had been out of jail for two years, and it had been over fifteen years since I had left the camps. Everywhere I looked, I still saw those high bars—imposing and keeping me contained. I would not die trapped. The only way for the sheep to gain freedom was to go forward.

"We go forward," I announced.

That was the end of the discussion for the rest of the drive. My heart never stopped pounding. The truck kept bumbling along the back country roads, leading to a community of Roma people tucked away in the middle of a valley. *Just another day, Avraham, just another day.*

47

Chapter 47

I could smell the open fires cooking rabbit stew in heavy iron pots. The earthy coat of hedgehog being cooked in clay as it baked in a pit, smothered in agrimony and sorrel. The cream cheese and noodles of Pirogo made my mouth get wet. I was home. That's what those smells meant.

We continued down the old dirt road leading to the community. I saw Long Jimmy's home. It was now a yellow Beetle. Pieces of brown metal laid at odd angles decorated the outside. His donkey Brianne, much older now, was still chewing a mouthful of grass, with her half-tail and a pink bow in her hair. How in the world this place had not been completely torn to the ground by the police was anyone's guess. I was still staring at Jimmy's donkey when Huey shouted. "Avi! Look out!" he yelled from beside me.

I yanked my head back to the road to see six massive gray and yellow wolves crossing the road. Their sharp eyes pointing in the direction of our blue truck. I slammed on the brake, spitting up rubble and grass as we came within inches of striking a bull of a wolf, a solid black giant. I leaned up, peering over the hood at the wolf, which almost came to the top of the front of the truck in height. The creature seemed to smirk right before it shimmered and within seconds, the fur of the animal peeled away like orange peels and there stood the gangly youth Bipin, now in his early twenties. His leather skin was as thick and red as his father's had been, with long black hair flowing to the crest of his back.

"Hiya, Avi." Bipin waved in all his naked glory as the other five wolves shimmered, then stood before us. Three other boys, and two girls with long flowing black hair, dark skin and wide noses looked at us with curious eyes. One of the girls still held what appeared to be a deer leg in her mouth. In the seat next to me, Huey had stopped breathing as I stammered for words.

"Uh, hi, Bipin—you've gotten big," I mumbled. "Do you guys mind putting on some clothes?" I asked, averting my eyes to the ground.

"Oh yeah," Bipin laughed.

48

Chapter 48

"Man, Avi, it's been years! How are you?" Bipin clasped me on the back as he pulled up his pair of jeans.

"Doing well, Bipin. What are you guys doing out here?" I asked pointing to his sister who had finally gotten dressed and was now taking the deer leg from earlier into a bag. The others had pulled out clothes from motorcycles that had been covered in heavy tarps. The bikes were remarkably well kept and though I had the feeling they were stolen, they looked to be cleaned almost daily.

"Oh you know, just running around, stretching our legs. Trying to keep these clowns busy, you know what dad used to say: 'ideal hands,' and all that good shit. The community has gotten a little bit overcrowded these days. We come out here to stretch and ride around," Bipin stated, pointing over the forest line that lead to where the camp used to be. I glanced at Huey. He was looking at Bipin's brothers and sisters as they started packing various different things into the compartments on the sides of their bikes, when he caught my glance.

Huey and I had decided that everything Tir and Bug had said was on some level most likely a lie. The thing we had to figure out was what were they lying about.

I looked at Bipin. His face was lightly marked with some acne and early signs of facial hair. I had trusted his father many years ago. I couldn't be sure if I could trust his son, though. A lot wasn't adding up. How were they still here? There were a lot of other questions that I needed to have answers to. Instead, I went with the simple approach: "Speaking of the community, Bipin—how are you guys still here?"

Bipin's face darkened for the briefest of moments. "I won't lie to you, Avi, but before I answer anything, can you be honest with me for a moment?" he asked.

I nodded. I knew this question was going to come up the moment I saw him turn from a wolf back to a young man.

"Shoot," I stated.

"Was it you that told the police where we were?" Bipin asked abruptly with a tone that was beyond the years of what he seemed to be. Everyone stopped what they were doing and looked at the two of us.

I sucked in a deep breath. "I had no other choice. Yeah, it was me, Bipin," I stated, feeling shameful standing in front of the boy whose father died directly because of my actions.

Bipin slowly nodded. "Yeah, dad would have said the same thing, regardless of what happened. He always liked you, Avi, not sure if you knew that. The way he saw it, you were the closest thing to our mother," Bipin stated.

That hit hard. Their mom had been able to turn into a wolf as well, but for some reason, her body just seemed to age decades in just a few years. Whatever was used to turn the others just didn't seem to work with her. She passed shortly after having Elder Ad's six pups—as he called them. "Your father was a good man. I never meant—" I started before Bipin held up a hand.

"It's in the past, Avi. Shit happens and then you move on. Just tell me why you did it? I was never as stuck on the absolute loyalty mentality that is in the community. Especially lately." He trailed off, looking at one of his brothers who had cut his hair to shoulder length, and spat when Bipin looked his way.

I took a deep breath, trying to keep calm like Huey and I had said the other night, when we discussed how we would handle the interactions once we got to the community. The plan was simple enough—find out where Dr. Joachim was, then find him and take him to jail. Let the police sort out what was happening, put in an end to the whole matter. Though part of me, the part of me that wasn't the wolf, disagreed with that plan. I wanted to devour that monster, for everything that he had done. The throwing in jail part hadn't been completely worked out either, but one step at a time.

I looked at Bipin. His face was young, lines sculpted to a charming and reliable face that suggested integrity without him having to speak. I wondered if my face had ever looked that way. I'd never considered myself to be dependable, even back then. It was hard—floating between every interaction like it was a dream and not actual reality. Most of the time, I felt as though I was a beaten piece of meat hanging from a hook that was completely forgotten about. I took a breath, shaking the sound of electricity snapping out of my ears. *I wasn't reaching through the fence again for Linor, I was back to a place I used to call home, trying to accomplish a mission. Keep grounded—stay in the moment,* I whispered to the hole inside my head.

"Bipin, how are you guys still here? The police raided this place. There's no way you guys could have made it after all these years. How are you still here?" I asked Bipin, walking toward the young man.

Bipin smiled, a crooked smile, turning his head to one of his brothers. "Tivian, get the tarps back out. Start covering this truck," he stated.

I looked at Bipin, perplexed by his plan, when he answered my thoughts. "You two are going to want to come and see this—no other way to explain this. Hop on our bikes. Every car in this town is completely known and tracked."

I nodded, the feeling in my stomach becoming worse, in too many ways that made me feel cold. The thought that someone knew all the cars and trucks in town—what was going on here?

49

Chapter 49

"Have you ever tried a yeti-burger, Avi? They're pretty good. They put an egg on top of the patty. Who would have thought that?" Bipin said to my ear, chomping down on a bag of pretzels. We were up on a roof across from the main police station in town, hunched over in the shade of the overhang. Huey lay flat on the hot roof, sweating bullets. I knew what he was thinking: a pair of crooks on a roof right across from a police station. No one can stay hidden forever, at least not if around other people.

"Can't say that I have. Haven't gotten into the burger craze just yet—I honestly miss some of the old stews—nothing like that good ol' Slavic cooking," I mumbled, trying to peer over the edges of the roof to the police station. I was scooted too far back from the edge to get a good look. My fear of heights would never change, but at least this time I only peed my pants once on the climb up here. In the distance, I could hear the loud roar of Bipin's brothers and sisters, cranking the engines on their motorcycles. The plan was for them to ride around, causing as much noise as possible, until the police came out to deal with it. We had been waiting on the scorching roof for about ten minutes. I was closer to getting a sunburn than having my questions answered at this rate.

I hated waiting around, but I kept the conversation going. "What about you, Huey, try anything good lately?" I asked him, keeping my eyes fixed on the doors of station.

"Anything tastes better than the crap we had inside. Besides, white people just don't have any good taste in their burgers. What kind of person doesn't put chili on their burger?" he stated.

"Good point—good chili takes time to make. You have to—" I started to say when the doors to the station finally opened. Out stepped Sophia. Her hair had been cut to ear length and blazed cooper brown in the hot sun. Her deep-set eyes were lidded with stress. Her being someone who had seen far more than they should have at her age was apparent. Like a hawk that was on constant lookout for other hooded killing machines.

She never had that look before, when we were younger, despite all of us having suffered through the camps. For the most part, none of us held the look of someone about to have their meal snatched away at any moment. Life was cold. I pulled my jacket a little tighter around me as I watched Sophia interact with the police. The sound of the motorcycles in the distance obscured their words—I did make out a few, though. "Yes ma'am, we will shut them down right away." One of the officers threw her a salute. Salutes, for a Gypsy Holocaust survivor? Now I had seen everything.

"Worry more about keeping the channels open for tonight's ceremony, sergeant." Sophia stared in the direction of Bipin's siblings, cupping her hands over the high sun. I ducked down when she swept her face back in the direction of the sergeant. The muffle of the massive engines circled back toward our location. That was the sign the police were giving chase to Bipin's family.

I looked back at Sophia when she had walked off. What ceremony was she talking about? Keep the channels open? Did she mean the police radio? If that was so, what was going on? Bipin taking me here to the station had left more questions than answers. I turned my head toward Bipin once the police had left the front of the building, "Bipin, we need to talk—can we get out of here?" I asked him, still whispering as the engines faded into the distance.

"Yeah, Avi, I figured you would ask that. Just needed you to see for yourself before I told you the next part," he stated. A nervous look played across his young brows, pulling his eyebrows in like they were balls of yarn that could be bundled in any direction.

I shot Huey a look. Huey nodded and begin to shimmy his way to the ladder we used to climb up the building. Bipin did the same and I followed suit. As I crawled down the ladder, beads of sweat rolled off my body. *Just look up, you scaredy cat,* I told myself as I descended to the lower ground. I made it, five pounds lighter from water loss, but in one piece. Huey held out a blue jacket and hat, and I took them, ditching my overcoat into a dumpster near the building we had climbed.

We were used to carrying around multiple pairs of clothes at this point. The only way to stay free is to never think you're free. That's what years on the run had taught me: you're only free as long as you can avoid the chains. Expect at any turn to be right back in the cage. The caged bird sings songs of freedom in hopes that one day it will be free. What the caged bird doesn't know, though, is that the world is one giant cage. *Sing away, pretty bird, you will never be free.*

We both quickly changed, donning our hats and following Bipin back to where we had parked the bike about a mile down the road. We found Bipin's bike behind a gas station that I didn't remember being on this street. In fact, as I looked around at the high-rise brick structures around me, even the skyscrapers in the distance, most of it was new. How much had things changed? I thought as Tivian, one of Bipin's sisters, pulled up beside us. "We lost them about a quarter of a mile back. They don't seem to be in the chasing mood—it's no fun anymore," she said, her voice ringing on every word. She cocked an eyebrow at Huey. Huey dipped his hat and I could have sworn I saw a dark man blush.

I patted him on the back as I came around to the back of Bipin's motorcycle. "Too young for you pal," I stated. Huey's eyes went wide as I slid behind Bipin and he kicked the engine to a roaring thunder. "Besides, you have that one lispy woman with weird hair back home," I joked.

Huey looked confused for a moment, "You mean Anna? She doesn't have a lisp, you skinny little—" Huey started.

Bipin punched his bike and we took off down the road. I held tight to the handlebars on the bike. Cars were one thing; bikes made me feel like I was a nuke waiting to be delivered to an unsuspecting city. "Happy thoughts, Avi. Happy thoughts. Drive slower!" I shouted as we peeled off onto a long black road in the golden sun.

50

Chapter 50

We were back at our truck, no worse for the wear, though Bipin had to change his shirt from the amount of sweat I had produced while we travelled. The whole time, the tarred road flew by like an endless river of murky pain full of creatures waiting to devour me with their teeth and bring the wolf out. I wiped my hands down and shook Bipin's hands once I got off the bike. Bipin killed the engine. I turned just in time to see Huey and Tivian come screaming down the road. She lifted the front of the bike high in the air, cruising with just her back wheel at speeds that made my heart pound just watching. I could hear both of them laughing over the sound of the engine. *Well at least one of us is having fun today.*

Tivian killed the engine and Huey hoped off, grinning ear to ear. "That was amazing," he exclaimed.

She smiled at my friend. "Anytime," she beamed back and gunned her bike down the road, disappearing at the edges of the woods like a flock of birds hightailing it south for the winter. Huey walked up to the two of us, still grinning when I stared him down. He wiped his smile, taking on the usual stoic calm that he always held.

I rolled my eyes, turning back to Bipin. "So, care to explain what we just saw?" I asked him, crossing my arms, leaning against the truck.

"This isn't going to be easy to say, Avi, but basically your brother has taken over," Bipin stated, with a frown and an uneasy look that borderlined fear.

I caught his look. "Bipin—" I said.

He held up a hand. "Relax—it's not like I am shitting my pants right now. Man, you have no idea the level of—I don't even have words for it, Avi. He's strong, very strong. I think even stronger than your wolf," he whispered.

Zevi was strong no doubt, but the wolf—that was a monster from hell. I gave Bipin a sad smile. "I wish that were so, Bipin. You never got to see the beast. Nor your father nor even my brother. Trust me when I say this—nothing is stronger than the wolf," I stated.

Bipin didn't look convinced. "I don't know, Avi, you're strong and all—just what he can do. It's not just strength; people are drawn to him. He is something else. It's hard enough for me keeping track of my knuckle-headed siblings. Trust me, if he gets talking to you, he could convince you that a fat man shimmies down your chimney once a year, and I ain't talking about your woman," Bipin gestured, crossing his arms as well, leaning against his bike.

"That doesn't answer how he controls the town, just that he might be a problem," Huey stated, moving toward Bipin.

"Trust me, guys, you don't want any of him. Look, my father left me to take care of the community, to take care of my siblings. When the police came, and boy did they ever come in force—we were still packing and trying to get out of Dodge. Your brother, though—he was a genuine demon. Combined with the other eight—the police got wiped out pretty quickly," he told us.

At the mention of the eight, my heart sank. In a small way, part of me wanted to know that Linor had gotten away. Surely she wasn't still in the community. Old grandmother or not, Linor was way too wild—too free. She was a songbird singing like the caged bird to be free. That was the Linor I remembered.

I shook my head. That flame was a long time ago, though it still burned in some part of my heart—but she had walked away from me at the end. Keep on walking; the story of my life. "Okay, so my brother and the others beat a bunch of bluesuiters. That doesn't explain how they didn't come back with the army, or how you're in this town still! I mean come on, Bipin. The town wanted us gone for way less than killing a police officer. What gives? Trust me, I am not here to get you in trouble," I stated.

Bipin glanced nervously around him, then at the truck. "No offense, Avi. My dad may have loved you like a seventh son, but my father is dead and gone now. I have to look after my siblings. I don't mind telling you—but let's just do this some place a bit less green." He contemplated, looking around again as if something was watching us. I quickly scanned the field. The forest line was hundreds of feet away, and all that was around us was the tall, green summer stalks of hay.

"Oh—yeah—Huey, let's take this conversation into the truck," I suggested as Bipin nodded and made his way to the truck. "It's a two seater, Avi," Huey stated.

"Well, don't anyone cut a fart."

51

Chapter 51

We were cramped in the front compartment of the truck, Bipin between the two of us. "Why do I have to sit middle? Avi, you screamed like a big baby on the back of my motorcycle," he jabbed.

I sighed. "First of all, I didn't scream, you just drive like a maniac. Second, this is my damn truck, and third, shut the hell up, kid!" I shot back, growling. Huey covered his mouth as a small laugh escaped. I debated letting the beast out, right then and there—maybe I could make an exception just this once.

Huey coughed. "As much as I like being next to two werewolves, can we get this over already?" he asked.

I looked at Huey—as far as I knew, he had never seen anything super-natural. For the most part, he was just some felon philosopher with some outrageous fighting skills. He took a lot of this in his stride. I would have to ask him about that later if he thought any of it was real or not.

"Oh yeah, my bad. Anyways, the thing is, guys—I mean, Avi. Your brother somehow convinced the police to not only stay away, but within a few weeks, he had the whole department looking the other way! It was crazy. He took control of the camp that night—Avi, seriously, something is wrong with that guy. He wore that damn creepy sack over his head. Anyone, I mean anyone who questioned him... well, let's just say you don't question him. If he knew you were even here, if he knew I had shown you what I had shown you, he would kill me and my siblings," Bipin whimpered, a slight quiver to his voice. Bipin may have been a kid, but he wasn't a liar. I've seen fear more than I ever wanted to see in my life; fear is the one emotion that breaks anyone down to below even animals. It snatches you like a current in a river, pulling you to the depths and drowning you in pure horror that leaves you trembling in your deepest misgivings. I was terrified of heights, terrified of anything that would bring out—*him*. Yet, when I had taken that knife to my wrist, all those years ago, I left the emotion of fear behind. Jitters and doubt plagued me at every turn. Something needed to be done. I had to do it, no matter how much faintheartedness I felt in that moment.

I had come because of what Tir and Bug had told me—it wasn't just that they had supposedly found Dr. Joachim. I still had my doubts on that actually being true and I had at the very least mixed feelings on the subject. But Zevi was my brother, and if he was in trouble I had to help him. Whatever was going on, I would have to sort out. Things were different now. I was far more reasonable then when I had been a teenager, and Zevi would be the same way. Though Bipin's story did give me pause. Zevi wasn't that crazy—why would he take over the town? It served no purpose.

I nodded at Bipin, trying to put him at ease. "Where is this ceremony taking place? Who's going to be there?" I asked him in the tight confines of the truck.

Bipin hesitated again, looking out at the fields. "Promise me, Avi, that you won't drag the others into this. Like I said, it's not just my siblings I have to take care of now. And the last time—no offense, things didn't go so well when you tried to help," he admitted, trailing his words off at the end.

He was right, though. That was the bitter part of doing what was right. Sometimes, things ended up worse than if you did nothing at all. Bipin looked a lot like his father in that moment, calm eyes set in weathered skin. "I promise, Bipin, that whatever is going on will stay between my brother and me," I swore, meaning every word. This time I would deal with my brother once and for all.

Bipin tilted his head toward me. "Okay. Well, first off, I don't know where the ceremony is taking place. They have these things from time to time all over town, and hundreds if not thousands of people show up. I mean seriously, it's nuts loud music and you can smell the weed burning for miles in the air. I've forbidden any of my brothers or sisters from going—I don't trust seeing a group of people dressed in all black and masks. Doesn't matter who or what they're selling, people shouldn't go around shouting in black and swinging bats and expect to not frighten people. Regardless—everyone will be there; I mean everyone, no matter what race or creed, man. It's a strange thing: they all come for miles to see the 'Prophet Zevi.' Really, if you ask me, it's just desperate people looking for answers in a person. Like dad always said, 'Look for the answers within, not in other people—people pee on people,'" Bipin told us.

"I like your dad," interjected Huey.

"Me too," Bipin replied, somberly.

"So, my brother is leading some kind of small group, and people are calling him a prophet?" I questioned, not believing the absurdity of Bipin's story. I still remember the chubby red head who could barely sweep the floor of our father's watch store. Sure, as we got older, we had drifted apart and Zevi was getting a little too big for his britches. We had been taught better, though.

"It's not a small group, Avi, I am telling you," Bipin almost pleaded with me. I stared out the windshield, looking at the field around us. Many years ago, we used this field to race through on the way to town—it held so many memories. How had things gotten to this point? We were a couple of stupid kids, sure, and we were actively hunting down those pathetic pieces of human garbage, but we weren't killing them. Before we found that American, we just—well, we beat them within an inch of their lives, then destroyed everything we could find of theirs. I wasn't proud of that; they were still alive. Then came that night—everything changed. In my heart of hearts, it had felt so wrong. We were avengers, not killers. But maybe that was where we had gone wrong in the first place. Maybe we shouldn't have sought those who had harmed us in the first place.

Prey stays prey when you let the predators wound you with no return, hissed the beast from deep within. I shook. Two years since I had last heard from him. He had gone silent and in all this time, I had almost led myself to believe he was gone—almost. Everything felt wrong, everything shook and my heart; there was this aching pain, a muddy river running dirty and wild, pushing the limits of the chambers of my soul. I shook my head venomously—there would be a time to address all of this later. Focus on the work, Avi. That was how you stayed here, that was how you stayed away from—

"Avi," Huey said sternly and I turned toward my friend. My knuckles had gripped the steering wheel so tight that they had turned the shade of a red tomato. Bipin was looking at me in wide-eyed terror, having moved what little distance he could away from me.

I took a deep breath before speaking. "Bipin, can you find out where this ceremony is?" I asked, catching my breath between each word as I looked down at the floor in shame.

"Sure, Avi. I can do that. There's some people that like to stay more aware than I do about what your brother is doing. You know how it is in the community; everyone knows everything except for—"

"Except for who stole the bikes," I smiled at Bipin, fondly remembering how closed-off the community really was. Yet the community always seemed to know what was going on in the greater world. Faster than the radio, faster than a steaming jet—talk within a Gypsy camp flew quicker than light. "Thanks, Bipin. Wait; is there anyone that you can trust, I mean, any of the others?"

Bipin scratched his chin for a moment, perplexed. "You know actually, yeah, I know one or two that haven't completely lost their marbles. But I am telling you, Avi, if word gets out that I told you any of this—we are dead men. Your brother—he hates Nazis. The stories I've heard, man... I think the meat packaging industry is a playground by comparison. The one thing he hates more, though, it's you, Avi. I mean he really hates you, worse than a dog chasing off the milkman."

In a way, part of me had hoped that Zevi had time to cool down all these years, to maybe come around to my point of view. It was still possible, I thought, a slim chance. *I should have dealt with Zevi a long time ago,* a cold wind whispered along my spine. *He is a festering beast, waiting to devour you. Only a fool would try and see differently,* growled the wolf. I didn't argue back. I wasn't entirely sure if that was possible or not. Everything seemed to choke on its way to anything that resembled a thought.

I opted for a small frown and remained quiet as Bipin went on, "You probably won't like who I have in mind," he stated.

"Get it out already, Bipin."

"Okay, but seriously, I think she's the only one."

"Bipin, if you're choosing this moment to fuck with me..."

"I'm not! It's just that, well Solly's a bit of a character," he said.

She wouldn't still be here if things were that bad. "Is Long Jimmy still going out on his benders?" I asked.

"I think so. I mean Jimmy is Jimmy, you know? If he's not drunk, he's trying to get drunk. These days he stays with Nanda Three-ears, you remember her?" Bipin gestured by his throat and I thought for a long moment about anyone that matched that description. "Doesn't matter, I guess. Anyways, Jimmy spends most of his time talking to her these days and isn't home much," Bipin explained.

"Okay, good. Tell Solly to meet there at nightfall, for us please, Bipin," I directed him.

He nodded slowly, sucking his teeth. "Yeah I can do that Avi. Only because, I don't know, man. My father was the best at talking, you know? He could sell water to fish," he stated.

"Only your father was never trying to sell anything," I replied.

Bipin nodded. "I just don't want to wake up one morning to find out that one of my brothers or sisters has ended up with those all black wearing weirdos and somehow gotten killed in the process. I am their protector. I am the eldest, you know?" Bipin asked.

I choked on my reply to a kid. Instead, I gave him a head tilt to avoid prolonging the conversation.

"I will tell her, I promise. Avi, try coming into the community if you get the chance—not everyone hates you. Just please be careful. I don't—"

"I promise, Bipin, this is between my brother and me."

He gave his sad smile again, turning toward Huey, "Nice meeting you, man."

"Likewise, kid," Huey replied.

"Stay away from my sister," Bipin remarked as Huey rolled his eyes, getting out of the front of the truck, opening the door. Bipin, slid past him, taking one last look at the two of us before heading to his bike. Huey waited until Bipin had made it down the street before speaking finally.

"Does any of that—at all raise an alarm to you? Because, brother, things don't sound good at all," he stated matter-of-factly.

"A lot of what he said bothered me, especially all the stuff about Zevi. Look, man—my people are—at the very least, dangerous. Are you sure you want to get involved in this?" I asked Huey.

He looked away for a moment before speaking. "We came all this way. Might as well see the end of it. Besides—a bunch of similar-dressed people in masks? Sounds like an army to me if I ever heard one. Not to mention the other stuff—that kid looked like he was about to piss his pants at the mention of your brother's name. To have that tight of a grip on anywhere, he must be one bad motherfucker," Huey stated.

"I agree."

"So what are you going to do about it?" he asked.

"I don't know—I think I am going to have a chat with him."

"What are you going to do about the doctor?"

"That's a whole other issue—I didn't think to bring it up. I have a feeling Linor would know," I replied.

"Linor—been a long time for you two. Going to be able to handle it?" he asked.

"Jesus, man, that was like fifteen years ago. I've moved on to greener pastures," I replied.

"You live in a trailer in the middle of the desert with another man. I think she's the one that probably has moved on by now or is, at the very least, in greener pastures," he stated.

"Ouch, sharp words, Huey."

"Don't be a baby—you need to hear this. Look, you turned in this community because of a hint of violence. To control the police—I won't say it, you know how powerful you would have to be to do that. Now we are back here on the word of two men you haven't seen in almost two decades, when we ourselves are wanted criminals. I am ride or die with you at this point, man—just I am feeling like we are getting deep already into something that we don't understand. Family or not, time separates us. We don't belong here," Huey declared.

I snarled, "They're my family, Huey!"

"Easy, man. I am just calling it as a friend. Besides, do you even know if you can trust what that kid said? he asked.

Huey made a good point—why would Bipin have shown us the police station otherwise? He had to have known that was the only way a couple of crooks would trust that the entire police force was bought off. Some cops are dirty—some ditches have trash. That was just a thing, not a wide statistic. What my gut was telling me was to not assume anything at the present moment. I looked at my friend. "I think we will know once we talk to Solly. For now, though, want to go into the camp for a bit?" I asked him.

"You think that is a good idea? We will stick out like a sore thumb there," he said.

"Gypsy camps are made of one underlying truth besides tent poles. They are a place for people that don't want to be found and want to stay that way. Us sneaking and hiding around will be a far better cover than anything else we can do," I replied, jamming my hands into my coat pocket as the day's events settled into my mind. It was like a big meal that was quickly taking up the room of everything else within.

Huey acknowledged with a grunt. I appreciated that about Huey; he knew enough about people to not push certain subjects beyond a certain point. Moreover, he would only do something if he thought the outcome wasn't going to be the two of us ending up in a body bag.

"Avi, say we find your brother, and he's as bad as the kid was saying. What then?" Huey questioned me.

"He's my brother," I stated.

Huey shook his head. "Why didn't you ask the kid about Linor if you trusted him? Don't bullshit me. I think you do view these people as your family. She's missing, and you still care. Otherwise you wouldn't have that sad ass look in your eyes," he stated.

I narrowed my eyes at him, sighing heavily. "Linor and I ran away all the time as kids—she had plenty of chances to leave. Why would she leave now? I sense something uneasy about all of this and if my brother is truly in danger and Linor is missing, I can only speculate that something deeper is going on. Zevi could have bitten off more than he could chew. He was a cocky little prick when I last seen him. I didn't ask Bipin, because I have my doubts he knows. Solly will know—if anyone knows at all, it will be her. Not to mention, you saw how shook up he was? The less he is involved the better. That answer all your questions, Huey?" I asked him, looking out at the field.

"I don't know if that is the best play here," he said.

"We don't have any other option here, Huey. Feel free to suggest anything you want."

52

Chapter 52

My mother once told me after she found me sneaking around the house, trying to get out early to play baseball, before my chores were complete, that only children rolled around in the dirt and it wouldn't help me become a man by skipping out on my work nearly every day. Where I disagreed with my mother was that only children rolled around in the dirt.

Huey and I had taken to the forest line, hugging the creek bed. We passed the location of where we had built a dam as kids. Green moss and algae had grown over the rocks we placed there, giving the dam an impression of looking like a small mountain that had formed in the middle of the valley—the green on the wet stones, swaying like fingers in the breeze, the stone smooth and lining clear trails through the miniature green forest.

We made it to the forest line. The woods had been remarkably well kept, to our disadvantage though—hard to sneak when you had nothing to hide behind. The woods here were only tall, long dark fingers reaching to the sky, but thin like tadpoles.

"Well—I never thought I would see you again, Avi, acting the maggot in the middle of these parts again," Solly joked from somewhere behind us. My blood froze. We hadn't even made it a hundred yards into the woods and we had been discovered. What was the point of having wolf powers and a veteran, just to get caught with our pants down at every turn?

"Now, the two of you turn around slowly. Keep yours hands high," Solly directed as we heard the familiar click of a bullet being chambered. We both turned around, still hunched near the trees. Solly's orange peel hair came into view only a few yards behind us. How in the blazes had she snuck up on us? She hadn't been here before we entered; I would have caught her a mile away daylight or not. Solly was now much taller and filled out in the ways that most models could only dream of being. She had the long perky nose of a redhead, but the angular cheeks of an elf. Hair that fell almost to her feet, punctuated by a neverending series of swirls, flowers, Nordic signs and shields tattooed over every exposed inch of her skin, save for her face.

"Wow, Solly, you finally let someone tattoo you, huh?" I asked raising my hands into the air.

"Did them myself, mate—impressive, right? I will cut you a discount after I shoot you full of some lead. You and that fine thing of a fella over there. I'm Solly," she flirted.

"Name is Huey," my friend said flatly—Huey had a hardline stance against using guns. I think it doubled when one was pointed at him.

"Nice to see you in this neck of the woods, Avi. Since when could you grow facial hair? That's a laugh. Wud ya get outta that garden!" Solly lifted one hand in the air, swirling it around above her head.

Both Huey and I kept our hands raised, not sure what was going on. Solly sighed, "Okay, not my best joke. Both of you, take a quick gander in here." She pointed toward the end of her rifle, the barrel seeming like a small black hole, when I looked down the muzzle. "Now—I don't really feel like shooting you two, I don't really feel like wasting any shells either. I would rather go home, pop over to your gaff later, and get completely flustered. So, in plain and simple language, tell me why I shouldn't shoot you right here and now, wolf?" she asked, putting her free hand back on the rifle, swaying the gun to my chest height. I had my doubts she would miss from only a few yards.

"For one, Solly, if I remember correctly, you couldn't hit the broad side of a barn when we were kids," I stated.

Solly responded by pointing her gun in the air, sending a loud boom into the quiet woods when she pulled the trigger. "We were using slingshots as kids, Avi. Don't think I am going to miss your big head from this far away."

"Good point—" I whispered.

"Avi," Huey whispered back.

"I got this, Huey. Alright, I will cut the bullshit. I came back—I came back to apologize." My heart shredded in that moment, not only because it was a lie, but because I wish it had been the real reason. Out of all the things that haunted me the most in my life, from the beatings, to the loss of so many people close to me, what got me the most were the things I failed to do. The things I wish I had done differently. I had already felt the debt of my life once it rolled out of my mouth. Lying was a simple thing—one that goose-stepped us into believing even our own tales that we spin. An endless yarn ball that is continuously rolling on and on, until it hits other balls and grows too heavy for even the Earth. That's the thing about a lie; it is predicated on the belief on some scale that we do it for survival. It's the other defense mechanism that came along with when we developed conciseness. We lie to get what we want, which is to survive, in whatever shape that takes. Only thing, though, we pay the price of the lie—the moment we forget what the price is, we've truly lost ourselves in a culture of make-believe.

Solly curled her red lips in, in a way that alone was enough to make my heart race. She was a truly beautiful woman, despite holding a gun that could easily take out Huey and me. "Really—Avi? Fifteen years and you're here now, to apologize after being caught sneaking in the woods. Come on, if you're going to try and give me a one-over, at least take me to dinner first before you tell me sweet little lies," she jabbed, pulling back the slide on her rifle.

"I mean it, Solly. I am here to apologize. If you had been in my shoes, would you have gone through the front door of the camp and announced, 'Hey?'" I asked her, my hands still in the air, my heart racing to reach higher than my hands would go.

I could see her face pausing to mull over my words. Solly wasn't stupid, she was also one of the few people in the camp that I thought wasn't that bad. She had never called me Numberless like the rest—but she also made it a point to only communicate with me when the others were around.

She finished deliberating with me, taking a deep breath, her alluring eyes traced me in the evening light. "You make a good point. Going through the front probably would have gotten you shot, to be honest. Avi, let me be right between the eyes with you. You weren't liked much before you sold us out. Now—I mean a certain German with a short mustache is only a few notches lower than you—do you understand? I don't understand you, Avi. You bought yourself a few more seconds. Now, please—stop stirring my pot and out with it already."

I gulped in some air, looking for an answer to her question when Huey spoke up, "Look lady, I don't really give a fuck what this nitwit did to you fifteen years ago. What's done is done," Huey stated.

"Hey now," I said.

"Shut up, Avi. What's done is, done. We are here because a hippie and some kind of strange, pasty, gray-skinned man showed up at our door in the middle of nowhere, claiming this moron next to me has family in trouble. That's the truth. If you have a problem with that, shoot us or do whatever it is you have planned. Frankly—stop wasting my Saturday. I didn't drive all the way out here to have a gun pointed at me by some ginger," he said flatly.

Solly blinked, then laughed, keeping the rifle pointed our ways. "He's an honest fella, unlike you, Avi. What gives? Is he telling the truth? You're here for your brother? You're here to help... him?" she asked, her voice dipping on the last question. With Tir and Bug, their story had felt like it had been rehearsed several dozen times before speaking to us. Solly asked her question almost like Bipin had, with a slight amount of fear in her voice—she was completely unsure. The fact that she hadn't shot me yet told me she was afraid of something far worse than a scared boy returning fifteen years later.

"If I am lying, I am dying, Solly. What he is saying is true, except for the moron part. Otherwise, yes. What is going on? Why did they contact me

after all this time and what is my brother doing out here? Where is Linor?"
I asked her.

She hesitated for a moment, finally lowering her rifle to her shoulder.
"Well paint my tits red and pull my hair. Fine. There's all kinds of strange
folks poking around these parts and we never know if it's not one of Zevi's
'Enlightened' come out here to cause trouble," Solly said, gesturing the
two of us to stand up.

"Enlighted?" I asked, confused by what she meant.

"Your brother has started some kind of cult, all black-wearing thugs
who claim to know the meaning of all this great clusterfuck that we call
existence."

I nodded, still trying to piece together how the two of us hadn't been shot.
It wasn't the first time I had skidded by my life from death, and probably
wouldn't be the last. "Tell us everything, Solly, please. We need answers,"
I asked her, stepping in her direction. She raised her gun slightly as I
approached and I stopped. "Please," I pleaded with her.

Uncertainty played across her face before she took a deep breath.
"Alright, alright, keep your knickers on. I can only give my part of the
story. Let's just say it didn't stop with that one unlucky chap from a few
years ago. We started out by beating up Nazis—remember that, Avi?" she
stated.

"Yeah—I remember," I responded.

"Well, it went beyond that after we killed that man. I wish that had been
the only one," she started to tell the two of us, in the green woods, a metal
mill looming in the distance, a rocky hill leading to an old home. Three
strangers meeting in the woods as the sun crest the afternoon sky, light
flowering out around us through the leaves, like spider webs forming over
the world.

53

Chapter 53

"Full disclosure: I am here because Bipin sent me out this way—honestly, you wanted me to meet you outside of Long Jimmy's place? With that big-ass jackass in the middle of the field? How romantic. Be honest with me, Avi. Why are you here? I'm not talking about what your friend told me. I have to know what would compel you to return," she asked as the three of us sat around a small fire in the woods. Even though it was still daytime, the fall in Washington could be clear as day—and brutally cold. I shuffled my hands in the pockets of my jacket. "I have a feeling it's not because you care about our community and you never had a taste for revenge, it seems. I could be wrong though," Solly said skeptically, eyeing me from across the fire. Her rifle lay across her lap.

"Those two knuckle heads said my family was in danger. This place, it may have been my home, but my community kicked me out, remember? I never forgot about my community. I won't do it now. Where is she, Solly?" I questioned her, meeting her gaze over the fire.

"Sounds like your family is still with a woman. That's sweet, Avi. Things change though, you have to see that. I don't know if you really are back for your family or not. I would believe it if you told me you were back for her. You were lovesick the moment you saw her at that fence line and shocked your little hands. I don't know where she is, Avi. I can tell you something though—she's been with your brother," she stated, pausing for me to reply.

I took her words in and tried to process them the best I could before speaking, "What do you mean, with my brother?" I asked, perplexed by that very idea.

"A lot happened when you were gone Avi. Things changed—people changed. Linor has been with your brother for a few years now," she finished.

Hearing that didn't erupt me in flames, nor make me feel compelled to attack Solly. Instead it was like a pebble being dropped into the ocean because it was not a pearl.

It's a bitter pill we all have to come to terms with at some point in our life, that someone we once loved has moved on. The bitter part is failing to realize that they had always been changing, as have you, and you just didn't realize it before they did. I took that pain and stuck it in somewhere deep inside me—there would be a time in a place to sulk and be broken later. Regardless, she was still missing, and my brother was in danger, that was the important part here. Not teenage fantasies.

Instead, I spoke to Solly, remaining calm despite the wound that was opening up. "It doesn't change anything, Solly—you guys are family. Zevi is still my—my brother. What do you know about Linor being gone?" I asked her, my voice unsure and weak as it carried across the small fire toward her.

"Gone? Where did she go? I mean, it's been a few days, but you know how Linor is. She just sort of wanders off sometimes. I figured she was just collecting one thing or another like always," Solly said, concern written over her face.

I knew in that instant that Tir and Bug had only told me that as a way to get me to come here. So, we were being played—played hard. Why though? Why go through all the trouble of tracking me down and then lure me out here? "I don't know. That's just what Tir and Bug told us. Solly, do you know where my brother is having his gathering tonight?" I asked her.

Solly looked perplexed for a moment before it dawned on her why I was asking. "No—why would you care to go? Oh—you mean to go check it out for yourself? I don't, Avi—I mean, I know where they usually have them at, but that's crazy. Your brother is—"

I held up my hand. "I am my brother's keeper. If he is in trouble, I have to go see him. If he is causing the trouble—I have to see him. Do you understand what I mean?" I stated, looking at Solly—unmoving and tense, despite the cold chill running up my back.

"Yeah I understand, Avi. I just think it's a stupid idea. If you're serious, you can't just walk in there all John Wayne-like." She replied to my stare with a fierce one of her own.

I looked at Huey, turning back to Solly. "Why not?"

"Are you that dense? If you said that Tiresias and Bug came all the way to see you, wherever it is that you've been hiding all these years, just to give you a cryptic lie that something isn't brewing? Come on, Avi, I thought you were always a little weird, but never stupid."

I sucked in my lips as my reply, and came close to shooting out before Huey said, "She's right, Avi. For all we know that Bug and hippie Tir fellow might actually be the ones putting your brother in danger."

Solly nodded. "I doubt that though. Tir and Bug are part of his crew—they're in deep. A few years back, the community had some... let's just say... disagreements with your brother—" she started to say.

I interrupted her. "Disagreements?"

She nodded again. "Your brother, he took over pretty fast after that night, Avi. In some small way, some of us, myself and a few others, thought you were right. Killing Nazis is one thing, but killing some middle-aged man who was probably asleep in his bed before we woke him up like some kind of hanging chicken from a meat hook..."

I bowed my head at the memory. We had seen so many people die, so many of us die like animals starved out or beaten to death. Engulfed in flames like a candlestick poured into oil, gassed like some kind of rodent. Yet, when it comes to taking another person's life—to cross that line is a point of no return.

Nodding my head slowly, I spoke up. "Solly, help me, help us. I can't change what happened in the past. I am here now though. I want to help my family this time, before it's too late. Zevi is my brother; he will listen to me, no matter what he's done," I stated.

"Avi, you have no idea what he's done. After he took over the community, he went full-on medieval, on anyone that dared to cross him. I have no idea how he was able to stop the police from blasting us into oblivion, but he did. We were all so grateful for him, then he started to get the younger kids going, you know? Got them cheering for him like he was the fucking Jewish superman. Then, it got worse. Pretty soon those petty little crimes we did escalated, you know? He started finding a whole lot more of the folks from that good ol' place we used to stay in. Wiped them all out, like toilet paper. It was brutal Avi, brutal. When it spilled over into the community and outsiders started showing up—well, that was the end of us as we knew it. Your brother did what everyone does when they get power: refused to give it up. It was never enough for him, and people in the community got hurt, Avi. People got taken away. That's why Bipin is so protective: he lost one of his brothers to Zevi's army," she told the two of us as the fire crackled into the darkening day.

"He is a monster, Avi. Anyone who follows him—isn't much better..." she trailed off, not meeting my gaze. I had no idea if what she was saying was true, if any of what had been relayed to me in the last couple of days was true or not. Was it better to assume to the worst here? Cast my family aside and admit that Linor was gone, that Zevi was gone? But there was no going back, no time machine to undo what had caused this with Zevi. He was my brother, and I am his keeper.

"I have to try Solly. We need your help. I don't know if what you're saying is true, take no offense in this, but I hope you're wrong. You and I have never talked about this—in fact, I never mentioned it to anyone outside of Linor. But the names you guys used to call me as a kid, the 'wolf?' It's true," I whispered.

Solly flushed red. "Avi, kids can be cruel. You aren't—"

I held up a hand to her. "What's done is done. There is a monster inside of me; it claws and bites at the edges of my heart every moment of my life. Even now, it would kill everyone here, the community over that hill, the whole city, before it was satisfied. It cannot be controlled. My brother, I don't know if he knows the full extent of what he is dealing with, that's why I do not believe he called me back for the wolf. I don't know what Zevi wants, I don't even know if he is in any kind of danger. It sounds like this army of 'Enlightened' you're talking about is pretty dangerous to the community. Maybe that is why Tir came. Maybe it isn't. I won't know until I speak to my brother. Will you help me? Will you help someone that has let you down, Solly?" I asked her as the wind put out the smoldering fire.

She was quiet for a long moment in the darkness before speaking. "Yeah, Avi, I can fucking help you. Just know we need a better plan. And a costume for you. Both of you."

54

Chapter 54

A Gypsy community is like any other community, if only in the sense that it has people gathered within it. That's about the only similarity you will find. Fifteen years later, the community was still abuzz with smells and strange sights. It was the start of fall. Every tree was covered in bottles, hanging from the limbs. As the camp fire reflected the lights, the night became filled with rainbows instead of stars. Tents made up of trailers, cars, signs, golf clubs, and even what appeared to be several taxidermy bears littered the walkways. It was good to be home, I thought as a group of kids ran past me, sparklers in their hands, flaring lights of popping greens and neon yellows. I pulled my hat down more, and my coat tighter. As much as I wanted to take in my old home again, that was in the past now. I was here to help my home, not return to my home. That was the price to be paid. This was as close as I could ever get; it might as well have been on the moon.

I turned around, looking at Huey to make sure he was following. He was, if you counted walking aimlessly flabbergasted like a shoeless man in the Holy Land. So much for blending in and looking like we belonged in the camp. Luckily, Solly was on it and nudged Huey. Huey shut his mouth and put his game face back on. He jammed his hands back in his pockets, and Solly locked arms with him. The two looked like a happy couple—good. It was one thing for me to return, it was another for outsiders to come into camp. Anyone can enter a Roma camp, maybe even stop by and get some food—most are friendly enough to feed someone, to trade a good or two. But look the wrong way, and you will end up in a world of pain; the camp kept an eye on people, even when it looked like no one was watching. I kept that in mind as I saw a man sitting on the remains of an old stump, carving an almost finished wooden lion out of a piece of iron blackwood. He appeared to be deep into his work, only his eyes were peering over the wood shavings as they flew, rolling over Huey and Solly, then over me. I dipped my head in his direction. The best way to stay hidden in plain sight when someone is looking at you is to stare back. People don't like a confrontation. He averted his eyes when mine found his—I called his bluff. Most people were just curious, curious to see who you were, curious to see what you were hiding under your baseball cap.

We pressed on and I kept walking down the trail leading deeper into camp. In the distance, I could see the old willow tree where I had made my last tent so many years ago. The uneven ground still causing my back to hurt as I thought about it, the shards of broken glass littered around its roots, the simple carving of my and Linor's names still in the base. It made my heart ache, seeing that tree, seeing my home. I had lost my home countless times in my life, so much that I forgot what it was like to have a place that I could settle in, a place where I could place my heart. That tree, that lonely, old, dying willow tree, was a place where my heart had been at home; it had someone there who helped me create a home. Now I was a homeless man in nearly every sense of the word. A man walking who had no home for his heart.

Just keep moving Avi, keep moving. Solly and Huey came up at that moment. Solly nudged my elbow as she whispered, "Stop being dense and hurry the fuck up, you gibbering ape!" I shook my head and let them take the lead as we walked to Solly's tent. My brothers "Enlightened" only met after a radio call, as Solly explained it. They were able to keep hidden by using a code. Instead of remaining in the woods to wait for her return, we decided to follow her out to the community. I needed to see for myself how things had changed, or for that matter hadn't changed. As we walked through, all I saw were fewer people than before. Loads of the elders, but no teenagers, not that many young twenty-to-thirty-somethings. Giving the camp the distinct impression that it was primarily made up of old people. Surely that didn't mean they were all joined up with Zevi? That couldn't be possible. That alone would mean at least a hundred followers. Maybe Solly wasn't exaggerating when she said an army of Enlightened.

We reached Solly's tent, her tattoo studio now under a wooden porch, the wood having been sanded down to a high mirror shine in the glowing lights of the camp around us. I could see her faded green working table, sealed-off crates around it, and an old pedal from which I could smell the oil and sweat seeping from the gears, from the many years of use that it had been through.

She caught my eye. "Still waiting to put a tattoo on you, Avi?" she joked.

"No thanks. I am still far too squeamish for such things," I trailed off, seeing a familiar group of trees and a signpost off in the distance. She knew what I was looking at. "Yeah, that's their place still. Hasn't changed a bit, has it?" she asked.

I kept my eyes on the twisted oak and red-flapped tent covering out front. They had added a few doublewides adjacent to their home. Trailers—meant to be a quick, cheap go-anywhere home, they ended up as luxuries for the middle class, honeypots for the poor, and easy building material for the Roma.

"Solly, I—"

"Just go. Me and your fella here will get the code. Be careful, though, Avi. I wouldn't say the old lady is too keen on anyone, especially you," she stated.

"Of course the old woman is still alive," I grumbled, walking off Solly's porch into the night. This part of camp had plenty of trees shielding the way from the miniature city's worth of lights coming from behind me. I stopped when I was in front of the lobby, a hanging sign on the front of the old oak tree, barely clinging by one nail. The previous "Don't bother knocking; in fact, just go away!" had now been replaced with "Go away!" scribbled in bold red above with the previous message which was marked out almost completely. I grunted as I took the nail out of the oak tree, holding the sign back in place where it used to be and shoving it back through with a few heavy moments of work. When I was finished, the sign looked like it was where it had been all those years before. *Same sign, different times though,* I thought as I approached the flap.

I paused before pulling the drawstring that I knew would ring a collection of balls throughout the modest home of Linor and her grandmother. After all this time, I don't think I had ever pulled it. I went to pull the golden corded string, when the tent flap was thrown aside and out stepped a hunched-over woman. Her hair had bled to an ashen gray with a few tussles of black entwined in her gray hair. She had her long, hooked nose, still hooped with a golden nosering gleaming from the candlelight, with a purple blanket that was draped around her, forming a borderline red wine color which encased her.

She now had glasses that drifted down her long nose, held up by a bronze and silver chain on both ends. "Wolf! You have a lot of nerve coming back here, fixing an old woman's sign in the middle of the night like you're some kind of dashing suitor trying to spring into my box. Well you're knocking on the wrong tent flap tonight!" she hissed brandishing a wooden cane.

I blinked, turning red as her words sank in. "I wasn't trying to get into your—"

"Don't be dense, wolf. Voices are listening at all times. It's better for someone to hear that than for them to hear something else, you imbecile. Hurry, come with me." She snatched my hand while I was still flustered over her comments. Her wrinkled hands held surprising strength, despite the knobs of where the ends of her fingers used to be so long ago. Linor had told me once that her grandmother had lost all the ends of fingers stealing bread before the war for her family. I may have hated the old woman, but she had seen and been through a lot in her years. She was a survivor even before the war.

She let go of my hand as I entered the dimly lit living room, with her drifting off into the darkness of her home. Linor's babies were still littered all over the home, vines of strawberries, grapes, and other plants trailed around so close to the walls and ground that I would have thought they were painted on the surfaces in the gloomy light. What caught my attention, though, was the collection of artwork on the walls. Linor's art had always consisted of dead leaves, flower petals, the leftovers of our many adventures together combined with shards of mirrors, glass, driftwood, iron wood, and whatever else she could find that was combined together in arrangements of fantastical colors.

Those paintings still remained, but the golden hues were gone now, replaced with deeper blacks on newer pieces. Less growth, twisted thorns of razor sharp jagged metal, combined with deep crimsons, giving the impression of veins bleeding out of her paintings like an exposed wound, festering and devouring the very canvas that they were painted on. I shivered at the thought of what had led Linor to painting such dark things in juxtaposition to her lighter ones. *That wasn't the Linor I knew, she didn't have colors like that—what could have caused such a change?* I wondered as her grandmother came back into the room, flicking a light switch in the dim light. The living room glowed a soft gold.

In a flash, her grandmother was sitting in a wooden rocking chair, its brown coloring chipped away in spots, and the arms showing signs of holding her elbows firmly in place for decades. A soft velvet cushion was draped underneath her and a thick checkered blanket was on the back. If I hadn't known better, I would have simply thought it was an old lady sitting in a rocking chair on a quiet evening. Only I knew better and though Linor's grandmother was approaching the twilight of her life, she looked anything but comfortable. Case in point, letting me into her place. After that night when she told me I was a wolf, all those years ago, she was the last person I ever thought I would run into again. Here we were, though, two enemies staring each other down in a living room adorned with paintings and other handcrafted pieces of someone that was important to us both.

"I—"

"Shut up, wolf." She gestured with her cane at me. I sighed. I was getting very tired of people telling me to either shut up or cutting me off. "I don't like you, and that fact hasn't changed." She spat in my direction before continuing on. "You're a wolf, plain and simple—in a lot of ways, what has befallen this camp is because of you. That brother of yours—he has poisoned the minds of this community. A bigger monster than even you!" she sneered and an angry pit opened up inside me. Who was she to be saying such things? In the end, it had been me who had liberated everyone from the death camps, it had been me who had scared the Russians into not killing the survivors. It had been me who saved everyone's worthless lives! I had never spoken it, but deep within, a festering resentment grew for everyone who had called me a wolf. I didn't ask to be the beast, to have a mark that meant whenever anyone called me an animal they were calling me a killer. Maybe it was time I just accepted that.

A cold wave washed over me and my mind came out of the pit burning within my body. Who was I going to take my anger out on? A bitter old woman in her rocking chair, in her own home? I shook from that thought as I just settled for a hard glare with her instead. To her credit, the old woman kept my gaze without giving an inch. "I wish I could blame my daughter's disappearance on you, but I can't, as much as I would like to." She spat again.

I fought back my retort before speaking. "I wouldn't be here, old woman, if it wasn't for your granddaughter. We are stuck with each other, so there. Now help me. I am assuming that's the only reason you've not gotten everybody's attention in this damn camp already," I retorted as she glared at me.

Snakes about to kill a mouse treated their prey with more remorse than she gave me in that moment. "This is all your fault, wolf. My daughter has been running around with that brother of yours like the rest of the young folks," she muttered.

I sighed. That was roughly what Solly had already told me. This was another dead end. I started to reply when she continued, "After you left, she was never the same. Didn't want to go outside, didn't want to paint anything that wasn't black. She talked a lot about how her food had lost all its taste and sleep was the sunshine of her day. Believe me, boy, I've been around long enough to have seen many people that have since died.

And the one thing that united them, no matter what the conflict was, was statements like that. When people give up the will to live, they just die. It's slow and painful. Drags out like the sun melting the snow in the winter. You know it's coming—you want it to come so that the things that the snow was covering will go away already, but it's taking its sweet time. About two months ago, your rotten brother's dimwitted fruitcakes came into the community to recruit youngsters. Tried taking one of Adahy's boys..." She paused, choking back tears on Elder Adahy's name. I averted my gaze. That was one staring contest I didn't want to get into.

"His eldest, the one with the same round and friendly eyes as Adahy, stepped in to get his brother back. Then the same thing happens every time any group tries to force another group to come against their will: one of them pulled out a gun and shot the poor boy. He fell hard and Adahy's eldest turned into a wolf himself, big as a motorcycle, all black fur and fangs, snarling and biting your brother's man. That didn't bode well for our community. Your brother came back wanting blood—and he made an example out of almost anyone that stood in his way. My daughter always had that heart. Such a useless and stupid thing, offered herself up to your brother and his army in exchange for him to leave the community alone. He accepted, and now here you are, back here in the flesh after all these years. Looking like a dissolved bum," she hissed.

Instead of getting mad, I pitied the old woman. She was just missing her granddaughter and had the courage enough to put aside her hatred of me long enough to ask for help. I suddenly felt very ashamed in that moment. Would I have been able to do the same? There had been a lot of people who had wronged me in my life. How often had I extended a hand toward them? It was easy to write off the overweight woman screaming at the casher as a raving lunatic, or demonize an addict. They were people that in some way disrupted our lives. They had wasted the precious moments of our small worlds, so therefore, in those moments, they were the worst people alive. In reality, we didn't know what was going on in their life, we didn't know that maybe that overweight woman might have exactly what we needed. Or that junkie was an amazing metalsmith who could fix the piping in our home very easily without having to call an overpriced plumber. Odds are it's not likely, but it takes a great deal of courage to ask anyone that we hate for help—to ask anyone for help, for that matter.

"How can we get her back?" I asked, opting out of any grand showdown with Linor's grandmother. She appreciated actions far more than any admission of love that I could make. She nodded. "That will be up to you to figure out, boy. Just bring her back to me—please," she mumbled through a strained voice that I could tell was on the verge of tears.

Anger, no matter how justified, is something that burns out like a candlewick. In the end, we are all nothing more than a bitter old woman in a dark living room, with a broken middle-aged man. "I will do my best," I responded weakly, hoping I could keep my word. I would do whatever it took to set things right, not only for Linor, but for everyone else.

I turned away, feeling much older than I had before coming into their place. "She always liked you, boy. For whatever reason that may have been, prove to me that she wasn't stupid, will you?" she called out behind me as I neared the flap covering their purple door. How they even managed to get the entranceway the exact size of the tent opening and the rest of the place the size of a circus tent, I would never understand.

I paused, looking forward. "I will," I grunted, opening the flap and stepping back outside into the cold night, a chill causing me to brush my arms, thinking about what was to come.

55

Chapter 55

I walked back to Solly's home slowly, looking at the soft dirt on the trail leading between the two locations. Footprints had long since eroded the road to a wide gap on both sides. I wondered if somewhere in the dirt there were the footprints from when we were kids. As I looked up and saw Huey and Solly's faces though, I realized how stupid that was. You could never walk the same way twice, not truly, at least. Time or the elements would break down the world to its smallest bits, then into even smaller pieces than that. That left me with one option really, to know that when I walked down a road, I was making the most of my moment on that path. I could never be that boy who was lovesick, following after Linor's steps. I could be my own person, though, make new tracks in the dirt.

I approached the two of them, preparing a joke to make the pair blush, when Huey's concerned face made me stop. "What?" I asked them.

They exchanged a look before talking. Huey cleared his throat. "We found them. It's not good, Avi. It really is an army," he stated, the nervousness leaving no doubt as to the total. I pressed on, "Ten-thousand or ten people, we still have to try and end this," I replied, with more confidence than I should have had.

"How did you figure it out, anyways?"

"Oh—that was the strangest thing." Huey pulled out from his pocket a saucer-sized dial that had a ring hoop attached to it. There was a series of rings within the saucer, all with various numbers and letters.

I looked at it for a moment then laughed, "Is that a decoder ring from a cracker box, Huey?" I asked him as he turned red in the shadows of the porch.

"I'm afraid so, they have a radio show they used to broadcast the coordinates. Not a bad idea, to be honest," he muttered.

I laughed in response. "Some army, using advanced technology from a popcorn box. I think we will be fine, Huey," I stated entirely to calm compared to the other two's uneasiness.

"I don't know, man. When the information came out about the location and the venue, it sounded like a lot. What exactly is your plan?" he asked me, his growing concern becoming more off-putting by the moment.

"The plan is pretty simple, the only two who have seen you and me are Bug and Tir. So, we avoid those two most of all. That leaves you as the emergency wheels out of there—if you're willing, Solly?" I turned toward her.

She had bitten her bottom lip, but nodded slowly. "Yeah I can do that—just what is your plan exactly? Load up and drive like a bat out of the frying pan?" she asked me.

"That is the exact plan. We get in, find Linor, and get out of there. Not do anything stupid. Trust me, Huey. We just need to confirm that she's safe and there. It will also let us know what is going on with Zevi. For all we know, Tir and Bug could have been warning us of something with my brother. Let's keep this simple and gather information. The two of us on the ground will be the quickest way in and out. No one will recognize us either; we just have to stay away from Tir and the others." I laid it all out but both of them still held reservation on their faces. "Come on, I need you guys to be on board with this," I almost pleaded.

"It just, you know, sounded like a lot of people on the radio," Huey said nervously. "I'm with you, man. Just don't expect me to be happy about it."

"That's fair. Alright, Solly, where are we heading?" I turned toward her. She pulled out a folded piece of paper and showed me what was written down. I read the address, perplexed, and not sure at all if I was reading that right. "Solly, this can't be right. That's right outside the mill in two hours—"

As if on command, a host of light shot off into the sky over the forest line leading to the baseball field and the old mill. It was followed by massive explosion of red and green in the night sky. "That's it alright, Avi. The only place where they can fit so many people," she warned, fearfully.

I suddenly felt far less secure than I had a moment before. We could never fully predict every possible outcome, so we were unable to secure ourselves from danger, but what we could do about it was choose how to face that danger. Now, something could be said to the extent that the three of us charging off into a horde of unknown danger in the middle of the night was most likely not securing ourselves from danger. We'd just have to make do with what we had and see this one through.

I thought of Zevi. What was he putting on such a show for? Another round of fireworks decimated the night sky. If he was capable of putting on such a display with so many followers, who in the world was he in danger from?

56

Chapter 56

By the time we got into the woods with supplies, the night was in full effect with the firecrackers maintaining a constant barrage above us. "So much for needing to decode their message," I grumbled.

Huey dropped a pack right next to where I knelt along the creek bed. "It wasn't a wasted effort. You said you got to talk to the old woman," he reminded me as he pulled out a can of red paint and one of Solly's black jackets. Long tassels of leather hung off at various places. I looked at it and sighed. The things I would do for my family. "Alright, bend your head over, dip shit," Huey gestured toward the ground as he shook the paint.

The plan was for me to go in looking like a young greaser. We had even picked up a couple of cans of hair product just for the effect. I hated it already. It smelled like something I would use to grease a lugnut on our truck's tires. Huey sprayed down my hair and I coughed, choking on the fumes from the spray can. Next, I popped open one of the gel tubs, spreading the jelly throughout my hair until I had more grease than actual hair. I messed it up in the similar comb-over I had seen some of Bipin brothers wearing their hair, and donned Solly's jacket.

"How do I look?" I asked, beaming in the dark woods.

"Like a jackass," Huey said simply.

"You're right. Got one for me?" I asked him as he finished rolling a cigarette.

He sighed, handing it to me. "Enjoy it man, while you can," he replied grimly.

"Don't be negative. Besides worst case, you will be in the crowd as well, and Solly is driving the getaway truck," I stated taking a drag from the cigarette.

"Trust me, Avi, when that many people are around you, you become lost at sea. Don't go deep into the crowd. Stay on the fringe—"

"Yeah, yeah I remember. Stay on the edges of the crowd, don't go into the middle otherwise it will be harder to get out. I got this, Huey, we will be fine." I finished the cigarette, dashing it, then stuck it in my pocket. In the darkness, I could make out Huey's face with the fireworks above. He looked scared. I had never seen him like that in the two years we had been together. That gave me pause. If someone like him was scared, after seeing lord knows what while fighting in the "bush," as he called it, then this plan must seem crazy. Yet, I had survived the closest thing to hell on Earth. A place where literally every day was an attempt to kill me or to dissect me, sometimes both. If there was anywhere I should have died, it had to have been there, in the tiniest and most remote parts of my mind. I wish I had. It was tantamount to admitting my own omission of giving up, and that's why I had locked those thoughts away, far in the back of my mind. However, I would be a fool to forget completely about those parts. We all want to give up from time to time, and take the easy road out because it is of course a road, which means it was supposed to be one that we could travel down. The difference was, though, that when we looked at the roads to choose where to go next, we always kept in mind we'd been down tougher roads.

I finished my outfit and looked at Huey, who had thrown on a similar black jacket and a floppy hat with bomber badges on it. He caught me looking at his hat. "It was from the war," he muttered. A lot of the younger people these days were in heavy protest against the war. Say what you will about the world, it certainly was being loud. We crossed out of the woods over the creek bed and through the baseball diamond. The old fence was still standing in place in a few areas. I pictured the many nights that we had played on the field. If I hadn't hit that ball that night, would Zevi had approached me after the game like he had? So much had occurred because of one decision. Where my life would be now, I could only speculate. It was too late to turn back the hands of time, to go back to before the glass shattered and the world rolled forward, indifferent to the seemingly monumental change which had occurred that night.

I lowered my head and took my eyes away from the field. I was unable to look away for long moments. Perhaps, maybe, I had just never left there, like I thought I had. As we moved past the dugout and prepared to cross the small railroad line bridge, we spotted other people coming out of the woods in that direction. Most were wearing all back like us, and some were wearing bright shapes showing places and things I had never heard of. A few women were completely naked, save for a wreath tied around their heads, followed by men doing the same right behind them.

"What in the world kind of gathering is this?" I pondered as Huey came beside me.

"You know, add some music, this would be a pretty good party," he stated, just as a loud rip from a guitar came from the other side of the towers at the mill.

I could see bright light spilling over the silos, the orange of fire meeting the rustic metal of the old mill, casting the world in some kind of crimson glow that teetered on the edges of becoming bronze. The light messed with my eyes, forcing me to close them. I turned, losing sight of Huey in the growing crowd of people around me. Where had they come from? More and more people where flooding from every direction. Some had made shops and campsites out of the abandoned concrete structures of the mill. At the intersection of walkway bridges above me, connecting between two towers, a sign had been hung in glowing lights, saying "Welcome all Enlightened, children of the Abyss," followed by two men downing a massive jug of what I could only assume was pure motor oil. My sense of smell was being overwhelmed by the many cigarettes, body odors, alcohol, marijuana, and sex. Festivals are not a kind place to someone with super senses. I covered my ears and kept walking, the push of the crowd surging close, swelling like hands reaching through the ocean to pull me under. The music rocked my eardrums, bouncing wooden hammers inside my head. Then, I realized the people around me had no faces.

They were lifeless shades, twisted and deformed, black husks of eyes and featureless smears, like someone had melted just the faces on a photograph. I flinched as one couple walked past me, giggling. Where was I? I wasn't in the crowd anymore; I was back behind the iron fences. Their spiked beacons shocking the air itself, like they belonged to a beast in the waters. Levantines of the damned, jutting out metal spears and a web of neverending steel rings, sealing me away forever. I was terrified, my heart beating faster than my breath could catch up. Where was the festival? Where had Huey gone? Snow fell around me, ashen and gray. No—not snow; it was the remains from the pits. Choking me, engulfing my sanity. The faceless begin to moan, a neverending sea of cries out into the day.

I opened my mouth to scream, finding no way out, as I collapsed to the ground. My shoes were a few sizes too big, my pants belonged to a dead man, and my hands ached like cracking metal under immense weight. I was breathing so fast, in sporadic gasps for anything as I tried to keep my head above the wave of nausea that had swept through me. I could hear the slide of a lock turning, the pull of a handle, a railroad door being slide back showing the furnace of hell...

And I threw up as someone patted me on the back. "Hey, you need to breathe. Just take a deep breath. It's alright, I promise. It's okay," someone said softly, their light touch on my shoulders, relaxing the explosion of tension in them. I tried to talk, but I opted to just let my mouth take a break for a change as my senses slowly came back.

"Linor," I choked out finally, looking up to see a caramel-skinned woman, concern written over her face, making her brown eyes light up like fresh honey from a jar.

She bit her lip. "Too much to drink, pal?" she asked me.

She reached for me, and I fell back, swatting at her hands, "Whoa, take it easy there!" she called out to me.

My senses started to recover and I noticed other people were starting to gather. I was drenched in sweat, my jacket close to falling off of me. I needed to defuse the situation and fast. "Let's rage!" spilled out of my mouth, shouting as loud as I could and doing the best impression of a bird trying to mimic a human. The woman laughed, as did several others, but it got them to leave me alone. I slid around the metal silo trying to catch my breath until Huey found me, hunched over, drooping almost to the ground.

"Are you okay, man?" he asked, pulling my shoulder. "Come on pal, I need you to get it together—we are on mission," he commented.

I slapped away his hand. "I'm fine, let's go." I stood up, shakily.

"No, you aren't fine man, not by a fucking mile. You look paler than a piece of white paper—you were already a pale white-boy before. Maybe we should—"

I held up my hand and cut him off. "Huey this is the mission."

We held a gaze for a long time and he nodded. Huey knew what it meant to have to do something, even if it was killing you. You stepped forward; that was all you could do.

"Let's finish this," he said, turning his back to me and drifting a few feet behind like we had discussed. We surged forward with the crowd, the music slowly settling down to more relaxed tempos. As we neared a wide field, I saw why everyone kept saying "army." Ahead of me was thousands of people, a sea of black jackets and masks. Flags sporting the logos of "The Enlightened" born out in bold colors, unashamed and unafraid. People of every race and background, men and women, and some older people along with the young ones. What had Zevi started? I was shaking at that thought. Could this really be the same chubby redhead from all those years ago? The illusion had been blown out the window when we were teenagers about Zevi being weak—but Zevi had seemed so angry, so confused, and lost just like the rest of us. In a lot of ways, I had expected Zevi to be no more put together than I was. This, however, the sheer amount of people still coming in, and people already lined up in the open field in the shadow of the aging mill, left me speechless.

At the end of the sea of people was a stage, rising high above the tallest individuals in the front. Cramming in to see what was going on didn't help my position at all, as more people flooded in, instantly making me feel trapped. *Just breathe, Avi, breathe,* I kept chanting in my head as the music suddenly died, along with the torrent of noise around me instantly.

A massive wall of a man, short in stature, but wider than most doorframes, waved at the crowd, a toothy smile played over his dour face and thick eyebrows that hung like slabs of meat on his face. His hands were cloven and he was completely bald, with hot pink skin that looked like he had just been blasted by a scalding shower. I recognized his cupped ears any day. It was Schwein in all his glory. His name was fitting at this point; he had gorged himself like a pig, expanding him to a size that I wouldn't have thought the human body capable of.

Next came Arnold. He had gotten taller in the years since I last seen him. Sandy blond hair had overtaken the dusty brown he used to sport. Unlike Schwein, he had grown taller, though, seeming to have lost the willpower to ever eat. The black jacket he wore swallowed him as he waved to the crowd. On his average face was a mischievous grin. I wasn't fooled in the slightest by him. A stiff breeze might have knocked him over, but it wouldn't be the same for his shadow, which I swore was moving in the shade of the lights on the stage. I shivered, remembering the face of his shadow demon. Hopefully I wouldn't have to see its deformed visage again.

Sophia strolled on stage to a big roar. Her face was passive, but that was the only thing passive about her. From her curves to her tone, she wasn't someone that you would want to cross. But where were Bug and Tir? Neither one of them was on stage. Maybe they were with Zevi? I looked around, apprehensive for my brother to show up. It had been fifteen years since we had last seen each other. That thought made me want to throw up again. Thankfully, I was too deep in the crowd now to risk doing it.

Then, the lights shone on my father—or I thought that, until I saw the green eye of my mother and his too-dark brown eye that looked like it was a square peg being forced into a triangle hole, as it appeared to be close to popping out at any moment. It was Linor's eye in Zevi's face—I felt great shame in that moment, realizing I'd never asked her about it. It didn't feel right—what would I say anyways? Why did you have my brother's eye while he had your eye?

The resemblance between my father and mother stopped there with Zevi. He had gotten taller, close to the same height as most truck tops. Thick corded muscle moved with his every step and yet he remained lean—like he was designed to be a hunter in the wild. He hadn't been lazy—and I had serious doubts that anyone could take him in a fair fight. I shook. Zevi was a beast that didn't need to transform; he was a beast without any boundaries.

Who could possibly threaten my brother when he was that strong and had so many followers? The trap that Solly and Huey had anticipated wasn't seeming so farfetched now. I turned, looking for Huey. We had gotten separated again by the crowds. *Relax—stick to the plan. Remember, once you've located Zevi, wait until after this crowd calms down, then start to figure out who could be after my brother.* If Zevi had gotten so big, it wouldn't surprise me if someone in this group was trying to harm my brother. We had considered a direct confrontation with Zevi, but I assured Huey that feelings between the two of us would take some ironing out. I didn't think Zevi would attempt to fight me; only a mad man would want to fight the beast; just that I was more concerned that I would ruin any chance that the two of us had at making amends. I still remember our mother's words, for me to look after him. I had done a piss poor job in the last—well, since I was given the job. I wouldn't make that mistake anymore. He pissed me off to no end, some of his actions I just couldn't understand, but he was my brother.

Solly also brought up a good point in reminding us that he had so many followers that it would be next to impossible to get anywhere near him unless he wanted you near him. That was miles away from being a reality at this point. No, the only way I was getting to Zevi was somewhere else, not here.

He waved to the crowd. The response was a roar that shattered the very sky, louder than the fireworks or band had dreamed of being. Only the impact of a bomb was louder—I thought maybe this was what I was actually seeing, a bomb going off around the world. Not the ones that end your life in an instant—the ones where everything else stops and you wonder what you've been looking at all these years.

Linor shuffled behind Zevi to an overhanging metal scaffolding that held the lights above. In those moments, when the lights radiated bright, she was far more beautiful and shapelier in the most symmetrical of ways that would make even the greatest math snob happy. Mostly because I could see her two different-colored tennis shoes, one red, the other black, with a tattoo of a fierce dragon fighting a massive winged crow. That was a new one. Her dress was modest, and her black jacket looked like it had taken a beating a few too many times to be worn by someone so thin, as her Rapunzel-length hair fell down, beaded and braided with an even bigger knife, from what I could tell, in its folds.

I laughed. How she even managed to do that without cutting a finger off I would never completely understand—what I did understand was how, in a dark sky, her hair was midnight and to me, that made me see only the daylight. An ache I'd had in my heart since this adventure had begun drifted away—both of them were safe. My family was safe. I gave a sigh of relief and relaxed the tension out of my body.

Sophia walked up to Zevi, handing him a loudspeaker boom phone. He smiled before he spoke, sending his voice out into the crowd. "Everyone having a good time?!" he echoed out over the large assembly. A swell of responses met him back and I fought to cover my ears over the noise. "Good! So, I would like to tell you a story, friends. A simple enough story. According to the earliest accounts of my life, my behavior sowed the seeds of what brought me here today. I often experienced periods of deep depression and despair, withdrawing from my family—my friends, to live this life in isolation and silence. And you know what I learned? Not a fucking thing!" he called out into the gathering to a roar of cheers.

"It's a strange and necessary thing, the capacity for self-delusion we can make, just because of a glowing feeling we carry within ourselves.

After all, this is my feeling—it makes me feel so much feeling that it seems semi-mythical, that would have you believing your own crafted mythology. And the truth is, I wake up every morning and still have to poop like every person here! Thankfully, I've been humbled by these times I've been alone.

"As you're all aware, I am a survivor of hell—just like many on this stage are as well. Just like all of you before me, beasts forged in the fires of this life!" he echoed out and I did my best to understand where my brother was taking his speech, as a roar of claps and cheers praised every word he spoke.

He continued, "Take solace in the rain, friends. Even though we live in a time when the propaganda is so far removed from events, everyone has such a beautiful story that can be hidden behind veils of malice, discontent, fear, anxiety, and whatever else we feed ourselves to hide. Truth is subjective. It falls prey to those who would like to distort it and those who would like to profit from it, but the fact never survives the process. It is changed, altered from its natural state, and once it changes, just like Humpty and his famous shell, it can never be put back together again. To that, I say: you find what truth makes the most sense to you in your life. I think that is why you all have gathered here! You've—discovered the truth to this life! That the world is masquerading as a public death squad in the open, with no repercussions for violence or cruelty. No concern for the hearts broken, the flesh that won't mend." The congregation booed in response to the last part of his words.

"I know, friends, it's not right. Not right at all, from public officials claiming they know exactly how you're supposed to feel, to your edgelord history teacher who is twisting the truth because they don't want to seem like a racist. We know the truth; we know the reality. That there are cruel fucks in this world who will say or do anything for a chance at power. And believe me when I say this: it doesn't take much before people start justifying torment and misery for others. Why do you care? There's a good movie on tonight. Or that fuck who controls everything? It's his fault. Yeah, he's the evil one. Meanwhile, let me go overtly flirt with the milkman. He's a man, or he's a woman, they're such and such doing such and such. Blame everyone else, complaining about the dirt, but where are their brooms? Where are their dusters and weapons against the filth? I tell you what, they say now that we are born this way into sin, that we evolved into such beasts of burden. To that, I say: You're right. We have been. However, if we can evolve into beasts, we can evolve into angels. That's right, folks, we can let the sun shine in on reality and be the honest change we want to see in this world. Now, you see others will be shifting the blame, shifting the heart away from truth. The truth is this world can only be fixed by honesty and cooperation. And we achieve that today, brothers and sisters of every shape and creed. We achieve that by killing Nazis," he finished and the crowd was animated with a heartened resolve that made me shiver.

I felt ancient, drained beyond my years, and I just wanted to go hide in a very damp cave. While everyone cheered around me, I looked for Huey, hoping to see his reaction to what Zevi had just said. As I turned my head away from the stage and turned it back, four chairs had been placed across the stage. I paused to watch as four people, whose hands were bound, were placed in the chairs. Three of them had hoods on. One had the shapely legs of a woman, and the others wore thick pants. I could make out their whimpers as the crowd started to die down with their noise.

The man without a hood; he looked familiar. It was Albert, now only older, skin not as refined, hair a little more ashen than it was. His top was a thick brown and he had a tussle of golden blonde hair. His face was older, his features guiltless and mature, leading up to a small button nose and a noticeable notch in his right ear that had taken the top portion away. Some would say he had a baby face. I remembered how cruel his face would be when he was taunting me outside of his cage, the many dark hours I spent crying in that small box. I cracked my fingers; venom surged through my blood.

"We have a special treat for everyone tonight: four Nazis!" Zevi cackled and the crowd cheered in response.

My heart deflated. This wasn't going there, was it? I knew the answer, though. Zevi wouldn't have gone through the trouble of bringing them

367

up on stage just to take them away. During my time in the meetings every week with Huey, I had learned a lot about other people. Heard stories from survivors and folks who had just had awful luck. The ones that stayed with me the most were when this one guy—Frank—spoke. Frank was a big man, and that was putting it mildly. He was closer to being a gorilla than an actual human being, and his arms were covered in anchors and other tattoos from his time in the navy, as he put it. When he spoke, his neck, which was the size of my leg, would cause his orange and blonde beard to twist to the sides, almost like it was being strained by some unseen force. Frank had spent some time confused after the war, joined up with a biker gang and as he put it, "raised hell" throughout most of the west coast. He ended up as an enforcer for a local biker gang, running guns and drugs for a few years until he got pinched. Long story short: Frank had killed, by his own omission, close to a twenty people. Brutally, and without any remorse, over a few lousy bucks.

Yet in those meetings, Frank was a screaming mess on the best of days. He explained how bowls of rice set him off. Anger, so much anger. Fury at everything and everyone, especially his wife and young daughter. He started drinking—anything to distract him from the pain he was feeling on the inside, when everything reminded him of that pain. A neverending cycle of music from a broken record.

One thing, though, was that despite what Frank claimed to have done, he was incredibly remorseful. He worked hard every day to make up for what he had done to people. Seeing Albert tied up on a chair liked that—it reminded me of Frank. Just a messed-up person, now an old man. I felt no righteous vindication against Albert. Rather, I wanted him to go back into the hole men like him came from. People aren't born monsters to each other; we go around long enough just fine, with no problem until something or someone turns us into monsters. *"Why, Avi, why not just hate Albert like the scum that he is? For all you know, he's been hurting people all these years. That was probably how Zevi found him. We rode around looking for the former Nazis. Albert deserves what is about to happen to him, doesn't he?"*

I was deep in thought when Sophia walked to Albert, sticking her fingers against his neck like a gun. The people were silent, and the world still kept on spinning as a man was about to die. Her skin around her hand phased out, becoming clear, until her veins glowed neon and a popping sound could be heard. A pull of energy and electricity flooded out of her fingertips, burning the flesh on Albert's skin. He started to cry, all shame gone as his pants slowly turned wet in front of us.

"I've always wanted to say this. Any last words—Nazi?" joked Zevi, whispering at face level with Albert, as the poor man peed himself and continued to cry. This was just torture. I was standing there, once again, letting Zevi lose his mind while someone else was about to get hurt. I had promised Huey and Solly that no matter what happened, we wouldn't react. We had to be sure what was going on, not be in the middle of it. If only Zevi and I had worked out our problems sooner, he would see what was wrong. He would stop this. I wasn't saying Albert deserved to live—not in the slightest. But he didn't need to be publicly executed just to make a point.

I wanted to throw up again, I wanted to get away. "*You coward,*" snarled the beast. "*Poor little Avraham; the world is so dark and I am so weak. Pity me,*" it continued.

Shut up, you stupid rotten demon! I shouted back into the confines of my mind. I can't even have a moment, just one moment, without your input.

With my attention given to the beast, I failed to notice that pop of Sophia's fingers. I saw the light though. An intense neon shot from the tips of her fingers, burning through Albert's neck, arching in a zigzag pattern. The light glowed an infinite amount of colors as it seemed to move like a serpent, striking the other three heads. I gasped as the crowd cheered. Zevi threw both his hands up in unison. Burning flesh and smoke drifted out toward us, as Albert's body sank forward. Sophia caught his body as Zevi produced a baseball bat. The simple wood was stained red in uneven patterns, with many splinters and dents in the wood.

"Oh no," I whispered as Zevi took a batting stance, rearing back his arms to swing. Sophia stepped out of the way just as soon as Zevi swung. A gust of wind erupted from his hit as the ball smashed into Albert's skull, sending it soaring over the crowd, only breaking into chunks as it hit the silos of the mill. I covered my mouth, fighting back a gag as Zevi smiled, happy with himself. He stepped forward to the next person in their chair, repeating the same process as before. This time, as the head lobbed over, bits fell into the cheering crowd as well.

I hunched over, sick from the display. Something else inside me had other ideas than throwing up. A spasm ran through me, thick and alive in a current of power. I was seized upward, dragged to the side like I had stepped into a raging current. My mouth opened wide and a stream of fire burst from my mouth skyward. It was the beast, the wolf. His growls echoed inside my skull. My voice was small as I pleaded for him to stop: *just please, don't do this. Just stop, stop this endless pain.* I felt the inside of my body shudder, my lungs filling with smoke, my mouth blistering and bleeding as the river of heat rushed from me.

After what could have only been five seconds, the flames suddenly stopped. I heard the snarl of the wolf as I opened my eyes and looked around me. The crowd had shifted far away, the air reeked of ash, and all eyes were on me.

"Hey there, *bruder*," cried Zevi from the stage. My body was stiff, I wanted to lie down and sleep until the end of time. "My friends, we have a very special guest here tonight, the one and only hell hound of Auschwitz, my brother—the beast!" Zevi bellowed, slapping his chest.

I heard shoving, quick footsteps, and Huey was standing beside me in a fighting stance. He glanced back at me. "What the fuck—was that?" he asked, not taking his eyes off of the nearest person in a black mask. It was a large man, his face hidden behind his veil, but his body language said he was ready to throw his size around.

My throat cracked as I tried to talk and I tasted blood. Everything stung. I was sure my chapped lips had melted down to my jawbone. I managed to croak a grunt as tears slid down my singed cheeks. Huey stayed, pointing toward the crowd that was already moving around us, forming a tight circle. I could hear my brother's laughter.

"Oh, this is an amazing surprise today, what a night! First killing some Nazis—now a reunion with my big brother. Yes!" he pumped his fists in the air, while in the back, I could make out Linor. Her face was in complete shock and I knew what she was thinking without her having to say it. I was back. After all these years without a single word to her, I had returned. I gasped for air through my burnt throat, wishing I could say something.

I healed—slowly, in an hour or two, I would be able to talk again. Though, at the rate the events of the night were unfolding, I was starting to wonder if I would live long enough to have my throat healed. Zevi started clapping his hands in excitement, drawing the crowd's attention, save for the big guy and his friends who were getting closer and closer to Huey, stepping forward inch by inch.

Zevi called out to me, "Hell of a way to show yourself back in our lives! My word, you could have just called—maybe even sent a letter." He suddenly stopped his jest and his face turned grave—then to malice. A liquid hatred that could flood the world in his gaze, I was suddenly terrified, like I had witnessed seeing a ghost. In a lot of ways, I was seeing a ghost, someone wearing the face of my brother—that wasn't him. He was monstrous in his every move, as cunning as a viper, and with oxygen slowly pouring back in my body, I had doubts that I wasn't in fact drowning at that very moment.

Around me were Zevi's followers. It was just my friend and I against a horde. Where was Solly? She was supposed to be our get-out-of-Dodge card in case this went south, which it already was. I faced Zevi as he gave me a deadeye stare, black and beady like those of a bear, not of a man. He snarled, "Show... me... the Wolf!" His voice echoed across the distance, silencing all noise like a gunshot. It was in that moment that I realized I had lost my brother for good and the idea of someone threatening him seem less and less likely.

I glanced around. The two of us were not getting out of here without a fight. The thing is, though, Huey and I had been running a sort of underground detective business the last two years. We had met loads of, well... characters, to say the least, and what I did learn very quickly was that people wore masks for a handful of reasons. It was either to hide, celebrate, or because they were cowards. I had a hunch, judging by the sound and voices of the few faces I could see that these were all kids. Scared shitless children, led astray by a smooth and charismatic talker.

They would go down easily. Knock out the big one and the rest would scatter like roaches under the fridge. Zevi flushed in anger, screaming this time, his face straining. "Show... me... the wolf!" *He's lost his mind; we have to get out of here.* I stepped forward, moving my winded body, tapping Huey's shoulder on the side deltoid, indicating through our system that I had his back. In that moment, the big man lunged forward, as Huey stood in place and popped out both of his hands, catching the man's shoulders while pinning his own head against the man's chest. Huey moved quickly to the side, his head pointed up, one leg either side of the man's legs. With a smooth jerk of motion, Huey drove his head into the man's chest and kicked out his legs, sending his massive bulk to the ground. In a blur, Huey placed one leg in the armpit of the man, and swung his other around the man's free arm. He sat back and clenched his legs tight around the man, and with his thumb pointed to the sky, Huey lifted his hips. I heard the pop of the man's shoulder before his scream.

Huey let go, rolling back over his shoulders into a fighting stance. One person rushed forward from the right, but I didn't rely on smooth moves like Huey. Instead, I kicked the person's knee from the inside, sending them sprawling to the ground, followed by a savage punch to their neck. They were down before I stood back up tall.

Groans came from both of them on the ground, but their friends' eyes told us everything we needed to know. We had scared them. Huey and I stayed tight together, moving slowly through the crowd. We had at the most thirty to forty seconds before they realized they outnumbered us again. They may have been young, but numbers give anyone a confidence boost—I didn't blame them either. I heard a growl come from Zevi as we both slowly edged our way through the crowd, hoping Solly was on her way.

Earth to the right of us started to shift, and mounds of dirt clods protruded from the ground. Then came a long limb, twisting and reeling, followed by a shape of a man. It was Tir, I though in a split second, before a wall of veins came shooting out of the ground, spinning like bullets fired from the dirt.

Huey was hit, grunting in pain, flying backward into a group of the masked Enlightened. I stretched to yell his name, but my throat still was scabbed over, and all that came out was a gurgle. I whipped my head back around to see Tir, covered in leaves and dirt, fly from the ground toward me. His fist smashed into the side of my face and I went down hard, clamping my mouth shut. *Don't bleed, don't bleed!* I shouted into the confines of my mind. I felt the beast stir again for a moment, heat emerging from my body—I shoved those thoughts down, remembering why I was here, remembering who I was. *I am Avraham, not a mindless beast. You do not control me!*

He snarled back weakly in response. I had never heard him that tired. Maybe that flame trick had drained him? Before I could dive deeper into my thoughts, veins exploded near my face on the way down, in the shape of Tir's fists and I was smacked hard on my left side. My eye was stung closed as my body was lifted from the ground.

I fell down in a cloud of dust, groaning as Tir stood over me, veins covering his arm, twisting into the shape of a long razor. He had been practicing in these last few years, and it showed. What in the world was happening? My head was spinning, I think Tir was smiling at me as he moved closer, the sharp edge of his arm gleaming from the lights of the stage. This was it; I was going to die, here right now.

I closed my eyes for a moment, opening them again to see Huey land a kick from the side into Tir's ribs, vicious and powerful, knocking the air out of him as he fell back. "Take that, twig boy!" Huey spat. One of the masked people lunged from the crowd, hitting Huey in the face, and Huey fought him off.

Leaning up felt like climbing a mountain, but I managed, just as soon as hands slid over me. I felt fingers tighten around my shoulders while

Zevi called out from somewhere, "Get him!" I felt another hard hit to my face, and my cheeks were so swollen that I barely registered that it had happened. More hands clouded my face as Huey in the distance fought to keep them off of me.

As my eyes drifted closed, crystalized hoofs landed next to me, flattening out one of the masked Enlightened. The world blacked out as it became filled with noise and somewhere in the distance, I heard a woman screaming. Her voice sounded familiar, belonging to someone that I had once known. It was funny. What was I doing here again?

57

Chapter 57

My head was on fire. That was the only explanation for the glaring heat that crackled, popped, and seemed to live like my skull was made of it. I groaned. I must have gone to hell. Not surprising: I had just never really bought the whole lake of fire thing. Come on, you didn't need to be flashy to torture people, just give them a weekend with the extended family and no beers. That did the trick for me every time. I rolled over, clearing my throat, leftover bile from my wounds healing. While my head wasn't pounding, I waited for the wolf to make a sound. None, just the emptiness of my skull. *That's good, right? Nothing too stupid going on up there right now.*

Can't be too stupid if no one can hear it. "That's right," I croaked, feeling like I had never used my voice a day in my life.

"I've always been right, Avi, thanks for finally agreeing," said someone soothingly. I snapped my eyes open and my fists shot out, as the memories of the field came flashing back. Instead I was in a well-lit room, sun coming in from out the windows. I was on a wooden bench, layers of blankets under me. A couple of pillows behind my head allowed me to see the room in front of me. Blankets were draped across the ceiling—while arrangements of flowers inside shoes lined the window.

"Linor?" I choked out.

"Just shut up, Avi, and drink this." As water was pushed into my hands, a long bendy straw jutted out of the water. I took a sip; heaven is iced water after a day like mine.

"Thank you," I mumbled, looking into the concerned face of Linor.

It flashed with irritation once we made eye contact, "You're such an asshole," she declared, keeping the cup by my mouth as I tried to talk again. "Haven't seen you in what, almost twenty years? And now you're back here, charging into a crowd like you're some kind of cowboy? To make it worse, you got your ass kicked and nearly died," she spat bitterly.

" I wouldn't say I got my ass kicked," I responded.

"You got your ass kicked."

I sighed heavily, "Yeah we weren't prepared for that in the slightest."

"That's the thing, Avi. You've never been prepared for anything in your life. You don't think and look where that has gotten you now," she stated, crossing her arms.

"I thought we would come back and help you," I defended as her eyes became ablaze at my statement.

"Excuse me, you came all the way to rescue me? Like I needed it! Help me because I can't take care of myself? I am doing pretty alright, Avi," she shot back.

"You know how I meant it—" I fired back at her.

She glared daggers into me, then rolled her eyes. "Some help, anyways."

"Yeah, some help anyways," I responded weakly.

We were both silent in the darkened room before she spoke up. "Avi—I'm just..." she started.

"Look, Linor, I will be honest here. I didn't want to come back to this place. I wouldn't have come back on the prospect of saving you or something like that alone. You can take care of yourself. I was told you were in danger, that all of you were in danger. I had no other choice. Now here I am," I told her.

She looked at the blankets on the ceiling for a long moment before replying, as if they could somehow tell her exactly what was going on in their stitches. "Funny how it's no longer 'We are in danger.' You've forgotten all about the community."

"It isn't like that."

"What is it like?"

I sighed again, rubbing my face. This conversation was heading downhill with every word. "I came back because I cared. Things can never go back the way they were—I can't—"

She waved me off. "Avi, I don't need you to explain how time works. You left the community years ago for your own reasons. I won't pretend like you will suddenly come back and we are kids again sitting on Pete's rooftop. Just don't pretend it was because you regret what happened to this community. You may have not made it worse, but you were the one that pulled the trigger—then you stayed gone. All of this came because of that night—terror at the hands of living under the thumb of yet another crazy person. Instead of apologizing, or at the very least writing a letter, you just stayed gone like a ghost in the wind. How am I supposed to take seeing you back after all this time?" she asked me as I bowed my head, thinking of a response.

"You have been thinking of me," I stated, letting my statement hang in the air between us.

She rolled her eyes and pushed my face. "Look, lover boy, it stopped being that kind of a story between us the moment you sold out the community and left," she replied, zero hint of remorse in her statement.

"That's fair," I replied humbly. She was right though. I needed a deeper reason for being back. I looked down, "There's not many days that go by that I don't regret what's happened. It's bad enough, having a beast inside me, but worse to think that I might be becoming the beast. I came back because you can't run forever, Linor. Even as much as I hate myself every day for things that are so far in the past that people don't even know their names anymore. I'm not here to leech off of you or anyone else. Just that this was my family—is my family—and I want to try and make a difference. I don't know what happened to Zevi or if he is truly a monster now. That's a whole other bridge we need to cross. For now, I want to help people, just for once in my life."

"If that means stopping your brother, what will you do?" Linor asked gently.

"I can talk him out of it. He can be—"

Her face said it all before she even spoke. "Avi, people cannot be the same person you thought they were on their road. Zevi is a monster. There is no changing that fact. It's not even Nazis anymore, it's everyone and anyone. He's crazy, Avi, he's gone." She stared me in the eyes, zero doubt in her look.

I looked away at the birds flying around in a thicket outside the window. Funny how much the world just didn't care about our problems. While I was losing my mind trying to solve the breaking of my family, the birds just flapped their wings and looked for worms. I wondered if it really mattered in the end, me coming back. I had to, though. I had tried leaving, I had tried running and it only became a neverending circle. Clocks winding with no direction until time ceases to matter altogether.

"When we were kids, Linor, I used to sneak off into the woods to try and kill myself almost every single night; while everyone slept or when people left to the bathroom, if there was a way, I was going to end it. But I never could and instead, my habit just came my life. None of us can find life again, it seems, not since we lost it in the camps, and every look comes off like a corner of that fenced-off hell we escaped from. I think the thing that bothers me the most about it all, Linor, is I just can't seem to get away from it all. It never stops, it never stops. I don't have the energy to shave or wipe my own ass, most mornings, yet I am still here. I don't care if you feel he is a monster; he is my brother, Linor. That alone is reason enough to try," I stated firmly to her.

"Avi—" she sighed, looking a lot older than she had since I first met her. Like an ancient sea whose waves have finally come back to rest on a sandy beach that had never been touched. "You've run away from anything and everyone your whole life—" she stated, leaving her sentence in the air between us. I fought back my response and tore the blanket from me, turning sideways off the bed I was in. My feet touched the hard floor of the wood paneling of Linor's grandmother's place.

How they had managed to get all the wood down so quickly on such uneven surfaces, all those years ago, still shocked me to this day. I was growing angrier and angrier at Linor's comments. *She is wrong, I know she is wrong. Just think about something more productive*, I told myself, breathing out a huge gust of wind. I rubbed my face, daring to go near my charred lips. They felt the same, just a little chapped, and definitely in need of some water. "Where are Huey and Solly?" I asked her, standing out of the bed, my knees popping as I stood. Since when was I the old guy with popping knees?

"They're in the other room. Avi, I didn't mean to... sound so cold. It's just... you've been gone for a long time. Things have changed, and we both know you left because of that night, because of what we all did," she said softly, tears forming in her eyes.

I found my shirt on the dresser next to us. I slid into it, facing the wall as I got dressed. "We were kids going around beating up strangers who used to torment us in a hell on Earth. It was only a matter of time before one of us did something stupid. I am surprised it didn't happen sooner. It just didn't have to be that man, not that night, not like that."

"He helped those tormenters, Avi. You can ignore that like you ignore everything else besides your damn self-loathing. That doesn't change the fact that if it had been one of the guards, you would have killed them just like your brother had. Ignore it, or deal with it. I don't care, it's already fucking done." She spoke bitterly, pushing back her chair as she started to leave the room. "Solly and your friend are with my grandmother. Don't stay too long Avi. Lord knows, you've been one foot gone since the day I met you." She left the room, leaving me standing there, with my mouth open, suddenly feeling far older than I should have.

"Good job fixing things, asshole," I muttered, finishing buttoning my shirt and heading out of the doorway into the hallway.

58

Chapter 58

"We shouldn't stay here long. This will be the first place they look," Huey stated, as Solly finished telling the story of the mad dash she made out of the assembly after picking us up. Apparently, Huey had managed to pull us both onto the back of Solly's crystalized deer form and she bounded her way out of the crowd as easily as skipping stones across a river. In the confusion, Solly had headed back to the community, figuring it would be too obvious for Zevi to think to find us. Turns out she had been right—for now.

"My brother is—my brother. He was never stupid, though. We just need to be smarter," I stated.

"No, we just need to get the hell out of this town. Tir was trying real hard to kill you two last night. In fact, I would say everyone there was trying really hard to kill us," Solly said gloomily, while sipping coffee. We were in Linor's kitchen. Linor was washing a cloth over and over again in the sink, having not spoken a word since the two of us had entered.

"Your friend is right, Avi. Your brother will be here soon. You need to leave. He hates this place almost as much as he hates the Germans," she stated, finally joining the room.

I wanted to say something more to Linor. How to approach her without putting my foot in my mouth was more complicated than I ever would have thought possible. "Speaking of that, Linor, you're the inside person.

What the fuck is Zevi doing?" I asked her. Without turning her back, Linor spewed smoke from her body. Colors of ashen gray and swirls of light brown formed a deer, stumbling to the ground with wooden arrows coming from its side. I regarded it for a long moment before clearing my throat. Linor continued to clean her rag in the soapy water of the sink. I looked at Huey and Solly. Huey seemed confused by the fact that smoke had created an image of a dying deer. I should have told him more about everyone's strange abilities. Solly looked like she had seen a ghost, her skin having gone paler than most paints.

"Solly," I whispered.

"You need to leave soon, Avi. Please," Linor stated.

Linor's grandmother walked into the kitchen once her granddaughter had finished speaking. "Boy—" she started. I turned toward her, already feeling drained from the coming fight. The old woman seemed to have aged a few years during the night, and her skin now dropped lower than before, bags under her sagging eyes were bruised to raccoon likeness. The night had been no more kind to her than it had been to us, if not longer, and must have been like reliving the nights in the camp.

I hated the old woman, but she was still part of the community. All the times she had tortured me and ridiculed me made more sense: she was afraid to lose her granddaughter to the big bad wolf. "Yeah, old woman?" I sighed, asking her.

"Thank you," she replied simply. The room seemed to draw its breath in, so much so that even Linor stopped what she was doing.

"I didn't—I had nothing to do with bringing her back," I mumbled. Linor dropped the rag and crossed the distance between her and her grandmother, taking the older woman into a deep hug. I stopped talking. This was a moment between the two in which I had no right to say anything.

Huey, however, was always the more objective driver out of the two of us. He would stay on task, no matter what came up. "I am glad to see you guys together, but we don't have time for this," he stated matter-of-factly.

"You were earwigging again, yes?" Solly asked my friend.

"What does that even mean?" Huey blinked at her.

"Means not minding your own business!" Solly stated, leaving Huey with a long face.

"No, he is right. Linor, we need to know, please: what is my brother doing? I cannot help anyone if you don't talk to me," I pleaded with her.

She stepped back from her grandmother, their hands clasped in their center before she turned back to me. "Did you know that Schwein has to eat so much to help with his teeth? Since they're always growing, he gnaws constantly—like some kind of teething puppy. And Bug, his skin is so pale now that he fries like a leaf during a brutal fall?" she asked me. Her face was turned slightly toward me, away from her grandmother.

I was borderline flabbergasted. She took my pause as a time to start talking again. "Your brother treats them surprisingly well; they would die for him—kill for him. He has an army, Avi. I know you. You won't do what needs to be done. You have to promise to kill him, Avi, if you even can. If you aren't willing to go the distance, then you won't beat your brother. He has rooted himself into this community as a protector," she stated.

I stepped back from the kitchen island. If I managed to make it through all of this, my stomach was never going to be the same. I felt a boulder roll into my stomach lining. "I won't kill anyone," I whispered to the room, my head held low.

"Maybe you should reconsider that position," she challenged.

"Linor," Solly said gently.

"No, Solly, he needs to hear this. A little bit after you left, I was walking home from work—we all had to get jobs like normal people after the police came. Zevi may have broken off a deal, somehow, but gone were the days of playing it fast and lose around town. Anyways—I crossed into a dark alley one night."

She trailed off and my heart busted open, like a door to a sub, deep underwater. Somehow and against all odds, something forced its way out into the crushing depths. I did not for a moment like where her story was going.

The whole room was quiet as tears rolled down her face. "They jumped me pretty quick. I fought back, but it was five on one and my abilities are just smoke creatures. Wasn't a whole lot I could do, so I did my best and fought back, made some pretty wild stuff. And you know what, Avi? It was your brother who came and pulled them off me. Some out-of-town asshats—either way, when they were bloodied and beaten, your brother simply offered them a place in his army. They accepted. I found out later he simply liked the way they fought, and it had nothing to do with what they almost came close to doing," she shouted.

I cleared my throat before speaking, "That doesn't mean that my brother is a monster. Everywhere has a few bad—"

"A few bad eggs? Okay, let me finish the damn story. Your brother knows his men do that—knows it and allows it. He may not pull the trigger, he may not be the one raping someone, but he might as well be, Avi. His men 'protect' this town by preying on people—harming anyone that they can get their hands on. I confronted him again about it later, and he gave me a blanket and told me to try not to kill myself. That's the kind of self-righteous monster you're dealing with! He's done far worse to far too many people. You're asking me to put my family at risk so that you can spare your conscience again? Get bent, asshole!" she screamed, storming off out of the kitchen. A wave of gray flooded the room, obscuring her as she went outside into the early morning.

All of us left the tent as tendrils of smoke shrouded Linor's home, like a living beast from the sea. She was gone. I had no idea which direction she had taken, either. I sniffed the air. There were too many scents for me to get a good read.

Huey was bent over coughing next to me when he stood up. "Not your finest hour, man," he stated, pulling out a cigarette from his front pocket.

I snatched it out of his hands and threw it on the ground. "We have to find her! She could be in danger," I told him.

His face looked doubtful at best. "I've known many women in my life. That's one subject that none ever take lightly. If you're going to get her help, you will need to drop every pretext you had before and just listen, man. Even if you said the right thing, it won't be. Just listen. Please, for God's sake, I am here for you pal. You don't have to lie to me. You still have the hots for smoke girl. That's fine. Don't lose yourself in the process though," he stated calmly.

"What the fuck does that mean?" I demanded.

"I think it means, don't be an asshole, Avi," Solly chimed in, coughing into her hand. Neither of them were much help in that moment.

"Where did she even go?" I asked, throwing my hands in the air. "I didn't even do anything!" I complained.

Linor's grandmother answered me, sternly. "I am only telling you this because I love my granddaughter. I don't like you, wolf. That still hasn't changed. She went to the old burnt-down church on the east side of town. She always goes there when she's that upset."

I nodded, turning to run off in that direction of town. "Hurry, Avi. We don't have a lot of time," Huey called over my shoulders.

"I know!" I fired back as I ran through the camp.

59

Chapter 59

My run had been quiet, save for the beating of my heart, as I flew like a jet through the eerily dead town. I didn't know what this silence meant. I was afraid even more now of what it would mean if I lost Linor.

An hour into my race after Linor, I had completely forgotten the direction to the old church. I wandered aimlessly through the backstreets, behind the fields and old factory buildings, until a farmer on a tractor came chugging down the road. I waved him down, wiping the sweat from my forehead, trying to appear somewhat presentable. "Greetings—young man. Don't think I've seen you in these parts before." The old man spoke through the side of his mouth, an unlit pipe jutting from the corners. He had chewed the wooden cobbler almost to a nub, giving me the impression he used to smoke a fair bit and had recently quit. Glasses perched on his wide nose and his ears seemed to sag, like the rest of his skin—victims of gravity, no longer able to fight. He squinted his eyes before waiting for my response. "Say—you wouldn't happen to be one of Zevi's boys, would you?" he asked skeptically.

Remembering what I saw last night, I cleared my throat and did my best to lie to the old man. I felt shame instantly, but I had no other choice, "Yes sir, I sure am. I am just looking for the old church on the east side. Can you point me in the right direction?" I asked back to the old farmer, trying to appear as if I was completely innocent.

He scratched his chin for a moment, sucking in on his pipe as if taking a long draw from the handle. "You're pretty close—just down that ways." He pointed slightly over his left shoulder.

I nodded. "Thank you, sir."

As I started to move around his tractor, the old farmer replied, "Anything for Zevi—that boy helped keep the debt collectors from taking my family's farm. All of us owe him. Tell him I said God bless." The old farmer powered on his tractor on, coughing a loud mechanical blotch into the air. I waited until the slow-moving tractor was out of my sight line before carrying on.

The church was in ruins. The roof had long since caved in, the stairs leading up to the rustic red chamber doors were nearly off their hinges, and the whole thing reeked of charred wood. I hesitated, wiping the sweat off my head. It had taken me a little over two hours to get here by foot. I had to risk running the roads, due to the fear of Tir somehow learning where I was by using the trees.

I walked through the broken doors of the church, opening the sun up to the crypt inside. Even though the roof was caved in, it still held surprisingly well. I called out, "Linor?"

She responded after a moment. "Avi? Avi." Linor stammered, her feet gliding over the burnt wood as if she weighed as little as a feather.

"No more bullshit, Linor. I want some answers." I entered through the archway, feeling my body tense and itch, ready to bolt from my own flesh, as if I was trapped in some kind of meat prison. I had to keep control. If I lost it, even for a moment, Linor was a goner. I hoped being direct with her was the best approach.

At the sound of my voice, Linor turned to me, her face a mixture of confusion that slowly shifted to genuine happiness floating through her eyes, as we engaged in what could be the last moments of both our lives in the slow decay of the scorched room. So much had changed with us—yet nothing at all, I thought, feeling regret for sticking my foot in my mouth before.

"I know. I know. You're right. And I always wanted to tell you but, I just... I can only remember a little and the rest is just gone! Like someone stole it from my head. Does it really matter now? I'm not blaming you for what happened, Avi. I just don't understand how you can think the way you do." She looked almost past me, as if staring off at an unseen performance of men and women on a backdrop stage, like we talked about as children. Putting on a play for all the world. But when the curtain was drawn and the lights were dimmed, what remained?

My anger deflated at that, here I was coming into the church, almost expecting a righteous call of someone who wronged me. *Not just anyone, you big monkey. She is someone that used to love you.* I lowered my eyes, searching for a moment in the blacked floor for an answer, when suddenly her hands took hold of my face. Although long and slender, they were powerful, firm, beaming with a strength I had no idea Linor could possess.

"You know what makes me want to take a knife and split you from end to end, Avi?" she snarled, her two mismatched eyes a blaze of fury. Even her green emerald, which first belonged to my brother, was as fierce as Greek fire burning on the sails of a fleeing enemy. This was not the woman I had fallen in love with. At least as her body moved toward me and her eyes hauntingly tracked my face, as it pulled mine inches away from her. But the monster I had feared had shown itself. *This is it, don't lose control.* I breathed. The beast crawled its way to the surface. I remembered last night's flames and I feared for her life; what if I couldn't keep it down again?

"I hate you! I have a safe of blood that oozes with every breath of air that you take into your lungs. I hate everything about you, Avi. How you could just walk away so easily, and now here you are again?" She twirled her left hand, ruffling her thick black hair. I shifted my weight back at her comment, causing a floorboard to creak beneath my weight.

She snapped back both her hands to my face, as if drawn like a baby from a mother's womb. Anger on the brink of a cruel world that was indifferent and would never be any different.

"I hate the way you frown and slump your shoulders. That quiver in your lips when you speak of anything. That way you remain aloof and blue; brittle as a bone being crushed by rocks!" She drilled me with her eyes, pulling my face closer to hers. "Most of all, I hate that you drape yourself in this cloak of sorrow. No, I'm sorry... entitled narcissistic cloak. Let me tell you something, Avi. The world is a very mean and cruel place waiting to devour all of us, in a slow grinding doom for all of eternity. Yet you! You prance around as if it's your God-given right to feel the saddest of them all. Never trying to change a smile or share the nectar of solace with anyone. No, instead, you stay imprisoned by what you are. No, I'm not talking about that animal inside you. What happened to you was barbaric and hideous. That's the thing though, Avi. You weren't the only one that suffered in that camp! You got out easy!" she screamed, detaching herself from my face and moving across the charred floor like a like a butterfly flapping through a field of flowers.

I put my hands at my side. She had me dead to rights. I lowered my gaze, tracking her feet as they glided over the floor, barefooted, but moving with grace despite the hardwood. In all the years I had known her, she'd never had shoes on, even in a place like this, come to think of it. The only time she wore them was in the camps. That was her thing, though, a chance to be rebellious against a world that did not care about us Gypsies and Jews. *Small holes can sink a ship just as quick as the big holes,* I reminded myself. I needed to start patching holes with my family. Linor had been suffering for a long time—longer than I ever thought possible.

She continued after a moment, her body freezing in place, now only feet away. I couldn't meet her gaze. "Do you know what it's like to have pieces of yourself stripped away, like the fat on an animal? Stolen from you, twisted and placed inside of another? Not just another, but inside the skull of a genuine animal? Then to have that person placed so deep inside you, so dredged inside you, that you can't shake the thoughts of a monster? Thoughts that aren't yours anymore, thoughts of violence, of terror, of this clinging, unstable devil that you hate so much that you would rather tear open your veins than to live with them. But you can't. Because when something is inside of you, so deeply, you can never remove it from yourself. It's a part of you, even if you don't want it to be. Once something is in you so deep, that hole is dug and you're just along for the ride. That's survival—that's my every day! You may not think your brother is an animal, but I've seen it, I can see it inside his mind!" She turned from me, weeping into her hands.

My words choked in my throat, the beast within me silenced. "Linor," I croaked. Her eyes shot opened and butterflies erupted from her mouth. A legion of crimson creatures fluttered around me, dozing me in thick goblets of blood. I knew they were fake, that they were just images she was projecting, smoke into the bottle of the world around her.

I still felt afraid. Only a truly lost man wouldn't shiver as the woman he loved broke down in pain, turning something as beautiful and as natural as the butterfly into a harbinger of blood. I just wanted to sit down for a long time, then take her with me and leave this place. Only that kind of relationship between the two of us was now over for good. Still, I cared for her and I wanted to do what was right, I reminded myself.

The butterflies disappeared just as quickly, leaving us in a room of total darkness. A gloom so absolute that I would have thought we were on different worlds, had I not felt her hot breath only feet away from mine. "You saved us... you saved us when were children. I know it hurts, I know it feels awful when you turn into that creature, but you have to. You can't beat your brother on your own and you know it. Why, I'm not talking about killing everyone in his army, just him. The only one, because he is a monster! Are you just that afraid, that gutless to do what's right?" she snarled—her lips trembling. Tears fell to the dark ground below us.

I snarled back. Linor knew perfectly well why I didn't turn into the wolf.

She sensed the anger coming from me. "Just him, Avi. Why is that so hard for you? That weird sense of antiquated morality that you don't even believe in yourself! You never believed in anything! Why start now?" she shouted at me, turning her body inward, covering her face.

"God almighty. No—it's never been hard! Every day, I feel this thing inside me that has been burning my insides and tormenting my dreams for years. Every day, I wake up wondering if today is the day that I finally lose control and everyone dies. If I feed that thing, stop trying to control it, that is the day that I am gone and there is no coming back," I whispered, looking at the floor.

"I am just talking about one person, Avi. One person. Because of what they did to your family. Please, if you ever loved us. If you ever loved me…" she whimpered.

"I'm sorry, Linor, but I can't…" I trailed off, not meeting her gaze. The room fell silent, and outside, birds chirped away the day as the two of us broke down into pieces smaller than the eye of a needle.

I sucked in a deep breath. I sucked in another afterward. *Think Avi, think for her.* That was the thing that I had been missing. Here, I was trying so hard not to let the beast out. *As if I had forgotten that the beast didn't make me the man I was!* The beast had helped shape me, but my actions now—that would only be a man playing at being a monster. Not the beast itself.

She genuinely loved me. She needed me to be strong and happy, to lead her through this pain; not remind her at every turn of the misery that we had been through. I had goose-stepped us into an endless night that stretched on forever. By not caring about anything other than my own pain, that was how I had become lost in my own pain, with almost no way out.

I felt shame as my lips began to move. I continued on, though. "We can never be whole, never again. It riles me, the way that we've allowed ourselves to become this. But that isn't the point. There is an undeniable amount of collective pain that we both share. That we all share in this life; but we weren't made to suffer. I don't think any of us were made to suffer in this world. We don't have to fight the whole world; we don't have to fight each other. Despite all the pain, it's exactly this grief, this sorrow that binds us. No one can tell us how to be in this world. I'm sorry I lead us down a path that is filled with so much shadow." I pulled my gaze up and stepped tenderly across the distance between us, until I felt my arms wrap around her. She flinched at first, pulling away from my arms. I held on, gently, and waited for her form to relax into my arms.

"We were made to love, Linor. I can't undo what this life has done to either of us. What it's done to anyone. I don't care how pathetic my words

390

sound to anyone else besides us—from now on, it's just you and me. There is nowhere else I would rather be than beside you. I think if the world created man, and man created so much suffering, then there's no reason why love can't create a better world. It starts with us; that is the easy part. It was never hard for me, and I'm sorry I wasn't seeing the monster that I was becoming. It's not about beating darkness. It's about curing the night; creating a star for all the nights to come. We cannot forget the pain, but we can find what makes us whole. Together," I whispered, cupping her chin into my own as I searched her eyes in the shadow of the room.

60

Chapter 60

Her face scrunched up, then blushed red before she started laughing. I held on for a few seconds before I dropped my hands. "What's so funny?" I asked her.

"You. You're pretty funny sometimes, Avi," she chided. "I don't think you're a monster, Avi. I've always thought you needed to get out of your own way, is all. I just want you to see that the rest of us need help from the big bad wolf, not just yourself," she stated calmly, twirling away from me.

She started to stretch in the darkness of the church. I watched for a moment before speaking. Linor was the only person I had ever known who could stab you with her hair knife right before taking you dancing. Other people would probably call her moody. She would tell you to shut the fuck up and would make gingerbread afterward. A truly bizarre creature—I liked her. I knew we weren't done with Zevi, not by a mile. I wasn't going to condemn someone on the words of others, especially not my brother. Even if it was looking and sounding worse by the second.

I decided no more lies and keeping to myself. I took a deep breath, "We need to get back to the others, Linor," I said softly.

She stopped her movement and looked at me. "Why do I feel like you've already retreated to that strange headspace of yours," she stated.

I smirked. "You know me better than anyone else in the world. What do you think is on my mind?" I asked her.

She sighed, "Probably something along the lines of still being undecided about your brother. All I ask, Avi, is that you recognize who's been your real family all this time. Think about how to help everyone else. Maybe then you can figure out how to help yourself," she stated, sweeping past me in the church. She leaned in, kissing my cheek softly. "Nice talk. Next time, just take me dancing instead." She lingered for a moment before leaving through the rustic doorway.

I shook my head, looking at the blackened stained glass. I think it had depicted an angel at one time. Now I could just make out a face and halo. Hopefully some angel was watching. We were going to need it. As I started to turn, the fire-stained glass splintered and cracked, dropping to the dark floor below. I stared blankly for a moment, not moving or breathing.

Please don't mean anything other than gravity, please. Would it be too much to settle this without anyone having to get hurt? I was so tired of seeing people get chewed up by this world as if they were dog meat. I knew though that was wishful thinking. And wishful thinking never got anyone through a fire.

61

Chapter 61

"Do you really think things will get better, or were you just saying that to get me to calm down?" Linor asked as we made our way back to the camp. Surprisingly, just like when we were kids, there were an abundant number of bikes littered around this town. Some things never changed, even in musky hometowns, where the bricks seemed to be older than the mountains that surrounded the town. As we rode, I thought about change, and how it never seemed to happen in a hurry at all—at least not while you were aware of it. But, like the turning of a light switch, it can all suddenly be different within a breath.

I smirked at her. "I would never tell you to calm down. Remember how that turned out the last time I did it?"

She beamed. "Yeah, I remember. Might have gone a bit overboard with the branch in your wheels thing."

"Just a bit. Left a lovely shiner. Lucky I landed in that dirty pond," I stated.

"That pond is still there by the way—still dirty."

"Really?"

"Yeah, really. Quit stalling, Avi. Answer me, please," she said softly.

I sighed. "Yeah, Linor, I meant it. Things can change."

"How do you know that? Like how can you believe things can change? That people will change?" she asked.

"Because time is like a river flowing forward always... but most importantly, I think the only way any of us can ever find peace with each other, with ourselves, is to change. Otherwise, what's the purpose of all of this? Ending up like the weird turtles in that strange pond off of the highway?" I gestured behind me at the highway leading around town.

Linor turned her head and looked at me. "I don't know. That all sounds well and good. Like something Elder Ad would have taught us," she stated.

I thought about it for a moment more. "How deep an answer are you wanting right now, Linor?" I asked her.

This time she sighed. "I know I am going to regret saying this. Sometimes you could answer things with just a yes or no, you know that? But this is the one time I won't complain about a long-winded answer, so go ahead," she replied, exasperated already.

"Because over all these years and after all the things that we've been through, when I saw you again, the rest of the world stopped. If love doesn't make things at least a little bit better, we are all fucked," I stated calmly.

Linor tilted her head down, thoughtfully, and the two of us rode in silence the rest of the way.

62

Chapter 62

Whenever I see smoke, even just a little, my heart always drops to the bottom of my stomach. Even from a candle I picture the unending gray that came from the chimneys at the camps, the feel of human ash falling on my cheeks. How light it is, almost like a snowflake, yet made from your brothers and sisters, mothers and fathers. Smoke meant something was burning; if it was on fire, it was either being used to create or to destroy. In this case, on a warm summer day, I knew that the smoke rising over the hill, like a thick blanket being draped over the world meant nothing good.

Linor immediately took off on her bike once she saw the smoke. It was in the direction of the community. I bolted after her, both of us quiet as our bikes tore through the thick woods on the way to the camp. We rounded the mounded hill and came to Long Jimmy's field. His home was an inferno, and his donkey lay on her side, the rounded holes of bullets sprayed across her body. Linor went faster, and I called out, "Slow down, Linor. We don't know who's out there!"

She ignored me and went even faster. I dug deep, pushing the small bike over the mounds of dirt. I looked down at one point—thick tire tracks and lots of boot marks. A lot of people had come to the community. It was clear—this had to be Zevi's men. But a small candle of hope for my brother burned even more. Around the bend, the first destroyed house of the community came into view. Fires roared on nearly every roof, every tent, and tree. Since most the camp was made out of scrap, I knew it was only a matter of time before the community went up into flames completely.

I trembled. But at least no one seemed to be in their homes. Even with the burning material, as we quickly passed each home, I could only smell the smoke of chemicals stored in people's dwellings. Burning food, but no burning people, thankfully. The smell of someone burning, it was a lot like pork at first. At first. Before the hair and the fingernails became heated; then it was nauseating, choking, terrible smells.

Burning rubber littered the air, causing me to pull my shirt up. I yelled at Linor, trying to get her attention. "Linor!" She turned, and I gestured for her to cover her mouth. She nodded, stopping long enough to tear off a long strip of her shirt, wrapping it over her mouth. I waited until she tied it before moving on. Every beat of my heart filled me with dread as we went through the many empty homes of the community. At the third trailer we passed, Linor got mad, ditching her bike, and she took off running in the direction of the huge oak tree at the outskirts of the camp. I followed suit, running after her.

Passing Solly's tattoo station as it went up in flames caused me to pause. Outside her place was a dropped shotgun and a pool of blood splattering the dirt and porch, near bullet holes in the side of her home. Someone had been shot, a few times to be exact. I just hoped it hadn't been Solly or Huey. I turned back to see Linor's home in complete disarray, spirals of flames licking over the cornerpiece oak tree, bark melting away like wet cotton candy.

Linor charged to the red tent flap, not pausing as she pulled at the zipper. She was mad—it was about to come completely down any moment. I could hear the cracking of the support beams through the sound of the flames. I rushed toward her, pulling at her waist, "Linor, stop. There's nothing you can do."

"Let me go, you, bastard!" she howled, I held on tighter, pulling us both to the ground in front of the burning wreckage. Nearly her whole life had been in that one tent. It had been a home for me as well, I realized, as she sobbed into my shoulders, a place where I'd gone to see someone I cared about every single day. I lowered my head in respect before standing, taking Linor gently with me.

"I don't want to go..." she trailed off, looking over my shoulders, as I walked us out of there.

"We can't stay here... besides, we need a plan," I responded to the flames as they danced all around us, haunting me, as fire burned away another home of mine.

No matter where I was or how old I seemed to get, the world just kept burning away my homes. There would be no rest today—not for a while.

63

Chapter 63

Safety for us came once I got us past Long Jimmy's place. The smoke from the community was reaching well above the forest lines. I walked us both to the field, my hands around Linor's waist. She had kept her head down the whole way, covering her mouth. The only sound she made was weak coughs. If it wasn't for the wolf, I wondered if I would have been able to lead us out of the haze—I could barely see my hand in front of my face our entire walk.

Linor coughed, her body still dragging along in the smoke. "Still think he deserves to live, Avi?" she asked me, weakly.

I ignored her, grunting as I focused on pulling us both to safety. *Get her clear first, then deal with Zevi,* I told myself. I sat Linor down gently against the side of mine and Huey's truck, in the field outside Jimmy's place. She looked awful, her skin coated gray from all the toxins in the air, and her face paler than ice.

I opened the truck door, rummaging for a bag in the back seat, thankful that Huey and I hadn't unpacked the truck. Ink stains were all over the steering wheel, I noticed, as I pulled a bottle of water out of the bag. That answered how Solly had got us back here.

I went to Linor, taking the cap off the bottle, and pressed it against her lips, tilting it back for her to drink. She coughed a few more times, before mumbling "Thanks."

I nodded back to her, leaving the bottle in her hands. In the distance, I could hear the roar of bikes; I jerked my head in the direction of the noise.

Just leave it out—they must be coming back to finish the job. I debated for a moment, shoving Linor in the truck and peeling out of there. How far would we get? Where would we even go? Before I could do anything, the riders of the motorcycles came into view, their faces lit in fury, but I gave a sigh of relief. It was just Bipin and his siblings.

They came to a stop, circling the truck, a mixture of fear and diesel permeating the air. Bipin's eyes were stained red, making the kid look far younger than I had seen him before. They must have gone by the community. In that moment, I saw myself in Bipin's eyes—just another angry kid who had lost his home; lost his life.

His fists were shaking at his sides and I took note that his siblings had circled Linor and me, not turning off their bikes, with far less control than Bipin. Most of them were twitching, squirming, and his sister was growling. The kid looked like he was going to jump right out of his flesh and attack me. Which may have actually been something possible—in this community, expect any super-powered feats.

We stared each other down in a High Noon-style face-off. I was too tired for the tough guy act, but I grimaced anyways. "Did you do this?" Bipin snarled in a low voice through clenched teeth. It wasn't a question and to him, there was the possibility that the guy who had turned in the community all those years ago, who could turn into a werewolf made of fire and hate, had finally snapped, destroying the community like everyone had always feared.

I regarded him for a long moment, not daring to lose eye contact with the boy. I recognized someone who was about to snap—I'd had the same wild look nearly every morning of my life. "No—I did not," I responded, keeping eye contact, while at the same time I moved my body at an angle in front of Linor. If things went south, I could at least shield Linor for a moment. Hopefully, the beast would leave her alone. In my experience with that creature, though, best to leave hope for the churchgoers.

He scrunched his face in deep thought. "How do I believe that?

You promised me that the community would be fine—that's what you promised," he hissed.

Ouch. The kid had a point, and exactly what I wanted to avoid by coming back home had happened. I destroyed things. That was my talent in life; we all had something that could be cultivated into a great sum. Mine was death, mine was destruction, ruination, and heartbreak. *Or maybe it is just self-loathing,* a small voice spoke up inside my head.

"Shut up you," both the wolf and I hissed into the confines of my subconscious.

"Your father would say to trust me or don't," I stated.

"Or act," he whispered, unclenching his fists and turning away to nod at his siblings. They all killed their ignition at the same time. I drew a breath, my legs shaking. I wasn't in the mood to fight the children of my mentor; of a man I had let down.

"You probably wouldn't have Linor right now if you had done it, and I doubt even the five of us could eat the whole community." He trailed off, lowering his eyes. I knew how much it hurt to bury your anger—put aside the desire to act. He would get that chance soon enough, hopefully, or else he would end up just like me. That I didn't want for any of these kids, a bitter person hiding from the world.

I stepped forward toward Bipin and his siblings hissed at me. Tivian was nearest and her hair was flaring behind her like a windmill. I had seen them transform many times when they were kids, into cute little puppies. Looking at their confidence, now, I would say they probably weren't as cute anymore. Whatever magic or force had given birth to the beast, had forever changed the world—in a weird way, that made me responsible for all of this. Zevi would have never gained this much power without his strength, without the help of the others.

I outstretched my hand, placing it on Bipin's shoulder. Bipin didn't react; he just stared at me blankly. I then threw back my meanest hook, catching him square in the face, sending the boy to the ground in a heap.

Tivian's eyes went wide, completely confused on how to act. Bipin sat up in the dirt, clutching his nose as a few drops fell down his face.

"What—the—shit was that for?" he muttered as the blood came down.

"Because, kid—let this all fucking go. You and I both know that my brother's goons have most likely been wanting to do this for a while. Armies like entertainment and judging by what I've seen and heard, they're an aggressive lot. I need you to focus—focus really hard on what I am about to say. Please," I added keeping my eyes fixed on him.

He hesitated, gesturing down to keep his siblings from ripping me apart.

"We are going to act, kid, I promise. This time, I will keep my word. But you saw the community—everyone is gone. If Zevi and his gang had killed them, there would be a lot more evidence than what was there. You know anyone in the community would put up a fight over a loaf of bread, let alone something like this," I stated. Bipin shrugged, clutching his nose.

"I need you to trust me that I am going to take care of this—with you. This isn't a fly-off-the-handle thing and kill all of them. If you want to do right by your community, I need to make sure you're firing on all the correct gears, and are not just angry. If you let that shit build up, it will stay with you long after you've done the right thing, then what will it matter what you did or did not do? You will loathe yourself too much, you might as well have been the one who set fire to all the homes. Let me tell you, kid, you don't fucking want that. So, I am asking you now, to help me in this. But I am calling the shots. We do this my way and we get our people back," I outstretched my hand toward him. He hesitated again, reasoning slowly setting in, and took my hand. I pulled the young man up, wiping the dirt off his back.

Tivian and his siblings surrounded him instantly. One of his brothers was already a massive wolf, close to the size of a small horse, easily weighing as much as their motorcycles. Long thick gray fur with a stripe of black down his back. As he passed me, a snarl ripped out between his teeth. He was almost at my chest level, so the sound reverberated up my body. I flinched. They weren't so cute anymore. Good, we were going to need that today. Tivian scowled at me from a distance. I left them alone to talk as I went back to Linor. She was up now, leaning against the truck, her face still too pale for comfort. "Are you, alright?" I asked her stopping a few feet away.

She looked world weary, watching the group before turning back to me. "You know—I was pretty sure you were about to get eaten there... Good call on punching a kid in the face," she joked.

I shrugged. "I would rather him dislike me than hate my brother and get himself killed or worse," I responded.

"What's worse than being killed?" she asked, skeptically as Bipin approached us.

"Being the last one left alive," I replied somberly.

"What's the plan then, Avi?" he said as the group pressed in around me. I had never liked being that close to anyone. As they neared, I felt like smoke in a jar. Agile enough in theory to dodge anything, but once trapped, smoke was just as caught as the rest of us.

I cleared my throat, tasting more of the burning community. I wondered how Linor was able to stand it, as her face had a sickened, ashen look. She needed rest. We needed to end this now. "Okay, I will be honest. I don't know where my brother took the community." That was met with a lot of groans and eye rolls. "Hey—let's look at what we do know. They brought a lot of people—enough to take well over a hundred people without killing anyone, even with some of the powers they have. It would still take a lot. So that's two. They have the numbers and they didn't kill any of our friends," I stated, holding up two fingers.

"So, basically we are fucked either way," Tivian groaned.

I sighed, rubbing my head—it was either the smoke or just the general insanity of my life, but one thing or another had seemed to cause me a headache every day since coming back to this community. I glanced at the group sighing heavily. "Not necessarily. My father was a watch maker. He spent his days in a shop toiling away at pieces of metal inside of tight boxes that he inherited from his father. One thing he often told me was the need to find where the pieces went. They always come together; we just need to figure out how. So, does anyone here for starters have any idea where they would take that many people—where they could be held?" I was asking a group of youths who could transform into werewolves, who spent their days riding around a community of Gypsies. Stellar people, for sure, but nothing in the way of what we needed at the moment.

Linor coughed behind me, tugging on my elbow as she stood next to me. "There's a warehouse that Zevi does most of his businesses at," she stated matter-of-factly. I looked at her, bewildered that she even had the strength to talk, let alone stand and move. Linor was tough. I smiled, glad to have her with me.

"That could be the place, depending on how far it is. Is it close?" I asked her. She nodded slowly. "Okay—here's what we are going to do. I have a hunch that my brother most likely knows that you will think to take us there. I believe the only reason he didn't kill the community is the same reason as last night: he wants something—or someone. Let's take advantage of that, break it down. Bipin, can you and your siblings cause a distraction? I'm not talking like last time. I mean something big—very big," I asked the young man.

He seemed thoughtful for a moment before saying, "Yes, I have an idea that should work."

I nodded toward him. "Good."

"That doesn't solve how we will get a hundred people out of a warehouse, Avi. Most are elderly and children," Linor reminded me. I looked at her, dreading what I had planned before I even asked. "We are going to need an image, Linor. Something really big. You have to turn the whole group invisible, like you did in the camps all those years ago for me." I looked at her, and part of me was hoping she would say no. She had been through enough over the years. I was tired of her suffering needlessly. I knew what kind of person she was, though, before she even answered.

Her look could have fooled a mirror, before she finally said, softly, "Yes."

"Thank you, Linor. And while every one of you guys is causing as much noise as possible, getting their army out of the building, I will make my move," I stated.

"By yourself?" Linor asked, concern evident in her voice.

"Yeah by myself. You aren't scared, are you chicken?" I jabbed at her.

A smirk ran across her face. "Scared? Nope, just sad I get to miss you sneaking around like a dumbass," she shot back.

I snorted. "Plenty of time in the future to show you my incredible skills," I replied.

She suddenly became very grave. "Avraham, you can't seriously think that you can rescue everyone inside a building you've never been to all by yourself. You will die, or worse, turn into that..." she trailed off. We both knew what she meant.

I was feeling awkward with all the kids around me. I tried to ignore that fact and responded to her, "I'm not some secret bad-ass, Linor, we both know that. My friend is, though. And Solly saved our asses the other night and your grandmother is too annoying to ever die." She raised an eyebrow at me for that last part. "My point is, if we come in there with guns blazing, then we will lose like last time. He wants us to come get them. Why, I have no idea. I don't want to know. This way, though, I don't think he will every suspect anyone could be that stupid to try. Call it a hunch, but Zevi has always been cocky. Let's use that hubris against him. I trust you guys can make enough of a distraction to give me time to get in and get out. If we act quick and hit them hard—I think it might just work. Otherwise, who else are we going to call? It's always just been us. We are the survivors of the *Shoah*. We're the Roma; we handle our own shit," I stated. That got a small smile out of her, but the concern in her eyes told me exactly what my shaky legs were telling me: *this wasn't going to work.*

It had to, though. I didn't see any other option. Linor looked as unconvinced as I felt, and so did Bipin and his siblings. I gulped. *This is going to be a long night—just for once, please, if anyone is out there listening, whatever force that may be, let this haphazard plan somehow work.* "Meet back here at nightfall, everyone. Let's get ready."

64

Chapter 64

I hadn't brought many pairs of clothes with me. I dug through the duffle bag in the back of the truck. Linor was sitting on the hood, twisting what looked like a bunch of flowers into a ring. I left her alone as I got changed. Both of us were completely covered in ash and other debris. I grumbled. When I had gotten out of the camps, one of the first things I'd done was buy sweaters, lots of sweaters. Every day felt like I was never warm enough again, like there wasn't enough fabric between me and the elements.

Nearing thirty though, to still have all my clothes fit into one bag made me wonder. Maybe, just maybe, I could finally stop this life and retire somewhere. I hadn't earned money in my life and I would never be able to have much of a "job." I did however, have good people that came into my life. That was worth me fighting for; worth only having a bag of clothes.

I pulled on a basic shirt and new pair of pants. They still hung loose and I had misplaced my belt just after taking it off. I rummaged through the back of the truck for my belt. Linor chimed in, interrupting my maddening search. "Look on the pants you were wearing, Avi."

I rolled my eyes, searching for my previous pair. Sure enough, my belt was still looped through them. I went ahead and poked a new loop in the belt with a knife. Still sort of loose—that should do, though. I closed the truck door and handed Linor a jacket. She glanced my way, taking the coat without saying anything. Careful not to drop her loop of flowers. "How do you always know where I put things?" I asked her.

Without looking up she responded, "Because I know you, Avi."

I took that for what it was. "Fair enough. How are you feeling?" I asked her.

"Same as the last dozen times you asked me. Does it really matter?" she responded.

"Fair enough—just, you know."

She arched an eyebrow at me. "What do I know, Avi?"

I muttered, feeling like everything I said was completely wrong with her these days. "We will get them back, Linor. We will, I promise."

"Don't make promises that you don't know if you can keep, Avi. We don't know what to expect."

"Fair—"

She cut me off, sliding off the truck and taking hold of my face in both her hands. "Stop saying 'Fair enough.' Nothing has been fair about any of this, alright? Just promise me, Avi, that you won't run away again, no matter what happens. You came back to help—I believe you, just see it through to the end, please."

She gripped my face in her hands, on the verge of tears. I nodded at her, and she kissed me softly while my blood rushed to my lips at her soft touch. We moved our lips. It was slow, rhythmic, and the kind of kiss that takes you away from the stresses of life, even if it's only for a moment. After a few more blissful seconds, we separated and Linor had turned back to her flower ring. I rubbed my lips, still feeling her on me, still smelling her.

I cleared my throat. "Let's get moving before Bipin gets worried."

"Fair enough," she replied, coming to the driver's door.

"I thought you told me to stop saying 'Fair enough,'" I stated as she turned the engine on in the old truck.

She moved the mirror into position, "Oh, you can say whatever you want. Just not those words," she responded.

"Okay—let me think what you can't say anymore," I pondered out loud as she reversed out of the field, fires from the community still trailing off into the distance.

"You can go fuck yourself, Avi," she jabbed, taking off onto the dark road.

"Fair enough," I muttered.

65

Chapter 65

She was smoking out the window, her cigarette hand cupping her chin gently, her other arm resting on the crease of her elbow. The wind causing her dark hair to sway like sails at sea. In the distance, thunder was crackling in the direction of the burning sky we had come from. Like the weather itself was crying out for what had happened. I punched the accelerator a little more, tensing up as we neared the warehouse destination point.

I was still looking at her when Linor said, "Can't you focus on the road, dumbass?"

"You know, something about watching you smoke—it's just probably one of the most sensual and alluring things I've ever seen in my life. Like a black and white movie, you know? The ones with the incredible woman in red, visiting the hard-boiled detective late at night in his office," I replied.

She smirked, dashing her smoke on the window and returning it to the ashtray in the truck. "I don't think anyone can be attractive while they smoke—but thank you, dumbass." She beamed.

"You're welcome, Linor," I smiled back, before letting out a long breath.

"What are you so afraid of, Avi?" she asked me silently as rain started coming down. She turned on the wipers. They needed to be changed, and the worn-down rubber scraped loudly across the windshield. I should have done that months ago. That was the thing about grief: such a dour and unending feeling, making simple chores become mountains, so that even changing windshield wipers or shaving my cheeks was almost too much to bear. Even though I had gotten better, it still felt like a long tunnel with no end in sight.

I shook my head before my thoughts got to dark. *Focus, Avi.* Hopefully this would put out some of the fires of the community—maybe there would still be parts that could be saved.

"It can't be saved though, you know it—Avraham," the beast said and I shuddered violently in my seat.

Linor caught it out of the corner of her eye. "Easy—everything is going to be alright," she stated.

I looked at her. She had one hand on the wheel, the other holding her head as the rain fell around us, splashing like tiny galaxies in an endless universe. "I guess—I mean I don't know what I am afraid of. Maybe I can't do all of this," I admitted.

She turned her head toward me, rolling her eyes. "Shut up, you little bitch. We both know you've never been afraid of stuff like this. Those kinds of fears are for people wetting their pants about following their dreams. We never got to have dreams, not like the normal dreams of being a baseball player or a doctor. But, be honest with me here, Avi. We may not be alive much longer. So what are you so afraid of?" she queried.

I looked at her, her face curved like the moon above, and I knew what I was afraid of. It was losing my home again. After all this time, I didn't want to live out of a bag anymore, to spend every morning and night worrying that today was the day I would have to pick up and leave again.

I hesitated to tell her. She looked at me, shrugging her shoulders as if to say, "Come on."

"I think—I don't know what I'm—"

She stared me down like she was going to reach across the seat and devour my soul. I thought better of finishing my statement. Instead I decided to be honest. That was the best play here. "I think I'm afraid that deep down, I never wanted a happy ending—I never felt like I deserved one. Not after so much was lost. The world has kept on spinning, so why should I in any way attempt to press my hold on it? I'm afraid, Linor, of losing another home, of losing what's left of my family. I am afraid of losing you. Most of all, I am just sick of being afraid," I told her.

She focused on the road and the two of us drove on in silence. The only noise being made was the heavy rain on the worn-down windshield wipers. Linor broke the silence between us after a while, just as soon as the rain parted and the night took back over, undisturbed. "Thank you for telling me that, Avi," she said calmly.

"You're welcome... I just—" I remained quiet, letting my words fall into the space between us.

"I can't promise you forever, Avi. I can only promise you the time I have left," she stated.

I looked up at her, taking her hand in my own. That would just have to do. None of the things I was afraid of losing had I ever been promised in the first place. Might as well stop acting like they were now. I squeezed her hand, as she drove us in to the night, the roads stretching endlessly, surrounded by pines.

66

Chapter 66

We had parked at a hill overlooking the warehouse below us. I knew somewhere in the woods, Bipin and his siblings were roaming as hulking wolves, waiting for their signal to cause a distraction. I could see a dark path leading through the brush of evergreens down the mountain, and knew that was the best way forward. Lights were on all throughout the massive building. It had apparently been used as the drop-off point from the old paper mill outside our baseball stadium.

It figured that Zevi would use something like this, a steel giant made of gray, locked away in the middle of nowhere. He probably thought it was funny. It was nostalgic, if nothing else. Linor came up beside me. The moonlight was weak, but the sky was clear though. I could tell she felt as uneasy about seeing that building as I did. Too many things had happened to us all inside buildings similar to that. I gave a silent vow in that moment: if I lived through this, I would make it my personal mission to clear away as many warehouses as possible. "What do you think?" she asked me.

I shrugged. "I think this is a bad idea and we are all about to die horribly, to be honest," I replied somberly.

She scoffed. "No—seriously, what do you think?" she persisted.

"I think I see a pathway leading down to the side of the building and only a few guards out front. Hopefully, you won't have to do too much for very long. I just wish I could see what those fools are doing on the far corner." I pointed, showing her a crowd of Zevi's Enlighted standing beside a collection of vans. They were laughing at something, and one of them threw a bottle. I couldn't hear exactly what it had hit—I did hear a cracking of a bottle, though. That made me concerned. Hopefully it was just drunk assholes littering. The path I had found was the easiest route to take to climb into the building and be done. My gut told me I needed to go see what was making that noise.

"I just see a bunch of his jack-asses outside. Avoid that please, Avi. I can make anything you can imagine, but I can't make sound. Hopefully, the wonder six will figure something out," she said. I tuned my ears in for a series of howls that would indicate that they were here.

"Listen, Linor—" I started before she waved me off.

"Please don't tell me not to go in, not when you shouldn't go either, Avi. I'm not stupid. If it looks too dangerous, I won't go. But if there is a chance to save everyone, I don't think one person sneaking in wearing a green sweater is going to be able to do much."

I looked down at my sweater, suddenly feeling subconscious. "I like this sweater," I muttered.

"Don't be so insecure, Avi," she teased.

"Don't be so vain, Linor," I shot back, while she beamed.

Both of us were only bantering because our nerves were shot. I was about to say another joke, when a long howl echoed across the woods, sending the whole night into an eerie silence that wasn't natural in these parts. Even the bugs seemed to know what was coming: no chirps, no clicks, no fluttering of wings tonight. Tonight, trouble had found its way to this small Pacific Northwest town. Another howl went up not long after the first, just as deep and as long, coming from a different direction. I noted that it sounded north of us. A series of four other howls came from other directions, all around the warehouse.

My heart stopped; that was the signal. I turned back to Linor. She was afraid, just as apprehensive as I was. Life had never given us much time to do anything; that was the same for everyone else, though. Instead of waiting, I leaned forward, kissing her softly. "Hurry back," she whispered and I nodded, bounding down the hill at a full sprint. A storm formed overhead, out of nowhere vast, moving like a serpent across the sky. I heard panicked cries as the world became a thick haze, like looking through cotton balls.

I broke the tree line at a dead run. A guard in front of me was staring at the thick fog that had suddenly come out of nowhere. I lowered my shoulder, ramming myself into him with all my strength. He hit the warehouse's metal paneling with a loud thud and groan, before falling to the ground. I tore off his bandana and jacket. They were a little big on me. That was fine; I never had clothes that fit anyways. I tied his bandana in the same way and dragged his dead weight to a nearby bush cluster.

"Don't wake up, pal," I muttered as I kicked him once more in the face for good measure. *Worry about the morality of it later Avraham. Save your family,* I told myself as I hugged the side of the building. Through the fog, I could hear nervous laughter and muttering. I made out the small cry of Solly though. That was her that they must have been throwing the bottles at. I tightened my fists. I could see the lights on the inside of the warehouse now. This was my chance; I couldn't leave Solly. I started making my way around the building, where more guards were circling the area. Some had flashlights out now, but most looked completely lost.

They're all just children. This isn't an army, it's children who don't know better. I continued moving slowly around the building, making my way to the collection of vans, when I heard the slide of a rifle being loaded. "You!" shouted someone behind me.

I froze in place. This was it. Not even five minutes into my rescue plan and we were already dead. I started to turn toward the voice. Maybe I could bluff my way out. Then I heard the rustle of a thicket, a quick scurry of massive claws over dirt and the muffled scream of a man as fangs dug into his face. I turned back to see a massive red and black wolf shaking the head of the would-be shooter violently, the creature easily weighing two hundred or more pounds. It looked up at me for a moment as if to say, "Go, you idiotic man."

I nodded and took off running around the building as more small cries came from every direction. "So much for disguise," I muttered, taking the bandanna off my face. Unsure how the guard could have even spotted me so easily in the dark—a small hand seemed to trace up my spine at that thought.

I scrabbled through the bushes, searching for the wall again until I felt comfortable that no one could come from my left. The fog increased in density, and it was becoming more difficult to see my hand even in front of me. Instead of panicking, I took a deep breath and started sniffing the air, opening my ears up to the sounds of the woods around me. I could hear quick breathing and heavy footsteps in a direction east of me. I could smell the sweat of at least three men, four women.

I kept sniffing and suddenly, my senses just stopped. I don't mean as in I lost the scent, but I mean they stopped. It was like a curtain had been drawn on a stage. I quit moving, peering into the gray. My eyes still worked, and a flutter of my fingers told me that they were still movable. What gives? I tried breathing through my nose again—no smells came. I stuck my knuckles in my nose and blew out—I heard the growl of the beast. *He was trying to cut me off!*

"Stop that, you son of a bitch!" I hissed. It had no effect and I could hear the deep rumble of his bark somewhere deep inside. *Just this once, please work with me.* He growled again and I fell to my side, a hot pain coursing through me. Was it trying to take control again? If he managed to do that, all of this was for nothing. I thrashed with all my might, willing my body to move. I started to sweat; fear was setting in. If I didn't hurry, the guards would figure out that this was a rescue attempt. I had only so long to go—so long before everyone could get hurt. They were counting on me. One more mighty push with everything I had and my right leg swung over. I was able to come to my knees.

"*Stop fighting me!*" The beast's voice cracked like a falling tree, causing me to fall down again and cover my ears. It worked out for the best, because at that exact moment, a guard came around the corner and stepped on my shoulder, pinning me down. I cried out, alongside the beast, which yelped loudly.

The guard was startled and fell back to the ground. *Stupid kid*, I thought as I sprang to my feet, the hold over me gone. I jumped up, pushing his knees forward, straddling one leg between mine, and when he kicked forward, I kicked my leg over, slamming both his knees in the opposite direction. I flung my body forward, placing my knee under him, and leaned my weight into him. He coughed out a gasp, as I slammed his arm into the ground. With the opening, I pulled his wrist down at an angle and swung my other hand under his elbow, and connected to my wrist. It was all over as I yanked, and the young guard cried out through his mask. When he shot up and I heard a snap of something in his arm, I let go, giving a vicious left elbow swing to his face, knocking him out.

I was breathing hard by the time I stood back up. My shoulder felt like one giant bruise. I knew though, that within a few hours, any damage would be healed. *That may not be true—look what that thing has done in the last two days.* It was true—I shuddered at the thought. I had less and less control over the beast within me.

"Feed the good wolf," I muttered as I searched the guard for anything useful. He had a wallet but the fog was too thick to see anything in it. I ditched the jacket. I had lost my bandana when I ran into the guard—so much for sneaking in and saving the day. A slow hand seemed to reach down my back at that point—I shook it off, remembering why I was here: to save the community and my friend.

I sniffed the air again and was able to pick up the previous scents from before. I followed them. Now there were only a few guards and a glowing deer hanging from its hoofs—thrashing in defiance and pain. I had known it would be Solly before I even got there. My heart still picked up in rage.

Now was the time to think, there were five of them and Solly was tied up. Using the light from her glow, I could see that most of them had weapons of some type or another. All blunt, though, like baseball bats and clubs. One guy had a knife. Around Solly lay the wreckage of a busted piece of wood. They had tried to break her outer shell. *Good luck with that,* I thought, her skin was tougher than almost any metal I had ever seen. When we were kids, I saw her run into the side of a truck by accident while transformed—her horns easily pierced the side, cutting a long jagged gash in the metal. That bought me a few extra seconds. She was going to be fine. It was me I was worried about.

Maybe Huey could fight five people and walk away relatively unscathed, but I had my doubts on doing that. Getting hurt would mean the beast would come out and all of this would have been for nothing. I needed to think fast and act fast—my thoughts were silence, but then a torrent of screams came out from the furthest man from the group. Followed by another one, then another, as a black wolf easily twice the size as the red one I had seen earlier swooped in through the haze, moving like a shadow over water, and taking the leg out from under one of the guards like they were just a child.

Shaking, tearing, and screaming entered the night and left as quickly. I sat on my haunches, wondering what had just happened. I blinked a few times and realized I was the only one there besides Solly. I got up, running to her side, and she reared back a powerful leg for a kick that would have surely killed me, "It's me, Solly—Avi. I am here to save you!" I whispered, frantically untying the knot.

I had gotten the first strap undone before Solly transformed back to her normal self. Her hard outer diamond like skin fell to the ground, dissolving into a puddle, splashing like a fish out of water. "No shit it's you, jack ass. I was just about to kick you because I knew you would say something cheesy—and what do you know, you did! I mean, really. Of all the lines..." she muttered, undoing the last strap. She fell down like a stack of bricks. I took hold of her and steadied her on the ground. I blushed hard when I realized she was naked and became instantly thankful that she wouldn't be able to see anything in the fog.

I turned away, listening to Solly rummage through the remains of the guards. When I turned back, she was sliding on a pair of boots from one of them, looking tired and wearing shredded clothes from dead people. She was no worse for wear, I noted gratefully.

"Thank you, Avi, I appreciate it," she stated.

"You're welcome, Solly. Where are the others?"

She jerked a finger into the direction of the warehouse. "Somewhere inside that thing, they took your mate and the others a couple of hours ago. I can't tell you where they are in there, though. Those creeps tied me up, and when I came to, I was helpless. They had managed to sneak up on us inside the community. Some of us tried to fight back, but that bitch Sophia started shooting everyone with her lightning and we dropped as fast as a frog in a well—and here I am," she told me calmly.

"So, Huey is alright? Why didn't they kill anyone?" I asked her, feeling more afraid of that answer than anything else tonight.

"Beats the heck out of me, boy—all I know is that brother of yours swooped in like he was some kind of medieval baron coming to slaughter some peasants, and poof—we all started following. Now your pasty white ass is untying me and asking all these questions," she stated and I rolled my eyes at Solly.

A couple of moments later, a very naked and surprisingly toned Bipin came out of the fog, he was short stature and his hair fell to his shoulders like his father, but he looked powerful. He smelled like wet dog, but I kept that thought to myself. "That should be all of them. The others are chasing down anyone who is left," he said, looking at Solly before blushing. "Hey Solly—sorry I'm naked."

"That's okay, lad—sorry I don't have a better light." She beamed.

"Children, please—no time for this," I muttered.

Bipin nodded in agreement, "What's next, Avi?" he asked me. Solly came up beside him, now dressed in the clothes of the guards as well. "I need you two to keep doing what you're doing—but Bipin, find a way to get the community out of here, somewhere safe that Zevi can't possibly know."

"Excuse me, jackass, I'm not just waiting by the car," Solly protested.

I sighed, "Solly—who else do you think they will follow—me? I need you to help Bipin get everyone out of here, and to also make sure Linor is okay. This much fog—she wasn't looking good before I asked her to do this. Please," I added to her.

She seemed to debate it for a moment before giving in and nodding.

"What are you going to do?" she asked me.

I looked at a vent that was above us. Solly followed my gaze to the vent. "You're kidding, right? You don't even know what's on the other side of that vent," she stated.

I agree—I didn't know. I had no choice. Time was up for anything else. The amount of noise we had made rescuing Solly, combined with the fog, Zevi would know something was afoot. "No other option here," I muttered and turned toward the building.

Solly came up behind me. "Don't clench, buttercup," Bipin said, taking hold of the back of my belt and one of my shoulders.

"Bipin—what the—" and I was thrown into the air like a child's toy toward the vent. I stretched my hands out, finding the metal grooves, and I reached exactly at the vent height.

"You better hold on!" shouted Bipin from below me. I was sweating—my fear of heights all too real, while hanging on the side of a building. I swore, pulling myself in through the small vent opening, until I could swing my legs through the door. Inside the vent, Linor's fog was shrouding the area, but it was not the same as it had been outside. That left very little time. I followed the direction of the air vent, sniffing, listening to anything and everything that could lead me out of here and to my friends. I felt like a mouse trapped in a cage, with metal walls only inches around me, as I moved slowly through the ventilation system.

Just keep moving, Avi, just keep moving.

67

Chapter 67

I had been crawling for at least five or six minutes by the time the first wave of smells hit me. This one, though, got a smile on my face. Only one person I knew smoked such cheap tobacco. It was Huey.

I crawled another few feet to an opening. Below me were Huey and someone from the community I didn't recognize. Their backs faced toward each other. A young man had a knife pointed at the restrained Huey, who looked less than impressed by the guard. "What the fuck is going on out there?" the guard snarled, his voice too shaky to intimidate a kitten.

Huey looked up as I pulled myself to the edge of the vent drop. I gave him the thumbs-up once he noticed me. He smirked. "I would be more worried about what's going on in here."

"What?" The guard asked, as I let gravity take its course and fell through the vent and landed in a heap on him. The poor kid went flat and wasn't moving by the time I got off of him.

I stood up, getting off the limp body of the guard and looked at my friend. "What's going on, man?" I asked him.

"I think I am done with this town—I never thought I would say this, but after all this shit, I might miss prison," he stated calmly. I took the knife from the guard and untied him and the community member. The man I untied was Chinese, slim, but with a powerful set of shoulders. He looked like he had spent much more time outside in a field than he ever had indoors.

"Where are the others, Huey?" I asked him, looking around the room we were in. It was a cluttered office, where chairs and tables had been pushed to the side. The windows to the office had been drawn closed, hiding whatever was on the other side. I handed Huey the knife and I started to walk toward the doors.

"Avi, what are you doing, man? We need to get out of here, now. Those fools came into the community and kicked our asses. Trust me, man, this isn't a fight I think we can win with some kicks and punches," he stated.

I got close to the door, opening it gingerly. "I hear you, Huey, but we have to get the others. When I open the door, take him with you and go find the others. Solly and Bipin are waiting at the north side of the building," I instructed him.

"Are you sure?" Huey asked, coming up to the other side of the door, gesturing for the man to lean against the wall with us.

"No—not at all. Just trust me," I stated.

"You got it," Huey replied, taking his knife into a defensive hold. I nodded at him and swung the door open, onto a massive warehouse that was surprisingly sparse. But it showed me a lot in a matter of seconds. First, we were on a scaffolding overlooking most of the community that was tied up. Second, my brother sat at a large redwood table, with four people tied down to their chairs and himself comfortable in the middle, with his bat from the other night laid out within arm's reach. Third, Dr. Joachim was scrubbing the floor in front of him, a long rope tied around his neck, leading back to my brother's hands.

A flood of emotions surged into me—anger at seeing that my brother had tied up the community. Confusion as to why the doctor was here, and why he was on a leash. I wanted to jump down from the overhang, charge over the table, and beat Dr. Joachim to within an inch of his life, to torment the man who had taken so much away from me—from us. *Malice coursing through me, I wanted to tear into that man with my teeth, my claws.*

At the thought of claws, I was able to see through the red haze that was building. *Not claws, Avi: fingers.* I looked at my hand to make sure they still were the same stubby fingers. After a quick flex, I let out a sigh of relief. I was still me.

I felt a hand on my shoulder and I fought the urge to swing. It was Huey with a finger to his mouth indicating to be quiet. I sighed, and nodded. He was right of course now was not the time to go crazy—that was going to come soon enough.

We crept along the scaffolding toward another room at the end of the walkway. I tested the door, pressing my ears to it. I could hear nothing on the other side. That made me more worried than putting me at ease. It was bizarre that Zevi hadn't noticed us, and even more odd that there didn't seem to be any more guards on the inside. I teased the handle once, twice—nothing. I looked behind me. Huey looked like he was about ready to jump out of his skin and the man from the community looked on the verge of passing out.

I turned back and opened the door, holding it barely open so the three of us could slip in quickly. The door opened onto a long narrow hallway, lights hung from coned ceiling lamps above us. The wallpaper was a putrid yellow, hanging off like it was melting from the metal in a sick way. It made our steps uneasy as we quickly walked down the way.

Halfway down the hallway, our path was blocked by Schwein.

The large pig-like man stepped around the corner like a shadow, impressive for someone his size. We were about twenty feet from him, but that was as close as I wanted to get to a guy like that. He had sweated through his grey shirt and pants, thick stains pooling at his pits. A wide toothy grin hung on his face. "Hey, Avi," he snorted, his words coming out like he was chewing on something rather large.

"Hey, Schwein," I said nervously, immediately looking for a way out. Schwein would always be like a dog for my brother. I had no doubt that might have changed. In a tight corridor like this, he was the dominant threat. I started to sweat with fear, trying to figure out what Schwein could do.

Schwein smiled an impossibly wide gap with his mouth that stretched his lips to a point where I thought the skin was going to tear apart. There was a cracking, a popping noise and a deep rattle came from his mouth, like pennies being shook inside a jar. A foul stench which made my eyes water even from this distance emanated, then the first set of teeth spat from his mouth, jagged, shredded and even some that were blunt, stained with stomach acid. They shot forward, peppering the three of us, some bouncing off, others coming close to breaking the skin.

The man from the community cried out, and Huey and I grunted. They were like miniature fast balls, hitting us with such a force that I swooped up my jacket in a vain attempt to try and cover myself. The hallway was filling fast with the almost endless amount of teeth that were now piling over my feet. Schwein was making gurgling noises, as the fangs ejected from his mouth like water being poured from a bucket, though that bucket was carrying a swimming pool's worth of teeth. I found myself having to pick my feet up to keep moving as the three of us instinctively retreated to the end of the hallway. My back was against the wall—a hard surface to think on. *So think, Avi!* I shouted inside my head as more teeth hit me, each one striking with enough force to feel like someone had just punched me. Any moment, one of those teeth was going to break skin. If that happened, then Schwein would be dealt with, but so would everyone else.

That meant putting some distance between me and everyone else, fast. I turned toward Huey shouting over the roar of Schwein. "Take him and get out the door!" I gestured toward the doorway. Huey nodded, grabbing the frightened man by the arm. The teeth were now up to my knees, putrid, hole-filled, and some stained to a deep black. More were coming in, at a rate that was unfathomable. I watched as Huey and the man drifted toward the door, their feet crunching on the ivory, like thick ice in the middle of winter. They made it toward the door before I was forced to turn back. My skin felt like one giant bruise as dentures now came up to my waist. I panicked, fighting the smell, making my way deeper into the hallway.

The sound was becoming deafening. Soon there would be no other noise except for the rhythmic tick of the teeth rebounding off the walls onto each other. I had made a mistake. Maybe I should have headed for the door. I was going to be crushed to death under a pile of pearly yellows as they slowly piled on me and bounced off of metal.

Metal! I shouted into my head, looking up and seeing another vent. That was my way out, I thought as I started to climb my way over the mound. The amount was well over my head now and was quickly approaching ceiling level as I climbed, scooping the teeth away from under me. I reached the metal vent and pulled with all my might. The wiring came free. I flung myself through with no time to look back. I smelled burning metal as I scrabbled through the vent. I heard a loud crash then looked back to see a small fire trailing behind, from where I had come. The wolf's fire was heating up the air, and the metal of the vent, and starting to burn me.

Oh no—that was going to make things infinitely worse. I had no time to react, as more teeth suddenly came spitting down the vent, through the flames.

One struck my hand, red hot, and burst through the skin.

68

Chapter 68

First, it starts with a small spark, like striking a stone against a piece of flint, a sheer blast of heat at such a small moment. Then comes the smoke, blistering and festering entrails that float out of the wound like a cloud made of red air. That is followed by the part that hurts, the part that transforms the very meaning of pain. Twisting, agonizing strikes of lightning—shooting up my body as if they had a mind of their own.

Every inch of my hand cried out in pain.

Like diving off a high cliff, the rush coming down was how it felt when the beast came out, springing forth like he was gravity himself. I felt the shift, my bones already elongating, popping out of place. "No!" I screamed in the air duct. If he came out now, everyone was going to die. My voice was cracking as a roar started to escape my mouth. I had only a few moments, a few moments to stop a transformation that I had never managed to do before.

I was in so much pain, endless and with no escape, a caged bird flapping to the end of its cell, only to find another cage, stacked on yet another cage. My pain was endless cages; there was no escape. I had to, though, I had to fight it. I had to figure something out. It hurt so bad—breaking, snapping, pools of my own leaking blood turning into smoke all around me. Everything was getting hotter, worse by the moment. I started thrashing in the tight space, my hands hitting a support piece of the vent and I let out a loud groan as the metal cut into my arm.

But I wasn't the only one who groaned when I did that. I heard a small snarl from inside as the metal entered me. *That was it: just like when the guard had hit my shoulder; when I was hurt, so was the wolf.* I shot my hand forward, my fingers already stretching to impossible lengths—the agony on the verge of blacking me out. If it continued, I would spasm, twinge, and then the misery would continue until the beast was fully in the driver's seat. *Not today!* I yanked the metal free and it cut my hand from thumb to pinky. The wolf and I both howled out in pain—the cries carrying down the shaft.

"This shit hurts you too!" I yelled in defiance, my body still twisting into itself. I felt his pull lessening, just for a moment. That was all I needed, just a moment. I crawled forward, outstretching my right hand. I could see fur bursting through the skin, spiking like a porcupine. With my left, I thrust down with the metal hard into the center of my right hand. Another cry of pain shot out of both of us. I spat blood.

Somewhere through the daze, I could smell smoke. The fire must have started to spread. Heat blisters started to form on any part of my body that connected with the scorching metal. I was going to burn alive in a dirty air duct if I didn't hurry. *Not today, not today,* I reminded myself, pulling the makeshift blade out, thrusting my left arm forward. A sudden jerk of motion snapped my elbow up, popping. I cried out, tears rushing to my eyes. It was fighting back.

"Fuck you, you son of a bitch!" I yelled once more, stabbing the knife into my left arm this time. We both roared in pain, my gums feeling like they were going to split, sending my teeth flying like popcorn from a kettle.

"It hurts you too!" I screamed, once more yanking the blade free and throwing my right arm forward, jamming the blade into my arm, sending blood-curdling screams which shook the enclosed area. A gauntlet of pain followed. I removed the knife and crawled forward for the space to plunge it deep into any part of my body that I could. The beast roared, snapping, chewing its way from my skin, fire under us roasting at my heels. Another stab, another few inches, another breaking of my body, a breaking of my sanity. I looked down at my arm. It was a litter of bones sticking through the skin, exposed, twisted at impossible angles, grinding like chunks of raw meat being packed into a shredder.

Sweat poured down my head endlessly. I tasted only blood as my voice cracked, straining to let both of our calls out at the same time. A shudder of pain rocked my skull, squeezing like a vice gripping my temples.

I crawled forward, nearly dropping the blade. I was almost out of strength. My fingers shook as I held it up. "This is my body—this is my life! I will not die a monster, I won't!" I screamed one last time, thrusting with everything I had into the center of my abdomen.

At that moment, the blisteringly hot paneling of the vent gave way beneath me, causing me to fall. I fell head first into another room, and I had just enough time to catch a sink as I hit it, shattering through the side, sailing to the hard ground below.

69

Chapter 69

"*Get up, little Avi,*" a voice snarled from somewhere above me. It repeated it again, causing my eyes to shoot open. "*Get up, little Avi!*"

I opened one eye slowly, searching for the loud voice that was speaking to me. An exit light bathed the small bathroom in a pool of crimson, splaying hues of deep shadows and blood reds in every corner. A snarl was coming from somewhere. It was uncomfortably loud, rattling my ribs on the cold floor. I shifted to move my hands to cover my ears, and found them stuck at my sides. I grunted, yanking them free, only to see the mangled lunchmeat that my hands, arms, and body had become. There was more blood than skin, bone showing through, lacerations, my flesh flayed out as if by a mad man.

The mad man was you, I thought as the pain came back like a train, running me over as if I was a sheet of paper. I whimpered in the darkness as the snarl continued. "*Get up!*" The beast drooled his anger—slavering over me, like a living hand reaching out from the shadows to strangle me.

I spat part of a tooth before speaking. "Stick a pipe in it, you wet fucking mutt."

In response, he roared, a deafening call that was louder than anything that could be heard in the natural world. An entire pack of lions on a hunting spree wouldn't compare.

That got me moving and covering my own ears, screaming back at the waterfalls of noise that were threatening to crack my skull from the inside. I stretched my voice to its limits until I was gasping for air, and still it continued. So much anger, so much hate coming from a living creature. That shouldn't be possible, it shouldn't be possible for so much malice to exist in the world. Yet it did. It was around us at all times, a constant reminder that just as much as love was floating in the fabric of everything we did. There was its opposite, its constant sibling. A neverending edge that tiptoed around in the darkness, walking like an elephant on egg shells—waiting for the chance to enter our minds, enter our souls.

What bothered me, though, was how he had become so hateful in the first place. The memory of the puppy in the flames seared its way back in my head. When I had seen the pitiful creature, I hadn't been afraid of it, I was more shocked that I was still alive. He was whimpering, he was crying—the poor beast was hurt. All alone in a strange place, eyes not even open, and the first thing he experienced was the hate of the world; a cruel painting of terror, an endless flame that promised to burn forever.

"You were born that day, in the fire," I stated calmly in the now-silent room, as I leaned my head against the toilet. The beast didn't respond. I cleared my throat of more blood. I was bleeding somewhere inside my mouth. "You were born in that fire—same as me, weren't you?" I asked the beast.

After a long silence, a gruff came out through clenched teeth. *"So what if I was, human?"*

I laughed, a small squeak, then it turned into a chuckle, despite being alone and bloody inside this dirty bathroom.

"What is so funny, human?" the beast snarled, ending the moment of levity that I desperately needed. More than anyone, I wanted to be driving down a long highway—hitting the gas and never looking back. I couldn't though, I was here. I had to do this. I had to save my family, to help them.

"You don't even know why you're doing this, Avi. You little rat! You never wanted to help anyone before. Why start now? A worthless, disgusting little creature wallowing in self-pity and low cunning. Why, those around you mock your very existence. They spit on you, as they should!" the beast stated, his growl barreling like a wrecking ball through a mountain, grinding rocks into pebbles.

That pissed me off. I leaned on the toilet, steadying myself in a sitting position. "Yeah, they can go to hell, and you can fuck off. I don't care what they said in the past—I'm doing this—" I paused, looking at myself in the mirror. I was a bleeding mess, my face completely soaked in blood, my body chewed like a dog bone in a pound.

All my life, I had been getting pushed by pain endlessly, restlessly, and with zero consideration to the value of my worth. So had all of them, the other kids. So much suffering brought on because the night was filled with hate. The beast was right; I didn't fully understand why I was fighting so hard for people that had given up on me long ago. I knew that in the moments when I could have made a difference, when I could have helped and I didn't act, those nights haunted me the most.

"I hate myself so much. Every day, I just want to crawl into my bed and cry. I can't shower without feeling shameful, I can't enjoy a meal without feeling the tug of everyone I let down. Ever scar is a storybook reminding me of how monstrously the world has treated me—treated others. I don't need to explain to you all the times I've spent crying in the darkest corner of whatever hole I could find—you were there for that, you were there for all those times in the camps, all the horrors done to me—to us." I stood up, shakily, my legs feeling numb, vertigo creeping in at every move. It was shallow steps, shallow breaths, as my hands collapsed onto the broken sink, looking into the dirty mirror.

"Hate is such a festering thing—it consumes us and becomes like an old friend, because at least it's consistent and there. Gives us so much power. I've been filled with it for so long, I am choking, I am dying from it. I don't know why I am doing any of this, but I do know I'm not going to die with all that hate inside me. If I can't find love and peace for myself, I will find it for my family. That's the sum of my life; that is why I am doing this. For them—for you," I said to the mirror.

I felt the beast's claws on my mind receding. He retreated back into his hole somewhere inside of me, giving a low snarl, not of rage, but one of fear.

I let my body shake after he was gone, the sink barely able to hold me with its broken pieces crumbling in my hands. I was alone again—I needed to get back to the others. There was no way Zevi and them didn't know we were here now. *Take a few deep breaths, then get back out there.* I was struggling to breathe, bubbles of blood continuing to come out of my mouth. Everything felt cold—the edges dark, my senses dimmed. *Breathe, Avi, breathe. You can do this.* I spat out more blood—noticing that the wounds on my arms were finally closing up—or at least clotting.

I blew out a sign of relief at that. It benefited us both for me to stay alive. If I could get hurt and cause him pain, it stood to reason that I could die and kill him as well. I looked up into the mirror again, not a confident young man—just someone who had seen too much shit. "What are you doing, man? You have heart, kid, but you know you aren't meant for this kind of story," I mumbled to my reflection.

I'd never wanted to be in any story—I just wanted to play baseball.

"Long way from those days, Avi," I stated, looking into the dirty mirror.

The shadows shifted in the lower corner of the mirror, I squinted my eyes to see a figure standing behind me. I had just enough time to register a glowing humanoid shape of a woman and her voice, before a wave of light struck me. "Long way indeed, Avi."

My body jerked in response to the light, an explosion of pain burning me instantly from head to toe. I felt my eyes close as I tilted toward the ground, hitting the hard tiles once more. Man, if I was going to keep getting knocked out, could it at least be in a clean bathroom? I thought as the world got cold, the curtains were drawn, and I closed my eyes for what could be the last time.

70

Chapter 70

"Avi, Avi," called my *muter's* voice.

"Just a few more minutes, please," I called back, rolling over in my bed.

"No, Avraham, time is up!" she shrieked, as a burning light hit the back of my neck.

I turned back to see a flame engulf my *muter* from head to toe, my bedroom lit with her fierce light, brighter than any star in the sky.

I jumped out of bed, my sheets still tight from when my *muter* had tucked me last night. They clung to my body as I wriggled free of their hold, though it nearly caused me to trip. My heart was beating so fast, I covered my chest to make sure it wouldn't fly out. My *muter* was screaming. I stepped back, hitting the closet wall.

"Mom!" I screamed back, covering my eyes with my free hands as the light coming from her charred body was getting closer and closer.

"Why didn't you do what you promised me, Avi?" she hissed and I felt myself weeping.

"I'm sorry *muter*, I'm so sorry!" I cried back as the lights blazed over me and I felt myself tumbling through a hole below me that shouldn't have existed in my bedroom. I landed hard inside my *foter's* watch store.

Patting down my chest, my heart was still there, even if I could swear I'd seen it almost coming out of my body just moments before. I looked around. The sun was coming through, irradiating the counters containing dozens of hand-crafted pocket watches, some older than the town itself, as my *zayde* used to claim. My *foter* had his back to me. He was cleaning a long golden chain, connected to a pocket watch, the coating nearly shined off after years of being used by our *mishpokhe*. My *foter* always told me he loved watches because of the feeling of timelessness it gave him, the gears in the *mishpokhe's* watch long since broken, as it stopped telling the correct time years ago. My *foter* could have fixed it; he chose not to. His *foter* had spent most of his life worrying about keeping the *mishpokhe* business afloat—according to my *muter*, my *zayde* had never been around for my *foter*, growing up.

As if reading my thoughts, my *foter* spoke, not turning to me, but focusing on his watch. "I never fixed this watch, Avi, because it is timeless. It's been in the pockets of my *foter*, and his *foter* before him. That is three generations of a watch staying in our family. It is unfortunate that I won't be able to give it to you, son. However, what this watch represents for our family, for us, is that no matter how long it takes, this family has love, no matter the age. That will never slow down in the passing of time. You have all the time in the world, my *zun*, you just have to see that," he stated, cleaning the golden chain with an oil that made the metal smell with such a nostalgic, metallic smell that I started to cry. I'd never forgotten that smell. I never would.

I stood up, still in my pajamas, walking toward my *foter* across the dirty floor. It was my turn to sweep the store. I had neglected it again. I felt ashamed of that—my father just wanted to teach me to value what we had. Playtime had always been more important. I would give anything to go back just to sweep those floors again.

"I don't have a lot of time, *foter*," I stated.

He half-turned toward me, a wide smile stretching all the way to his eyes shown under his deep facial hair. "We have all the time we need, son, it's just our heart gets in the way. Remember, it's timeless, stretching further and deeper than anything else we can possibly understand," he said calmly.

His words confused me. What was he meaning? I was pretty sure the warehouse was on fire and assuming I was still alive, I was trapped inside a bathroom. No closer to saving the community, to saving my *bruder*.

"*Foter*—I—I..." I looked down at the floor, sighing, "I am so sorry—for everything," I teared up, choking on my words.

He suddenly stopped what he was doing, setting his watch down carefully on the counter, turning toward me. He knelt down, placing one hand on my shoulder, the other on his knee. "Avi, can we go back in time?" he asked sternly.

I looked at him, his face a picture of stoicism, emotions completely untraceable in his thought lines, slowly creeping into deeper curves as he aged in a way that was unreadable. I stammered. "I don't think so—you always said that could only be done when we wound our watches, otherwise there was no going back."

He nodded in approval. "That's right. What's done is done. There is nothing to apologize for. You did your best, my *zun*. All I asked was for you to protect your *bruder*. You can still do that," he stated calmly, standing back up and resuming cleaning his pocket watch. I was perplexed at that. Whatever this was, my *foter* didn't know how Zevi had turned out. For that matter—I was struggling to understand my *bruder*, while everyone around me wanted me to give up on him. Why hadn't I done the same?

Because even if he has proven to be the monster they say he is, it changes nothing about your promise. I knew that was the reason as soon as my thoughts rolled out. "What if Zevi is a monster?" I asked my *foter* quietly, unsure of my thoughts.

Without turning he added simply, "Then you keep your promise and protect your *bruder*, Avi. Protect yourself. We cannot protect ourselves from danger, *zun*, or the way the rain falls on our faces, but we can decide how we deal with that. You can choose to pull out an umbrella, or simply smile in the rain. Either way, Avi, only you will know how to protect your *bruder*. Now, it's time to go—I know you will make me proud."

And that was the last I heard of his voice as the edges of darkness left, replaced by bright orange and yellow lights, combined with the slow hum of machines churning along, doing their job endlessly, as the rest of the world forgot theirs. I tilted my head down.

My brother had his sack mask on, his bat at his side. We were at the table, with the addition of Linor, bruised but alive, her head lowered as she sat next to him.

"Welcome back, older *bruder*. You look like shit," Zevi beamed.

71

Chapter 71

"Look who's talking," I replied back to Zevi as the full force of the world came crashing down in an instant around me. Not only were both my hands tied down, but I was facing in such a way that I couldn't see anyone behind me. I strained to listen, but my hearing seemed to either still be deafened, or the room was completely empty, save for the scared people sitting at the table, and Zevi.

I could, however, hear brushing, the slow rhythmic push of something being drawn across a concrete floor. Was that Dr. Joachim? It had to be him from earlier. Why was he here, and why was my brother forcing him to clean a floor? Since coming here, I seemed to be asking endless questions that never bothered to be answered by anyone. They just kept piling on—one after another.

Zevi's smile hadn't broken since he had said hello. He just stared at me, from behind his sack, the corners pulled up, showing a huge grin underneath. Asking him why he was doing this seemed like a waste of breath. Instead, I shot for what I thought was a better question. "What is the point of all of this, Zevi? You had Bug and Tir come and find me in Arizona on the word that you were in danger. Now that I am here, you're smashing people's heads off with a bat, building some kind of crazed fanatic army, and have—I don't know—one of the worst people who's probably ever existed casually scrubbing a floor!" I shouted.

The brush stopped. Zevi's smile faltered for a moment. "I didn't say stop," he snapped at Joachim behind me. The brushing resumed.

He pointed his arm to someone behind me. "Show my brother who is all here," he directed to a person behind me. I looked at Linor. her head was still hanging low, blood dripping into her midnight hair like roses tossed in the black sea. That ticked me off on a whole different level—up to this point, I had kept my emotions in check to the best of my ability. Maybe, maybe it wouldn't be so bad to indulge it and kill every one of them. I remembered my promise, though, to protect my brother. That seemed more and more impossible with every moment.

A guard came around the table, she seemed young, her dark face behind a red mask, long brown hair flowing down her back. She stepped to the nearest person in a chair to the left of Zevi, taking off the sack that was on their head. It was Joseph, frightened and older, his hair now replaced by a shining bald spot and a few moles that had more hair than his sideburns.

He wore round glasses now, that were crooked and bent from the sack, a double chin replacing the once-fit German solider and the unmissable weariness that comes from a father who cared more about his family than looking good. He bore that pleasant sort of happiness that suggested he was comfortable with a fuller frame, if that meant time spent with his family—as I noted by the large golden ring that sat on his hand.

I looked around as the guard removed the sacks from the heads of the other three. They were a young boy and girl, both with deep blond hair, streaks of brown waiting to come in with age, the boy on the verge of his teenage years, while the girl appeared to be up past her bedtime as her scarred face drooped from exhaustion. Finally, the last sack revealed a plain woman, with a round and guileless face, flowing curly brown hair, broad shoulders, and a matching golden ring. One look told me this was Joseph's family.

My heart sank—no good could come of this. I was in Zevi's game and I was going to learn just how much humanity was left in my brother. A long time ago, we snuck out of the community to go hunt down these kind of people, people like Joseph who had tortured us. I couldn't live with the idea of actually killing them—having hunted men, eaten them, been sick with their consumption. I couldn't subject anyone else to the meat grinder that is our world. I looked at Zevi with a cold stare, one that I hope summed up all the animosity I had toward him in that moment. If he did this, there would be no going back for him.

"What the fuck is this, Zevi? Let them go, now!" I snarled, straining against the ropes on my arms until they bit into my already shredded skin.

He shook his head. "We both know that option isn't on the table. This much death—there would be hell to pay. I don't feel like sparing my consciousness just to save the lives of a Nazi and his kids," he stated calmly.

I stopped fighting the ropes and looked at him. I had strained so much that the ropes were starting to bleed— what little blood I thought I had left was coloring the rope a deep brown. No flames, no anger—I suddenly felt very alone in that moment. In a way, since the beast had joined my life, I was never alone. He was on the fringes of my mind, like a festering bug bite that lingered. Reminding me of its burning existence in every moment, every breath, every decision. Now, though—nothing. I felt a profound emptiness. I was facing a monster—all by myself. There was nowhere for me to run, nowhere for me to go, and lives depended on my every word. I broke out in a sweat instantly, as the realization came onto me how aloof my life had become—or maybe had always been.

"Zevi—stop this." I strained weakly, doing my best to maintain strength, as I fought for an out from this situation. I just had to think, something would come to me. Did anything ever come to me when I was in the camps? Like plunging into an endless frozen lake, my mind shook—I had never figured my way out of any situation. Someone else had always saved me. The only idea that had ever occurred to me was unsealing the beast, but now he was gone, and it was just me. I fought for time, deciding to ask the dumb questions. *Feed the monster, keep your brother blind to what you might be doing.* "Why are you doing this, Zevi?" I asked him.

He smiled through his mask. In a weird way, I felt that Zevi was enjoying this. This was his moment.

"There's too many voices to describe how to feel. Too many sounds and images to tell me how to love. Cartoons drawn to shine a light on the truth, political intellectuals screaming to add their views to the hierarchy. Why am I doing this? Well, it's for truth, *bruder.* Truth is subjective. It falls prey to those who would like to distort it and those who would like to profit from it, but the facts never survive the process. The truth is changed, altered from its natural state, and once it changes, just like Humpty and his famous shell, it can never be put back together again. Me, I'm just me. I'm the guy with the bat who knows what he wants. I'm the guy who is going to blow up everyone in this room very soon," he stated matter-of-factly.

"Then what's the objective truth, Zevi? What can this kind of behavior possibly uncover for you?" I asked him, hoping Linor would wake up. I realized she was the only way out of this. My heart was beating like the seconds of a clock; I hoped it wasn't in sync with the bomb that Zevi claimed was in here. Could he really be serious, blowing this place up with all of us?

The children started to cry, pleading for help, when Joseph said, "Please—just let my family go. They did nothing wrong. Just let them go."

I regarded Joseph for a long moment. He had done such horrific things to me many years ago, but now, here he was, restrained and at the will of my brother. This was wrong. I felt no desire to harm him in that moment, only to help him and his family. Maybe he had been a monster before, but no one deserved this; human beings are not animals. If we keep tying each other up, inflicting such atrocious acts upon each other, we are worse than animals. So much awful shit committed nearly every day—and for what? A chance to cause the exact same harm again? This was what Zevi was causing with his behavior. A repeat of what happened to us, a stranger destroying our family.

This time, something ugly flashed over Zevi's face for just a moment, I noted as he turned toward Joseph. With a deep eye roll through the sack, making it appear like he had sprouted horns under the cloth he said, "Will you shut up. This is a situation that you surely have to see by now is beyond your control. Even if you could escape, there's still the variable of getting

439

your family out of here and then somehow surviving a life on the run. Considering how easily I found you—I wouldn't bank on such fantasies, Joe," Zevi stated.

Poor Joseph looked as if my brother had just slapped him. His faced puckered and turned a bright shade of pink, while his wife started to weep. If any of this was having an effect on my brother, I couldn't tell. He simply remained completely calm.

He was used to it, I thought. That was chilling—not to mention disarming. It was hard enough trying to figuring out how to escape, but now I had to worry about an unknown bomb and getting Joseph's family out of here. "Leaving here is not the important question that needs to be asked, anyways," Zevi stated, turning his head back to me. "Isn't that right, Avi?" he asked.

"Look this is between you and me, Zevi," I searched for a leverage of any kind, every second causing me to doubt our escape chances more and more. *Don't think that way, Avi. The more you doubt the plan, the less likely you will be able to come out of this. Buckle down, and think. Take away pieces off the board, take away Zevi's power. Clearly he only ever wanted you.*

"Let them go, Zevi, let them all go," I stated. Zevi's lips sucked in like he was sucking on a lemon. I stated my demand again; "Let them go, Zevi; they were only following orders."

"Yeah, that's right—" Joseph chimed in. Zevi in a blur slapped him across his face, causing him to fall to the ground in the chair.

The kids called out and his wife snarled, "You bastard."

Zevi regarded me for a long moment, staring in my direction before doing anything else, as if waiting for some kind of reaction from me. Instead, my jaw hung open, gasping at the apparent futility of the situation. "Ma'am, I already tied you up against your will, what makes you think I won't get up and slap you as well, slap your children. If both of you do not shut it, right this instance, far worse will happen," he said to Joseph's wife as if there wasn't a care in the world to him.

With a tiny whimper, she was quiet, and Zevi nodded in approval. "Now, back to the rather asinine statement made by my silly older brother: 'Just following orders.' Are you really going to defend them with that kind of comment?" he asked me.

I racked my head for an answer, still shocked at the speed at which Zevi had slapped Joseph. It had been an unreal burst, that even my eyes had trouble tracking. Once more, Joseph was completely out cold on the ground. Had I just caused the last few moments of this man's life over my stupid comments? *No, Avi, because you're going to figure this out right here, right now.*

That's right, I thought with no real conviction, *I am going to get us out of here.* I just had to figure out how. I regarded Zevi with a long look before replying, already tired of this game between us. "That's right, Zevi, you're going to just kill them because of a group he used to belong to?" I gestured toward Joseph on the floor.

"No, Avi, I'm not going to make that kind of generalization. The world will. Nazi iconography and historical revisionism will see to it that all Germans will be demonized no matter what I say here and now. Truth is, many were desperate and had nothing to do with the atrocities at the camps, some worked in the camps and tried to help. People are the shitty ones, not necessarily the groups."

I stumbled on my reply after Zevi's statement. "Then... why... are you doing this, Zevi? Is this some kind of game? Do you enjoy this?"

Zevi looked at Joseph passed out on the floor before responding. "This man did horrible things to you. He did worse things to me—to the others. What do you think happened to us when were taken into the other rooms, every morning? How do you think I ended up with her eye?" Zevi pointed at Linor, who's headed was still dipped low.

"I didn't—" I started before Zevi held up a hand to end my statement.

"Save it, Avi. Like your 'following orders' conversation, I am past that. Life is all about letting things go; growing and becoming something better and new," he stated calmly.

I still had no idea how to get out of the situation I was in. A sinking suspicion told me that the beast wasn't going to come out, no matter how much I cut my wrist. I'd never felt more drained in my life until today—I had to go on, though. Sunrise doesn't come until the night is finished. Shine a light and push through the darkness.

"The truth is—in a lot of ways, what this scum next to me did, and what that fool scrubbing my floor accomplished, made me the man I am today. I feel so, so complete." Zevi gestured with his hands toward his face, as if he was eating a truly enjoyable meal.

That made the hair on my neck stand up as I stammered out. "What do you mean?" I asked, fear creeping up my spine like a raging river bursting through a dam.

Zevi smirked with a look that you would expect to find on a python about to strike their prey and wrap them in a deep constriction, crushing and choking the life out of them, one whimper at a time. I shivered at his look, doing my best to see through the red-dotted eyes of my brother's mask. He had been wearing it since we were kids—a memento made by our mother. Mother, father, all of our family—if they could see Zevi now. My fingers dug a quarter of an inch into the wood handles of my chair, my thumb bleeding as I shook with anger. This *punk* had the nerve to wear our mother's mask—no, to *dishonor* our mother's mask—by doing all this shit. I clenched my teeth in rage.

He finally answered my question. "I think human conscious has a word limit. I think we all have only so long before words become hateful and we start to lose every semblance of what it means to be human, dear brother. It all becomes like a race, one giant step outside to see who can push the limits. Who has suffered the most, who is the most privileged. The biggest problem with this idea is that the very notion becomes twisted. If you think you're born to suffer, if you're alive in this world—you're born to die. How can anyone of us hope to learn any amount of integrity or goodness? Naturally, that will push anyone for survival, that will lead to groups forming and one seeking to claim a higher spot over another group. Therefore, how can anyone possibly know how much anyone else has suffered, when they have not experienced the same pain?

"Some will claim if you have not experienced it, then it cannot be explained to you, and you simply cannot understand it. This flies in the face of rationality. If an argument cannot be explained, then maybe the person who holds it cannot understand it themselves, or maybe it is just wrong. And this is the most important part, because morality is almost always brought up in discussions as an excuse to avoid having to explain a point: claiming that since you are unable to understand someone else's pain, then you also cannot understand whatever point is being discussed. And since morality is defined as cognitively invisible, then by definition, you can never understand it, and any argument against it can be waved off as 'uninformed'. It is simply a new way of saying, 'Believe what I say and do not question it.' We know what that's like, don't we Avi? To have someone tell us that we are animals, to treat us like animals. Slaughter us down to every man woman and child. What I learned from these men is simple: the world cannot escape pain. However, it cannot grow to heal itself if it's not pushed. Ages of comfort will come and go, one by one growing softer. Pain will wrap us all into tight little balls, screaming for help. I am simple, Avi. People need terror—it reminds us that we need to love. The world needs monsters, Avi; I'm just part of the ecosystem." My *bruder* finished speaking and the whole room drew one long collective breath.

"What the fuck is wrong with you, Zevi?" I asked my brother, a cold realization that I had no argument against him. He was right, the world was full of pain, and he was part of it.

He chuckled, placing his hands over his belly and letting out a long roaring laugh. "That was funny. I needed that. Thanks, Avi. Tell you what, do you read comics any these days? Probably not. From what I heard, you spend all your time living in a trailer with some strange dude doing kicks in the early hours—no judgment here. Anyways—there's this thing that always annoyed me, where the antagonist would lay out the reasoning for their convictions to the protagonist, while the antagonist would wait for an answer. What ends up happening over and over again is that the protagonist doesn't say anything; they simply fight, bad guy loses and boom, it's all over. So, I am asking you a question—and remember: tick tock on the clock, *bruder*; things are going to blow at any moment. Why do you think I brought you all the way here, just to see me?" he asked me casually as if it was a simple pleasantry at the dinner table.

I thought about it, twisting my head around, searching one last time in vain for anything, a sign, something that showed me the bomb. Zevi couldn't be that crazy—could he? I had no time to test that, too many lives were at stake here.

I spotted Joachim. He was thin—thin as the ghosts he had created in the camps. His skin drooping from the massive amount of weight his body had shed. His eyes were sunken in so deep that I could no longer tell the color. His hair was wispy strains at best and his wrinkles were so deep they could stop a runaway car dead in its tracks. It was his stench that curled my nose the most, though: he smelled like he had spent months living in his filth. Judging from his appearance, as he fell out of his oversized shirt, that was probably the case.

I felt nothing toward the man who had killed my family—I felt suddenly very old. He was more animal than man by this point, scrubbing the floor in his dirty underwear. Clothes too big for his small frame. He wasn't the man I still had nightmares about, who woke me in the middle of the night with a cold fury and a desire to end him, to destroy everything he held dear in his life, and to end him. Now he was little more than a leper cast out, pitiful at best, lower than a common rat. Did anyone deserve that kind of treatment? Maybe so, but I never enjoyed being the one to decide such things. I wanted to lock him in a deep cage everyday—but not turn him into such a feeble creature.

My life had never been easy—I never wanted to see such things; to have to debate such things. In a lot of ways, the memories of the things he had inflicted upon me would stay forever, but the things I kept failing to do, those were becoming nightmares even with my waking eyes. The thing about nightmares, though, is that sooner or later you wake up. Sooner or later the dreams end and a new day arises. A new day had come, many days after the endless terrors. I had a chance to wind the watches, to move the hands forward. They could never go back, but I could decide on the time from here on out.

I growled at Joachim, and he averted his eyes. I still didn't like the man, and allowed myself one little jerk moment—the situation allowed for it as some much-needed levity. I smirked, turning back to my brother. I was tired of playing madman's games for their entertainment.

"If I had to take a guess, you want me in your army, hence Joachim. You probably thought I would lose control and kill this man. I won't. I won't be harming a hair on his head. You know what else, brother? You won't either," I stated calmly.

Pure rage flashed across my brother's face, before he settled into his own smirk, matching my own—if not more sinister. He was still in control, got it? That was his game here; I just had to take his control away. *Find the bomb, Avi, subvert his plan before he has a chance to cause further harm.*

I went after his weakness, his plan: "Frankly, I don't even care that much about Joseph either, but you're going to let his family go right now—along with Linor and Joachim," I demanded.

"Oh, why would I do all that after going through all this trouble?" He pointed around the room.

"Because you got what you want: I came back here. You have no need to do any of this now," I replied.

He seemed to ponder it for a moment, before lifting his hands up, removing his sack from his sweaty head. His copper red hair was a tangled mess; his eyes shifted around the room constantly. Zevi extended his arm out with his mask holding it out toward my face. "Our *muter* made us this mask—I must say, I loved it the moment I saw it, not because it protected me from danger—we both know a sack doesn't do that. What it does allow is a place to think in peace—little fibers of thoughts wrapping around me all over the place. Pennies and dimes, flings and whims, I love to zing," Zevi sang out, laughing in the silence of the warehouse, causing my smirk to falter. He cut his song and screwed his mask into his hands, turning the last remnant of our mother into a tight ball.

"You still don't fucking get it—you never will, Avi. The world needs monsters, don't you see? I am making this town better—I have brought order to this place. No more suffering for a town full of Gypsies! Can you believe it, police not shaking down minorities anymore? No longer getting hassled just for having a different skin tone, for being poor, for being culturally misunderstood. And I did it all, by reminding the world that the world is full of monsters. I am a monster, Avi, no doubt. However, what kind of a monster forgives those that killed his family, then leaves his family?" he spat at me, snarling in anger. "A worse kind. At least I am serving a purpose here, at least I am making our town better. Making this place better," he stated.

I fired back, "Burning down the community huh? Sounds like a real hero, huh, big man. Just a child hiding behind a mask."

Zevi slammed his hands into the table, causing the wooden frame to crack under the weight of his blow. "I will burn it all the fuck down! Watch every tree go up like a candle, see every river dry, burn everything down to ashes if it means a chance to bring a little bit of order to this clusterfuck of a misguided evolution, to bring this poor social experiment down. I don't have to explain my reasoning to you—you who has no conviction, no values," he spat again.

"Only a lunatic wants to see the world in skulls, Zevi. I will give you one last warning to let them go before I break every bone in your body if I have to. Stop this shit, please. I beg you," I growled.

Zevi reared back his head like I had just punched him in the face before speaking. "You think for even one moment that you have any idea what I've been through, Avi? What any of us have been through? You had your powers from the get go—we had this done to us!" he pointed at his eye.

"I didn't have the powers—I think I was given them; I don't know—but it hasn't been easy with this thing inside me!" I pointed, sticking my fingers up to point at myself, the rope biting into my skin.

Zevi curled his mouth inward, grimacing all his teeth at me. "So, you think you were given them, huh? Sure wish I had been given them; I would have saved our mother!" he hissed.

I hung my head in shame. He had me there and I knew this conversation had been coming. I just wished it could have been easier—dealing with bereavement is never meant to be an easy conversation and no matter what I said, I always conveyed the worst message. After all, they had lost someone; they had died right along with that person, and all I was doing was scratching at the door as they built a house of grief.

"I'm sorry I wasn't there for them. Sorry I wasn't there for you, Zevi. I don't know how to help you," I mumbled back to Zevi. I just wanted to dig a big hole, covering myself in enough dirt to devour a mountain. Anything was better than facing my brother in such a way.

His lips pulled back into a tiny frown before he replied, "I don't know what bothers me more, Avi, the fact that you killed our mother or this bizarre antiquated morality of yours that insists on both disagreeing with what we are doing here, yet clearly you hate the good doctor there. Come on, Avi, you mean to tell me you don't want to eat a nice sandwich out of him—out of any of these people?" he gestured around the room and sniffles went up from one of the kids.

I responded with my heart to my brother, not knowing what to say anymore to him. "I want a lot of things—too many to count. But these people didn't harm me. Let them go," I pleaded.

Zevi snarled again, rolling his eyes deep. "I mean tell me lies, brother, tell me sweet lies. That's fine; the clock is ticking. How about this: the good doctor tells me they could never figure out how you turn in to that lovely demon of yours. Care to share?" he asked sheepishly.

Just like that, the pieces fell together in my head. Zevi had gone through all the effort of bringing me here just so he could build an army of Enlightened superpowered freaks. That thought terrified me. Just a few of us had taken over this small town in Washington. I didn't want to imagine a couple thousand.

I had no idea how Dr. Joachim had even managed to turn the others into what they were. From my understanding, they could only get my blood once from me—the original transformation. The other times, they were terrified of unsealing the creature. That was a saving grace, I realized then at that moment. If I hadn't had the beast inside me in the camps, I wouldn't be here now. I would have perished in the bonfire, just another stack of kindling in a neverending fireplace that had burned so many, just to keep a few warm. Or worse still, I could have also been one of his experiments.

"It will never work. I won't tell you how I can become the beast," I stated, locking eyes with my brother, his mask still tight in a ball in his fists.

He uncurled his hand and looked at the mask, "You know why I like this mask, Avi? It helps me, you know, have a separation from the bullshit. I can't escape the mask; I still need it. You however, don't even know you're wearing one. If you did, maybe you would see that I already broke the thing behind you scrubbing my floors ages ago. He made me what I am today, by taking something from you. That is what I 'want,' whatever it is that is inside you, Avi."

I leaned my head back to look at the doctor. He had peed himself as Zevi looked at him. Which meant, Dr. Joachim didn't understand it himself. I was still unsure if it was magic or what it was that caused the powers to manifest. The truth was: I didn't care. It was a curse, a mark that could never be wiped away. There would be no good playing with such unnatural forces, with something we did not fully understand.

I opened my mouth to speak, when I noticed Linor's head dip forward, a small groan coming from her. Zevi followed my glance. Seeing her stir, a mischievous smile went wide across his face, "Well, now..." he said, almost giddily.

"Zevi—don't you fucking—" I shouted.

A click went off from directly below the table, buzzing like a great tree falling to the hard ground below, thousands of years growing in a space of dirt that had seen more ages than anyone could ever truly understand, suddenly falling; all those years now completely done in an instant. A click, signaling the end, before the popping and crashing of the witness of the ages comes crashing down.

That's what I heard, a click, just before the turning of a mechanism and unknown chemicals filled the air. Suddenly, my senses were back and more, as I screamed, planting my feet into the ground and jumping with the chair toward Linor. As I flew through the air, several things happened

448

at once. My brother's eyes lit up brighter than the sun, and a deep rolling laugh came from between his clenched teeth.

The bomb was centered directly under the table. Flames tore through the wood like it was made out of matchsticks, igniting almost instantly. All of this happened as Linor looked at me, her eyes wide, and a silent truth went through both our minds in that instant. This was it; there was no saving us. Bright light hit me as I flew across the table, propelling my trajectory upward. I felt my skin flay away as if the flames were a surgical knife cutting me free of my skin. The beast roared, my bones snapped, and the world went black while my brother laughed.

III

Part Three

"It is man's peculiar duty to love even those who wrong him."
Marcus Aurelius, Meditations

72

Chapter 72

I was under pressure—there was no other way for me to describe it. Only that wasn't entirely right; it wasn't pressure that was forcing me down. It was a weight that I felt cracking my very skull, my legs burning, shoulders splayed out to their limits. An inconceivable amount of weight that should have flattened me to a piece of bread. How was I alive, how was I doing this? I knew when I opened my eyes through a darkness, a haze so deep that even gloom was unable to compare to the night. I was seeing through a mirror, a mirror I had never seen before. My reflection showed me a charred slab of meat wearing the remains of a red dress, midnight black hair almost completely gone on one side.

Was she... I couldn't finish the thought. *I won't.* I stared through the mirror. I shifted my eyes, the overwhelming pressure collapsing on my body, like rows of dominos falling down in succession. I had never felt such tension before. One twitch of my muscles, one misstep and whatever I had on my back was going to end Linor. That wasn't going to happen. I roared, blowing the hair on her head wildly.

"This is a lot of weight—it would be easier to just let it fall," said the beast. For the first time, he sounded as if speaking with a normal tone.

Startled, I replied, "No!" and my voice echoed as if I was stuck in some kind of giant vase, shocks of sound coming back just as quickly as they left my mouth.

That explained it. The beast was in control. It must have been the bomb. Which meant that whatever it was holding was most likely the roof of the warehouse. "Give me a reason why I should care about what you want, Avi," the beast told me, his horns casting dark shadows in the space I was occupying.

I flinched. Seeing him this close made me back up until I hit a wall. Wherever I was, it was small, tight, and as my senses returned, I took it all in. I was trapped in a black void, no ceiling in sight. Like a cage, so cramped with no room to move, but boundless in the inevitable fact that I could never leave. I had been here before, I realized, once when I was a boy—when meeting a small crying wolf puppy, and at other times, when I was devouring the flesh of men and women. This was the place where the beast stayed; this was his home.

No wonder he was always so mad. I took in the edges in the darkness, and I steadied my mind. *He can't hurt you again, Avi, not now at least. It's not here.* That wasn't true, though—he was in control, a wild flame dropped in a wooden world. I feared what he would do—this thing that I carried each and every day; my heart of darkness, my mask of the light.

Through the mirrors, I could see a huff of hot air escape its mouth, breathing on Linor, her burnt cheek absorbing his breath like wind hitting a mountain. "Please!" I begged, feeling like there was no way out of this situation. It snarled in response. If there was one thing I had learned about the beast, he enjoyed blood. It mattered not who it was, he just wanted the blood.

I was afraid, terrified. This thing was going to kill Linor and there wasn't a thing I could do about it. I started to speak again, when a glow came from behind me. The beast shifted a leg and the pressure impressed upon us, weighing him down with a snarl and a groan. I looked on in horror until I realized the glow was coming from behind me. I turned around, covering my eyes. Linor was sitting on a massive iron safe, a simple dial near one of her dangling feet showing a number set between one and ninety-nine. Her skin had returned to the moon pale, long flowing black hair with no signs of burns. She simply looked concerned, and wore only red panties.

My face went the same shade as what she was wearing as I averted my eyes and coughed.

"What's—how are you here? And why are you dressed like that?" I asked her.

She gave me a sad smile. "Seemed comfortable enough. Just for once, stop complaining. Just listen, please. I don't really have a lot of time, I'm afraid," she said somberly. I thought about her burns. Was she referring to those? They had looked awful, but I hadn't got a good enough look. They must have been worse than I thought.

"Don't worry, we—"

She held up a hand, silencing me before I could finish. "That's not why I am here, Avraham. I wish I could stay here and chat for a lot longer. You know I do, you will always have me, for as long as that is, but I told you it wouldn't be forever," she stated and I felt my eyes get heavy at the implications of the thought.

I was going to lose my best friend, I was going to lose the only person I had ever loved and there wasn't a damn thing I could do about it. That was death, though. Like it or not, one day, time was up—it wasn't for you to decide, it wasn't for those that cared about you. Whatever cosmic force there may have been in our world, Linor would live or she would die. There was no changing that fact now, no way to mask what was coming. She seemed to be accepting it though, and as I finished the thought, with tears streaming down my face, I knew I would have to as well. The longer I stayed around in such a farce of reality, the colder I was becoming, each day a step away from being my own barren desert, coated in ice.

Linor said again, "You made a promise, Avi, that you would save the community. I believe you; I always believed anything you told me. You need to take control," she stated again.

I lowered my head, whispering, "I can't."

"Can't what?" she asked.

"I can't. I'm trapped in here, this place. I've been here before. That thing is in control," I responded, meeting her deep eyes, pools of green in one, the other as shiny as smooth marble.

Linor sighed, tossing her legs over the massive metal safe, and dropped to the unseen floor of the space we now occupied. She walked toward me, gliding over the floor as if she floated on some unseen force, propelling her over the world's bleakness. When she was within range, she slapped me, the sound echoing in the small room. I covered my cheek, the skin raw and red from her hit already.

"Stop saying that shit, alright Avraham? You're stronger than that and you know it. You're the strongest person I've ever met—there's a reason why you have that creature and none of us do. No one else could have kept it from controlling us. After everything that's happened, here you are worrying about turning into a monster. Out there, your brother just blew up a warehouse full of people," she gestured out of the mirrors before continuing. "Avi, you can do this, you just have to believe you can," she told me softly, placing her hands on my shoulders.

I shuddered, feeling her warmth on them, wondering if this would be the last time I would ever feel her touch. More tears started to come as I spoke, my voice cracking, "What can I do, Linor?" I asked her, dumbfounded at the situation.

"You can face it, Avi, you can take control of your life. You were never a beast, Avi. You were my friend. My love, my hero. You just have to believe you can," she said.

I was having trouble standing. She steadied me, moving us toward the safe. "How are you doing this right now, Linor?" I asked her as she held on to my elbow.

"I can do this because you want me to do this, Avi. I'm always going to be here, okay?" she replied, almost intimately.

We reached the safe, and she placed her hands on the dial, putting in a combination I could not make out, even with the glowing light coming from the room. "Fight the monsters, Avi, rage against them until you have nothing left—just keep on fighting, keep on going forward," she stated.

Terrified, I trembled next to her at the prospect of what was coming next. Whatever was inside that safe, it was full of monsters—it would be me against them, against the shadow that had been behind me at every turn. Every edge of the black hole that never ended, sucking in the light, a void of endless joylessness. Was I really about to face that all by myself, me, who couldn't even take a day being sober without pissing himself?

Linor smiled at me in the darkness. "Oh, Avi, it's okay to be afraid. You know that there is something to overcome, to become stronger than. Trust me, you will grow strong—very strong, because you've always been the toughest fucking knucklehead I've ever met. Go kick its ass. You just have to believe—don't be afraid." She pulled open the safe door. A gray light busted through, showing a dim and barren field. I stepped to the safe's door, covering my eyes.

"I love you," I whispered to Linor.

This time she cried, "Don't be afraid—Avraham."

I dove through the door of the metal safe, plunging to the dusty field below.

73

Chapter 73

Dust filled my mouth and I groaned, spitting out bits of debris. "Why is this shit always happening to me, or at the very least, can it happen some place nice, for a change?" I grumbled, sitting up and looking out at the vast world around me. The barren land stretched like a gray sheet crumpled over an impossibly huge bed, thick hills and rolling waves of gray sand in every direction.

I started to get to my feet when I heard growling, freezing me in place. I turned my head slowly. Nearby in the shadows, the wind hit a wall of muscle and anger. The beast was crouched. His marble horns curled in tight swirls like massive shadows. A broad body, taunt with muscle, raven-colored fur thicker than any blanket I'd ever seen spread over the creature's body. Alarming, gray eyes, the size of my fist, burned like the ash-colored streak going down his chest. Rows of sheared teeth filled its muzzle, which were complimented by its four powerful limbs, bulging with power and claws. It was the beast that had haunted me since I was a boy, the beast that I had found as a puppy, once upon a time, in a pit of fire. Easily bigger than two of the Bipin siblings transformed—this was a true monster of the night, a creature that belonged to the darkness.

My legs trembled, as from his mouth, he spewed a black ball, covered in drool, which rolled toward me in the gray dust. It was a simple ball, the treading worn down from time and being chewed on by such a massive beast. The ball rolled until it was halfway between us, which could have only been the distance from first plate to home plate. *What are you doing, Avi? Don't think of the distance; think of getting the hell out of here. That thing is going to kill you.* I stepped to my left and it growled, one stout leg slamming into the dirt. *It was my imagination that had felt the ground rumble,* I told myself. I stood no chance. I had to run, and yet—facing the thing, that thing, my shadow—despite how much my legs shook, I couldn't pull myself to leave. If I stopped now, it would win. The beast that had stalked the edges of my heart after all this time would win.

"Boy—you're just a beast, a no-good beast!" snapped Linor's grand-mother's voice in my thoughts.

Others joined in. "Show me the wolf!" cried my brother.

"You're more wolf than boy," shouted Dr. Joachim.

Finally, my mother called softly, "You promised you would protect your *bruder.*"

Their voices continued to repeat endlessly, causing my legs to tremble. I needed to bolt—I had to go. My body was drenched in sweat, my clothes nearly falling off from my heat, salt in my eyes. I felt used, like a tire that had been driven over an endless mountain, only to be patched and rolled back again.

"It's not too late to save him, Avi," my father whispered.

"I know, *foter*—" I whispered as I felt the warmth from Linor's hands on my shoulders.

She whispered softly, "Don't be afraid, Avi."

That stopped the fear that was eating its way up my back. This cold ocean that would reach up and take the heart of me, if I let it. I wasn't going to do that, no more. I looked at the beast, growling and drooling, as he looked upon his next meal. "Just a big fucking predator looking for a snack. Lunch isn't coming so easy today, pal." I shouted at the creature.

It responded. Without moving the massive lips covered in teeth. "Feeling pretty brave all of sudden, little Avi," he hissed.

"Oh yeah? You think this is your body and you control me, knowing every little fear I have?" I stated.

"That's right! I see every sniveling little quiver you make. Every sad cry you produce. I know you, inside and out, Avi. You're a coward, a tiny insignificant weakling!" it growled back.

I looked at my dirty shoes. Almost thirty years and I could not remember the last time I'd had shoes that fit, or the last time my feet weren't dirty. I had seen a lot in my life, done a lot—I was here to take this thing down, that was why my life had led me here—to this place of shadows and pain.

"I'm taking you down, wolf," I growled back.

It tilted its head back in response, roaring into the day. All the hair on my body stood up, my ears popping from the noise. Why was he getting so mad? If he was so confident, the beast wouldn't even be worried. *That was it*, I thought, as the idea hit me like lightning on a metal pole. *The big bad wolf was afraid of me.* Just like in the vent when I had stabbed myself and it hurt him. "It hurts you too," I whispered as I dug my feet into the ground.

"If you think little scum like you can possibly take me down, go ahead, be my guest," the creature roared. "What makes you think that you can even do anything against something like me?" It snapped its teeth, clacking at a rate that I knew had the force to easily break my bones to pieces.

I stood tall suddenly. "Because I am not a beast," I stated, bolting forward and digging my feet into the ground.

Flashes of the games we played as kids flew through my head. We grew up not knowing what baseball was. We only had the radio to go off, and what magazines that found their way into our small Polish town said about the game. I would imagine myself inside colosseum-sized stadiums, crowds watching me as I ran across the bases, my head down, my legs and arms pumping against the very air, moving me through it as if I was fighting off an invisible force trying to hold me back. in those games we played, I ran with everything I had. Just like I did when I was in the camps. I would stare out through the bars, imagining a world beyond them, where I could be running free—just the ground being pushed away from my feet, my face going toward an unknown destination.

My life as an adult, in and out of jail, looking out every day from a window that showed either a locked-in cage full of other men, repressed and lower than beasts, or the calls of people in the community, afraid of the creature that was inside me. All those times, I had run, doubting myself, hurting so much inside. An endless circle, a cycle that I could never break. But that was never true—it had never been my destiny to run the loop until my legs could go no more. I was running, because all my life I had finished my race. I would break the circle; I had everything I needed. *I am not afraid.* As I propelled my body toward the ball, the beast pounced, closing the distance between us at an alarming rate. I breathed deep—my lungs burning as I felt the fear leave my body.

I had a beautiful *muter* who loved me and my *bruder* dearly. A brave father, who guided me and believed I could take care of our *mishpokhe* when he was gone. The love of a woman who could possibly be the most insane person I'd ever met, but would love me no matter what I did. Over the years, despite people being afraid of me, I had made friends like Huey, like Bipin, Solly, and others who walked with me, who believed in me. I wasn't going to let them down. *In their eyes, I am not a beast.* I wasn't going to lose to this creature, so I vowed to win right here and now.

Every muscle in my body strained as I ran harder than I'd ever run in my life. My vision narrowed, red showed at the corners of my eyes. I was going to reach that ball—or die trying. The creature was blazing across the distance, easily faster than me, its legs kicking up mounds of dirt in every direction.

Big beast, I thought as I came within three yards of it, two yards, and then one yard. I bet it doesn't stop easily, I thought, as I slid my legs down, and glided across the dirt. One massive limb shot forward, a paw the size of my chest reached over where my body was. I slid, taking the slimy ball in my hands and coming back to my feet. Just like I had done during all those games as a kid, I had run forward toward the person on base. Regardless of how fast or strong they were, I was going to run.

Once on my feet, it occurred to me finally I had no idea where to run now. I had a split second to register before the beast pivoted its massive body and turned toward me with way more grace than a creature that size should have had. I flinched as a meaty paw took me to the ground like a kitten playing with a ball. I punched the toes of the paw holding me with my free hand. If it had any effect, the beast didn't show it. Inches away from my face it snarled. Thick drops landed on my face, covering me in an ocean of drool.

Well I gave it my best shot—I am about to be eaten, I thought. I closed my eyes and a memory of a hunt with my *bruder* and me came back into play.

74

Chapter 74

Our *zayde* trudged a few steps ahead—walking slowly, not snapping twigs and leaves. Moving like he was made in the forest. By comparison, my *bruder* and I must have sounded like a bull in a china shop: we hit every branch, crunched every twig, and grunted from the bags our *zayde* made us carry. At some point, our *zayde* leaned his rifle against a tree. "Boys, hold up for a moment. We are going to take a break," he stated casually, walking around a tree.

Zevi and I took that as the exact moment to drop our bags and fall to the ground. I groaned, wiping the sweat from my forehead with my sleeve, wondering when would be the next time that I got to see Linor. As I looked through the light coming between leaves, splaying the world in a golden snow, I felt very much like taking a nap. *Zayde* would have us out here for a few more hours still—long enough for him to tell us more fantastical stories of bears and other creatures that used to stalk the land when he was a boy. Things that Zevi and I had our doubts actually existed.

At the thought of my half-pint little *bruder*, I rolled over, looking for him. The little guy was being unusually quiet. Looking next to me, Zevi's pack lay in the grass undisturbed, but I couldn't see my *bruder*. I bolted up, looking for my *bruder*. My *zayde* was still behind his tree, but I couldn't see Zevi. My *muter* would kill me if I lost Zevi again. It seemed like every time we went anywhere my *bruder* would find a way to get lost.

I panicked, not because of Zevi possibly being hurt, but rather that our *zayde* would punish us both for this. I walked the tree line where we had stopped, looking for a sign of my *bruder* coming through the woods. I found his small shoe prints in the mud, broken twigs everywhere. Thankfully, he never picked up his feet when he walked, making this much easier. I kept walking, my eyes staying glued to his prints, when the ground suddenly shifted at a forge. I had just enough time to register the earth was parting before I fell forward, rolling down a hill.

My mouth was opened wide enough to scream as I tumbled, hitting every branch from trees growing on the hill, every limb and trunk. The most I could do was grunt when I finally landed on the hard surface of moss. It was hard to breathe, and my chest felt like I was a balloon that had been squeezed flat. My eyes were closed, and when I could finally open them again, I looked around me, seeing a part of the forest I had never seen before. A thick canopy of overgrowth, jutting rocks poking from the ground like teeth, and lime-green trees, splashed together so thick that the sky itself seemed to be choked out—leaving me in almost total darkness, despite it being midday.

I bounced to my feet, kicking leaves in every direction. "Hello!" I shouted, trying to see a way up the steep hill I had fallen down, but a sheer rock face was on both the left and right side of me. It was a miracle that I had gone off the grassy center. I would have to go around, judging from how steep it was. My thoughts began to flutter, faster than my beat of my heart that had forgotten that moments ago it had very nearly had the life squeezed out of it from the fall.

My legs were shaking, kicking up dirt and twigs, so I didn't hear the footsteps approaching behind me until I felt hands go around me. Instantly, like a light switch, my legs returned to normal. Tiny, dirty hands were wrapped around my stomach. I turned around, seeing Zevi. He was covered with mud, and streaks in the dirt near his eyes showed that he had been crying. His deep green eyes appeared iridescent in the low light coming through the canopy.

Zevi held tight, burying his head in my stomach. I was just as thankful to see him. I would never say it, but I was just as terrified as he was, if not worse. "Alright, enough of that," I said after a while, stepping away from him. I placed my hands on his shoulders, kneeling down. "We have to get moving now, Zevi. Why did you have to run off again?" I asked my little *bruder*.

He looked at the ground, muttering, "Promise you won't make fun?"

"It's just the two of us, partner," I stated back to him.

"I was chasing a butterfly—and well, fell down the hill," he stated.

I snorted. "Some butterfly it must have been."

"You fell down here, too!" Zevi shouted at me. I covered his mouth with my hand, holding up a finger to my mouth until he stopped fidgeting. I whispered, "What's *zayde* always telling us when we go out? We don't know what is out there when we are lost, so don't waste our energy yelling until the right time. Okay, Zevi? I am going to take my hand off now." I released my little *bruder*, and his eyes watered up.

"I got us lost, Avraham. We are going to die!" he sobbed into closed fists.

I sighed, "We aren't dying today, little *bruder*. You know why?" He shook his head. "Because we have each other. And because *zayde* taught us everything we need. Just remember to punch the big predators inside the mouth, okay?" I feigned shoving my fist in my mouth. Zevi let out a nervous laugh—that got him to be quiet, which in turned calmed me down. I could always beat him up later for getting us into this mess.

75

Chapter 75

"Punch big predators inside the mouth," I whispered, as the overwhelming strength of the beast pressed down on my ribs. I felt a crack, followed by a pop. I grunted as more than one rib broke. It loosened the pressure just enough for me to roll slightly to my side. The beast brought his mouth into a gesture that suggested he was done playing with his meal. Now he was going in for the kill. I shouted, roaring at the creature, as my hand holding the ball punched up toward that gaping mouth full of jagged knives. My *zayde* was correct in what he had told us as children: punch big predators inside the mouth.

As the beast's jaws opened, my hand with the ball shot deep into his mouth. Hot saliva, that burned my skin almost like acid, stung my arm as I plunged elbow-deep into darkness. I felt his scaly tongue just before hitting the end of his throat with the ball, before I heard the first gag. He recoiled, like a rubber band, coughing and sputtering worse than mine and Huey's old truck. When my arm was free and his massive paw lifted off my chest, I rolled to my feet, coming up quickly, knowing I had only one chance, while the beast coughed on the ball.

I stuck my hands into its fist-sized eyes, forcing it to reel in pain, flinching back as it closed the lids in an attempt to protect itself. The beast staggered. I wasted no time, grabbing its massive horns, smooth to the touch, just before I drove my knee into its snout repeatedly. It bucked on the first hit, barely more than a sneeze to such a large animal, but I continued, over and over, hitting the creature's nose. Blood shot from the creature's nostrils, and I continued to kick with my knee. I heard a crunch, causing me to shout out. That was all it took, and was long enough for the beast to swing one massive paw, swiping wildly, nearly bowling me to the ground.

This is getting me nowhere fast, I thought, as I dodged another close call with its paws. His eyes might have been shut, but it was only a matter of time until he either got lucky or sniffed me out and I was a goner. There was no way I could beat something that would make a grizzly bear nervous in a fist fight. What I could do? I heard it cough once more on my ball. It was making it that much harder for big-and-ugly to breathe.

I locked around its horns, spinning over the neck, saddling the beast. My left hand covered his bleeding nostrils, my right went in for the choke. I pressed forward with my hips and chest—using all my strength, and held on. The beast reacted immediately, bucking wild, kicking up huge clods of dirt in every direction. Holding tight, I did my best to get my legs around its broad shoulders and ended up straddling the creature's thick neck. I clenched my knees, locking my feet.

At some point, I started screaming. I shut my eyes as I felt a thick gush of wind as the creature leaped into the air, landing hard, sending me shuddering forward. I held for another few heartbeats as my fingertips began to burn. I removed my hand from the beast's nose just in time as a torrent of flames came roaring out of its nose and mouth, along with the ball burning into pieces right before my eyes.

"Oh, no," I muttered, just as the creature bucked one last time, sending me over its horns, landing me in the dirt.

I looked up at the black fur of the monster, the gray streak on the front making the creature's fur almost appear blue. It gagged, spitting out chunks of the ball, then with a deep breath and a growl that could only mean a painful death, the beast turned toward me.

I sat up, groaning from the fall, until I came at eye level with the beast. "I'm not afraid of you anymore—do your worst!" I shouted at the thing, throwing a handful of dirt for good measure.

Wide teeth slipped out from its gums, long and sharp fangs that looked like they belonged inside a shark devouring the ocean's fishes. The beast was the same as a shark, though, I thought as its heavy paws moved the dirt near it, as if it weighed nothing.

It really is a shark, just a different kind, I thought. I prepared for the worst as the beast neared me. My heart was exploding in my chest. This must have been how rabbits felt just before they were about to be killed—something big approaching with no way out. Only thing left to do would be for their heart to explode. *It beat being eaten any day of the week*, I thought as the world went black and the creature approached me.

76

Chapter 76

I'd woken up far too many times not remembering what had accrued the night before; usually to some erroneous assumption that I had just gone to bed without having caused any problems. More often than not, I was completely wrong. This time when I opened my eyes, I was momentarily confused as to where I was, when I saw the massive head of the beast only inches from my face.

I closed my eyes for a moment, hoping that the sharp teeth near my face were just part of a dream, and I rolled over onto my side, searching for a cold spot under my pillow. But instead of a pillow, my hands found dirt: lose, grainy sand like dirt, which was nothing like my simple bed. My eyes snapped open and I rolled back to the grimacing face of the wolf. I was a goner—beast or not, the snout of something that big with so many teeth would make anyone almost wet themselves. I wouldn't have been surprised if I did.

The beast grunted at me, his snort from his bloody nose causing the hair on my head to be pushed back, as if I was standing near a plane taking off. I thought about raising my hands to fight; I had none left in me. My arms felt like one hundred pounds of lead, while the rest of my body was double that. I opened my mouth, croaking on my words before spitting dry blood out, "Well, get it over already."

The wolf simply stayed sitting on its haunches, in a manner that if I hadn't known better, I would have said belonged to a dog and not some massive monster that appeared humanoid, mixed in with a demon. I started to get up, and the beast growled, curling back its lips, exposing more of the jagged teeth. I rolled my eyes. No point in being polite to the big bad monster, "Come on, man, I am tired, you look like shit. Just get it over with—I don't have the energy for this game anymore."

Then the monster did something I thought it would never do. He stretched out his front legs, bending forward, and dipped his head. He smacked his lips breathlessly and stuck a long ruby-colored tongue out, as if tasting the air itself.

I blinked in surprise and slowly shifted my weight until I was sitting up. As the wolf stretched, his gray eyes stayed on me all the way up to standing. I brushed the dirt off me. "That was a good fight, by the way—I totally kicked your ass. Just saying," I goaded the creature. He either didn't hear me or was as unimpressed with my taunt as the rest of my body felt.

He sat down, his head resting on his paws, black horns gleaming in the bright sun. The perfect image of someone taking a nap. That was just rude. "Hey, now asshole, get over here and kill me," I gestured toward the beast. One of its massive eyes popped open and regarded me with about as much interest as a person looking at an ant.

It snorted at me in response. Furious, I shouted at the wolf, "Hurry up and do something! People are dying! Linor is dying and you just sit here, like a big fucking dog."

That got through him, and in a flash, I was pinned to the ground under one of his paws again, which was nearly wide enough to span from shoulder to shoulder. "Watch your mouth, puny human. I am no crooning pet," it snarled, the words carrying into my mind like a bomb. It lifted its paw after a moment, standing on two legs this time, and walked toward a small mound of dirt, planting his body back into the ground with the same disinterest from earlier.

This is just getting annoying, I thought, as I brushed the dirt from my clothes. Odds were if I called him "dog" again, I had my doubts he would be as polite. This time, I decided something different. Something you could only learn after being in prison for the majority of your life. Make friends with people you never thought you would, just to survive. No matter how different the beast and I were, we still occupied the same space. That was something, at least, a commonality that I had to capitalize on.

I approached the beast. He opened one eye, watching me with a feigned disinterest. *He's waiting for me to make the first move.* I came to the mound of dirt nearest the beast and I sat down. It let out a loud puff of air in response.

"Yeah well, I don't like you either," I muttered. I went on after a few more moments of the beast lying there in the dirt. "You're the big bad wolf, that's for sure, but I suspect the only reason you haven't popped my head off yet and drunk my insides is because it would kill you. That about right?" I asked him.

He remained silent, his eye glued on me, unnerving me with every passing gaze.

"That's probably the truth, but maybe it's for another reason. Maybe you're no more bad than any other do—creature out there," I stopped myself from calling him a dog as his lips curled up at the "d" sound.

"That was you, all those years ago in the bonfire, wasn't it? That tiny puppy," I stated and the beast growled again. "You saved my life—I don't know how, but you did. I guess—I never thanked you for that. Thank you," I said softly, as a cold wind blew around us. Both of us remained silent.

"Alright than—" I started, before the beast spoke into my mind.

"What do you want, little Avi?" He spoke in what could for the first time ever not be considered a head-splitting neutral tone.

I seized the moment. "What I want is for you to help me get whatever is weighing us down off of us and save Linor, please."

He snorted again, turning his head to look as if he was sleeping once more. "Why would I do that? It's a chunk of roof on my back. It would be easier to let it fall. None of those people ever liked me anyways," the beast stated.

Countless times growing up, people in the community would call me a beast just at sight, even those that weren't part of the community when

I first got there. When I had last transformed, who knows how many had perished in the flames from the beast. I shivered, thinking about the memory, of my youth spent with this thing inside me.

"It wasn't easy being inside you, you know. All the times I saved those people's worthless lives. I could have just let them rot inside that cage," he growled, the usual anger coming back to his voice. In a way, that was less unsettling. At least I was I used to him being that way.

But it all made zero sense to me. Why was he bothering to tell me this all now? Was I to believe that this monster had somehow been hurt by all the comments said about him over the years? That could be it, though. When I had crawled through the ventilation shaft, stabbing my body repeatedly, the creature had roared, growled, and hissed. He also yelped; he even sometimes cried. "It hurts you too," I whispered. The beast remained silent in response.

Making sense of our past is a very difficult thing to do, if not impossible. For several reasons beyond painful memories, even when we try to recall what happened during an event, you can never put words to the feelings. You can recall how you felt, maybe even describe it, but in my experience, how can you feel that way again after so much time had passed? Yet, all those memories, that trauma shook me to my core, and kept me up nearly every night. That was something I could never forget.

I thought about those memories, those times that I would sneak off at night, and do anything just to escape the memory. The memory was long gone in some cases, just a candle wick nearly at the end. It was the feelings that had stayed, an intangible force, clouding over everything in my life.

The beast must have felt it the same way. It must have felt conflict over the same things that happened. I wondered for a split second if he was the reason I turned away from killing myself on occasions when I couldn't calm down. I shuddered at the thought.

I now realized fully that this was true; the beast had felt everything I had, from the beatings to being locked up. We had both experienced those things together. We had suffered together, bled together, grown together. I thought of all the times I had been shivering in the woods when I was younger, looking for my way. "That was you, wasn't it? All those times when I was freezing and I somehow didn't die. I never could get a fire going that first year or so, but I somehow survived a winter in Washington with just a few blankets. Yeah, that was you—it had to be."

The beast didn't respond, as placid as ever. I hung my head for a moment. So many things I thought I had been sure of in this life. Not a single one had I ever ended up actually being right on. The problem with the grief I had experienced for so long—it made me blind to those who did care. I wasn't sure if the beast really gave a shit or if he only looked out for me for self-preservation reasons. Either way, the beast had been with me since the beginning. Even though carrying him had been a curse, he was always there. My shadow was a part of me, not something I could cast away.

I understood in that moment what Elder Ad had told me all those years ago. It wasn't just about feeding the good wolf—I always would have both sides in my nature. The only way to make peace with those wolves was to feed them—it was time for me to take care of my shadow.

"Thank you—for everything you've done," I stated. The beast simply lay on his front paws, not moving or making any kind of agreement to what I said. Just as well—it was worth a try, and maybe it would keep him from trying to kill me.

After another long moment between the two of us, the wolf grunted.

"What do I call you, beast?" I responded to his grunt.

I flinched back, expecting another swipe from one of his mighty paws, but instead he replied, "I've been around for more ages than you could ever understand, tiny human. I appear to those that are in great peril. For a group that has been done a disservice so unjust that there is only one hope: me."

I nodded. In a strange way, that made sense. On the train to the camps, prayers were the only words spoken, pleas from those about to face a faith that was far worse than anything they could imagine. I shuddered. The smell of the ash that night wafting back into my system.

Now that he was talking, that was progress. "So, you were living inside that old Rabbi before me, correct?" I asked him.

He turned his head and shook his horns once. "Yes—he was the being that cast the final prayer that was needed."

"Prayer, huh. So you're so kind of angel? Boy—all those demon comments must have really rubbed you the wrong way," I jested.

The beast growled, "I am a reflection of the hate in this world—not the trivial kind that a being such as you would ever understand. Such simplistic words," he snarled.

"Easy—just trying to piece it together. You can't blame a guy. You've tried to take me over... how many times? Not to mention what was done to everyone when you did take control—" I stopped when the beast stood up, looking at me.

"Pain to you is like a shock to my entire body. You're such a fragile and worthless thing... I would kill anything that causes you harm," the beast growled.

"So, you do care? I get it," I sighed. I continued, "Like it or not, we've both done things bad to each other, I suppose, that's the truth of it."

The beast stood to its full height. A wave of muscles lined his body, unnatural and thick bulges hanging at impossible angles. He easily had to weigh five hundred or more pounds. And stood at a height well above my head. A snarl came from his mouth. I pressed on, despite the urge to run away from that spot as fast as I could. Facing him, I came to the creature's chest, but I looked up. I was going to stare this demon in the eyes. "All those times—all those people you killed. Was that to protect us? Well I need your help to protect more than just us, now. I need you—I need your help, beast," I stated.

The beast let out a howl. That made me cover my ears. His horns seeming to shimmer in the light, pulling the sound around them.

When he was finished I uncovered my ears and pressed on. "Help me," I demanded.

The wolf shot out an arm, pushing me in the chest. I was sent flying back five to ten feet. I landed hard, dirt in my mouth, but the creature did not approach. "Why would I help you, you insignificant rat?" he berated.

I mumbled out a curse word in the dirt before standing to my feet. The wind had been knocked out of my chest. I had a feeling that if he wanted to, that shot would have killed me easily. "Because for twenty years you've been stuck with me. Twenty fucking years. All those times you tried to take over, tried to stay knocking at my door. Why is that, I wonder," I pondered, fighting the urge to put my hands up. Even though I had little doubt on what that would actually do to protect me from a monster such as he.

The wolf spat, a long trail of saliva and lord knows what else, bigger than my head, landed on the ground. I was never eating again, I decided, as I tracked my eyes back to the beast. "The only reason I have not killed you, human, is because you carry me, otherwise I would grind your bones to ashes—"

"And drink my blood. You've used that line on me already. Seriously, cut the shit, man. I kicked your ass and you know it. You owe me that much at least," I yelled at the creature.

He roared, hissing out a small trail of thick black plumes. "Fine, I will cut the shit, as you say. I've shared a body and mind with you for twenty years. More intimate than any lover you ever had. Every thought and feeling you've ever passed through that witless skull of yours, I've been privy to. It's exhausting, honestly, the amount of time you people spend doing other things besides hunting and fucking. You don't need to eat so much.

"But you've had a habit of picking a lot of fights for someone so meek—someone who runs so much. Any conflict that by all rights, you should have run from, you were there still scrapping. I like that. It takes guts to face a foe, knowing they're going to win, and still go through with it. I've had plenty of hosts—some truly selfish, and some were monsters that the depths of hell couldn't create. You, Avi, stayed fighting, despite the odds," he stated.

I thought on that for a moment. *What he was saying wasn't wrong. It was progress. Just hold on Linor, I will get you soon, I promise.* I took the time to speak during his pause. "You mentioned you come in a time of need. Well I imagine my time of need was in the camps; why are you still here, wolf?"

I asked him.

I swear the big beast rolled its eyes before dropping down to all fours and gingerly making his way to me across the gray sand. It had to be my imagination; I was pretty sure the earth was shaking as he shuffled toward me. He sat down on his haunches, and this time, he was only slightly above my eye level. I faced him, unsure what was about to happen.

"My name is not Beast, or Creature, or Wolf, and it's not Monster. My name is Ascher Feyer Valf," he said in perfect Yiddish.

I blinked, doing my best to hide my surprise at that. "That is a mouthful. How about I call you Ash for short?" I asked the wolf.

He growled. "How about I call you Toothpick For My Teeth?" Ash snarled.

"I would rather you not. You still haven't answered the question. Why are you still here?" I asked him.

"I am here because I am still needed. When my time is up, I will cease to exist until the next time that I am needed," he stated calmly.

I looked down at the dirt. If what he was saying was true, I had spent most my life treating him as a curse living inside of me, both of us feeding off each other's hate. Another thought occurred to me in that instant. "Do you have any idea what my brother wants with us, so badly?" I pondered.

This time, the beast's eyes grew wild, angry, like a predator had just caught the scent of something dangerous nearby, about to steal its kill. "I do not like your brother—that is a vile, savage man," he stated.

I kept my head down. "Maybe. He is my brother," I whispered.

He hissed at me. "If you had recognized your brother for what he is, you wouldn't be in this situation anymore," he stated.

There were some elements of truth to that. My brother's actions today suggested he was a long way gone. Beyond just my father's promise, a lingering thought kept chewing away at my brain: if I gave up on Zevi, how could I ever defeat my own darkness?

"I know exactly what Zevi is—I will deal with him."

Ash remained silent. I thought he was going to ignore my statement before he finally replied, "I suspect that the reason your brother wants me

476

is what my blood does. It makes you an aspect of myself, drawing from my body and creating something new when you drink it. You've seen what a small amount has created—imagine a whole army," he stated.

I shivered at the thought. It made sense. Zevi had most likely found Dr. Joachim, tortured the poor man until he revealed how they stumbled across what they learned. What bugged me the most, though, was why not have come sooner and just beaten me in my sleep? Sophia easily knocked me out. Once more, super powers or not, Zevi had managed to take over this small town all on his own. I wasn't sure what terrified me more, the reality that the wolf's blood gave people powers, or that my brother was trying to build an army of crazed people with the wolf's blood.

"Does my blood give them any powers?" I asked the wolf as he still stayed upright, stoic in the cold wind that blew around us. The temperature was dropping, I noticed. Wherever we were, the sun was falling. I hope that didn't translate to the real world—*hold on, Linor. I am coming, I promise.*

"No, it is mine that does it. What the doctor figured out in the camps was that when you bled, it brought me out. What they failed to do was to harm me." He almost seemed to smile when he said it. That was just horrific and caused me to take an involuntary step back. "Do you have any more questions?" he asked me.

"Will you help me, please?" I pleaded to him.

"I have spared your life because you showed your bravery against me. Knowing full well you could not harm me, you still fought anyways. In many ways, you're a gallant human. I see no reason why I should ever help another human again. I am used as a weapon, nothing more and it's always the same: point me at your enemies to devour their marrow. Condemn and lock me away until the next cycle. It's always the same; humans are just filled with hate. Therefore, I am hate. It does not change, so I am done doing that," he stated.

I challenged him. "I don't believe that for a moment. You wouldn't have protected me all those times," I stated.

"I only protected you because you stood your ground. You were put into positions that no one should ever have to deal with. That alone is why I protected you," he stated.

"Then protect me now. If you're truly here to help, to right an injustice, help me. I know you've been let down and I know you feel that the world has treated you as a monster and that has created so much hate inside you. I get it, things like that, things that burn your blood and just eat you away until there is nothing left but a deep hole. I am so sorry for not talking to you sooner, for not bridging this sooner. I now need your help—I need it. So, please, Ash, help me. Because when I am finished settling this shit with my brother, one day, I am going to come after all that hate inside you," I stated.

The beast cringed back, almost as if I had struck him before speaking. "I've seen your thoughts, your mind. Why should I believe that you want to do anything for anyone else, Avi? Your female was right. You've been a runner all your life," he replied.

"Because like the times when I should have run, I stood my ground. I'm through with letting this fucking world decide how to think. How to feel, how to love, how to hate. I make my own way from here on out. I am choosing to protect the only *mishpokhe* I have left—I will do it with or without you." I turned my back and started walking off into the gray ocean around me. It dawned on me after a few steps that I had no idea how to get out of here.

The beast trotted next to me. In a smooth motion, he dipped his head and flipped me onto his back. "That's not the right way, dumbass."

77

Chapter 77

I blinked. I was back in the room as before. Linor was buried, and all that remained was the mirror on the wall. Looking down, I could see her eyes half opened, as if she was squinting from a bright light. "Hang on, hang on. We are going to get you out of here, Linor," I shouted in the confines of the room.

Ash growled in response, bracing his back up. I could hear shifting coming from above us. Steady grunts came from the beast as he attempted to move the rubble from on top of him. Small chunks of stone and roof fell down around us. A piece hit Linor's badly burnt cheek. "Hey watch it, we need to move this without crushing Linor." I panicked, pointing at the mirror showing me the images.

"I know!" he responded, grunting under the exertion.

The weight of the roof was overwhelming, I realized. I could somehow sense what the wolf was feeling, the grit of his teeth, the crushing strain on every inch of his back. *He can't lift it—this is it, being crushed under the rubble of a warehouse roof.* Looking through the mirror, I couldn't tell if she was breathing anymore. My heart sank as I held her tender form in my eyes. I could be lost in her a daze of her black hair for she truly was flawless to me. But it was more than simple vain beauty—she was *mishpokhe.* I would never let *mishpokhe* down.

I placed my hands against the walls of the room. They were cold to the touch, a slippery surface that had a bit of give when I pressed into them. "Alright, please work," I prayed, closing my eyes and thinking of what I was fighting for. I was fighting for Linor, for Huey, Solly, Bipin, the rest of the community... and for Zevi. With a roar, I cast all that energy, my fear, my anxiety, my history with all of them. All the good, all the bad that life had saddled us with. I reached out through the wall, until I felt the mind of Ash. I imagined this was how he seemly knew exactly what I was thinking. "Please, work," I muttered once more, as I grunted, propelling all my thoughts through my hands.

It took me a moment to become aware that both the beast and I were yelling. Weight begin to shift from his shoulders, burning tension being released all at once. He grunted, roaring as he his height slowly started to rise. "That's right, fucking fight, this will not be our end!" I cheered for the beast, and he roared back in reply as chunks of the roof started to shake down. I felt both his palms go flat against the debris. "Keep going!" I shouted once more.

The beast gave one final roar, sounding like a volcano exploding for the first time in millions of years. His roar was true, fierce, and exactly what was needed, as the roof was dislodged and the chunk thrown off his shoulders.

A cold breeze replaced the warm air instantly. I could feel it brushing over the beast's fur, like wearing a wool coat in the middle of a snowstorm. He let out another roar in exultation. I kept my focus down, though, looking at Linor. Now that we were clear, moonlight was giving me a better look at her. The bomb had done far worse damage than I had expected. Her skin was now stone-like in appearance. More black and red than her normal olive-colored skin, I couldn't see her hand, either, on the left side. The only thing that appeared not to be completely burnt off was her hair and part of her face. She was in bad shape—we needed to get her to a hospital.

"Ash, we need to save her, now!" I shouted at him. He pointed his head down, grunting in reply as his hands stretched out around her, picking her up as if she was a mere child and not an actual adult. "Be careful, please," I said gently. He grunted, turning, leaving the broken building, heading into the woods.

78

Chapter 78

I set her down gently on the cold grass. A howling wind was blowing and I shivered as I looked at her, but it wasn't from the wind. It hadn't taken long for Ash to run us a few miles into the woods. We were deep enough that I heard only animals in the distance, a few calls as the night bugs came out to mate. I needed to get Linor to a hospital, but that made me wary. I wasn't sure how deep Zevi's hold on this town went. After learning what I had about the police force, it wouldn't surprise me if nearly everyone in this city was a part of his army. The way he spoke when we were in the warehouse, he fancied himself as some kind of demagogue with a silver tongue that knew all.

I put off thoughts of my *bruder* for a moment to think of how to best help Linor. I had no medical knowledge; I had never needed it—I simply would heal. I spoke to the beast inside my mind. This time, he was in the room curled up in a ball. There, the surroundings were now lit up, in a hazier yellow, which allowed me to see better. "You wouldn't happen to know anything about treating burns, do you?" I asked almost frantically, trying to keep the fear out of my voice.

He signed before speaking. "Avi, I have fangs and teeth. What do you think I am to know?" he asked.

I growled, punching a nearby tree, both of us yelping in pain at the same time.

"Watch it! Just because you're mad doesn't mean you can fix the problem that way."

I cradled my hand, the bone slowly mending. I was healing again; the many stabs I had inflicted upon myself earlier were clotting finally. Ash said he could heal from most things, so I could now as well. However, it had its limits and as the mending to my body took place, tissue growing back, wounds scabbing over, I felt like I had run a double marathon.

I knew why he had also told me to be careful. The easiest way for him to die was if I died. We were both now aware of each other's weaknesses. It was hard, though, to keep a clear mind and think about the best way to handle the situation, even with us together. Every moment we spent out here, Linor was closer to dying.

I was just about to punch the tree again when I heard motorcycles calling in the distance. "It's Bipin!" I exclaimed. "Quick, switch places with me," I told Ash.

"Why?" he asked back.

"Because I need you to get his attention." I gestured toward the bikes. "Do that flame thing you did again," I stated, my nerves all but shot by this point.

"That won't do any good. You won't be able to talk for a while, remember. You will need to let me out, Avi," he stated.

I thought about it. My hesitation wasn't that the beast would run rampant, it was that the transformation always ripped my body to shreds—the most painful meaning of the word pain. But it was for Linor and would be the fastest way to save her.

"You still have to be wounded for me to come out, and it must be fresh, blood for blood, Avi. Just don't go overboard. No need to cause any more damage to your body—a little will do," he informed me.

I started to growl, my body trembling. I felt so powerless—so weak to change what was happening to someone I love; what a horrible feeling, to be powerless to save someone. I refused to think this was the end; there had to be a way. *Just keep thinking, there has to be a way.* "What about giving her your blood? She already has been powered up once by you. Why not do it again? I remember in the camps how many bandages Bug had—he seemed to survive it somehow," I stated.

Ash clicked his tongue. "It's a good idea, but it won't work. My blood supercharges the body—transforms it, twisting the foundation. It is not a natural growth, what is inside me. An adult, especially in her state, would die from it—I wouldn't risk it," he informed me.

"I trust you," I muttered.

There was nothing else for it. I ran to the nearest tree and punched the trunk as hard as I could, neglecting exactly what the beast had just told me. My fist jammed into my hand as my wrist shook from the force, and the skin around my knuckles shot in different directions as if it was made of splinters. Red smoke poured out of my hand instantly, I began to sweat, my bones popped all along my body. My mind was breaking like glass thrown from a tall building.

I whispered somewhere through the pain, as my skin peeled away, my body becoming unnaturally long, "Please, hurry."

Snapping, tearing, popping, and a long moment of suffering eventually passed. I was back in the room, looking through the mirror, and smoke still radiated all around me. The grass the beast stood on was burnt away for many feet in every direction. The beast didn't wait for me to take it all in. He tilted his head back, and a warm sensation flew out from his unhinged jaws, before a long blast of fire rocketed over the tallest trees.

The fire left ashes falling down like snow on the beast's skin. In the distance, I heard several other engines roaring as the motorcycles changed direction toward the source of the fire. It was worth it, I thought. Even if someone else might have seen that—this is for Linor. "We need to switch back," I stated to the beast.

He grunted in reply. As the shift back started, I was sucked out of the room and the beast's fur fell off like cotton from a flower top. At least this wasn't as bad, I thought.

I worried that there wouldn't be a path through the woods to us. I just had to trust that Ash had made the right decision bringing us here—wherever we were—in these thick woods.

79

Chapter 79

I had just finished coming back to roughly human proportions when the first headlights settled on me. I squinted, the lights burning my eyes. A pair of van lights came into view with the rest of the bikes. My heart gave a silent "yes" as I heard the familiar chug of mine and Huey's truck. I waited until their lights hit me—like the lights from the camp when I first came off the train. Lights after being in the dark for so long mean change. However, what I've learned from change is that it's unbiased. The futility of nature asserts that change must happen over and over again—whether the change bodes something fruitful or sinister, nevertheless, the world is going to change.

The lights from the bikes and van held me steady for a moment, before they were abruptly cut. Some got out of the truck holding a lantern. I knew it was Huey before I even saw him. I could smell the kerosene and tobacco. It was a comforting smell after the night's events. He walked toward me, casting the orange light on my shivering form. "Man, you look like hell—why are you naked?" he asked.

I pointed behind me. "Never mind that. Do you know anything about medicine? Does anyone here?" I asked frantically.

Huey peered behind me at the burned form of Linor. He nodded gravely. "We might—we got most of everyone out before the whole place went up in flames. It wasn't... you know...?" he asked carefully.

I looked at him sharply in the orange lights. "No—it wasn't the beast, it was a very different kind of monster—my brother," I stated.

80

Chapter 80

Huey gave me a change of clothes from the truck and I quickly got dressed in silence. Behind me, most of what was left of the community was huddled around Linor. When I got my pants zipped, I ran back to the small circle of people. One of Bipin's brothers nodded to me and moved aside as I passed. Linor's grandmother was bent next to her, the old woman looked like she had aged another forty years since I had last seen her, her silver hair almost vanishing before my eyes. Her face was sorrowful, lines formed so deep that she would never be able to smile again. She held Linor's hand in hers. When I approached, she turned back, looking my way. I expected her to blame me this time, but her eyes only showed one thing: please. She was desperate for help, as was I.

Solly spoke from beside me. "I passed along to everyone what was happening inside the warehouse—thank you, Avi. We are... you... this wasn't the wolf, was it?" She asked just like Huey had.

I noticed then that the collective group was staring at me. No anger this time, just fear. Fear from a group of people who had suffered a lifetime of loss. They were at their wits' end, and a stiff breeze would probably be enough to defeat even the stoutest of hearts. I took a deep breath—it was hard for me to ignore that for most my life, these people had viewed me as a monster, viewed Ash as a monster. After we had saved them from the camps, saved them from much worse. But their fear was not misguided, and after all that the beast had brought, it wasn't farfetched to believe it. What they needed was hope, just like the beast. Hope that all the suffering they had endured would one day come to an end, that good things did exist.

I cleared my throat. "There is nothing that hurts me more than to see those I care about suffer. We've all suffered for so long—for so little return. This was not me, this was my brother. I swear." I let my words sink in as I turned around in the group. "Choose to believe me, or choose not. I don't care—all I care about is saving a person I love. So, I am asking you, if anyone can help at all, now is the time."

I looked around the group, but all I saw was crestfallen faces. We were defeated—there was no other way to put it. My hands shook with rage. After all of this, Linor was going to fade away, like wind through a keyhole.

"I took a couple of pre-med classes before dropping out of school," said Tivian. I glanced her way, my heart stopping as the young woman looked around nervously.

"Can you help?" Linor's grandmother pleaded.

Tivian nodded "That's a maybe—I need supplies, and someone's help," she stated.

Huey cleared his throat. "We need to get something on her, out of this grass," He took off his coat, laying it on the ground. "Solly, get the van pulled around now. Bipin and anyone else, take a corner. We need to put on an application of solutions, of silver compounds or salts," Huey directed. Solly sprang into action running toward the van. Bipin went to the coat, along with one of his brothers, and his sister and Huey took the other end.

I approached Huey. "What do you need me to do?" I asked him frantically.

Huey glanced down at Linor, his face deadly grave. "I need you to be calm, Avi. You look like you're about to lift a truck over your head. Secondly, I need you to get to the grocery store and make sure it's clean."

I nodded, taking one last look at Linor before I turned to run into the woods. The whole community slowly lifted Linor, and she let out a small moan. I faltered for a step. She was alive! I quickly shot back to my thoughts though. *She won't stay that way if you do not hurry.* I put my head down and tore off my clothes again, slamming my elbow into the nearest tree. "I am counting on you, Ash."

The beast growled in response as smoke flew out of my body and my screams filled the night as I quickly endured pain again. For my family.

81

Chapter 81

We were on top of the roof overlooking Pete's when the van pulled up, along with the rest of the community. I blew out some air. "Thank you, Ash," I said to the beast.

He grunted. "I'm going to stay in control for a while. Just in case," he stated.

I nodded. "Yeah that is probably for the best." The van doors opened, and I saw Huey directing Bipin to get the shop doors, as they carried Linor into the store. Somehow, in a way, I was glad to not be down there helping. I would only get in the way right now; my anger was far too great to be controlled. Fortunately, the beast seemed to remain stoic, an immovable object in a world that seemed to always be shifting. Still, the feeling of uselessness couldn't be shaken: my fingers twitched, my hands burned with a desire to hurt.

"Avi, you must relax. There is nothing more we can do," Ash advised.

"Actually, I think there is," I muttered, facing the wall, unable to see any more of the almost empty town. It was like the whole place had been deserted, drawing their breath in for the coming storm. And a storm *was* coming, I could feel it in my bones, shaking me, driving me onward. My teeth were gritted, fire was building inside me, choking rage at the futile sense that was growing, like vines over an abandoned home. "We can find Zevi, and end this now," I whispered as the words trailed out of my mouth.

The beast was silent. He was looking up at the moon, hanging in the sky like a crooked toenail as the crest blasted light upon our small little world. "I am a warrior, Avi. That is my purpose. I have grown in hate because of the reproach and treatment I have been given. But I have never questioned what I am or what my purpose is. Can you, though, Avi? Can you charge off into battle, to fight the fight that needs to be done? Butcher work is coming—that is what it is, do not mistake it for anything else. I can do all the work, but can you live with it? We share not only the same mind and body, but the same heart. You will die from this, if you're not ready," he stated.

I growled back. "I'm ready." I turned with Ash as he readied to leap from the building. As we pivoted, Huey faced us. Ash stopped mid-turn, snarling, toward my friend. "Easy, Ash, its Huey," I stated.

"Where are you going?" Huey asked. Ash growled in response.

"Ash, switch," I said, as I felt myself falling forward again through the mirror. My skin burned, my bones popping, as my body slowly came back into being.

I was breathing heavily, working hard to catch my breath when Huey faced me. He had a cigarette in his hands, a wide-eyed expression on his face. "That looked extremely painful. Where are you going, Avi?" he asked again.

"Why aren't you with Linor?" I snarled, stepping toward him. Huey neither moved nor seemed to react. He just took another long drag before speaking. "We've done the best we can for her—at this point, I don't even think regular doctors could do much more. I haven't seen burns like that since—since the war." Huey trailed off, looking over the side of the building.

I stopped my rising anger momentarily, remembering how hard it must have been for Huey to have been involved with treating her. "Thank you," I whispered, not able to face my friend as the words left my mouth. I knew if I stopped, if I went down to the store and saw her again, that would be the end of me.

"I've known you for, what, two years now? I would say we are friends.

You don't have to lie to me, man. Where are you going?" Huey asked me.

"You know," I replied to him, solemnly.

Huey shook his head. "You and I both know that is what your brother would be expecting. For you to fly off the handle, hot-blooded, looking for revenge. I can only guess that—if that explosion had been your fault, you would have already run, am I right?" he questioned.

I just gave him a long look until he got the point, not trusting myself to speak.

"Yeah I figured that was the case, or else you would have eaten me alive just now," he stated calmly.

"You're awfully calm for facing down the beast," I stated simply.

Huey shrugged. "Call it a little bit of faith and mostly blind luck. Look, man, I get it. This isn't the way, though. If you leave now, you may not even win—or worse, you do win and you have to live with it," Huey stated.

Exasperated, I sat down on the nearest ledge, my body facing toward Huey as I avoided looking over the edge. "I think the best someone like me can ever hope for is peace. Beyond that, that's it. When you've been brutally broken down to your smallest bits, all you can ever learn is to love yourself. How can I ever love myself, Huey, when everyone I know keeps falling through my fingers, like I am trying to hold onto smoke?" I informed him.

I leapt forward from the ledge, sweating from the toll of the night. Then, I finally leaned over and vomited off the rooftop. Huey came up beside me with a cloth, handing me the material. "Thanks," I muttered.

"I'm not going to tell you what to do, Avi. At the end of the day, these are not my people. If it was left up to me, I would be running my ass out of here. A little bit of advice from a friend who's seen enough of your habits to know you—you aren't made to be a butcher. Me, on the other hand—I was born to do this." Huey held out his hands, as if some invisible weapon was in his grasp that only he could see. "You asked me once what happened. Well, now I am going to tell you. Maybe that will give you some insight into what you're thinking about getting into."

82

Chapter 82

"I don't know, man—something about putting cinnamon on my spaghetti makes me want to vomit," I told Jackie as we made our way through yet another dirt road, deeper into the foliage, which seemed to reach out towards us. I gulped, sweeping my eyes back to my position in the clearing. Don't think about how some of the leaves looked like green hands—hands that wanted to take hold of you and pull you deep into the jungle forever. I shivered, despite the constant humidity. I could probably drink the air itself, I thought, as I signaled for the rest of the patrol to stop.

Jackie was still recounting his tales of terrible food from Ohio, and so distracted that he ran right into Tex, our radio man, who had stopped his search when I halted us. "Jackie, shut your damn mouth for five seconds and watch were you're heading—you up'dee cow," Tex drawled in his long accent. Tex looked at me, his square face and thick eyebrows leading down to a heavy chin. He wasn't handsome by any stretch of imagination, but he looked like a man who spent his time working on a ranch. Wide shoulders, traps bigger than most men's chests. Tex was about a foot taller than Jackie—*it's that corn they feed folks on the farm*, I thought. As I watched Tex and Jackie argue, their antics distracted me from the heat just for a moment, while I sat down on the dusty road.

"Gimme a break, ev'thang you mention from that city gonna make me hurl. What you need is some big ol' Texas barbeque, not that weird chilly shit you eat, right boss?" Tex asked me, turning his head my way with a long smile.

I pulled out rolling paper and a pinch of tobacco. I'd never smoked before the military—in the jungle, people will do anything to stay calm. For me, it was cheap tobacco and if I was lucky, five minutes to think of a beautiful woman rather than my three sweaty squadmates.

We had been out on patrol since 0400, walking the dusty roads near camp for about eight hours now. We hadn't seen shit, just dust and the endless green inferno, like flames of iridescent devouring the countryside. It was a boring day; I was more than alright with that. Soon, our point man Johnson would return and we could head back. Only, what was starting to bug me more than the bush was how long Johnson was taking. We'd sent him ahead 20 minutes ago—he hadn't returned. I wiped my forehead, doing my best to ignore the stinging fear that was racing up my spine. Johnson was either taking a shit or getting into shit. Out here, it was more likely the latter of the two.

I sighed, dashing my cigarette, and I stood, about to tell Tex and Jackie to knock it off, when a shot boomed in a forest line just beyond our spot. As the shot carried over the jungle, all went silent, from the bugs to our heartbeats—bullets meant only one thing: someone had just died.

Instinctively, we all dove into the ditch and pointed our rifles toward the forest line. I was sweating bullets as I searched the trees with my rifle. Snipers were impossible to spot. The tension in my back got tighter. If it was a sniper, he'd done a piss poor job of not killing three stationary men in the middle of the road. Which meant it was an ambush.

Just who was getting ambushed? I waited five slow breaths before signaling to Jackie and Tex. They both nodded as I stood up slowly and advanced my way through the overgrowth. I swept my rifle from side to side, all the while moving slowly. *Just keep stepping, heel to toe, heel to toe, Huey,* I thought as I made my way into the jungle. A moment later, I heard the snapping of twigs and Tex's heavy steps as he and Jackie followed. Their presence only made my heartbeat slightly more normal.

Each step was like taking a walk into a fire, the ground dissolving under my heavy combat boots, twigs and vines lashing out onto me as if trying to make me become part of the jungle. It was tough not to panic; it was everything I could to not curl into a ball and call out for my mother. I had no choice: it was walk through these woods and find Johnson or die. I wasn't going to lose a brother of mine. Not like this, not to this green hell. I had very little in this life these days—a smooth drink would be nice, maybe finally a bed. But, when you spend so much time with people day in and day out, comforts like that stop mattering. Instead, you just want your people to be alright, to make it home to their mothers and fathers. However, the longer I fought in this war, the farther from home I felt.

As I was lost in my thoughts, I failed to notice the jungle clear, before we arrived at a big field, clear of trees and only tall grass that came up to my knees. I held up my fist to indicate *stop* to Jackie and Tex. They did, coming to a halt right behind me. I scanned the field. Johnson was leaned against a tree, his head hung low, his rifle pointed at the ground. A lone tree in a field of tall grass, a bloodied man missing from his patrol.

I knew it was a trap; I think part of me did, but the three of us ran frantically towards our friend. Jackie was the smallest out of the four of us, so he reached Johnson first, despite my shouts for him to slow down.

I saw Jackie's hand shake Johnson before the flames blew his hand towards Tex and me. The tree was engulfed in flames, and Jackie danced screaming in the field. Tex reached Jackie before I did, stripping off his shirt and smacking Jackie down as the young man burned. I did the same once I reached them. It was too late. Jackie's skin peeled off like paper, but the man was dead. He was on his way home.

I sat back, looking at the carnage of my troops, my friends, my brothers. Too stunned to feel anything, the toil too great for me to pay, as the tree burned and Tex cried.

I bolted upright and heard a similar click as well, directly under my foot, obscured by the tall grass. The trap was now completely set and we were losing the game. I looked down, seeing the familiar "x" of the toepopper. I swept the grass with my rifle, doing my best to not shake my leg, as I saw hundreds of the M14 mines spread all around us.

My heart stopped at the realization of this. Either the enemy had taken the time to set up an ambush with our own mines, or we had fallen victims to friendly fire. Either way, we were in trouble.

"Boss," Tex whimpered and I looked at the big man. He was on the verge of tears.

"Don't panic, I am pretty sure these are the ones with the steel washers on the bottom. They can be disarmed. You just need to relax. The smoke from the tree will have other patrols here soon enough," I told Tex, wondering if what I was saying was really true. In any case, Tex nodded his head and the two of us stood like stone statues in the grass.

Time passes like paint drying, when you're that close to dying. Or maybe we were already dead, I thought as I looked at Tex. The big Texan was drenched in sweat, his body dipping slightly. We'd both thrown our rifles down an hour ago. I felt naked and alone in the field as I looked at my rifle. It was useless in this situation. Tex had tried using our radio a while ago as well, but somehow, when the explosion had killed Jackie, our radio had been hit. We were stranded, as the black smoke danced above us.

Where were the other patrols? We weren't that far from base camp. My question was answered as a group of 20 men came out of the tree line on the other side of the field. They were dressed in similar camo to ours, but their weapons were wrong. They looked Russian and they were far too tall for any Vietnamese.

"Mercenaries," I muttered as the group slowly made their way across the field. Their movements were spread apart, moving swiftly, but steadily, keeping a wide berth from the middle of the field. They knew where the mines were. Which meant they had been the ones that set them. That explained why the field was filled with our mines.

I gulped in fear as one of them stepped towards me. His head was shaved smooth, as if hair had been a poison on his skin and had to be removed no matter the cost. The rest of his face was the stuff of nightmares. The skin had been peeled back, like someone would a flay a deer. His eyebrows and eyelashes missing on the scar side of his face. He approached me with a calm that was unnerving. There were two dead men near Tex and me.

Their bodies still smoldering.

This man looked bored. "Clearly, this was a trap—you should have left your man on his tree," he stated calmly. I growled at the man, doing my best to keep my legs steady. He looked down at my foot, blowing out a whistle. He had a strong accent that sounded like every word he spoke was from the back of his throat. "That is—unfortunate." The man gestured towards his men, and one approached, brandishing a knife. The man looked at the soldier who had just handed him the knife. He rolled his eyes and stabbed the man who handed him the knife. I stood gasping, and Tex whimpered.

The rest of his men stood like trees in the field. "There's two of you. But he only handed me one knife. I don't have time for that kind of incompetence. I hate this country—but I love the war. You know what I mean, don't you, son. What is your name?" he asked.

"I'm not your... son. And it's Huey. What's yours?" I spat, and the man smiled.

"Pleasure to meet you, Huey. Dreadful situation you've found yourself in. Tell you what, I hate these kinds of things. Unwinnable and just not fair, not at all. I am going to give you this knife. You can use it to kill yourself, or you can try and free yourself of that mine you find beneath your foot. I would hurry, though. It's almost nightfall and this is their land," the man said.

Flabbergasted, I stuttered before finding my voice. "Tell you what, you can shove that knife up your ass. If I find out you had anything to do with—"

"You'll do what? Nothing. You're trapped on a mine, dear boy. I found myself trapped out in the woods once as a young boy, with no food or tools. I would have starved. A hunter found me, and taught me the most valuable lesson when he left me a knife. I could either live, or I could die. And you only have so much time left. Stop wasting it," he stated, before turning and gesturing towards his men. They slowly started to leave the field.

Before he could leave, I risked shouting at the man, fury gripping my heart in a hold I that I never knew could exist. "What's your name?"

The man simply stated, "Hans."

I snarled back, my whole body shaking with fear. "I will find you Hans. I will kill you," I shouted.

He nodded as if it was an ordinary thing for me to say. "Good luck." He turned, walking away.

With him and his men gone, the bravado was gone. Reality was setting in, nightfall was coming, and both Tex and I were deep down shit creek, almost out to the ocean.

Huey trailed off with his story staring off into the night before speaking again. "I got myself out from that minefield, even made it back to base camp," he rasped in a whisper.

I gave him a moment to breathe. "What happened to Tex?" I asked.

Huey remained silent for a while. "All that matters is, Avi, don't forget your brothers. I will never do that. I will find Hans," he stated.

83

Chapter 83

"I did find the man who killed most my team: Hans. He got away time and time again. And as you know, I kept ending up in and out of jail," he told me again.

I rolled my eyes after wiping my mouth on my sleeve. "What's your point? You already told me this story. It's what got me to train with you for two years," I stated.

"Then you will understand that for a long time, that life on the road, just like yours living every day on the run, being hunted, that was my life. Here is the thing, though: I was choosing it. A number of years ago, I came across a rickshaw puller in Calcutta. One of the most awful things in the world, a human being doing the work a horse should be doing; pulling other humans in a heavy car. What I learned from this rickshaw man was that his lifespan was about ten to twelve years on the job. They catch tuberculosis most of the time, then die very painfully. The man I met already had TB. To help his family, he had sold his skeleton for after his death, for a few lousy bucks from a local gang. This poor man never had a chance. He was asked how long he had been working, and once he told them the truth, they went ahead, giving him money. Rickshaw workers don't have anything to lie about: their life is pulling that car—pulling in the money for their family. Once he died, they would take his body from his wife and kids. Yet when I asked about his future, the future of his family.

He simply responded, 'Well, I'm doing the best I can, but the rest is in the hands of God.'

"That is a man who knew what he was, knowing full well what his actions would lead to. Hans got away when I found him, because I wanted to pull the trigger, but I wasn't a killer. So Hans didn't die. So, I ask you, Avi, after all the tears you've shed, are you resolved to your fate, just like the rickshaw man? Because if you are, then brother, I am with you, until the end. It's your choice, but know what you're getting into and know what that means. Can you really put down your brother? From what I am seeing, I don't see any other option, and I can't be the one to do it," Huey explained.

I looked at him and fell over, naked on a rooftop in Washington, covered in my own vomit.

Huey walked over to me, offering a hand. Just like before, I hesitated. Once, when I was a boy, two men would offer me their hands from inside a metal cage. One hand would be peace, the other would be pain. Now both of them were gone, in brutal and terrifying ways. I didn't think there would ever come a day when I wouldn't hesitate to take a hand, as a result. Dwelling in the stew that was my mind, a thick endless pit that would hold me there shivering on the roof no matter what, part of me really wanted to do that. Just stay on the roof, or just let Ash handle everything. That was what would turn me into the beast. Using him to solve my problems, rather than facing them on my own.

I was terrified; I wanted to run. Still, I outstretched my hand, taking Huey's as he pulled me to my feet. If I couldn't face what was coming alone, I had no other choice than to face it with friends. I nodded to Huey, he nodded back, turning away. "I really wish I could stop seeing you naked every five fucking seconds," he grumbled.

"What are you talking about? No one has a problem seeing a pasty white starved man naked on a rooftop," I joked.

"I just feel bad for bird watchers and the newspaper boy. They're going to be scared for life once they catch a sight of you," he jabbed, making it to the ladder.

I took a deep breath and followed his descent as well. On the way down, what he joked about concerned me. It was nearing the witching hour by now, but the whole town seemed dead. In fact, I hadn't heard a car since we came back in town. I was hoping it was just a result of this being a small city. "Not likely," I mumbled as I climbed down the steps. "How big is this town's population now," I asked no one as we reached the bottom. I gave one final nervous leap and landed hard on the road below.

Huey answered my question, and my heart knew he was right as soon as he spoke it. "I would say about the size of the crowd we had at the assembly down by the mill the other night. Too many," he stated.

Those kind of numbers didn't bode well. Wolf or not, sheer numbers is an advantage. This wasn't going to be easy—I was glad I had my friend, only, I didn't want him to die for my cause. "Huey—wait," I stated.

He turned toward me, sighing deeply. "I know what you're about to say: probably something stupid. You always look someone just kicked a puppy when you make that face. If it's about letting you do this alone; think again. You don't leave teammates behind. So, don't bother asking me that—just ask me what the plan is and whose car are we taking," he stated, simply walking past me in the direction of Pete's.

"Oh, one more thing. For fuck's sake, find some pants, man."

84

Chapter 84

I came over to the small crowd at the front of the grocery store once I had pulled on the last pair of pants and shirts from my green bag in the truck. Well, this was all or nothing, I thought; there was no return trip after this journey, I realized. That was okay with me. When I had packed my bags days ago, part of me had known that one way or another, my life had just changed. Change is constant, change is here. I wasn't escaping that; we are all enrolled in the cosmic play of whatever divine creation there might be out floating in the mystic reaches of our imaginations. I only ever needed one pair of pants, anyways—this was just keeping me humble, I thought, when I approached one of Bipin's brothers, Bina. He gave me a slow nod. I nodded back and passed him slowly.

Linor lay flat on the checkout counter, bags of ice placed on almost every inch of her skin. Periodically, Tivian instructed someone to move one of the bags from a part of her. Her clothes had been stripped away, replaced by a seemingly endless roll of bandages, which made her look more like a mummy about to be sealed in a deep dark tomb than the beautiful woman I had known all my life.

She was coated in something that made her already plastic skin look even more waxy—I hoped whatever it was, it would do something. I had my doubts, though. My hope was seeing her chest slowly rise and fall. I was thankful for that, thankful for Tivian.

I scooted next to Tivian, silently whispering, "Thank you."

She said nothing at first, staring off at the wall beyond Linor. "Don't thank me yet, there wasn't much Huey and I could do," she muttered.

"You did something though. That counts. Sometimes, that is all we can ever ask for, someone doing something," I stated.

I felt the dull ache crawl over the heat building in my belly. *Soon. Soon, I would be able to use that heat—not yet though.* Tivian cast her head down. I approached Linor. Her grandmother was at her side, clutching her hand. The old woman looked like she was one foot in the grave already, having aged another ten years since I had seen her last. My heart sank most for that; she was dying, right along with her granddaughter. She turned, looking at me. I braced myself for the mundane wave of insults that she strung at me in these situations. Instead, she did something different. She placed Linor's hands at her side and walked up, inches from me. With a smooth gesture, she reached up, slapping me across my right cheek. My face rolled away, stinging from the hit, but as I turned back, she pulled me into a tight hug. So much power in such a frail body.

I hesitated, then I hugged her back. A tension in my shoulders suddenly fell down like ice hanging from the gutters at the end of winter, in one loud crash of emotion. She whispered, "You dumb ass—thank you."

Now I knew it was the end. Linor's grandmother was hugging me without trying to stab me through. I cleared my throat. A thank you seemed so out of place. After all, I hadn't saved her granddaughter from dying. "I'm sorry," I whispered back.

She pushed away, wiping her tears. "Don't make me slap you again—boy. My granddaughter made her choice, and you risked your life for her and for the community. None of us would be here otherwise." She gestured to the crowd of about thirty people. Some faces I recognized, some I had never seen a day in my life. They all looked scared, defeated, but grateful to be alive. That was the power of the Roma: throw us against any wall and we would come right back.

Everyone was quiet, piercing me under their gazes, when I realized they were waiting for me to say something. This was in no way shape or form my strongest skill. I felt shy—extremely out of place and wondering what they could possibly expect me to say. Huey stood near Solly, on the fringes of the store. He nodded at me, while Solly just looked concerned. I scanned the crowd. Long Jimmy was there, his overalls smoked to a coffee black, his face hidden behind layers of grime. I could tell he was angry; his fists shook at his side.

Next to him was Bipin. The young man was reserved, a cold steel in his eyes. He was ready to do what needed to be done, no matter what it cost him. By comparison, his siblings looked like rockets all about to go off, one by one. I had known these people since first coming to America. Some were black, white, red, and every other color under the sun. Short, tall, wide, young, and the old. We were society's rejects, constantly pushed aside to parts of the world that no one wanted to go to.

With that, though, we were survivors. We were those who had seen the worst and the best of days, coming out on the other side still ready to fight; still ready to live. They needed a win, they needed a break, they needed their freedom. We had left the camps twenty years ago, and in that time, we had never really got our freedom, not what was taken from us. The fire that burns; the thing that keeps the nightmares away, that helps us taking those steps, even when the ground is lost at our feet. I put my hand on my stomach. I could feel a burning warmth near my navel. Glancing at my arm, the wounds from earlier tonight were coated over into puffy sacks, nothing more than scars now.

"Ash, can you hear me?" I thought, closing my eyes, until the wolf appeared before me. We were both in the yellow room now, Ash lying on his paws, stretching his long body.

"I can hear you. What is it that you want, Avi?" he asked, yawning at me. I was annoyed at that yawn, though thankful for once that it wasn't a snarl or a comment about grinding my bones into dust.

"Promise me that no matter what happens tonight, that you will fight for this community. Please promise," I begged the wolf.

He straightened up, both of us remaining still until he finally broke the silence. "I promise," he stated.

I nodded at him before opening my eyes again and looking out before the community. "All of us had our homes taken, our families taken, the very thing that made us human—stripped away. The world has tried to knock us flat on the ground, covering us in dirt until we are buried. I say: they bury us standing, because I am sick of assholes messing with my life. My brother has an army; he might even have some of us with him."

I looked around at the size of the crowed and compared it to what I had seen earlier. Not everyone had been in the warehouse, so maybe Zevi had kept some of the community. Either way, he needed to be stopped.

I continued, "My father once told me that time stopped for no one. If that is true, then I suggest we use what time we have left and take back what was stolen from us. This isn't about revenge, this is about taking back what we lost—about standing up, and moving forward." A few more eyes held my gaze now. I seized the moment. "Fuck grand speeches, I will just say this: who wants to be buried standing? Who wants to be put in a grave?" I asked the crowd.

No one moved or said anything until Tivian spoke up, next to Linor. "Bury me standing, just like my father and my mother. I am with you, Avi," she stated.

Bipin soon nodded. "I am with you," he chimed in. I gave Bipin a silent nod.

Others around us started doing the same, putting in their own vows to help. After a moment, the whole group had decided to come with me and fight an army of fanatics. The thought sank in—but what else could we do? Leave, and I had a feeling Zevi would never let the community go. He had been playing with them, and he wasn't protecting them. He was only using them just to lure me back in. That left us with only one thing: that left us to fight the darkness.

85

Chapter 85

Fighting the darkness was going to be easier said than done, though. I looked around at the group forced into a tiny grocery store on the edges of an old town. It really was maybe thirty of us total, excluding children, that made about seventeen fighters—some of the older people toed the line between being too old as well. I sighed heavily, rubbing my eyes. Blood flakes peeled off over my lids—it was my own blood, I realized. I must have looked like a mad man to them. But we were all dirty—blood can't be washed away.

The memory of the first man I'd killed hit me like a ton of bricks, nearly causing me to fall over, my hands shaking like they did that first night on the train. I had killed that man, without knowing anything about him—family or not, I'd killed him. That I couldn't get over, yet I couldn't live with myself for not saving Albert, Joseph, or even Joachim. Maybe it was because I'd gotten to see that they had families of their own now. Time—I wondered if it truly cleared someone of a crime or not, or if it would ever clear me. My punishment was what befell my family. Despite whatever good I thought I might accomplish by taking his life—I would still pay in the end.

Which was what I wondered. Would they pay for this, tonight? The people following Zevi couldn't have been all bad. They had their own families and friends, just like the community. That was the problem with revenge: it would only lead to more death. I took a different approach before breaking down the plan. I needed to galvanize them—hopefully spring into action without losing their souls. I opened my mouth to speak again.

Huey cut me off first, igniting a cigarette, which made everyone turn their attention back toward him as calmly smoked, taking a deep breath. "Good speech, Avi. Now let's go kill some assholes," he stated.

Many heads nodded. They were with it, repercussions or not. It wasn't my choice to make, it was theirs as well, I realized. I lowered my head for a moment. "Okay, first things first, before we even start breaking down fighters. How many weapons do we actually have?" I asked the group.

An assembly of calls went up with confused faces. "I got me a long rifle; two, in fact. One double barreled, the other, a Springfield from the war," Long Jimmy spat.

I looked at Long Jimmy, perplexed. I had no idea what kind of guns those were. I nodded and muttered, "Good man."

Linor's grandmother from behind me said, "I have my father's pistol," I shook my head at her. "Someone needs to watch Linor—I know there's no one else here who would fight as hard as you would," I stated.

The old woman looked crestfallen before shaking her face, back to the mask of pacifism. "Then take my father's gun, at least." She pulled a small bronze-coated gun that had a wooden handle, big enough to extend almost to her elbow.

"I think that thing will kill whoever shoots it. Hold on to it, and give it to Linor when she wakes up." I turned down to the gun, handing it back to her. Her eyes watered and she stepped away.

"You have our fangs and claws, all six of us." Bipin pointed at his siblings. A cold look was brewing in his eyes. A snowstorm about to freeze the world.

"Thank you," I told the young man.

"What about you, tough guy? Bring any guns in that truck of yours?" Solly asked Huey, the two of them tucked away in their part of the store.

Huey dashed his smoke on the ground. "Nope—no need for such things," he stated calmly.

"Well a bright fucking fart that does any of us here. Avi, you better believe that your brother will have more than just the guns at the police department—he has Bug and other freaks; more importantly, he's had time to plan. He doesn't strike me as the type to let go that easily," Solly declared to us all.

I exhaled. "You're right, it would be foolish to assume he doesn't have a massive armory to go along with his many people. We will have to draw his attention with something." I turned away from the group, walking to the doors, peering out at the empty streets around us. The town was dead—well, the town was alive. It was with Zevi. Two guns and some wolves wouldn't be enough to defeat an army.

"There is the local gun and pawn store off of 5th Ave," Bicka stated.

We all turned back to the youngest sibling of Bipin. The boy was the same age as the rest of the pack, but he looked the most fragile, small in stature and a mop of curly hair. It made me realize how young Bipin and his family were. Kids, fighting in a war. Oh what a long way gone we were all now.

"Bina, go now with Bicka and a few others in the van. Go get as many guns and whatever you can collect in thirty minutes. Come back here afterward. Be quick and if you see anything, anything at all, come back here," I directed.

Bina nodded. "I'm on it." He headed out the door with Bicka following close behind him. I pointed at the three nearest people of the community. "Go with them." They all jerked to standing tall and filed out behind them. I shook my head; we were going to be working with what we have, I reminded myself.

They exited the store, and a blast of cold air came bursting through. I hoped that wasn't a sign for the rest of the night. I turned back to the group, "Listen up—all of you kids, and anyone else that doesn't want to fight. Stay here in the store with *alt froy*." I pointed at Linor's grandmother.

"What is wrong with you dumbass? It's Isabella," the old woman stated from behind me.

I shrugged. "Been a rough night. We are learning a lot about each other, old woman," I stated. She smirked at me and I turned back to a few of the parents that had kids. Some fathers and mothers, along with their kids, went and stood next to Linor's grandmother.

Counting the wolves, Huey, Solly, and myself, it made seventeen fighters of almost all ages. "And only two guns," I muttered, before looking at Solly finally, in answer to her question. "I will just have to distract them. No other choice," I said resolutely.

Solly shook her head. "That won't work and you know it. That many bullets hitting you, I've seen that thing you have—while it is impressive, it won't be anything more than a sponge out there," she stated.

I slapped my hands to my side, exasperated. "Well, what do you suggest that we do, then?" I asked her.

"Know your resources, love," she told me calmly, before taking a step forward. Her whole body shimmered briefly, like a small sun exploding in the grocery store, before diamond-colored coated bones burst from her skin, enveloping her quickly in a seemingly impenetrable skin.

Before me was her deer form, glowing lights bouncing off her in every direction. "Impressive, truly. But can it stop bullets?" I asked her. Solly dug a hoof into the tile of the grocery store. "What are you trying to tell me, Solly? I don't—"

"Oh, fuck off already dumbass. My granddaughter is screwed if you're the best she has," Linor's grandmother stepped forward with her pistol, shoving it under the deer's head and squeezing the trigger. I blinked in surprise as the loud boom inside the small store made everyone close their eyes, before I screamed, "No!"

Solly simply flicked her head, no visible damage done to her hard exterior. "See? Problem solved. Back to figuring out the other problems," the old woman stated simply and went back to Linor's side.

I stood dumbfounded for a few moments before turning back to Solly. Her deer form slowly fell from her body onto the dirty tiled floor, hitting the ground in a thick sludge of mush. I looked at her, and she appeared completely normal, not a hair missing on her red head. "See? Good as new. Only a tickle, she smiled."

I gave her a skeptical look. We had no other choice. I was pretty sure the beast could only take a few shots—everything that bleeds must die at some point. "Right, so, does anyone have any idea where my brother and his people are at? We don't have the time to split up and look," I stated to the remainder of the group.

Solly answered my question. "If you were a psycho, where would you go?"

I scratched my chin wondering that myself. It had to be somewhere large enough and convenient enough that all of his people could get in and out quickly. But, knowing Zevi, he always liked attention. That was why he would go for sucking up for *muter*, rather than our father. *He likes attention*, I repeated to myself as I looked out the window. *Where is a place that matches all that, bruder?* A dim light shone from the light pole, shining like a beacon... shining like a city hall. *That's a perfect place for someone like my bruder.*

"Anyone here have a map?" I asked the community. A quick shuffle of looks were exchanged before a short-statured man in the back raised his hand. I debated saying something about his hand raising, but cooler heads prevailed. *Another time, Avi.* "Shoot, what do you got?" I directed at the man.

He had narrow shoulders, thick glasses, and a receding patch of black hair that somehow suited his offset shoulders. "I used to work for city planning before—well, before things started getting weird here and I ended up with you people," he stuttered, pointing at the rest of the group.

He must have been pressed into that warehouse because of his knowledge, and now he was in a grocery store talking with a bunch of strangers, planning a takeover of the current establishment, that had stolen their power from the previous government. This was a very strange decade. Confusing times indeed.

"Okay, that is something. Welcome to the Roma people. What's your name?" I asked the man. He held up his hand again. I rubbed my nose in response.

"My name is Evan," he stated.

"Hi Evan, welcome. Alright everyone, gather around. I have a plan."

86

Chapter 86

Twenty minutes later, I was sitting outside of Pete's, drinking a beer. *Two years of sobriety gone right there*, I thought as I took another drink. Good as time as any to start back. I drank another sip before spitting out the rest. I wasn't going to waste two years—tonight wouldn't be the end of my story. *Whatever fucked up story I may be in, it is still my story and I won't let the pages end tonight.* I just wish I believed that, I thought, as Huey came out of the grocery store, leaning on the wall near me. He handed me a smoke. It was lit, and I drew heavily and blew out a smoke ring. He sparked one of his own.

I signed heavily, suddenly, rubbing my head, bent over against the wall. "Man, I'm no soldier, spouting out all that back there, as if I really knew what I was talking about. I just don't know if I am making the right decisions or not," I admitted.

"Probably not," stated Huey.

I gave him a long look. "What do you mean by that?" I asked him.

"Means there's no telling if you ever have the right plan doing anything. To be honest, everything I've ever attempted in my life, I never had it fully formed. That's not why we do it. In your heart I think you know why we do it," Huey declared.

"Oh, boy. Driving toward certain doom without even a hint of what to expect in the end. How reassuring," I joked, trying to keep a hysterical laugh from leaving my throat. "Why do you seem so calm?" I asked him.

"Because I trust my friend. And mostly because sooner or later, something will fuck you in this life. Might as well choose what that is," he stated.

"Yeah, well, in case you haven't noticed, life has been fucking us both pretty hard for a long, long time," I stated.

This time, Huey sighed. "You know, I've come to get used to certain level of hubris, Avi, but my God, man, read the signs around you. You've done your best for everyone since I met you without a second of wasted time. It had nothing to do with guilt; you just knew instinctively that you could help. Get out of your own way! You have soul, and that's all that matters with all this shit," stated Huey, dashing his cigarette against the red brick of Pete's. "I swear just for once I would like one of these to taste good right before I die. Whichever asshole started that rumor that last anythings are always amazing is full of it." Huey walked off, heading toward the side of the building, his hands in his pockets.

"Where are you going?" I called after him as he neared the corner.

Without turning around, Huey called back, "I'm going to spend time with a pretty woman. I suggest you do the same."

He disappeared out of sight. I stood up tall, brushing my hair out of my face in the reflection of the store windows. Had I really gotten that old? I had more than a few days of stubble, a slow lining of gray starting to pepper the edges of my hair. My eyes seemed to sag, as if I were older than time itself. A few turns of my hair and I was satisfied that it wasn't a complete lost cause. "I look almost like dad now," I whispered as I looked at the grocery store windows. The crows feet stretched in a neverending race toward my ears.

It was time to go see Linor. I had been avoiding her since getting back into Pete's. "Hey, Ash, care to ignore what's about to be said between us?" I asked the wolf.

I heard a hearty yawn in response. "Your conversations never interest me, human. Shut up so I can sleep," he growled.

I beamed in the cold night, as snow started to land around me. "Thanks,

Ash."

87

Chapter 87

Bina still hadn't made it back yet. That was okay with me. Gave me a few more minutes. I walked toward Linor. Only the two of us were inside the store. I took deep breaths, every step feeling like I climbed an endless mountain. I made it to Linor, and her skin was even paler than before. She looked like a—like a corpse, I thought, pale skin grayer than the ashes from the countless cigarettes I had smoked. Linor appeared more lie a wax figurine, locked behind glass, a sad observation of the cruelty of the world on display.

I shoved down the burning feeling again, my stomach about to burst from the amount of anger that was growing. So much hate—I wondered if I would die from it. I would if I kept at it like this.

I took her hand. It seemed so normal, the delicate lines tracing down her hand, a small crown tattooed on her index finger, wings on her middle finger. I smirked at that—she loved her tattoos. I wished now that I had taken her up on the chance to get matching ones at least once. There were so many things I'd never got to say to her—but saying those expressions of "I love you" now, when she was almost gone, felt cheap and more like a consolation that was not earned; an ostensible gesture, nothing more. If I had cared enough, I would have just said it—love never has to be complicated, you're either dancing to the same beat or you're not.

So, instead of regaling her with words about how I should have told her

I loved her, I would tell her about the exact moment I fell in love with her. She had me at dumbass. I gripped her hand as the memories from fifteen years ago came flooding back into my mind.

88

Chapter 88

Our lines were cast and lures sank deep in the rumbling creek on a sunny afternoon. Linor sat against my leg, my back propped up against a massive rock behind me. "Isn't this just lovely, Avi?" Linor beamed, pulling on her line, dancing her lure in and out of the water. It was just a top piece where I had taken out the core on the sides, to form something that kind of floated in the water, if you constantly moved it. We were fly fishing and so far, neither of us had done much more than catching rays of sun.

"Huh, yeah, it sure is pretty out here—I guess. I think it would be even better if we had some base—" I started before Linor rolled her eyes.

"Avi, just for once, not everything needs to have baseball involved. Come on, just enjoy the moment, child of doom and darkness. Enjoy it here. With me," she stated, turning toward me.

"I mean, I would enjoy it more if you didn't have so many clothes on, but that's just me," I joked.

She rolled her eyes dramatically and smacked me playfully in the chest. "Hey now, this is a date, not your fantasy. Though I am glad you didn't suggest me dressing up as the 'Babe' and hitting pitches from you." She emulated hitting a ball with a smoke bat that she made appear out of thin air.

I laughed. "Then why do you have his jersey?"

"You dumb ass," she jabbed.

Linor stood up, shoving me playfully, the bat disappearing, a slow bleed coming from her nose. She hid it, wiping it off with her hand first, before plunging it deep in the running water of the creek. I pretended to not see her do it. Linor was getting better at what she could make—but it worried me, seeing her nose bleed like that. I left it at that, though. For the most part, if I didn't ask her, she wouldn't ask me about the things I did.

She waded into the water, coming up to her ankles. She hiked her dress up, making a face at the cold. "Come in, Avi, it's not that bad," she stated.

I replied by coming to my feet, and dipping my feet into the water. A cold bite went half way up my foot before I yanked it out. "No thanks, I prefer to keep all my limbs," I called out to her as she stood in the waves like the statue of Rhodes, a golden beacon above the waves, guiding sailors home from their long trips at sea. I smiled at her, watching her play in the river, the day flowing by—but the moment lasting forever.

"Come on, stop being such a baby," she joked.

I called back, "Nope, can't convince me that easily!"

"Suit yourself square. I will have all the fun myself." She turned away, feigning hurt, before turning back quickly, dipping her hands under the water splashing me with the cold drops.

I covered my face, pretending to be angry. "Oh, you're so dead," I called out to her, jumping into the water. I sent a rushing jolt of water, and she covered her face before splashing water on me. Before I knew it, we were both laughing.

Which was why we didn't hear the sounds of tires pulling up to our favorite secluded riverbank. Nor the doors being closed, nor heavy footsteps as drunks made their way down the hillside. My nose picked up the booze first, before I smelled the stench of unwashed hair and sweat-ridden clothes before I turned my head. Three heavily intoxicated men swayed toward us. Their clothes ruffled, heavy stains around their armpits, and twigs sticking out of one man's beard. They each wore some type of overall, brown jackets and blue jeans that were closer to gray now than actual jeans.

Every alarm in my head was going off at the sight of them. Thick necks, barreled chests, biceps the size of my legs—that all made me nervous, but it was their smell. They had a lust about them, one that I know was directed toward Linor. The strength was overwhelming, more so than even the beer they had been drinking, or the marijuana that the smallest and thinnest in the back had smoked right before pulling up. They would do bad things to her, if they could.

That wasn't going to happen, not on my watch—not without killing me first.

"Can I help you?" I asked the nearest one, his sunglasses almost sinking into his doughy face, a thick sunburn making it seem as though he had no eyes, and instead had slits of deep, neverending black.

"You're a pretty girl." He ignored me and stepped toward the shoreline.

I instinctively put myself between Linor and them. I walked toward the man, closing the distance. The other two were either really confident or drunk, but no one reacted as I got within a few feet of the man. I slowly moved my right foot out of the water, placing it on a slippery stone. They still made no notice of what I was doing. I decided to bluff one more time.

"Can I help you?" I asked him, this time louder. That did the trick. He shook his head as if coming out of a deep slumber and focused on me. "No... boy... move along. This is—" he fumbled his words as I shot my leg out and kicked him in the balls. The man let out a grunt, falling forward like a hot air balloon. I brought up both my hands and swung them into his face. He fell to his side, into the creek. The other two snapped out of their trances. Charging forward, I threw a wild punch, hitting one them somewhere in soft tissue. I heard a crunch as the other took me down. I landed hard under the waves, his hand around my throat. Darkness swam into my eyes as water entered my mouth. This was it; I was going to die.

I was almost dead when a light went off overhead. I blinked as some kind of massive snake glided over the water toward the men. He suddenly released me. I shot out of the river gasping for air, holding my throat as the three men ran toward their parked truck.

"Yeah, you better run. Assholes," I croaked, spitting out water. I stood up tall, struggling to get to my feet. I held on to my throat. I looked for the serpent, and it was nowhere to be found. Linor. My mind shot back to the moment, and I turned around looking for her. Blood was streaming from both her nostrils, and she was bent over, about to fall in. I panicked and waded my way through the waves toward her.

I thrashed through the water, not nearly quick enough, as she fell into the river. The current, if I remembered correctly, was about in her area, sweeping her away like a straw. She was pulled under the water as if by an invisible hand, devouring her in a watery grave. I jumped right in, without looking or with concern for my own wellbeing. It was not a question, nothing I had to decide. The water was murky brown. All I could see were pieces of the woods and other small bits floating before my eyes.

I dove my head above the water as the river began to pick up speed and power. A hundred yards or so from me, Linor was coming in and out of the water. Her eyes were closed and I could see a nasty gash on the top of her head. She must have hit a rock when she went under. I dove under again, propelling me in the direction of where I had last seen her. I had only once chance, I knew, as I felt my body being rocketed by the current.

My sense of smell and hearing—all my senses, really—had always been above normal, and I wasn't entirely sure why. However, as I tried to smell in the water, my nose quickly filled up. I felt myself running out of air quickly as a result. Dumb idea, I chastened myself.

Through the haze and darkness, I made out a hand in the water—just a glimpse. That was all I needed, and I swam harder than I thought possible, my body straining, the cords in my shoulders feeling as if they were about to pop like ropes stretched too taut. I reached Linor's hand after five counts of my heart pounding in my ear.

Taking hold of her body, I cradled her against me as I navigated through the river toward the shoreline. The water was bitterly cold, the current having long since zapped my strength, like a cold icy glove sticking a hand on my spine, and breaking the bone. I caught an overhanging limb in the water and held tightly. I pulled forward, gritting my teeth. Linor was slumped over in my arms, her dead weight making the already tough task seem even more impossible.

The thought of Linor drowning, of her being pulled away like a branch in the water, frightened me. It steeled my heart away from the cold long enough for me to cry out and pull us both closer, into the shallows. We were finally free of the worst of the river, and I started up the embankment. Coughing, spitting out mouthfuls of water with nearly every step. A few more moments and straining with effort, and I got us to the shore. I lay Linor on her side, spitting out more water. I had no idea what to do at this point. I had seen in a picture show once how someone had done mouth to mouth, but that looked a lot more complicated than awkwardly kissing.

I settled with hitting her on the back. I whispered, "Sorry," before striking her in what I thought would be her lungs from the back.

Nothing happened. My heart beat faster, the water crashed around me; I struck again. This time, I heard a pop, followed by a gurgling sound coming from Linor as she spat out water, opening her eyes.

She was breathing so fast, I thought she was about to cut herself off. "Take it easy. Just breathe," I whispered to her, holding her back, "Just breathe, baby, girl, just breathe." We sat that way on the shore, Linor coughing up water slowly, me doing my best to rub her back.

The sun started setting—I started to shiver. Both of us were still in our underwear. "Just stay here for a bit," I stated to Linor. She waved me on, content against her tree, her head still hung low like it was setting for the last time. I dug through a bag I had brought with us, and within a few minutes, after gathering a buddle of sticks, I had a fire roaring.

Sunset was blasting hot rays, warming my damp skin as I brought Linor both the towels, placing them around her as we sat with our backs toward the fire. I shivered. It may have been summer, but Washington isn't a place for anyone to be dancing around wet in their underwear. "You can have one of these—I'm fine now, thank you," she said softly. I turned toward her, almost unsure it had been really her who was talking. Since falling into the river, she hadn't spoken a word, just chattered her teeth and occasionally coughed.

"That's okay, you keep it. I will get warm soon enough," I lied, stretching my hands behind my head. The wet stones felt lifeless and arctic against my legs, reminding me of the cage bars in the camp. I hated metal, I hated stone—just cold tools used to imprison me. Draining the very warmth out of the air, like happiness couldn't exist around such things.

"Stop being tough, big guy. You're cold," she whispered, taking the towel wrapped around her shoulders and placing it around mine before I could protest.

It was damp, but I instantly felt better than I had before. "Thanks," I whispered.

She nodded. The fire behind me was burning to ambers, no matter what I seemed to do. It was because the wood was green. As soon as Linor was ready to travel, we would need to go. She needed just a bit longer, though. Looking at her, her lips were still blue, and her skin looked like it was about to slide right off of her thin frame. I was watching the sunset behind the tree line when she wrapped her arms around me.

I put mine around her, and we stayed that way, looking at the gold as it flew over the world in light. "Do you think we will ever have more moments like these?" she whispered, barely above the sound of the river.

It took me some time before I turned back to her, trying to match her tone. "Sure hope not. You nearly died and those three were some pretty bad folks."

Linor rolled her eyes, "No—you know what I meant," she stated.

I sighed, I was fatigued, wet, and really in need of a nice bed. Thankfully, the three drunks had driven off as quickly as they had arrived. Almost losing her made me want to never let her go, nor leave my sight, even for a second. She had been there, though, looking out for me—that counted for something on this long road of ours. I hesitated once I saw the tears swimming in her eyes. So often, I just wanted to say the right thing, to do the right thing. But no matter what I seemed to do, it never felt like enough. Like I was a complete stranger, knocking at her door, like she had no idea who I was either. Maybe that is what love is—knocking on each other's doors and deciding if we wanted to spend our time shivering together, down by a river, watching golden sunsets.

"I think we will never know for sure, but any time you want to have one with me, I will always be there," I stated, wrapping my arms tighter around her.

"At least you didn't butcher some poet with a baseball analogy—dumbass," she joked.

"Speaking of which, have you heard about how when a ball is hit—"

She sighed deeply but nonetheless listened, kissing me on the cheek at some point.

Yeah, I liked spending sunsets with her.

I floated in the memory of our time together for a bit longer than I should have, because I hadn't noticed Linor sitting next to me now in the store as I held her hand. I blinked as I suddenly realized how it was possible. I gently set her hand down on the counter and turned toward the image of Linor. "You aren't really here right now, are you?" I asked.

Linor held a small smile on her face before shaking her head. "Nope, but I can hear you—I can feel you." She reached out a hand, placing it on my cheek. Her touch felt like air being blown on me while I was covered in thick blankets. I could feel something there, but it wasn't a force that could do more than just let me know it was around.

I felt my eyes water up at her touch. It was a cruel thing to be so close to the person you loved the most in the world, but so far away. Yet, that thought was selfish. I could physically touch Linor's charred body on the counter at any moment. I just wanted her to return that touch so badly. It was a wretched thing; the things we forget about at the end, when all we do is wish to stay in sunsets. Doesn't always work that way. It can't stay sunsets by the beach forever, but sometimes—I just wished it would.

So, instead of a grand speech, Linor just said, "Hey dumbass."

"Hey stinky," I replied, standing up. "How are you doing this, right now?" I asked her

"I figured it was time I leant a hand and all, considering what you're going up against," she stated.

I thought about it for a moment. "You know Zevi knows your abilities inside and out. Probably everybody's," I stated.

She beamed. "Not everybody's," she replied.

"That's something more, at least—how long will I have you for?" I asked.

Her face crunched in for a moment. "Long enough, Avi."

I suppose that was all we'd ever had anyways. Just long enough.

89

Chapter 89

Bina and the few he had taken with him had arrived about ten minutes ago. I had them hand out rifles to those who could join in and shoot. Huey refused one, simply stating he didn't need it. As they were loading up, I spoke to Linor's smoke behind the truck. "I'm not sure if hiding from everyone else is the best idea, here. You know your grandmother would—" I started to say, before I saw the heartbreak in her face.

I sighed, regretting my words as they left my mouth. Linor didn't need to say anything. This was her goodbye; she didn't want to drown it out with even more misery. Not to mention a sinking feeling I had from the smoke image she was using—Linor was only able to keep them out for so long, and for so far.

"We don't have much time together, Avi, just the time we need. Use it. You've always been brave by default; don't change that now," she stated, drawing away from me. With a quick jolt, she turned into a small raven and perched on top of the van. None were wise to her presence.

I came around the van; it had been close to forty-five minutes since I had instructed everyone what our plan of attack was. Every minute seemed to be against us; every minute that Zevi was secure was our only chance.

I spotted Linor's grandmother—she was staring at the raven with a keen interest. I cleared my throat. "That's a nice raven."

She regarded me for a moment. "Strange seeing one at this time of the year, all alone. Means bad luck in most cases," she muttered, turning away from me.

I stopped her, pulling her elbow. Something like that with the old lady before and she would probably have shot me. Now she just turned and gave me a long look.

"Just because something appears to be a bad omen doesn't mean it's bad. It could simply mean it has a message—that could be good or bad. If I was to bet, I think the message would be simple: Linor is glad that you're safe," I stated.

The only woman looked between me and the crow before nodding at me. "Good luck, dumbass," she stated and disappeared inside Pete's.

I turned back to the rest of my "crew." Everyone at least had a gun now. I viewed a group of uncertain, everyday people, covered in smoke and grime.

We all stood there for a moment longer before the town's clock tower started signaling midnight was here. I looked at Linor, speaking to the crowd around me. "Look for me to make a move," I stated calmly as Solly came up behind me, her diamond skin glittering like a snowflake under the street lights. I mounted her as Huey and the others piled into the vans.

Bipin and the siblings tore off their clothes. Six hungry and massive wolves stepped out in their places afterward. They bolted behind the store, running to get into position. The vans pulled off, and Linor flew above us until she was out of sight.

I shifted my weight on top of Solly. Her rough armored skin caused uncomfortable bites to form, entirely too close to places I would not want jagged rock next to. "Please don't hit any bumps," I whispered.

Solly snorted in response and started galloping.

90

Chapter 90

The capitol building came into view, massive columns supporting a lime green dome top, flanked by two heavily windowed stone buildings. The windows had all been busted out and replaced with boards, covering the outside in thick pieces of wood and spray paint. A beautiful building where I remembered from my youth thinking that places like this must have been where gods and goddess worked. Now it looked like some assholes had shacked up and decided to make a statement on a building. Either or, I suppose. Solly slowly moved along the straight road leading to the front side of the capitol building.

I could smell them before they came into view. The town was assembled out front, their masks obscuring their faces. Weapons brandished like swords on some kind of ancient battlefield. To my horror, it looked to be more than just the front line had weapons. The rest had baseball bats and whatever else they could find. Our only hope was that everyone was already in place on top of the buildings that lined the sides of the streets leading up to the capitol.

There was no way of knowing now, though. I coaxed Solly into stopping. "Remember not to pop out until they're about to fire," I whispered to her. She skipped her legs and ran off down a side street.

I stood alone then, only a couple hundred yards from my brother's army. That's when I saw Zevi sitting on a lawn chair, one hand tucked under his chin. Sophia stood leaning on a door near him. Bug was on his right, Tir on his left. I couldn't see Schwein, but I was more concerned by the heavily scarred man behind him wearing all black, save for his face. He was still bald and his forehead looked like someone had tried to scrape his hair off completely, long ago. It was Hans. Three long scars now covered his face, his nose missing down to the bone, flat with only scar tissue remaining.

At that, my heart started beating like it had when I saw the blade he had given me. In a lot of ways he had saved my life, judging by the grimace on his face. The fact that Zevi did not have him tied up told me everything I needed to know. I had never seen Hans work. I had seen Huey go to town in a fight once—if someone scared a man like Huey, who spent his days training that much, it was cause for alarm.

"Address the first problem, Avi—all the people pointing guns at you," I muttered, walking down the center line in the middle of the road. I stopped once I was between two four-story buildings that flanked me on both sides. I had no idea where the rest of the crew was at—I had to hope that they managed to get into a safer place. Staring now at all the barrels pointed my way, I could see that Zevi had been busy—very busy.

We stood no chance if we didn't take care of this problem right now. That was why we had picked a full frontal assault—we thought that Zevi wouldn't be expecting a show of force. This only confirmed that he knew I had survived the warehouse. I wondered, though, had he taken into account the others surviving the warehouse fire, or did he simply not care? I had found out from Linor's grandmother that the fire had miraculously seemed to fade away from them when the bomb went off, almost like the blast had been drawn to the beast. They had managed to crawl out from the rubble, the few that survived. It wouldn't have happened, if not for everyone's help.

It was getting real old fast—people in this life discounting someone because of what they wanted outweighing the usefulness of people. I opened my hands wide, using the boosted courage from my anger—or in this case, general insanity. They were the only words for taking on the sheer amount of people against us.

"Hey—Zevi—you're an asshole," I shouted at my brother over the people before me. There were a few snickers in the crowd and I could almost feel Sophia's eye roll from this distance.

Zevi stood up smiling from his lawn chair, arching his back, stretching as he flexed his arms upward. I noticed now his bat had been replaced with just a chunk of wood, with tape along the bottom. It was more club-like now, thicker and with a few dents in the wood already. The yellow sides stained brown on one side, near the top hitting area. I shuddered at the thought of how many people had to be hit with that in order to cause such coloration.

"Hey, brother," chided Zevi. "Glad you can make it. Welcome to our humble-la-ba, do you like it?" He gestured toward his army.

I shook my head slowly. "Not really. Personally, I prefer my town to be a little less—what's the word—dictator controlled? Maybe not so militant. That's just me," I stated, gesturing back toward his army.

Zevi grinned at me. The night was silent, except for my legs shaking like a straw in the river. It was coming; I could feel it in my bones. A reminder that I was dragging people into a conflict against my brother. *We can't possibly win*—I thought. Then again, I never once thought I could win any of the other moments in my life. Most of the time, it was floating through from one moment to the next, but I was always there, always fighting. Tonight would be no exception.

"So—I didn't get to see much of that thing inside of you when the warehouse burned down. Was too busy looking at you trying to save Linor. Pity that. She was really useful. Bug can only help so much with noise. Whereas she—she can do some awesome convincing of a lot of numbers. More so than just a simple gun." He gestured behind him to Bug.

I let a growl come out of my throat, a warning to Zevi. The nearest member of his army started shaking, his rifle rattling in his hands.

Zevi suddenly ran forward to the marble stairs leading up to the capitol building. "That's what I want! Show me the wolf, brother!" his voice cracking from the pitch and the prospect of seeing the wolf.

No—Zevi wants to fight the wolf, he's always wanted that. I had spent my whole life running from the beast, and here was Zevi wanting to go toe-to-toe with a creature that had indirectly given him his abilities in the first place. Surely he wasn't that off the deep end, I thought. Judging by his smile, he might actually have been.

"Oh, I will show you the wolf, Zevi," I snarled at him, as all the weapons in front of me placed their target. "That's not good," I muttered, as Zevi's face changed to a grim resolve.

"As much as I want that fight, this is the part where someone gets overconfident and ends up losing it all. So, instead, I am just going to shoot you," Zevi stated casually.

I blinked for a moment before Ash roared inside my head: "Move!" And I did, turning to bolt toward the nearest building. I made it maybe two steps before the first crack of the rifle broke the silent night. If I got hit, I couldn't tell. I pumped my arms and ran faster, knowing that the odds were against me. Sooner or later, one of the people shooting would get lucky. I was fairly confident I could take getting shot, but even the wolf had his limits.

Another step, another shot. This one I felt the wind on, as three more were fired in succession, followed by the first series of shots coming from behind. I closed my eyes, readying myself to get shot, when a glowing light hit my face. I opened them to see Solly dashing toward me at incredible speed, her hooves seeming to glide over the paved road as if she was skating on ice.

Instantly, all the shooters forgot about the skinny man dashing toward the building and instead focused fire on the diamond-colored stag running toward them. Bullets bounced off of her like rocks hitting a windshield—but like rocks hitting the glass, every bullet was taking a little out of her. Solly's eyes periodically closed, wincing in pain from the hits. I caught flecks of diamond-coated skin falling to the ground as she flew past me. I suddenly felt guilty for running. I pivoted, turning to run back toward the crowd, when hundreds of Sollys appeared from nowhere and the whole scene quickly descended into a warzone.

A black raven flew above the battlefield, as all the Sollys lunged toward the shooters like falling meteors hitting an unsuspecting forest below. Screams came from every direction, and wild shots zoomed into the night with no target.

Somewhere above me, I could hear small arms fire open up as the team started firing. I smiled—there was no running now. I bolted in the direction of the firing line, punching a masked man who was taking aim at one of the Sollys. Flames erupted nearby me, lobbed from some kind of bomb, that washed over the group as if they had plunged in an ocean of fire. I shielded my face from the hot flames.

Another person in a mask approached me, their gun waving around as they took shots. I winced, but none hit me, giving me just enough time to tackle the person to the ground. Their mask slipped off, showing an old man. He covered his face. "Please don't hurt me—I had no choice. He said he would kill my family if I didn't join," the old man blubbered.

I growled at him, letting some of Ash's roar come out as I pulled him by his collar. "Then I suggest you stop shooting us and get the hell out of here—now!" I snapped, pushing him to the ground.

The old man wept, nodding as he picked up his rifle, slinging it over his shoulders and taking off, running from the group. The area was in disarray. Bullets littered the ground as if it had snowed bronze and gold. Dozens of people lay either dead or clutching themselves from bullet wounds. It made me sick. I wanted to throw up, but I kept my eyes on Zevi.

The honk of a horn made me snap my head back as a massive semi-truck came roaring down the street, followed quickly by six bikers. I could see Long Jimmy was driving the truck, smashing into the nearest group of Zevi's army as if they were bowling pins. He came to a stop at some point, having gone deeper into the group than even Solly. Jimmy stepped out, shotgun in hand, and started blasting into the nearest crowd.

The six bikes stopped, and with a shimmer, six massive and unnatural wolves charged down the center. The truck tail bed went up, and out stepped Huey and four other fighters from the community. Huey looked sick as he saw the dead littered around the truck. He had never wanted this; neither of us did. We never escaped our wars—all that time and effort we took to distance ourselves from the past and look where we were now, driving over people that were as much afraid of Zevi as the rest of us.

Or maybe we could escape our wars—we could lay down our armor and swords... but that seemed like a distant dream, a ring in the heart of darkness that seemed to contain only the blackest of holes, never aging, turning the night sky into a dusk of gray.

I snapped out of it as a bullet tore into the shoulder of my jacket, punching a hole into the wall behind me. That got my attention and I charged forward, kicking at the nearest person in a mask. Luckily for me, none of these people knew how to fight much more than I did. As the pandemonium kicked into full throttle, I became aware that most of Zevi's forces no longer had guns and were resorting to clubs and anything else with a sharp or blunted end. I dared to have a little faith at that and kept fighting forward.

Somewhere overhead, I heard the raven caw out at the crowd below, and so did Sophia. With a quick step, she shimmered to an array of neon colors, firing bolts of lightning across the wide array of people, taking aim at the crow. The illusion of numbers wouldn't fool Zevi for long—he knew what each of us could do. What he didn't know was where Linor was. I had no doubt that they thought she had to be dead. I gritted my teeth and tackled another person to the ground, punching forward with all my might.

"Avi, it is almost time for me to come out," Ash whispered into my head.

"Are you completely healed up?" I asked the wolf, dodging a woman's wild swing with her bat, which only narrowly missed me because one of the wolves lunged at her, biting into her throat. On the ride here, Ash and I had decided to wait for him to completely recover before he came out. During the fire from the warehouse and the strain of moving the roof, he had absorbed enough heat and pressure to crush a boulder down to dust.

"Almost. Try not to die," he snarled. I laughed at the absurdity of that as Sophia fired more bolts of lightning, still missing the raven. She should know better that Linor couldn't transform, only project illusions. However it had to be the case that they didn't fully understand her powers. Knowing Linor, she had probably given them the barest amount of information.

I smiled at that as a vicious punch took me in the right cheek, sending me sprawling to the ground. I looked to see a man holding himself in a boxing stance—he held himself with the confidence of a fighter. I wiped the blood from my nose and rolled, standing up, chest out, my body squatted down low.

Moving forward, I dropped a knee to do a takedown. He sprawled back, striking an elbow that got me square in the nose, easily breaking the bone. I recoiled from the hit, my eyes watering uncontrollably. He wasted no time swinging a jab that hit my left eye, spinning my head back. Before I had time to process that hit, an uppercut caught me under the chin, knocking me on my ass.

I sat down, my nose bleeding and my face feeling like the leftovers at a butcher's shop. "That fucking hurt," I spat as the man squared off in his boxing stance. I smiled at the man. His chin untucked and he risked looking behind him... only to see the raised legs of Solly kick forward, jamming through his body as easily as pencils through paper.

"Thanks, Solly," I mumbled, climbing to my feet. She nodded and took off back into the fray. I blew blood out of my nose and charged another masked fighter, and continued a series of blows as rainbows of lightning shot above me. Lakes of fire exploded and people died screaming in the night.

I vomited at some point as I pushed forward, bullets shattering all around me. I wanted to curl up in a ball, every time I kicked or punched someone. I hated the way my fists rattled, the way my body reacted to strikes, moving like a snake out of the way with expert ease. I watched in horror as the young wolves ate people who they may have ran into in this small town on numerous occasions, people they probably stood behind while they collected their mail.

It was never going to end, this hell, this crust on the pie of doom, baking in the fires of the damned. My ears were ringing, I was taken to the ground by a group of masked men, and as I landed, I was back in the hospital bed in the camp. My hands tied down, doctors and nurses all around me, rushing to get a tube down my throat. I thrashed, kicking and screaming, gnawing at one man's skull, spitting out the hair onto his face. He screamed, and I announced terror into the night. I was not going to be tied down, never again. I was never going back to that place, that place of isolation and horror that took pieces of me day by day. I was shattered glass at that thought, a scar that would never close.

I punched up at the nearest masked person, hitting their teeth as their bite dug into my knuckles. With a grunt, I twisted on whatever I could get ahold of. A long tongue came out as I was shoved back down to the ground, a fountain of blood spraying over me. I kicked my legs out once more, and threw as many wild punches as I could, my strength failing with every blow.

I jammed my eyes shut, doing my best to shield any more blood from coming in. Somewhere I felt a bone break in my right foot. Another vicious blow to my mouth. I spat out a tooth, hoping I had hit one of my attackers in the process. That gave me some level of smug satisfaction as I was hit once more, rattling my skull.

Through the red haze that was forming under the weight of each hit, I could hear the beast: "Just hang on, Avi, a little bit longer," he said urgently.

My thoughts lacked even the strength for a reply as I felt another kick to the face. This time I saw stars, even in the darkness of my closed eyes.

I don't think—I can't hold on much longer, my thoughts drilled into my heart. I started to hear my blood shake, and my head became trapped under water as I felt the edges of a deeper blackness than any I would ever understand start to corner its way around me.

In that darkness though, a light reached out. I snapped my eyes open to see a flock of ravens strike at my assailants. They swatted their hands in confusion, cursing and screaming into the night. It was Linor; she was saving me.

I grunted, willing myself to stand. It took all my effort to get on one knee. Gasping for air like a fish out of water, I stood. The ravens continued to peck at the men's heads. I had maybe a couple of seconds before they realized that the ravens weren't actually pecking them. I spotted a crowbar lying near me.

The heavy metal felt wrong in my hands; or maybe it was because I was about to use it for something other than cracking open a door. *Oh well, box or skull: same thing when you're pissed.* I lunged at the nearest attacker with the curved end, sinking the metal deep into his skull. I pulled the bar out and had it swinging as the attacker to the left of him realized what I was doing. He was too slow and I cracked him in the jaw, crunching his face with the metal.

The other two must have felt outgunned by the birds, or maybe it was me standing over their friends with a bloody crowbar. Either way, they took off screaming into the night, away from the battle. I spat after them and turned back to one of the smoke ravens.

I started to smile at the bird. "Linor, tha—"

That was I could get out before the bird suddenly vanished along with the Solly copies. Around me, the insanity of the battle subsided, and I was left holding a crowbar covered with blood. I felt the swell of a broken heart as my home—my family—slipped from this world.

91

Chapter 91

The exact moment the bars slid free and I stepped out of my cage, that was when Linor's raven disappeared before my eyes. In a way, the anger I'd felt, all these years, had never gone away. It was a nasty cough that lingered, itching at my throat, urging me to spit up a world of black void. When you're finally free, you expect there to be cheers. Just like the cough, so much force is put into keeping the bile down. Freedom should be the same.

It's not though, it's absolute silence. I now knew what it meant, and it was deafening, it was complete, it was all the sound I would never hear again. My heart beating from seeing her, my lips stretching to contain the smile she brought to my lips. Freedom now meant giving into the beast; I was going to kill these fuckers, each and every one of them. I shook the fire in my belly, now becoming an inferno of conflagration spinning out.

I let it happen, I unhinged the rage. "Ash, do your thing," I whispered as his roar shook the skin free of my body. I cried out as my eyes bulged to impossible sizes, my skin ripped to shreds, and all that made me a man ceased to exist, under claws and fangs.

Two men stepped forward with automatic rifles, big drums under their long barrels, and began to fire into me. The bullets took out chunks of my skin in no time, and my scream was a mixture of the wolf and my voice, crying out not from the pain, but for what was to come. When their guns started to smoke and click empty, I smiled. "My turn." I howled, my mind coming to inside the room with the mirror.

Ash stepped over my pile of clothes and skin, snarling at the two men. They screamed, dropping their guns. He responded with a gun of his own, opening his mouth wide as a torrent of flames laced across the road, engulfing both of the men in a screaming mess. They danced on the way to the ground. A small voice wanted me to look away—I was too far gone for that now.

I no longer cared; kill them all. "Kill them all, Ash," I whispered. He roared, landing on all fours. He punched, landing in a group of the masked fighters that were close to landing on a now-injured Solly. With a roar of brutal strikes, caving in the chests of men, breaking the backs of others, the beast howled our hatred into the night.

Solly looked at the beast, her diamond skin cracked in hundreds of places like glass that was waiting on a stiff breeze to break her into millions of pieces. She was terrified, trying to move her small body away from the wolf, her movement making her sound like glass sliding along the road. Ash let out another mighty roar, shooting flames into the sky, higher than the buildings themselves.

The wolf is unleashed in a field of sheep; it's hunting time. Ash charged forward, bowling the group of masked men and women over as if they were dominos before a tsunami. Flames, roars, cracking of bones, desperate shots, claws, and all manner of blades broke across the night—like a terrifyingly marvelous spray of shooting stars in the night sky.

Ash moved like the wind, pausing only long enough and to strike with his mighty paws, or even to ram someone with his marbled horns. One man he gored so hard with his horns that he went through the door of a car as it was thrown onto its side. A snarl left both our mouths at that, as the two of us stopped being separated and became a being of rage, of malice, of hate.

With his head pointed at the capitol building only a hundred yards or so off, I could see a look of pure panic on Sophia's face. Bug was darting into the building. Zevi simply smiled, then his face turned into a grimace as he pointed at Tir and Arnold in my direction. Tir took one look at Ash—I could sense his fear. Arnold was either brave or stupid. He summoned his shadow beast.

The ape-like creature roared his challenge into the night and leapt from the stage, with Arnold following close behind him. With a roar and a blast of inferno that melted away all before him, including a truck, down to molten stumps, Ash charged forward, making the very ground shake under the power of his feet. Arnold's shadow emitted a shriek that caused those nearby to cover their ears. I stayed focusing on Zevi in the distance, as did Ash.

The big creature stepped forward, swinging a massive spiked arm at Ash, who caught it with his horns, twisting it away. He followed up with a heavy swat of his arm, flinging the shadow creature into the side of a building, through the walls, and crashing into the interior furniture on the inside. Arnold's jaw dropped. He fell to the ground, backpedaling out of the way and covering his face.

Ash snarled at the man, then pressed on, charging as Tir came out of the ground, a cluster of roots shaped around his fist like a harpoon, striking Ash in the jaw. Ash's head snapped up, and blood spilled from the wolf's mouth. I could feel the red hot anger blaze in him, like someone had poured gasoline on a bonfire. I agreed with that anger, understood that anger, and added my own into the fire.

With a quick snap, Ash tore the roots from around Tir's arm. Tir flinched back, shooting more roots in place. He was far too slow. The beast gripped him in one of his massive paws, his fingers curling around Tir's neck. As Tir struggled against the grip of the beast's hold, Ash roared one last time and breathed a lake of fire onto the man, until he broke like a dry leaf through fingers, into thousands of small pieces.

"Goodbye, Tiresias," I whispered as the beast charged past him, going forward, a steam engine that was too big to be stopped by anything, once he set to rolling. The eater of the dust, the cry of the night, he was the big bad wolf, and nothing would stand in his wake.

The wolf kicked away the ashes of Tir, a friend I had known since being in the camps—one of us. But he had lost his place the moment he betrayed the community. Ash continued on and I caught myself looking behind at Tir. Had he really earned that death? Had any of these people deserved such brutal ends? I had turned in Zevi once, unaware that the fallout would bleed over into the community for fifteen years.

Then I had run off, after a good and dear friend was shot, for fear that the beast would come out. For fear that I had been wrong for stopping Zevi. In that instant, the truth became apparent finally. I had harmed my family, in those times as a child when Ash had taken over, when he had run wild. I knew now that that mostly had to do with him being just as scared and as hurt as I was. He hadn't meant to hurt anyone or destroy the camp. Very likely Ash had even tried to cause a lot less damage because of that.

Yet, my heart still held this aching pain, through the blood red haze, through the strikes of bodies that flew like freshly cut grass around me. I felt my anger pinwheel from out from under me and I suddenly felt sick to my stomach. Sheer death all around us. I had no idea if Tir had deserved death. I had no idea if any of the guards in the camps had, or if anyone deserved to be chopped to pieces like this. Whatever lay beyond the black rainbows of tears and the looming shadows, I knew one thing for certain: we weren't coming back. At least not the same, not in the same way or place, or even in the same kind of love. That frightened me to no end, and I just wanted this night to be over. It wasn't, though, not by a long shot. Then Hans stepped forward with a long pole in his hands.

The pole stopped at just under his chin, it was rigid in the center and otherwise looked to be about the width of a broom handle. Ash stopped momentarily, before charging forward toward one of the old torturers of my childhood. Toward the one man everyone in the room had always averted their eyes from in fear.

As we approached Hans, I soon found out why he commanded such respect. With a surfboard-smooth sidestep, he pivoted out of the way of Ash, bringing the far end of his metal bar smashing into the side of Ash's face. The wolf let out a grunt as Hans swung his metal weapon again into

Ash's face. Ash roared, striking with a meaty paw, breaking the metal staff in the center.

"Yeah, that's right," I screamed, but it was premature triumph. Hans took a piece of both the metal staffs and started expertly striking Ash. Whenever the wolf went to strike, Hans would dodge, skipping to the side and striking at Ash's paw or his face. The hits weren't heavy, though would have been enough to kill a grown man. I could feel the frustration of the wolf as Hans expertly dodged any attack made by us.

"He's kicking your ass," I stated. Ash roared in reply, spouting flames from his mouth which consumed a building where Hans had been standing just moments before. It went up in bright orange light. Ash roared again, snapping at Hans, who popped him in the jaw hard enough to make him bleed this time. Ash snarled, stepping forward slowly. A small fighter could do a lot more damage than you would think, with a couple of well-placed hits and fancy footwork—as I had seen Huey do hundreds of times. Hans was a man who had dedicated his life to killing—that was obvious in the way he moved, the way he glanced at us with no fear, never telegraphing which direction he would strike in next.

Ash went to lunge forward again, and we suddenly found ourselves standing with three of the wolves. A massive black wolf, a smaller red and white one with a curled tail that I suspected to be Tiva, followed by a golden and brown little wolf. I wasn't sure which one that was, but our sheer numbers made Hans finally look unsure of himself.

Ash stepped forward, leading the attack, when Arnold's shadow came storming out of the wreckage of one of the buildings, taking the golden wolf by surprise, lifting the smaller wolf in the air. Before the wolf had any time to react, Arnold's shadow creature hissed, bringing down the wolf on its knee. With a loud crack, followed by a yelp, the wolf let out a cry and started to return to human shape. But only the upper body managed to return to human—everything below his spine stayed in wolf form. Furious, Bipin and Tiva attacked Arnold's creature with a savage fury, forcing it to back up into the nearest building. The power was still on. The creature had gone into a bar, where a pool table was in the center, with a well-stocked counter containing one-seater chairs flanking us on almost every side. Ash prepared to charge as well, when Hans struck hitting the side of his face.

He snarled, and I snarled as well. We were getting beaten by an old man with a stick. Hans prepared to strike once more, when Huey flew past us like lightning, catching one of the metal pipes in his hand and twisting it free. Hans stepped back, snapping a kick at a speed similar to a jet taking off, as Huey brought up his arms, defending the kick.

With a quick jab, Hans shot the other bar toward Huey, who again deflected it, but not before Hans landed a vicious thigh kick. I had never seen Huey struck before. Even the beast paused long enough to watch the two fight. With a grunt and a twist of smooth motion, like water flowing down a river, the pipe hit the ground. In an instant, the fight turned in a much different direction as Huey and Hans exchanged a flurry of parries, strikes, kicks, and expertly timed dodges. Their limbs blurred before my eyes, neither men wasting a single movement.

At some point, Huey lunched his forearm into Hans's face, but Hans countered by landing a knee into Huey's gut. With a blast of air, Huey stepped back, joining myself and the remaining snarling wolves. Arnold came to stand next to Hans. They were on the far side of the bar—during the course of the fight between the two men, we had drifted into the store. Bug came out of the back room, brandishing a small shotgun at his side, the long barrel sawed away. Ash snarled at Bug, who flinched.

Without facing me, Huey called back, "Avi—take off now. Go get your brother. We got this," he stated as the two wolves came to his side. Ash hesitated for a moment, but Huey waved him on and bolted forward, pulling a pool stick from the billiards table and lunging it like a homing missile, striking Bug in the face. Bug fell flat to the ground, his shotgun sliding away somewhere into the bar.

"Holy shit!" I yelled inside of Ash's head. Ash pulled away as Arnold stomped, shaking the bar like a juggernaut of pure rage. Bipin and Tiva shot like bullets from a gun, easily clearing the billiards table, and attacked Arnold.

"Good luck, guys," I called, as Ash pointed himself forward and jumped back into the hell of the fight around us. More of the masked people cleared out and ran in every direction, like ants fleeing their home after a boot steps on them. *That is what Ash and I are right now.* The memory of one of Bipin brothers, contorted and dying on the floor, hit me hard enough to rekindle the fire in my belly.

"Let's kill them all, Ash!" I screamed as Ash roared, pouncing on a man foolish enough to come at a beast like Ash with nothing more than a baseball bat.

92

Chapter 92

Shots rang overhead, and the fire seemed to be neverending, no matter which direction we moved. I tasted more blood than actual air, as Ash hummed along, moving through our enemies like a well-oiled machine.

Solly pulled up beside us, her diamond armor almost completely gone around her shoulder, showing her frail human flesh beneath. I wanted to shout to her to get out of the area, but there was no way to do it. Every second, explosions rocked the whole place, causing Ash to stagger on his way toward the capitol building. In the chaos, Zevi had disappeared. Masked men and women fled in every direction; their numbers were getting smaller—good. Shots were still ringing from somewhere overhead, which meant that Jimmy and his gang were still laying down fire. They hadn't run out of ammo, yet. As Ash scanned the outer buildings, the remaining wolves nipped at the heels of those fleeing. It always amazed me just how much control they had over their wolves; they didn't seem to have the growing pains that Ash and I had.

Lighting shot from somewhere ahead, bolts of neon yellows and universal purples, nearly taking Ash's head off. He fell to the ground, glancing behind him to see the bolts strike a building where some of our people were based, laying down suppressing fire. I screamed, "No," and Ash roared in response, going to all fours quickly, and galloping toward Sophia, who was hunkered down behind the remains of a car. Half her face was splashed in red crimson blood. She glanced at Ash, then redirected the bolts flying from her hands into us. Ash had maybe a second to dodge. He wasn't fast enough, though, and a lightning storm engulfed us.

We both roared out in pain as hot laces of fire shot through our body, shaking every inch of our skin. I felt the shift start—I was being pulled from the mirror room. I twisted in agony as the electricity raced over every inch of my skin. It was to no avail, I was being pulled out like a new born calf, kicking and screaming.

With a shattering cry, both of us switched places. My jaw returning to normal portions, my body arching and going limp, in impossible shapes, as I felt my mind stretch to its breaking point. Ash's fur fell from me, and my arms returned back to their normal size, flesh regrouping over the thick muscles of the beast. He roared, cracking, biting, howling in the night; the lightning continued. I blacked out several times, spit drooling out of my mouth into an ocean. When I was back, one of my eyes refused to open. I had a moment of reprise from the lightning, long enough for me to see Sophia walking toward my frail body, as I lay like a baby bunny rather than a wolf. She was breathing hard, her fingers glowing, her skin barely even there anymore, as her veins glowed like the bright lights of Vegas. I readied myself for another volley, but lord help me—that was the most painful thing I had ever experienced. I wouldn't be able to survive another one of those attacks.

She prepared to fire. My eye closed again and reopened to see Solly completely out of her armor, throwing wild punches and kicks at Sophia. Sophia caught a blow to the jaw, then she stepped forward, placing a heel behind Solly's, and she tripped her to the ground. Solly's head hit the pavement hard. I could see blood spilling out from a cracked skull as she lay still on the war-torn ground. *This is fucking ridiculous, we had come here only to be beaten like this? Why does every single one of them know some kind of martial arts?*

I pushed myself up, my chest raised as she neared me. Her fingers glowed, veins popping out of her face. "Avi, open your mouth!" roared the beast. I was too tired to argue. I opened my jaw wide as flames danced out, like the tongue of a frog. It caught Sophia by surprise. Her eyes went wide as the flames struck her face. The flames continued as my lips burned, and my throat started to choke off, until I fell forward, gasping for air.

I attempted to vomit—nothing came out save for blood. I was starting to wonder what my limit for pain had to be. Sooner or later, you reach your breaking point physically. I pushed off the ground at that thought. I was going to die long before then.

Sophia was nowhere to be found. Solly groaned in the distance. I crawled my way over to her. She was as pale as a snowflake, and had bruises covering nearly every inch that I could see. It must have been all those shots: they had been really hurting her. *Damn it Solly.* Solly groaned again. I tore part of her shirt, tying it around her head. She woke up at some point, coughing before settling on speaking. "Why... are... you... naked, Avi?"

I regarded her with a long look and pointed at my burned mouth. It felt like there was no longer any flesh on my mouth, as the hot air around us kissed my face. A dawning realization sprang into her face, and she understood; with a grunt, I helped her to stand. There was no time to linger. She threw her arm over my shoulder and we made our way out of the hellscape that was still unfolding around us.

So many rounds were being fired; screams as long as the blackest of nights. I no longer had any idea who was on our side and who wasn't. *Just stay alive, guys—that's all I ask, please. Just for once, don't let any more of my family die*, I prayed as we approached the marbled steps, chips of rocks missing, the rail almost completely torn down.

93

Chapter 93

The power was out in the capitol building. Most of the windows had been blocked off with piles of wood and various other furnishings. I had never been in a building as nice as this one; I imagined that before Zevi had moved in, the place would have looked like a home for a king or queen, with soft sofas and unnecessary chairs placed everywhere. Now, the building was daubed with paint, trash piled in every corner, and windows were smashed, spilling glass everywhere. Many sleeping bags, and various pots and pans were stacked in the corners of nearly every room, haphazardly placed. *They had left in a rush*, I thought, walking forward into the total darkness. Solly gripped my right shoulder—her hand crystalized, shining a small light.

We had agreed to keep the light from her hand low—more as a last line of defense, and instead, we opted to use my senses, with extra power granted by Ash. I was still unable to talk, and my throat was blistered shut. It took Solly and I a few minutes to relay a plan using just gestures—but we knew we weren't alone in the capitol building.

Somewhere in here was Zevi and all manner of the devil knew what. Every step in the darkness made me feel uneasy beyond belief—this was exactly what my brother was wanting us to do. Be lured back into his dark cave like we were a prize fish swimming after a hooked worm, unsuspecting of what was about to transpire. "Stay calm, Avi," Ash whispered inside my head. He was back in the mirror room. I closed my eyes and let my nose guide me for a few steps as I concentrated on Ash, until we were both in the mirrored room.

Drenched in blood, guts, and smelling of smoke, Ash lay on the floor of the room, his head resting on his paws. I noticed that one of his horns was chipped, and the curled end appeared to be broken off. A huge swath of his under-hair had been burned away, combined with multiple bullet holes. Ash looked like he had been put through a meat grinder. I felt the tenderness of my throat; it stung to the touch. We were both nearing our end. "Thank you, Ash for saving me," I stated to him. He kept his eyes closed and blew smoke out of his mouth. I smirked. That would just have to do for now with him. After a moment, Ash said in a low voice, "I will need to sleep for a bit to regain some strength. Healing your throat and my injuries is going to take some time."

I shook my head, "Don't worry about healing me—if we run into Sophia or Zevi, we are goners," I stated.

"You think too lowly of yourself, Avi. Besides, even worms like yourself have allies. Use them. You have that redheaded woman by your side," Ash replied, with a voice that was close to near-fatal exhaustion.

Ash opened one large eye, before sighing. "You've convinced them to follow you here; you even asked for their help. So use it and trust that they won't let you down," he groaned, before stretching out in a manner which was—although I wouldn't dare say out loud—cute, kind of like a big puppy. Albeit a puppy that could kill you with just one slice of his razor-sharp claws.

I sighed, leaning against the walls of the mirror room. I was getting more and more tired as the night dragged on. I wanted a good night's rest, but that wasn't it; it was something a lot deeper. It wasn't just a lack of faith; every step would take me into a confrontation with Zevi. Running, for once, wasn't an option. For once, I would just trust that someone was out there trying help me. Which was good, as I wasn't much by myself anyways—way too prone to getting my ass kicked.

I left the mirrored room and pulled Solly's other hand. "Follow me this way," I gestured, as we made our way around the dark corridors.

94

Chapter 94

Solly and I continued down the hallway. My throat had started to clear up by the time we reached the second floor. Ash had fallen asleep, leaving me with the sensation of a blank spot inside my mind, like a brick had been taken out of a wall. I suppose this was how he felt whenever I went to sleep. I had Solly put out her light completely—we hadn't seen anyone yet, but that didn't mean this wasn't a trap.

"I think they're most likely running for the hills by now—if they had any lick of sense, that is," Solly whispered nervously.

"Not likely. This is his endgame—he knows it, we know it," I croaked, coughing to clear my throat. I would never let Ash breathe fire out of my mouth ever again.

"Why? What could he possibly stand to gain at this point? He already has an army—what's left of it. Either way, we are all fucked, sooner or later," she stated.

I turned toward her, not knowing what she meant. She felt the shift in my shoulder as I now faced her in the dark. "What do you mean?" I asked her.

"Avi, we just... we are still fighting in a warzone. It's a testament to Zevi's control that the whole town isn't swarming with every single person in the government as we speak. Face it, Avi, even if we win here, we're fucked," she said.

I turned back to the darkness, wishing she was wrong. It was true; there was nothing that could be done about that. Maybe the best thing we could have done was just leave. But Zevi made it clear that he wanted me—what did that mean for the community then? Easy: he would have hunted them to the ends of the Earth if it meant a chance to catch me. Like it or not, this was the point of no return. Although for me, that had been crossed the moment Linor was blown up inside a warehouse. I cracked my knuckles in an attempt to drive out the anger that was rising inside me. All of this, just so my brother could cause more pain and suffering. I slumped against a wall for a moment, and Solly rushed to my side. "What is it, Avi?"

My hands were shaking, moving as if I held a drumstick, banging on a hard surface. With a deep breath and the strong mental thought of *stop*, my hands quit moving. I kept chugging down air as Solly put her hands on my head, her cool fingers helping to ground me. "You're on fire, love. We need to get you some water now," she stated, pulling me off the wall. In the darkness, shapes came out, faces of those I thought lost long ago to the fires of the camp.

Shades begin to whisper in my mind, and the darkness of the building stretched for miles. Every time we bumped into an object I flinched, jolting to the other side of the hall, unsure if I had stepped on a body or if I was about to be struck by some unseen force. At some point, Solly found a bathroom for us. She had risked coating her hand in her bright diamonds.

I couldn't tell her to douse it, as my mouth seemed to lock down and the only thing I could manage to do was stutter. She pulled on my arm, and globs of sweat dropped off me as we entered a stuffy bathroom. My vision came in and out, as I did my best to just close my eyes and try to ignore the overwhelming feelings stacking up like tiny rocks until I could no longer be seen.

"Come on, lazy bones, get to dancing," Solly grunted, pulling me toward the sink. She turned the knobs, and surprisingly, water came out after a few coughs and strains from the sink. "It must be what's left over from before the power went out. You can take being shot—I think you can handle some dirty water," she stated, cupping her hands and splashing me. I could smell dirt in the water, but nothing that would worry me. The water helped, soothing away the fear of the shadows.

Those things are behind you, Avi; you know this. You're only feeling fear because that is your fallback. Don't be afraid. Solly pulled the diamonds from her fingers, stacking them on top of the sink counter. The bathroom had three sinks and four stalls directly behind us. I blew out an air of relief when I realized that the room was fairly clean.

Blue light from Solly's diamond-coated skin bathed the giant mirror before us. Solly was covered in ugly yellow bruises, some deepening into a velvet purple, seeming to expand as if some horrible liquid monster wanted to pop from her skin.

I didn't look much better. Although the time I had spent training with Huey—training for the first time since childhood—meant I finally had weight on me, I was still on the lighter side. My father's beaked nose had been passed along to me and my hair was cut short. The rest of me, however, was completely ridden with scar tissue. I had rough ridges, and rows of scars that went so deep, the bone would poke out if I moved around too much. I hung my head, letting beads of sweat drip down my face.

"Let me see if I can't find something at least to put on your feet. The whole floor is covered in shards of glass," Solly stated. I looked down, pulling my feet toward the light of Solly's rocks that she had stacked up. I had no idea she could take her diamonds off. If Linor's grandmother had known that... I smirked at the memory of the charcoal and peanut butter as I sat up, pulling small pieces of green glass out of my left foot.

This actually saved my life; it gave me enough time to catch the sudden shift in light as a neon orange blistered in the mirror. I ducked as the electricity fired from behind me, destroying the mirror in thousands of molten hot razors. On the ground, my mind kicked in full panic mode and I shot to my feet on my way toward Sophia.

In the dim light, I could make out that half her face was simply gone, replaced by obsidian-like skin. She was going to fight to the death now. I put my head down to take her to the ground, hoping that Solly was in flight as well. I made it maybe three steps before a meaty arm shot of the darkness and I ran right into it, rolling backward as I fell on my ass. I groaned, looking up.

His smell wafted from him before I even saw his cloven face. "Hey, Avi... Zevi said I could eat you," Schwein snorted, thick globs of snot sliding down and landing on my face. I gagged. The smell of it alone was enough to make me want to give up. *That wasn't an option*, I groaned, pushing off his leg, using the globs to slide along the floor.

"Hi, Schwein," I muttered, coming to my feet as I massaged my throat. The big ugly pig stepped toward me; I would need to talk to Ash next time about sharing some of that super strength with me before he ever decided to fall asleep.

I risked a quick glance. Solly was wrestling for control of Sophia's arm, the bolts readied to be fired again. Sophia may have been a good fighter, but she had lost half her face—then again, both women were completely exhausted. That made three of us. Schwein lumbered his massive body forward. I was easily able to dodge it as his meaty fist struck the bathroom wall, breaking a hole in it.

He grunted. I pivoted, stepping to the side and kicking down at his knee as he was bent over. With a loud crunch and a squeal of pain, Schwein yanked his arm through the wall and destroyed one of the sinks. Chunks of metal flew at me. I covered my face, sliding back across the floor. He hadn't used his teeth on me yet—it must have been because Sophia was in the room with us.

I wasn't a great fighter, and I was way too banged-up to fight someone as big as Schwein this close. But I had Sophia here—perhaps that was to my advantage. I looked over Schwein's shoulders, seeing bolts of electricity shoot into the ceiling above, bringing down dust, and a heavy fog of dirt cloaked the room. *Take out the lights*, I thought as I took hold of a broken piece of the sink. I saw Solly's diamonds providing the only light in the room. I took aim, launching the piece of broken sink, watching as my throw completely missed, banging against the wall with a thud. Schwein turned his head, laughing at my efforts. That gave me enough time to jump to my feet and kick the pig man between the legs.

Schwein tilted forward, and I kicked once more until I heard a crunch. For good measure, I kicked again, and Schwein slumped forward, whimpering as I turned toward Sophia and Solly. Sophia swept a leg under Solly, bringing my friend to the ground hard.

"Bitch," snarled Sophia as she pointed her fingers at me, the ends turning a bright yellow. I covered my face. I heard a shriek, though, as her fingers stopped crackling the air around us. Solly had stabbed Sophia in the leg with another piece of the broken sink. That was enough for me. I ran forward and barged Sophia to the ground. She squirmed, landing a few punches to my jaw that would have easily taken me out, had Solly not helped me restrain her. We pulled her to one of the stalls. Solly yanked out her belt and tied Sophia's wrists around the door, trapping her.

"That's for calling me a bitch, you hateful drug-addict-looking vein-head!" Solly snapped, kicking Sophia in the ribs.

I stood back, catching my breath. "Thanks Solly," I stated through clenched teeth.

"You're welcome... Avi, look out!" shouted Solly, pushing me out of the way as Schwein shot forward with a heavy thrust of his arm, punching a hole through the tile floor. He opened his mouth, stretching it to the size of my chest, and I could hear his teeth popping like cornels of corn. I knew it would only take a few seconds for the room to be filled to the top.

Sophia spat at me. "Die, you coward," she hissed, her fingers glowing. Solly reacted before me, wrenching Sophia's hands up just in time for them to shoot into the gaping mouth of Schwein. The pig man shrieked enough to make a slaughter house depressed. His head burst into flames and his body dropped forward. I could smell burning flesh as the whole room filled with noxious smoke.

"Solly!" I coughed as I saw the lights go out from Sophia's hands and the thud of something hitting the ground hard.

"I'm fine. Come on, Avi," Solly shouted, pulling my hand. I was holding onto something glossy and cold, then I realized it was her diamond-coated armor in my hands. She led us out of the bathroom, and we came out gasping for air. Solly slumped over first, against the furthest wall. I turned back to the bathroom door, where the room was thick with smoke. "We can't leave Sophia in there like that—we can't," I started to say.

My eyes adjusted in the dark, making out the sweat on Solly's face. She looked gray as she slid to the ground. Without hesitation, I moved to her side. The glow from her arms disappeared, not before showing me that her hands had both been burned down to stumps. I hunkered down, pressing my hands against her forehead. "You aren't looking too hot, Solly," I said soothingly, trying to figure out the best thing to do.

Solly smirked. "Look who's talking. Can't blame the cold, small fella," she joked.

I laughed, feeling my eyes get heavy. "Hang on, Solly, I will get you out of here," I stated as I started to lift her.

With her shoulder, Solly shook me off. "Just tie off my hands and get to stepping after your brother already. Finish this, will you?" she stated, her eyes struggling to stay open.

I nodded, tearing off a piece of her shirt, bandaging both of her wrists. She whimpered, but remained awake. "Solly, thank you for everything. When you wake up, get out of here," I whispered as her eyes closed and her head dipped. I watched her chest rise and fall before I was satisfied.

I let out a low growl at the situation. I was naked, alone in the dark, with no one to help me now. As the anger surged through me, I focused—I had someone who was going to pay for all of this. Maybe it was self-preservation that had caused me to run all those times when I was a kid. I'd never done anything with all my efforts—generally, I was too afraid or lost in my own cage. I wasn't going to let that be the case any more. I didn't care what happened after tonight. Just for tonight, I was going to settle this thing between my brother and me. Right here and now.

95

Chapter 95

I found a pair of pants that only stayed on my hips after looping a belt nearly twice around. I had dragged Solly out of the hallway, placing her near an open window at the end of the hallway. Her head still felt warm to the touch and her skin wasn't faring much better. I went back for Sophia, but the smoke had already killed her by that point.

I still dragged her and Schwein out into the hallway. Maybe none of this would have ever happened if we hadn't ended up in the camps. People aren't born to be monsters; we all start out generally good, until life presses us just enough, beats us in just the right ways, until the difference between staying alive and doing the right thing is murky as the waters of the Black Sea. It wouldn't have happened, I thought, but we had our nights stolen from us, our sunsets ripped away, our days turned into haunted shades.

I thought of what Elder Ad had said: "Feed the good wolf." That caused me to stop as I moved through the capitol building. That simple statement had been haunting me my entire life. What it really meant, I questioned in moments like this. The choice had been made this morning, long before I ever realized that I would be leading some kind of war against my *bruder*, struggling in the dark.

I had chosen to do this. I needed to be whole; there was no way that I could do this split in so many grains. I stopped when I reached an open hatch that lead to the roof of the capitol building. Light and noise in the distance showed the way through. Just like in the cage, all those times where I thought escape would somehow lead me to a place far worse. Was this the same situation? The part of me that wanted to run, go back to howling in the woods, completely agreed with that.

It wasn't right, but I was still afraid. I stopped, leaning against the wall. I closed my eyes and reopened them slowly. Three figures had appeared in front of me: a brightly lit man, a shadow, and a small figure of a boy. The shadow stood across from me, tiptoeing around the light coming from the opening, until he stood inches from me. He was a silhouette made only of lines in the shape of a man. Nervously, I examined the boy standing near me as well. He was wild. His clothes were little more than tattered piss-stained rags, held together by strings. He looked as old as fifty, and his skin in some areas showed signs of what I thought was scurvy. Blotches of dirt, huge bruises, and oil-black hair that was so clumped together, no parent could ever untangle it from the frail boy. He was more skeleton than actual kid, I thought, as tears ran down my face.

The wild-eyed boy stepped away from both the shadow man and the light man, standing opposite me, but off to my left. The shadow continued to move closer until he was inches from my face on the right.

The light man stepped out of the darkness in a tailored suit that made his shoulders look like he took care of himself and ate well. His chest was spread wide and proud; his composure was of a man at peace. The same fierce eyes, beaked, hooked nose, and narrow cheeks that were a little bit more puffed out than my own. He held a golden pocket watch, hanging from a breast pocket, that caught the light like a miniature sun. I knew it was my father's watch—just like I knew all three of them were me.

"Well, shit, boys. Welcome to the pity party," I stated dryly to the group.

96

Chapter 96

The shadow moved closer to me, a dark anathema that every instinct in my mind told me to stay away from. I slid down the wall, deeper into the light from the roof. The shadow version of me just shook his head. "Mate, I think you misunderstood what Elder Ad meant so long ago on many different levels. You have two wolves inside you, not just the good," he stated.

I growled at him. "I know, feed the good wolf, and all that shit."

He shook his head. "No, it's not just that: you have two. It's true that you have decided who's in control each morning, but even more true is that you need both in order to exist. You can't just go and pick and choose which side you want to have," he stated.

I slapped my legs, falling down the wall. "Look, I am feeling pretty exasperated here. If you're real, just get whatever you're about to do over with. If you aren't, then please, explain to me why I should listen to a creepy outline, some dapper dude who looks like he stepped out of a budget porno, and a very sickly child." I replied, casting my eyes on the well-dressed version of myself.

The well-dressed me blew out his lips and turned toward the other two. "We are here because you need us, Avraham. You called us, not the other way around. At all times, people carry everything about themselves: the past, the future, and the shadow. You can't be a human without the four," he stated again.

I thought about his statement, then blew out my lips as well. "Glad to know that the future me still hasn't gone to school for math—there's three of you, asshole."

"Four!" pointed the young me, his voice coming out as little more than sandpaper, like a growl. My heart sank looking at him. I turned my head away—seeing him so little, so frail. Had I always been that thin?

"There's four of us, Avi. Your future aspirations"—the well-dressed me pointed at himself—"your past"—he pointed at the little boy—"and your shadow, which is everything that you do not like. Before you say anything, we are all assholes. Get over it," he stated. "And finally, your present." He pointed at me.

I sighed. "So, what, are you the Ghosts of Christmas Past, here to warn me about changing my ways? In case you haven't noticed, I am a long way gone from what I used to be!" I gestured to the little boy, still not wanting to look at him directly if I could help it.

He shook his head, "No, Avi. At the end of the day, we can't tell you anything that you didn't already know yourself. Your mind fills your head with billions of thoughts a day, and none of that will ever tell you anything about yourself more than what you decide for yourself. People are always changing everyday—every moment, and you can't possibly know everything," he informed me.

I sat on his words for a moment. The night had been long and I just wanted to curl up in a tight ball and sleep until the end of days. Life doesn't work that way; I had chosen to take part in all of this, and I would have to see it through. Even if the future was starting to seem like a reflection of light, not a real place.

"I appreciate the feedback, but how does that help me now?" I asked the future me.

The shadow was the one that responded, his voice cracking like a whip. "Because... your... life... depends... on... it..." he stated, and I stepped back again as he moved closer.

"Because others depend on it," stated the future me calmly.

"How, then? Just tell me. If you're here to help, then help me," I stated to the three of them.

It was silent under the hatch of the roof. Outside, the noises were starting to quieten down. What did that mean? Had we been wiped out? That thought terrified me more than facing my brother.

"You worry about too much shit out of your control, Avi. What can you do about it anyways? You still have more than one person to face," stated the future me.

I looked at him, confused. "What do you mean, more than one?" I asked him.

He smirked at me. "Start with the past, there, Avi. All the bad that has happened to you, all the bad that you've done. Then, make peace with the future. There's a lot that you just won't understand—all you can is face it with a certainty. But none of that will matter if you're still ignoring your shadow." He gestured toward the shadow moving in the darkness, only inches away from me now.

I was becoming flustered with every moment—the emotional toll of coming here was sinking in, I decided. When I'd left Arizona, I hadn't planned to be caught up in such events, and I hadn't planned on seeing Linor again, or talking to anyone from the community. I certainly hadn't foreseen fighting this many people.

As my shadow came into view, I could make out his features. He wasn't just an outline of a thing I had never seen. Instead, he looked like me, exactly like the man I had seen in the mirror down in the bathroom. Same long nose, deep eyes that only seemed to know sadness; and then I understood what they wanted in that moment. I had made the three appear, and this was my mind telling me exactly what I needed. I already knew the answers; I just had to walk forward and face them. The things we hear, when we finally shut up—those are things that just make sense when everything else is senseless.

I walked forward and held out my hand toward my shadow. "I no longer care which of us is the 'good one' or the 'bad one.' Either way, I've lead myself here to this place on my own," I stated. Then, I looked to my past.

"Little boy—Avi, you get out of the cage at some point, and there's no more cages when you start to fly." The boy looked at me quizzically, but remained silent.

Finally, I looked at the future me. I nodded and walked forward toward a long ladder, leading to a rooftop high above the city. I still hated heights, and that wasn't going to change. But the funny thing about change is, you never know when it will occur, you never know what will happen if you just start climbing.

"You know what to do, Avi," stated my future self.

"Haven't got a fucking clue, my man—but I'm not afraid," I replied, climbing the steps of the ladder.

"Good luck," whispered my past self. I looked at the little boy, with his wild eyes, and I wondered at what point it was that they were no longer round. That they failed to catch a gleam of a smile anymore and became pools of endless mud. My mother had told me once she loved my eyes most of all—that wasn't true, as she also loved Zevi's green eyes and red hair. She did always tell me that I had the happiest eyes, but those weren't my eyes any more. Mine were the eyes of a boy who had seen too much, lived too much. Now those boy's eyes were my eyes, whatever those might have been.

I ascended the ladder, and a cold wind caught me before I went through the opening, nipping at my back. *That wasn't the cold,* I told myself as I went into the light.

97

Chapter 97

The moon was heavy in the sky, a blast of golden rays even in the middle of the night. My brother's back was turned toward me, on the flat roof of the capitol building. The roofing was a tin green metal that had been shielded from sight by enlarging the ledges to make the building appear as though it was one solid rock going across the front of the building. Had to cut corners somewhere, I guess.

I stepped onto the metal, and it popped, bowing under my light weight as I moved out onto the roof. My brother was staring off into the distance, but doubtless he knew that I was coming. Gunshots were becoming more and more spaced apart below, as the moans of the wounded drifted up toward us. So many people were dead or dying for no reason. I flexed both my fists. I wasn't going to kill my brother, but it didn't mean I couldn't hit him in the face a few good times over.

We both remained silent, the wind picking up slightly, pulling on my jeans, wrapping around me, as if toward the conflict that was about to come, just before ceasing altogether. The world was holding its breath. The night devoured the day, while the moon smiled on all the horror below.

I decided to break the ice finally. "Kind of reminds you of all the games we used to play as kids huh? The rockets going up into the air, the burning of our neighbor's lamps so we could play into the late night," I stated.

Without turning around, Zevi chuckled, which under even normal circumstances would have sounded disturbing coming from such a deep voice. Now, I had never felt my spine shiver so fast. "Yeah—it kind of does, doesn't it? Isn't it marvelous though, brother? A cosmic play of God, acted out right before our very eyes." My brother spread his hands wide as if he was a rocker, showing off for his adoring fans. Another chill ran up my spine as I slowly moved my body into a fighting stance.

"Ash, are you there?" I called out to the mirror room. I could see the great beast slumbering on the floor. His body was no longer bleeding thick globs of blood, but his eyes still looked airtight and in general, he still had the look of a haggard, wounded animal. "All alone on this one, I guess," I muttered.

I called over to Zevi, hoping that I could sway him. If I could convince a beast such as Ash, I could convince my brother, bring him back before the tide pulled him out onto a sea from which those who sell their souls into the fire can never return. "There's nothing marvelous about watching people rot out and die, Zevi," I stated to him.

He still had his arms stretched above his head. "Is it any different to what we find anywhere else, Avi? Do the hands that hold this world soften, just because we aren't rejoicing in the destruction? If that was so, were they ever gentle to begin with?" he replied.

"What, you have a problem with God now? A problem with the world? Get over it, Zevi. There are countless things that are unfair and unjust in this world. That doesn't mean we can right all that by celebrating conflict. We should be trying to end it—we should be trying to be brothers again," I implored to my brother, walking closer.

I heard the quick snarl of his voice before it returned to the mask of control. "I *am* fighting the wrong in this shitty fucking place, Avi. I will create the conflicts. I will fight back the real monsters. You think I am terror? The doctor who tortured you as a child did far worse to your dearly beloved, mutilated me, mutilated her. I am now what this virus-filled planet needs. Something to scare it back into position. Everyone here has become worse! How is that even possible, with so many people dying every moment! It's infuriating! A morality meter about as long as a goldfish's memory! No, I am exactly what this world needs, dear brother. By becoming the nightmare to the monsters, I can bring people back to seeing the pretty lights of baseball fields and hot popcorn after the fair in our hometown. Give people unity, so there will be no more pain. When they forget, step out of line, then I will simply be the world's monster. Yes, brother, I remember all the good. But I remember how it was all taken, and I will never allow that again. Give me the beast. Help me and stop this foolishness," Zevi almost sounded like he was pleading as he lowered his arms.

I thought of Ash, how he had saved my life tonight, how he had saved all of our lives. He was no beast. He was a product of the world that Zevi described, but he was my... my friend. Not a monster to be used as a weapon. I wasn't going to let that happen, not after all we had been through. I had to find a way to stop this, before it got out of hand. "What then? I give you the beast, then you're suddenly going to let it all go. Please, you will never leave the community alone," I yelled at him.

He whipped around for the first time, a snarl on his face, making him appear more demon than actual man. "I would have let them go. They had suffered enough, but after this, after what you did here... I will spare no one. I will build a new world, brick by brick if I have to. Give me the beast, brother and I will make your and their suffering quick. No more pain, no more tears, just a world that is being fed what it needed so badly: hope," he countered.

I fired back. "Hope, you say? How will you do that? By building an army of brainwashed juiced-up blood bags to cause mayhem?" I challenged my brother, swiping at the distance between us.

He turned completely, tilting his head back, and let out a laugh that was louder than bullets. "Yeah—that's about the gist of my evil plan. Shut the fuck up, Avraham. I know all about your little monster inside of you. You see, unlike you, I've spent some time using my life wisely. I didn't spend it chasing a dead bitch and hanging out with men in trailers while you cried your eyes out. *Boo hoo, no one can understand my pain. Look at me. Boo hoo. I run away from anything and everyone because I am a selfish piece of human garbage*," he growled.

I snarled, fuming. "Don't... you... ever... call her a bitch... you hear me? Don't you ever say that again," I was holding on my whole body, feeling like a bomb ready to explode.

"Bitch... bitch... bitch." He beamed at me.

I cracked my knuckles, pushing in on my index finger so hard I felt the bone break. The pain caused my eyes to water. It was enough to calm me down, though. If I lost control, even for a moment, someone was going to die. Everyone else had given up on Zevi—if I worked that hatred through now, we were both goners, regardless of who won the fight.

I kept growling, snarling as drool fell from my mouth and my whole body shook.

"Boy, you really are an animal, huh?" he jabbed, swinging his own fist between us. We were now only separated by a few feet.

He goaded me with a smile, but I resisted, hearing my father's words, "Promise me, Avi."

"I promise, father," I said through clenched teeth.

When he realized I wasn't going to respond to his taunts, Zevi stood tall. "I read that your beast comes to those who are in a great need, that he is reborn anew each time and bestows blessings upon his allies, upon his enemies. I need that—I deserve that power, Avi. I won't waste it like you have. Our enemies are still out there; the descendants of their ideas still plague this Earth. The creators of their hate still roam free," he explained.

"How will going around killing anyone be any different from what you're supposedly trying to fight? Do you really think this is what everyone in the community wants? That they somehow didn't just want a place where the cops weren't throwing them out of their homes every day? Our parents—do you think they would want this? Mother, father?" I challenged my brother.

Zevi widened his stance, growling. "Typical—so I have to acknowledge your world views because they don't line up with your code? When it's my views that have brought sanctuary to the community. When it's me who would have saved our parents, would have saved everyone!" he spat at me.

He has to acknowledge my world views? What did he mean by that? Telling him I cared wasn't going to work, pleading with him about the past and his actions seemed to only make him defend himself more.

I bowed my head, spreading my feet into a fighting stance. "I wish it had never come to this, brother; right now, you must feel trapped. You must feel far lonelier than a fish out of the seas. I understand that pain; I get what it's like to be so filled with hate that there can only be one release of the great inferno building up inside you," I stated.

I paused. Zevi's face was now covered in veins and I had no idea if he was even hearing me anymore.

I continued, "But I will do what I must—even if I have to break every bone in your body, I will stop you right here and now. Please, Zevi, don't do this. It is wrong what happened to you, truly. In the end, though, all that will ever truly matter is what we do with our judgment of the things that happened to us."

Zevi laughed again, holding onto his ribs like they were going to fly away from his laughter. It was a truly spine-tingling sensation, that was juxtaposed with the violence below us. I needed to put an end to this once and for all. War just created more Zevis—more Avis. I wasn't about to let that happen anymore.

"Then I will do what I must," I muttered, moving toward my brother, my feet spread apart at an angle, hips squared and shoulders rolled back.

Zevi laughed again. "I've waited a long, long time for this. Show me the wolf, brother!" he cackled, taking his own stance, before switching back to standing normally. He had his arms at his sides, his body facing toward me. I paused. He wasn't taking me seriously. I flinched from that, now that I was within striking distance. I threw a quick jab, and Zevi took it right in the face. His cheek turned, but everything else stayed still, as if only a stiff breeze had hit him.

Frustrated, I threw a right hook. I knew Zevi was strong, but he was still flesh and bone. Brittle and breakable like anything else. I half-stepped back, throwing a right kick, twisting my hips. Zevi stuck out his hand, catching my ankle in his hands, like someone had just thrown him a ball of yarn. His face appeared disinterested, then he snarled in rage. In a blur, my one leg still on the ground was swept out from under me.

I fell hard, the wind escaping from my lungs. Gasping for air, I started to roll forward. Zevi countered, pushing his hand into my neck, dragging me across the ground with enough force to strip the metal off the roof. A long trail of blood led behind me as I fought for air. His fingers were like steel beams.

We came to the edge of the roof, and he lifted me off the ground like a child slamming his toy into the toy bin. My back hit the concrete overhang, smashing through it until my head was hanging off the side of the building. I couldn't feel most my back, and my shoulder felt like a giant placeholder for where my arm used to connect.

I groaned as he let his fingers lose enough for small amounts of air to escape through. Now he was grinning. "I really thought you would be a better fighter than that, Avi. You were always the meat head out of the two of us," he teased.

I spat, coughing up blood on his hands, feeling my back as a raw section of naked pain. That let me move my legs, without telegraphing my plans. I kicked my right leg up with all the force that I had into his knee. Zevi let out a breath, falling forward with one arm dangling enough for me to take hold of it. I climbed his arm, instead of falling off the capitol building.

Taking advantage of his pain, I struck again with a knee in his groin. Super-strong or not, he was still made of flesh and bones. Still a man. This was a fight with a complete asshole; nothing about it needed to be fair.

Zevi coughed, leaning forward. I took hold of his face and went into the next series of the move, ramming his face into my knee. I regretted that immediately. His face was like jamming my knee into a brick wall. *Stick with the original plan.* I went back to striking Zevi in the groin, vicious kicks over and over in the same spot. Huey and I had trained heavy bag kicking, and those rounds would last anywhere from a minute to five minutes. My brother was about to experience a world of pain, I thought, as I continued to kick. He attempted to stand, then I clapped both his ears with my hands, causing him to curse, spinning his head wildly in every direction. I moved us forward, away from the edge to the center of the roof, continuing to land as many heavy blows on Zevi's soft spots as possible.

He rolled forward, coughing out, spitting up blood on my feet as I was about to go for his nose. He shot his arm upward, lifting me from my feet and sending me spiraling into the air toward another building. I blacked out within an instant, when I smashed down onto the roof, falling heavily.

I was somehow still conscious as I watched Zevi bend his knees and propel himself from the capitol building. He was sailing through the air toward my roof when Ash finally woke up. "He's kicking your ass," the beast growled from somewhere in the furthest reaches of my mind. I grunted my reply, unable to move any part of my body, my jaw feeling like a ball of heat.

A valve hissed, releasing a thick red haze of smoke around me. I couldn't feel the transformation, but I managed to tilt my head down to see my arm extend, fur appearing slowly, violently breaking its way through my skin. All of this happened in the moments before Zevi landed in front of me, while a blood red haze still swam around me. Ash roared, a long cry that shattered the glass nearby us into pieces, shaking dust loose from the building, as it vibrated under the vicious roar of the wolf.

98

Chapter 98

Zevi landed, and a wide toothy grin spread over his face, so the blood from the wounds I had inflicted made him look like a deranged monster. I was back in the mirror room, lying against a wall. My body was aching, drenched in sweat as a warm heat moved up me. I was healed enough now to fully move my head and neck, though my jaw felt like a glass bowl that had been taped back together.

I still couldn't talk, but as the heat ran up my body, bones snapping back into place, I watched what unfolded.

Zevi stood tall, his hair falling from his head in thick clumps like a sheep being sheered. Muscles somehow enlarged before my eyes and I swore that something was moving under his skin.

Ash finished transforming, standing to the height of Zevi, his strong legs curling beneath him.

"Hello, wolf," smiled my brother. Ash, roared, kicking his legs out into Zevi's chest, like a catapult. This time, it was my brother's turn to go flying into another building. I watched as Zevi jetted through the air, the beast jumping right after him. Flames pooled around Ash; I could feel a dragon rising inside his stomach as he blew fire from his mouth like a jet from a firefighter's hose.

The blast melted the wood and stone of the capitol building in an instant, destroying the foundation in a world of destruction. Ash landed in the smoldering wood, a long growl escaping his mouth. There was fire and smoke everywhere, and I couldn't see anything in the darkness besides dancing flames. I strained my ears as Ash did, searching for Zevi in the heat. Shimmering surrounded us as Ash walked on all fours, sniffing through the smoke.

I wondered, then, if his nose was strong enough to smell through this much, but that didn't seem to be the case, as he shifted through a pile of burning wood. My heart fell. Maybe we had burned my brother to nothing, a smoldering pool of debris.

A rumble came from beneath us, and Ash jumped back, landing against the remains of a burning structure piece, grunting from the heat. An explosion came from the ground. My brother jumped through the hole that had opened up. He was bathed in flames, his clothes and hair stripped away like a newborn. His eyes, though, were suns of hate; a devil in the ashes.

I choked up—in a lot of ways, I had always seen the devil in the ashes, but it wasn't me. It had never been me. The devil was there before me. Waves of malignance and vindictive hate—an evil that would never quit until it had consumed us all. For a moment, I panicked. I would have continued panicking before today; the old me would have pleaded with Ash to take us running as fast as possible. Instead, now, here at the end of things, I was alive again. If my brother was the devil in the ashes, I was born of them too, I decided. Since the firepit in the camp, since my flesh had melted from me, I had been crucified by the past.

I was alive now, in the fight to stop the spreading of the darkness. Ash roared a challenge to my brother, who was no longer laughing. The smile was gone as web-like horns grew from his back. His skin became as barren and gray, absent of the blue skies of life, becoming the color of death. Death is not black; it is gray—the combined leftovers of life and death. A shaken dusty silver that is a vision of nothingness. The most terrifying color, the image of falsehood itself.

His head was spiked at the top. It looked to be a medieval torturer's wet dream. His fingers became more knife-like. He hissed, a mouth full of shark teeth, double rowed, with only one true meaning: to devour.

We both had beasts, I realized, but whose was the stronger one? Ash charged forward, bounding over the distance between us in an instant. He growled, swiping with a massive paw that Zevi dodged by jumping back, swinging his fist into the side of Ash's face. Ash was carried through the walls like they were sheets of paper.

After blasting through six or seven drywalls, we stopped, slamming into a wooden desk. Ash growled as Zevi almost seemed to materialize in front of us, his speed quicker than the shadow of the moon. He threw a punch, his long knife-like fingers burying themselves deep in Ash's shoulder.

With a roar, Ash took hold of Zevi's arm and tossed him over his shoulder through the connecting wall behind us, out onto the chaotic street below. *This wasn't going to end well*, I thought, as Ash jumped down to the bloody streets. He pulled in air, a hot molten feeling rushed into our stomach, and out came fire from Ash's mouth.

Zevi was up, dancing away from the fireballs, until he stood next to a truck. With an effort, he seized the back end of the delivery truck, crushing in the top roof and bottom like it was a can, and smashed it into Ash.

We were jolted back into the lobby of the capitol building, which was quickly burning down. I grunted inside the mirror room, my jaw still reforming, but my back was somehow better and I could stand. I wondered then if Ash was wasting energy healing me. Through broken lips, I wheezed, "Ash—stop. Focus on him."

He came back a moment later, pushing the wreckage of steel and wood off. "I am using everything I have on the both of us. If you die, I die. It is two on one, remember," he stated, and I beamed. *That's right; I wasn't alone in this fight.* "Kick his ass!" I howled.

Ash roared, meeting Zevi mid-stride through the lobby with a ram of his horns into my brother's chest. Ash had coated himself in some kind of flame cloak, dancing around him like he was a bullet shot through flames. Zevi was launched back out of the lobby to another building on the other side of the street. Small arms fire was exchanged in our general direction. Something hit Ash's ribs, and he grunted as he jumped into the building

Zevi was in. *Good—someone was still fighting.* I gave a silent prayer as the fight with my brother continued on.

Zevi was moving, jumping from building to building as we gave chase, Ash shooting balls of fire, Zevi just managing to dodge everyone with ease. It took me a moment, but soon I realized that the direction Zevi was heading in circled to the end of the battlefield, near a huge building that was being constructed in our downtown area. A dark tower, unfinished, and covered in cranes, loomed before us.

Zevi tackled Ash into the lot of the constructed building, tossing him over steel beams as long as a truck, thick as trees scattered all around us. Ash tackled my brother, clawing and biting at any exposed piece of Zevi.

He cried out as he was bitten, then countered with a quick jab to our jaw, knocking out teeth. The blow caused Ash to roll over, and Zevi kicked the beast in the mouth, sending him sprawling through the unfinished lobby of the building, knocking over metal poles that were haphazardly placed across the floor.

A loud ring went through our heads, causing both of us to cry out, covering our eyes. Zevi sprinted toward us, a huge section of skin missing from his right shoulder, claw marks all over his gray flesh.

With a quick twirl, he pulled one of the metal poles off the ground and smacked Ash, breaking the metal into pieces, ringing our head again. Ash was flung back into the yard. He staggered when getting up, and I had the feeling that a few more hits like this, and even he would be put down for the count.

That's when I noticed the long shadow from a wrecking ball crane, the massive ball looming well overhead. "Up there, Ash." I pointed Ash's eyes toward the ball. He knew right away what I meant and leapt the fifty or so feet to the ball chain. Breathing fire, he melted the chain as if it was a dry leaf. The ball fell, and Ash caught the remainder of the chain in his mouth, spinning himself and the ball quickly. Zevi had just exited the building as the ball came whirling from the air, smacking him flat into the ground.

Dust shot in every direction as Ash landed on the ground, breathing hard from the strain of the ball. It had to weigh a couple of tons. Ash spat out a few fangs, blood coming from his mouth.

This was over; there was no way Zevi could have survived that. Ash limped on his paws to the side of the ball. Zevi's arm stuck out from underneath. We walked around the ball, the rest of him hidden by the girth of the massive ball.

I had breathed a sigh of relief too soon, as Zevi's arm shot up, gripping the ball and rolling it off him. He flew out from under the ball, his nose broken, blood coming from both his mouth and eyes. "Not bad, brother, not bad at all!" he cackled, standing tall, looming over Ash. "My turn," he spat as he took hold of the wrecking ball and flung it at Ash. Ash sailed over the ball easily, but it was a feint, and Zevi came from on top, gripping Ash's horns, and flung him into the building. He crash-landed, destroying the unfinished walls and piping structures before coming to a stop at the end of the room.

Rising to his feet, Zevi came through the wreckage again, punching Ash hard enough to twist his head around. Ash jerked back in response, flinging a wild strike with his paw, and met Zevi's forearm. Ash's claws were stuck in Zevi's arm, as my brother laughed, spitting more blood on us.

With a roar, Zevi punched into Ash's horns, breaking off the end piece. Ash screamed, a howl of pure pain, and collapsed to the floor as Zevi took the broken horn, stabbing it through the paw that was stuck in his arm.

Swinging his other arm around, Zevi took hold of Ash's horn and flipped him into the adjacent wall. Ash was whimpering, growling between the yelps of his pains. In a quick gesture, Ash bit down on the horn in his paw, pulling it free. I watched the wounded skin fizzle over, as white fur grew back instead of the usual jet black.

"Ash," I croaked. My voice suddenly sounded raspy and far older than it had before. I reached up, feeling my face. My facial hair had grown halfway down my face. The dark night of my hair was now flecked with long strands of silver. My arms looked thinner; veins that had never been there before crisscrossed far clearer than ever. We both had aged years—was it related to losing so much blood?

It was possible. I looked on for another moment and saw that Ash's black fur was coming back. My skin started to tighten back up again. My beard was becoming its normal stubble again.

"Ash, what was that?" I asked, terrified.

He replied with a grunt. "I can only heal so much—too much and I begin to age. It's part of the magic. Nothing on this planet is supposed to live through everything. Even I have my limits. This will be the last time I can restore us," he stated.

I noticed then that his left horn was still broken, and although his wounds from before though closed, they appeared to be fresh scars instead of the usual patches of fur. Zevi approached, bloodied but unbowed. He was not stopping, and neither would we. Ash pressed his teeth together, unleashing a long trail of smoke, plummeting the room into a deep night that seemed to have no corners of light. Somehow, though, Ash could still smell Zevi, and struck my brother as he staggered, lost in the darkness.

Ash leapt forward, taking Zevi's legs out from under him. Ramming Zevi's body was like ramming a tree, and Ash's bones seemed to rattle. With a fierce roar and all the claws that could be mustered, Ash struck into Zevi's body. My brother didn't stay blind long. He kicked and punched Ash into the walls as the two fought like mad Titans, two mountains colliding, the union of two tidal waves crashing down in a small hallway.

Blood flew in every direction, bits of skin, even fragments of bone. It was making me sick, and seeing my brother's finger in Ash's mouth, I leaned against the wall. Zevi's eyes were black coal, more beast than man. The fight continued to the elevator shaft, the door already broken in. Who threw whom down the shaft first, I was unable to tell. I only felt Ash's pain as his leg broke from the fall. We were back in the lobby of the building. In the distance, shocks of electricity shone yellow light, illuminating the two beasts, as they continued to fight like ancient Spartans. There was no retreat for them. No going back. It was the unspoken law amongst predators: when they finally meet, it is to the death, no matter what.

It wasn't always like this, I thought as I watched the two rip each other to shreds. *Once, the two of us had been brothers.* But now, every swing, bite, claw and vicious attack Ash made on Zevi, I felt. I felt my hands hurting my dopy little brother. The damn ginger who once got us lost in the woods, in our grandfather's woods, only a couple of miles outside of town.

99

Chapter 99

It was only a day's drive from my *foter's* watch shop. *Foter* used to say it was the best thing about inheriting the watch shop of his *mishpokhe*. He got to be closer to everyone, but he was also at least a day away, at the most. It was a weird old people's joke—there was nothing good about being so close to *mishpokhe*. Especially when it's your dopy little *bruder* stinking of pee and hunger, while the two of us made our way through the thick woods, completely lost.

I was still mad at him for getting us lost again and again. He always had to wander off, had to look at things he wasn't supposed to. Now, I was stuck in *zayde's* weird woods. I stopped, turning around to look at kid. He was shivering, and his coat was soaked through from the freezing mud. His hands looked like resin that had set in the sun for far too long, and his green eyes were as deep as moss.

I sighed, pulling off my own muddy coat, and placed it around my little *bruder*. I was almost eight; he was almost seven. Our *foter* had asked me to protect him no matter what. Sometimes, I felt like my *foter* didn't understand how hard it was with this kid. If he spent less time making me sweep that old watch store and maybe more time playing ball with us, he might have known how weird Zevi was, and how out of my depth I was when looking after him. Point in case: us now walking in the woods, as rain started to fall, first like tiny speckles, but soon much larger drops. I made us stop, taking shelter under the long limbs of a nearby evergreen. We were still shivering, cold under the limbs, but a little bit dryer at least.

At some point, we ended up hugging under those limbs, trying to hold together what little warmth we could. During the fall, I had lost the flint *zayde* had given us. I still had the knife, so before the sun had gone down, I cut more branches and stuck them in the mud to keep the wind away. *Zayde* had taught us that: soon we had a somewhat warmer place and as the night fell, we both drifted off to sleep.

The creature's breathing is what woke me. Not the way he seemed to almost move the Earth with each laborious step. *Nighttime plays tricks on you*—that is what my *muter* would tell Zevi when he couldn't sleep. She'd say that anything he was seeing wasn't really there, and that the night had a way of tricking the mind. I rubbed my eyes at the outline of the creature moving in the shadows nearest us.

It was impossibly large, swaying in the darkness like a moss-covered tree. I felt myself wanting to call out in fear, wanting to scream. I knew, though, that would only cause it to charge us. I slowly inched my way toward the knife in my pocket. The blade would pop out if I flicked the release on the side, but it would also make a pop that would tell the creature we were awake—if it didn't know already.

Loud breathing came from its snout. I could feel huffs of hot air in the cold. It was a bear, large and covered in brown fur. Huge front legs that towered, heading in our direction slowly. The beast wasn't worried about me as a threat; it was just seeing what we were. *More curious than dangerous*—I remembered my *zayde's* words. Staying calm is a lot harder to remember when the beast is so close to you in the dark, and you had nothing that could be used against it. I slid my free hand over Zevi's face until I found his mouth, and clamped my hands over it.

He stirred almost instantly, mumbling under my hand, pressing against my fingers. The rest of him started to move, but I did my best to turn his head toward the bear which was only centimeters away. It took Zevi's eyes a few moments before they adjusted and he stopped moving under my hand.

The bear grunted, moving closer, sniffing the air for our scent. My heart pounded, watching him get within inches of us now. He spread his mouth wide, and huge teeth and a long tongue met me. It kicked the dirt, and I had the feeling that the beast was going to attack us. There wouldn't be anything that the two of us could do. My reaction to the bear would have been to start screaming, to pee my pants, but I think it was because Zevi was with me that I hadn't done so already.

He was such a big creature—*zayde* would speak a lot of nonsense that I thought would never actually be useful. One point he always drove home was how big predators couldn't swallow. I had one chance, and as the bear opened its mouth once more to roar, I popped the knife from out of my pocket and shot forward, thrusting my arm into its mouth and down its throat. The bear yelped, gagging on the blade, pulling away and heading back into the darkness of the woods from where it had come.

I let go of Zevi's face. My right arm was covered in the bear's saliva. Zevi said nothing, and he just hugged me. I placed my arms around him, staring in the direction of where the bear had been. The two of us stayed in the darkness. The surrounding forest was filled with beasts, us boys still terrified to move even an inch.

100

Chapter 100

I thought of those moments with my little brother in the dark woods. If he hadn't been there, I wonder if I would have been brave enough to face the bear that night. As he and Ash continued to destroy the building with their fight, I tried to stay focused. Both Ash and I were at our limits.

Zevi must have sensed this. He capitalized, taking Ash by the horns, and threw him into the wall. He straddled the great wolf, pinning him down with his weight before cocking back his massive fists, whaling on Ash's face, over and over again.

Ash shot a paw forward. but Zevi rammed the broken piece of horn down into Ash's paw, pinning it only inches away from a power cable that was shooting sparks of blue in nearly every direction. Another punch; this time, Ash's head was rocketed back, digging into the concrete. More blows came down quicker, each one shaking my skull under their force. I felt, somewhere, a lessening—like a seal had been pushed broken. Ash didn't have much time, not while he fought such a... such a beast. That was what my brother was now, under his gray-coated skin and horns, he was a beast.

"Big beasts have trouble swallowing!" I shouted.

"What?" Ash called back weakly from inside the mirror room.

"Never mind that, switch with me, please!" I shouted at Ash.

He hesitated. "I don't think that would be a good idea at all, Avi," he replied.

"Just trust me, Ash, please," I begged the beast. "When have I lied to you, Ash? I promise. This time you won't get hurt, buddy."

"You're different from any other host I've ever had. Humans use me as a tool, but you're the first to learn my name, for good or bad," Ash said.

He was silent for a moment, before I felt the pull of the switch and my body started to convert back to its normal shape. The sudden change had the effect I had hoped, and Zevi hesitated, not throwing any more punches. With my arms still elongated from the change, I wrenched my hand off the horn fragment that pinned it down, and screamed as I reached for the power cable.

In a smooth motion that I would never be able to accomplish ever again, I jerked the power cable free, thrusting it into Zevi's chest. Big beasts tend to overlook surprises—especially when they're about to get the kill, as my brother was expecting.

The shock lifted Zevi off me and he reeled in pain, squirming on the ground, kicking out his legs and arms. I held the cable into him as long as I could. His gray skin flaked off, onto the floor like frosting from an old cake, along with the spikes, as Zevi fully shedded the monster.

Zevi was coughing, spitting up vomit as I got to my feet. He was lying on the ground, and I kicked him in the face, making his head shoot backward. I stumbled over to my brother's bloodied body on the ground. The cable was sizzling as I dropped it on the cold floor.

My mistake was taking my eyes off Zevi as I stood near him. He gripped my heel, yanking me to the ground in an instant. I cried out as my head hit the ground, and my brother expertly flipped to a sitting position on my chest. He proceeded to keep punching me in the face. His blows now lacked the indescribable strength they had before, but were still enough to kill me if he kept it up.

That's what he was trying to do. Kill me and be done with his brother. But we were still brothers, and I would never see him any other way as he pounded my face. One of my eyes closed over, and I saw my dopy little *bruder* in the woods, when our grandfather found us and broke down in tears. I saw the way our mother had hugged us both when we got back to our grandparents' home. My father was mad of course about us wandering off. I told him it had been me, sparing Zevi from getting in any more trouble. The look my father gave me implied that he had his doubts.

Later that evening, after Zevi had fallen asleep, the house quiet, I remember my father telling me that he was proud about what I did with the bear. I don't think they would have believed me if not for the gash that one of the bear's teeth had left along my arm. It was my first scar, a small thing, but as my father had pointed out to me, "Scars exist to remind us of what the world will never do to us again."

Another hit sent stars in my vision. I could see that Zevi's knuckles had already started to burst and dislodge from the assault. His face was only rage, as if there had never been any other emotion that could have been there. There had been, once, when he was a boy. Still anger, for sure, but he had also been a kind and shy kid.

I saw my scar from the bear that had attacked my brother and me during the night. It existed to remind me of what I would never do again: I would never abandon my family again. Through the years, my body had become a maze of scars, just as many on the inside as on the outside. Though they mounted up, I knew that they had a purpose—that in a world which seemed to be just designed to kill people, something still existed as hope. Clarity came back to my mind, even as I continued to be savagely beaten.

Ash chimed in, concern evident in his voice, as if he was afraid. "Avi! Can, you hear me? We need to switch, now!" I heard his exhaustion through the fear. I knew that all the fighting had taken its toll on him. I opened to the part of my mind that held the mirror room. He was an old wolf now, covered in white fur and limping. His face was drawn into deep lines, heading toward his snout.

I responded simply, "I got us."

His face contorted before turning into a doggy grin, and he dipped his snout.

I was back facing Zevi. I smiled, and my brother hesitated for a moment. I could see the wheels in his head try and find the pavement again. I shot up and headbutted my brother as he hesitated, while also kicking myself up, sending him sprawling over. I felt the give of his nose bone as my head broke the weak cartilage.

I reared back my fist and gave Zevi a few well-placed punches. He resisted with his hands weakly as I continued to pound his face. One...two... three... he finally dropped his hands, his face covered in blood. He looked at me, and his pond green eye stared at me with a dull light. I dropped my hands, sitting on my brother's chest, distributing my weight against him. I opened my mouth and let Ash's roar come out, and I felt a wave of power overtake me. Somewhere in my mind, I felt the wolf go to sleep. "Get some rest, buddy," I thought as I turned my attention back to Zevi.

"Just finish it," he stated softly.

I gave him a long look, doing nothing. My brother's eyes started to water up, the swell of a current that only he could see, one that was sweeping him out to a long dark sea. "Please," he begged as his eyes started to water. Even monsters all had a human heart, once upon a time. And I didn't think my brother was a monster, just lost in the darkness. Both of our candles had nearly burned out their wicks. The truth was that the darkness would always be there, a force surrounding the light of the candles. Though the flames might be small, they still made the night afraid. All it took was a reminder to the candle that the flames would always burn; just light them and let them catch fire.

I kept my fists to my side and slid from Zevi, sitting next to him. "I should have said this sooner," I sighed. "You're my *bruder*, Zevi; no matter what happens, I will always protect you, I will always love you." I stated this calmly in the darkness of the basement, the two of us inside a lonely building that would now have to be torn down before it could be repaired. A steel beam lay twisted nearby. The metal seemed to be sliding out as it was still scalding hot.

His eyes pooled even more, before a fiery heat hit them. "Shut the fuck up, Avraham!" he lurched up before falling flat again. His body was done, and all that was left was his hatred to drive him. Zevi sat up partially, before falling back down to the floor once more. He gasped, breathing in heavily. Both of us sounded like chugging old engines firing to life after so many years. "There you are preaching to me about love? Fuck you! There's no such thing! Just a bullshit way our *muter* got us to go to sleep, Avi. And look where she is now? Just fertilizer in a field! Why the fuck do you even care?" he screamed, choking on his words.

My own tears started to slide down my face, landing on the dust below us. "You're my brother—that's why," I stated, getting to my knees slowly. I stood on shaky legs. One of them gave out and I fell to the ground, grunting. A bone stuck out just below the knee. It burned—it would heal soon enough. Things heal with time, or they at least lessen enough for you to make peace with it.

But the ache I felt in my heart for those who had gone before me would never truly go away; they occupied a space that didn't let people go. The only space outside of time's control. And this wasn't how my father and mother meant for us to live, beating each other to death. Hunting down people we thought deserved death. Brothers, killing each other—it all ended so twisted in the end, and neither of us even knew why.

I smiled at Zevi. He was my brother and that was something to me. It was true that I should have given up on him. Anyone else would have. But when the dust settled, and the room became empty, I knew there would be nothing more than what I chose to do with my life. I wasn't going to let it be written that all I had ever done was drown in my sorrows. I was someone who protected those that I love, even if I hated myself to the end of time and they was as truly selfish as they come. I could still do my best—lessen someone else's suffering because fuck it, that was my motto. It was better than running. I had done enough of that.

"I tried... to kill you... to take your blood. I killed... so many people." My brother's voice broke.

I smiled sadly at Zevi. "I didn't say you were perfect or even a good person, jackass. Just that I am your brother. We are going to get through this, even if I have to kick your ass again and again. I am your *bruder*," I stated again.

Zevi turned his head away from me, looking into the darkness. "You actually forgive me? Even when I held so much against you..." he trailed off.

I smiled again. "It never cost anything. We've lost so much already. I would like to see for a chance if there is anything left to gain," I pondered. My knee was really starting to ache. I wished Ash was awake and this would heal already.

"I grew up envying you, you know that?" Zevi stated, his head turned away from me still.

I sucked in a breath at that. Zevi had seemed to hate everything about me growing up. I had picked on him too much for it to be any other way.

He continued, "I envied the way father seemed to give you more attention—always talking about your work and never mine. How mother—mother doted on me to make up for it. The other kids liked you more, and you were so good at baseball. And after the camp, while the rest of us went to shit—you never changed, Avi. You stayed the same. Pain changes people; but it didn't change you..." He trailed off weakly. "Just let me go, Avi. I've done—awful things." He broke down and started to cry, long tears flooding endlessly.

"Now you're going to have to work awfully hard to try and fix this shit, brother."

He turned back around, his eyes wide. "You really aren't trying to kill me? After everything that has happened," he stated.

I sighed. "You're my brother. You're just trying to find your way. I'm done fighting—maybe that's been my problem my whole life. I've been running away and becoming a slave to it all. Mostly just imprisoned by my own walls—my own fences. I won't anymore. This is my life, God damn it, and I will see this shit through. No one is dying a monster here today. Let's get out of here, Zevi. Take one strikingly beautiful and astonishing step at a time—no matter how much it hurts or how hard it is to breath; we just keep moving. This meat grinder called life is not our end."

I extended my hand toward him. He took it and we both stood on shaky legs. He wrapped one arm around my shoulders and I one around his waist. I did my best to stay up with my arm around him.

We started to walk, slowly, both of us grunting, trailing blood in our wake, as we made our way to the entrance of the building. I smelled the smoke first, the metallic burning of metal, like rocks made of blood. Then came the smell of crumbling rock, burning wood. Loud cracks started erupting around us, and the building gasped almost for air, sending out puffs of dust in every direction.

"This whole place is coming down! We need to get moving, now!" I urged as I started to hobble faster in the direction of the broken doors. They lay in pieces of scrap metal. We were still easily thirty yards or so, and as we moved, the ceiling started to fall, the floor cracking open.

"Please, Avraham, I won't change, I won't stop," my brother whispered weakly in the darkness.

I had no doubt that he would stop. His convictions had led him here. Just as my path had led me to holding my brother as the world was falling around us. I thought of Linor, of Ash, Huey, Solly, and even myself. We all had made it, in some form or another, despite the filth that was thrown at us. There is a light in this world, and it comes out when we see infinity—the infinite love that we can find in ourselves, and bring to others. That thought stole my breath away. I paused long enough to tell my brother the truth. "We can deal with all that later. Now move your legs, dumbass."

We aren't going to make it. Move faster! I screamed to myself, cursing my leg as it flowed with blood, which dribbled off into the cracks in the floor, like some kind of drain leading to the underworld. Pieces of the broken tower sliding to the ground, which rumbled like an invisible river as the very earth shook.

Zevi suddenly stopped. I almost fell from the suddenness.

"What are you doing? Come on, we need to get out of here, Zevi."

He gave me a long look before a small smile appeared on his face and he shook his head. It dawned on me, like the Judgment of Solomon had just been made by my brother. "Sorry, Avi. I will always love you," he stated, before kicking me in the chest.

I started to shout "No," but the wind left my lungs and I was sent flying through the falling debris of the crumbling building.

My brother was smiling at me in the darkness, as the world seemed to collapse in on him. I stumbled back through the entrance before blacking out. The last thing I saw was my brother smiling, tears in his eyes and then the building fell, and all went to the color of ashes.

101

Chapter 101

I could feel warm heat on my neck, my whole body aching as I heard Ash's voice. "You did good, kid," he said softly.

I groaned, opening my eyes, moving back from a burning tire that I had landed next to. The wafting smoke caused me to cover my nose. Looking at the remains of the construction building, my heart sank. Mounds of rubble and steel beams jutted from every direction. Heaps of broken bricks remained stoic in the orange flames burning all around me. The world was burning, and I was watching it. It wasn't a joke; I didn't find the punchline. I just wept for my brother.

When I was done, I looked down. My knee bone had gone back into place. My body still felt like I had been run over by a truck, then two to three more after the first one had backed over me. I decided to respond to Ash. I closed my eyes and appeared in the mirror room. His fur was no longer deathly pale white snow, but he was not healed back to midnight black fur. He was streaked with multiple lines of gray—in fact, he now appeared to have the coating of a gray wolf, with a little bit of black mixed in.

He sighed as if reading my mind. "Even I can only take so much—this is how I will remain. You saved my life, Avi," he stated. I sat down next to him, placing my hand on his shoulder as he lay on his paws. He opened one massive eye and regarded me for a long time. I hesitated, then proceeded to pet the big wolf. We both didn't talk; we both knew what we had done for each other. He was my demon that I had carried for almost twenty years, and seemed to always be a part of my life. He was my friend. I wasn't sure what I was to Ash, but for the first time since we had been forced together, he wasn't trying to eat me.

However much longer it may be, we were together as one, the good and the bad wolf. No, not quite that—we were just the wolf. After a while, I left the mirror room and reopened my eyes to the burning town that used to be my home.

The police were going to arrive—the army even, I figured. This much destruction and carnage, it was only a matter of time. The community would never be able to rest now. They would all be branded war criminals or terrorists at the very least. Huey and I would probably be shot without question if we were found.

I started to stand when a voice hissed at me from behind. I turned around seeing a broken Hans pointing a gun at me. "I fucking hate you—wolf. I came all the way to this shitstain of a country, this worthless town, just to have you destroy it all again! No amount of money is worth this. I am tired of some asshole floating cash and pretending they can morally change the world. Here's the truth, wolf: power is fucking worthless! We are all meatbags and there isn't any changing that. Don't know why anyone tries to make it more complicated." He pulled back the hammer on his revolver, his one arm pointing the gun shakily, the other arm hanging uselessly at his side.

I covered my eyes, until I heard the groan. I opened them to see Huey standing over Hans, who was now on the ground clutching his crotch. Huey had a black eye and was bleeding out of both his shoulder and mouth. He wiped his mouth. "I've waited a long time to do this." He kicked Hans again, in between his legs, and the old German guard cried out.

Huey kicked Hans's gun away sending it clattering down the street before kneeling and punching Hans in the face. The old solider closed his eyes. He was knocked out and wouldn't wake up for at least a few hours. "Enough people have died because of you, asshole—I won't be your next victim." He then turned toward me, painfully making his way through the destroyed brick that littered the area.

"You look like shit," he stated as he pulled me to my feet.

"Likewise," I grunted as I got back up. "What happened there? Thought you were the zen kung-fu master?"

Huey gave me a long look. "The pecker head cheapshotted me as soon as I spared him the first time. I tried to kill him, I really did." Huey looked defeated, his hands shaking at the side.

"But you spared him the second time. Let it go," I stated, catching his eyes.

Huey nodded a few moments later, hitching a thumb behind him. "We lost two of the wolves—less of the community than I thought we would. But still," he said glumly.

"Yeah. We survived."

"Won't be for long—you and me, you know we can't hide from something this big, Avi," he whispered.

"Did you find Solly?" I stated, just as miserably.

He sighed before speaking again. "Found our foxy redhead. Tough gal. Hands are completely gone." He sounded devastated.

I nodded, turning away from him, "Get the others, Huey. Get them out of here. Go back to the community and have them stay there. Then you need to get lost for a few months. I got a plan on how we can get out of this," I stated.

Huey's face was flabbergasted before understanding sank in. "No, Avraham—" he started before I cut him off.

"Bunch of dead bodies destroyed small town? I am betting that Hans didn't work for my brother alone. I will tell the police that it was Hans, a terrorist group acting on their own, and turn myself in as well. Only way to clear us. Don't worry, I've been electrocuted before. I will think of it as a mini vacation. They can't hurt me. Not now, at least." I smiled at Huey.

Huey frowned. "That's just the way this is—they will frame you as a mass murderer, a survivor of the Holocaust who destroyed a town to get a bunch of former Nazis. It's the only way, though. Any survivors of Zevi's gang will point to him. Unless you... pin it all on yourself," he stated matter-of-factly.

My smile weakened, but I couldn't think of anything else for us to say and do. "That's the way it is. Get out of here, Huey," I said as my friend gave me a hesitating look.

He turned and trudged away through the rubble, before stopping and turning around again. "Stay out of trouble Avi." He waved goodbye.

"Likewise," I called back, before speaking to my friend one last time. "Don't tell me where the community goes, Huey. Wait a few months before contacting me," I stated.

Huey knew what I meant. Nodding solemnly, this time he left. I went and sat down next to Hans as he groaned in his sleep, for good measure, I kicked him in the ribs and heard a small moan escape. "Choose to live or die, asshole," I muttered, as I could see a helicopter flying in the distance. I wish I had asked Huey for a cigarette. This was going to be a long night.

102

Chapter 102

"I've always seen the devil in the ash. Even now," muttered my cellmate as he looked out the window, hogging the light that was coming through our bars.

I sighed, leaning up in bed, tucking in my messy shirt. Rollcall was about to come, and this guy was smoking our last cigarette. I smiled at him. "That sounds pretty dark, man. Will you just pass it already?" I stated as the doors to our cell automatically opened and guards begin to call out around us for our morning count.

I yawned, covering my mouth as I scooted off the double bunk, tucking Huey's latest letter into my pants pocket. I had been incarcerated going on a year now since that night in the small town just outside of the Tri-Cities area in Washington.

Most of my life had been spent fighting and running from anything and everything, especially myself. *Those days are over.* I smiled as I thought of Huey's last letter. In exchange for the Nazi war criminals, the community was finally granted citizenship and allowed to stay in the boundaries of town without the police chasing them down. I had doubts that the public perception of them would change—it was a step in the right direction, though. Huey assured me that Bipin was leading them well, though they had decided to pick up and move deeper west. That was for the best: stay in the wind—that was how the Roma survived.

True to his word, Huey never said where they moved to, and I never asked. My family had done enough to that community. It was the bitter price to pay.

Huey had found Zevi's files on all the war criminals that he had located and the location of those who had died. Turns out around a hundred or so had come with Hans, and close to seven hundred had been tracked down by Zevi's gang over the years. Those who had joined him were slowly being rounded up, for a laundry list of crimes, and most would never see the outside world again. Hans had got the chair last week—nothing lost there. How Huey was handling it I would have to find out later. Sometimes, we just don't get to put our demons to rest; but Huey would make peace with that, I knew he would.

I was in for life, spared only because of the evidence I brought forward. Zevi's crimes were placed at my feet. Instead, I had framed him as someone who tried to stop me. It wasn't much; it saved my brother from being hurt worse. Zevi—it was the best I could do for my little brother.

For my sentencing, turns out putting a former Holocaust survivor on parade and possibly getting the chair made people very uncomfortable—it was the only time in my life those nights in the camp had become useful. So instead, it was metal bars and bright lights for a while longer. Nothing I wasn't used to.

As I walked down the metal scaffolding that would lead out to the yard, the cool fall air hit me, and I beamed. Huey had asked me when I was planning on leaving in his letter. I told him I was liking the weather, so maybe in a few months. I stretched my hands behind my head, secure in the fact that life was continuing, despite everything that had happened. I had lost so much; I had so much left to gain.

Yeah, I always saw the devil in the ash. That was true. Turns out, it was just seeing myself free from the fires—freedom from all that gray. I had no idea where I was going to go; I still got the shakes when there were too many people. Sometimes, I would forget where I was slightly. Loud noises made me jump. It was different now, because those moments passed me by, and I just smiled through the pain. That was enough to keep me walking forward, to keep on burning like a candle, even in the darkest of storms.

103

Chapter 103

"That was it? That's all we were doing? Just sitting and watching them like some kind of kid with an ant-farm?" I asked the man in shadows. We were both standing above the carnage that had unfolded in a small city in Washington. A cold chill was passing through the night. I stuffed my one hand inside my pocket and waited for his reply.

He took his time—always drawing out everything into a nebulous speech that seemed way more complicated than it needed to be. "This world got saved, thanks to you kicking a troubled kid out of a car: yes. It wasn't our place to interfere, just steer in the direction it was supposed to go," the man in shadows stated. He sheathed a red-coated dagger, which seemed to have a moving black eel dancing along the blade, twisting in the light of the flames from a nearby rooftop.

"Okay, fair enough. But you still haven't explained why any of this is important. You literally just had us spend a few nights in jail, then pulled out that blade, and boom, we were here. Like teleporting genies in a magic lamp." I gestured with my hand, exasperated.

He gave me a long look, sighing. "Look, James, you ask way too many questions. Which is fine. Just wait for them to be answered. Your part in all of this is just starting," he stated.

"How was it determined that this place was going to end anyways? How could you know that?" I asked the red-eyed man.

The man in shadows sighed heavily before speaking, almost like he was conversing with a child. "Because the higher-ups determined it so," he stated matter-of-factly.

I growled, tempering my anger. We had only been together for a few days. That was long enough to learn that I stood no chance against him, that he could travel to anywhere and any when. But, most importantly, he'd said that somehow, if I followed him, I could... I could get Holly back. A cold slab of ice froze over my anger, like a snowstorm in the middle of spring, reminding us of the horror we had escaped could come back. We had to work for the spring, work for a summer that would outshine the darkness.

"Whatever it takes," I chanted to myself. Whatever it would take to get Holly back. I would not stop until I had her back.

"What's that, James?" asked the man in shadows.

"Nothing. What are we going to do now?" I asked him.

He pulled out a purple and blue dagger from inside his jacket pocket. I could see six more of his oddly colored daggers. Each one seemed to do something different.

"Now we are going to the hourglasses, James. We are going to meet the bosses. They hold everything. Then we must go find us another," he stated.

I shivered at that thought. "We have to watch another planet destroy itself—already," I whispered.

"It is the way the universe works, James. A life for a life; a balance. It may seem cruel—it is cruel. Everyone in every dimension would be dead without us. But no. Before that, we must find another helper of sorts. There must always be two of us—remember that, James. I won't be around forever," he stated, smiling.

"Soon it will be your turn to save the universe—to ensure that everything is perfectly in place, scaled to as many lives as it's supposed to have," he said. I nodded, agreeing with a genocidal murderer who had already let countless die. I would do whatever it took to get Holly back, even if it meant losing my soul. It was already gone anyways.

The man in shadows pulled on the blades, playing a song, and a portal opened. I looked behind me at the carnage below. "At least he made it. Don't waste it, Avraham," I stated.

104

Chapter 104

I was smoking in bed, humming a song—one I had heard my *muter* sing often when I was a child. I didn't understand it then, but I think I had got it now. You never really understand a love song until you've had your heart broken, until you've loved. A slow tear slid down my cheek. I smiled as I understood my *muter* a little more.

My singing was interrupted. An explosion rocked me from my bed, sending me to the ground. I panicked, my heart racing. "Ash—what's going on?" I asked the wolf, the demon monster that inhabited the deepest reserves of my mind.

He growled back, "They're coming."

"Who's coming?" I asked, as my cell door was blown off its hinges. Sirens rang in the distance, men screamed all around me, and I could hear the thundering of the guards' boots clattering over the cold metal walkways in a frenzy.

Smoke filled the small cell. I covered my eyes, squinting as two figures approached. One was a tall woman with long, flowing, copper-red hair, deep blue eyes, and high cheeks. She had on a white cowboy hat, dirty overalls from a long-passed era, and enough guns around her waist to make an arms dealer blush. Two of which were in her hands as she smiled at me.

"Found him at last," she stated cheerily, holstering one of the pistols in her waistband.

"We need to hurry, Holly," urged the smaller woman, with long black hair and tan skin.

"Get your panties out of a wad, Winona: I have to say it first," Holly replied.

"Please, no. Seriously, not again, Holly, we don't have time for this." Winona slapped her head, looking around urgently. I noticed then that her skin wasn't tan. It was utterly black on one side, pale milk on the other. Like a line had been drawn down her.

I blinked at the two, taken aback. I stuttered, "Who the hell are you?"

The woman in the cowboy hat smiled. "Avraham, we are here to ask you along on an adventure to save all of existence," she stated.

"What?" I exclaimed.

She sighed, blowing out both her lips. "Oh my God, he's stupid. Okay, no matter. Some people don't want to do a little thinking. Why not listen to the person saving your ass? It's always a million questions," she muttered, pulling out a silver pistol with a big barrel. She aimed it at me. "Come with us if you want to live, cocksucker," she beamed.

The other girl slapped her own face hard. "You just have to say that every single time, don't you?" she yelled at the other woman with the big gun.

"It's a good saying—you just don't understand culture, Winona," she countered.

"How could he even know what you're talking about? I never know what you're talking about. We have to go Holly!" she yelled; a thick accent similar to Elder Ad coming out as she pointed down the hallway. I could hear the guards shouting now in the distance.

Holly put her gun away before extending her hand toward me. "Fine, no one seems to want to have a little fun, saving the universe and all. What do you say, Avraham? Want to come with?" she asked.

I was utterly bewildered. "Come where?" I asked her.

"Where we can save everyone," she stated.

About the Author

I am traveling the road for a bit—goodbye, everybody! I will update on the next one.

You can connect with me on:

🌐 https://www.jonathanblazer.com

🔗 https://www.instagram.com/jblazerwriter

Also by Jonathan Blazer

Out of the Night

James is your average everyday father; he loves his wife, he loves his daughter, he's happy with his lot in life. All of that will change in an instant, thrusting James into a never-ending battle for his sanity—a war for his soul. "A father protects his family; he will lose it all for his family." That's what James tells himself as his city falls apart and ghosts become the new population in his once proud home. To live in a world that is quickly fading into shades of apparitions; while cradling the lines of what it means to be alive: in a world that has become a ghost, will he either stop at nothing to save his family or become a memory along with the rest of the world.

Made in the USA
Columbia, SC
15 April 2022

59046733R00362